THE ASH PARK SERIES, BOOKS 1-3

FAMISHED, CONVICTION, AND REPRESSED

MEGHAN O'FLYNN

Copyright 2017

This box set and every novel herein is a work of fiction. Names, characters, businesses, places, events and incidents are either the products of the author's imagination or used fictitiously. Any resemblance to actual persons, living or dead, or actual events is purely coincidental. Opinions expressed are those of the often disturbed characters and do not necessarily reflect those of the author, though she does agree that Ash Park may not be the safest place to put down roots.

No part of this book may be reproduced, stored in a retrieval system, scanned, or transmitted or distributed in any form or by any means electronic, mechanical, photocopied, recorded or otherwise without written consent of the author—nobody likes a thief.

All rights reserved.

Distributed by Pygmalion Publishing, LLC

IBSN (paperback): 978-1-947748-03-3

ALSO BY BESTSELLING AUTHOR MEGHAN O'FLYNN

STAND-ALONE THRILLERS
The Jilted
Shadow's Keep
The Flood

THE ASH PARK SERIES
Salvation
Famished
Conviction
Repressed
Hidden
Redemption
Recall
Imposter
Composed

SHORT STORY COLLECTIONS
Aftertaste
Listeners
People Like Us

DON'T MISS ANOTHER RELEASE!
SIGN UP FOR THE NEWSLETTER AT
MEGHANOFLYNN.COM!

FAMISHED

AN ASH PARK NOVEL

For my father, who raised me lovingly—and quite normally—and who should not be blamed for the twisted nature of my work.
I love you, Daddy.
Always.

SUNDAY, DECEMBER 6TH

Focus, or she's dead.

Petrosky ground his teeth together, but it didn't stop the panic from swelling hot and frantic within him. After the arrest last week, this crime should have been fucking impossible.

He wished it were a copycat. He knew it wasn't.

Anger knotted his chest as he examined the corpse that lay in the middle of the cavernous living room. Dominic Harwick's intestines spilled onto the white marble floor as though someone had tried to run off with them. His eyes were wide, milky at the edges already, so it had been awhile since someone gutted his sorry ass and turned him into a rag doll in a three-thousand-dollar suit.

That rich prick should have been able to protect her.

Petrosky looked at the couch: luxurious, empty, cold. Last week Hannah had sat on that couch, staring at him with wide green eyes that made her seem older than her twenty-three years. She had been happy, like Julie had been before she was stolen from him. He pictured Hannah as she might have been at eight years old, skirt twirling, dark hair flying, face flushed with sun, like one of the photos of Julie he kept tucked in his wallet.

They all started so innocent, so pure, so ... *vulnerable.*

The idea that Hannah was the catalyst in the deaths of eight others, the cornerstone of some serial killer's plan, had not occurred to him when they first met. But it had later. It did now.

Petrosky resisted the urge to kick the body and refocused on the couch. Crimson congealed along the white leather as if marking Hannah's departure.

He wondered if the blood was hers.

The click of a doorknob caught Petrosky's attention. He turned to see Bryant Graves, the lead FBI agent, entering the room from the garage door, followed by four other agents. Petrosky tried not to think about what might be in the garage. Instead, he watched the four men survey the living room from different angles, their movements practically choreographed.

"Damn, does everyone that girl knows get whacked?" one of the agents asked.

"Pretty much," said another.

A plain-clothed agent stooped to inspect a chunk of scalp on the floor. Whitish-blond hair waved, tentacle-like, from the dead skin, beckoning Petrosky to touch it.

"You know this guy?" one of Graves's cronies asked from the doorway.

"Dominic Harwick." Petrosky nearly spat out the bastard's name.

"No signs of forced entry, so one of them knew the killer," Graves said.

"*She* knew the killer," Petrosky said. "Obsession builds over time. This level of obsession indicates it was probably someone she knew well."

But who?

Petrosky turned back to the floor in front of him, where words scrawled in blood had dried sickly brown in the morning light.

> Ever drifting down the stream—
> Lingering in the golden gleam—
> Life, what is it but a dream?

Petrosky's gut clenched. He forced himself to look at Graves. "And, Han—" *Hannah*. Her name caught in his throat, sharp like a razor blade. "The girl?"

"There are bloody drag marks heading out to the back shower and a pile of bloody clothes," Graves said. "He must have cleaned her up before taking her. We've got the techs on it now, but they're working the perimeter first." Graves bent and used a pencil to lift the edge of the scalp, but it was suctioned to the floor with dried blood.

"Hair? That's new," said another voice. Petrosky didn't bother to find out who had spoken. He stared at the coppery stains on the floor, his muscles twitching with anticipation. Someone could be tearing her apart as the agents roped off the room. How long did she have? He wanted to run, to find her, but he had no idea where to look.

"Bag it," Graves said to the agent examining the scalp, then turned to Petrosky. "It's all been connected from the beginning. Either Hannah Montgomery was his target all along or she's just another random victim. I think the fact that she isn't filleted on the floor like the others points to her being the goal, not an extra."

"He's got something special planned for her," Petrosky whispered. He hung his head, hoping it wasn't already too late.

If it was, it was all his fault.

TWO MONTHS EARLIER

THURSDAY, OCTOBER 1ST

THE KILLER LOOKED at the ceiling, listening for the call of a night bird, a cricket, a barking dog. But the cemetery was silent, save for the moaning of the wind and the whispering rustle of leaves outside. These were the noises of the dead.

The one-family mausoleum was made of thick white bricks turned gray with age and reinforced with mortar and stone. The walls were a barrier against the outside sounds of gunshots and throbbing bass lines emanating from cars with rims larger than their wheels.

The walls also muffled any sounds that might have tried to escape the small room.

The silence shimmered through his lungs, focusing him. Soon the burgeoning sunlight, birthed from a vast bloody womb, would announce that today was the present and it was time to move beyond a past that seemed so close in these early morning hours.

He closed his eyes and let her image come rushing back at him. Would she still look the way she did inside his head? On the surface, it was a simple question, but it toyed with him, stirred his curiosity and roused an unbridled rage that seared his very soul. He could see her face as clearly as if she were standing before him now—her alabaster skin, the vibrant green of her eyes, iridescent like the Mediterranean Sea.

Bitch.

He looked down. This girl was a poor substitute. The slab of concrete bearing her weight was barely wider than her hips, so it had been no burden to cuff her wrists and ankles to the sturdy wooden pillars beneath. Families had once placed the ashes of their loved ones here for a final goodbye before stuffing them into the wall for all eternity. Now it was a real altar, heavy with sacrifice.

Her eyes were unseeing and blank in the dim light. The creamy white of her skin would eventually become translucent as death took over, blending her flesh into the gray stone upon which she lay.

But not yet.

He ran his fingers over her breasts, flattened from years of malnutrition. A roadmap of abused veins ran the length of her arms. Her drooping mouth gaped, a string of drool dripping down her wasted face. Dried tears streaked her cheeks.

He had never understood tears. In her case they seemed all the more repugnant as he'd merely finished what she had already been doing to herself. They all tried to deny it at the end, but every one of them wanted this. Even the one he hadn't killed. His neck muscles went rigid, as stony as the altar. He had done everything she had ever asked of him. Would have continued to if she hadn't gone.

This is for you, cunt.

He trailed his eyes down the girl's chest to the yawning gorge that had once been her belly. The skin lay peeled back, revealing his prize within the emaciated cavity.

He touched the stomach and it slid like a nest of maggots, writhing away from the light. The still-warm jelly that surrounded her innards sucked at his hand. He slid his fingers over the shiny glass exterior of the organ, gripped it gingerly, and pulled. Resistance, then release, as the surrounding tissue gave way. He bent closer and palpated the surface, pinching, prodding until he felt the familiar firmness, the proof that she was just as disgusting as he'd suspected.

Then the scalpel was in his hand, and there was only the dissection, reverent and precise, the taste of iron on his tongue growing stronger with each inhale. His brows knit together in concentration. The blade sliced cleanly, smooth as a finger down a lover's cheek, as he opened the tissue, inch by inch, toward his prize. Then it was free, writhing in a gooey mass of greenish-yellow mucus and reddish-brown tissue, toxic with her essence. He removed the wriggling creature slowly. His mouth watered.

There you are, you little bastard.

RADIO SILENCE. Then static, like a thousand locusts humming in my ears. The pillow was ripped from my hands and someone screamed, the sound strangled and choked. It was me. It was always me.

I opened my eyes in the dark, panting, clutching at my chest, shirt balled in my fists, the panic hot and white and unrelenting. Next to me, Jake snored softly, oblivious. I watched the covers rise rhythmically with his breath. A demonstration of his ability to not give a crap about anything.

I rolled away from him onto my side, knees hugged tight against my wildly hammering heart. The skin of my arms and legs was dewy with sweat. A scar on my ankle throbbed and stilled just as abruptly.

You're not back there, Hannah. You're here. You're here.

But I wasn't here, not all the way, not ever. Even on my best days, I could still hear him, my first love, my only hate, whispering in my ear *I'll find you, you little whore*. I could still smell him—the stink of sweat and some musky, dirty, vulgar thing lingering long after the nightmare, trying to choke me as I lay in the filmy pre-dawn gloom.

I raised my eyes and blinked back tears as the alarm clock swam into focus. Five-fifteen. Two and a half hours until I had to leave for work. Two and a half hours to get myself together and not be so fucked up, or at least find a way to act less obviously crazy. But acting was hard. Most days, I'd rather just disappear into the background. I fantasized about slipping from view, a lithe mass of dark hair, wide mouth and green eyes fading to a transparent whisper, then only the scenery behind, as if I had never existed. If I could force this disappearing, I would. Then maybe I could stop running.

I sucked in a deep breath, my heart expanding and jerking sharply like an agitated blowfish in my chest. Slowly, carefully, I dragged myself away from Jake to the edge of the bed, keeping my eyes on the door in case someone burst through it and grabbed me by the throat. At least Jake would wake up and help me, or I hoped he would; I was counting on him for that part. Probably the one thing I could count on him for. I hoped I was worthy of at least that much.

I swung my feet off the bed, toed around for the slippers below, and crept to the bedroom door, cringing against the chill on my clammy skin, alert for the slightest sound. *Nothing.*

Panic's chokehold lessened to a subtle pressure. *Jesus.* If neurotic freaks ever ended up being cool, I'd be ready for the red carpet. I crept down the hallway toward the living room, pretending I was Scooby Doo on the trail of a creepy amusement park owner. Silliness wasn't the only way to chill out, but it was one way. And it worked ... sometimes.

Other times the panic ended up strangling me.

I paused in the hallway, listening, and flicked on the light. Shadowy, amorphous shapes solidified into a familiar scene: the couch, the table, a pack of Jake's cigarettes. I scanned the apartment for the slightest movement. Nothing, not even behind the window curtain. No noise outside. A hint of Jake's lingering cigarette smoke harassed my nostrils and the dusky memories shivered away.

I checked the window lock anyway, snaking my hand behind the curtain and pulling it aside so I could poke at the tab with a trembling finger. Below me, the street was empty, the patch of frosty grass along the sidewalk glowing amber under the streetlight. I dropped the curtain, picked my way back through the living room and groped the deadbolt on the front door. Locked.

My purse sat on the table. I pulled my phone out of it and my heart seized and restarted as I tapped in my code. No creepy text messages. No threatening voicemails. Nothing.

I pushed my purse aside and jumped at the sound the strap made when it slid and hit the table. In the kitchen, the overhead light bounced off the refrigerator and cast a weird, flattened circle of light on the floor. I concentrated on it as I waited for my heart to shrink and drop out of my throat.

Cake. I should bake a cake. Because isn't that where everyone's mind goes after a horrible recurring nightmare and panicked lock-checking? But I was being practical. Now I wouldn't have to stop at a bakery on my way from work to the women's shelter, and Ms. LaPorte would get a nice birthday surprise. I still owed her. Probably would for the rest of my life.

I shuffled to the cabinets and carefully pulled out cake-making supplies. Once the mix was emptied into the bowl, I cracked the eggs and zoned out, there but not, baking on autopilot. People got over stuff, right? They left it behind them. Eventually I would forget how the clasp on my duffel bag jangled as I ran for the bus station, chest heaving with sorrow and loneliness and abject terror. Eventually I would forget the way his calloused hands felt against my windpipe. I grabbed the whisk and attacked the mixture in the bowl. Each ingredient added brought the batter one step closer to something better, just like each day took me one step farther from where I had started. I wasn't as delicious as cake, but I was surely an improvement on who I had been five years ago.

Ten minutes later the cake was baking and I was on my way to the shower. I got ready in the dark, easing drawers open and closed to avoid waking Jake. Unless I startled him, he wouldn't be up until well after I was gone and his first cigarette would kill any lingering vanilla in the air. Which was good, especially today. He had no idea where I went after work and the cake would raise more questions than I ever wanted to answer.

THURSDAY, OCTOBER 8TH

ON THE MORNING of his forty-ninth birthday, Edward Petrosky awoke with the remnants of liquor thick and woolly on his tongue. The dawn had brought a gray film that settled on him like fingerprint dust. He stretched, hauled on his clothes, and tripped over frayed carpet to the bathroom.

The mirror over the sink revealed a weathered forehead topped by thinning hair the color of salt and shit. In blue jeans, sneakers, and a gray button-down shirt, he probably looked more like a retired gym teacher than a detective. But that was appropriate; he hadn't felt like a detective in a long time.

Petrosky brushed the fuzz off his tongue, willing his bleary mind to connect with his legs, and headed for the kitchen. In the living room, the suede sofa sat, scuffed and battered, against one wall. Next to it stood a wooden end table, its cigarette-burned top hidden under a tattered copy of some fitness magazine he'd stolen from the dentist's office, and a half-empty (aw, hell, three-fourths-empty) bottle of Jack Daniels.

He ignored the itch to grab the bottle and hauled himself through the doorway into the kitchen, where his daughter's old princess night-light lit up the stovetop in rose. He swallowed away the ache in his chest and flicked the light switch. Cabinets that had glowed dusty pink now showed their true state, covered with nicks and dings over top of the three refinishing jobs completed at the behest of his ex-wife. She had left the month after Julie's death—before the last coat of paint had dried—still screaming: "Why can't you find who did this to her?"

Julie's thirteen-year-old body had been found broken and mangled after being ravaged for two days by feral dogs. She'd been strangled to death and discarded like a piece of trash. Petrosky had left the room before the coroner could finish with the details—probably the only reason he was still functioning at all. His ex-wife certainly hadn't helped him stay sane. Or sober.

"If we didn't live down here, this never would have happened!" had been her favorite assault because she knew it cut him deepest. And she was right. That shit happened far less to rich folks. He should have worked harder. Now he had less reason to. He fucking hated irony.

He grimaced at the cabinets and shut off the overheads. On the wall, the night-light flickered, the only candle on his pathetic cake. Petrosky grabbed his keys.

Happy birthday to me.

His unmarked Caprice smelled like stale fries, old coffee and resentment, like any respectable cop's car should. Through the windshield, the clouds were pregnant with rain—or maybe snow. You never could tell. October around Metro Detroit was a crapshoot: sometimes warm, sometimes frigid, usually miserable. In the distance, the sun peeked through heavy layers of cloud cover and bathed the street in light. But Petrosky saw the sickness the sun illuminated. The sun's rays couldn't wash away the grime that covered humanity, couldn't conceal the barbs in people's brains that led them to strangle their children, beat their wives, or leave their best friends lying in the gutter, life shimmering from their limp bodies through the manhole covers. By now, the blood underneath the city probably flowed like a hematic river.

Out the passenger window, the Ash Park precinct grew larger, two stories of the dullest dirt-colored brick, home to donuts, pigs and paperwork. On the other side of the street, a matching building proclaimed *Ash Park Detention Facility*, only partially visible behind the lake fog that crept over their tiny part of the city every morning.

He swung into the lot in front of the precinct—an acre of cement, and not one close spot. *Typical.* Stray pebbles crunched and spun from under his tires as he drove to the back of the lot and parked under a streetlamp. It blinked out for the day as he killed the engine and opened the door.

Petrosky glowered at the light and shoved his keys into his pocket. The air brushed at his cheeks with damp fingers, the wet seeping into his sneakers as he clomped toward the building.

On the sidewalk, two familiar silhouettes stood close—not close enough to arouse the suspicion of the masses, but Petrosky knew better. Shannon Taylor was a firecracker of a prosecutor with a perpetual knot of blond at the base of her neck and an ice-blue stare that could cut you in half. Severe black and white pinstripes covered a bony frame that could probably use more home-cooked meals, or at least a few donuts. She wouldn't get either of those with Curtis Morrison.

Morrison was a rookie in the detective unit and still wore pressed blue slacks, though he'd at least traded in the traditional blue uniform shirt for a black crew-necked sweater. He'd relocated from California after getting some fancy English degree. Since they'd met last year, the guy had spent their down time trying to feed Petrosky granola and hounding him to join his gym. Petrosky was perfectly content with carrying twenty years of stake-out donuts around his waist. He assumed he would continue to decline until he finally retired, and then it would be too late to give a shit anyway.

Not that he gave a shit now.

Petrosky stepped onto the curb.

"Leave my rookie alone, Taylor," he barked.

Morrison jumped like he'd heard a gunshot. He was more physically imposing than Petrosky at a chiseled six foot one, but he had a surfer-boy smile in a perpetually tanned face, and blond locks too long for any self-respecting cop. Perfect for beach going, though. All that was missing was the bong.

Taylor smirked. "That still works on him, eh?"

"Still."

Morrison grinned. "I always get jumpy when I see that ugly mug of yours."

Taylor leveled her gaze at Petrosky. "I was just filling in your better half on Gregory Thurman."

"That asshole needs to go away forever," Petrosky said.

"He won't. Few months maybe, based on the physical evidence we had. Child abuse, but not rape."

"I gave you the girl! What the hell happened?"

"She told *you* he raped her every day for five years. But she won't tell me, and she sure as hell won't tell a jury."

"Fuck." Petrosky glanced at a stray piece of concrete near his shoe. He fought the urge to kick it.

"You have a way of getting female vics to talk, Petrosky. If you figure out a way to keep them talking, let me know."

Petrosky glared at her. In his peripheral, Morrison opened his mouth, closed it again, and looked at his shoes.

Taylor adjusted her bun and brushed imaginary lint off her suit jacket. "Speaking of talking, I've got a date with a working girl later. She'll serve some time. Keeps asking for you, Petrosky. Says you bailed her out before, thinks you'll do it again."

"I didn't do shit."

"You don't even know her name."

"I plead the fifth."

"I have the paperwork."

"I'm sure she was innocent that time. And anyways, sex isn't a crime."

"It is if you get paid for it." Taylor glared at him. "And it's dangerous. If we get them off the streets, we can help them."

"How very utopian. But it isn't her fault when someone else is abusing—"

"I prosecute the abusers too."

"Right. Sometimes." Petrosky's phone buzzed in his back pocket. He ignored it in favor of watching Taylor's left eye twitch.

"If you want out of sex crimes, bailing out working girls is the way to do it," she said.

"Who says I want out of sex crimes?"

Taylor crossed her arms as Petrosky's back pocket buzzed again. He snatched out the phone, glanced at the text message and jerked his head from Morrison to the direction of the parking lot. "We've got a call. Get moving, California."

Morrison nodded goodbye to Taylor and stepped off the curb. Petrosky followed.

"I'll be down in a little while to get your working girl, Taylor," he called over his shoulder. "Do me a favor and have her ready, would ya? And remind her to put the wrong address on her paperwork so she's harder to find when she skips bail."

"Fuck you, Petrosky." Her heels clacked away until the only sounds against the pavement were Petrosky's sneakers and Morrison's rubber-soled somethings, probably made out of hemp or whatever the hell they made shoes out of in California.

"Consorting with the enemy, Surfer Boy?"

"She's on our side, Boss."

"That she is. But she's still a fucking lawyer."

"I guess." Morrison didn't look convinced. "So what kind of call did we get?"

"Some kids found something over on Old Mill. If we hurry we'll beat the medical examiner."

THE CEMETERY WAS in an older part of town where residents had started demolishing abandoned homes and raking up the dirt to plant gardens. Across the street, a defunct workout facility sat next to a Chinese food restaurant, each furthering the need for the other, yet both one step away from being turned into a cabbage patch.

Petrosky parked in the road. The entrance gate to the cemetery hung from one hinge and shrieked as Morrison pulled it open. Petrosky winced. *Whispering Willows, my ass.* The gravestones were cracked and crumbling, etched with faded epitaphs about the beloved deceased: *William Bishop, forever in our hearts*, though the barren grounds around the plots suggested that poor Mr. Bishop had been very much forgotten. Through the fog, toward the center of the grounds, stood a small stone building—a poor man's Taj Mahal.

Crime techs milled about in the brown grass outside the building, tweezing bits of dirt and leaves into baggies. One—a kid with insect eyes and boy band hair—saw Petrosky and Morrison and waved them over. "You won't be able to get in with anyone else. It's pretty small."

Hooker heels and a tiny swath of cloth, maybe a tube top, lay discarded outside the door. Probably the reason they'd called him. Sex crime or not, no one else cared about prostitutes.

Petrosky ducked into the building. The air was thick, heavy with the tang of metal and rotting meat and other noxious fumes he didn't want to consider. A row of tiny doors the size of apartment mailboxes, presumably niches for ashes, lined the back wall, keeping silent vigil over the cement room. Below the niches sat a waist-high stone table on concrete pillars, probably used for flowers. But there were no flowers today. Only the girl.

She was on her back on the slab, arms and legs bent awkwardly and tied together between the table legs. Her swollen tongue protruded over blackening lips that pulsed as if she were trying to talk, but that was only the maggots, writhing in her mouth. It had been a few days. How long exactly would be determined by the medical examiner, but he was guessing at least four or five days based on the lack of rigor mortis and the blisters on her marbled skin. Deep gouges that looked more like knife wounds than split flesh scored her arms and legs. Someone had beaten her badly before killing her. If she had been untied then, they'd at least get some skin samples if she had slashed him with her nails.

Someone's baby girl. Petrosky's stomach roiled and he patted his front pocket for a spare antacid but came up empty. He inhaled through his nose and clenched his jaw.

The knife wounds continued onto her torso. Her abdomen had been torn apart. On top of her thighs lay coils of intestine, some of them shredded like strips of bacon. Another organ, black and jelly-like, sat on her chest, the side wall torn, fluids oozing from beneath it.

Petrosky bent to examine the restraints binding her wrists and ankles. Metal cuffs, easy to come by, though forensics would have more on the specifics later. Dark stains dripped over the slab and onto the floor, which appeared clean, or at least bore no discernible prints. She had bled a great deal in that little room. Hopefully she had been unconscious.

From the doorway behind Petrosky, Morrison's camera phone clicked. "Holy shit."

Petrosky straightened. "Suck it up, California, this is the job." Not that Surfer Boy would be getting the full brunt of the smell halfway outside the room.

"Got it, Boss." Morrison aimed the phone again and snapped a photo of the letters on the right wall, inky and dripping.

A boat beneath a sunny sky

> Lingering onward dreamily
> In an evening in July-

"Is that paint?" Morrison asked.

"I doubt it." Petrosky backed out into the cool, muggy air.

"Detective!" The bug-eyed tech stood near the corner of the building, holding out two plastic bags. "Got a purse with I.D. We're dusting the area now."

Petrosky noted the purse, laying on the ground next to a tube of lip balm and a pen. "Needles?"

"No, sir."

"Pills?"

"No, sir. Just some condoms, a little makeup. And this." He held up one of the bags.

Petrosky peered through the clear plastic. "Meredith Lawrence. Morrison, you got your notebook?"

"You know it, Boss."

"Seventy-three eleven Hoffsteader, apartment one-G." Petrosky nodded to the tech and headed up the path toward the car.

Morrison fell into step beside Petrosky, hippie shoes squishing through the grass. "You think it's like ... a psychopath?"

"Maybe. He's calculating. Aggressive. Not what you'd normally see in a crime of passion. I think we can be certain that he took her here to kill her since he had the cuffs. And there aren't any clear signs of struggle around the building. Even the clothes by the door are in one piece. Either she knew him and trusted him enough to follow him in, or she was already unconscious when they got here."

"What would motivate someone to—to cut her open like that?"

Petrosky shrugged. "Whatever she did, she didn't deserve this."

"I can't imagine anyone does."

Petrosky ground his teeth and studied the mournful clouds.

THURSDAY, OCTOBER 8TH

It's okay, Hannah. Just breathe.
  I breathed. It didn't help. Probably because there was a big difference between entering employee files into a computer database and telling someone to get the hell out.
  The paperwork rustled with a thick swoosh that sounded like the whisper of a thousand jerks before me getting rid of inconvenient people. It was the swoosh of the executioner's axe over Marie Antoinette, the swoosh of Hitler throwing a swastika like a ninja dagger at a disobedient soldier. Though I was probably nicer than Hitler. I hoped.
  I pulled the phone to my ear and punched in the numbers. "Mr. Turner?" My voice quavered. *Darn it.* "We need to see you down in HR … yes, I will meet you here … Thank you." Clunk went the phone receiver, like Marie Antoinette's head.
  Turner was one of seventy or so engineers the Harwick Technical contract house employed, and one of thousands we contracted out worldwide. He would be at my desk in five minutes, or as long as it took to get from his floor of big projects and design deadlines to my tiny piece of Hell.
  Human resources: where happiness goes to die.
  I rustled through the papers one last time, stood, and took a step toward the entrance of my office.
  Well, not really an office. Unlike in the rest of the building, where you could touch your neighbor from your desk, the cubicles here were spaced for privacy—little islands in each corner further segregated by chest-high opaque acrylic. The partitions were low enough that you could still see who picked their nose while they typed. You could also tell who liked their dogs, who had children, and who was in that awkward

in-between phase where a new child made a previously devout pet owner decide that it was just a stupid dog after all, leaving them to tuck Chihuahua pictures behind fresh shots of chubby babies. Maybe it made them feel less guilty about their shifting priorities.

The wall to the side of my desk was covered by an old cork board. I had put it there just in case I ever got a dog, though worrying about Jake was enough for now. On my side of the room, my best and only friend Noelle stared at the computer in her corner. Across the room from Noelle, Ralph's bookish glasses wobbled as he attacked an acne eruption on his cheek. In the corner behind Ralph, Tony was nearly invisible, his chalky skin and pale blond hair disappearing into the white of the room. I had never spoken to him, not once in four years. When I'd first started at Harwick, I tried smiling at him, but he swiveled his chair away. Noelle had said he was autistic—but maybe I just had spinach in my teeth. Neither would have surprised me.

The only other person in the room was Jerome, the security guard, who was summoned on an as-needed basis to our part of the building. His ebony skin and shaved head glistened under the fluorescent lights. I often wondered how much trouble I would get into if I were to rub his head like a shiny Buddha, but I didn't have the guts to find out.

Jerome watched the door, Noelle watched the computer, Ralph glanced at the fingers he'd pulled from his pimply face, and none of them noticed me and my shaking hands. Maybe I had already started to fade.

Through the glass wall between my office and the hallway, David Turner approached the door. Turner was tall, with protruding eyes, a beak-like nose, and thin lips pulled into an uneven line. In contrast to his unimpressive face, his gray suit and tie were neatly pressed and impeccably matched. He strode with the confident gait of a man who knew his own worth.

He would not maintain that confidence for long; they never did. It was like watching a balloon deflate every time. I usually deflated with them, leaving me feeling spent and hollow.

Turner pulled the door open and looked at the other workers, who steadfastly pretended not to hear him or know why he was there. Clearly unaware of the nature of my job, he smiled at me and marched to my cubicle.

I drew myself up to my full five-foot-four inches. I wished I were taller. Magic beans. I needed magic beans. Or an earthquake. I paused, hoping for some catastrophe to strike, so someone else could pick this up later. Nothing.

Figures. Way to go, Michigan.

He sat, and I did too, lest I end up looking like even more of an overbearing asshole. My heart scampered around like a pissed-off weasel. I cleared my throat, readying my speech from the training manual script. "Mr. Turner, unfortunately your services are no longer needed. As of today, you will no longer be an employee of Harwick Technical Solutions. We will mail your final paycheck to the address on file. You will have fifteen minutes to gather your belongings and make your way to the parking lot. Security will assist you."

The color drained from Turner's face. "But ... I haven't had any complaints since I've been here. I have a wife, two kids. There must be a mistake."

I averted my eyes, hoping he'd think I was giving him time to process, but my motivations were selfish: I needed to focus on something else before my heart blew up. In the middle of the desk was a corner of paper I must have torn from the folder earlier in a subconscious attempt to curb my anxiety. Across the top of the desk, the three ceramic owls that usually stared at me quizzically were glaring like I had shit on their waffles. My favorite was a horned owl missing an ear. I had stowed the ear in a desk drawer, intending to glue it back on, but had since decided I rather preferred his one-eared imperfection. Plus, it made him look less smug.

"Is there anything I can do?" Turner's voice cut into my owl assessment. "If I understood the problem..."

I blinked. His frustration was palpable, his fists clenched, and I resisted the urge to duck. A bruise on my arm throbbed.

You've got this, Hannah. You're okay.

Turner's eyes flicked to the security guard.

I followed his stare, relieved to see we had Jerome's full attention. Jerome always made me feel safer, like he could somehow shield me from anything that might come through the doors. If only he could protect me from the psychos in my past. My heart lurched drunkenly against my breastbone.

Jerome approached the cubicle. "Mr. Turner, you will have to come with me." His voice was the texture of wet silk.

Turner stood slowly.

I pushed the papers toward him. "I need your signature at the bottom of this form."

Turner signed it, barely glancing at the few lines of text, and walked from the cubicle toward the main doors. In seconds, he was eclipsed by Jerome, the guard's gleaming bald head the sun to Turner's gray misshapen moon.

I took a few deep breaths. Human resources wasn't the perfect job for me, but the guards and the locked entrance made it safe enough. And it was far, far away from ... *him*.

Lovers ain't nothin' once they go south. I couldn't remember where I had heard that, but it was more poignant than most of the nonsensical songs about true love and happiness and beauty and bullshit.

I looked at the clock in the lower corner of my computer screen. Half an hour. Would my chest palpitations ever relent? Maybe I should pound on my breastbone, gorilla style, to subdue my heart. But I'd just end up looking like an idiot.

"Hannah?" Noelle leaned over the partition. Her blond hair floated in silk strands over blue eyes and full lips made even more supple by pinkish gloss. Men followed her with their eyes, if not their actual penises.

Even I couldn't help staring at her sometimes.

I forced a smile and moved my hand from my chest to the desktop before Noelle thought I was playing with my boobs.

"I'm going to grab a coffee, then take some dismissal forms back to the filing room," she said. "Do you have any more?"

"Sure do. I'm the most popular person here today. As long as popular means everyone wants to punch you in the throat."

Turner's dismissal papers required my signature as the bearer of bad news. It was like signing a death certificate, as if before that moment, nothing had happened that couldn't be taken back. Adding the final signature always made me feel like the biggest douchebag. Maybe coroners felt like that too, with their endless parade of dead-on-arrival cadavers.

I scrawled my name on the form.

Rest in peace, Turner.

Stop thinking crazy shit and say something.

I looked at Noelle. "I like the pink gloss, by the way. It looks like you blew a dude made out of cotton candy." *Crisis averted.*

"Cotton candy doesn't talk back. Hey, you going to the company picnic tomorrow?"

"Oh ... yeah, I think so."

Noelle squinted at me. "What's up with you? You look like someone just killed your dog."

"I don't have a dog."

"Something happen with Jake?"

I pulled my sleeve over my wrist, folded the cuff into my palm and tucked my fists into my lap. My sweaty handprint remained on the desk top.

"Did he find a job yet?"

Is littering the house with fast food wrappers a job?

Noelle stared at me.

"No. It's not Jake. It's just ... this." I nudged Turner's termination papers on the desk.

Noelle nodded, her silver earrings swinging. "You want to go out somewhere tonight? It'll take your mind off of it."

"Nah, I told Jake I'd be home early."

Noelle's eyes darkened, and my breakfast skittered around in my stomach.

"Soon, okay?" I said.

"Sure. Here, I'll take those papers." She smiled and I watched her go, swaying her hips to unseen music.

I turned back to my computer and glanced again at the clock. Twenty more minutes and I'd be on my way home to the man I loved, or at least, was pretty sure I loved. And he loved me back, as long as I didn't make him mad, which happened more than I wanted to admit. But he was the lesser of two evils. No matter how much of an asshole Jake was, he wouldn't kill me. That had to be enough since I couldn't take Jerome home. Maybe I did need a dog. Not a Chihuahua though. Those things are yappy jerks.

I set my jaw, pulled the keyboard closer and went back to work.

DOMINIC HARWICK SAT at his desk, his manicured fingers tapping on the keyboard as he finished reviewing the newest batch of engineering resumes. It was a menial task, beneath him, but it was necessary; each individual represented a dollar amount he would not forget.

He had begun a startup engineering staffing firm fresh out of Harvard. When the recession hit, he put his inheritance to work for him, buying up property in California, Texas and New York. But he'd finally settled on Michigan as his home, unable to convince himself to abandon the glorious buyer's market that had developed in the blighted Detroit Metro area. A few years later, Harwick Technical Solutions had acquired international acclaim by securing a staffing contract from a large aeronautical corporation, prompting local papers to ask, *What Recession?* when covering the construction of his ultra-modern, four story contract house.

His father would have been proud, though he'd have gotten nothing more than a curt nod from Rupert Harwick. Dominic could still picture his stocky legs, his barrel chest and the salt and pepper hair he had kept buzzed close to his scalp. Even if he had let it grow, no one would have dared call him anything other than 'Colonel,' 'Mr. Harwick,' or 'Sir'.

Dominic reviewed the last resume, made a note, and shut down the computer. The screen lowered into a special compartment inside the desk, leaving the opaque glass desktop perfectly pristine. Across the room, leather-bound books sat next to gleaming modern sculptures on custom glass shelves, all now cast in the orange glow of twilight from the floor-to-ceiling windows behind the desk. An oil painting of Duke, his Great Dane, hung beside a door of the thickest oak money could buy.

While the rest of the building was full of glass walls and low partitions to encourage openness and cooperation, his office was shut away from everything and protected by a bulldog-like secretary who let no one enter without his approval. An army of assistants kept his life just as he wanted it: uncomplicated, predictable, and efficient.

Dominic glanced at his Rolex, stood, and walked to the window. On the glass near his right hand, a smudge left behind by the cleaning crew sullied his view. He frowned.

Distasteful.

Dominic peered past the offensive blemish. Below him, a large employee parking lot ended in an expanse of rolling hills that sloped down to meet the water. By day, he could see the lake peeking from behind the tall oaks, maples, and firs that surrounded the five-acre complex. At dusk, the west-facing windows provided an overture to day's end. But these were not the reasons he had chosen this space for his office.

For several minutes, all was quiet. Then he saw him.

David Turner emerged from the building carrying the contents of his desk, his jacket, and, from the look of his hunched shoulders, his pride. He fumbled with his keys, popped the trunk of his car and hoisted the box into the back. As he closed the trunk, he wiped his eyes with the back of his hand.

Yesterday, Dominic had overheard Turner bragging to a fellow worker about his track record at the company.

"Six years of service," Turner had said, "and not one complaint."

People who got too comfortable became unimaginative workhorses and rarely came up with anything new. They were bad for business. Sometimes when Dominic fired people like that they seemed relieved, leading him to suspect an inherent boredom with their daily tasks. Turner did not strike him as that type of person, but Dominic suspected the man had some type of emotional connection to the company beyond a simple paycheck, something that would keep him there regardless of his motivational level. And he knew it wasn't Turner's wife, whose makeup-covered split lip at a fundraiser last week spoke volumes about her ability to influence her husband.

Turner would have no trouble landing another job, and quickly at that. Yet, the man was crying. If allowed to, he would have stayed well past his usefulness.

The idea made Dominic's back tense. He turned from the window, plucked his briefcase off the floor, and left the office, each step on the open stainless steel staircase echoing his departure like a drum roll.

Near the bottom floor, another set of footsteps sounded. He paused in the stairwell and watched as Hannah Montgomery appeared around the bend and hurried toward the glass doors to the parking lot, hair flying behind her, feet tapping at a nervous pace against the tile. Despite her constant deer-in-headlights demeanor, he had never once regretted hiring her. She was quick. Predictable. Reliable. Efficient.

Unlike Turner. Dominic smiled and continued down the stairs.

She startled at the sound of his footsteps and dropped her purse. By the time Dominic reached her, she was on her knees scooping items back into her bag. Practical things: a wallet, car keys, sunglasses. She avoided his gaze as he bent and handed her a standard issue blue checkbook. Their fingers touched. She snapped her hand away as if he had shocked her.

They stood and she shouldered the bag.

"How are you this evening, Ms. Montgomery?"

She met his eyes, then looked at her shoes. "I'm fine."

She was an intriguing girl.

"I got your email the other day in response to my request for new ideas in staffing recruitment. You had some great suggestions."

She looked at him again, and this time her eyes lingered on his face. "Really? I mean, thank you, Mr. Harwick."

"I am already implementing some of them. As you know, I believe that the people who work for me are the lifeblood of this company. There's nothing more crucial to its continued success than quality hires. I'm glad to have people like you on the team."

Her face and neck reddened, as did the small swath of chest near her clavicle. "Thank you, sir."

"Have a great night, Ms. Montgomery." He watched her disappear through the glass doors to the parking lot and headed for his private garage below the building.

Hannah. It was a lovely name. He wondered if her skin felt as satiny as it looked.

DOMINIC WAS STILL CONSIDERING her when his Aston Martin crunched up the limestone drive to his expansive home of white concrete and glass. In front of the house, life-sized marble nudes looked forlornly over the grounds amidst a sea of lilies and vibrant red bee balm on its last blush of the year. Not a single weed, as it should be.

He entered through the mudroom and removed his shoes to avoid marring the white marble floors that ran the length of the first level. The lights flickered on as he strode past a roomy half bath, through the kitchen, and into the living room, where a four foot high blown glass sculpture in blue sat on an iron table between convex white leather sofas. No coffee table. A television was hidden in the ceiling, though he usually had better things to do with his time. The Colonel had admonished those who spent their days on frivolous pursuits. Not that Dominic had ever argued with him about it.

He took the open steel staircase at the back to the second floor master suite which was as open as the first floor, save for a bathroom and a gym at the back. He changed his clothes, returned to the mudroom to tie on running shoes, and took the door to the back porch.

Like everything else, the black paint on the porch was a conscious decision—even the door to the outdoor bathroom where he cleaned off after running was the same deep, sooty color of his Great Dane.

Duke had been a pup when Dominic had taken him from his dying father. Nothing makes a man more trustworthy than a dog, the Colonel had said. As always, his father had been spot on.

Instead of running circles around his four acres of meandering waterfront property, Dominic jogged through the gate, down his drive and into the road. Duke followed at his heel, keeping pace through the quiet streets as the sun painted the sky with stripes of violet and fuchsia.

A young mother pushing a baby carriage piled high with blankets smiled at him as he passed. He nodded in her direction. A few blocks later, an elderly man tending to some end-of-season gardening gave him a friendly wave. Dominic waved back and the chill air kissed his exposed hands.

A few blocks from his home, open wrought iron gates welcomed him into the neighborhood park. The breeze off the manmade duck pond brought with it the scent of dead and dying cattails, and with them, the memories of summers on Lake Michigan, his father at the helm of their sailboat.

He headed toward the pond, watching the withered grass along the side of the walk. Winter was coming early, but Dominic felt no anticipation for the upcoming holidays. There would be no tree, no gifts, no family gatherings. Those days were gone.

As he passed a wide curve in the path, a woman came into view. She leaned over to stretch her legs, her spandex pants leaving nothing to the imagination. Diamond and amethyst rings sparkled on her fingers and a small dog yipped around her heels on a ridiculously tiny leash.

Dominic did not recognize her face or the perfectly symmetrical breasts that swelled under her zippered top. She must live elsewhere, and from the way her gaze lingered on his expensive running gear, he guessed she probably lived in a less affluent subdivision.

He ran past her, three steps, four steps, five, giving her time to start running, then glanced back and feigned surprise, both that she was still watching him and that he had been so unfortunately caught in his stolen look. He turned his face forward again and slowed his pace to match the *thwap thwap* of her approaching sneakers behind him. She bumped his elbow. Cheap perfume and another, undeniably female scent cut the earthy aroma of decaying foliage. Her lipsticked mouth turned up at the corners, playing coy.

He didn't buy it. "Hello," he said.

"Hi."

Their sneakers beat blithely against the pavement.

"Do you run here often?" she asked.

She was into clichés. He could do that.

"Yes, Duke here seems to love it. Well, that and the lovely animals he finds to play with."

Nothing made a man more trustworthy than a dog.

"Yeah, Tootsie enjoys that as well." She gestured to the tiny dog at her heel, scrambling to keep up.

Tootsie. He kept his grimace to himself.

"How about you? Do you like the view out here?" She winked.

Dominic tried not to sigh at the stale innuendo. "Yes. I have a thing for Pisces women."

Her eyes widened. "How did you—"

"Something in the elegant way you carry yourself." *And the birthstones on your fingers.* "Sorry if I was staring, but you are exceptional."

She smiled. She liked that.

They always did.

TWO MILES AND A SHOWER LATER, Dominic took her out to a small Italian bistro. Women were all the same in the way they expected him to impress them. He did not disappoint. He bought her wine while he drank sparkling water and regaled her with witty anecdotes and tales spun to show how interesting he was, with an emphasis on his financial success. When dinner was over he stifled a yawn and took her back to her house, ten miles from the park.

"I don't usually do this," she whispered as she pulled him through the front door.

They always said that. Why, he wasn't sure. It wasn't as if it would alter the outcome—or what he thought of her.

He watched her carefully, determining her likes and dislikes before she verbalized them. It was basic science, the flush of blood in certain areas of the body, subtle arching, accelerated respiration. When she began to scream his name, he pushed her further, heightening the experience to an art form as he drove himself into her. He raised his face to the window as she panted her way through her orgasm.

Later, as she slept, he went into her bathroom. Soap scum ringed the tub. Spots blemished the mirror. He stepped into the shower, turned the water to scalding, and scrubbed his body until his skin was raw. Then he pulled on his clothes without drying himself and walked out of the house. By the time he climbed into his car, her name was barely a memory.

FRIDAY, OCTOBER 9TH

PETROSKY GRIMACED at the man in front of him.

Preliminary research indicated that Meredith Lawrence didn't have much in the way of friends, jobs or family. All she had was recently eviscerated organs, her blood on a mausoleum wall and this asshole in the doorway.

"What do you mean she's dead?" Ronnie Keil stood blocking the front door of his apartment, staring blankly through Petrosky with the beady eyes of a reptile. The sweet haze of recently smoked marijuana wafted around Keil's pasty face from the room behind him.

"Mr. Keil, I know this must be difficult for you, but we need to ask you a few questions about your girlfriend."

"Questions about what? I didn't do it."

Petrosky exchanged a glance with Morrison. "No one said you did. But, we do need to know where you were yesterday. You sure weren't here."

Keil's snaggletooth scraped against his fat bottom lip. "I worked all day at the shipyard. After that I went to the bar on Rosenthall for my cousin's birthday."

Petrosky had verified Keil's work information the day before. "What's your cousin's name?"

"Gerald."

"Last name?"

"Keil, same as mine."

"Phone number?"

He told them.

Morrison flipped a page in his notebook.

"Tell me about Meredith. Anything you think might help," Petrosky said.

Keil's eyes were blank, more than marijuana stoned. Pills, downers, maybe. Down the hall, a door slammed and someone cursed. Morrison glanced toward the sound. Keil stared, slack-jawed.

"Mr. Keil? What can you tell me about Meredith?"

"Oh uh ... she was real pretty. Nice to most people unless they looked at her the wrong way."

"Had she mentioned meeting anyone new recently?"

"I don't think so." He paused. "She was kinda bitchy sometimes. You think someone killed her for that?"

"I doubt it," Petrosky said. "Did she ever go out to clubs?"

"Nah, nothing like that. She mostly just hung around here. Do you think it was someone she ... like ... knew already?"

"We're just covering all the bases, sir."

"Oh, well, she didn't know that many people anyway."

"Did she have any family? Any friends?"

"Her mama died when she was little. Never had a daddy."

No daddy. Not that a daddy would have been able to save her. Petrosky popped his knuckles against his hip and grimaced at the empty pocket where he used to carry his cigarettes. "No parents? Was she in foster care in Michigan?"

"Yeah. I dunno for how long or where, she didn't talk about it."

"How long were you together?"

Keil looked at the ceiling, thinking. "Maybe four years. Not quite."

"And in all that time she never mentioned where she grew up?"

He scuffed his foot on threadbare carpet. "Once she said she had a foster father who beat her up, and she ran away. That was before she met me."

"Brothers, sisters?"

"Just the kid but she hasn't seen him since we gave him up."

"A kid?" Petrosky's eyes snapped to Morrison. Morrison shrugged and shook his head. "What kid?"

"She was pregnant when we met. Had the kid, kept it here for a little, but she wasn't cut out for that. She took him to the church downtown, I think. The one where they have the orphanage."

"What was the child's name?"

"She called him Jessie, but I don't know if it stuck. He was only a few weeks old."

Morrison's pen scratched frantically against the notepad.

"The date?"

"No idea. Late August, maybe? September? She talked about needing to get the kid warmer clothes because it was getting cold. But we didn't, just put him in a blanket with all these little ducks on it and then she took him." His bottom lip quivered. Either the drugs were wearing off, or the police presence was shocking Keil into sobriety. Or he felt guilty about the kid.

"Who was the father?"

Keil swiped at his eyes. "No idea. She didn't either."

"So, a boy. And she took him to the church?"

"Yeah the big one right down the way. With all those troll things. I think it was the only one she could take him to. Not all of 'em take kids." He sagged against the door frame. "She's really dead?"

"Yes, sir."

"Like, dead, dead? I just thought she found an overnight. She was happy when she got one of those."

"I'm sorry for your loss."

"Aw, shit." Keil put a hand to his chest.

"Do you need to sit down?"

Keil lowered his hand to the doorframe and gripped it until the knuckles turned white, but he shook his head. "No. I'm okay."

"We'll make this as quick as possible, Mr. Keil. We need to know where she was the night before last. Who she was with."

"Working." Keil glanced at the wall and dragged his eyes to the floor, looking everywhere but at them.

"Mr. Keil, we have no doubt she was working the street. What I need to know from you is where she was standing when someone picked her up and killed her."

Keil's jaw worked, but sluggishly. "I'm not sure. Maybe Ventura? She was usually up there. If she went anywhere else, I dunno."

"Tell me about the overnights."

"Every now and then someone would pay her for the night, to stay there. Rich assholes with hotel rooms, I think. She always came home not worried about money for a day or so."

"Any idea who they were?"

He shrugged. "No, it was never the same person."

"When was the last time that happened?"

"It's been months."

"She have friends that she hung out with? Anyone you knew?"

Keil shook his head.

"How did she not have any friends?" Morrison asked.

Petrosky cleared his throat and kept his eyes on Keil. "Often in domestic violence situations, women are isolated from their friends and family in order to keep them from revealing the situation."

Keil stared at Petrosky, but said nothing. Morrison turned back to his notepad.

"Anyone she might have seen that night?"

"I don't know, man."

"Where were you the night before last between the hours of twelve and three a.m.?"

"Um ... I think I was here."

"Anyone with you?"

Keil looked over Petrosky's shoulder, into the hallway. "Yeah... uh ... Darcy."

"Last name?"

"Evans."

"Who is she?"

"A ... friend."

"Meredith know you had a special friend, Mr. Keil?"

He stared.

"Did your girlfriend like poetry?" The bloody poem on the mausoleum wall was a wild card Petrosky didn't want leaked, but Keil would be too nervous to tell the press ... if he even remembered the question later.

Keil's eyebrows lifted. "Poetry?" He shoved his hands in his pockets. Keil probably had cigarettes. He'd probably let Petrosky bum one.

Petrosky narrowed his eyes. "Where does Darcy live?"

Keil raised an arm, feebly pointing to a door three apartments down from his. "Wait ... uh, just wait a little, man. Her husband's home. Saw his car out the window."

"That doesn't bother me any," Petrosky said.

Keil's jaw dropped. He took the card Petrosky offered, but his eyes darted nervously toward the door across the hall.

"Sorry for your loss."

Keil looked once more down the hall and closed the door. The lock clicked into place.

"What do you think, Boss?" Morrison asked as they walked toward the other end of the hallway.

"He's a dick, but he's telling the truth. Popping pills and coming off downers will make a person honest, if not a little confused. Good for us. He mentioned her overnights, then freaked out when we asked what she did. And the kid thing ... he'll probably regret sharing that when he sobers up. We'll find out in a minute if his alibi checks out."

"I liked the way you snuck the poem in." Morrison lifted the knocker and dropped it. In a neighboring unit, a dog barked and someone yelled at it to shut the fuck up.

The man who answered the door dwarfed them both, his dark shoulders as wide as the doorframe, button-down shirt stretched over biceps that would make Hulk Hogan jealous.

"Afternoon, sir." Petrosky flashed his badge. "I'm Detective Petrosky with the Ash Park PD. I'm looking for a Darcy Evans."

The man's brows furrowed but he backed up and waved them in. "Of course, officers. Come in."

A black leather sofa sat against one wall beside a gleaming glass table with a Tiffany lamp that looked nice enough to be real.

"Darcy! Some visitors for you!"

Petrosky studied a series of black-and-white photographs on the wall that appeared to be the insides of abandoned buildings. *Interesting.* Perhaps they had some photos of abandoned mausoleums.

Petrosky turned from the wall as a woman emerged from the back room, her black hair braided in neat rows. Her smile faded when she saw the badge. "Isaiah, what's going on?"

Isaiah shrugged his beefy shoulders.

"We're looking for information on Meredith Lawrence, your neighbor across the hall," Petrosky said.

Evans's shoulders relaxed. "Oh thank God. I thought someone had died."

"She did, ma'am."

Evans covered her mouth with her palm.

Morrison stepped forward, touching Petrosky's elbow. "Do you think we should do this in private?"

Her hand dropped to her chest. "Why?"

"Because it concerns Mr. Keil," Petrosky said.

Evans shrugged. "I don't know what you're getting at, but there are no secrets between me and my husband."

"Then let's jump right in," Petrosky said. "Ms. Evans, were you with Mr. Keil the night before last, between the hours of twelve and three?"

"In a manner of speaking—if you count him lying passed out in the hallway and me trying to wake him every twenty minutes as being together. I finally got Isaiah around three and he helped me get him into the house and onto his own couch. Though I think he slept through that part."

"Mr. Keil seemed more than a little concerned about me coming over here today."

"I can take this one," Isaiah said. "The one time we spoke, I told him that he needed to get his shit together and stop worrying my wife before I came after him. I wasn't ... serious. I just hate to see her upset. She'll sit up all night, thinking he's going to die of an overdose outside our door."

"Did you know Meredith Lawrence?"

Isaiah shook his head. "Not at all."

Darcy sighed. "Not really, just in passing. We talked occasionally in the laundry room, but it was mostly complaining about the laundry machines not working and stuff. She was usually coming in when I was going out to work."

"And you work where?"

"I'm a photographer. I keep weird hours sometimes. Just ask my poor husband. He usually comes home for lunch so we can spend some time together."

Isaiah put his hand on the small of her back.

"What do you do, sir?"

"Molecular biologist."

Petrosky glanced around the apartment.

"You want to know why we live here? With guys like Keil? Student loans. We're saving for a house. And Darcy wants to write a book."

"Anything else you can tell us about Meredith, Mr. Evans? Mrs. Evans?" Petrosky watched them as the silence stretched, but there were no sudden shifts in movement, no alterations in breathing, no wandering eyes. Only slouched shoulders and furrowed brows—worry, but not defensiveness.

"The only thing I can think of that was different is that she seemed ... sad," Darcy said finally. "Not a normal life stressor kind of thing, but real, deep sad. Something in her eyes. I take lots of pictures, so I notice that stuff. I just wish I knew why."

Isaiah wrapped his arm around her shoulders and pulled her to him.

Petrosky held out a card. "If you think of anything else–"

"Thank you. I hope you find who did it," she said.

Isaiah opened the door for them.

"We'll do our best, ma'am," Petrosky said.

TWO MORE HOURS of door knocking gave them nothing new. Apparently, Meredith Lawrence had been invisible. Hopefully her baby wouldn't be so elusive. If they could find the baby's father, all the better, particularly if he felt that Lawrence took his child from him. If Petrosky ever found the person who took his little girl, he'd do worse than slice them open and paint the walls with their blood.

Morrison clicked his seat belt. "So anyone can just drop off a baby and leave?"

"Safe Haven laws. You leave a baby in a safe place, like a fire station or a church instead of a dumpster, and you're not under obligation to answer questions. After a few months your parental rights are terminated and they set the kid up for adoption. Don't they have those laws in California? You'd think surfers would be first in line to drop off kids so they could get back to playing ukulele or whatever the fuck you people do."

"Yeah, they have the laws. But I never played ukulele, so I never paid much attention."

Petrosky ignored the smile in Morrison's voice and watched the sky roll around them, the clouds heavy and dark. He glanced at the temperature gauge on the dash. Forty-two. No snow today. Rain. Tomorrow was supposed to be warm, and when the sun came out, everyone would grin and talk about how glorious the weather was for October, as if this didn't happen every goddamn year.

Beside him, Morrison tapped on his phone as the church came into view. Through the windshield, gargoyles reached for the sky on stone spires above church doors that looked too massive for human use. Petrosky wondered if maybe you had to build 'em big to invite God in, but he wouldn't know anything about that; God had abandoned him a long time ago.

Petrosky pulled into the parking lot and took a space in front of the main door. Their footfalls crunched against the grand stone stairs. Above them, stripes of stained glass arched toward the thunderclouds, reflecting muted blues and greens and pinks. Morrison pulled the front door open with a *whoosh* and Petrosky followed him in.

The air inside burned with the sickly sweet aroma of incense. Walls and windows repeated their footsteps back to them as they walked between the rows of pews toward the altar.

A door opened and shut behind the pulpit. A bald, rotund man with white eyebrows approached them, shoving his glasses up his bulbous nose, a white robe and long purple scarf swishing in his wake. "Can I help you gentlemen?" His voice was whisper quiet, perhaps a testament to years of sitting in a confessional.

Petrosky flipped his badge and stuck it back in his pocket. "I'm Detective Petrosky, and this is Detective Morrison. We're looking for information on a child that may have been dropped off here three years ago."

"Dropped off?"

"Part of the Safe Haven law."

The man pushed his glasses up his nose. "I see. Why don't you gentlemen follow me to my office and we'll see if there is any way I can help you." He turned, and they followed him through a back hallway, past ornate bronze and gold fixtures and oak walls glistening with furniture polish. At the last door, he stopped, unlocked it and waved them in.

An intricately carved oak desk dominated the red-carpeted room. On the top corner of the desk sat gold-plated wax stamps, blotters and sheets of rolled parchment. Stained glass windows bounced chartreuse light off a gilded Jesus crucified on the back wall, wrists bleeding gold, mouth agape in an eternal scream.

"Quite the place you have here," Petrosky said.

The priest lifted one corner of his mouth and settled behind his desk, pressing his fingertips together. Petrosky and Morrison sat in red wingbacks across from him. The chairs felt like satin. From the roof above, the muted rattle of rain began and intensified until it rang through the room like buckshot on tin.

"As you surely know, gentlemen, those who leave their children with us are not required to give information, and often don't."

"Understood. We're just hoping."

"For what exactly? Most of these children have gone on to successful placements with adoptive parents, some within this very congregation."

"We're not looking to take the child back," Petrosky said dryly. "His mother was slit open from end to end and we have reason to suspect that the father may be responsible."

The priest's jaw fell open and his hands dropped into his lap.

"Your name, sir? For our records," Petrosky said.

"Ernest Bannerman the third. Father Bannerman to our parishioners."

"Mr. Bannerman, can we get a look at those records?"

The priest pushed himself to standing and walked to a squat file cabinet in the back corner of the room. He slid out the bottom drawer, retrieved several thick folders, and returned to the desk where he flipped the top one open.

"We haven't had many, that's for sure. We've been lucky, I suppose. Only about twenty since the law came into existence." He scanned the top sheet, turning it over on the desk. "Do you know if you're looking for a boy or a girl?"

"A boy. Jessie. About three years ago, late summer or early fall."

"Ah." Bannerman replaced the page, closed the top folder and slid it and the second folder onto the desk. The bottom folder rasped as he pulled the top cover off. One page turned. Then another.

"Hmm."

"Got something, Mr. Bannerman?"

"No, no, not yet. We had two girls come in three years ago October. Another in December." He flipped a page. "I don't see anything else from that time. No boys, no Jessie. Are you certain of the year?"

Petrosky looked at Morrison, who nodded.

"Let's do a quick check of the other years," Petrosky said. "Four years up to two years ago."

Bannerman paged through another file, opened a third and paged some more. He shook his head. "Most of these are older boys, winter or spring, a couple more girls."

Petrosky scowled. "We'll need a copy of that information for our records."

Bannerman's eyes went steely.

"I can get a warrant, but taking all that extra time won't help me find a killer who is still on the loose."

"I'll jot the information down for you." Bannerman pulled a sheet of stationery from his desktop and a pen that appeared to be made from an animal tusk. All God's fucking creatures. Apparently that one wasn't worth saving.

"Any other places around here that she could have taken him to?" Petrosky asked as Bannerman wrote.

"Downtown there's a fire station on Anderson that's listed as a Safe Haven." Bannerman made a final note and handed the paper to Petrosky, who folded the page into his pocket and stood.

"Thank you for your time, sir."

"Father." Bannerman straightened his shoulders.

"Whatever," Petrosky said.

Outside the church, rain sheeted, rattling the glass and making the stark tinny sound Petrosky had heard in Bannerman's office. He pulled the collar of his jacket tight against the wind and hustled to the car, littering the dash with tiny spots of water from his coat as he climbed in and jabbed at the heat controls.

Morrison was silent, tapping on his phone.

"You doing that texting thing with Taylor? None of that hanky-panky shit during work."

"No, Boss." Morrison didn't raise his eyes from the screen.

Petrosky turned onto the main road and watched the gothic church give way to a similar building that now belonged in equal parts to a legal practice and a bank. They passed a lot full of weed-ridden gravel. Then a gas station. Then a fast food joint. Only eight more restaurants to go and they'd be at the precinct. He stopped at a red light.

"Baby boy found dead on October twenty-third four blocks from Lawrence's apartment," Morrison said.

"Lots of babies are found dead, Morrison. But we'll follow up."

"He was wrapped in a duck blanket, according to the news reports. They ran a picture of the blanket instead of a dead kid."

Petrosky squinted at the grainy image Morrison held out to him. He could barely make out a tattered blanket covered with yellow and orange ducks, graying with filth.

Petrosky turned back to the road. "Looks like we need to haul Keil back in for questioning."

"He gave us an awful lot of information for someone trying to hide the fact that he left his girlfriend's kid to die three years ago," Morrison said.

"True. But not all killers are smart." Petrosky tried to picture Keil in the mausoleum, dopey eyes staring at the wall as he painted words in blood: *A boat beneath a sunny sky, Lingering onward dreamily* ...

Petrosky shook his head. "If she was the one who left the kid, daddy might be pissed at her. So far, Keil's the last one to see her alive and he might know more than he thinks he does."

Above them, the light turned green and Petrosky hit the gas. "There's a burger joint up here on the left. We can get it to go, hit the precinct to look up that poem, and head back to Keil's place."

"You want soup and salad?" Morrison looked up. "I know a place with awesome vegetarian chili."

"Unless it has dead cow in it, I don't want it."

Nothing but the pitter patter of sludge on the windshield. Petrosky glanced over.

Morrison stared at his phone, brows knit together in a mask of concentration. Probably a California thing, worrying about poor, abused cows. Maybe. Petrosky craned his neck to see the screen.

Morrison lowered the phone and Petrosky straightened and stared out the windshield.

"We don't need to stop at the precinct. I've got it."

"Got what? You sending PETA after me?"

"The poem. It's from *Through the Looking Glass*. Circa eighteen-seventy-one."

Petrosky raised an eyebrow. "Rare?"

"An original copy? Maybe. And our guy might have one if he's that into it. But the poems are available anywhere as evidenced by me pulling it up in two minutes on the web. I read it at some point in school, probably undergrad. One of those what's-the-meaning-of-all-this-shit kinda thing. I think I read it younger, too."

"Younger?"

"It's the prequel to *Alice in Wonderland*."

In Petrosky's mind, the gory letters on the wall morphed into a children's book, pages fleshy and oozing. "We'll hit the libraries tomorrow, make some calls, and see what we can come up with."

"Crazed professor?"

"Doubt it, but they might know something about the literature angle that we're not thinking about, even with your fancy-ass English degree."

Morrison didn't take the bait. "The words at the Lawrence scene are only the first few lines. The poem has seven verses, Boss. That worries me."

"It should, Morrison." The rain relentlessly hammered the car, as if the clouds were attacking. Petrosky pressed harder on the gas.

Six more. That worried him too.

THE CLOCK GLOWED five minutes until quitting time. Robert Fredricks popped his knuckles and studied the three-dimensional quarter panel blueprints on his computer screen. The design wouldn't win him any awards, but it was what his lead had asked for. And the job was a prime gig even if his asshole boss found something wrong with this design the way he had last time.

The call had come unexpectedly: "Can you come to Michigan?" Robert didn't remember signing in with the head hunters at Harwick Technical, but he assumed he must have. Even if it had been a paperwork mistake, he'd figured it was about time for his luck to change. He had packed up his basement apartment of meager belongings and taken a bus that same week. He wasn't in the main building on the lake, but it had only been a couple years. You never knew what might happen tomorrow.

At precisely five thirty, he stood and threaded his way through the array of cubicles, down the elevator, and to the parking lot. His Nissan stuck out in the sea of Chryslers. The taupe and black granite building behind him cast a long shadow over the lot.

"Hey!" Thomas Norton waved his hands, a cheerleader above the rows of cars. Thomas had a cubicle in the same department, across the aisle from Robert. When Robert had started at Harwick Tech, Thomas had been the first person in the room to say hello, loping over on stocky legs with his mop of sandy hair shellacked to his head like a helmet. Thomas hadn't stopped talking since, though that wasn't what bothered Robert. It was Thomas's eyes, big and brown and all-knowing, the kind that seemed to peer into your soul. Robert hated that feeling, even the merest hint that someone could guess his most private thoughts. But, if Thomas had even the faintest idea what went on in Robert's head he wouldn't be smiling as he approached. And the women—shit, if *they* knew what Robert was thinking they'd run screaming into the night.

"Yo, Jimmy! We still on for drinks later?"

Idiot. Robert smiled. "You bet."

Thomas grinned like a fifteen-year-old girl with a cock in her ass. "I'll have a seat waiting."

Robert climbed into his car. *Jimmy. Ugh.* He hated the name, but it was necessary now that he could no longer use his own. The world was not a friendly place for ex-cons. Not that it had been particularly friendly before his arrest. He gritted his teeth and pulled from the lot.

He had always been bad. There had always been a filthy wrongness lurking within him, despicable and abhorrent, waiting to be exposed. He could remember the exact moment he discovered the truth of it.

He had been adopted into a pious family in southern Mississippi where the air was so thick in the summer it was like breathing underwater. Their old plantation house was surrounded by gnarled oaks—"hanging trees" his father called them, because of the slaves who had once strangled to death in the boughs. As a child, he often watched the wind rustling the branches with rapt attention, squinting until he swore he could see the bodies swinging. Even walking to the bus stop, something ominous always tainted the air, a wisp of energy not yet departed from the place, a tingling on his back whose origins he couldn't quite pinpoint.

Especially under those trees.

Sometimes he could feel the weight of the whole place bearing down on him, concentrated in the glare from his father's eyes. They were the eyes of a prophet, an angel even, at least if you asked the women of their congregation.

His father was not those things.

Despite his unknown heritage, Robert possessed those same eyes. He also had thick black hair and a finely boned face with a jaw wide enough to be attractive, or so he had assumed from the way the girls at school watched him. He wondered if they knew fornication was a surefire path to Hell. Desire was a manifestation of the Devil, his father would say, a ploy for the souls of the weak-minded.

Then it had happened to him, an unfamiliar tingling in his thighs as he watched his sixth grade teacher write Shakespearean verses on the blackboard.

> But there's no bottom, none,
> In my voluptuousness: your wives, your daughters,
> Your matrons and your maids, could not fill up
> The cistern of my lust.

Since then, his lust had never been sated, each libidinous thought weaving into a frenzied net set to wrench him kicking and screaming into the ring of fire. As a child his fingernails had gouged into his hardened flesh at these thoughts, bringing him pleasure and pain and pleasure again. Even then, he'd dared hope he might be normal someday. But then he'd been caught, hand on his body, palm still working, and his father had entered the room solemn-faced and carrying a willow switch.

"Train up a child in the way he should go: and when he is old, he will not depart from it," his father had said over and over again, a mantra to excuse the suffering he would inflict.

When his father yanked him from the bed and slung him to the hardwood floor, Robert knew there would be no absolution, particularly when the first blow from his father's fist landed hard against his spine. When his father ripped his shirt from his body and he heard the singing rod as it whipped through the air, he knew he was a dirty, rotten sinner. And when the willow slashed deep into the delicate skin of his back, over and over again, he cried out, because in his core, he knew God would have no mercy on someone like him.

He was bad. Disgusting. Unlovable. Unforgivable. There was no hope.

And without hope, there was no longer any point in fighting his carnality. Then oh, how it had grown. Like a beast in his belly, filling him, consuming him, eating him alive.

A car horn blared, startling him back to the present. Robert's erection was turning his pants into a prison.

Someday he'd find The One. She'd forgive him his thoughts, his actions, his deviousness. She'd understand his lust and appease his demons. She would save him from himself.

The light was green. The horn honked again. Robert waited for yellow and gunned it just as the light turned red, clearing the intersection amidst the bleats of horns belonging to other angry motorists.

He glanced in his rearview mirror and adjusted his zipper. Heat spread through his lower body.

He had to find the girl.

SATURDAY, OCTOBER 10TH

THE SUN WARMED my face and turned lake water ripples into a carpet of glitter thrown by an unruly child. The outdoor end-of-summer picnic at Harwick Technical was a vast improvement on the conference rooms we'd turned to last year when the picnic had been rained out.

Noelle sat alone with a plate of food at a table overlooking the lake. Closer to the building, children giggled on inflatable bounce houses. Their parents talked amongst themselves, feigning calm, but poised like meerkats ready to leap at the slightest indication of danger, or, more likely, hair pulling and unauthorized spitting.

I took my plate to where Noelle was sitting and claimed a spot across from her. Ribs, potatoes and corn, the best picnic food money could buy. At least I assumed that was true; I was certainly not a picnic connoisseur. If such a thing existed, that would be my new occupational goal. It would have been better than typing up employee files between bouts of crushing people's dreams.

"You don't have to look so pissed to be here," Noelle said. "I mean, you need to get out of the house sometimes, right? Explore the world. Get away from Ja—"

"I'm not pissed. Just hanging out." I took a bite of corn on the cob, feeling a little pissed. "Besides, Jake was busy today. He went over to his mom's house." A corn kernel escaped my lips and landed on the table. I wiped it away, pretending it was Jake's mother, the real reason I had told Jake this party was mandatory. At least he hadn't wanted to come; having Jake around would have made me feel extra horrible when my boss's presence turned me into a blubbering imbecile. I scanned the field for Mr. Harwick, but that sinewy mass of handsome was nowhere to be seen. Bummer.

"Gotcha. Well, see? You wouldn't have been doing anything anyway." Noelle speared a piece of chicken. "Can I ask you a question?"

I shrugged. "Shoot."

"Why do you put up with that guy? He sits around all day, visiting with his mom and who knows who else, while you work to—"

"I love Jake for things besides money."

Noelle cocked her head. "What, like his cooking? Didn't he once cut the tops off the broccoli and serve only the bottoms?"

I winced. "He tried."

"I guess you must love him for his brains."

The corn rolled around in my stomach. "Everyone deserves a chance, right? And he's there for me when I need him."

Noelle snorted. "Like a faithful lap dog, only way more expensive."

"Faithfulness is important." My ears warmed. "Besides, it's his other attributes that keep me coming back." I winked and hoped it didn't look forced.

Noelle glanced across the field and back at me. "He must have a golden dick, then, for all the shit you put up with."

"Nothing golden now, but believe me, we tried. That sparkly paint was way too itchy."

"Jesus, Hannah."

"Jesus would never do the things I make Jake do to me." My ears cooled. The corn settled. I set the half-eaten cob on the plate and grabbed my fork.

"You're probably right about that. Plus he always had all those apostles following him around."

"He has a long staff though," I said. I smiled, and this time I meant it.

"So I hear." Noelle stared past me and straightened her shoulders, her boobs torpedoing toward someone at my back.

"Good afternoon, ladies."

I startled and dropped a forkful of potatoes at Mr. Harwick's voice. *Nice going, Hannah.*

He stepped around to the head of the table, his eyes deep blue oceans flecked with a lighter shade of gray. His aquiline nose cut through the middle of his face above lips that were just shy of pouty, now twitching up in amusement. The blue suit he wore was immaculate, right down to the silver cufflinks and navy-striped tie. Did he ever wrinkle? Each element of him registered, but separately like the flickered images from an old silent movie.

"Afternoon," I said. Noelle said it at exactly the same time, ensuring that we sounded like wannabe twins, or maybe synchronized talkers. Synchronized talking, an Olympic sport like synchronized swimming, only way lamer. If that was a thing, I had another job aspiration. But I couldn't think about potential jobs or anything else when Mr. Harwick's eyes were staring into mine and making my world disappear, which was probably totally unhealthy but I didn't care. Such was the nature of fantasy men, right? I waited for him to walk away like he always did. He had probably heard that little crack in my voice. Shit, maybe he knew about my weirdness.

But he was still there, staring at me with that amused expression. God, were his eyes always like that? They were *sin*-sational. Was that a word? I wondered if I could dive into them and swim around for a while. And if he'd notice me taking a dip in his eyeballs. And how Jake would feel about that.

Maybe Jake can come too!
That's what she said.
Christ. Stop it, Hannah.

"Enjoying the party?" he asked. His eyes twinkled and I wanted to touch them. But eye poking would surely hurt him and make me look flat-out crazy.

"Very much. It's pretty nice of you to feed the whole place," Noelle said.

He turned to her, and the hold he had on me disappeared. I fought the urge to slump under the table and hide.

"I appreciate the things all of you do," he said. "Might as well show my appreciation with coleslaw and chicken." He looked back at me and rubber bands wrapped around my chest, like that rubber-bands-around-a-watermelon trick where you add more and more until it blows up. If I exploded, it wouldn't be as hilarious as the watermelon thing. But it might make it to America's Best Home Movies or whatever that show was called.

Noelle nodded. "Yeah, the chicken is pretty good."

And there were those eyes again.

"How are you enjoying it?" he asked me.

"Nothing *fowl* about it," I said, and fire spread from my cheeks to my neck. *Nice. Super classy.*

Mr. Harwick laughed. My heart somehow managed to speed up and slow down at the same time.

Noelle cocked an eyebrow at me and shook her head. She cut into a potato with a plastic knife.

"I even got real butter, because with butter there is little *margarine* for error." Mr. Harwick winked at me.

I was a fish gasping for air; I couldn't close my mouth.

"Have fun ladies." Mr. Harwick turned in the direction of the building.

And there he goes.

"He's fucking delicious," Noelle whispered. "Weird sense of humor, but delicious." She was watching me closely, eyes darting from me to his receding back.

I'd like for you to stay, but I love to watch you leave. Damn, someone else had said that right? It wasn't me. I would never think such a thing. I had a boyfriend, and I loved him.

I swallowed hard and nodded at Noelle.

When the event wound to a close, I skittered to the back of the parking lot, rubbernecking for signs of danger like an inquisitive—or extremely paranoid—giraffe. To my right, a woman with a baby on her hip unlocked her car. Beyond her the lot was gloriously empty.

Clear.

My Buick's windshield was the only shiny element of the vehicle, the luster from its burgundy paint long ago stripped away by years of winter salt. I slipped the key into the ignition, pulled out of the lot, and headed for the freeway.

A few times a week I was a goddamn liar. Jake would throw a fit if he knew I still volunteered at the domestic violence shelter instead of working late like I kept insisting I was. I had been staying there when I met him, ruined and lost, stocking shelves at the drugstore where he worked. Maybe he wanted me to leave that part of my life behind as much as he wanted to leave behind the fact that he actually worked when we got together. And though I might have chosen a more creative name, I couldn't let The Shelter go. They needed my help. Plus, it was hard to feel sorry for myself in the midst of so much suffering.

I clicked on the radio.

"—in other news, a local woman was found murdered in an Ash Park cemetery. Police have identified the woman as twenty-one-year-old Meredith Lawrence. If you have any information—"

I wonder what she did to make him mad.

I clicked off the radio with shaking fingers. *Well, fuck.*

I could almost hear his voice oozing like pus from some hidden corner of my brain: *I'll find you, Hannah. Don't ever doubt it.* And the weasel was back, sprinting around in my chest like he was on meth. I squinted through the windshield, waiting for his snarling face to appear against the glass, his nose irrevocably twisted from the lumber yard accident, his eyes that looked just like ... mine.

Get it together, Hannah. He would have found you by now if he was looking.

I glanced down at my purse, searching for protection. I needed to pick up more pepper spray, though someone in my apartment building would surely complain; the last one dropped and broke in the stairwell, leaving everyone with runny eyes for days. Could lip balm be a weapon? Maybe if he startled me in a parking lot somewhere I could whack him over the head with my journal. My therapist thought writing was a good way to get in touch with my feelings—had the woman known more about my history, she might have prescribed more than a pencil and paper.

I pulled a deep breath into my lungs and held it. *I will always be broken.*

Broken but funny. Well, maybe.

Dominic laughed at my joke.

On my dashboard, a one-armed panda bobble head gave me a jiggly nod as I veered off the freeway. Litter-strewn residential streets crackled and crunched with empty Faygo pop two liters and broken beer bottles. Beside the shelter loomed an abandoned school, plywood windows surrounded by crumbling red brick.

The shelter itself was a lump of gray, but the back facade was covered with bright, lewd graffiti—as if a deranged city planner with a can of spray paint had walked up and said, "You know what this place needs? A giant orange dick."

I parked in front of the tangerine penis and got out, surveilling my surroundings for crooked noses hidden in the shadows.

Crack! Something snapped at the back of the lot, where trees were steeped in evening dim.

My elbow smashed against the car door and I pressed my back against it, trying to do that hold-your-keys-between-your-fingers-like-a-weapon thing. It didn't help. An icicle shuddered up my back. I squinted into the trees.

Not a movement, except for a few rustling leaves.

I locked my car with my key-claw, dashed into the building and punched in the code to quell the alarm.

"Hannah!" Ms. LaPorte's swishing eighties pantsuit almost glowed, the electric blue and white as unabashed as their wearer. A whitish-blue perm rose from the top of her head like a snow-capped mountain peak.

The ice in my back thawed. "Hi, Ms. LaPorte. How are things tonight?"

"Good. We have a few new girls, but it's been pretty quiet. I was just getting supper on."

"I'll help you. Brandy still sleeping?"

"Yes, dear."

Brandy Lovelle was Ms. LaPorte's one full-time employee; green hair atop a thin, bird-like frame, wiry arms sleeved in tattooed ink, lip ring glinting when she pulled her mouth into one of her ready smiles. She worked the overnights, starting around ten o'clock when Ms. LaPorte left to go home. Brandy was usually asleep in the evenings when I came by, which was a bummer because I suspected she was all kinds of awesome.

I followed Ms. LaPorte down the narrow hallway and into a tiny but functional kitchen outfitted with scuffed appliances. One wall had a hole cut in it for serving food, the chest-high opening finished with a large piece of plywood and covered with a floral tablecloth.

"How's Mario?" I asked.

"He's fine, dear. Just watered him."

I stepped to the makeshift counter and ran a finger over one waxy leaf of the philodendron. Mario was poisonous inside, but if you just admired him from the outside, he was beautiful. Kinda like some people.

I'll find you, Hannah.

I shifted my weight, let go of the leaf, and peered down the hallway toward the back door.

Ms. LaPorte hustled to the stove and cranked off the heat. The huge pot spluttered protests and speckled her shirt with reddish-orange. "Chili night. I should have known."

I grabbed the faded apron from the hook on the wall and held it out. "You take it, Ms. LaPorte."

"No, dear, I don't want you ruining your pretty sweater."

"I have a backup." I tugged off my sweater like a bored stripper just trying to get to the point, revealing a long-sleeved T-shirt underneath. *Bow chicka bow wow.* "Problem solved."

Ms. LaPorte's smile was cut short by wailing coming from the front room. I handed her the apron and walked through the open doorway into a space that resembled an elementary school cafeteria, right down to the row of metal cafeteria tables that cut through the center.

Dragging those tables from the school next door in a moment of anarchistic fervor had been my proudest episode of vandalism. Then, in a decidedly un-thief-like way, we had painted the walls a sunny yellow, knowing full well the nature of our work meant that the place had never felt truly friendly. Still, we tried, and that's what mattered.

Around the perimeter of the room, women talked in groups of two or three. A few had small children clinging to their legs. Two little boys sat on the floor running matchbox cars over the linoleum, their mothers looking on silently.

A tight mewl sounded near the front door—another little boy, about six. He gave me a sidelong glance and buried his face in his mother's leg. She watched me with a mix of desperation and practiced suspicion.

"I'm Hannah," I said softly as I approached. "Do you need a doctor?"

The woman poked gingerly at her head. Her black hair would have been lovely had it not been caked with dried blood. "No."

"Do you need the police?"

Her features twisted in anger. "They's the reason I got this." She gestured to her head. "Trey didn' like that I called 'em on his ass yesterday. Shoulda never done it. Wasn't even that bad."

The child sniffled again, and the woman bent and whispered in his ear. He wrapped his bony arms around her and she picked him up and cradled him against her chest, his head resting on her unbloodied shoulder.

I waited, feeling like an intruder, heart aching. There was so much hurt in that embrace, but there was love too. I envied them that even as I reminded myself that I was there trying to help people not get their asses kicked. We didn't receive state funds and weren't under obligation to report, but seeing guys get away with hurting these women made me stabby. She looked back at me and I realized the other women in the room were watching me too.

I swallowed hard. "It's up to you," I said. "We won't force you to file a report. We're here to provide temporary sleeping quarters and a night-time meal." I lowered my tone. "But if you need to get away from someone, a police record may be helpful."

The woman shook her head. "It ain't gon' do no good."

"Down here they never show up until it's too late anyway," called a gruff voice. Behind me, the short, squat woman who had spoken sat with her hands folded over her protruding abdomen. "Then he's back at you before the next day is done."

The other women nodded their agreement and I resisted the urge to nod along.

Ms. LaPorte emerged from the kitchen, wiping her hands on the apron tied to her waist. "Thirty-three minutes is no kind of response time at all," she said. "Let's have a look at you, dear."

The words echoed in my ears. It was the same thing Ms. LaPorte had said to me nearly five years before when I had arrived at the shelter with two T-shirts, a pair of jeans and a fluttering in my abdomen that wasn't nerves. *Do you have a game plan?* She had asked. I'd nodded. *Yes. And it needs to happen soon.*

Let's have a look at you, dear.

My knees wobbled. *Relax, Hannah. No one knows who he was. Not even Ms. LaPorte.*

If he knew where you were, you'd be dead already. My hand shifted to my stomach as if the kid was still in there, waiting to eat me from the inside out like a fleshy Pacman.

The woman and her son disappeared with Ms. LaPorte into the communal bathroom. I trembled all the way to the kitchen. *Deep breaths, Hannah. Deep breaths.*

I ladled chili into bowls and placed them on the counter, trying to still my shaking hands by repeating to myself, "I'm not cold, I'm just a little chili," but the mantra helped very little. When all had been served, the women sat and talked amongst themselves in solemn camaraderie connected by an unspoken need for peace. They were almost friends, the pain they shared a tenuous alliance that still left them disconnected enough to feel lonely.

I understood. In high school I'd hung out with an eclectic mix of misfits: Marianne with her sausage arms and cherry red eyeglasses, Jillian with her flaming orange hair, and Monique who wore long sleeves in the summer and a smile even when her eyes were bloodshot. All of us had been hurting, but hiding it, while we tried to belong somewhere. The best thing we had going was when I'd tell them the jokes my dad taught me.

"Why don't cannibals eat clowns?" I would ask excitedly. "Because they taste funny!"

Thanks to my father, I also knew all the dirty jokes. Without other prospects for friendship, my mismatched group wouldn't tell on me. But I still kept the nastiest ones to myself. The cleaner jokes I told with an air of conspiratorial secrecy.

"An airplane is about to crash, and a lady jumps up and says, 'If I'm going to die, I want to die feeling like a woman,' and takes off all her clothes."

I would pause, gauging how effective the joke was by the vibrancy of Jillian's cheeks.

"When she's naked she says, 'Is there someone on this plane who is man enough to make me feel like a woman?' A man stands up, removes his shirt and says, 'Here, iron this!'"

Their giggles always made me smile. But our relationships were as fragile as those in the dining room now, especially since we never saw each other outside of school. These women would never see one another again. Did they have someone at home like I did back then? When my mother put in extra hours at the dentist's office where she worked, I at least had my father to play Monopoly with, though he never gave me any indication I was good at the game.

"Don't worry about it, darling. You're just not quite smart enough," he would say, and I would nod, sure he was right. And when I would admit my hurt over never seeing my friends outside of school, he would smile knowingly and put his arm around me. "I understand, honey, but no one can ever really love you the way I do. You don't need anyone else but your old man."

And I would giggle and tell him that he wasn't old. It was also true that his protection and love would never have an equal. My friends did not appreciate me the way he did, and the rest of the school didn't even know I was there at all. So I would throw my arms around him and kiss him, vowing never to disappoint him.

It was a vow I had broken. Terribly. Irreparably. But I had real friends now, or at least one.

I should get Noelle a present. Maybe new earrings. She had been there for me from the day she started at Harwick Technical Solutions. She'd probably even listen if I ever got the guts to talk to her about anything important. Friends mattered, even when they had awesome torpedo tits and hated puns.

I watched as the women pushed aside their trays, cold, faraway expressions barely disguising the hopelessness they probably felt at the thought of leaving the shelter, or maybe at the thought of leaving their mates.

They weren't good enough. They had disappointed someone. Probably themselves.

I grabbed a rag and attacked the counter. *I will not turn into this.*

DRIVING from the shelter to my apartment was usually the most relaxing twenty minutes of my day. In fifteen miles, downtown caved to suburbia, with libraries and apartments across the street from professional buildings, all decorated with only moderate amounts of penis graffiti. Signs for gas stations and fast food restaurants twinkled on either side of the road, the colors on the signs crisper than they'd been in the heat of summer when they had to compete with the fog of muggy air. I passed the comic book store. Lucky's pizza. A cell phone repair shop. And there it was: the little apartment building that could.

Somewhere along the way I'd gotten stuck in five stories of red brick, six units to a floor, a place that just about screamed "I'm here for now but not forever"— at least that was what I'd told myself when I moved in. The building sat on a residential street across from some kind of second hand kiddie clothing store that I had never ventured into and probably never would. In the back, the parking lot bordered another road and yet another gas station. Because what city is complete without four gas stations per block?

I parked in the back and ran up the cement steps, the October air chilling my bones even after the heavy door had swung shut. The smell of onions and old socks permeated the stairwell and hallway on the third floor, much better than my pepper spray, but still gross. I hoped the smell wasn't coming from my apartment.

The door latch clanked. On the television, tires shrieked and a woman yelled something unintelligible. Steam rose from a pot on the stove.

"Hey, babe!" Jake said from the couch. "I was just going to make some of those noodles you bought the other day. I brought pasta sauce from my mom's."

I scanned the apartment, mildly concerned his mother might jump from behind a chair, howling like a banshee, dripping cigarette ash all over the carpet. I glanced at a burned spot on the rug. Like mother like son. "Thanks for starting the water. It's been a long day."

Jake nodded, his eyes on a reality show about wrestling crocodiles. A plume of smoke billowed from his nostrils. "Yeah, sure. Hey, I was talking to my mom and she says we should move down by her after we get married."

"We can't afford to move right now, Jake."

"Well, yeah but one day we might be able to." He didn't raise his eyes from the screen.

"It takes time to move up at work," I said to the back of his head. *Plus you could get a job, too. You know, like you've been promising to do for months.*

"Yeah, I guess. Can you get the plates? I'm beat."

I slid dry noodles into the water, poured the sauce into a pan and set the table. Jake kept his gaze on the TV. I resisted the urge to hurl a plate at his skull. Sometimes I hated the way he acted, but having someone next to you made you harder to strangle; at least I assumed that was true. I stalked back to the kitchen to test the sauce. Hot, but store-bought.

Jake was at the table when I returned with the meal.

"Thanks, hon. I love you, ya know."

"I love you, too." I clutched my fork tighter than necessary.

He's always been there for me, even when I was difficult and crazier than I am now. Maybe I should just agree to marry him and get it over with.

What was I waiting for, anyway?

Mr. Harwick's smiling face popped into my head, telling me I was a great worker, helping me pick up the stuff from my purse. I tried to distract myself from the warmth in my lower body by shoveling pasta into my mouth.

I DID THE DISHES ALONE, half listening to the murmur of Jake's television program.

I love him. I need him.

The pasta did a nervous dance in my abdomen. Jake's mother was probably trying to poison me. Very Snow White-ish except I didn't have any knee-high friends to mine coal or help me with the goddamn dishes.

I dried the last dish and walked into the living room. My mouth was dry.

Jake stared at the screen.

I love him. I love him. I love him.

Prove it.

I sat and put my arms around him. He turned, gripped my shoulders and pushed his mouth onto mine, prodding my tongue like an imbecilic iguana. His tongue tasted like stale cigarettes and Pabst Blue Ribbon. I fought a gag and waited for a tingle, heat, something. I felt nothing. Not that I ever did. Not that I had any reason to expect better.

I wondered how much that case of beer had put me back.

When Jake came up for air, I pulled off his T-shirt and felt a twinge of guilt when Dominic's face flashed in my mind again, helping me, complimenting me, smiling at my lame jokes ... No, not Dominic. Mr. Harwick. I grabbed Jake harder.

I love him.

Jake pulled away and yanked at our clothes, tossing them into a pile on the floor. His member jutted from his body like a thick diving board. Well, not that thick. Let's not get silly.

You're going to poke someone's eye out with that thing.

I wanted to giggle, but couldn't because he was pulling my head toward his crotch. I tried to plaster on a seductive smile but only managed a muted sigh. Not that he would have noticed either way.

I bet Dominic would be better at this stuff.

Mickey Mouse would be better at this stuff.

Nothing sexier than bestiality.

Shut up, Hannah, and get it over with.

I closed my eyes and opened my mouth.

EVEN AFTER ALL THESE YEARS, Robert could hear the priest's voice in his head, louder than the girl's anxious breathing: —*and the sinners shall pay for their transgressions, the adulterers, the fornicators, the scourge of the earth in their filthy enterprise burning for all eternity* ... But the priest was not there now, and, if he were, he would be on his knees screaming unanswered prayers to the heavens.

The girl sat on the bed, her legs wrapped around Robert's hips. Her ash-blond hair was demurely braided over one slender shoulder, resting at the top of two perfect breasts the color of cream. He imagined her skin would taste like cream as well, rich and velvety on his mouth, her sweetness intensifying as he trailed his tongue lower, seeking the heat of her being, each flick making her moan in ecstasy—

The priest's voice got louder, accelerating in pace, like a crescendo toward damnation—*the heathens who do not know God are doomed to succumb to earthly sin, to embrace lust not honor, passion not holiness, Hell not Heaven*—

Robert took a breath, trying to ignore the words and pretend, just for a moment, that he was a good person, a person worthy of compassion. Perhaps this new girl would find him worthy in a way others never had. He began a poem for her inside his head.

My heart expands at your nearness,

Like a balloon begging to be broken,

Yearning to spill our love over the world in rivers of happiness.

Hope lit in his chest, hope that this creature would forgive him, that she might be an angel who would help him purge his sins before they swallowed him forever. He thrust into her, deeply, slowly, savoring every inch of her.

She moved against him. *I forgive you.* She didn't say it, but Robert felt it, saw it in her glistening eyes. He caressed her face and rotated his hips, each thrust bringing him closer to salvation.

I forgive you.

He stroked her breast gently, thanking her for her mercy.

She winced. *Winced.*

She was one of them. She'd be pleased at the thought of sinners thrust down into the pits of Hell. Sinners like him.

Rotten. Unlovable. Unforgivable. He might as well embrace his true nature, enjoy his lechery, for there would be no enjoyment in eternity.

Not for one like him.

Robert pulled himself from her depths and plastered his palm over her mouth before she could vocalize her judgment. Pimples ripe with pus reddened across the bridge of her nose.

Fucking cunt. She will pay. And dammit, she will like it.

Robert grabbed her hair and yanked her forward, off the bed. He kicked at her shins until she knelt before him, worshipping him in the way others worshipped their God, a God that would condemn him and torture him until he could take no more, an agony to be repeated for eternity.

He forced that agony on her, slapping her, splitting her lip. Her sobs echoed through his brain like music, hypnotic and rich. As the blood ran into her mouth he shoved himself into the opening, moaning as she cried, accelerating his pace until he choked her with his seed.

—and the righteous shall rise again, pious on the Earth until they are embraced into the kingdom of Heaven.

He pulled the whore's head back, and she stared up at him, lashes wet, freckled skin stippled with hatred, each pock mark like a mouth brimming with accusation. Her glassy eyes told him all he needed to know.

He raised his hand. She would not forgive him. She would not absolve him. His fists clenched, his muscles aching for release of a different kind.

She cringed and turned her head.

No. Not now. Robert brought his fist down on the bed behind her and smiled when she yelped. *Stupid fucking whore. This was all her fault.* He tossed money at her and went to take a shower.

She would not be there when he returned. They never were.

SUNDAY, OCTOBER 11TH

Rotting garbage and animal urine curdled the air. The silence resonated with the eerie heaviness of a ghost town, if you were prone to fanciful bullshit. Petrosky wasn't. He squinted at the house.

The building was beyond repair, part of a housing project long abandoned by any developer or landlord. Even panhandlers would not come out this far to squat for a night when they had to trek five miles back in the morning to beg for their breakfast.

So why here?

Behind him, rubber soles on gravel crunched closer.

"Morning, Boss."

"California."

"I brought you some coffee and a protein bar. I'll get them after we finish up here."

Petrosky grimaced.

"Come on, Boss. You'll like it."

"That's what you said about tofu. I will take the coffee though. Later." Petrosky walked up the front steps, Morrison at his heel.

"He killed another one pretty fast, didn't he?" Morrison said.

"Too fast." Only ten days between murders, highly unusual even for a serial killer. They ducked through the front door, kicking up dust and mold that sat, itchy, in Petrosky's throat.

"I don't like this."

"I bet she liked it less." Petrosky glanced around the living room where pieces of roofing tile had tumbled haphazardly to the splintered floor. He followed the low hum of voices and the phosphorescent ricochet of flood lights down the groaning basement stairs, and inhaled deeply when he reached the lower floor. The scent of mushrooms and dank earth clung to the back of his tongue. A dull sheen lit the basement windows from the outside, the sunlight struggling to illuminate through years of filth.

The woman lay prone on an old dining table, wrists and ankles each bound to a different table leg with leather restraints. Blond hair fanned around her head, mussed as if she were merely asleep, but there was no mistaking the vacant death stare in her hazel eyes.

A few techs bustled around the dim space, tweezing and bagging and scraping. Petrosky ignored them and scanned the victim's extremities. Graying skin covered her arms, and the fingers of her left hand were contorted like a claw on the table. Stiff. No maggots yet. She hadn't been dead for long. "Do you have a positive ID?" Petrosky asked no one in particular.

"Jane Trazowski," someone behind him said. "She's in the system, got a couple charges for solicitation of prostitution. We need the family for a positive ID but Connors here recognized her from a domestic violence arrest where her kids were—"

"Fine." Petrosky said. He cleared his throat and dragged his eyes over her belly. Her abdomen had been hacked apart revealing gelatinous blobs of organs and the slick sheen of intestine. Like the first body, the long whitish tube was splayed open, a sheet of bloodied tissue, more torn and gnarled in some areas than others. Either their guy had been pissed, or the rats had gotten to her already. Petrosky squinted at the ruin. Probably both.

"Damn. I feel bad for them." Morrison's voice was irritatingly nasal.

Fucking surfers. They always sounded high. Though maybe he was just trying not to breathe through his nose.

"You feel bad for who? The woman or her kids?"

Morrison's face went red. "Both."

Morrison would have to cut out that blushing shit before he was allowed to handle any perps. Too much visible emotion and suspects would eat him alive.

The stairs wept behind them with a shuddery *scree*, and Petrosky and Morrison turned to see Brian Thompson, the medical examiner, coming down the last few steps. He was tall and lanky with perpetual five o'clock shadow and teeth like a mule. He nodded at Petrosky and approached the table reeking of cigarette smoke—good tobacco, none of that pepperminty menthol bullshit. Petrosky's mouth watered.

"Suspect used standard metal clasps to keep the skin peeled back while he worked." Thompson circled the table, gray eyes wandering like he was bored as fuck to be there. "You can get them from any hardware store. Usually these guys are perfectionists. While the dissection is pretty meticulous, there is a brutality to it that goes beyond the simple cuts themselves. See this here?" Thompson gestured to a series of scrapes visible along the underside of the body. "Splinters in the skin. Looks like she was rubbing against the table, trying to escape."

Petrosky peered at the cuts. "You think she was captive for a while before—"

"Yeah, like the first. He didn't just murder her and then play around with her insides. She was probably alive when he removed her organs, though I will need to complete the autopsy to confirm abdominal surgery as the cause of death."

Upstairs, the telltale clank and rattle of a wheeled gurney approached the basement steps. *Can't put it off any longer.* Petrosky swallowed over the knot in his throat, bent and craned his neck to see the underside of the table. Copper stung his nose as he read the poem, each line written on a different board in block script. Here and there, the splitting lumber had skewered a chunk of something dark and gory and almost alive. Rotten wood. Perhaps a piece of paintbrush. Maybe skin.

> Children three that nestle near,
> Eager eye and willing ear
> Pleased a simple tale to hear-

Petrosky straightened. Evisceration, shock, death. This fucker had tortured her. She'd been in agony. She had begged for her life. Julie probably had, too. An invisible rope tightened around his throat.

Children three that nestle near ...

"How many kids did she have?" Petrosky asked.

"Three," said the tech from the floor.

"He knew this one," Morrison said.

"Or of her. Maybe Lawrence too." Petrosky let that sink in. "Let's find out where these ladies spent their time."

THE SHELTER WAS in a shitty part of downtown, but it looked surprisingly well-kept if you ignored the spray paint. In the back parking lot, a spry sixty-ish woman broomed debris from the walkway. She looked up as Petrosky and Morrison approached.

Petrosky flashed his badge. "Ms. LaPorte? We have a few questions—"

"Our girls lives belong to them alone, sir." Her lips were a thin line.

Petrosky stiffened.

"Ma'am, we're following up on the murder of a woman who spent some time here. We were hoping you could help us," Morrison said.

LaPorte's free hand clamped over her mouth.

Way to go, Surfer Boy.

Morrison shrank under Petrosky's glare.

"Who? When was she here?"

"Jane Trazowski." Petrosky tried to keep his voice non-threatening.

"She was here last week, Thursday. We think she may have left Friday morning."

LaPorte shook her head. "I wasn't here, had a touch of the flu. You'll have to ask Hannah or Brandy. Brandy's out at an appointment but she'll be back later."

They followed LaPorte down a back hallway to a small kitchen. A thin woman stood at the counter, shoulder blades visible through her shirt on either side of a long dark ponytail as she scooped macaroni and cheese from a metal dish. She turned toward them.

Cotton plugged his throat. *Julie. Jesus fucking Christ. No, not her, but—*

Everyone was looking at him. He nodded at Morrison. *Take it, California.* There was no point trying to speak; his tongue had become a useless dehydrated mass on the floor of his mouth.

"Good evening, ma'am. I'm Detective Morrison and this is Detective Petrosky. We're trying to get information on a Jane Trazowski who may have been here a few weeks back."

She's not Julie.

The girl, not Julie, the girl, bit her lip. "I'm not sure. I don't always get names."

Petrosky pulled a picture from his folder and showed her. Her mouth fell open. "Yeah, I ... what happened?"

"She was killed."

Petrosky winced at Morrison's bluntness.

Hannah froze. It was the type of shock Petrosky often saw when he told someone their loved one had died, but it seemed an overreaction in this circumstance. Unless this girl was closer to Trazowski than she was letting on. *Interesting.* Petrosky tried to wet his lips with his tongue but his mouth was dry.

LaPorte put an arm around Hannah, who seemed to be having trouble taking in air.

"I ... she had some really nasty marks on her. Bruises and ... stuff. She said it was from a bad—" Hannah's eyes flicked to the officers.

It was a guilty look. *Very interesting.* "She's beyond trouble at this point," Petrosky said, low but even. "Help us catch the person who hurt her."

Hannah took another breath and blew it out. "She said it was from a guy she slept with. He paid her enough for her rent, but she was afraid to go home because he knew where she lived."

"Do you remember anything else about him? A name?"

She looked at the ceiling, the way lying perps sometimes did. It was how they accessed the creative center of the brain. But what would this girl have to hide?

You're just fucked up and imagining shit, Petrosky. This girl wasn't a suspect. Whatever she was hiding had nothing to do with this case.

She met his eyes. His stomach jerked against something sharp, like he had ingested barbed wire. *Those eyes. She's not Julie. Julie's dead.*

She shook her head. "No, no names. It never got that deep. Sometimes they don't ... want to talk."

"Do you remember exactly what she said?"

"Um ... some rent-check mother ... um ... got caught up in something. I'm not sure. It wasn't that, but something like that. I can't really remember." Beneath her nose, her lips quivered and stilled.

His arms ached to hug her and tell her it would all be okay. Petrosky ground his teeth, returned the photo to his folder and pulled out another. "How about her?"

LaPorte and Hannah stared at the image, frozen.

"Ladies?"

"Is this another one? Another ... victim?" LaPorte asked.

Questions, no answers. That didn't sit well with him. "It is, ma'am. Do you know her?"

LaPorte shook her head.

Petrosky turned to Hannah.

Hannah bit her lip, eyes radiating uncertainty as she glanced at LaPorte. "No."

"Are you sure?"

"I ... think so. I mean, we see so many and we don't always get IDs or whatever. Some of them are really scared."

But were they afraid of their exes or of someone else stalking them, hunting them down? "Scared?" Petrosky asked. Clean and non-specific. Sometimes it was what you didn't say that tripped people up.

"You'd be frightened too if someone you loved was beating on you." LaPorte stepped in front of Hannah, her finger jabbing at the air between them. "You'd be afraid if the police didn't help you when you called them. These ladies are allowed to be afraid."

Faces appeared at the hole in the wall behind Hannah—some clean, some battered, all inquisitive.

"We'd like to ask around here, if you don't mind."

LaPorte bristled. "As a matter of fact, I do mind. You have no right to go poking around into these women's lives, and I'll be damned if—"

"Let me rephrase: This is a police matter. We will be interviewing everyone here in an attempt to trace our victim's movements."

LaPorte's spindly fists formed balls. Beside Petrosky, Morrison stopped writing.

"Do you have a room we can use?" Petrosky asked.

LaPorte walked to the door. "Do your dirty work out back."

If a voice could cut flesh, Petrosky would have been on the floor with a severed jugular.

. . .

THEY DROVE to the precinct in silence. Eight women in the shelter. Three identified Trazowski from her visit earlier that week. One recognized Lawrence, but wasn't able to identify where she'd seen her.

And then there was Hannah. He could still almost see her face—strained and pale. Shocked, but more than shock. She was afraid. Someone had died, yet he hadn't given her a reason to think she'd be in danger any more than losing a loved one signals that you might be next. So what was she so afraid of? He yearned to know, to fix it, to take away the fear.

Cement barriers whizzed by the window. She looked so much like Julie—how Julie would have looked if she had been allowed to grow up.

Too bad you couldn't save her.

Get it together, asshole. Bury that shit.

He could almost taste the whiskey, feel the fiery comfort of it in the back of his throat. But a drink was the last thing he needed. He had a job to do.

Morrison swung into the lot and tossed Petrosky the keys, heading through the glass door to the precinct. Petrosky huffed up the interior flight of stairs after him, vowing to smack the shit out of anyone who dared suggest he go to the gym.

On the top floor, a hallway to the left led to the chief's office and a series of conference rooms. The rest of the place crackled with the controlled chaos of too many crimes and not enough cops. Detectives and plain-clothed officers sat at the dozens of desks in the bullpen, filling out paper reports and typing frantically on old PCs, trying to get the fuck out of there because they'd promised their wives they'd be home in time to see the kids off to bed. Petrosky had done that too, before Julie was taken from him. He'd give anything to do it again.

"What's up, Morrison?" A short, stocky man in police blues smiled and clapped Morrison on the back before shooting a nervous glance at Petrosky. His teeth were too small, like someone had buzzed them off halfway down.

Morrison shook the guy's hand. "What's up, Pete? See Annie this morning? I think she was looking for you on the Jackson case."

"Oh, really? I'm on it." A final goofy grin lit his mahogany face, and Pete something-or-other was gone.

Petrosky started for the center of the room, for his desk. "How do you know all these people?"

"I meet them in the gym."

"That where you get your girl talk in, California?"

"Pretty much."

The chair squealed under Petrosky's ass as he sat. Morrison grabbed a chair from his desk across the aisle and plopped into it looking like a lap dog: eager, inquisitive, expectant. Might as well throw him a bone. "Morrison?"

"What's up, Boss?"

"LaPorte come off confrontational to you?"

"Sure did. I think maybe she's had some bad experiences with cops. Type of place, maybe. Protecting the girls."

"Maybe." Petrosky's fingernails beat a rhythm on the desk. "Maybe something else is going on."

"Boss?"

"Two girls, similar backgrounds. One definitely stayed there, one possibly around before her death, and you don't cooperate?"

Morrison cleared his throat.

"What is it, California?"

"I thought it was weird that LaPorte didn't ask about safety. If I found out that someone who stayed at my place had been murdered, let alone two people, I'd worry about the guy showing up again. Even store owners sometimes ask about extra police protection after a robbery, or at least request a few drive-bys. Why wouldn't she?"

Petrosky stopped tapping. "Nicely done."

"Thanks, Boss."

"What's your take on the girl?" Petrosky's stomach twisted. He needed a bottle of Jack Daniels. He jerked open a drawer and pulled out a roll of antacids instead.

"Jumpy, probably in shock. Wanted to help, but I don't think she knew much. I'm sure she's seen a lot over there."

"Agreed." Petrosky unwrapped an antacid and popped it into his mouth. It coated his tongue with chalk.

"So you think there's something fishy about LaPorte?" Morrison said.

LaPorte was fiercely protective of those girls—she hadn't killed one. But to refuse to cooperate in a police investigation, knowing the victim had been there? Something was happening at that place, something everyone there was nervous about. Including Hannah.

Petrosky frowned and swallowed the mess on his tongue. "Let's find out."

TUESDAY, OCTOBER 13TH

Noelle sipped her coffee, willing the caffeine to enter her bloodstream ASAP. The morning had been shitty enough already. The second she'd walked in the door, her manager had come over to interrogate her, giant teeth flapping in the breeze.

"I noticed you had a few files left the night before last."

She'd sat straighter. "I thought I could finish them the following morning. I didn't have too much lined up, and the work day was over."

"The overseas offices are on a completely different time zone. Some needed those reports to begin the next day and you put them another day behind." His beady eyes had radiated disapproval.

"I'm sorry, sir." She'd hung her head.

"Don't let it happen again. There are plenty of people who can do this job." He had marched away, clenching his ass as if he were trying not to shit his pants.

Noelle's cheeks were still burning from the episode. She took another sip of coffee.

Hannah poked her head over the cubicle wall. "Everything okay?"

No, I'm just blowing everything. As usual. She was ashamed to admit it, but Hannah's willingness to pick up the slack was probably the only reason Noelle was still employed. And Hannah's support in her personal life was probably the only reason she was still sort of normal. Sort of.

Noelle loved her. Maybe more than she should.

"Everything's fine," Noelle said, drawing her lips into her best smile to prove that it was true. She held the manufactured grin until Hannah nodded and went back to her desk.

But everything wasn't fine. She didn't want to lose this job. She couldn't go home to a customer service job in a small town where nosiness was written into the charter. She could hear the meddlesome locals now: "I'm so sorry about your mother. How are you holding up?"

She would have to bite her tongue to keep from responding. Those assholes just wanted the story. Noelle's father being unfaithful was juicy enough, but her mother swallowing a bottle of pills over it was delectable.

Here in Ash Park, no one knew, not even Hannah. Noelle's life before Harwick Technical belonged to someone else, shoved into a closet in the corner of her brain. That was also where she hid Mr. Cantonelli, big shot attorney with sausage fingers and breath that reeked of sauerkraut and coffee. New York: where the buildings were as high as the crack addicts and stiff as the boss's cock, especially if you were desperate enough to do *anything* not to have to return to your nosy hometown and your father's disapproving stare.

Things had fallen apart as quickly as they had come together. She'd worked hard both on and off her feet, and Cantonelli had still given the promotion to some redheaded bitch.

He had paid for that one.

Noelle had brought him coffee that night for the last time. "Just so you know, Harry, I'm pregnant. I'm pretty sure there's a case there for sexual harassment, right?"

His face had gone from disbelief to outright terror.

The next morning she had clicked on the television. "And in breaking news, a local attorney was found dead late last night in his office by the cleaning crew. Foul play is not suspected."

She had faked a resume and gotten in at Harwick Technical before Mr. Cantonelli's body was in the ground. Faker or no, there was no one to dispute her credentials.

Not anymore.

Noelle's heel was doing a wild dance under the desk. She closed her eyes and saw Cantonelli behind her eyelids, his bulldog face contorting in ecstasy above her.

I'll make sure you get that job, honey.

Then Harry's face turned into her mother's, eyes open and vacant, vomit on her pillow like the day Noelle had found her.

Fucking slut, her mother said.

You weren't any better, Mom.

I got a house and a family out of it, her mother sneered. *What the fuck do you have?*

Noelle opened her eyes. Her boss walked by the glass doors.

She picked up her coffee cup and wondered if it would smash through the window and actually hit him if she threw it hard enough. Her fingers tightened on the mug, as if all her fury was pooling in her hands. She was going fucking insane. Noelle slammed her cup against the desk and coffee splashed over the brim.

"Noelle?" Ralph, her coworker across the way, was wringing his hands next to her cubicle.

"I was wondering if"—his eyes dropped to the floor—"if you might want to go out sometime? I mean, I know I've asked you to do stuff before, but I just keep ... hoping?"

Noelle took in Ralph's nerdy glasses and weak, vulnerable gopher face. Her first day there, he had watched her breasts as she panicked at the stack of paperwork. Her jaw clenched in anger.

"Sure," she said, trying to look excited.

Ralph's face lit up. "Really? I mean, great! Let me know where I can pick you up." He almost skipped back to his cubicle.

Asshole.

THE NEXT NIGHT, they ate at a small Italian restaurant off Orchard Lake Road.

"So what do your parents do?" he asked.

"They're in real estate."

"Cool. It's a good area for that. They live nearby?"

"No. They live in Texas," she said, hoping she would remember the information later.

"Oh."

After dinner she let him walk her to the elevators in her building. "Good night, Ralph," she said, pushing the button as she turned her back on him.

"Good night."

THE FOLLOWING WEEK he took her to a Tigers baseball game. His excitement was palpable as she sat with him behind third base. She stifled a yawn.

"Do you like baseball?" he asked.

"Sure," she said.

"My ex hated it. But then again, she hated me, too. Thought I was unstable, when really, she just couldn't keep up with me." He had a laugh like a donkey's bray.

Couldn't keep up? *Right.* Noelle kept her eyes on the first baseman as he reeled back to catch a ball and missed it.

Ralph cleared his throat. "My brother always liked to play baseball. Do you have any siblings?"

"No." She wondered what her brother Steve was up to these days. She hadn't spoken to his self-righteous ass since he'd called to tell her their father had died. She had hung up on him before he could tell her about the arrangements.

Ralph cocked his head. "You okay?"

Noelle plastered a smile on her face. "Of course. Why wouldn't I be?"

Ralph followed her to the lobby again that night. She let him kiss her softly on the cheek. "Good night, Ralph."

"Good night."

Later that week he took her out to dinner at an Indian restaurant downtown. The coconut curry was delicious.

"Where did your parents meet?" Ralph asked.

"A real estate conference."

"Was it love at first sight?"

She tried not to look bored. "Yes," she said.

When dinner was over, he took her back to her apartment and walked her through the lobby to the elevator again. She saw the affection in his eyes, the ache, the longing, the adoration. He was in deep enough to suffer.

"Well, I guess this is good ni—"

She put a finger on his lips. "Would you like to come up?"

Desire brightened his eyes. "Yes," he said, breath already ragged with anticipation.

She awoke at three the next morning with the weight of his arm pinning her to the bed. Her skin crawled where his arm made contact with her flesh. She shimmied from underneath him, padded into the kitchen and sucked down a glass of water at the sink, considering whether she should wake him and throw him out, or just wait until morning when he would leave on his own.

Her mind wandered to the night before, and how he'd been so willing and eager to put his tongue between her legs. She smiled.

I'll wait until morning.

Monday morning, Ralph approached her as she entered the office.

"Hey, Noelle!" He moved closer to put his arm around her.

"Hello." She sidestepped his hand and walked past him to her desk. The blank computer screen reflected her perfectly curled hair and smooth features. Not a hint of exhaustion as in previous weeks.

He followed her. "Is everything okay?"

She turned on the computer. "Yep." She watched her reflection morph into the Harwick Technical logo and stared at the sign-in window until Ralph finally walked away.

Hannah poked her head over the partition. "So ... how'd it go this weekend?"

Noelle shrugged. "You know, same old same old."

THE NEXT DAY, there were flowers on her desk when she arrived at the office. Ralph stood by the water cooler, waiting for her reaction. She dumped the flowers into the trash and watched his face fall.

THURSDAY MORNING, Ralph was waiting for her at her cubicle. His face was drawn and there were bags under his eyes, but his mouth was set in a furious line.

"Hey," he spat.

"Hey." She turned on the computer and stared at the screen as it booted up.

"Did I do something wrong?"

Two priors:She could see his fists in her peripheral vision, clenched at his sides near her desktop.

She shook her head. "Nope."

His breath whistled through his nostrils on a long, deep inhale. He sighed it out. "I just ... I really like you. I thought we had something good going. I mean, I know it was only a few dates, but—"

"Yeah, sometimes things just don't work out."

"This is tearing me the fuck up," he said.

She shrugged, refusing to look at him.

"Can't we just try again?" His voice rose. "Maybe dinner? A movie? I feel like I'm going insane. I can't think about anything else. I'm on Xanax for Christ's sake." He was practically yelling, loud enough for everyone in the office to hear him. Not that Hannah would be all judge-y about it. And Toni never said shit.

"No thanks, Ralph. I don't think you can make me happy."

But as she heard him stomp away, she did feel a glimmer of satisfaction. Not happiness exactly, but close enough. Good old Ralph ... that boring fucker.

Maybe the next one would be more interesting. Find the right guy and you could get him to do anything.

Anything at all.

Hannah peeked into her cubicle. "Xanax, huh? Are you okay?"

"Yeah, I'm fine. Sometimes, they just like you a little more than you like them, right? Maybe one of these days we can go out, take my mind off all this."

Hannah nodded uncertainly and disappeared behind the partition. Noelle turned back to her computer and tried to hide her smile.

FRIDAY, OCTOBER 30TH

PETROSKY STARED across the cherry desk at Dr. Stephen McCallum. The department psychiatrist was Santa Claus in the off season, at least two-hundred-and-fifty pounds, with ruddy cheeks and a head full of curly white hair that matched his beard. No red coat, though; McCallum's green button-down shirt and brown tweed jacket strained against his bulk.

"Do your victims have any common acquaintances?" McCallum asked.

"Nope."

"Any promising physical evidence?"

Fuck no, there wasn't. No fingerprints on any of the restraints, but tons of random prints all over the crime scenes, probably from kids smoking dope or squatters. "At the Trazowski scene, we found fingerprints all over that basement from some guy who had a previous arrest. Crack addict, says he slept in the basement once, shit in a corner. The restraints are expensive and the dissection meticulous enough that I don't think corner-shitter is our guy."

McCallum nodded. "Agreed. What else?"

"No sexual assault, no murder weapons found, and no witnesses. Trazowski and her kids were pretty much ghosts; I've got nothing on her movements until she arrived at the shelter, and less than a day after she left, she was filleted in the basement of a house she has no connection to. The father of Trazowski's kids is currently doing four years in New York on a series of B and Es and he didn't know Lawrence." So not a pissed-off father situation. That would have made his life too fucking easy. "As for Lawrence, she had an abusive boyfriend with eight previous arrests for domestic violence, but he's got an alibi the night of the murder. She had two priors: one for domestic violence and another for prostitution. Then there's her abandoned kid."

Petrosky blinked hard against the headache that was taking root in his temples. "The kid died of hypothermia, no signs of violence, but I turned it over to the prosecutor's office in case they feel like going after Keil. I don't think much will come of it."

McCallum leaned forward in his chair and folded his hands on the desktop. "That bothers you."

"Of course it fucking bothers me."

"Because you'd give anything to have your kid back, and here people are throwing them away?"

"Because it's fucked up, that's why." Petrosky had seen McCallum himself after Julie died. Mandatory leave, they'd said. Fucking bureaucratic bullshit.

"Has the anger abated any?"

"Goddammit, McCa—"

"I'll take that as a no. Remember, anger can be a symptom of both depression and complicated grief, but it's not something to ignore. Drinking still under control?"

"Everything's under control," Petrosky said tightly. He rubbed a hand over the stubble on his cheek. "Let's get back on track here."

"Fine, have it your way. Lawrence, then."

"Lawrence. No family and no friends that the boyfriend mentioned." A lack of acquaintances wasn't uncommon in these situations, but it made Petrosky's job far more difficult. Fewer friends around, fewer ways to trace a person's movements. Fewer leads. He sighed.

"Okay, so not much to go on there. Anyone else who might provide you with some leads?"

"Maybe," Petrosky said. "What's your take on LaPorte?"

"Her file is very interesting. The early arrests for protesting and civil disobedience aren't especially concerning given the time period. However, when paired with other symptoms, trouble with the law can be a sign of antisocial personality disorder, the clinical diagnosis related to psychopathic tendencies. The later arrest for the murder of her husband certainly fits that bill."

"It was dismissed as self-defense. When a man stabs you with a kitchen knife, you're allowed to bludgeon him to death with a tire iron."

"I happen to agree," McCallum said wryly. "And running a non-profit shelter for abuse victims speaks to empathy and a history of victimhood as opposed to someone with antisocial personality disorder. Whatever attitude made you suspicious of her is more likely related to her protecting those under her care than an admission of guilt."

That much was true. LaPorte wasn't a suspect. But between LaPorte's defiance and Hannah's anxiety something still felt wrong.

"What about the poems left at the crime scenes?" McCallum asked.

"From what I understand, that poem is open to interpretation, and hotly debated. The whole book is a psychedelic Freudian's dream."

Petrosky had gleaned as much from Morrison's assessment last week: "The poem he's using is from the end of the book. The whole thing's pretty weird, so it's hard to tell what he's saying. If I were him, I would have used the Walrus and the Carpenter. All those poor oysters."

"So you're saying you're the Walrus?" Petrosky had asked.

"Koo koo ka choo, Boss."

So much for a fancy-ass English degree.

McCallum laced his fingers on the desk. "The poetry is a conundrum, but the typical profile for this type of crime still fits. White male between the ages of twenty-five and thirty-five. A planner, intelligent, probably well educated in this case. Someone shrewd, calculating."

Petrosky nodded. "Could the dissection be related to the fact that both were mothers?"

"If he were dissecting only the uterus, the reproductive organs, I'd say yes. But according to the medical examiner's reports, he dissected the stomach, the intestines, and in one case, part of the esophagus. Almost as if he's looking for something there."

Petrosky pictured the gaping hole in Trazowski's abdomen, envisioned someone rummaging around, hands submerged to the wrists, forearms coated in gore. His gut clenched. "What would you look for inside someone's stomach?"

"Something he fed them, perhaps, or maybe he wondered what their last meal had been. Or maybe he's just interested in the mechanics. While the dissections were deliberate and rather precise, there were some small tears around the incisions, so I'd guess that he simply lacked the medical knowledge to complete the job perfectly. And the fact that they were alive when he cut into them speaks to an underlying rage or past slight. You might be looking for someone who was hurt by a maternal figure. Lack of attachment in these cases is prominent."

"So our guy had a shitty upbringing?"

"Possibly. But some psychopaths are born without the ability to emote, while others only show sociopathic behaviors after severe abuse or neglect. Either type can end up killing people in fairly horrific ways. It's hard to tell which category this individual would fall into since the presentation is generally the same."

So their killer was likely a younger male, not a physician, who possibly, but not certainly, suffered childhood abuse or neglect. The abused became the abusers, if they lived long enough. Everyone had a motivation. Not that this excused leaving a murdered child to be torn apart in a field. Petrosky's chest tightened and he settled into the anger, letting it focus him. He needed a lead. He needed to think.

How did the killer choose his victims? Both women had a history of arrests for prostitution as well as drug charges. They were similar physically, with thin bodies and blond hair, though that wasn't hard to find.

Petrosky cracked his knuckles and the noise startled McCallum's hands off the desk. *Jumpy motherfucker.* Petrosky eyed him, but he recovered quickly, leaning back and steepling his fingers beneath his chin in official shrink style.

"You know, this guy is a goddamn stereotype. Kill the hookers. Like that hasn't been done."

"Whether it's the prostitution thing or not, there's something about these women," McCallum said. "They remind him of someone. And whoever it is, he's killing her over and over again."

"You think he killed the original?"

"Perhaps. But maybe he couldn't. She could have died of some other cause. Or maybe she got away and he doesn't know where she is."

"Let's hope someone got away." Petrosky stood. "The next one won't unless we find him."

McCallum shrugged his fleshy shoulders. "That's your department, Ed. Not mine."

McCallum walked him out, huffing as he tried to keep up.

Petrosky kept his eyes on the hallway in front of him. He needed to find a more solid link between the victims, or at least someone else who knew something. It was either that, or wait until the guy chopped up someone else and left a clue. If he left a clue. Hannah Montgomery, the young woman who had been a spitting image of Julie, flashed through Petrosky's mind. He pushed the image away and opened the door.

Icy air brushed his face, but the wind was laced with the smell of grass and earth, a stubborn summer still rasping its final breaths.

"Later, Ed. And I'm here to help you work things through, on this, or—"

"I know, Steve. I know."

Petrosky flipped his collar against the breeze and headed for the precinct.

"Petrosky!" Shannon Taylor's long jacket flew behind her like a cape as she hurried toward him across the lot.

"You looking for my rookie again, Taylor?"

She stepped onto the curb. "Yeah. Where is he?"

"Out. Tracking our vics."

"He's good, Petrosky. Got an eye for details."

"I know. But he'll be better."

"You're taking a lot of time with him. You feel bad because his dad died, or—"

"Did you need something, Shannon?"

"No 'Taylor' anymore, huh?" She smiled. He didn't.

"All right, so I have a defendant in holding across the street. Former or current prostitute, arrested on domestic violence, claiming self-defense."

"And? She need someone to bail her out and you thought you'd ask me?"

"She says she's been over to the shelter. Knew one of your victims—Trazowski. Kinda shaken up about it."

Petrosky squinted toward the street. The detention center hulked in the background. "You been pulling information from my rookie?"

"Just talking."

"How long's she got?"

"Transfer later today to the William Dickerson facility. I told her we'd probably cut her some slack if she cooperated with your homicide case."

"I'll check it out."

Taylor started toward the precinct.

"And, Taylor?"

She turned.

"Don't mess with Morrison."

"I'm not messing with him. He's nice. And unlike you, he doesn't try to hide it from everyone."

"Thanks for the helpful tip, Taylor. I'll let Baker know you said she needs to plead the fifth and focus on changing her name before you lock her ass up."

"You're such an asshole." She turned on her heel and walked away, cape-coat flapping behind her.

It was the same goodbye every time. He smiled at her back and crossed the street toward the Ash Park Detention Center. Halfway across the road, an oncoming Chevy honked at him. Petrosky stopped in the street, forcing the driver to halt with a squeal of brakes. He flipped open his badge. Deciding that asshole looked appropriately chagrined, Petrosky left the street for the detention center where a lady cop with a bored expression checked him through the metal detector inside the front door.

Inside, the waiting room looked like the DMV but felt more miserable, if such a thing were possible. Behind a counter surrounded by Plexiglas, a man with ghost-white skin and a face flat enough to have been run over with a steam roller raised caterpillar eyebrows, too indifferent to bother asking what Petrosky wanted. *A. Cook* glinted off the badge on his chest.

"Cook."

"Petrosky."

"Need a form. Got a few questions for one of your detainees."

Cook pulled a yellow carbon sheet from a drawer and slid it through the Plexiglas slot. "You make them sound like they're on their way to Guantanamo."

"Some of them might as well be for all the good this place'll do them."

He scrawled on the form and Cook pulled it back through the slot, a yellow tongue retracting into a Plexiglass lizard.

"Give me ten."

Petrosky moved to the blue-upholstered chairs, set in rows across the middle of the room. Three seats away, a mother with stringy orange hair fed gummy bears to an overwrought toddler, probably waiting for daddy to be brought to the visiting area so they could pretend they were a family for thirty minutes. Behind her, a woman in a business suit picked at a hangnail with a faraway look on her face. Waiting on a brother or a father, Petrosky thought—someone far removed from her own station in life, but whom she just couldn't let go.

The door next to the Plexiglass-enclosed counter clacked open and the previous round of visitors emerged, all from different walks of life, but all wearing the same expression: forlorn, defeated, depressed. Behind Petrosky, the exit whooshed open and closed, open and closed, bringing with it fresh bursts of misty winter that he could barely smell over the stench of hand sanitizer, dry toast and cheap perfume.

He took his place in line with the others, behind the woman in the business suit. She'd abandoned her hangnail and was now twirling her short, dark curls with such ferocity that Petrosky expected one to snap off in her hand. The toddler was wailing somewhere in the back, a warning siren for his mother to run for the exit before whomever they were seeing sucked her down too. She hushed the child as they walked single file through another metal detector and into a holding pen between two bulletproof doors, then into the sterile-looking interior hallway that led to the visitor stalls.

A young black officer with a drawn face and a full beard stood in the aisle holding a list. "Chapman, second stall," he said, gesturing with the paper toward the first hallway. The woman in the business suit raised a hand, stumbled forward and disappeared down the aisle.

"Baker, end of the line."

Petrosky followed the officer's finger to the last stall, where Sarah Baker stood waiting for him on the other side of a chest-high cinderblock wall. He peered at her through the thick black mesh that ran from the top of the wall to the ceiling. She was thick and stocky, the kind of girl you'd want on your side in a street brawl.

She edged her face forward and squinted, as if trying to get a better look at him through the mesh screen. "Who are you?" Her voice had the low husky quality of a lounge singer.

"Detective Petrosky. I heard you might have some information on Jane Trazowski."

"Oh, that." A wet slap, the pop of bubble gum. "I met her at the shelter over there on Hamerstein."

"LaPorte's place."

"Yeah, her and me were talking at dinner one night. She was real beat up. Bruises everywhere. Couldn't hardly eat on account of her lip, all busted up. Even had those marks on her wrists, the kind from rope or whatever."

"She'd been tied up?"

"Yep. Said the guy paid for the night but he was into some kinky stuff. Gave her twice her normal."

"Did she describe him?"

Pop. "She said tall, I think. Not muscle-y like, but tall."

"Hair?"

"I don't remember. I don't think she said."

"Eyes?"

Pop. "She just said tall and that he was an asshole. Told him to stop and he said he already paid her so she couldn't say no."

Entitled fuck. "Sounds like an asshole, all right."

"So was it him? The one that killed her?"

"We don't know. Where'd he pick her up?"

She shrugged. "Didn't say."

"Tattoos? Anything?"

"Nuh uh. Nothing like that. Just that he was mean and she was afraid to go home because he might know where she lived."

"So he picked her up close to her house, then."

Pause. "Well … I dunno. Maybe. Or maybe he dropped her off. I'm not sure."

"How long were you there with her?"

"She left the day after I got there. You can only stay ten days at a time, but I think she was only there one or two."

"Where were her kids?"

"I dunno."

"Why didn't she bring them with her?"

Pop. Pop. Pop. Petrosky waited.

"I only really talked to her that once at dinner. Didn't even know she had kids."

"What'd you have?"

"What?"

"For dinner."

"Burgers." *Pop.* "They were good. The assistant toasted the buns and stuff."

"Assistant?" LaPorte had called her "Hannah" at the shelter. Now his file referred to her by her last name. "Ms. Montgomery?"

"Uh … yeah, whatever. She was real nice."

Ms. Montgomery, the assistant, not Julie, his daughter. His stomach tightened anyway as he remembered the shock of the resemblance. "I'm sure she was nice. I'm sure they all are."

"Sometimes they aren't on account of them being hurt. It makes people mean. Some of us anyway."

"Hurt?" Heat flared in his chest. He clenched his fist against his thigh.

"Yeah, that girl—"

"Ms. Montgomery." *Not Julie*.

"Yeah. She had a few bruises on her wrist. She covered them up real good, but I know what it means when you have concealer rubbing off on your shirt sleeves."

"She ever mention who hurt her?" Petrosky asked.

Baker squinted at him though the screen. "Why? Is she dead too?"

FRIDAY, OCTOBER 30TH

I CHEWED my cheek and typed in another batch of dismissals. Engineer Ernie Smack was not nearly as intimidating on paper as his name suggested he'd be if I tried to fire him in person. Luckily, Noelle had let him go this morning and I was just helping her play catch up on her files. Not that I minded; I needed something to keep my brain busy so as not to end up in a padded room.

So far, my efforts were working. Over the last week, things had been so quiet at the shelter that my panic had finally subsided. And it was looking like the first victim was completely unrelated to the shelter or to me. When I saw her unfamiliar face on the news—bleached blond hair and polar bear white skin—I was so relieved that I didn't even mind when Jake snapped the channel back to his lame car race.

This ride on the paranoia train happened all the time, and I wished I could stop buying tickets. I once freaked out for three weeks after the news reported a tall man with dark hair had strangled a female store owner whose face kinda looked like mine. Which obviously meant that he was trying to find me and got confused. I tend to be a paranoid jerk and not the cute kind that can feign innocence about it. At least I'm aware of it, I guess.

The horned owl on my desk glared at me. *I should break his other ear off. Or get a plant for him to hide under.*

I looked up at the sound of heels clacking on the floor. Noelle stood at the entrance to my cubicle, smiling, her lips shiny from a fresh coat of gloss. "What's up?" she said.

Just contemplating torturing an inanimate ceramic figurine. Also, someone might be after me and killing girls I work with at a place you don't even know I go to.

"Not much. Crushing people's dreams and occupational aspirations with the touch of a few buttons."

"Eh, I'm sure Dominic has a reason."

I stared at her, trying not to think about lying beneath Jake's naked body the other night, eyes squeezed shut, swallowing Mr. Harwick's name while Jake moaned in my ear. "You're on a first name basis?"

"Well, no. But hopefully I will be soon." Noelle winked.

My face grew warm. Subject change time. I nodded at the other side of the room and lowered my voice. "How are things with Ralph? He seems bummed, and he's been watching you all day."

Noelle shrugged. "He wasn't what I was after, I guess. Boring, you know?"

There was something else in Noelle's eyes, but it passed before I could get a handle on it.

"Anyway," Noelle said, "how about we let off some steam after work? There's a club downtown that I've been dying to check out. They keep sending me ads. Maybe it will give me a little practice for the boss, or at least help me find someone more interesting than Mister Excitement over there." Noelle jerked her head in Ralph's direction.

I needed to stop chewing on my lip before I ate it clean off my face. One day, Noelle was going to get tired of asking me to go out with her. Maybe she'd even go find another friend altogether. *Shit.*

"I'm not sure ... I mean, I don't know if Jake—" My wrist throbbed. I cleared my throat. "I can't."

"Girl, it's fine. Next time, okay?" She waved her hand in that universal shooing-a-fruit-fly gesture.

Ouch. I hoped I had better than fruit fly status—buzzing, fruit-stealing, poop-eating, assholes. Did fruit flies even eat poop? A biologist I was not.

"Yeah, next time," I said to the owls since Noelle was already gone.

My cell phone rang. I grabbed it out of the bottom drawer.

"Hey, baby. What's up?"

Jake was chewing on something, and the wet crunch of chips or pretzels made me want to gag. In the background, the television chattered about leasing a car.

"Just working," I said. *Like you should be doing.*

"My mom wants us to come over for dinner tonight," Jake said.

"By 'we' do you mean 'you?'"

"Why do you always do that?" he demanded.

I took a deep breath. He was right. I was in a horrible mood and in no shape to be around his mother. Not that my heart ever swelled at the prospect of sitting in her living room, choking on cigarette smoke, watching her glower at me. *I should run off with Mario, my silent but poisonous plant—or Horny the rage-faced owl.*

"Sorry, I just ... don't think she likes me very much."

"She likes you fine. I just think ... I dunno, I think maybe she wishes we'd gotten married before we moved in together."

I'm pretty sure she just thinks you can do better. I rose and peeked at Noelle, on the phone in her cubicle. Maybe making plans with someone less fruit-fly-like. My heart squeezed. "Actually, I'm going to work late tonight. I'll get dinner before I come home. You go ahead."

"Fine," he spat.

Don't be mad, don't be mad. "There's some extra money in the drawer in the kitchen. Why don't you grab some drinks and dessert for you and your mom? I won't be too late."

The channel changed in the background. Game show. Judge show. News show.

How do you get your boyfriend to do sit ups?
Put the remote between his toes!

There was a pause, then a sound like Jake was rummaging in a drawer. The shuffling stopped. He must have found the money.

"Well, okay." His voice was softer. "Don't spend too much on dinner."

"Okay." *Like you should have any say where I put my money.* "See you when I get home. Tell your mom I said hello."

"I will. Love you."

Not mad. Thank goodness. "Love you too."

The line clicked, taking the chatter of the television with it. I tossed my cell back in the drawer and headed to Noelle's cubicle. "Change of plans," I said, my heart twitching with nerves or maybe ... excitement.

Her hand pressed against her chest in mock surprise. "You mean Little Miss Goodie Two Shoes is actually going to go out and absorb some nightlife?"

"I guess so. I just need to make sure I get back early. Like, maybe dinner, and then we can stop in at the club but head out after an hour or so."

"Aw, but no one's out at five, Hannah."

Jake's mother usually slugged back half a dozen beers and smoked a pack before she took Jake home. Last time I went to visit her, we got home at midnight—not because we were having a blast, but because his mother had fallen asleep on the couch and Jake said she'd be angry if he didn't say goodbye to her. "If we can get out of there by ten thirty, I should be fine."

"Okay, Cinderella, I will return you home punctually and as virtuous as when you left." Noelle's eyes said she would do anything to break that promise if I was willing. She smiled. "You won't regret it."

Robert ate a late dinner at Johnny's, an Italian pizza kitchen around the block from his house. The food was good but not great, eaten over a nondescript tablecloth and served by a nondescript waiter. Despite his obvious boredom, the waiter looked expectant when he handed over the check, like he thought he deserved a tip.

He's going to be disappointed.

The car ride was no better. Every accident within sixty miles was clustered along his route to the club. Robert bit back his rage as best he could, though it didn't stop him from aiming expletives and obscene hand gestures at an elderly woman in a neighboring car. Her horrified eyes improved his mood considerably.

Thomas was waiting for him at the entrance to the parking structure a block from the club, eating something fluorescent from a small plastic bag in his palm.

As Robert approached, Thomas held the bag out in offering. "Gummy bear?" Thomas's tongue was green.

Imbecile. "You look like a fucking leprechaun," Robert said.

The drone of music and lively chatter swelled as they neared the club. Each drew IDs for the muscled door attendant who was hulking behind rope chains and currently squinting at the license of a skinny blonde wearing stilettos and a miniskirt that left half her ass hanging out. *Slut.* The bouncer waved her through and stared Robert down over the top of his fake license. Robert stiffened.

"Twenty apiece, pay at the door." The guard handed Robert's ID back and nodded at Thomas.

They walked to the entrance, handed the cover charge to a grim-faced skinhead with barbed wire tattooed around his left bicep, and entered the club.

Inside, the warehouse-like expanse stunk of stale smoke and the rank tang of sweat. The place was already teeming with bodies, a mix of men and women in sharp business attire as if they had come straight from work, and casually-dressed young people who gave off "regulars" vibes. A few slouched men in cargo shorts and women in spaghetti straps scrutinized other patrons as if deciding whether anyone there was worth fucking.

At the bar, a young woman in a tight halter dress approached a stodgy Tom, Dick, or Harry in an expensive suit. She rubbed her breasts on his arm and whispered in his ear. Robert narrowed his eyes in disgust. The succubus always found her prey early.

"There's a table near the back," Thomas said. "It must be our lucky night."

They threaded their way to a small table with a wraparound leather bench across from the bar. The polished wooden tabletop was littered with empty glasses and wrinkled napkins. A few tiny stirring straws were set up in a tic-tac-toe formation in the center.

"Wanna play?" Thomas gestured to the straws.

"Nah. I hear leprechauns suck at that game."

Thomas stuck out his tongue and it glowed eerily yellow under the black lights. He really was an idiot.

A redheaded waitress appeared wearing tight pants and a harried expression. Her lithe hands scurried like rabbits, clearing the table into a brown bin. She set the bin at her feet and whipped out a small pad of paper from her back pocket. "What can I get you?"

"Vodka and Red Bull," Robert said.

Thomas shrugged. "Whatever you've got on tap."

She scrawled the orders, shoved the pad into her pocket, and flashed them a tense smile. "Be right back, guys."

Robert watched her over Thomas's shoulder as she walked away, her hips sashaying more than seemed necessary. Maybe that was for his benefit. Maybe not. He frowned as she disappeared into the back with the bin and their table scraps.

Thomas was focused on the televisions behind the bar. Robert glanced at the screen where a common-looking woman in a blue suit yammered into the camera about something surely as tiresome as her flaring nostrils.

"CNN, huh?" Robert said.

Thomas met Robert's eyes and grinned. "Nothing says it's time to party like stock market updates."

Robert looked past Thomas again, but the redhead did not reappear. When he drew his gaze back, Thomas was staring at him with knowing eyes, and Robert resisted the urge to throttle him.

"You looking for our waitress?"

Panic chilled Robert's marrow. "Yeah, I'm thirsty."

"Aw, come on, man! You were staring at her when she walked away. Not that I blame you." He winked, tarnishing her.

No, he could not let Thomas take this away from him, not if she was The One. There was no time to dwell; Robert felt her return in every cell of his body. She emerged through the doors, eyes alight with passion and the promise of resurrection, of atonement, of a chance to prove himself worthy and noble. He had been noble once.

He could do it again.

For love.

And he had loved her, if only for a day during his senior year in high school. Mindy Haliburton. Each twist of her fingers, each bite of her lip had been a sure indication that she was trying to control herself. But she was Reverend Haliburton's daughter.

They were in the Reverend's basement when Robert had pushed her to the floor. "Don't worry, Mindy. I understand," he whispered

Of course he'd understood. He understood that by fighting him, by making the lust his alone, she might absolve herself of guilt and save herself from Hell. He understood that her thoughts were as deep as his, or she wouldn't have asked him there. And he surely understood that she wanted this, no matter what she had to say to protect her reputation and her soul. Each desperate sound she made mirrored his own desperation, their mutual desire mingling with fear of repercussions, their need for one another overriding their terror.

"No! Robby, stop!"

But he heard what she really meant: *Yes! Robby, harder!*

When it was over, she lay still, eyes bloodshot, face ashen and laced with tears. He stroked her cheek and ran his tongue over her bottom lip.

You're welcome.

He had admitted to the rape, despite their mutual need. He had saved her from her own sins by sacrificing himself to hordes of inmates who had offered no remorse, no leniency, no forgiveness. There was nothing more noble one person could do for another.

Pride welled in his heart.

"Here you go, guys."

Robert refocused his attention on the redheaded waitress as she set Thomas's glass in front of him. She had a tinkling voice that grew a little hoarse as she increased her volume to be heard, as if Pollyanna were trying her hand as a phone sex operator. Robert met her eyes. She did not look away. He touched her wrist as she put his drink down, and electricity zipped up his arm, through his chest, and down into his groin. She pulled her hand away, too quickly. Her eyes, once warm, now emanated surprise and fear—and revulsion.

She knew. She could feel it in his touch.

"Can I get you anything else?" she asked, her voice suddenly not so much sultry as irritating. Robert shook his head.

"No thanks," Thomas said with an idiotic smile, oblivious to the whole exchange.

But Robert was not. *I am a doomed man, and she knows it.*

The waitress picked up an empty cup, her eyes wide. Watching him. Marking him. The mark of Cain.

No one will ever offer me forgiveness. He kept his gaze on her, memorizing her features as she retreated.

Especially her.

"Earth to Jim! You hear what I said?"

Robert blinked at Thomas.

"Two just walked in, our age, both of them gorgeous. The blonde looked right at me."

Robert ground his teeth together. They'd surely sense his wickedness and mark him like all the others. But if there was any chance, any at all …

His jaw relaxed.

"They're in the booth next to us. We should say hello."

"Yes," Robert said, plastering on his best come-hither smile. "It would be cruel to make them wait."

THE HANGOUT WAS A POSH ESTABLISHMENT, but the bouncer shooed Noelle and me in without asking us to pay the cover, which made me feel attractive and also a little like a prostitute flaunting her wares to save twenty bucks. The music pounded through immense speakers and strobe lights pulsed flashes of red and yellow, green and blue, in time to the music. Noelle stood on her tiptoes to scour the seating situation, then dragged me to a back corner booth across from the bar. The vacating couple was still collecting their drinks when she clambered into the seat. I waited until they disappeared into the crowd, and sat as our waitress approached.

Noelle ordered a daiquiri. I got a cranberry juice with lime.

"I better take it easy on these," I said when the drinks were delivered. "I don't want you to have to carry me out of here."

Noelle laughed, but it was hard to hear her over the music. I watched her face, trying to decide if I was supposed to be making conversation as she scanned the room. I settled for working on my drink.

Within minutes, the booth began to feel like a prison. A gopher in my chest clawed at my rib cage. I pictured the rodent from *Caddyshack* and squinted at the subtitles on the muted television behind the bar, half expecting Jake's face to leap onto the screen, eyes radiating disapproval. *I really need to get out more.*

"Hey, need some company?" Two men stood next to our table, drinks in hand. The one who spoke was blond, with chiseled features and a wide mouth. His taller, darker companion looked like he had just stepped off the cover of G.Q. His eyes were sharp like a hawk's and ringed with aqua, the unique coloring visible even in the dim light of the club. As our eyes met, a pang of memory flittered across my mind and disappeared. My breath caught, but I could no longer remember why.

"Sure." Noelle scooted toward me in the booth and the blond slid in beside her. I moved to the end to avoid being squished.

"I'm Thomas," the blond said, offering his hand. Noelle took it and smiled at him.

"I'm Jim," said Mr. G.Q. He was watching me, presumably waiting for me to tell him my name, but my mouth was too dry to speak. When I said nothing, he parked next to Thomas.

Noelle raised her voice over the pounding music. "I'm Noelle, and this is my shy friend Hannah."

Thomas waved, and it was so exaggerated and goofy that I almost smiled. Jim bowed his head once. "Nice to meet you, Hannah."

I picked up my juice and put it to my lips instead of responding. Social awkwardness was a bitch. *Dammit, Hannah, act normal!*

Noelle glanced at me and turned back to the guys. "So, Thomas, what do you do?"

"Yoga." Thomas's voice was strained, speaking over the music, but it was still mellow somehow. Calm. "I also play on the jungle gym whenever possible. Buy catnip. Not for me, mind you, but that doesn't make it less true."

Noelle laughed. "No, for work."

"We're both in the automotive industry," Thomas said, pointing to Jim. "Being in the Motor City, it was between designing cars and starting a Motown boy band. But I can't dance."

Noelle's eyes were on Thomas's face as she shifted toward him and put her hand on his arm. "Original. Most guys just go for 'I'm a big-shot lawyer' or 'I'm an engineer.'"

Thomas's smile was infectious: straight, white, genuine. "I have to play to my strengths. I'm better at creative dialogue than dancing anyway."

Noelle laughed harder than I'd ever made her laugh and a pang of jealousy hooked my stomach.

"Did you go to school here?" Noelle asked him.

"Yep. University of Michigan," Thomas said.

My head throbbed in time to the music. I set my glass on the table next to Noelle's.

As if remembering there was someone else at the table, Noelle took her hand off Thomas's arm and sat back in the booth. "How about you, Jim? Where did you go to school?"

Jim sipped his drink and watched me like he hadn't heard her. It was probably my overactive imagination, but it didn't stop the niggling at the base of my skull. There was hunger in his fixed stare, like he wanted to eat me alive.

"Cal Tech," he said finally.

I turned my head and looked across the way, behind the bar, toward the television again—anywhere to avoid Jim's eyes. The view wasn't any better over there. On the flat screen, a spunky young newscaster feigned seriousness while, behind her, police officers walked by with a black body bag on a stretcher. It was the same shot that had been on replay for weeks as the media exploited the murders of two young women. Jane and what's-her-name. Meredith. I winced.

"Scary stuff," Jim said.

I turned toward him but kept my eyes on his forehead.

"Don't worry, they'll catch him," he said.

"What makes you think it's a him?" Noelle asked.

Jim's head cocked to the side. "It always is, isn't it?"

Noelle's face darkened so briefly that I thought I

imagined it.

"Things aren't always as they seem," Thomas said, and his voice was solemn, all trace of humor gone.

The hair on my arms stood.

Jim painted an abstract in the condensed water on his glass. "I mean, it's always some dude who is so fucked up in the head that no one else wants anything to do with him. Look at Dahmer. Same story, different guy."

Noelle elbowed me lightly. "Hannah, you okay?"

I cleared my throat. "Yeah, I guess I ... feel a little sorry for some of those guys. Not the murdering part, but the part where they're so desperate that they think their only option is to kill someone."

There was a pregnant pause. *Did I just say I feel sorry for murderers?* If only I were a magician so I could disappear. Behind us, the black lights flickered off and neon strobes swept over the room, like searchlights seeking to highlight my stupidity.

"Hey, how about another round of drinks?" Thomas asked, summoning the waitress with his trademarked goofy wave. Noelle giggled and nodded her agreement.

Thomas was my new personal hero. *I'll call him Captain Awkward and he can come to my rescue in ridiculous social situations.* It was an ingenious plan. So why was my skin still crawling?

I twisted toward Noelle but she was whispering in Thomas's ear. In my peripheral, I saw Jim, openly staring at me, his eyes alert and sharp and ... famished. My heart backflipped. *No. Don't panic. Not now.*

Too late. I couldn't breathe. I grabbed my cranberry juice to loosen my vocal cords and the cup slipped, splattering juice down the front of my shirt.

"Shit."

Well, at least you can still talk. "I'll be right back," I croaked like someone who had just turned from a princess to a frog but without any of the royal pizzazz. I squeezed through happy women, angry women, and dancing couples to where a hand-painted wooden sign decreed *Ladies* above a little stick figure of a person in a dress. I was wearing jeans. I considered using the men's bathroom to make a point but jerked open the door to the ladies' room.

The bathroom was crowded but only for the stalls. In an alcove off to the side, I found a place at the sink and scrubbed at the stain with a wad of wet paper towels. The stain spread. I scrubbed harder, trying to avoid the buttons so I didn't tear them off. Other women walked by to the other sink, but none acknowledged me. I kept my eyes on the bleeding stain.

Why couldn't you just have a vodka tonic like everyone else?
Because you can't handle being out of control even a little bit.

A little more water, some soap, and a ream of paper towels later, the spot had faded from maroon to a sickly pink—still visible, but better. My heart had slowed as well. I looked into the mirror.

Shit. Under the florescent lights my cream-colored blouse was almost completely see through. *Shit, shit, shit.* At least the stain had covered my undergarment. Now, the outline of my bra was clearly visible to everyone.

I stepped to the hand dryer and jabbed the button, half squatting and stretching the blouse as best I could to get the fabric under the airflow. The dryer stopped humming. I pushed the button with my elbow and frantically tried to get the material back into the perfect place before the hot air stopped again. By the sixth round, I was smashing the button, less worried about the shirt and more consumed with the desire to kick the dryer into space. Why couldn't the thing just keep going? Like anyone's hands really got dry in one push!

"Hannah? What are you doing?" Noelle stood in the doorway, eyebrows raised. I desperately wished for a sudden power outage so I could make a groping, awkward run for it.

"I was ... trying to get this blouse to work again." Out of the corner of my eye, I caught a glimpse of myself in the mirror: hair askew from the errant dryer wind, cheeks flushed with exertion, and that fucking shirt stretched and hanging off my front, a disarray of transparent ripples.

Noelle began to laugh. I joined her, and once I got going, I had no ability or desire to stop. Tears rolled down my face and mingled with the sweat of panicked shirt drying. Three other women walked into the bathroom and tossed each other knowing looks. *Wow, look who's already had one too many*, their pursed lips said.

I wiped my eyes with the back of my hand. "Can we take off, please? This is enough excitement for one night."

"Aw, come on! We've only been here for an hour! Plus, with your invisible shirt, you're finally in something club appropriate. Maybe you'll even get laid when you get home! Nothing like a little ooh and aah to make the embarrassment worth it, right? Though I'm not sure Jake knows how to get you to make those noises anyway."

Point taken. "What's the difference between ooh and aah?" I said.

Noelle raised her eyebrows.

"About three inches."

We collapsed into laughter again. Noelle was the first to catch her breath. "Let's get our stuff. I already got their numbers, but I want to say goodbye. Here, take this."

She handed me her cardigan. I pulled it on and followed Noelle out of the bathroom toward the table. The guys stood when they saw us—impressive, actually—but it didn't change anything.

"I'm sorry, gentlemen, but we have to head out," Noelle said.

Thomas's face fell. "But it's so early! Is there anything we can do to change your minds?"

Noelle shook her head. "We had a little wardrobe malfunction."

Their banter faded in my ears. Jim's eyes roved over me, as engaged as if I had suggested we strip naked and hula hoop. The prickle of goosebumps I'd felt earlier returned with renewed ferocity. I touched Noelle's arm and jerked my head toward the door.

"Hopefully we can get together again soon," Jim said.

I tried to force a polite nod, a grin, some kind of acknowledgment, but my body was shouting *no way in hell*. Noelle and I weaved toward the exit through throngs of club-goers smelling of Axe Body Spray and desperation. It wasn't until we reached the street that I felt my body relax as if an invisible wire had been cut.

"Why the hell would it be okay for you to go to a club?"

My face was on fire. "I wasn't there for long and I didn't dance or anything like that."

"Did you talk to anyone?"

"Well, yeah, but—"

"What the fuck is wrong with you?"

Why did you tell him, Hannah? "The club was next to the restaurant. I just—"

"Who'd you go with? Are you fucking around?"

I put a hand on the table behind me to steady myself. "No! I ... saw Noelle, this girl who works with me in HR. She always asks me to come out with her, and I always refuse because I know you wouldn't want me to. But I was right there. I thought she might get suspicious or something if I said no."

"Suspicious?" A flash of understanding. Not enough.

"I mean ... I don't know." My back was dewy with sweat. *The table. Focus on the table.*

Jake stepped toward me, face inches from mine. "Are you fucking listening to me?" I could barely hear him over the thudding of my heart.

He grabbed my arms in both hands. "Look at me, goddammit!"

"I'm sorry, I'm so sorry, Jake, I just thought that—"

"Why do you make me do this to you?" He released me, violently. My tailbone hit the table and I yelped.

Just get it over with. Be done.

"I need to get the fuck out of here to calm down," he said. "You're fucking worthless, you know that?"

I watched him stalk into the hallway. The door slammed.

You're worthless. I am the only one who appreciates you.

Let me show you how much I care about you—

I ran through the living room to the bathroom and dropped to my knees in front of the toilet. One of Jake's pubic hairs stuck to the seat.

My stomach muscles lurched, but nothing came up. The world wavered. I gripped the sides of the toilet bowl.

In, out ... in, out ...

I shouldn't have told him where I had gone. No, I shouldn't have gone somewhere that I wasn't supposed to be. I was a damn liar and nowhere near clever enough to do the right thing or avoid pissing him off. Maybe I should stop working at the shelter too, before he found out and had another reason to get angry.

A scar on my ankle throbbed wetly. In the past, it had been worth bleeding the dejection from my veins with a straight razor. The pain had worked to clear my mind because it released calming endorphins, though I suspected the hurt also served as a distraction from my shitty life. But I wasn't that girl anymore.

Maybe if I did just a little. It wouldn't take much to make my head stop spinning.

I won't go back.

I stood on wobbly legs, leaned against the counter and stared into the mirror. Pale cheeks, like Casper, but not as adorable. See? As long as I could crack a joke, I would be okay. I smiled shakily at my reflection.

You're okay, Hannah.

I splashed my face with cool water, toweled dry, and walked out to the living room. All was silent except for the television that had been left on low. The whole place felt utterly abandoned. I touched a large brownish stain on the armrest of the empty couch. *Sticky.* I sighed instead of crying.

Beer bottles and old magazines littered the coffee table. I was bending to pick them up when a cold chill shivered down my spine. Someone was watching. I jerked around, envisioning a figure emerging from the shadows, but the room remained empty.

Outside. The curtains were open, window cracked—probably so Jake could smoke a bowl without me knowing—but now the darkness beyond taunted me with far more terrifying unknowns. I clasped the papers to my chest and moved closer to the window, peering down at the empty street below. What would happen to me if Jake left for good?

Get it together, Hannah. There's no one there. No one's going to come after you, you're not that important.

I was important enough to him. And I'm sure I made him furious. I slammed the window shut.

The living room took half an hour, the bedroom another forty minutes. When all was tidy, I finally felt like I could breathe again. As I brought dirty rags back to the kitchen, I stumbled over my purse on the floor and grabbed the wallet off the top. But I already knew—my cash was gone.

Famished

THROUGH THE GLASS FRONT DOOR, the man saw Jake rush out of the stairwell and into the lobby. The man had no time to escape across the street without drawing attention to himself, so instead he grabbed the front door handle as Jake emerged.

"Pardon me," the man said.

Jake glared back, his stained T-shirt showing beneath his wrinkled, open jacket.

"A friend of mine is having a party here tonight, but I seem to have left the address at home. Can you tell me where Sandra Henson lives?"

Jake snorted. "How the hell would I know?" He scurried down the walk without waiting for a response.

The man held the door, watching Jake's back until it was swallowed up by the night. Then he let the door swing shut and crossed the street to a building that had once been a family home, but was now a tailoring service for children's clothes by day and vacant every evening after six o'clock. He ducked under the awning and considered the boyfriend.

An unexpected encounter, but not concerning. Jake would be less apt to think it strange when they met again.

And they would.

His breath hissed steadily in and out, merging with the brisk, dry air and the twigs that skittered across his path. A short distance from his shoes, the grass shimmered under the glow of the streetlight. He wore the shadows without concern for passersby; she lived on a street populated with people who went to bed early. Was it by chance, or by her conscious design? Probably the price. And the fact that there were fewer people to hear her boyfriend yelling at her like a Neanderthal.

And then there she was, a silhouette against warm lamplight, moving, almost dancing as she wiped the glass. She had stayed up late, as if she knew he'd be there.

He inhaled the crisp scent of leaves and musty earth. Interesting how quickly he had found her once he began looking in earnest. It was equally intriguing that he wasn't yet sure whether he would kill her, whether he would pull out her insides and watch her writhe like the others.

Usually, he knew a woman's date of death from their first meeting. This time he felt the question throbbing between his ears, wrapping his mind in a conundrum.

"Hannah." He let the name play on his tongue, tasting the syllables, savoring this single piece of her he now possessed. Hardness strained against his zipper. He watched closely as she spun from the window, clicked off the lamp, and disappeared into the blackness of her apartment. Satisfaction tingled around the edges of his brain.

The night birds squalled as the light in Hannah's bedroom turned on. She did not pass the windows, no more bustling around trying to forget her useless boyfriend, not even a shadow as she dressed for sleep.

Perhaps she was already in bed. The wind pulled at his jacket, the cold sharpening his focus on her window until the song of the night birds faded in his ears. He could almost hear her breathing. And still the light remained.

Hannah must not be sleeping well. He suspected it was because of him.

MONDAY, NOVEMBER 1ST

What a difference a weekend makes.

On my desk, a vase of tulips brightened my cubicle with silent but sincere apology. Three were already wilted, but they did their job all the same, even if they had been bought with money from my purse. At least I hadn't had to pay for the deliciously long back rub that had lulled me to sleep last night.

I should pick up something special for him on the way home. Maybe condoms.

I was the most romantic girlfriend ever.

Also on my desk, three stacks of new hire packets fluttered in the dry heat from the vent. I blinked hard to wet my corneas and an eyelash stabbed me in the eye. I tried to blow it off. It stuck. I brushed at it until the stubborn bastard came out, then finished entering the last of the new employee data from the second stack.

I took my completed work to the filing room and found Noelle already there, shoving personnel files into the cabinets with practiced precision. "Hey there, stranger! What's been going on?"

"Same old, same old," I said, trying to sound casual but feeling guilty as hell for not calling Noelle back this weekend.

She squinted at me. "You okay? What happened?"

"Jake was a little pissed about the whole clubbing thing, but we made up. No biggie."

She wiggled a file into place. "I just don't understand what you see in him. I keep thinking about what you told me when my dad died. All that stuff about it taking more than blood to build a relationship, so I wouldn't feel bad for hating his ass. But all Jake ever gives you is grief, and you don't even—"

"I really do love him." My pulse quickened and I swallowed hard.

"He's had a tough time finding work so I think he's stressed." I just needed to talk to him more. Be more understanding. At the least, I could avoid intentionally doing things that I knew would make him upset.

Noelle touched my hand. "Hey, I'm sorry, okay? I didn't mean it. I'm just a little tired."

My heart slowed at her backpedaling. But ... Noelle, tired? There were no bags under her eyes, and the whites were clear, probably more clear than mine after my renegade lash incident. She looked ... peaceful. Happy, even. "You're tired? Why? Did you go over and mess around with Ralph? He looks like he could go all night long." I tried to smile.

"I went out with Thomas last night."

Jim's creepy, weirdo eyes flashed across my consciousness and disappeared. "How did it go?"

"Dinner was good." Her words caught almost imperceptibly, like a leaf hitching on a breeze that doesn't ultimately possess enough power to change its course. Noelle closed the drawer and bent to open the one below it, but kept her face buried in the files. "He's an interesting guy. Really ... different from any other guy I've met. He's funny but not like he's trying to be."

"Did you ... you know?"

Noelle closed the file drawer and straightened. "Nope. He came back to my apartment but he didn't even try to get in my pants."

"Really? I mean, he likes women and everything, right?"

Noelle laughed at my joke, but not as hard as she had laughed at Thomas's. "Yeah, he likes women. He's just ... nice. Cautious, you know? Respectful. Plus he's kind of a homebody. Would rather hang out in the woods or at home than be out partying."

I took her place in front of the cabinet and opened a drawer. Noelle was happy with a homebody? She wasn't determined to drag him out clubbing with her?

Or is it just ... me that she needs to take out? Am I not interesting enough on my own?

I stuck a couple folders into the drawer. "So what did you do at your apartment?"

"Talked for a few hours. And ate ice cream."

I closed the drawer. "Come on, Noelle. You have to do better than that. How else am I supposed to live vicariously through you? I need details!"

"If you feel like you need to live vicariously, then that just proves you're missing something in your real life. Jake seriously needs to step up his game. Or you need to make better friends with your vibrator."

HANNAH LAUGHED, but her eyes glazed over as if she were thinking something she didn't want to say. Noelle's stomach clenched.

Note to self: Don't talk about Jake. Just the mention of that jack-off made Hannah's mouth tighten up.

Noelle ground her teeth together to keep from screaming at her friend to kick his ass out. She knew Hannah wouldn't, and she no longer cared why.

"Good enough," Noelle said. *Good enough if you don't care about being happy.*

She avoided Hannah's eyes.

There has to be a way to get him away from her.

I TOOK a bite of the roasted vegetables I had made for dinner. "I just can't believe I got everything done today. I'm glad I was able to sneak out of there on time."

"Well, I know you're good at your job. You're good at everything you do. I appreciate the way you always take care of me."

His words softened a touch of the frostiness I had felt when I walked in and found beer bottles all over the kitchen counter and the garbage overflowing. But being angry at him wouldn't push away this feeling I had that someone was after me, and it certainly wouldn't help if I pushed him away and ended up alone. I stared at the table and wielded my fork like a bayonet as I finished my veggies. Better the carrots than a person. Probably.

I should buy myself some more flowers.

After dinner, he slothed off to the living room, though sloths are cuter than the face Jake makes sucking on his after-meal cigarette. Maybe instead of Mario the philodendron I would get a tree, so Jake could hang out in the branches all day on his machete claws, looking dull. Doing nothing.

I washed the dishes with irritation burning in my chest like a nasty infection you couldn't scratch lest you make it spread. I tried to picture the flowers on my work desk. I should have brought them home so I could be more easily reminded of the good things. Things like the way he used to hold me when I was too afraid to sleep, though he thought I was just an insomniac. And the compliments, used sparingly, so I knew he really meant them. And what about that time he spent all day cleaning the apartment after he got angry and … well there were other good times, too. Lots of them.

When the last dish was clean, I poked my head into the living room where Jake was glued to the TV, eating what looked like a fast food apple pie from a paper sleeve. "I'm going to get the mail." My voice dripped annoyance, but if he heard it, he didn't acknowledge it.

"Mm-hmm."

He even talks like a sloth. I rolled my eyes and yanked open the apartment door, but glanced back toward the living room once more as if really expecting to see a sloth lounging on Jake's recliner. The television droned on, flashing lights on his face as he chewed with his mouth open.

I squared my shoulders and hurried down the hall and downstairs to the wall of mailboxes. A slip of white paper poked from the corner of my box, probably an advertisement for housekeeping services. Or pizza delivery. Maybe a new takeout restaurant. My keys clattered against the metal doors as I unlocked the box and grabbed my bills and the rogue paper. A scent like lilies wafted into my nose, but it was sharper, more acidic. Citrus. Oranges, maybe. *Weird.* Perhaps I'd be a scent detector if this thing at Harwick didn't work out. But they already had German Shepherds for that. Doggie jackasses, stealing all the good jobs.

I opened the mystery sheet.

Jake

Miss you, babe! Come down tomorrow after she leaves for work. I picked up that lingerie you like and some whipped cream. xoxo
~Me

Jake? Snakes in my stomach awakened and writhed. Acid climbed to my throat. Behind me, someone entered the building, and the blast of bitter air turned the dew on my skin to ice. I fled to the stairwell. My feet on the metal stairs thudded like an executioner's drumbeat.

How could he do this to me? I reached my floor and grabbed the door handle, but it was heavy, much too heavy.

No one else will ever put up with me the way Jake does. Maybe I shouldn't say anything about it at all.

I let go of the door and collapsed on the top stair, face against the dilapidated railing. My tears tasted metallic.

Just leave. Run. Start again.
Stay. Don't say anything. It's not worth fighting.
I won't make it on my own.
So what? What have you got to live for anyway?

My hiccuping gasps echoed around me, then, from the phone in my pocket, a text message plink: *Baby, where'd you go?*

The snakes lashed themselves against my esophagus. I wiped my tear-stained face on the sleeve of my shirt and stood, fist clenched around the letter. Lingerie. Whipped cream. I had never had a chance.

THE APARTMENT DOOR clicked softly closed behind me. Sometimes the beginning of the end was a whisper. I resisted the urge to throw myself at his feet, begging him to stay.

"Where'd you go?"

I stared at my shoes, the wall.

"What's in your hand?"

"The ... mail." No use delaying the inevitable.

He snatched it from me. "What the fuck is your problem?"

Paper rustled. I walked around him into the kitchen, and turned back to face him, my butt against the dining table.

"What the hell?"

Jake flicked the letter with two fingers. "I have no idea who this is! It must be for someone else." His face was flushed, neck corded.

Don't talk. Tears slid down my cheeks. I swallowed back bile.

"Baby, it isn't for me! Someone is fucking with you. I want to marry you! I've asked you a dozen times!" His hands clenched into fists when I didn't respond.

"How could you even ... so what, it's over now? We're not going to get married? I have to start all over?"

I clamped my lips shut, stealing glances at him, gauging his distance.

I'm sorry, forget I said anything, please don't hurt me!

I don't care who you screw, please don't leave me alone!

His knuckles were white. "You're going to believe some stupid note over me?" His voice grew louder with each word, escalation steeped in rage. "We've been together for years and you're just going to throw it away on this shit? What the fuck is wrong with you?"

Don't speak. You'll make it worse.

Jake's fist unclenched and everything around us slowed until there was only the motion of his hand, reaching along the counter. A weapon? A knife? My heart slowed too, then seemed to stop, the throbbing of my chest replaced with white noise so deafening I couldn't even hear what he was shouting, though spittle flew from his moving lips. Then movement, sudden as lightning. He grabbed a plate from the stack of drying dishes and I flinched, preparing for the pain, for the shattering glass to embed in my skin. It flew past me and the breath from the hurtling dish whispered in my ear: *Run. Run away.* I flattened myself against the table. *Don't move. Watch the wall. Nothing but the wall.*

Footsteps pounded toward me, reigniting the furious beating of my heart, and then he was there, his breath hot with rage and reeking of tobacco. His fist slammed into my temple with a dull, wet thud. Stars exploded behind my left eye and I was falling, plunging over the edge of the table, crashing against the linoleum. Pain roared up my side.

He panted above me, breathing fast, much too fast. I curled into a fetal position and squeezed my eyes shut. I waited. No more blows landed.

"I'm done. I'm fucking done," he said. I heard footsteps stomping away from me, and then the door slammed.

As my tears puddled around my throbbing head, I wondered if I would survive without him.

It was dark, as it had been in his younger years, though he no longer waited in patient silence for the feathery kiss of tiny legs to climb over his dirty bare feet. Nor did he listen for the disembodied groans coming to him through the closet door, or the wet *thwack thwack thwack* of skin-on-skin, those strange songs that had once held a faint promise that maybe he would eat tonight.

He stretched his eyes wide, adjusting to the gloom. As a child, he had once wondered if he could develop superhuman sight if he strained hard enough against the dark; comic book super heroes certainly had no less outlandish ways of acquiring power. But he had dismissed the idea just as quickly, even then. Most children will believe anything. He'd believed nothing.

Moans filtered through the memories and snapped him back to the present. The drugs must be wearing off. The man on the table groaned again, louder this time. He could get as loud as he wanted; no one would find them here.

The cement building had long been abandoned, each stinking puddle of rat urine a tribute to all the wretched lives that had once spent time in these rooms. Crumbled walls, crumbled dreams. From the windows on the upper levels, a power plant lit by feeble floodlights was visible in the distance, belching eerie clouds of grayish smoke into the obsidian sky.

Cities like Ash Park were punctuated by isolated pods of despair where the silence was so complete that even vagrants seemed to avoid them. Here, a child could go undiscovered for weeks on end before anyone in the apartment building noticed the smell of their mother's rotting corpse. These streets felt like home and beckoned that quiet child back into focus.

But he was not a child anymore.

Around him, the basement room had retained its shape, unlike the rubble-strewn rooms on the above floors. A lantern in the corner cast the floor and ceiling in amber. His captive was on his back, supine and naked, stretched across a four-by-four-by-six concrete table constructed from cinderblocks and covered with a clear plastic tarp specifically for this occasion. The filthy gray cement made Jake's pale skin stand out in striking contrast, though he was still jaundiced by the yellow glow of the lantern. Above Jake's head dangled a single, unlit fluorescent light bulb in a battery-powered goose-necked lamp. A flick of the switch turned it on.

Jake opened his eyes in the sudden blinding light and worked his mouth behind the duct tape, squinting like a woman readying herself for a beating. As his mother had. As perhaps Hannah had. But there would be nothing so trite as punching happening here tonight.

With latex-covered fingers, he reached for the small instruments he'd lined up on the floor. Scissors, chest clamps, nails, scalpel. *Scalpel. No, stopwatch.* How could he forget? He reached for it and pushed start, betting on fourteen minutes and twenty-two seconds with a forty-five second margin of error before Jake stopped screaming. Only once had he miscalculated, but that had been enough.

He grabbed the scalpel and held it up. Jake's eyes bulged. Behind the tape, his captive leaked a whining screech, the squall of a bird seized by feline jaws.

He moved the scalpel to Jake's clavicle and slowly, slowly, sliced rib cage to sternum. A bright red line appeared and swelled to a garish stream that gushed down Jake's sides and formed slick puddles on the plastic tarp. Grunting and huffing, now fully alert to the precariousness of his situation, Jake strained against the cuffs—arms, then legs, then both in a helpless dance.

He peered into Jake's eyes. The expression was familiar, and he stopped mid-cut, the scalpel buried in hair below Jake's belly button. They all made that same face at the end. Fear? Anger? Maybe the look of recognition when someone realizes they are about to die. Desperation, perhaps.

Desperation would not save him, though. Nothing would.

He returned to his task, cutting the thin skin of the abdomen and cleaving slowly through flesh and fat and down to the muscle. The struggling man shivered as the muscles split under the blade. He set the scalpel aside. Jake's muffled howling disintegrated into thin yelps and squeals.

It won't be long now.

He peeled the layers of skin back and secured them in place with hardware nails, then pressed his fingers into the cave of Jake's belly, prying the ruptured muscle back to expose the cache of organs beneath. He wrapped his fingers in a coil of intestine and pulled.

Jake panted through his nostrils. His eyes rolled back in his head, his breath erratic and fast.

No more screaming. Satisfied, he dropped the spiral of intestine and pushed the stop button on the watch, leaving a bloody fingerprint on its face. Thirteen minutes, fifty-eight seconds. *Still within the margin.* He smiled and picked up the scalpel.

Drawing his attention back to the tangle of organs that had once been a man, he picked up a length of intestine and sliced it open, watching the yellowed, pus-like contents drip into the open abdominal cavity. The scalpel slid smooth as silk—not the slightest hesitation in the tissue, as if it wanted nothing more than to give up its treasures.

But no insect.

This time he had waited several hours after forcing the roach down his victim's gullet, so perhaps it had already made it through the small intestine. He should at least be able to spot the legs and shell; roach exoskeletons were admirable in their ability to remain at least partially intact through the duration of the digestive process. He remembered that well enough from his childhood, along with the way they smelled: that oily, musky odor that set his mouth watering even now.

It was an amazing thing, how a human being could survive and function on so little nourishment. How a handful of cockroaches every day and the occasional loaf of bread could sustain a child for years at a time.

Simply incredible.

He ran a finger over the soft, slippery tube of intestine as if it were Hannah's cheek, envisioning her face when she heard the news: her eyes getting hazy, then overflowing, her arms reaching for him.

She might cry out of genuine sadness.

He dismissed that possibility, giving it twelve-to-one odds in favor of tears of relief—if she cried at all.

Jake was a waste of a human. It made no logical sense for anyone to miss him.

TUESDAY, NOVEMBER 3RD

Dawn's light shone sickly and dim against the windowpane. I dressed and applied makeup over the deep purple bruise that stained my temple. Then I went through the house and filled a box with Jake's things—so he would have no reason to go through the rest of the place—and left the box in front of the door where he'd trip right over it. If he came back at all.

I can't turn into one of those women.

News flash: you already have.

Decisive actions, but everything was foggy, confusing. I blinked back tears all the way to work. At the office, my fingers sat leaden on the keyboard until I forced movement, and even then it was slow. Each file I entered brought me another minute closer to the end of the day and an empty apartment.

"Hey, girl!" Noelle was smiling when she poked her head into my cubicle, but her eyes widened when she saw me. "What the hell happened to you?"

I looked away, the explanation catching in my throat, blocked by shame. A tear escaped from under one lid. I swiped at it with my sleeve.

Then Noelle was there beside me, her hand on my shoulder.

"It's almost lunch time," she said. "Come with me."

I stood unsteadily and followed her from the room.

We sat at the picnic table near the lake. The sun had been swallowed by deep clouds. Frosty air blew off the ice that was creeping along the edges of the water. I shivered. "He's ... cheating on me. I found a note."

"That's why he hit you?"

"Yes."

"But this wasn't the first time."

"No," I whispered.

"When did it start?"

"He never did it until after I moved in with him." He used to be so supportive, so kind. What had happened to that guy?

"Why didn't you just leave the first time it happened?"

"I don't know. I should have. I know I should have."

"Oh, no, it's not your fault, Hannah."

But it was. "I just kept pushing and I knew better. I tried not to say anything about the note, but he knew something was wrong and I just—"

"Jesus, Hannah, would you fucking listen to yourself?"

What's wrong with you, Hannah?

You're an idiot, Hannah.

Angry bees swarmed my stomach and stung my heart. I hung my head.

"Aw hell, Hannah, I'm not trying to get on you. You just shouldn't blame yourself. You need to leave him."

"I think he's gone for good. He said he's done with … me." My tears were hot in the icy breeze. He'd never said anything so terrible, even during our worst fights. But there hadn't been another woman before either.

That I know of.

Oh god, that's probably where he stayed last night.

"I put his stuff by the door so he could grab it and take it over to her place," I said. My rib cage felt constricted. I pulled frigid air through my nose. "I don't want to be there when he comes back."

Noelle walked around the table and wrapped me in a bear hug. It felt good, safe, even though bears were more known for their mauling than their hugging.

"Hannah, I am so sorry." Noelle had tears in her eyes. "You don't need that worthless asshole."

If he's worthless, what does that make me if I can't even hang on to him? Noelle's sympathy made it clear that she was oblivious to this point, which only made me feel worse.

She held my hand. "Come out with me tonight. I was going to meet Thomas and Jim downtown at The Mill at six. There's an art show down the road. Jim was going to bring someone, but she cancelled."

My mouth dropped open and I tasted lake air on my dry tongue, metal and mud. "I … I can't just go out—"

"What are you going to do? Sit at home alone and wait for him to come back all pissed off? Be out of the house. You can even sleep at my place if you want. If he's really leaving he should be back to get his things while you're gone. And if not, the extra day will give him more time to cool off."

We'd broken up less than twelve hours ago and all I wanted was to curl up in my bed and cry. But as Noelle watched me, the throbbing of the bruise on my cheek was slowly awakening something else: rage. I could feel it bubbling under the fear and the loneliness. And I didn't want to be alone in that apartment. I found myself nodding. What kind of a person does that? Maybe I was destined to be a tramp.

Noelle beamed. "I'll get you some makeup before we head out. We'll need to do better with that eye."

"Or I can just go with the raccoon look. Quick, punch me in the other eye." My voice cracked.

Noelle gave me another one-armed hug.

I visualized angry bears again, and somehow that comforted me.

Noelle looked like she wanted to maul Jake.

WE MET the guys at The Mill and ordered two pizzas topped with pepperoni, onions and extra cheese. I hadn't eaten all day, but I was still surprised when my stomach grumbled.

Jim raised his eyebrows at me. "So, are you totally single now?"

Noelle stiffened beside me.

I froze, a pizza crust halfway to my lips.

"It's just that I thought I remembered Noelle telling us you were involved with someone. It's none of my business, really—"

"We ... broke up." The words felt foreign on my tongue and I realized I had never had to utter them before. I took a deep breath. The pizza in my stomach lurched around like it was alive and angry at being trapped.

"Sorry to hear that," Jim said, but the twinkle in his eyes said he was anything but.

Placid. Think about the lake. Or Botox. Maybe I should get that. I'd look chill all the time. "These things happen," I said over the thumping of my heart. I grabbed my root beer, glanced at my yellow blouse and wondered if this restaurant had better hand dryers than the club we'd gone to. I set my glass down again.

"If you ever need someone to help take your mind off it, I would be happy to oblige," Jim said.

I shot a panicked look at Noelle. She rolled her eyes.

I turned back to Jim and cleared my throat. "I might need a little time, you know?"

He inclined his head, but slowly. "Of course."

"So how many artists will be at the show tonight?" Noelle said.

The men took turns answering her questions while I sagged against the plastic booth. I wanted to kiss her for changing the subject. Still, she had been right; this was preferable to sitting at home on my kitchen floor, trying to forget my own worthlessness while listening for the creak of the floorboards in the hallway.

ROBERT LIKED the way her mouth moved as she spoke, the minute quiver of her lips that she probably hoped no one else noticed. The faraway look in her glorious green eyes. She was sad, perhaps conflicted, but not a single tear. That was admirable. He had underestimated her strength the first night they met.

Her sadness would surely escalate in the days to come as she worked through her loss. And he would be there to pick up the pieces, to analyze her desires and become them, making her ache for him, driving her to the brink of insanity and back again before she collapsed desperately into his arms.

But slowly, he cautioned himself. He couldn't push her. She wasn't like ordinary women, wonton and shameless. She was better. She was pure.

He smiled.

What could he do to repay her for the wonderful thing she was going to do for him? What gift was there for the salvation of his soul?

He turned to Noelle. Her hair fanned as she tossed it over her shoulder, her sweater struggling to restrain her creamy breasts as she moved. He smiled more broadly.

Noelle smiled back.

What a whore.

WEDNESDAY, NOVEMBER 4TH

Petrosky threw the newspaper down hard enough to spill his coffee. This media bullshit wasn't going to help him any.

In the last week, he'd spun his wheels questioning everyone who knew either of the murdered women, but he'd gotten nothing more than a few vague details he could have figured out on his own. They had both suffered some pretty violent beatings at some point in the weeks before they had died, but that was commonplace with prostitution. There were no leads on common acquaintances, dealers, or johns.

He dropped his eyes to the paper. Front page. Two days old already.

> In an update on a recent story, the killer responsible for two murders in the Ash Park area may have used even more horrific methods than first speculated. According to an anonymous source, the victims were surgically opened while still alive, enduring the dissection of intestinal walls, and possibly the stomach, before perishing. Police have no strong leads. If you have any information, please contact the Ash Park police department.

Now they needed someone to cover the false confessions from the crazies. Fuck it, he'd have Morrison get one of his buddies to do it. Or he'd just give the crazies the number to the goddamn newspaper office.

Petrosky slammed his fist against his desk. "Hookers are killed every day, and they pick my case to publicize? Why do they care all of a sudden?"

But he already knew. *If it bleeds it leads*.

Morrison looked up from his desk across the aisle and shrugged as his phone rang.

Petrosky righted his upended coffee cup. "I swear to God, if I find out who the hell—"

"Petrosky!"

He startled at the strain in Morrison's voice.

Morrison was already out of his chair and pulling on his coat. "We've got another body."

"This doesn't fit, Boss."

The building was a skeleton of a factory. In some places, towering pillars of cement and steel reached toward the sky; in others there were only piles of rubble. Petrosky grimaced at the steel ribs as he passed underneath, wondering how much jostling it would take to make them fall.

The basement seemed sturdy enough, at least for now, with steel support poles like the kind found in an underground garage. The concrete roof was cracked in places, but intact, blocking the elements and protecting anyone inside from the falling debris of the upper stories. Off the main area, smaller rooms with cement walls offered even more privacy—probably why their killer had chosen it, along with the building's distance from the more populated areas of the city. It was dumb luck that some homeless man had snuck down here during last night's snowstorm and found the body.

Petrosky followed the murmur of voices to a back room. In the center, a man lay on a bloodied plastic tarp on top of more cinderblocks, his eyes closed, his mouth open in a silent scream. At each of the four corners of the makeshift table, bolted-in metal cuffs secured the man's wrists and ankles. A straight cut ran down the center of the body. The man's intestines were piled on his scrawny bird chest in filmy coils.

Crime techs bustled around the concrete blocks, dusting the restraints with fingerprint powder.

"Got an ID?" Petrosky said.

A dark-haired, darker-skinned tech stood from where he'd been crouching behind the concrete block. "Jacob Campbell. Wallet was in his pants pocket."

"He's not wearing pants, tech."

"They were in the corner, *Detective*."

Petrosky glowered at the tech until he crouched behind the cement wall again. "Any sign of a poem? Lettering?"

Another tech, who was working on something on the floor, shook her head without looking his way.

Petrosky peered at the ceiling. "Too far away for anyone to hear much. But to know the basement was down here … he knows the area. Gotta be a local."

Morrison nodded stiffly.

All of this was shit they knew already. What they didn't know was why they had a new victim who didn't fit the original pattern. Looked like McCallum was wrong about their killer having a type. What else had he been wrong about?

The medical examiner arrived with a stretcher and acknowledged Petrosky with a twitch of his bristly jaw.

"Wait a second." Morrison said it so softly that it took Petrosky a minute to figure out who had spoken. Morrison rifled through his notebook, brows furrowed, until he tapped a sheet with his index finger. "Got it, Boss. His address is the same one I pulled the other day from the domestic violence shelter file."

"Why was his address in the files for a women's shelter?"

"His wasn't. It was the girl we talked to there, a" —he ran a finger down the page— "Hannah Montgomery."

Shit. Since meeting Hannah at the shelter, Petrosky had been wrenched from sleep night after night, sheets soaked through with sweat. Each nightmare was the same: a trail of blood leading him to a field where he came upon Julie and Hannah, arms around each other, throats slit. Fuck it, he wasn't going this time—seeing Hannah was the last thing he needed. His brain was already hazy enough from the midnight shot of liquor he'd used to lull him back into a tortured sleep.

Petrosky slipped out of the room, Morrison scrambling after him.

"Who've we got that can go to Montgomery's place?" Petrosky said.

"Boss?"

"She's not a suspect, Morrison. We don't need to do recon on the bereaved." Their shoes echoed along the cement hall. A breeze blew down from the open ceiling.

Morrison stopped walking. "But—"

Petrosky's footfalls were heavy, angry. "We just need someone to let her know what's going on, keep an eye on her. I'm going to follow up this afternoon after we check out the apartment building and get a little background on Campbell."

On Campbell. And on Hannah Montgomery, the girl who knew two of the victims, one intimately. She had to know something, even if she wasn't aware of it. Petrosky pushed away an image of Hannah's wide, frightened eyes. She wasn't as ignorant as she pretended to be.

She was in danger. And she knew it.

THE APARTMENT MANAGER was a wiry man who looked to be in his sixties, though time may have just been remarkably unkind. Dark brown khakis and a button-down shirt hung from his gaunt frame. His shiny skull was speckled with patches of brown age spots, some of which looked too dark not to be malignant.

"Detectives? I'm Samuel Plumber." His thin lips parted to reveal teeth the same yellow as the whites of his eyes. Liver failure, perhaps, and yet he was still wandering the halls of this shithole.

Petrosky and Morrison followed him into a tiny office. The room was messy, but in a neglected way, not a busy way. The particle board desk was piled high with folders and crumpled papers, the wastebasket overflowing. No photos, no coat hook, no boots in the corner. Petrosky wondered which unit Plumber lived in, or if he lived there at all.

On the wall above the desk were two small television screens above three VCRs. The recording equipment looked as old as the desk and the cracked vinyl chair, though a crocheted afghan slung over the back of the chair appeared relatively new.

Plumber sank into his seat and Petrosky and Morrison crowded in behind him to look at the television screens. "I tried to get them as close as I could to what you were looking for. You're lucky you called when you did; I reuse these tapes every three days."

"We'll be taking the tapes with us." Petrosky squinted at the grainy images. One screen showed a stairwell, and the other, the mailroom right outside Plumber's office.

"Is that him?" Petrosky asked as a dark-haired man sprinted down the stairs.

Plumber nodded. On the other screen, the man emerged from the stairwell into the mailroom and disappeared from view in the direction of the front entrance.

"He's in quite the rush," Morrison said.

Plumber stayed silent. He pushed a button and the clip froze on the empty mailroom.

"What about the outside of the building?" Petrosky asked.

Plumber shook his head. "I just keep an eye on things in here. I expect the cops to take care of things out there." He picked up another tape. "I did find some with his girlfriend, though." But he made no move to insert the tape into the VCR.

"Problem?"

Plumber looked up at Petrosky's question. "It's just that she seems like such a good girl, and—"

"Mr. Plumber, Ms. Montgomery is not a suspect at this time. We just need to put together a chain of events for the evening. This was the last place Mr. Campbell was seen alive."

Plumber pursed his lips. "I must admit, he was trouble. I got calls about him yelling and carrying on all the time. Even yelled at other tenants in the hallway."

"He yell at his girlfriend?"

"Yeah. One time, someone heard glass breaking or something and I went up there. She said she dropped a bowl. But ain't no reason to cry over a bowl." Plumber sniffed and turned back to the screens. "That boy didn't do anything good for anybody, from what I could see."

If Campbell was a shit-head, that could be the beginning of a motive. But the girls? It didn't feel right. The set of Plumber's mouth was off as well, stubborn, almost defiant, not a trace of regret. Petrosky's back stiffened. "Mr. Plumber, are you implying that Mr. Campbell deserved to die?"

Plumber looked up at him, his eyes earnest. "No, sir. It's just that I don't know of anyone who would be worse off at having lost him."

THE TAPES SHOWED Hannah rifling through the mail, then fleeing up the same stairwell that Campbell had run down several minutes later. She had cried on the metal stairs for what seemed like an eternity before going back inside her apartment.

Petrosky was not sure what to make of her actions, but seeing her broken up like that tugged at a tender place in his stomach where this morning's coffee was still trying to settle. He vowed to think about it later. Or never. For now, recon.

He and Morrison started at the top floor and worked their way down to the residents on the ground level. Many of the apartments were empty this time of day, and Morrison used his notepad to track who would need follow-up calls.

The few residents who were home were of little assistance. In one unit, a young woman in a white tank top and dirty jeans stared blankly at them until they thanked her for her time and left. In another apartment, an older woman with a set of reading glasses on her head and another set of glasses on a chain around her neck asked them four times who they were before shuffling off to her living room. Petrosky closed the front door for her.

"What do you think, Boss?"

"All it takes is one neighbor to hear something. This last floor won't take too long to finish up and then we'll head out."

"You think Campbell was killed by the same guy who killed our female victims?"

"Looks like it. But with the press leak on something like this you never know if you're dealing with a copycat. It's not likely—but it's possible. It happened once about twenty years back, some tweaker beating the shit out of dealers with a flathead shovel. Press got wind of some of the details, but not all, and a week later we had a crack dealer beaten to death with a spade. Small differences, but enough to find the second guy and clear him of the first few crimes."

"What about the first guy? The serial?"

"It's probably still in the cold case file."

Morrison pulled open the door to the ground level hallway. "It's disconcerting that no one knew either Campbell or his girlfriend."

"If he was roughing her up, that isn't a surprise."

"I got that. Sickening."

"Life's not all rainbows and surfboards, California."

Morrison's mouth tightened. Instead of responding, he rapped hard on a door.

The knob turned, the door opened. "What the hell do you want now?"

Petrosky balked and recovered.

Janice LaPorte wore a pink and yellow flowered housedress that undulated around her thin frame like a pair of parachute pants. Her thin mouth was done up in a horrible shade of maroon.

"Ms. LaPorte."

She frowned.

"We have a few more questions."

She stepped aside. "Fine." Her voice was as stiff as her shoulders.

Petrosky and Morrison followed her into a sparse, but clean, living room with flowered furniture in shades of green and orange, still covered with heavy duty plastic furniture covers. The wooden coffee table was old but polished to a mirrored sheen. She waved them to the couch and the plastic squealed in protest under their butts. Morrison pulled out his notepad.

She sat across from them in a wingback armchair with a lacy crocheted blanket draped over the headrest like a doily. LaPorte saw Petrosky looking at it and fingered a corner. "Made it myself."

"It's nice," Morrison said.

Petrosky glared at him until he turned his eyes to the notebook. LaPorte watched the exchange with narrowed eyes.

"So did you meet Ms. Montgomery here?" Petrosky asked her. "Pretty coincidental that you both live in the same building."

LaPorte's jaw stiffened. "No. We didn't meet here."

"What about—"

"Is this about that poor girl again? I haven't seen anything since we last spoke."

"Ma'am, this is about another resident of the building. A Jacob Campbell."

"Hannah's Jake." LaPorte's eyes hardened. Her voice was cold.

"He was found dead this morning," Petrosky said.

Her left eye twitched, and Petrosky's hackles rose.

"I ... I had no idea."

"Anything you can tell us about the night before last? Anything out of the ordinary with either Mr. Campbell or Ms. Montgomery?"

LaPorte shook her head. "Not that I recall."

"How were they as a couple?"

She hesitated. Petrosky saw a flash of agitation in her eyes before she looked away. *She's a killer. Don't forget what you're dealing with.*

"She doesn't open up much." Her face was a blank slate.

"Did she ever mention Mr. Campbell?"

Morrison's pen scratched. LaPorte stared.

"Ma'am?"

LaPorte shook her head again. "When she did, it was in passing. I remember thinking she might have been afraid of him."

"Fights?" Petrosky asked.

LaPorte looked away from him, toward the window. The hairs on the back of his neck danced, though Jacob Campbell hitting his girlfriend was hardly a revelation. And why was Campbell dead? If their killer was picking off abusers, he'd have taken Meredith Lawrence's boyfriend down instead of Lawrence herself.

"She never fought with him," LaPorte said. "He yelled at her sometimes though. Just him. I never once heard her yell." She sighed. "Poor dear." Her voice was soft, but tight. Irritated.

Morrison's pen froze.

Poor dear? *What do you know, Ms. LaPorte?* Was LaPorte in danger here? Was Hannah? Were the other girls at the shelter? Petrosky shifted his weight and lowered his voice. "Poor dear, as in Mr. Campbell, the man who was brutally killed?"

"If you ask me, officers, anything that happened to him he brought on himself."

I BLINKED sandpaper from my eyes and shut the desk drawer for the fourth time. I should have brought my cell phone to work. I probably would have if I'd thought I was strong enough to ignore Jake's calls. If he ever called. So far, he hadn't even come by to pick up his things.

What's the difference between boyfriends and condoms? Condoms have changed. They're no longer thick and insensitive.

The office phone rang. I jumped.

It's him!

It's not him.

It rang a second time. I grabbed the receiver.

"Ms. Montgomery?" The voice was deep and gravelly—familiar, but I couldn't place it.

My back tensed. "Yes, this is."

"Detective Petrosky. Ash Park PD. I would like to speak with you as soon as possible regarding Jacob Campbell."

"Jake—"

Oh God. Someone must have called the police about the other night after all the yelling ... or maybe about my eye. I stared accusingly in the direction of Noelle's cubicle but only saw the empty cork board, which wavered as my vision blurred.

Shit. He's going to be furious.

"Ms. Montgomery?"

"Yes. I ... can I just drop the charges over the phone?" I gripped the receiver harder.

There was a pause on the other end of the line. "Ma'am?"

My hand cramped. I tried to loosen my grip. "I mean, everything is fine, I just ... I mean, I'm fine. I don't want to press charges."

This time the pause was longer. Dread thickened in the pit of my stomach. Maybe I was the one in trouble. Maybe it was all my fault. Maybe the cops already knew that.

"Is he there with you already?" I asked. "If it's about his stuff, he can come get it. I wasn't trying to, like ... steal it. It's all by the front door."

"Ma'am, Mr. Campbell is dead. I'm sorry, I thought someone had already been by to tell you."

The room expanded around me, then vanished as if it had been an apparition. The suddenly thin air didn't want to fill my lungs. The phone clattered against the desk and dropped to the carpet, but the sound was muffled, as if I were underwater.

A hand on my back. "Hannah?" *Noelle.*

A small, tinny voice buzzed from the receiver. I reeled it in and put it back to my ear. Everything vibrated: my chest, my legs, my hands.

"Ms. Montgomery? Hello? Are you there?"

"Yes," I whispered. Noelle squeezed my shoulder.

"I know this is difficult, but we need to speak with you. Can you make it to the station, or would you like us to meet you at your home?"

"Um ... I don't ... the station." *Where all the cops are. Where it's safer.*

"Can you come now?"

I nodded.

"Ma'am?"

Oh, right. "Yes. Yes, I can come."

"Do you have someone who can look after you?" His voice was softer now—kind, even.

I met Noelle's eyes. "Yes."

"Good." The line clicked.

I dropped the receiver and fled the office.

"Hannah!" Noelle's voice faded halfway down the hall. I threw myself into the bathroom, locked a stall door and sat on the toilet seat. The stall pulsed around me in time with the knifing beats of my heart. My breath wheezed out of me, dissipating, disappearing into the air, and I was jealous, so jealous of this ability to ... vanish.

I'm safe right now.

You can't stay in the bathroom stall forever.

I pushed my hair from my face with shaking hands.

You have nowhere to go.

The room went black at the edges.

He's found me.

Petrosky considered Hannah—Ms. Montgomery—through the two-way mirror in the interrogation room. She seemed fragile, dwarfed as she was by the large metal table.

She looked just as innocuous on paper: Hannah Montgomery. Born in Vermont. Parents: divorced. One sister. Employment history began five years ago at an Ash Park convenience store, then at Harwick Technical. No arrests, no warrants. Not even a speeding ticket.

Beside him, Morrison toed the linoleum, face drawn up with just the right amount of sympathetic concern. Petrosky crushed his empty coffee cup, wishing he had something stronger to drink, and reread the notes off the file in his hand. It had taken two hours for her to arrive, which had given the medical examiner extra time to get his shit together.

There were significant differences between this crime and the others. This one had used metal cuffs instead of leather restraints, and nails instead of silver clasps to hold the skin back. There was no note. They had also found a pair of tread marks in the room, though those could have been left behind at another time.

The two hours had also given Morrison time to go poking into Montgomery's whereabouts over the last week. What he had told Petrosky was interesting to say the least.

"You think she's got something to do with it? That whole double dating thing is pretty coincidental," Morrison said.

Petrosky stared at the notes in his hand, written in the flowing script you'd expect from an English major. "We'll see. You did good, California."

"Thanks, Boss."

In the interrogation room, Montgomery folded her hands in her lap.

She's just a grief-stricken girlfriend.

She was on a date hours after he died. The facts won't go away just because you don't want them to be true.

"I'm going in. Watch. Take notes. You're good at that."

"Right on, Boss."

Petrosky tossed the cup into the garbage and entered the interrogation room. Montgomery straightened, her dark hair falling over her shoulders. He had tried to braid Julie's hair into pigtails once and she had ended up looking like Medusa. *Fucking hell, Petrosky.*

He cleared his throat. "Thank you for coming, Ms. Montgomery. Do you know why you're here?"

"Because Jake—" She shivered, closed her eyes, then opened them again. "You said you wanted to talk to me."

Petrosky nodded. "I'm sorry for your loss."

"Thank you." Her lower lip quivered and Petrosky smothered the rush of warmth in his belly that tried to well up for her.

Focus. He stood on the other side of the table and put his hands palm down on the top. "I need to know about his movements in the days before his death. Tell me anything you can remember."

"I think he went to his mother's. Dinner the night before, maybe." Her brows furrowed. "Everything is so ... fuzzy."

"Try."

"I think dinner with his mom. That's all I know about. He ... I...I work during the day. I don't really know what he did when I was gone."

"Why didn't you report him missing?" Petrosky kept his voice even, trying not to scare her into silence. Three days was a long time not to notice he had disappeared.

She shrugged. "I didn't know he was missing, I guess, not really."

"Neighbors say you had a disagreement the night he disappeared."

She stared hard at her lap.

"Quite the bruise you have there." He waited for a response, and when none came, he switched tactics. Maybe he'd surprise a real answer out of her. "How did you not think he was missing when he didn't come back home for three days?"

Finally, she met his eyes. "He was moving out."

"That must have made you pretty upset."

"I ... I don't know," she whispered. A tear dripped on the metal tabletop where it formed a shiny little bead.

Petrosky wished he had a tissue. He pushed the thought away. "You were angry enough to go out with someone else the day after he disappeared."

Her eyes widened with surprise. She choked back a sob and gripped the sides of her chair as if she were trying to hold herself upright. "It was just a friend thing. I didn't want to go home."

Guilt jabbed at his chest.

Do your fucking job. He balled his fists behind his back. "Where were you on the night of October tenth?"

"October tenth?"

Petrosky froze. Repeating phrases was a classic sign of lying.

"I don't know," she said "I mean probably at home with—"

"How about the first of October?"

He waited for a telltale twitch, a flash of guilt. She just shrugged.

"Anyone else who might have seen you on those dates in October?"

Montgomery shook her head. "Maybe at the apartment? I don't know."

"I'll look into it. What about your friends?"

Silence. Again. *Talk to me, dammit.*

"Anyone else who may have wanted to hurt him?"

Montgomery jerked her head up and her eyes were brighter, her mouth open in stunned realization. "Maybe. He had another girlfriend. She sent him a letter the night he left."

That was what she had found in the mailbox that night, the note that had sent her sobbing to the stairwell. "What's her name?"

"I'm not sure."

"But you knew he was messing around on you?"

Her face crumpled.

Petrosky wiped his own face with a beefy palm. *She's not Julie, for Christ's sake. Get it together, Petrosky.* "Do you have the letter?"

"Um ... no, I don't think so. He took it."

"Did you look at the postmark?"

"It didn't have one. It was just slipped into the side of the box." She was gripping the chair hard enough to turn her knuckles white. Her eyelashes were wet.

Petrosky looked away. "I'm going to look into your alibi and check some security tapes. I'll also need to look through his things, check out your apartment."

She stared at him. "All his stuff is in a box by the door."

"He do that?"

"No. I did." Her voice shook.

It sounded like she couldn't get away from him soon enough. "Do I have your permission to search or do I need a warrant?"

"You can look."

Petrosky pulled a page from the folder and unclipped a pen off the cover. "I'll need your signature here. Until we sort this out, don't leave town."

She left without another word. He strode to his desk and rummaged in the top drawer for a pack of cigarettes and a lighter. They had been there for six years, since the day he'd promised Julie he'd quit.

They're bad for your health. His daughter's voice echoed in his head. He could almost see Julie, her face tilted toward the sun, her dark hair shining. He wondered what she would have looked like had she been allowed to grow up.

Probably a lot like—

He ground his teeth and tore open the pack on his way to the parking lot, trying to shut out the voice that told him he had just badgered an innocent girl. Julie had been innocent, too. She had died innocent.

He walked out into icy drizzle, feet squelching on half melted snow and parking lot sludge. He yanked a cigarette from the pack and lit it. Acrid smoke burned his throat.

Sorry, honey.

SUNDAY, NOVEMBER 8TH

Some days I missed him so terribly I could almost taste the despair. Other days, I hated myself for feeling relieved that Jake's murder was connected to the others. "Serial killer," the news said. I still cried myself to sleep, wondering if my actions had caused him to leave, caused him to die, but the idea that he was killed by a stranger and not as a direct result of my past made me almost giddy. And my guilt at this almost giddiness weighed on me like a ton of rock. It was a vicious cycle.

If I weren't so paranoid, so afraid, would I have wanted him to die?

This morning, as I applied makeup over my still-bruised face, I was thankful to the person who had taken him even as I feared that the creaking footsteps in the hallway outside would stop at my door. It was all too much. I could almost hear the moment I shut down and separated from myself, like the clank of a bank vault.

The detachment accompanied me to the grave of my murdered almost-ex-boyfriend. I stood still and silent in my black funeral attire with dry eyes and a fluttering in my chest, like a sparrow trying to escape, though it was someone else's chest, someone else's bird. Beside me, Noelle clasped my numb fingers, and though I gripped her back, it still felt like she was holding someone else's hand.

Jake's mother stared daggers at me across the gaping hole in the frozen earth as they lowered the casket. The hem of my wool dress flipped in the breeze, and arctic air bit at my ankles. I smoothed the dress and pressed my feet together in a halfhearted attempt to warm them.

To the side and a dozen feet behind Jake's mother stood Mr. Harwick, solemn in a black suit and wool overcoat. He raised his eyes from the casket, focused on me, and my mouth went dry. I looked away.

The casket found the bottom of the hole and the straps kicked up ice and sludge as they were removed. The *shh* of the straps on the ground sounded like the earth trying to breathe.

A wailing, like a wounded animal, split the air as Jake's mother threw herself on the ground at the graveside, tearing at the dusted snow with her fingernails. The priest tried to restrain her. I looked away, dropped Noelle's hand, and stepped back.

Noelle raised her eyebrows. *Want me to come?* the look said.

I shook my head and escaped across the cemetery. The wails faded, replaced by the crackling of frozen leaves. I was halfway to the car before I realized that I wasn't alone. Another set of footsteps ground ever closer, stalking through the snow behind me. I stopped. I was too far from the gravesite for anyone to see us, but maybe they'd still be able to hear me scream and send help. I whirled around, hands fisted at my sides.

"I didn't mean to startle you." Mr. Harwick's ice blue eyes met mine, kind and sincere.

I relaxed my hands, heart still in my throat. "No, it's okay. I just didn't know it was … you."

"I gathered. Shall we?" He gestured to the gates and I nodded. Our feet crunched across icicles of grass, leaving a trail of brown footprints.

"I was saddened to hear of your loss, Ms. Montgomery."

"Yes … I mean … thank you." What the hell was wrong with me? I tried to avoid looking at his mouth. I failed. A branch caught my foot and I was falling, the ground growing closer, my arms windmilling—

Strong hands under my arms righted me and sent currents of pleasant electricity through my chest. "Oh, uh … thanks," I said as he released me. So much for electricity—my face felt like it had been seared by a blowtorch.

He met my eyes. "If there is anything you need, you know where to find me. And you are welcome to take some time off past the bereavement period. Just apply and I will approve it."

"Thank you."

He nodded once and turned toward the front entrance once more. I watched the back of his head as he walked over the hill and through the wrought iron gate at the front of the cemetery.

Behind me, new footsteps drew closer, but their rhythm was familiar, as was the clank of Noelle's jewelry.

"What was that all about?" Noelle asked.

"Wanted me to know I could take some time off if I needed it."

"You going to?"

I considered my empty apartment, Jake's toothbrush moldering in the bathroom, the prickling of my spine every time I passed the living room window, the heart palpitations every time a floorboard creaked.

"No. I'll be back tomorrow."

MONDAY, NOVEMBER 9TH

PETROSKY'S DESK chair groaned as he leaned back in it. He tapped Morrison's smartphone and rewound the video again. Morrison had taken Plumber's apartment surveillance tapes and installed them into some fancy ass thing on his phone. *An app,* he'd called it, which wasn't even a whole fucking word, and yet the damn thing was working pretty well.

Petrosky tapped play and squinted at the tiny screen as the wall of mailboxes appeared. Then came the girl—at least he thought it was a female. Small, lithe and fast. She wore a long jacket with a hood pulled over her face. Dark blue or black jeans. And she was watching. Back and forth, scanning, nervous. What was she scared of? Was she looking for Hannah, her lover's girlfriend, afraid of getting caught? Then the letter from a coat pocket. He zoomed in. She wiggled it into the slit in the door of the box and pulled her hood tighter over her face, shielding herself from the camera. She had known where the camera was; knew her actions would have consequences. It would be tricky without a face, without even a hair color, but they'd find her.

Morrison rushed into the bullpen and headed toward him.

Petrosky tossed him the phone. "Nice work, California. Now to find out who she is."

"I'm on it. But we've got a situation. Jacob Campbell's mother is here."

Petrosky followed Morrison down the stairs to the public section of the building where citizens came to whine about their neighbor's dog. Ms. Campbell stood in the middle of the waiting room wearing a pink muumuu over a black tank top, the straps cutting into her bared, pudgy shoulders. No coat, despite the snow. She had a cigarette tucked behind one ear.

Petrosky approached her. "Can I help you, ma'am?"

She turned glassy eyes in his direction. "Yeah, you can fuckin' help me. I need to know how to get around this shit." She thrust a sheaf of papers at him. "It's like all the government wants to do is fuck over good tax-paying citizens while they give everything to those bitches and their welfare babies."

Petrosky took the papers and gestured toward a door that led to their interrogation rooms. "Follow me, ma'am."

Morrison sat at the head of the table. Ms. Campbell sat across from Petrosky and glowered at him as he looked over the paperwork. It was notification of a monetary settlement to be paid to Mr. Jacob Campbell. The amount was nearly thirty-six thousand dollars.

"I'm not sure I understand what you're trying to do, Ms. Campbell."

"What I'm trying to do? That money should belong to me."

Petrosky turned the page, trying to figure out why she was there instead of at her lawyer's office. But he'd be damned if he suggested she get a lawyer before she told them something useful. "Why didn't Mr. Campbell have the money before now?"

She shook her head. "It's in there somewhere. There's a bunch of shit."

Petrosky passed half of the pile to Morrison and they spent the next few minutes looking over the information. Morrison spoke first. "It looks like there's a provision to turn the money over to Mr. Campbell when he gets married or turns thirty, whichever happens first."

Ms. Campbell shrugged. "Yeah, what the fuck ever."

"And in the case of death, all monies go to the closest living descendent or relative," Morrison said.

He and Morrison looked at her.

"Ma'am, you did realize this is a motive for murder?" Petrosky asked.

"For who?"

"For his closest living relative."

She gnashed her teeth. "It isn't me. It's his fucking kid."

Petrosky set down the papers. His kid?

"He always said that bastard wasn't his, but she put his name on the certificate. Now the lawyers want to give the money to him once he's big enough."

Petrosky's mind raced.

She pulled the cigarette from behind her ear and stuck it in her mouth. "So, what do I have to do to get my boy's name off that fucking birth certificate?"

Shellie Dermont lived just outside Pontiac on a side street carpeted with last season's leaves and the oily residue of hopelessness. Even the house she lived in appeared to be frowning, its filthy awnings drawing furrowed brows over sagging window eyes, its front door a yawning howl of a mouth. Tax forms indicated she was broke, but stable, supporting herself working two waitressing gigs in the area. Still, people killed for a lot less than thirty grand.

Petrosky stood in the living room. Dermont sat on the couch, paperwork on her knee, finger moving in time with her lips. "I don't understand what this is." The black ring in her nose matched the heavy metal T-shirt she wore. In the next room, a boy rolled a toy truck back and forth under a rustic dining table right off the cover of one of those shabby chic magazines Petrosky's ex-wife used to read.

Morrison pulled out his notepad and sat at the table. Petrosky glared at Morrison until he stood, then turned back to Dermont. "You've never seen this before?" Petrosky asked.

"No." She held the papers out to him. He waved them back and she laid them next to her on the couch.

"It was sent certified mail to an address on Carper," Petrosky told her. "But it was never signed for."

"I only lived there for a few months. There were roaches in the cupboard and the landlord ... I guess you don't need to know that, huh?"

"When was the last time you talked to Jacob Campbell?"

She laughed. It was a melancholy sound. "Not since Jayden was born, so around five years. He came to the hospital to see us. Took one look at him and bolted. Never even held him."

Petrosky waited for Morrison's pen to stop scratching on the notepad. "So you were separated before the baby was born?"

She nodded. "He was ... mean sometimes. I didn't know I was pregnant when I left, and after I found out, I couldn't bear the thought of—" Her eyes moved to the boy who was now lying on his back, feet in the air. "Anyway, I told him about Jayden and he wanted a paternity test, so I had one done."

"Did you file for support?"

She shook her head. "He never had a job while I was with him and I didn't expect that he would suddenly get one after the baby came. I didn't want him around, anyway. He was always pushy, always asking me to marry him, especially when he found out I was pregnant. He got mad when I said no. It was kinda ... scary." She shuddered.

"In what way?"

"Just the way his eyes got. Like he wanted to hit you."

"Did he?"

"A few times. After the last time, I left."

"Good for you."

A sad smile flashed and was gone.

"Hear anything else about him? Through mutual friends?"

"We didn't have mutual friends. When I was with him I didn't have friends at all. He kinda made sure of that."

Typical abusive bullshit. "I see."

"I know, it was stupid. At the time I just didn't ... it's hard to see when you're in the middle of it, you know?" She looked at her hands. "To be honest, when I saw the story on the news, I wasn't all that ... sad. I mean, it was a shock, but not all that sad."

There was a scuffling sound behind Petrosky as the boy ran to his mother and put his head in her lap. She stroked his hair. "Hey, Care Bear, you want to go get a book? We can read before I have to go to work."

"Stay home, Mama."

"I can't, baby. But Ms. Ross is coming and you always have fun with her, right?"

He shrugged. "I'll find the dog book."

"Okay." She watched him scamper off down a back hallway then turned back to them. "What else do you need to know? I have to get ready for work soon."

Petrosky and Morrison exchanged a glance. "We're almost done, Ms. Dermont," Petrosky said. "Were you aware that Mr. Campbell had an insurance policy that reverts to your family in the event of his death?"

Her eyes narrowed. "I don't understand."

"Mr. Campbell had an insurance policy from his father. He was to receive thirty-six thousand dollars after he got married."

"That's why he wanted to marry me?"

"I don't know."

"Well, I didn't marry him, so—"

Jayden skipped into the living room carrying a book and leapt into his mother's lap. "Found it, Mama!"

She smiled and kissed him on the cheek.

Petrosky waited until Dermont looked back up. "In the event of his death, that money reverts to his closest living relative."

"His mom, huh?" She smirked. "She always hated me, but she'll be happy now."

"Not the way it's written. In this case, children get precedence over parents."

Dermont stared at Petrosky, open-mouthed. "Wait, are you telling me that ... that Jayden ..."

"I am. Which is why I need to ask you a few questions about your whereabouts on the days around Mr. Campbell's death."

She sniffed. Her face had gone tomato red. "Ask away. I'm never anywhere but work or here, and I have a few neighbors who can verify. Ms. Ross lives across the street. She watches Jayden when I'm at work and keeps an eye on everything and everyone the rest of the time." Her voice was choked with emotion. A few tears slid down her cheeks and onto the top of Jayden's head.

"Hey, Mama! Stop! Stop! All wet!"

She held him close to her chest.

"You're going to college, baby."

Ms. Ross was old, wretchedly mean, and honest. She wouldn't let them in the house, but she had plenty to say: the kids in the neighborhood were too loud, Morrison's hair was too damn long, and there was no way that Shellie Dermont was anywhere but where she'd said on the nights in question.

Petrosky was quiet as he slid behind the wheel.

Morrison cleared his throat. "You think our killer believes he's helping people?"

"Helping?"

"Yeah, like offing people who are getting in the way of other people's happiness?"

The car's engine grumbled to life. "I doubt the families in question would have chosen that path," Petrosky said.

"Well, obviously they wouldn't have. Maybe that's why he intervenes; he thinks he knows what's best for everyone else. Like a nosy old lady." Morrison nodded at Ms. Ross, who stood on her porch in her bathrobe glaring at them.

"If we've got a killer out to rid the world of assholes, he'll have to kill a lot more."

"As it is, I don't see him stopping," Morrison said.

Petrosky put the car in reverse and nodded to Ms. Ross who squinted harder at him but touched her door handle like she was considering going inside. "No, he won't stop."

Their killer had planned this. Chosen a poem. And he'd gotten off clean so far, which would only whet his appetite for more slaughter.

"The killings are coming fast," Petrosky said. "But this one with Campbell feels ... different. We're missing something."

"Besides the poem?"

Petrosky's hands tightened on the wheel. Yes, the missing poem. Between the poem and the restraints and the type of victim, there were too many differences. That didn't sit right, and it intensified the disquiet already eating at him. "If we don't get a handle on this soon, we'll have another family to notify."

"At least the next family might not cry, if what we've seen so far is any indication," Morrison said.

Petrosky braked hard enough to lock the seat belts. "You a fan, California?"

"No, Boss. Just saying."

WEDNESDAY, NOVEMBER 11TH

Just another month and you'll have enough cash to get out of here.
You don't really have to leave. This has nothing to do with you.

From my desk, roses and lavender filled the air with a subtle sweetness. The elaborate vase had come after the funeral and graced my workspace every day since, a constant reminder that Jake had never given me anything so beautiful. That I was really better off without him. I had cried fat, guilty tears at those thoughts, but it hadn't been enough to make me remove the vase. It was enough to make me toss the note, though:

If there is anything I can do to be of assistance, please let me know.
  In sympathy, Dominic

I had torn the note from the vase the day I got it, both in panic that I might have to take off work, and out of fear that I'd spend my life rereading it, extracting meaning that had never been there to begin with. Plus, I worried that if someone came to search my place again, they would misconstrue his words.

Let me be of assistance. I want to help you.
Yes, sir.

"Hannah ..." Noelle's trembling voice floated over the top of the cubicles. I followed her gaze. Detective Petrosky was at the glass doors to the office, staring in at me.

He thinks I'm a murderer. I walked to the door on shaky legs, my stomach trying to dance a jig and succeeding only in making me want to vomit.

"Ms. Montgomery." He nodded.

"Detective Petrosky."

"Can you spare a moment or two? Maybe take a fifteen-minute break?"

I glanced back into the office. Noelle was staring openly at us. Ralph wandered past, pretending not to look, but failing miserably.

"Maybe ... um ... a walk," I said.

WE SAT at the picnic table by the lake, my face toward the water, his face toward me. Half a dozen mourning doves crooned by the lake's edge, pecking at icy thistle and casting hopeful glances at us.

The detective's face did not look as hopeful. "I'm sorry to bother you at work, Ms. Montgomery. I just had a few follow-up questions."

I swear I didn't do it! Ask someone else! "Okay."

He pulled two pages from the folder and slid them across the table. Photos, black and white and glossy, of someone in a hooded jacket. "Do you recognize this person? Maybe the coat?"

"I can't see their face." I leaned toward the pictures and plastered them to the table with my fists when the wind tried to whip them away. *Was this taken in my mailroom?* "Is this ... her? The girl who left him that note?" Hopefully, the detective would understand if I puked on his shoes.

"I think so, ma'am."

I touched the photo, her hood, her shoulder. *What did she have that I didn't? What made her so special?* I could feel my heartbeat in my frozen ears.

"Ms. Montgomery?"

"You think she was the one who ... did it?"

"We're looking into it. You're sure you don't recognize her?"

"No, I don't. I doubt she would ever have wanted to meet me."

He took the pictures back and put them in the folder. "Were you aware that Jake had a child?"

My mouth dropped open. Jake *was* a child. "I ... No, there must be a mistake."

The detective's expression remained deadpan like he hadn't just blindsided me. "No mistake. He had a five-year-old son."

"But ... he never said anything. I don't think he ever paid support—" My neck muscles went rigid. "You think this has something to do with his death?"

"Not the child support, but perhaps the inheritance from Jake's father."

I shook my head, hard. Now I knew they had it all it wrong. "He never knew his dad—"

"Maybe, maybe not. The money was to be paid when Mr. Campbell got married or when he turned thirty, whichever came first."

Let's get married, baby. I want to take care of you.

Maybe we can just go see the judge. You know I love you ...

It had always been about money. My jaw clenched.

"Something wrong, Ms. Montgomery?"

"No. I'm just ... I'm starting to feel like I didn't know a lot of things about him." Like the fact that he had an inheritance. That he had a fucking child. Maybe he'd always preferred store-bought spaghetti sauce to the homemade shit. All bets were off now.

Petrosky's eyes were soft. "Don't feel too bad," he said. "This is not information that many others had."

"Did his mother know?" Of course she did. No wonder she was pissed that we didn't get married before we moved in together.

"Yes, but she didn't think the child was his."

I blinked back the sting of tears. They had all known. Everyone except me. "But the baby is his? For sure?"

"He is. We have the tests to prove it."

I stared at the doves, who were obviously not worried about anything but preening their feathers. Petrosky's voice came to me in snippets, something about keeping this quiet, not leaking to the press.

I met his gaze. "Why does this even matter? Wasn't Jake killed by the same person who killed those women? That's what they keep saying on the news."

His eyes darkened, like he was angry at me for asking. "We don't know."

The ice swept through my chest, hardening my lungs. "What do you mean, you don't know?" *No, no, no. This could still be my fault.*

"There were inconsistencies with your boyfriend's murder. We can't rule anything out."

His face swam, blurring in my prickling tears.

I thought of the eyes on my back as I walked around my apartment, heard the crunching of footsteps in empty alleys behind the shelter. I blinked hard to hide the fear that must have been written across my face.

I'll find you, baby. We will always be one.

"So Jake's killer ... might not have killed the others? He might have just killed Jake?" My voice cracked. "If you thought it was all connected you wouldn't be asking me about some woman in a picture, right?"

Petrosky searched my eyes. I resisted the urge to close them.

"Just covering our bases. Have you given any more thought to who might have wanted to hurt him?"

Jake's dead because of me, and knowing it makes me an accessory.

I don't want to go to jail.

"No, sir. I can't think of anyone."

Petrosky stood. "Thank you for your time, ma'am. If you think of anything else—"

You already know more about the man I lived with than I ever did. I nodded at the tabletop and waited, my heartbeat wild and hot inside my icy body. His footsteps crunched over the snow toward the parking lot.

I looked back out at the water, took a final deep breath and stood. *I hope I can save enough to run again before he kills me too.*

It had been hours since the police came to their office, but Noelle was still unsettled. She assaulted her fingernails with her teeth and winced when she drew blood.

Through her windshield, barren maple trees cast clawing shadows on snowy lawns that rolled up to neat, uniform houses. The homes were red or gray brick behind small cement porches and topped with aluminum-sided second floors.

Thomas's house was in a cul-de-sac at the end of a winding asphalt road. Bay windows protruded from brown brick on either side of the entrance. It was a nice home. A *family* home. But you couldn't just take a house and magically make a happy family any more than you could take just any self-centered jackass and make him a good father.

He opened the door before she knocked, his smile wide. "Hey! You found it!"

"I did."

He grabbed her hand and led her into the house. "You smell good. What is that, lemons?"

"Orange-mango."

"I like it." His lips were frozen in a permanent grin. "Come on in. I was just feeding the cat."

Noelle's boots squeaked over the light oak floors. The foyer walls were painted a deep green. A narrow table sat against one wall of the entry, topped by a small, sickly plant. Brown leaves littered the tabletop.

Thomas saw her staring at it. "Wolverine's kind of a jerk to plants."

They entered a large cheery kitchen with matching white appliances and light oak cupboards. He opened one and grabbed a bag of cat food.

She followed him through to the living room. "Holy shit."

"Oh, yeah. I forget that not everyone is a fan."

The entire room was painted a deep electric blue, making the light floors and suede couches seem larger. Small wooden tables topped with glass sat on either side of the sofa, and a leather chair faced the television on the wall to her left. The TV on the wall was at least sixty inches, flanked by large black speakers that looked as if they could blow the house apart if Thomas got carried away. Behind the couch, the far wall was entirely covered in a stretched canvas painting of huge, muscled-up green giant charging into the room, fist outstretched as if in attack, face twisted in a grimace. Droplets of cartoon saliva flew from his half-open mouth.

"It's ... interesting." Violent and angry, but interesting. "I didn't even know you could get art like that."

He laughed. "I painted it. It was that, or tack up a poster."

"You painted it?" She studied it more closely. *He's kinda good.*

"Yeah, like I said the other night, I needed something to do with my time instead of football. Plus, the Hulk is more reliable companionship for a geeky kid than school buddies anyway." Thomas stooped and poured the cat food into a glass dish. "Hey, there he is!"

A fat orange tabby entered the room from a hallway in the back corner and slunk toward them, staring at Noelle with suspicious green eyes. Thomas scratched him behind the ears. Wolverine purred like a rumbling motor.

Thomas righted himself and offered his arm. "Shall we?"

She took it. "Lead the way."

He is never picking the movie again. Noelle glared at the screen. *Seriously, who cares about this superhero bullshit? I mean, except ...*

Thomas's face was a mask of childlike excitement. Even the way he wiped fake popcorn butter on his khakis was endearing. What was wrong with her? Was she falling for him? Maybe it was the way he just seemed so damn happy all the time. He had probably had the perfect childhood outside of that whole being-small-and-bullied thing.

Maybe that's why he likes this stuff. She pictured him as a small, dejected boy in a Spiderman T-shirt, poring over comic books, losing himself in another world where he was more ... well ... *super*.

Noelle's phone vibrated with a text message. She pretended not to hear it, though it seemed impossibly loud in the sudden quiet. On the screen, a guy in a neon blue leotard pressed himself against a brick wall. Very incognito.

She yawned and rested her head against Thomas's shoulder. He smelled like shampoo and something that could only be cat hair. She sneezed.

"Bless you," he said.

"Thanks." Her phone vibrated again.

"Do you need to get that?"

Noelle shrugged, fumbled in her purse for the phone, and checked the messages.

You're such a bitch.

She sighed. Ralph had been going back and forth from *I hate you* to *Please forgive me for whatever I did to upset you* for weeks. He had even left her a six-minute voicemail telling her that he knew she lied about having a brother, like she gave a shit.

"Everything okay?" Thomas whispered.

"Everything's fine." She turned the phone off and vowed to change her number tomorrow. He'd get tired of harassing her soon, if he was anything like the others. Their anger never lasted forever. She wondered if anything did.

Thomas put his hand on the armrest. She covered it with hers, leaned her head back against the chair and closed her eyes.

"You're missing the best part," he whispered.

She dragged her lids open. "Oh, I was just—"

"I know, resting your eyes." He chuckled. "Hey, there's no accounting for taste. Or for people staying home because they're afraid of a little snowstorm in the forecast." He nodded to the nearly empty theater. "I think the reviews were pretty bad, though. That's the first thing Jim said when I told him where I was taking you."

Noelle glanced at the screen, where two guys were engaged in a seemingly intense conversation about what it takes to bring down a superhuman. She rolled her eyes. Maybe next time Jim would get through to Thomas and save her from this nonsense.

"How's he been? Jim, I mean."

"Good. On a blind date. I get the impression he's just wasting time until Hannah is ready to go out with him. Every time I mention that I'm seeing you, he asks about her."

Poor Hannah. Noelle's stomach roiled. An explosion lit the room as the hero threw a car. Then he tripped over a fire hydrant and went sprawling, his blue leotard making him look like a flattened smurf. Noelle laughed and her stomach settled. *Okay, this isn't all bad.*

Thomas beamed at her, teeth shining in the light from the screen. "Maybe we can double with Hannah and Jim, once she's ready. I'll let you guys pick the movie."

Her stomach gurgled again, hot with equal parts guilt and fury. She had been glad when Jake and Hannah split, excited that her letter had the desired effect. She had not been sorry when he died.

But—

He was not supposed to hit her. She hoped his death was horrific. And slow.

Thomas was still waiting for an answer.

She squeezed his hand tighter and watched leotard guy leap from one skyscraper to another. He brushed his lips against her cheek. Her heart slowed.

"Noelle, you okay? I'm sorry if you hate double dates or something. We don't have to do it if you don't want to."

"No, I'd like to double. Hannah might be upset for a while, though. She's pretty torn up."

"Maybe." Thomas shrugged and turned back to the movie. "Who knows? Things aren't always what they seem."

Noelle wasn't sure if he was whispering it to her or to himself.

THURSDAY, NOVEMBER 12TH

I CHEWED ON MY CHEEK, trying to ground myself in the pain of it. The thought of leaving tonight and having to find another shelter in another city made me sick to my stomach. I just had to save a little more cash so I could legitimately start over, on my own two feet. Because whether or not Jake was killed by the same person as those other women, *someone* killed him. Someone who could be watching me right now. I felt like I was losing my mind. Maybe I was paranoid, but that didn't mean that someone wasn't out to get me.

The owls smirked at me from under my pointless blank cork board. No puppies, no babies, and I had never even picked my nose behind the partition. I should start, so that when I was old and gray in a rocking chair on a porch somewhere with an owl on a perch next to me, I would at least have this one small thing I could say I took advantage of when the rest of my life fell apart. I looked at my finger.

"Ms. Montgomery?"

The finger disappeared under my desk.

"May I sit down?"

"Yes. I mean, yes, sir." My heart quickened and slithered up my throat like an agitated python.

He took the seat across from me, his black suit and lavender tie too good for here. He stuck out like a penguin at a Bar-B-Que.

An incredibly handsome penguin. Do people fuck penguins? That seems ill advised, and yet ...

Weeks of subpar sleep were creeping up on me and manifesting as slap happy absurdity.

"Something funny?" he asked.

I had not realized I was smiling. *I really am losing my mind.* "No, sir."

"Please call me Dominic."

"Yes sir ... I mean, Dominic." I put my fingers to my mouth to stop the goofy-ass grin.

"I hope you have been able to cope with the events of the last couple weeks satisfactorily."

"Uh ... I've been okay."

"I notice you didn't take any time off. I was frankly surprised that you came back so quickly."

"I know, I just ... feel better staying busy."

"If you need more time, a week, a month, the offer still stands."

"Thank you. Thank you for the flowers, too. They were gorgeous." *Oh my god, Hannah, stop babbling.*

"Is there anything I can do to help?" he said.

Yeah, teleport me out of this state. Maybe out of the country. Or off the planet. "No."

He studied my face. "Let me know if you think of anything," he said quietly.

"Yes, sir. Thank you."

"Dominic." He smiled. His teeth were the straightest I had ever seen.

"Dominic."

And as abruptly as he'd arrived, he was gone. My stomach dropped a little. I told myself it was hunger and not disappointment.

"Hannah! What did he say?" Noelle's head appeared over the cubicle. Would she miss me after I packed up and left? Maybe I would call her one day, years from now, from another state. From another life. More likely, I'd stare at her number and wonder what ever happened to her.

"Hannah?" She was watching me, eyebrows raised.

"He didn't say much. Just wanted to remind me that I could take time off if I needed to. You know with all the ... stuff that's happened."

"He came down here personally for that?"

"I guess."

Noelle pursed her lips.

"He's just being nice. He cares. He's a good boss."

"Yeah, he is. But the way he looks at you is a little more than standard employee appreciation."

"It's not like that." But something flitted around in my belly as I said it. Excitement? Fear? Hope?

Noelle reached down for the owls and tapped Horny on the top of his fake head. "You still have these things?"

"Yes, I—" My sinuses tingled with something subtle and sweet and familiar. The back of my neck was suddenly very hot. "New lotion?"

Noelle put a hand to her nose, apparently unaware of the quaver in my voice. "Yeah, you like it?"

A hornet in my ear buzzed angry violent songs of love notes and cheating and perfume. Noelle had always put Jake down. Always tried to get me to go out, knowing it would make him angry, knowing it would pull me away from him. Because she was ... what? Sleeping with him? But that didn't make sense.

"Hannah, you okay?"

"I—" *No.* "Not really. I feel sick."

"I know you've had a rough few weeks, but come out with Thomas and me tonight. Jim will be there too. Maybe it will get your mind off of everything."

"I can't." *Last time I went out, someone filleted my boyfriend.*

"You're going. Don't leave me with two strange men at a dark Greek restaurant."

Sweat leaked from under my bra and trickled down to my belly button. "I can't, okay?" But uncertainty nagged at me. Noelle was dating Thomas. She hadn't been after Jake. She hated Jake. And already Noelle had the same look that acquaintances got in elementary school when I told inappropriate jokes. I could see it like a rocket ship countdown: confusion, irritation, disconnection and *bam*! I was alone.

I couldn't lose her, not yet. Not before I had to. Surely it was possible that a skin care company might have made more than one tube of citrus-scented lotion in an insane attempt to turn a profit? I mean, *duh*, as the kids would say.

A few more weeks, that's all I needed. A few more weeks to suck everything I could out of our friendship so I could wrap the memories around me like a blanket when I was in some new, lonely place. If I made it that long.

Noelle pulled her hand back and the smell of oranges bombarded my nose like someone had thrown a bushel of them at me. My heart ached from pumping so furiously.

It was crazy anyway, to think Noelle would ever do something like that. I needed to stop looking for reasons to mess up the few good things I had left. God knows I had messed up enough already.

I inhaled through my mouth. *It isn't her. It wasn't her. And going out is safer than hanging out at home, right?* I pulled a pencil from the drawer, trying to hide my quaking hands by tapping it on the desktop. "You know what they say about the Greeks," I said.

Her eyes danced. "Big kabobs, small olives?"

"You got it." I swallowed hard.

"I'll pick you up at eight."

I watched her walk away, convinced I was finally, officially, going insane. I needed help. I glanced at the owls, and they glared back. I flicked Horny in the head and watched him topple over the edge of the desk. We were all just one good push away from breaking.

"You're sure I'm not crazy?" I asked, though I knew the answer and further knew that Tammy Bransen, shrink extraordinaire, didn't have enough information to make any kind of accurate assessment at all.

"Magical thinking, anxiety, depression." Tammy ticked them off on her fingers. "They are all part of the normal grieving process and you need to give yourself permission to move through those feelings. You need time to heal. Your wounds are still fresh." She pushed her horn-rimmed glasses up her nose and tucked a lock of straw-colored hair behind her ear.

We had met at the shelter, after one of the monthly group sessions Ms. LaPorte arranged for the women. Ms. LaPorte had thought it might help me after the abortion. Her relief when I agreed was a good enough reason to show up. Sometimes I even felt good coming here, like I was doing *something*, despite the fact that I hid the stuff that really mattered.

"I just feel so ... paranoid. About everything."

Tammy shook her head. "Hannah, it is expected that you would have strange reactions to other people, what with the way your relationship with Jake ended. The fact that it was a sudden death makes it all the more difficult to bear, and the type of demise, and the police questioning, well—"

"The whole thing just seems so unreal. Like tomorrow I'll wake up and find out it was all a nightmare."

"How has your sleep been?"

I sighed. "Not great." It was never great. And I still wrote about it, every morning, waiting with bated breath for that notebook to help me the way Tammy had promised me it would.

"Have you noticed any patterns in your sleep journal?"

"Nope, just the usual crappiness. It did get worse after Jake died, I guess. More trouble dozing off, more waking up scared."

Tammy nodded sympathetically. "That's quite common after experiencing such a loss. All very normal."

"Is it normal to believe your best friend tried to steal your boyfriend?"

Tammy raised her eyebrows.

Oh, Jesus. "Hypothetically. I have the craziest thoughts sometimes."

"Racing thoughts are normal. They're from the anxiety, and they're, by definition, irrational. So is the magical thinking thing."

I squinted at her and waited.

"Magical thinking is where bereaved loves ones convince themselves that they were responsible for the death. They feel like a final argument, or a missed phone call, somehow triggered the event. Again, irrational and completely untrue, but very common."

The room swam behind my tears. "I need it to stop. I just want to be normal." Not that I'd ever been normal.

"It takes time to heal, Hannah. Don't rush it."

"I just feel so nervous around other people lately. I feel like I always want to run."

You have a good reason to run.

No one else knows that.

You don't have a reason. It's magical thinking.

That doesn't mean you shouldn't pack up and leave.

Another nod. Maybe Tammy's head would wobble and detach, roll over to my shoes and spout off semi-supportive drivel from the floor.

Tears fell on my clasped hands. "I'm so tired of being so scared."

Tammy walked around the desk and offered me a box of tissues. "Don't push too hard, but allow yourself room to find a new normal, a new way of doing things that will benefit you. You may need to be around others to prove that people are not as frightening as you think they are. Go out if it helps, show yourself that there is nothing to be afraid of. Do whatever you think you need to do to heal. Don't just sit at home alone in the dark."

That struck a chord. *I hate the dark.*

By eight thirty I was fiddling with my fork and inwardly cursing Tammy's stupid face. *It's all part of the healing process. I just have to stick it out and prove how silly this all is. And when that doesn't work, I'll pack.*

We ate lentil soup that I could barely taste while Noelle and the guys chattered about their favorite restaurants, and recent movies, and which of their current supervisors were dickheads. I listened halfheartedly and avoided Jim's penetrating gaze.

They quieted as the waitress appeared with plates of garlic paste, hummus and warm pita bread. My mouth watered despite my initial ambivalence about dinner, and the food proved to be savory and spicy and just plain awesome. Had I really not eaten a full meal all week? *That's about to change.* I reached for a grape leaf and accidentally brushed Jim's fingers. Electric current zinged up my arm, and all my hair stood on end.

Next time I went to therapy, I was going to punch Tammy in the nose.

It's all part of the process, I told myself.

But I didn't believe it.

FRIDAY, NOVEMBER 13TH

PETROSKY GROUND his teeth together to avoid calling Chief Castleman a fucking asshole. Next to him, Morrison was stiff, the muscles in his jaw working in a decidedly un-surfer-like way.

"You can't be serious," Petrosky said.

"Detective Petrosky, Detective Morrison, this is not an attempt to freeze you out." Castleman squared his chubby shoulders. "But we have a serial killer on our hands and the Mayor doesn't want to take any chances. A screw up is the last thing this city needs right now."

"And I'll screw it up?"

"This has the potential to go national, Petrosky. The only reason it hasn't yet is that someone bombed a bus down south and killed a bunch of grade-schoolers. But that story won't stick around forever. We don't find this guy, they'll crucify us ... and you."

"I understand, but—"

"No buts. The FBI has far more resources at their disposal. And it turns out that Meredith Lawrence was the royally fucked-up niece of a radio show host up in Dryesdale. He's making a big stink."

"A radio show host? How the fuck does a radio show host get to tell us—"

"I expect complete cooperation on this. Agent Bryant Graves is waiting for you in the conference room with his men. Get down there and give them what they need."

Dismissed, Petrosky left the chief's office and stalked down the hall, Morrison beside him. Framed photos of dead cops stared at them from the walls with solemn expressions, as if they knew that one day he and Morrison would be underground too, their snapshots also mounted like prized deer heads. Petrosky wanted to mount Chief Castleman on the wall too, along with Agent Bryant fucking Graves.

"Was Graves the one in charge of that case in Frankfurt last year?" Morrison asked.

"How the hell should I know? And how do you?"

"Heard about it from Zajac over in traffic. He used to live up there. The name sounds familiar, but I could be wrong."

Petrosky stopped. "You hang out with the traffic boys, too?"

Morrison stepped past him, leaning against the wall under a picture of an officer with brown eyes and an arrogant expression. He pulled out his phone and tapped a few buttons. "I met him at the gym ... okay, same guy." He pocketed the phone. "Zajac said the case was a couple of kids making pipe bombs. Burned two teenagers and a father unlucky enough to open his daughter's mail. Turned out that the kid making the bombs was the mayor's son. The evidence was pretty substantial against him, but they ended up shifting the blame to the kid's friend. There was a lot of suspicion within the department that Graves might have taken a bribe to keep quiet about it."

"Sounds like a winner." Petrosky glanced at the conference room and drew himself up as tall as he could. "Let's go meet this asshole."

BRYANT GRAVES STOOD at the conference room window, phone to his ear, eyes narrow with concentration—or rage. "What do you mean, no one asked before?" He stared at Petrosky and Morrison as they sat across from two other men, presumably, Graves's agents. The bald one exchanged a knowing look with the asshole with a buzz cut. Petrosky hid his clenched fists under the table.

"Call you back." Graves slipped the phone into his pocket, his eyes radiating accusation. "Detectives." He nodded to Petrosky's side of the room. "Shall we skip the niceties and get down to business?"

Graves gestured to the white board at the head of the table, where pictures of the three victims stared at them. Solemn mug shots for the girls, and a photo of Campbell in a red sweater from his mother, grinning at them with a much more optimistic expression than any photo in the hallway. "Meredith Lawrence, Jane Trazowski and Jacob Campbell. Since this type of killer does not usually have such wildly different victims, there must be something that connects our working girls to Mr. Campbell. The first two had similar lifestyles and drug habits. Jane Trazowski and Jacob Campbell were both connected to Hannah Montgomery in the last six months."

Petrosky's temple throbbed. "Trazowski showed up at the women's shelter after an altercation with a john. Apparently he roughed her up pretty good; she was scared enough to leave her apartment."

Graves glared at him. "Have you found the john?"

"No."

"How about any connection between Hannah Montgomery and

Meredith Lawrence? They may have met at some point due to Ms. Montgomery's position with the shelter, particularly in light of Lawrence's extensive domestic violence history."

"We weren't able to find any connections."

"Then we're missing something."

The throbbing wrapped around his forehead and expanded until Petrosky could feel his heartbeat in his eyeballs. "We questioned Montgomery about it, but the night of Trazowski's murder she was working at the shelter. We verified it with the woman she works for and with another woman who was staying at the shelter that day."

Graves's lips tightened, nostrils flaring like he smelled something foul.

"We also have video of her apartment building. She was inside the night Campbell was killed," Petrosky said. *Reading a note from her boyfriend's lover and sobbing.* But he'd let these haughty fuckers find that out for themselves. "She's not a suspect here."

"No one thinks Montgomery is a suspect, detective." Graves leaned forward and put his hands on the tabletop as heat rose in Petrosky's face. "But just because she didn't do it doesn't mean there's no connection to her. We need to go over everything again."

Of course she wasn't a suspect. He was letting his emotions fuck with him. *Goddammit, Petrosky, get your shit together.*

Graves stood. "Hernandez!"

Baldy straightened, light reflecting off his scalp. "Sir."

"Find out what you can about Trazowski's background and see if there are any more questionable activities we should be aware of."

Petrosky stiffened. "That information is in the—"

"Paulson!"

Gray buzz cut turned toward Graves expectantly.

"I want more on Campbell. Friends, exes, family members. And double check the movements of Meredith Lawrence in the weeks before her death."

Paulson nodded.

They were wasting time. All of this was in the file. Petrosky met Morrison's eyes and Morrison raised one shoulder, maybe acquiescing, maybe feeling helpless, or maybe wanting to punch the condescending look off Graves's face.

Graves turned to the other two men at the table. "I want you to research the poem and double back on Shellie Dermont. And see what you can find out about Montgomery. Since two of the victims knew her, we may do well to keep a tight watch on who she sees and talks with. There may be a link between her activities and the way the victims are being chosen."

Graves turned to Petrosky. "Coordinate with these guys and fill in the gaps. We'll need your knowledge of the area and any insight you may already have. Let's get it closed before this ends up splashed all over the national news."

"Or before he kills someone else," Morrison said.

Silence. Graves turned away, toward the window. "Yes," he said finally, voice softer and lower and thick, like a perp making a confession. "That too."

SUNDAY, NOVEMBER 15TH

RADIO SILENCE. Static. Then the pillow was ripped from my hands.

His face was red, split by a flash of white teeth.

Panic tightened around my throat like a scarf. *Run.* But I was pinned beneath him.

"No, please—"

He put his mouth to my ear. "Shut the fuck up, you little slut. You've been coming on to me for years, and now you tell me that it's wrong? That I don't have a right to give you what you've been begging for?" Droplets of saliva clung to my cheek, hot and wet.

I am a slut. This is all my fault. "Please, I'm sorry, I—"

His hand smashed into the side of my face. My ears rang. "Shut. The. fuck. Up." It was the quiet, husky tone he'd once used with my mother and it had made her sit motionless on the couch until he'd left.

I tried to stay still like she had, tried to focus through the wavering orange that had settled across my eyes. I felt my pants sliding over my thighs, but distantly, as if in someone else's nightmare. He forced my legs apart with his knees. *No.* I kicked in a futile attempt at freedom.

"You wanted this. Don't you ever fucking forget that." He leaned close to me, his breath warm and putrid.

The world twisted and faded. He forced himself into me and the hurt pounded through every part of my body, hot and sharp and raw, until I was nothing but the pain. He laughed and heat in my chest exploded into furious panic.

"Stop! No! I'm going to tell!" *No! Shut up, Hannah! You'll make it worse!* I bit my tongue until I tasted blood.

"If you want them to die too, go ahead," he whispered in my ear. "Just ask that bitch of a mother how her new husband is doing."

"You killed mom's—"

He sneered down at me. "You'd do well to keep that to yourself. Just knowing about it makes you an accessory. Between jail and death, I'd pick door number three." He moved his hips. I felt like I was being ripped in two. "We will always be one, Hannah. I won't ever let you go. And if you leave, I will find you. And I will fucking kill you."

Numbness seeped in where I once held only adoration. I floated outside my body near the ceiling, looking down at my prone figure draped in the angry profile of my father as he raped me, tearing the tapestry of trust and love and kindness that had taken my entire childhood to build. Blood-tinged semen dripped onto the bed. I prayed to a God I didn't believe in, but understood that help would not come, not now, not ever.

Nothing would ever be the same again. And it was all my fault.

I jerked upright, the air cutting like shards of ice into my sweat-covered skin. My shirt was soaked through. My teeth chattered.

The nightmares. I had thought they were over. I was wrong.

On the end table, the clock glowed three-fourteen.

I should go see my shrink again, maybe on Monday. But I had no words to describe my pain. And when I didn't know what to say, Tammy would say something like, "Let it out. Openness leads to less difficulty over time." Complete bullshit. There was no faster way to screw things up than to open your mouth.

Maybe I could tell Tammy about my mother leaving us for her boss, the dentist, the summer before I entered fourth grade. And about her husband's death the following year from ingesting something he was allergic to, and how my mother never came back to visit, even when she didn't have some mouth-poking, tooth-filling, wrinkly man to climb on top of. Maybe I could tell her how I had retreated to my father's room, wanting to ease his heartache. How some days he seemed happy and I rejoiced, as if finally there was something I could do correctly. But what would she say to what came after?

The night he put his hand on my thigh, I had not resisted. When his mouth found mine, I had brushed aside the nervous tingling at the base of my skull and reminded myself that he was the only one who believed I was worth anything. When his fingers parted me gently, I wasn't sure it was wrong. It felt weird, yet somehow nice. And as I lay naked and felt the searing, intense pain of him deep inside me, he had held me and whispered in my ear: "It's okay, baby. Daddy's here. Everything is okay."

I had believed him, from elementary school and all through middle school, though to say that out loud now seemed insane. Even more so when I considered that the more often I found myself in his arms, the more I knew I was completely and totally in love, a notion that was not contradictory to what I'd been taught in rudimentary sex education classes. Sex was for people who loved one another. Check. Sex happened between people in committed relationships. Check. Sex needed to be based on trust. Check. It all made sense.

In the teacher's defense, it was unlikely she suspected anyone in the class would be fucking her own father.

It was great until it wasn't. Sometime in high school, awareness crept up on me like cold centipedes on my arms, a million tiny legs groping me. It was in the way he avoided hugging me in public like other fathers did. The way he hid the cordless phone in his pocket and never let me answer it. The way he sometimes called out my mother's name when he came.

I knew there were legal penalties for adults who engaged in sexual activities with minors, but I also knew I was already in too deep. It was too late to go back.

I was not normal, and never would be. I loved him too much. And I had to remain silent or he would end up in jail and I would never see him again. At some point, panic gave way to dread that settled in my chest like a stone, growing heavier with each passing day until I knew it would crush my lungs.

And then I talked. It was such a simple question he'd asked: "Hey, Hannah banana, what's wrong?"

I could have said I was tired. That I was worried about a test. That I was on my fucking period. Anything. Instead, I sobbed into a pillow.

"You ... we're not supposed to—" I had choked on the words, as if saying it out loud would somehow make it true. *You're not supposed to have sex with your daughter.* It was applicable to everyone else in the world, but not to us.

Then radio silence. Static. And the pillow had been ripped from my hands.

Honesty gets you nowhere. Openness is fucking crazy.

Focus, Hannah. He's not here. Not now.

I peeled myself out of bed, the wet top sheet still clinging to my skin. Every night home alone seemed worse than the one before it. Maybe tonight it was because of that electricity I'd felt when Jim's fingers brushed against mine. Or maybe it was the knowledge that I was now completely and utterly alone. Vulnerable. Small. With no one to help me if he finally came sneaking in from the hallway with that awful hungry look on his face, lips peeled back in a sneer, eyes dark and glittering with excitement. Maybe he even knew about the baby.

Maybe he was pissed. More pissed than he'd been at mom's husband, and he'd poisoned him, right?

My breath caught in my throat and I tried to think of something that would make it better, make it funny, make it bearable, but there was nothing besides the fear and the urge to retch as if I could purge all this vile stuff from deep inside.

I left the bedroom, made my way to the living room window on jelly legs and drew back the curtain. Below, the streetlight cast ghostly shadows onto sidewalks covered with wisps of powdered sugar snow. Empty as it always was, but hell, I was a paranoid freak, right? It had been five years, surely he wasn't coming tonight.

I dropped the curtain.

Stop, Hannah. Just stop. I kept my hand on the couch to steady myself, then the counter. In the kitchen, I pulled a lonely Pabst Blue Ribbon from the fridge and drank it in front of the sink in case it made me throw up. I gagged once, but swallowed again and again, and tossed the empty can in the sink. That would buy me four or five more hours of sleep and tomorrow I'd jot down notes about my shitty night, just enough to make Tammy shake her head and say: "Mm-hmm. And why do you think that is?"

I staggered back to my bed, the room wavering at the edges, and pulled the blanket up to my chin. Beside me, the deserted spot where Jake used to lie felt like a living thing, breathing into my ear.

Alone. So alone. But did I miss him or just the body that provided some respite from being so vulnerable? Had I ever wanted him or was I a terrible person who just needed someone to be there because I was so fucking afraid?

Probably the second. In a perfect world, I would have chosen someone more supportive. But that didn't mean Jake deserved to die. My eyes filled and I wiped them on the blanket. If I'd just held my tongue, Jake wouldn't have left that night. Though he'd still be here if he had been more ... calm. Patient. Understanding. Or if he hadn't fucked someone else.

Let me know if there's anything I can do ...

Dominic's flowers were still on my desk, probably wilting and filling my cubicle with their sickly sweet perfume. I'd have to get rid of them soon, though I didn't want to. How dead would they have to be before Noelle began to tease me for holding onto them?

I closed my eyes, pictured Dominic's face, and slipped my hand into my panties.

There must be something I can do for you, Hannah. His voice in my head was deep and smooth and reassuring.

Maybe if you just stayed here, just for a night, I could get some sleep.

Shall I sleep on the couch?

No, why don't you stay with me in the bed. I'm sure we'll both be more comfortable ...

I ground my hips against my fingers. Nice, but not earth-shattering like what you read about in those Cosmo-type magazines. I focused on the mellow warmth of the alcohol coursing through my system. Not orgasmic, but sort of nice.

Panting and nauseous, I rolled over and glanced at the clock. Four thirty. I needed to sleep so I could head to the shelter later. One of the only places outside of work where I wasn't as alone, wasn't as afraid, wasn't as fucked up.

I STIFLED a yawn and knelt before a little boy who was bouncing on the balls of his feet. Ash blond hair glinted above huge brown eyes and cherub cheeks that I would have pinched if it wouldn't have made me look like a huge weirdo. He was the kind of kid you see and think, *aw, I could eat you alive!* but you try to keep that to yourself because it's super creepy to talk about eating children.

"What's your name?" I asked him.

He smiled broadly. "Timmy."

"Nice to meet you, Timmy." I held out my hand and he took it. "Would you like a hot dog? Your mother said it was okay."

"Yessssss!" he said, drawing out the word as only a five-year-old can.

"Follow me, sir."

He skipped behind me to the cafeteria tables, clambered onto a bench and grinned up at me as I retrieved a plate of food from the kitchen. "You're pretty," he said.

I froze, though I wasn't sure why. What the hell was wrong with me? I swallowed hard. "Here you go." I put his plate and fork in front of him and went back to the kitchen to take care of the women who were waiting patiently for their plates.

Hot dogs, baked potatoes, canned green beans. Hot dogs, baked potatoes, green beans. Dogs, potatoes, beans.

Timmy's mother, Antoinette, stood next to me, efficiently wielding a pair of tongs. The bruise on her cheek and the gouge across her lip had almost healed from the altercation that had brought her to the shelter last week. Her blond hair was up in a clean ponytail, and freckles were visible along her nose and at her neckline. A pair of perfectly matched bluebirds on either shoulder aimed inwards toward her collarbone. Antoinette twisted to grab another stack of plates and there was something in the set of her shoulders—high and straight—that suggested she hadn't been born into a life of abuse. What had changed for her?

A little voice piped up from behind the counter. "Momma, can I have another one?"

Antoinette stood on her tiptoes and peeked over the partition. "Did you eat the beans?"

"Um ..." Timmy scampered back to his plate.

"Kids," Antoinette said with a grin.

"He seems sweet." I set the last plate on the counter.

"He really is. He's an angel."

"Momma, all done!" He was back with his empty plate.

Antoinette put another hot dog on it. "Here you go, hon."

He frowned. "Ketchup, please?"

She smiled, squirted some on the hot dog, and he ran off, eyes on his food.

"So what do you have planned for next week?" I asked. Unless no one else needed the rooms, women could only stay one week. Right now, we were full.

Antoinette shrugged and took off her apron. "I think I can go back to my old apartment."

I nodded uncertainly. "I hope it works out. But if it doesn't—"

"I know where you are." She wiped her hands on her jeans and went to the front room to sit with Timmy.

Out the front window, the last of the dying sunlight had faded to dusky black, making everyone in the dining room stand out in stark contrast. I watched Antoinette ruffle Timmy's hair and kiss his cheek, and my stomach turned like I had eaten something bad. I turned away and headed for the dishes in the sink.

The back door clanged open. I lifted a frying pan like a club and held it at the ready until I heard the pecking beeps of someone entering the alarm code. Then Ms. LaPorte entered, hugging three paper grocery bags to her chest. I rushed to her side and grabbed them from her, still gripping the pan.

"Thank you, dear." She shrugged out of her down jacket, hung it on a hook and opened the fridge by the stove. "I got everything for tomorrow's breakfast. Even found some bacon on sale."

I set the bags down and handed Ms. LaPorte a gallon of milk. Her hands were warm and comforting, but my stomach was still tight. I took a deep breath.

"Everything going okay here?"

"Dinner's winding down. Nothing else to report. Pretty quiet, actually." *Quiet and gloriously boring.*

"Ah, we can all do with some quiet nights." Ms. LaPorte bustled back and forth between the fridge and the cupboards. I started on the pots and pans with a stainless steel scrubber. By the time I set the third pan on the sideboard to dry, my stomach felt almost normal.

"Hannah, why don't you go home for the night?"

And the nausea was back. My hand shook. I dropped a clean pan onto the sideboard and it clattered like it was going to break the counter. Ms. LaPorte shoved something else into the cupboard and either didn't notice or didn't mind the racket I was making.

"I'm okay for now." I fought to control the tremor in my voice. "I figured I would help clean the after-dinner dishes."

"You've been here all day, dear. Time for you to get home and get some rest. Everything will be fine. I won't take no for an answer."

Everything will be fine. Of course it would. It wasn't like I could live at the shelter. I set the last pan on the sideboard. "I'll be back early tomorrow evening. Right after work."

"No hurry, dear. You take your time."

I exchanged my apron for my coat. "Like I said, I'll be back early."

I cast one more glance at Antoinette, who was wiping Timmy's mouth. She saw me looking at her and waved. I waved back, zipped my coat and exited the building, letting the door swing shut behind me with a clang that echoed through the deserted lot. No ... not deserted—

I dropped my keys but I was frozen, unable to retrieve them.

A figure crouched next to my car with a long slim object.

A knife!

My lungs stopped working. *No a ... coat hanger.*

He's trying to get into my car!

He jerked upright and made a break through the trees at the back of the lot.

His gait. The way he walked. I had not seen his face, but I didn't have to. I knew.

He was going to get in and wait for me ... and then— My insides turned to water. I thought of Jake, of those women. I did not want to know what my father had planned for me. And if he was here ... maybe he had killed those other women too, just to scare me.

Or to practice.

I could never come back here. Ever.

I am not crazy.

Detective Petrosky's sad bulldog eyes flashed in my brain. *He thinks I'm a murderer.*

He's right. Knowing who killed Jake makes me an accessory.

It's all my fault.

I retrieved my keys and leapt to the car, my heart shuddering in my rib cage, my mouth dry as I gasped for nonexistent air. I was out of time.

What the hell am I going to do?

MONDAY, NOVEMBER 16TH

Scorched air huffed from a vent under the psychiatrist's desk. Petrosky had been there five minutes and dampness was already creeping around his armpits.

"The change in victim is concerning," McCallum said. "It doesn't fit the mold. Not only do you have a completely different victim, but you have a completely different type of restraint system. Then, there's the fact that there was no writing at the scene." He grabbed a pen out of his desk drawer and clutched it in his meaty fist.

"We purposefully withheld the poems from the public in the first two murders. It suggests copycat, but with the similar dissection styles it's hard to say. We're still pushing the same killer to the public either way, though. One is less scary than two."

McCallum nodded.

But Campbell was killed by his guy, Petrosky could feel it. So why would he vary his pattern? And why Campbell, some loser nobody, with no connection to the other victims?

"Let's hash this out. I need to think." Petrosky leaned forward in his chair. "If we're dealing with the same killer, he had a very specific reason for choosing Campbell. I just can't figure out why. Did Campbell piss him off? Did he see something he shouldn't have? I could get behind our guy just being in the mood to slit someone's throat, but he had all his dissection shit with him. It was premeditated."

Petrosky's gut was a hot mess of too many chili dogs and too little Jack Daniels; the nip he'd had before coming here wasn't nearly enough.

McCallum tapped the pen on the desk. "If we're looking at the same killer, there's clearly some connection between the third death and the first two. If Campbell knew something, he'd have to have been there to see something, or know someone who was. Did he go out much?"

"Nope. DUI a few years back, no license, no car. He does have one common acquaintance from the shelter, but she only knew one of the female victims, not both."

"This girl ... is she a suspect?"

"No. I mean, I don't think so."

McCallum's eyes bored into him. "You're worried about her."

Petrosky sighed. "Yes." It sounded dirty to say it out loud—dirty but honest.

McCallum set the pen down. "Do you have reason to believe she's involved?"

"Not really. I can't see a motive for the women, and we have the tapes of the lobby, so she has an alibi for Campbell's murder. Unless she went out the window."

"What's your concern?"

"I'm ... not sure." His stomach roiled.

"She's not Julie." McCallum's voice was low but he might as well have shouted it.

"I know she—"

"I understand, Ed. Julie's on your mind. Always will be. It's grief. It's trauma. It's complicated. But it's a mistake to assume that any suspect who looks like Julie must be innocent. You're generalizing, maybe even seeing resemblances that aren't there because you *want* them to be there. You want to save Julie and you can't do that, so you're trying to save someone else. But not all these women deserve your sympathy."

"She just lost her boyfriend. She deserves something." Petrosky wiped a hand over his forehead. It came away wet.

"Katherine Delacrois deserved your sympathy too, right? I'm sure you remember her."

Petrosky clenched his jaw. Katherine had been just as lovely, with the same huge eyes and dark hair. She had been soft-spoken and tearful when he questioned her, and he'd felt so guilty about making her upset that he defended her to the other officers. A week later she had quietly, and just as tearfully, admitted to brutally stabbing her boyfriend thirteen times in the chest.

"This isn't—"

"No, it's not. But it wouldn't hurt you to remember that *this* girl is not *your* girl either."

"I don't have all day to bullshit about old news." Petrosky clenched his fists under the desk, something sharp as a fish hook tugging at his heart. "I need to figure this out before he kills someone else."

McCallum sat back in his chair, eyes tight but not surprised. "If you insist. Back to your case."

He tried to ignore the twitch at the corner of McCallum's mouth, but his back tensed anyway. "I need to look at the victims more." Maybe there were similarities he had missed, not that he'd ever give Graves's the satisfaction of admitting that.

"Their attraction for your killer may not be as obvious as it seems."

"The attraction to the working girls seemed pretty obvious until Campbell."

McCallum put his hands flat on the desk. "Look deeper."

Petrosky stood and started for the door.

"Ed?"

He turned back.

"You know what you need to do. Find the links between the victims and you'll figure out how he's choosing. You can't focus on things you know aren't leads; you can't focus on this girl. As you said, you don't have the time. He's out there. And he's hunting."

All night I sat at the dining table, staring at the door with a kitchen knife in my hand, imagining I'd be ready the moment I heard him picking the lock. While I waited, I considered my options. One: leap into the car and run with the couple hundred bucks I had in my wallet. But I wouldn't get far. Two: take the bus with that same money and probably get farther. But since he obviously knew that I had stayed in a shelter the first time, he'd surely look at shelters this time and find me right off. So that was out, and I had no idea how I'd find an apartment without someone like Ms. LaPorte looking out for me. I had never even used my name to open a credit card. Three: there was no three. For the life of me, I could think of nothing else to do.

The next day started on autopilot. My hands trembled as I lathered my hair, but I still washed it. My stomach lurched at the thought of food, but I still made toast. And when the hallway creaked ominously outside my door, I threw on my shoes, peered into the hallway and raced for my car like I was running from a burning building.

At least at work my heart could relax to a dull roar in my ears, white noise instead of the heavy metal drummer that had blasted away in my skull all the way to the office. I'd never been so grateful for the guarded doors, the security locks, and Jerome, somewhere in the building looking out for shady characters.

But I couldn't stay here for the rest of my life, in this building, with the incessant clacking of fingers on keyboards to help me keep my composure. I peeked over the partitions at Noelle but the back of her head wasn't very comforting. Nor was the way Ralph was leering at her from across the room. I collapsed back in my chair and tried to lose myself in my work, punching in information as fast as I could until my shaking fingers refused to type any longer.

Let me know if there is anything I can do. His words rang in my head until there was nothing left but his voice, and the hope trying to seed itself within me.

I shoved my chair back. File folders crashed to the floor.

Maybe he can help.

No, certainly not.

Tell him a joke! He likes those!

Not like you have anything to lose.

I threw open the office door too hard, caught it, and closed it gently, glancing over my shoulder through the glass wall at Ralph and Toni and Noelle. No one looked up. I ran to the staircase and ascended, my shoes on the metal steps almost as fast as my heartbeat.

The top floor was another world—leather armchairs and cherry wood furniture, and abstract art. Doubt seeped into my chest like a river of burning oil. Desperation burned hotter.

What's the worst that can happen?

He'll think you're crazy.

So what?

He'll fire you.

Joke's on him—I quit!

The secretary had steel gray hair and black-rimmed glasses like an old-fashioned schoolmarm. Her bony fingers kept typing away on her keyboard even as she stared me down.

I smoothed my hair. "I need to speak to Mr. Harwick, please."

"Name and appointment time?"

"Hannah Montgomery. I don't actually have an—"

She smiled, but her gaze was one you'd give a naughty child. "Then I am afraid he cannot see you."

My body felt suddenly heavy, like I was wrapped in a wet blanket of hopelessness. *Of course he can't see me.* I was an idiot. "Can I make an appointment to see him today?"

The woman punched a few buttons on the keyboard and squinted at her screen, eyes flat and disinterested. "How about three weeks from tomorrow?"

I put my hands on the desk to steady myself. I couldn't breathe.

I'll be gone by then.

Or gutted like a fish.

"Please, I just … please—" My voice rang shrill, foreign, hysterical. Black spots floated around the edges of my vision. My lungs were on fire.

"Ma'am, you're going to have to—" The secretary's voice grew distant. My fingers, splayed on the cherry wood, slid toward me in slow motion as I gasped nonexistent air and fought the haze at the edges of my vision. Everything went black.

He held me, cradling me like a child as he walked me to my bedroom.

Shhh, it's ok, baby ...

I opened my eyes with a start. I was half lying, half sitting in a leather armchair, knees over the arm. Near my feet, a sculpture made of colored glass reached toward the ceiling with intertwined bands of red and yellow.

"You're awake." Mr. Harwick rose behind an enormous desk of glass and stone.

I tried to pull myself up, but my sweaty hands slipped on the leather.

"Just relax for a moment."

I stopped struggling and wilted in the chair.

"Are you hurt?"

I shifted in the seat. My legs were asleep, but I only felt pins and needles, not pain. My elbow stung with what was probably rug burn. My lungs were working again. Nothing felt too sore or wrong, though I did seem to have a mass of creepy crawly things teeming in my stomach.

Then everything came back to me.

I need help. My father killed my boyfriend and it's all my fault.

Shit! Don't say that!

He perched on the arm of the other chair, concern etched across his features.

I swung my feet to the floor.

Tell him.

I don't know what to say.

"I ... need help." It came out a whisper.

"What can I do for you?"

His cologne was biting, earthy, masculine. "Uh ..." In all the hoping I'd done I had not thought to plan out what to ask of him. I wanted to punch myself in the head.

You can't tell him.

You have to tell him. You can always deny it later if he tells anyone.

"I ... my um ... father ..." I looked down. "He wasn't very nice when I was growing up. I ran away." *Why are you still protecting him?*

I took a deep breath. "I ... I'm afraid he may be trying to find me. I am ... I don't know what to do, but I can't ... I think he's been following me."

"Did you call the police?"

My heart caught in my throat. *They'll arrest me for not telling them who killed Jake.*

"No. I mean, I think I might be in trouble too. I ... uh ... took some things from the house when I left." *Yeah, like your clothes. Look at you, super thief! First your clothes, then an old cafeteria table, and tomorrow a bank so you can actually manage to avoid homelessness wherever you end up.*

His forehead wrinkled. "I see."

"Maybe ... maybe I can take out a loan against my next paycheck? Or I can just borrow a little bit so I can get started in another state? I'll pay you back, every cent. I'll work two, three jobs if I have to. I just need enough to get away and set up somewhere else."

Here it is. Now he'll tell me to get out and I can go pack my apartment.

"I can help you."

You can ... what? I blinked at him.

"You don't have to leave, Hannah. If he found you here, he'll find you there. Then in another year you'll be back in the same position. Let's give it a week or so to assess the situation."

"But—"

"Did he come to your home?"

Not yet. "He will."

"I can help you get an apartment in another name."

"He's been following me. He knows my car." *Oh, God.* He probably knew where I ate dinner, where I shopped for groceries.

"I'll drive you, or I will have a car sent."

I did a double take, heart twitching. "What?"

"Or you can stay with me for a few days. I've got an alarm and a big dog."

You can't help me, no one can help me. You'll die just like Jake did. "Mr. Harwick, I—"

"Dominic."

"Dominic. We don't even ... I mean, we don't know each other all that well."

"I know you're scared, but I can help you. And if in a week you still want to run, I will give you some cash and a new license plate."

Something was obviously wrong with my ears. *He doesn't understand the gravity of the situation. If he did—*

"Are you sure you don't want to call the police? We can do it from here." He reached for the phone.

"No! I mean ... I don't know."

They'll lock me up too, just for knowing about Jake. They'll blame me. Would Dominic?

I had nothing to lose anymore. My eyes filled with tears. "I just feel so ... broken. Like I don't even know what to do to be normal anymore."

His eyes were far away. "My dad always used to say, 'Pretending to be normal is the best way to make people think you are.'"

I wrung my hands, every nerve in my body twitching. Pretending, I could do. It was what came after the pretending that worried me.

"You're strong. You'll get past this." He touched my arm softly. "Everything will be okay."

Everything will be okay. Was that true? *Everything* encompassed so very much and it felt like it was all flowing through me in that moment—the unrelenting stress of the past few months, the pain of my childhood, the guilt and the grief and the panic—until I feared I would burst or lose my mind completely. *Everything.* I needed everything to be okay, if only for a moment.

His eyes bored into mine. "Hannah, you're shaking. It's all right. I'll help you." He was so ... confident, his eyes calm, patient, understanding.

I threw myself into his arms and sobbed into his shirt as he stroked my hair.

"I ... thank you."

I'm safe here.

Then, there was more than gratitude. It began like a fire in the pit of my stomach and crept lower, heating the space between my thighs. *Something's wrong.* I pressed my legs together, but the smoldering ache swelled and spread.

I tilted my face upwards and he captured my mouth with his, silencing the remnants of fear. But then the fear reemerged, burning panic mingling with something feral, clawing at me to get out.

I can't do this.

I put a hand on his chest, prepared to pull away, but he wrapped an arm around my back and liquid warmth spread through me.

He'll hurt me too.

But his hand in my hair was soft, gentle, kind. He did care for me. Maybe he always had. I could hear my heartbeat in my ears, feel the throbbing of it between my legs, sweet and unrelenting.

He had come to the funeral. Not for Jake, not for just another employee, but for *me.* He'd sent me flowers. Came to see me in the office. He cared, and not because I was an employee, not even because I was pretty—I surely hadn't been ten minutes ago with snot streaming down my face. No, he cared about ... me.

I clutched his shoulders as if letting go might cause him to disappear and I would be left desperate and lonely again. I was so focused on his mouth, his scent, the hardness of him against my pelvis that I didn't feel him moving me toward the desk, but there I was, the glass top cold under me as he laid me down and guided my arms above my head. Then my mouth was free, my lips still swollen with the taste of him, as his tongue trailed along my jaw, down the side of my neck, over to the top button of my blouse. He unbuttoned my shirt slowly and brushed his lips against each patch of newly-exposed skin. I closed my eyes.

Everything will be okay.

He put his hands on my knees and moved upward under my skirt, each stroke leaving tender, tingling flesh in its wake. A low moan escaped me, primal and hungry, a sound I didn't even know I was capable of making. The past months—all my worries, all my mistakes—

vanished. There had been nothing before this moment. Here, with him, it was safe to be born again.

Everything will be okay.

Then he was inside me, filling me, and I raised my hips to meet him. His tongue flicked against my nipple, and I could feel every gentle suckle in my loins. I wrapped my legs around him as if I could erase everything else by pulling him deeper into me. He thrust, again and again, his fingers stroking me at the apex of my thighs.

Everything will be okay.

An unfamiliar sensation took over my body, and there was no more control, no time to be shocked, only pulsing, shuddering waves crashing over me as I clung to the desk and screamed Dominic's name. He covered my mouth with his, joining the two of us in blissful silence that spoke volumes. He cared about me. He wanted me. And I wanted him back, desperately, furiously, in that moment, and for as long as he would have me.

He will protect me.

Yeah, as long as he never knows how fucked up you really are.

Swallowing the thought, I wrapped my legs around his hips and fastened myself to him as if he were an anchor, one steady thing in a sea of hurt.

WEDNESDAY, NOVEMBER 18TH

Robert seethed. *This is not possible.*

He sat with Thomas at the deli down the road from their office. A ham and Swiss sandwich too big to fit in his mouth sat untouched on his plate. The completely oblivious bastard across from him was making short work of his own turkey and cheddar.

She betrayed me.

It was a simple thought, one that shouldn't have surprised him, and yet it did.

Women are whores. Liars. Vile.

But not this one. This one was supposed to save him. With every part of his being he rejected the idea that she had left him before granting him absolution.

"When did this happen?"

Thomas shrugged. "This week, I think? Apparently, Hannah just packed up and moved out of the blue. Noelle was totally shocked when she found out."

Robert cursed himself for biding his time instead of actively pursuing her. But a sudden move did not seem like typical behavior for the demure woman he thought he knew. The girl he needed would not have given herself so easily to anyone. And it was not possible that one could change so suddenly.

He sat up straighter. What if she had been tricked? Perhaps she was merely the unwitting victim of a cunning adversary. He could save her from him, give her a gift, and in return, she would cleanse him, grateful for his selflessness.

A pastoral voice sounded in his head.

Therefore, confess your sins to each other and pray for each other so that you may be healed.

Without her there was no one who could absolve him. He felt himself sliding into the grips of desperation, each breath more difficult than the last.

Thomas bit into his sandwich and chewed, the sound wet and thick and infuriating.

"Who the fuck is he?" Robert asked as soon as he could speak.

Thomas's eyes were boring a hole into him and Robert wanted to rip them out of Thomas's skull.

"That's the craziest part. The boss man."

Robert squinted. "The boss? Like, the head of Chrysler?"

Thomas laughed. "Nah, I don't think she aimed quite that old. The owner of the contract house we work for. Harwick."

Robert leaned back in his chair and gaped. He had worked there for years and had never even met Harwick. "I didn't know they knew each other."

"Yeah, I think they work in the office with him," Thomas said, nonchalantly, clearly missing the blinding rage and despair emanating from the man across from him.

Dominic Harwick. Robert clenched his teeth together, jaw aching with the pressure of it.

She is my only hope of salvation.
I cannot fail.

WEDNESDAY, NOVEMBER 18TH

He crouched underneath the table, not because he was scared, but because she had screamed at him to do it. The john didn't want him in the closet while they were in the bedroom. There was apparently no worse buzz-kill than the sneeze of a small child.

He waited while the moans from the bedroom accelerated and finally stopped. A shirtless man walked out to the table, kicked under it until his foot connected, and left the apartment.

He watched the door close behind the john and rubbed his throbbing shin.

Then her face appeared, nearly purple with rage. She reached under the table to grab him, as he had expected, and jerked him into the open. The splintered linoleum tiles slashed at his legs as she dragged him across the floor. She slapped him in the face and his cheek lit up with pain. Her foot connected with his stomach. He tried to breathe but the blows came too quickly.

Still, he remained impassive, yielding. It was better this way, faster too. Maybe he'd even pass out. When he came to, it would be over.

"You prolly just cost me fifty bucks, you little piece of shit."

Her words were slurred. She kicked him hard in the thigh. The air returned to his lungs. Much better. Much more—

He was weightless for half a second. Stars shot into his vision as he struck the cabinet with his head and crashed to the floor on his stomach. There was a loud snap as a bone in his ribs gave way. Pain flared in his chest. He gritted his teeth and lay still.

The front door slammed.

He struggled to his feet, panting through his nose as the ache in his side intensified. In the bathroom, he climbed gingerly onto the sink and peered into the mirror. Blue and green marks stained his skin. He touched his side, swallowed the pain, and watched his face. His eyes stayed as empty as the kitchen cupboards.

He brought the edges of his mouth up like the hero did in the comic magazine he had found. He frowned.

That wasn't it.

He tried again, willing the corners of his eyes to move as well.

The door slammed. A man's voice muttered something. Then a clink of glass—they'd stopped in the kitchen. He scrambled from the bathroom sink, gasping against the stabbing pain in his side, and ran to the bedroom, into the closet.

Maybe if she came for him again, that smiley face he'd been practicing would help him. It certainly seemed to help the man with the cape.

He shook his head at the long-ago memories. Superheroes never lasted, nor had that vulnerable boy who had once dreamed of becoming one.

She wouldn't last either.

The woman paced the alley on legs run through with purple veins. Her stomach was too thin to have seen anything but blow in the last week. He wondered if the boy housed in the apartment upstairs was as malnourished as she was. He could almost smell the child, dirty and sweating, hiding in a closet, cowering in a corner. But no matter. Soon the boy would be free of his bitch mother.

Her artificially yellowed hair shone under the single streetlight like a beacon as she tossed it over one shoulder. Business was good tonight; he could tell it by the bounce in her step. So much the better. Her good mood would make her that much more trusting.

Fucking idiots. Like oysters led to their slaughter.

He emerged from the shadows and let her see him. She grinned, revealing yellowed teeth with wide gaps.

"Hey, honey, you looking for something?"

He nodded, feeling the cool wetness in the hand he held behind his back. Chloroform always made the taking easier. Plus, it let them awaken for the best part.

He squinted, beckoning another face into focus, a reminder from the past.

There you are, bitch.

She walked toward him on precariously high heels.

He readied himself, pulling his lips into his best superhero smile. Though she was not the one he wanted, for today, she would do.

No one would miss her. No one at all.

THURSDAY, NOVEMBER 19TH

When I opened the door to my apartment, the first thing I saw was the box. Jake's box, brown and sad and lonely. *Forgotten.* That seemed the worst kind of slight. The air itself seemed itchy, like someone was picking at my skin.

"Hannah?" Dominic set a stack of pre-folded boxes against the dining table and straightened. His khakis matched the boxes. His sweater brought out the subtle flecks of green in his eyes. I wondered if he'd done that on purpose.

"Oh, sorry. I was just thinking, I should bring that box to Jake's mother."

"I'll have it sent." His eyes scanned the kitchen and the living room beyond. "You've had company."

I followed his gaze to the kitchen, where white powder dusted the cabinets. Two of the upper doors still hung open. By the fridge, a piece of blue tape clung to the countertop.

"They were already in here right after Jake died," I said uncertainly. They must have come back for ... something. What had they been looking for that they didn't find the first time?

I scratched at my arm, too hard, but stopped short of drawing blood. Maybe they knew my father was after me. Maybe they knew he'd killed Jake. Maybe they'd be back to arrest me any day. I stared at Jake's box and tried to avoid retching.

"I'm sure it's just routine. I heard the FBI is taking over the case, so I bet they're double-checking everything."

Of course. It wasn't all about me, was it? I was as narcissistic as the world's most irritatingly self-centered rappers. Maybe I'd even name my child after a direction in honor of the kid's importance, so whenever anyone said, "Go left" I could hear, "Go, Left!" and rejoice in the universe's unrelenting support of my child.

"I'll take this box to the car and let you get started up here."

"You're leaving?" *But you're supposed to protect me!*

"I'm walking to the car, Hannah. I'll be right back."

"But—"

He closed the distance between us and hugged me tightly to him. "Everything is fine. You haven't even been here in three days. No one is crouching in a closet waiting for you to show up."

Something in my chest writhed and tightened around my lungs.

"Have I steered you wrong yet?" He let me go and peered down at me. "Have I done anything inappropriate or even remotely dangerous?"

Inappropriate. I took a deep breath and could almost feel it crackle over my dry tongue, like winds across a desert. Was sleeping with me inappropriate? If so, I wished he'd been *more* inappropriate. The past three nights I had slept snuggled against his back and he hadn't even tried to touch me. *Why doesn't he want me anymore?* Maybe something was wrong with me. Maybe he realized that he had been a total dolt bringing some strange girl home with him. Or maybe the sex just hadn't been as good for him as it had been for me and he was loathe to repeat it.

And yet, sleeping next to him, I had felt safer than I had in years. Tammy would be thrilled at the change reflected in my sleep journal. I'd even occasionally wondered if all my fears had just been me being crazy about nothing. Maybe the man in the parking lot had just been someone trying to steal my car stereo, as Dominic had suggested. This possibility did seem more likely than my father showing up at the shelter. Too much coincidence. And if they thought the killings were related to dear old dad, wouldn't the police have called me to get some information on him? As Dominic said all the time, logic ruled. I wondered if Dominic would kick me out if I decided to stay in town after all. Maybe he'd kick me out just for being nuts.

"Hannah? Do you trust me?"

I swallowed. Nodded.

"Good." He hoisted the box to his shoulder. "I'll be right back to help you finish and we'll go out to lunch after. I know a great Italian place."

I watched him go, licked my parched lips, and tossed an empty box onto the kitchen floor. Plates and bowls. Silverware. Cups. Some got wrapped in paper towels. I picked up Jake's favorite mug, the one he had always chugged beer out of while I cleaned the kitchen. I left it on the counter. Noelle would have thrown it in the trash. *Noelle.* I should call her.

The door clanked and packing tape squeaked.

He came back!

Of course he came back.

"I'll set these next ones up and secure the bottoms," Dominic said, unfolding a box. "I'll tape that one when you're done."

"It's done." I pushed the box toward the door and Dominic taped it shut. "Thanks."

One box of choice items was enough for the living room, too. In the bedroom, I stared at the dresser drawers, sighed, and upended one after another into a cardboard box before turning my attention to the bedside tables.

The bed hulked in the middle of the room, a reminder of things I didn't want to think about—and much closer to the dresser than I remembered. It was like the room had gotten smaller, collapsing in on itself now that the world was missing Jake's energy. But I wasn't sure I missed him. I took his pillow from the bed, put it to my nose and inhaled the faintest trace of cigarettes. I threw it against the wall.

Footsteps approached, but there was no menacing squeal of rubber, like that which accompanied the shoes my father wore, only the soft clack of moneyed leather.

The tension drained from my neck. I flipped the cardboard box closed. "Last one."

He scooped it up in one arm. "I can send someone for the furniture."

"Don't bother."

"Are you sure?"

It won't fit in my car anyway. "Too many memories."

I followed him to the front door and down the stairs, calling quiet goodbyes to my life here; the hallway, the stairwell, the smell of socks and putrid onions.

"Did you want to invite some of your friends to lunch? You haven't seen anyone in the last few days."

My toe caught on a stair. I righted myself on the railing.

"Are you okay?" Dominic stopped and turned back, the barest of smirks on his beautiful mouth.

"I'm fine. And no, I don't want to call anyone. They won't even miss me yet."

He started back down, shoes lightly smacking the stairs. "I just want to make sure you're staying in because you want to and not because you're frightened. I'm sure Noelle misses you."

"Maybe." My face heated. "Lately, I haven't wanted to hang out with her."

"Why?"

Because I suspected her of screwing my dead boyfriend and now I feel guilty. "I—I'm not sure."

"I see."

He shifted the box to his shoulder and held the lobby door for me. The room was barely brighter than the stairwell, dust particles playing in a beam of sunlight that shone through the tiny window.

"I find being around people is helpful during trying times," he said. Tammy said things like that too, but the words felt different coming from Dominic. Almost... believable.

I glanced at the mailboxes, ominous and dark, and remembered the letter. *That girl.* Jake had probably been thrilled every time I left. *Maybe Dominic wants me to go out, too.* "Do you want me to make plans to get me out of the house?"

"Of course not. I just don't want you to feel like you have to stay home all the time." He smiled and I forgot the mailboxes.

"Okay. But just so you know, I don't usually make big plans. The only thing I did on a regular basis was volunteer, and I can't go back there."

"The place where he tried to get into your car?"

"Yes."

"You think he'd be brazen enough to do it again?"

"I ... maybe."

"I can hire someone."

"Hire someone?"

"To check the lot. Or to drive you. Either way, you can't let fear hold you back. And it's not too late to call the police."

I shook my head. "No. Thanks, but no."

He opened the door to the parking lot. "Hannah, I just want you to live your life normally. You need to do the things that make you happy, not spend your life afraid. I'll help you."

A beam of sunlight fell on my arm. "Why are you doing this for me?"

"I made you a promise. I'm keeping it." He shoved the front door and it opened, screeching in protest.

Air blew against my face, cold, crisp but somehow sweeter than it had ever been.

I made you a promise.

I followed him out into the sunshine.

FRIDAY, NOVEMBER 20TH

PETROSKY DUMPED coffee grounds into the filter, his gut heavy with old hurt and yesterday's donuts. Julie's night-light glowed over the sink.

Fix this. Save someone else's girl. It's the least you can fucking do.

He ran over the cases in his head. The women had been young, urban prostitutes who used their hard-won funds to feed drug addictions. Jacob Campbell had been a white boy living in the suburbs with a pretty girlfriend and an absentee kid who was taken care of elsewhere. It didn't fit. But that wasn't the problem.

The killer was methodical, intelligent. Maybe angry.

He has a plan. So why wouldn't he leave a message at Campbell's scene?

Petrosky punched the countertop, relishing the ache in his knuckles.

The clamps. The nails. The dissections. There was a reason for everything. Had to be.

The scene had been scoured by crime scene techs and FBI agents alike, and each board and piece of trash had been examined. They had printed and moved and touched and tagged. Yet they'd found nothing.

Did he run out before he could finish the note?

Petrosky shook his head at the thought. They would have found another body if someone had interrupted him.

Look deeper.

Fuck. He yanked the night-light off the wall and hurled it in the sink next to six empty beer bottles. The coffee pot percolated like a lazy asshole. Petrosky walked back to the bedroom and jerked on a pair of jeans and a sweatshirt.

Halfway to the car, he stopped in the driveway and stared at the ground, then returned to the kitchen and retrieved the night-light. He wiped it on his shirt and plugged it back in.

Sorry, honey.

He shot the half full coffee pot one final glare and kicked the front door shut behind him.

"What are we looking for, exactly?" Morrison stared at the cinderblock mass in the center of the underground room where they had found Campbell's body. Small chunks of cement had been chipped away, probably by their forensics team.

Petrosky knelt at the back corner of the room and ran his fingers along the line where wall met floor. "Not sure. Anything different." He hated the strain in his own voice.

"Different like what, Boss?"

"Different like ..." Petrosky stood and wiped his fingers on his jeans. "Shit, I don't even know anymore."

Morrison prodded the side of a cement block with his thumb. "It's crazy that there was a body on here. It doesn't have blood on it or anything."

Anything different ...

"There was a tarp here, right?" Petrosky pictured the blood-stained table in the westside basement and the cemetery concrete that would forever smell like copper. This guy had never used plastic before. There had to be a reason now.

He knelt and laid his head against the floor, exploring the bottom of the structure with his fingers, then heaved himself upright and sat back on his heels. "There's no way. A cement mass this size has to weigh, what? A thousand pounds?"

"I doubt it," Morrison's voice echoed against the concrete. "I worked construction in college. Cinderblocks are usually hollow."

Petrosky stared at the table. "Hollow, but still pretty heavy."

Morrison bent down beside him. "Yeah. He'd have to be strong to shove it even a short distance. Or he has a partner."

"No, no partner for our guy." Petrosky stood, rubbing his forehead with his fingers. *How did he do it?*

Wait. The treads. *Of course.* "He had a dolly. And he didn't shove it. He needed a way to lay it down without marring the words." If there were words. There had to be words.

"There's no way he lifted this whole thing with a dolly alone."

Petrosky squinted at the rows of cinderblock that made up the top. "Could you hold those top pieces up with something besides other blocks?"

"Metal supports, secured internally and run from one side to the other could do it." Morrison stared at the concrete. "Do you think the killer put it together himself?"

"In this whole place, there isn't a single other intact structure. I can't believe we missed that."

Morrison frowned. "But if he painted words in Campbell's blood under there, he couldn't have done it before he killed Campbell. And he couldn't have built the structure underneath the body afterwards—the blood splatter on the tarp and the surrounding ground was consistent with Campbell being killed where we found him."

Petrosky walked around the cement table, probing the mortar between blocks. "All this was dry when we were here, right?"

"It was. I talked to the techs and they pulled samples from the blocks, side and top. Someone would have noticed wet cement in the crevices."

Petrosky's chest was tight. He kicked at the base of the block in front of him. Solid. He took a step to the right and kicked again. No give.

Morrison lowered his eyes and followed suit. *Kick, pause. Kick, step. Kick.* "Boss?" Morrison disappeared below the side of the structure.

Petrosky stepped around the blocks. Morrison was pressing on one of the lower bricks with the beefy part of his palm. "There's a little give. Not much, but the bottom should be the most solid and there's definitely some wiggle here."

Petrosky knelt on Morrison's right, pulled his Swiss Army knife from his back pocket and scraped at the mortar, where a hairline crack was already widening. A chunk of mortar fell, revealing dead space between the bricks. Were they all like that? Mortared thinly on one side to save dry time? No. That tricky fucker had left himself a way to get in, then patched the outside to make it look solid. You don't do that for no reason.

Petrosky shimmied the knife into the mortar over the brick to the left, but the mortar there was thicker. Morrison pushed at the first brick. A crack appeared down the left side. Petrosky followed suit on his side until the block was free of the rest of the structure, but there was still no room to get his fingers around it.

"How would he get in there to write?" Morrison said. "The space is too small to even see what you're doing."

Petrosky shoved his knife into the space between the bricks and pried, heart hammering in his ears. It shifted, but nowhere near enough to free it. *Shit.* They were so fucking close. If only he had a sledgehammer.

Morrison stood and positioned one bull shoulder against the table and gripped the top with the other hand.

"What are you—" Petrosky began, but Morrison's face was already reddening, his fingers white against the structure as he heaved his weight against the top row of bricks. Petrosky followed suit, shoving the side with his shoulder until the mass lifted, just enough for Petrosky to get his fingers around the brick and slide it out with a grating sound like an angry rattlesnake.

Morrison grunted and lowered the table.

"Looks like all those gym visits were good for something, Surfer Boy. We didn't even need the dolly."

Morrison sat beside Petrosky and pulled his phone from his pocket, wiping his brow on his sleeve.

"Who you calling now?"

"Flashlight, Boss." He tapped a few buttons and handed Petrosky the phone, which now glowed from the top with a single beam of LED light.

Petrosky set it next to the opening to illuminate the inside and lay on the floor, his belly fat crushing his organs. The concrete dug into his cheek and cooled his fiery forehead. He scooted closer and pressed his face into the opening, the sound of his labored breath raspy in the tiny, hollow space. Above him, the metal rods Morrison described held up the tabletop bricks. Their guy had built himself a structure after all. And he'd left his card behind: a single sheet of paper, reflecting the brilliant white light.

Petrosky jerked a glove from his back pocket, lifted himself onto his elbow and pulled the paper out, disgusted by how much his hand was shaking. The poem was printed in the same block script as the others, the words the deep carmine color of dried blood.

> Long has paled the sunny sky:
> Echoes fade and memories die:
> Autumn frosts have slain July.

Sweat dampened his neck. He handed the note to Morrison and pushed himself to his feet. "Call Graves and get some techs over here. There's a reason this one was special. We need to figure out why."

SATURDAY, NOVEMBER 21ST

I love you Daddy, please ...
You'll like it. It won't hurt if you just lie still.
I struggled against him, but he held my wrists tight, his face contorted in a grimace. He pushed closer. I cried out, yanking at my hands, throwing my knees up, gnashing my teeth when he lowered his head.
No, not again, no, no, no ...
"Hannah, stop."
The voice was not his. *Daddy? No ...*
My eyes flew open. Someone was on top of me, pinning my wrists to the mattress. My breath came in ragged gasps.
"Stop." His face swam into focus, nose inches from mine. Dominic.
He'll help me get away. I was still trying to hit him. I stilled.
Dominic released my arms and climbed off the bed. His skin glistened under the waning moon that shone through the skylights as he headed for the bathroom.
Daddy.
Dominic.
I touched my face. It was wet, but my heart was slowing.
Stop. It didn't work when Tammy said it, or when I tried to tell myself to knock it off. But somehow, it was different coming from Dominic.
He returned, stretching an arm out to me. "Come on."
"What?" I took his offered hand and let him lead me across the room, around the stairs and into the weight room. A chill brushed my damp shoulders and I shivered. "What time is it?"
"Doesn't matter. Put your shoes on."
"I think they're downstairs."
"I put them here, where they go." He gestured under the bench.

What the hell? I tied them quickly.

"Treadmill."

I gaped at him.

"Trust me."

I got on, sleepy muscles protesting.

He stood at the head of the machine and pushed the button. It hummed to life. "Start slow and tell me when you feel warmed up."

I walked, faster, faster, shrugging and rolling the tension from my shoulders as the stiffness in my leg muscles eased.

"Ready?"

I swallowed hard. "Yes."

He punched the button. I ran, breasts flopping all over the place under my tank top. Thank goodness I didn't have torpedo tits or I'd give myself a black eye. Maybe he liked torpedo tits. Maybe that's why he didn't want to touch me. But I couldn't think about it because the track was flying beneath me.

Sweat poured down my back. I gasped for breath.

"Dom … I … maybe—"

"You can do it. Keep going."

I can't.

He stared hard at me. I stared back and ran until there was nothing else, nothing but the treadmill and his eyes.

The machine beeped twice and skidded to a halt. My heart thudded in my temples.

"Weights."

"I've … never done … weights before," I panted.

"Good time to learn."

"In the … middle … of the night?"

He shrugged and held out a barbell. "You're stronger than you think."

Am I? He kept saying it, so maybe it was true. I took the weight and let him lead me through a set of curls. And another. My muscles shrieked and burned.

"Last ten."

I pushed harder.

"Now squats."

"Dominic, I can't."

"Stop saying that and do it."

I did. One. Another. Ten. Twenty. My jelly legs threatened to buckle.

"Stop," he said, and my muscles seemed to skid to a halt in response to his voice.

"How do you feel?"

"Like a bowl of pudding. And now I want pudding." I rested my face on the glass and saw his eye twitch in the mirror. Saw the smear on the glass from my sweaty face. I peeled my forehead from the mirror and stood. "Sorry, I'll get that later."

He nodded and held out his hand.

What now? Much more and I'd pass out.

"Shower. Then bed. I doubt you'll have more dreams."

My dream. I had forgotten all about it.

Under the shower's hot spray, my muscles melted. He stood behind me and soaped my hair. I leaned back against him.

"Turn around." His hand slid over my breasts, down my rib cage, between my legs. Another hand teased my nipple, flicking until it was hard. A fire rose in me, an intense liquid heat that spread through my belly and settled between my legs, pulsing and wanting. So this was passion. Real passion, something I had never experienced, something I had been so worried was just a onetime fluke in Dominic's office. Somewhere inside me, a dam was breaking. His fingers slid into me.

I moaned and turned to him. He lifted me by my thighs and pressed me against the shower wall. The spray from the dual showerheads caressed my hair and sent rivulets of water down my body, awakening the nerves beneath my skin. And then he was inside me, hard but so gentle, so warm, massaging me from the inside. He captured my mouth with his.

I felt. I felt him. I felt everything, every wave crashing over me, every beat of our hearts throbbing in time to my lower body. My insides convulsed, shuddered, released. I screamed his name, over and over again, unable to close my mouth, unable to think.

I didn't feel the shower turn off. I only vaguely felt his hands wrapping a towel around my back, carrying me to the bedroom, laying me on the bed. The cotton felt like silk against my back as he climbed in next to me and stroked the tender nub between my legs. Even in the dark, the colors of the world seemed brighter, each muted shade of gray more vibrant than I remembered. Through the skylight, stars glimmered, dazzling but nearly unrecognizable as if every star I had seen before tonight was a different, duller breed. My eyes prickled in spite of myself.

Dominic stopped touching me and shifted his weight to the side, moving his hand near my shoulder. "Are you crying?"

I wiped my eyes. "I worried that it was just luck or something. At the office."

"Luck?"

"No one has ever made me ... well, you know."

He touched my cheek, trailed his fingers down over my neck to my chest and circled my nipple with his thumb. "They've been doing it wrong." He climbed between my legs and slid into me. My hips rose automatically, seeking him.

He put his mouth to my ear and rotated his hips, slowly, sensuously. "Had I known you had this concern, I would have proven it to you before now. I assumed you wanted to get acclimated to your surroundings." His breath was feathery against my earlobe.

He had been waiting for me to be ready. He cared. My feelings mattered. "And today? Now?"

He rose above me and smiled. "I thought it might help."

"Oh, it did." I really did feel okay with him. I wasn't sure exactly what that meant, but it had to mean something.

"I'm glad the shower helped you feel better," he said. "It didn't do anything bad for me, either."

"Well thank goodness for that."

He thrust slowly, deeply, every inch of him exquisite, then faster, more urgently. I flung my legs wide and let him take me, clinging to him, pleasure surging through me until I was sure I would burst. When I could take no more, we fell asleep side by side, my leg hooked over his hip.

When Dominic awoke, he was alone in the bed. He sat, listening. Not a sound save for the gentle tapping of rain or sleet against the skylight, a wake-up call far preferable to the muffled crying and swift kick to the groin that had woken him last night. The skirt and blouse he had laid over the chair last night were gone. He climbed from the bed and padded into the weight room. Her face print had been wiped clean.

Curious.

A clatter arose downstairs. He followed the noise to the kitchen.

She was standing at the stove with her back to him wearing a pair of flannel pajamas and fluffy yellow socks. The dishwasher stood open, but empty.

Hannah turned as he approached, her cheeks flushed with the heat from the pan, a spiral notebook clutched against her chest. She slid the book onto the counter behind her back, eyes locked on his. "I was making a spinach and mushroom omelet for you. Looks like you're up too early for breakfast in bed."

"Looks like I'm awake too early to pick up the clothing from last night as well."

Alarm flashed across her features. "Sorry I—I like things clean." She looked down as if that were something to be ashamed of—as if the world wouldn't be a better place if everyone picked up their shit.

More curious.

"I do too," he said simply.

She grabbed a spatula, cut the omelet in the pan and slid two almost symmetrical halves onto a pair of plates, then put the pan in the sink.

In the dining room the table was already set with orange juice, coffee and sliced melon.

Yes, he could get used to this. Perhaps he'd let her stay forever.

MONDAY, NOVEMBER 23RD

It's quiet here.

An hour from Petrosky's usual domain, far from the brick and mortar of the city, the howling wind lashed against fields of dead grass and grain. While nearby areas were covered with higher-end condos and lakefront housing developments, this town just outside Lapeer had peaked and declined well before his killer had made the trek out here.

The run-down barn was tucked in the back corner of an abandoned wheat field, at the end of a gravel drive. To his right he could make out a trailer park in the distance, though it was too far for anyone to have heard much.

I'll question them anyway.

In the middle of a pasture on his other side, an enormous metal chicken loomed, the only thing around that appeared to be in good repair, despite deposits of graying snow on its beak. *Fucking country folk.* Maybe his killer had a sense of humor.

The barn itself was missing boards, like many of the other barns in the area. Through holes in the ceiling, frosty sunlight speckled the straw-covered floor. The air was redolent with damp hay and the iron scent of freshly spilled blood.

The girl was laid out on a wooden table at the back of the barn. Like the other girls, her wrists and ankles were secured by leather restraints which had been fastened to the table legs. Her stomach had been sliced neatly in half, like two sections of a broken heart. The pieces lay on top of her chest, the remnants of her last meal teeming with ants. Jumbled corkscrews of intestine dangled from her belly down onto the sawdust and what might have been the top of an ant's nest below the table—they'd probably been hibernating when they were disturbed by the dripping of warm bodily fluids. The techs bustled around the perimeter of the room, either done with the table or simply avoiding the mess.

"The location is different," Petrosky said finally. "This rural thing isn't his style."

Morrison's face was green. *Rookies.* You never knew when they were going to lose their cool, or their lunch. Here it was probably the bugs, the way Morrison was staring at them.

"Well ... yeah, Boss, the location is different, but the building is just as dilapidated. And the place itself probably has the same number of people within a two mile radius as those old housing projects. The modus operandi is consistent with the first two as well."

"Modus what?"

"It's Latin. It means—"

"I don't give a fuck what it means, Surfer Boy. And breathe through your mouth before you throw up."

A winter bird, blue and orange, squalled and fluttered out through a gap in the ceiling above. Petrosky watched the bird disappear into the frigid sky.

"Maybe our killer ran out of places in the city," Morrison said.

Or he's escalating, broadening his territory. "They know who the girl is?"

Morrison looked at his notes. "Working girl, same deal. Bianca Everette. Her driver's license was under the table. Not bothering to hide their identities, is he?"

It was a dare, a tease. "This guy's fucking with us," Petrosky said.

"We've got something over here." A tiny wisp of a woman with a tattoo behind her ear and short-cropped platinum blond hair waved a flashlight from the front corner of the barn.

Petrosky headed her way, leaving Morrison by the body.

"What've you got?"

She pointed near the corner where a splintered piece of plywood leaned against the wall. "Behind it. I was dusting above the board and touched it to secure my tape, and—"

Petrosky squinted in the dim light. "Show me."

She pinched a corner of the board and lifted it away from the wall. He peered into the space, past threads of cobweb strung with sawdust. There were marks there, uniform, deliberate.

"Need a bigger light over here!"

The crime tech slid the plywood out of the way.

Morrison shone a thick flashlight beam onto the words, dark brown now, hard to read against the grime. With a blood tracking LED, they'd light up like Christmas.

> Children yet, the tale to hear,
> Eager eye and willing ear,
> Lovingly shall nestle near.

A tech behind him snapped a picture.

"What do you have?" Graves ducked into the barn, boards squeaking under his shoes.

"Poem, in blood, like the others. He's trying to tell us something, but I just can't—"

"ID?"

"Bianca Everette."

"Where's she from?"

"Close to here according to her license."

Graves whipped out his phone, tapped the screen and put it to his ear. "Hernandez? I need you to do a background on a Bianca Everette. Look at newspaper ads in the Lapeer area and anywhere nearby. And I need someone to pull all escort services in a fifty mile radius. Have something for me when I get back." He slid his phone back into his pocket.

Petrosky's muscles vibrated with tension. "What the hell was that about?"

"They're already in front of a computer, Petrosky. Tricky guys. Can crack into anything to get what we need in ten minutes."

"So can my guy, Graves." He gestured to Morrison. Morrison straightened, jaw set.

"It's under control, Petrosky."

Rage burned in Petrosky's chest. "This is bullshit."

Graves glowered at him. "If you're so anxious to make yourself useful, go to her house. Find her next of kin. Go talk to her mother. Get us something we can use this time."

Petrosky sucked down three cigarettes in the six miles to the Everette house. He tossed the last butt into a swath of pine trees in the front yard. The house was tiny, maybe eight hundred square feet, with two windows—the one on the left probably for the living room, and the one on the right belonging to a single bedroom, as evidenced by a pillow and a stuffed bear smashed against the inner screen. From the front porch, Petrosky could have reached out and touched either one.

Morrison stood behind him, as irritatingly calm as he'd been on the drive over. Apparently, year-round sunshine made you care less about FBI shitheads. Petrosky breathed through his nose like a bull and fantasized about goring Graves, or at least breaking his jaw. It almost made him forget that he was there to give a mother news that would fuck up her life irreparably. Fast and direct. That was the best way to do it. Coddling wouldn't make a kid any less dead. Still, he felt like a truck was sitting on his chest. *Dammit.*

He knocked.

The front door opened to reveal a woman with papery thin eyelids and a strawberry bun streaked with white. A boy of about four sat on her hip, his thumb in his mouth, his shirt dirty with the remains of breakfast. The wind huffed freezing air at them through the open doorway and the kid buried his face in her neck.

"Donna Everette?" Petrosky said.

"Yes?" Her voice was low, soft, cautious.

He flashed his badge. "Detective Petrosky. We need to speak with you, ma'am."

She blinked rapidly. "Is it Bianca?"

"It is, ma'am."

She put the boy on the floor. "Go play in the room."

He clung to her leg.

"Gavin, now!"

Gavin let go and scurried away.

They squeezed into the living room with the one window. She sat on a futon behind a large electrical wire spool topped with a plastic bowl of milky Cheerios. No other chairs. Petrosky stood across from her, Morrison in front of the door.

"What happened?" she asked finally.

"We found your daughter this morning in an abandoned barn off of Chickesaw."

"By the hen?"

"Yes."

"Is she—"

Fast and direct. "She's dead, ma'am. The local coroner will have you make a positive identification, but her wallet was found with her. I'm sorry."

Everette's face didn't change. "Will I have to go to the courthouse to identify her, or do ya have a picture? I don't have time to be driving all the way to town right now."

No surprise. No sadness. Petrosky clenched his jaw to keep it from dropping.

Morrison pulled out his phone and turned the screen to Petrosky. He'd gotten a shot of just the face—pale and dead, but none of the grisly mess. Petrosky nodded and Morrison handed the phone to Everette.

Her face was impassive. "That's her." She handed the phone back.

"Gramma?" Gavin stood in the doorway, eyes wide. "When's Mama coming home?"

"Get in the room, now! Ain't you got no sense?"

Morrison startled and dropped his phone on the carpet. He bent and wiped it on his shirt before sticking it back in his pocket.

Petrosky watched the boy walk backward into the bedroom and close the door. "I take it you two weren't close?"

"How could anyone be close to that?" Her eyes narrowed. "You shoulda seen the things she did."

Disgusted by her own daughter. His killer would be smart enough to at least act upset, but Petrosky wanted to haul her ass down to the precinct anyway. "But she did live here?"

"Sometimes, when she couldn't find somewhere else. I didn't see her much."

Morrison's pen scratched on his notepad.

"Anything unusual in the last few weeks?" Petrosky asked.

Everette cocked her head as if she had no idea what that sentence meant.

"Any bruises? Mentions of anyone violent? A boyfriend?"

"Oh, she had boyfriends all right, but never for more than an evening. Some of 'em beat her, some didn't, but I don't think she cared as long as she got her money. Not that she ever brought it back here."

"Where did she go when she wasn't here?"

"Hell if I know. She just left."

"What about friends?"

"None that I know of."

Something hit the bedroom door and thunked against the wall.

"Is Gavin her child?"

Everette snorted. "*Her* child. She pushed him out all right, but ain't never bothered with him since."

"She didn't support him, then."

"Nope, she sure didn't. She didn't even know who his father was. Didn't do much of anything except sell her crotch to the highest bidder. I used to hope she'd get smarter, better, but she was just always bad."

"Maybe she was just always desperate."

She glared at him, lips tight.

Petrosky gave her a card. "If you think of anything, ma'am, please give me a call. We need to do everything we can to find the person who did this to her."

Everette crumpled the card in her palm. Petrosky nodded to Morrison and they let themselves out.

"What was that all about?" Morrison asked as their shoes beat against the frozen earth. "You think she hates her own kid?"

"Don't know, but McCallum suspects that whoever is doing this had a disaster of a childhood. Mommy issues." Not that they could really check. Most abuse went unreported, and even foster homes were a crapshoot when it came to safety.

"Do you think Graves knows—"

"Don't worry about that asshole," Petrosky snapped.

"Boss?"

"Fuck him, Morrison."

"Yeah, Boss. Okay. But this is important."

Petrosky yanked the car door open. "What?"

"The poem. It's out of order." Morrison pulled out his phone, tapped it a few times and handed it to Petrosky. "We're missing one verse."

> Still she haunts me phantom wise,
> Alice moving under skies
> Never seen by waking eyes.

Petrosky passed the phone back and slid behind the wheel. "We're not missing a poem. We're missing a body."

MONDAY, NOVEMBER 23RD

THE ITCH WAS BACK. Robert had felt it as a child when he rolled around in the grass under the hanging tree, picturing the bodies dangling precariously above him as verdant blades irritated his skin. But he had not been back there since high school. And this itch was not one he could scratch.

He would have been what she needed. Whatever she needed. And now he couldn't get to her.

Thomas sat on an adjacent bar stool, staring at him like an idiot with dopey eyes in a dopier head. Robert wanted to punch him. Probably would punch him before the night was over.

"What's going on, man? Sounds like the boss has been getting on your case. You need help?" Thomas sucked back his beer, too righteous to wait for an answer before he tended to his own needs. He'd be doing the same thing if Robert hadn't been there at all.

But Thomas's question made him uneasy. Robert needed to slow down, get his head straight. Two in the last week, poor substitutes, but he'd had no choice. It was the only way to release the pressure.

He spent every waking moment obsessing over Hannah. He lost himself in her eyes even as his boss berated him for mistakes on his projects, mistakes he never should have made. He couldn't even recall designing the projects in question, let alone fucking them up.

"I just need to concentrate. Been having some trouble sleeping. Too much coffee."

Lies. He was turning into an animal—growing claws and teeth, almost rabid with desire. He shook with the constant, desperate need to find the next, to take her, to slake his lust, lest he implode before he could beg Hannah to love him, to forgive him.

He had waited too long. Someone else had taken his Hannah.

Thomas raised a finger to order another round. "Maybe the beers will help, eh?"

Robert plastered a smile on his face, the face he needed to have to survive, to fit in. To keep them from knowing. "Perhaps."

"I'm meeting up with Noelle in a little while. You want to join us?"

"On a date?"

"Kinda. We're just going bowling. But you seem a little down, like you could use some company."

So, Thomas wanted to share his woman. Use her, throw her to the lions, watch her squirm. "I'm sure she'd love that."

Thomas grinned.

Imbecile.

"Maybe if you show her how charming you are she can hook you up with Hannah. You keep going out with all these other women, but you never see them again. What's not to love about blond hair and tight pants? What'd they do to piss you off?"

The itch. His back crawled with the prickling of a thousand needles. "How do you know that?"

Thomas sipped, swallowed. "Know what?"

"What they look like?"

"I know you. You've got that photo on your desk of some woman."

"Are you crazy? That's my mother."

"Yeah, your mother. They say we all look for someone like our moms."

"Who's 'they'?"

"I dunno. Scientists."

Behind the bar, the television flickered, taunting Robert with laughing newscasters. He looked away, heart hammering, half expecting Thomas to turn on him after some prim news anchor flashed his photo with a list of his sins laid bare for the world to see. And if Thomas saw his picture and was warned, Hannah would also see his face staring at her, telling her to stay far, far away from him.

He needed her more than ever. He could not lose her.

The thorny sensation on his back subsided. Perhaps if he found his way to someone close to her, someone she loved more than her abominable ex-boyfriend, he had a chance. He would be careful. Very careful. His efforts had not been tenacious enough, methodical enough. She had not been hurt enough to fall into his arms. She'd need to hurt in order to see. It was the only way she would find her way to him.

"Bowling sounds fun," he said.

She'd hurt. He could make it hurt.

And then she would be his.

TUESDAY, NOVEMBER 24TH

ICICLES SEEPED from the metal table through the thin gown I wore. I shivered, wrapping my arms around my exposed abdomen. The child would be cold too, if I didn't leave.

A woman walked in rolling an expensive-looking ultrasound machine, her eyes bright with animosity. An elaborate array of blue, green and yellow cables sprang from the front of the machine, and next to it sat a television monitor and a white cord attached to a small paddle.

The woman grabbed a tube of bluish jelly and squeezed a frigid glob onto my abdomen. "Watch the screen." She shoved the wand against my belly. I bit my lip and tried not to shrink from her piercing stare.

"There's the heartbeat," she said, not even trying to hide the disdain in her voice. "Still beating right now."

Please ... please stop.

"Here's her head ... her feet."

The world was closing in. "Her?"

The woman kept her eyes on the screen. "Sure you want to go through with this? You can still change your mind. There are other options."

Want to? I *had* to. And I had to do it now before it was too late.

Through a veil of tears, I nodded. "I'm sure." I was prone, captive, and totally vulnerable. And I was nothing to her.

The woman thrust the wand back into its holder on the machine and started for the door. "The doctor will be in shortly. God bless that poor child." She made the sign of the cross and softly closed the door behind her.

I didn't notice the doctor entering, but suddenly, there she was, only a jet black ponytail visible between my knees. I stared at the ceiling, removing myself from the pain as I had so many times in the past. When

I couldn't pretend any longer, I let the tears fall, soaking my hair with salt.

One final surge of suction, and I heard a familiar voice: "All done."

I watched in horror as the doctor stood, but it wasn't the doctor anymore. It was *him*, holding the tiny child, my child, by the leg, its face grotesque and bloodied, its scrawny arms and legs flailing against my father's wrist. He wrenched the child's head, snapping her neck bones in one fluid motion. He laughed, and it echoed through the room, inside my head, even when his mouth stopped moving.

I scrambled backwards on the table.

"You thought you'd get away from me that easily, did you? You will always be a part of me." My father lunged toward me, extending the mangled infant slick with my blood. "We're a family now, Hannah. Take her, love her the way I loved you." The child's skin brushed my face. Cold, so cold.

I screamed and bolted upright, shivering from fear and the cold sweat that soaked my T-shirt. My hand settled on my flat abdomen. *A dream. Just a dream.* Just another shitty night to write about in my notebook.

I felt his gaze on me before I saw him, seated in a leather chair in the corner, obscured by shadow. The nightmares were surely too frequent for him to ignore. How often had I woken him up in the last week?

I crossed the room and settled awkwardly on the arm of the chair. "Sorry."

He shrugged, his face impassive.

"Did I wake you?"

"Yes," he said, like he had just agreed to a bologna sandwich. Did he not care about being awake or did he not care about ... me?

I'm going to lose him. Spoors of panic took root in my chest and multiplied, crushing my lungs and ribs. It had been acceptable for Jake to think I was a little nuts—he had been a jerk either way. But, Dominic was genuinely kind. And he actually cared. I didn't want to push him away by keeping things from him.

So tell him.

Is damaged better than crazy?

I stared at the floor, the words rushing out before I could stop them. "About five years ago, I ran away from home. My father ... he ... I was pregnant with his child. I aborted. I had no idea what else to do."

"And you wish you had done it differently?" His voice was neutral, serene even. He was probably relieved that he had a good reason to kick me out.

"No." My voice cracked.

"Deciding not to carry an infant you know you can't feed seems perfectly rational. What were the other options? Force the child and yourself into a life of poverty? And for what? If anything, you did everyone a favor, including that incest-derived embryo whose mere presence would have served as a constant reminder to you of all that is wrong with the world." He stood and took my face in his hands. "Would you like something to drink?"

I stared at him. "Uh ... sure."

"I'll be right back."

I barely noticed him leave the room. Had he really just said that the things I'd spent a lifetime hiding were ... acceptable? I must have misunderstood.

"Here you go." He was back already, handing me a glass. "Orange juice. I thought you could use the vitamin C. With all that worrying, you're going to end up sick."

Was I dreaming now? *He doesn't hate me?* I sipped, despite my lurching stomach. Sweet, with a slight bitter tang of peel—probably fresh squeezed. The good stuff.

He looked at me, almost expectantly, but I wasn't sure what he wanted me to say.

I lowered the cup. "I'm sorry."

"For what? Everyone has a past. Children have only so much control."

My stomach churned, hot with shame. "I mean ... it's a lot to take in. I've never told anyone. And I wasn't a child when I had the abortion." I waited for him to say something, anything, but he just squeezed my hand and watched me. "Don't you feel anything about all this?"

He shrugged. "Not really."

And when I searched his eyes, I saw no disgust, no anger. He understood. Calm, pure and blue, ran through my abdomen where stabbing anxiety had held me prisoner for so long.

He doesn't hate me. He doesn't think I'm a terrible person.

He led me to the bed. I lay there, wrapped in his arms and let the tears fall as years of pain melted into acceptance.

As I fell into sleep, I wondered how I had gotten so lucky.

IT'S TIME.

Robert stood at the bottom of the bed. The whip unfurled at his side, dangling over his shoulders like the cross he bore, the leather warming with his body heat. His knee squeaked against the plastic mattress cover. He jerked his wrist and a noise like a firecracker reverberated through the room.

She screamed, but all that came out was a muffled whine. *Pathetic.* Handcuffs clanked against the metal headboard. He cracked the whip again and shook his head in disapproval. She stopped moving, her face a mask of fear behind the duct tape that held her lips together.

She knows. And she hates me for it. The knowledge of his exposure swarmed his brain like a cloud of locusts, gnawing away at his self-control.

They all knew. Except one. Except *her*.

And she's with him.

He brought the whip down against the whore's rib cage. She flexed and moaned. *Crack! Crack!* Slices appeared in the shaved skin at the apex of her thighs.

The fear in her eyes drew out his own.

I'm a marked soul, every mistake inscribed on my face. But love can erase it all. Love can save me.

He needed Hannah. And soon.

His heart rate accelerated. He cracked the whip harder and watched a long line of blood weep from beneath pale ivory as skin gave way. She wheezed a ragged sigh through her nose.

He brought the implement down, again and again, crosshatching the skin of her thighs, her breasts, with oozing red.

She would bear the marks too.

Satisfied, he tossed the whip aside and climbed between her legs, positioning his face above hers. Pancake makeup dripped down her face on beads of sweat.

Look at me, bitch.

She did, as if she could hear his thoughts.

He ripped the tape from her mouth and thrust into her roughly, feeling the resistance that she couldn't will away, even for the money he was giving her.

Pinpricks of crimson on her lips grew until the blood trickled down her chin.

"Please, stop—"

"Close your fucking mouth."

"But—"

Robert only wanted the words of one woman. *I forgive you, Robert. It's okay, Robert. I love you.*

"Please—" Her voice was nasal and petulant and vile. And she was not Hannah.

He backhanded her, the sting on his hand and the clack of her teeth offering some comfort, some consolation, though not enough.

"Anything else?" he said.

She stared at the wall.

Robert squinted, blurring his vision so her thin face dripped away like a Dali painting, oozing, shifting, reforming, solidifying. *Hannah.* Dark hair swirled around her lovely face, the green of her eyes pulling him into her.

She smiled at him. *I forgive you.*

He moved his hips faster, with renewed passion.

I can take the pain away. I can help you.

Over and over he thrust, feeling *her*, smelling *her*. When she moaned louder, the screams were Hannah's as he brought her to the peaks of passion with him, rewarding her for saving him, for loving him, for releasing him from a lifetime of dread.

Shaking, he wiped tears from his eyes with the back of his hand. His knuckles burned. The whore's sweat and blood clung to his skin.

He climbed from the bed and left the room, careful not to look at her. He did not want the reminder that *she* was not there with him.

"Soon," he whispered.

She'd be with him soon enough.

WEDNESDAY, NOVEMBER 25TH

"They froze me out." Petrosky resisted the urge to kick McCallum's desk.

"I heard. How did that make you feel?"

"You know how the fuck I feel about it. They didn't even call me. Just went out there themselves and ran the scene." From what he'd heard, Alice Putrus had been found under a manhole cover, her stomach torn open, a dog gnawing on her bloody shirt. She'd been there for a few days, definitely killed before Everette. And his guy had done his homework—there was no way her name was a coincidence.

"Where's Morrison?"

"Getting what he can from the brass. Or from his workout buddies."

"He's better with people, isn't he?"

"Doesn't take much to beat me at people pleasing."

"There's some truth to that."

"How insightful. Some shrink you are." He paused. "I'm going to solve this fucker."

"That's why you're here?"

"Yes."

The doctor raised an eyebrow. "No other reason?"

"Goddammit, McCallum, knock it off. This isn't about me. This guy is good. Meticulous. He might not be the best at dissection, but he's certainly the best at getting in and out of there clean. Even used a rake to obliterate his footprints in that Lapeer field."

"So we're left with what?"

"The type of victim. The poems." The poems bothered him more than he cared to admit. Especially Campbell's. Had their killer hidden the poem on purpose to throw doubt on his identity? If that was the case, why write it at all? Maybe he was messing with their minds. Or maybe it was as simple as them missing the fact that they could move that brick.

"The other poems were hidden too, but not nearly as well," Petrosky said. "I mean, he actually risked bringing a large piece of equipment in to lift the cement and hide the paper. He used different restraints, too. There has to be something special about that killing."

McCallum nodded. "I agree, though the reason it matters might not be as deep as you think. Have you found anything to indicate that Campbell knew any of the other victims?"

"No."

Just her.

"McCallum tapped his pen against his desk. "If he hadn't gone right back to the old pattern, I would say it was a sign of escalation; a game. But he just picked up where he left off, though he's clearly accelerating his pace."

Petrosky resisted the urge to grab the pen and hurl it across the room. The dull throbbing in his temples was turning into a full-blown ache.

"Anyway," McCallum continued, "the similarity in the victims before and after continues to scream past slight. I would bet that Campbell's death was for another reason. Either he knew something he wasn't supposed to, or he was getting in the way somehow."

Petrosky gritted his teeth. "How would he get in the way? He never did anything! He didn't work and hardly left the apartment except to walk down the street to get cigarettes. He didn't even have a car to get close to any of the places the killings occurred."

McCallum shrugged. "Maybe he had something the killer wanted."

"We've considered the money route, but the only people who would have benefitted are his ex-girlfriend and her son. They have alibis."

"Plus, one of them is five." *Tap. Tap.*

Joke it up, asshole. Petrosky clenched his fist to avoid shoving the pen through the doctor's twinkling eye.

"Money isn't everything. Your killer had something to gain by Campbell dying." *Tap, tap, tap.* "Figure out what it is and you'll be one step closer to solving this case."

"I'm doing my best." Petrosky stood.

"Where are you off to?"

"Staff meeting." He pulled his coat off the back of the chair and hauled it on, one of his shoulders creaking in protest. "Might as well make an appearance before Graves tries to throw me off the case altogether."

"You and I both know that wouldn't stop you, Ed."

"Yeah, probably not. But it'd sure make getting into the donuts more difficult."

. . .

Morrison was already in the conference room. Petrosky sat next to him and swallowed bitter precinct coffee, casting envious glances at Morrison's stainless steel mug. He always brought the best joe from home. In the front of the room, someone had transferred the victims' photos to an oversized cork board, neon green sticky notes tacked beneath each picture, connections between victims outlined in thread. Next to the cork board, the original white board listed their victims:

>Meredith Lawrence: October 1st
>A boat beneath a sunny sky
>Lingering onward dreamily
>In an evening in July-
>
>Jane Trazowski, October 11
>Children three that nestle near,
>Eager eye and willing ear
>Pleased a simple tale to hear—
>
>Jacob Campbell: November 3
>Long has paled the sunny sky:
>Echoes fade and memories die:
>Autumn frosts have slain July.
>
>Alice Putrus: November 18
>Still she haunts me phantom wise,
>Alice moving under skies
>Never seen by waking eyes.
>
>Bianca Everette: November 22
>Children yet, the tale to hear,
>Eager eye and willing ear,
>Lovingly shall nestle near.

Graves stood at the front of the conference room, his eyes much too cool for the occasion. *Prick.*

"As most of you know, Alice Putrus was discovered this morning on the eastside, hidden under a manhole," Graves said. "Preliminary data indicates that she died around November eighteenth. Our killer is moving faster. That means more chances he'll make a mistake."

Graves looked out the window as if he expected to see the killer grinning up at him from the parking lot, holding a dead hooker and waving a bloody Q-tip. But their killer wasn't going to trip himself up. Not this guy. Petrosky pushed his coffee away as his stomach soured.

Graves turned back to the boards and pointed at Campbell's picture. "At the Campbell crime scene, a note was recently found underneath the table. It appears to have been placed there using a dolly to lift the blocks after the killing. Like the others, it was written in the victim's blood."

Petrosky bristled. *Was recently found*. No recognition for his discovery, not even a nod in his direction. Looked like Graves didn't want everyone to know his guys were goddamn useless.

"Why it was hidden is still uncertain. He may have been trying to lure authorities into thinking we had a copycat, at least until the writing was discovered. The different restraints may have been a part of this. Officers are looking into the November second press leak, in the off chance the information was leaked by our suspect to encourage the confusion."

The off chance. It wasn't an off chance. The killer was fucking with them. Bloody words smeared themselves across Petrosky's brain. There was a reason for everything. There was a reason for Campbell. And if there was a reason for Campbell—

She's in danger. It was a gut feeling he couldn't shake.
Maybe she knows more than she thinks.
Don't focus on her or you'll blow the whole thing.
Graves was still talking but Petrosky was no longer listening.
One last visit can't hurt.

HANNAH SAT WAITING for him at the picnic table, her face as placid as the glass pond. He crunched toward her over frost-streaked grass and the occasional frozen leaf.

"Ms. Montgomery."

"Detective Petrosky."

He stopped walking, his back stiffening, but not with cold. Her squared shoulders and erect posture were a far cry from the skittish demeanor she'd had at the shelter. Something was different. *She* was different.

He sat across from her, tense and wary.

"What did you need to see me about? Did something else happen?"

He shook his head and watched her, gauging her reaction. Her features stayed even. Detachment, maybe? Had everything become too much to bear? "I understand you've been cooperative with the FBI, answering their questions about the other victims. I thank you for that."

She nodded. Not speechless, not nervous, just matter-of-fact.

Muscles along the back of his neck tightened and cramped. "We have recently come across new information. I was wondering if you might have some insight."

"I'll help any way I can." She looked him straight in the eye, not past him or at the lake like she had before.

"What I am showing you has to remain confidential."

"Of course."

He pulled out the list of poems, watching her face for a hint of recognition or understanding. "Do these words mean anything to you?"

She took the page, scanned it, and met his eyes again. "No."

Not a single anxious twitch.

"Are you sure?"

"Positive."

He appraised the calm of her face, the evenness of her mouth. "If you happen to think of anything else—"

"I'll call you."

Maybe she didn't need help after all.

He felt her eyes on his back as he walked away. Her boyfriend was gone, but as both LaPorte and Plumber the apartment manager had said, she certainly didn't seem worse off having lost him.

THE VERY AIR I breathed was different, lighter somehow, as if a suffocating fog that had always been wrapped around my face had suddenly lifted. Even the snow on the pond seemed to sparkle through the detective's questions about a poem. A poem he insisted was connected to the killings. My father didn't know anything about poetry, but that wasn't what made my heart soar.

It was all because of Dominic. He knew my secrets now, and he still accepted each and every part of me, even the parts I had once thought appalling. I felt like a whole new person.

A better person.

I practically floated to the filing room to finish up a few things before our monthly staff meeting. If I could find a way to float to the meeting, Dominic and I could giggle all night about the shocked looks from his other employees. *Oh no! It's a ghost!* In my current state, I'd make the least terrifying apparition ever. Which was kind of okay.

Noelle crouched by the bottom file drawer and squeezed a folder into place. "Morning!"

A twinge of guilt pricked my stomach. I'd been awful to suspect her, to avoid her the way I had. But that was in the past. It was all in the past.

"You getting a jump on the filing, too?" I asked.

"Yeah, I want to make sure I get out of here on time tonight. Got a hot date." She closed the drawer.

"With Thomas?"

"Yep." Her cheeks flushed. "Though I must admit, I don't usually let myself get carried away like this."

I knew what she meant. It was both exhilarating and terrifying when a guy could make you feel drunk and giddy at the mere thought of him. I opened my mouth to tell her how I felt about Dominic, how fast I'd gone from a crush to adoration, but there was no way Noelle would trust my judgment about relationships—after all, I had chosen Jake and professed my love for him even when he was causing me pain. "Looks like you're falling for Thomas," I said instead.

"Yeah, I know." Noelle squinted at me. "Hey you've got something on your—" She gestured to my chest.

I looked down and brushed off a few dark hairs. "Duke, Dominic's dog. He's almost always just wandering around the backyard, but we were wrestling this morning before work." I closed the drawer and it latched with a soft *click*.

"Quite the happy family over there, aren't you?"

"It could be worse." *She had no idea.*

Noelle stared past me at the wall. "Yeah, it could definitely be worse," she muttered.

We both turned as Ralph entered through the open door. Noelle coughed and slid past him out into the hallway. He watched her go, shoulders slumped.

Ralph always looked so ... hurt. Sad. Maybe I could talk to her about making amends with Ralph. Maybe she'd trust me about him. No one could say I didn't understand what it was like to be hurt.

I followed Noelle, trying to ignore the tightness in Ralph's eyes as I passed him. Looked like he wasn't taking nearly enough Xanax.

BY THE TIME our staff meeting was over, I had almost forgotten about Ralph and his agitated gaze. Perhaps it was the conference table loaded with coffee and pastries. Maybe it was the banner behind the podium that demanded *Imagine!* in rainbow colors. Or maybe there was simply nothing as relaxing as listening to your supervisors drone on about teamwork for an hour.

Well ... almost nothing.

The phone on my desk was ringing when we got back to the office. I raced over and snatched up the receiver, glad my hands had finally steadied.

"Harwick Technologies, Human Resources, this is Hannah," I said in the higher pitch that I hoped screamed customer service.

"Good afternoon." Even on the phone his mellow baritone gave me chills.

"What are you doing calling me at work? My boss will be terribly irritated." I couldn't keep the amusement out of my voice. I hoped he could hear it.

Dominic laughed on the other end of the line. "I won't keep you. I just wanted to know if you were free Saturday evening. I have tickets to the symphony downtown. I thought we could go to La Roseo right down the street first."

"I would love to. But ... I'm not sure about the symphony."

He was silent for a moment. "Do you have other plans? Maybe another kitchen reorganization?"

"I thought you liked my mad organizing skills!" I wondered if anyone else in the office could feel my happiness radiating out at them, tickling their backs.

"I do. Just don't organize my man cave."

I rolled my eyes. Only Dominic would refer to a workout room that way. "I wouldn't dream of it. I just don't have anything to wear to the symphony."

"That is not a problem. We'll go shopping first. Maybe hit the salon. On me."

Shopping? The salon? I usually trimmed my dead ends in the sink. "That's ... I mean, I don't want you to have to pay to dress me." Even as I said it, my uncertainty dissolved.

"Trust me, dressing you would be my pleasure."

I'm sure you'd enjoy undressing me more.

"Do we have a date?" he asked.

I had a choice. I had control. And he cared about me. Maybe. Probably. My heart was as full as those jelly donuts. "It's a date," I said.

"Good. And I'll meet you out front at five-thirty. I'm making dinner tonight, so don't be late. You've done enough cooking this week."

I smiled into the phone. "I don't mind."

"Neither do I. And I'm pretty good at it, if I do say so myself."

HE WASN'T LYING about being able to cook. The smell of warm butter and garlic permeated the air as I entered the kitchen later that evening. Dominic was putting the finishing touches on two plates.

"What's all this?"

"Pan seared duck with rosemary, roasted potatoes and caramelized beets with green salad."

I watched, high on endorphins from an hour on the treadmill, my hair still wet from my shower. A spark of apprehension twittered in my chest. I was falling too fast. We had not known each other long enough. But I couldn't help it; I was completely and totally smitten, and all he was doing at that moment was spooning potatoes onto a plate. He hadn't even minded when I set up Romeo, my new philodendron, in the kitchen and accidentally smashed his crystal vase. "These things happen," he had said.

"It looks amazing," I told him.

He put a sprig of parsley on top of the potatoes. "I hope it tastes amazing. I spent an hour on it."

"Sounds like someone needs a hobby."

He abandoned the plates and wrapped his arms around me. "I have one now."

We ate by candlelight in the dining room, each bite more delicious than the last. When I could eat no more, I sat back and stretched, yawning.

"You sure you're okay?" He laid his fork beside his plate.

"Just a little tired."

"I'll make sure you sleep well tonight."

"I bet you say that to all the ladies."

"I am an expert in putting women to sleep. It's my electric wit." He smiled around his glass of sparkling water.

"Or ... this." I raised my foot under the table and rubbed my bare toes against his crotch.

"Just what every man wants to hear. 'Darling, your penis puts me right to sleep.'"

"The sleep is just a happy byproduct. And what woman doesn't love a nap?"

"I think we can do better than napping. And I don't need to use my penis to relax you." He stood. "I want to show you something."

"I'll bet you do."

"No, not that, though I'm sure I could be persuaded later." He led me through the living room, past the right archway and opened a large wooden door that I had assumed was a closet.

I followed him inside the room and gasped. It was humongous, like every other room in the house, but it felt like another planet: cozy in spite of its size, and rich and majestic like an old library. Wait ... it *was* a library, the entire back wall covered by floor-to-ceiling bookshelves. The other walls were paneled with deep wooden planks each about a foot across, their rough surfaces dull despite the stain. I ran my hand over the surface and feathery splinters pricked my palm.

"The wood came from a turn of the century barn that was on my father's property," he said. "The people who wanted to buy the house after he died were going to demolish it."

"It's ... beautiful. All of it." I glanced to our right at two perpendicular leather couches. Between them sat a coffee table fashioned from an enormous piece of driftwood topped with a carved chess set, the pieces arranged haphazardly on the top.

"You play chess?" I asked.

"No."

"But—"

"It was my mother's."

"Sorry. It looked like you were in the middle of a game."

"We were. That was the last move she made." He touched a pawn. "I was six. Cancer. My father died of cancer also, just a few years ago. He went quickly, in line with his wishes. He believed that pain was not an acceptable end to a life well-lived."

"Dominic, I'm so—"

He continued as if he hadn't heard me. "My mother loved chess because it was full of possibilities. The plays themselves may not fall the way you think they will, but they always work out the way they should, especially if you're paying attention." He straightened. "I've always thought that this still board is like a version of the end in and of itself. No one else will ever play on it, but all the pieces are where they should be if you just accept them."

Acceptance. Healing. His parents had taught him well. And now he was teaching me.

He walked to the bookcases that covered the back wall and pulled a book off a shelf. "How do you feel about Rabindranath Tagore?"

I raised my eyebrows. "Who the what now?"

He smiled and sat with me on the couch. I relaxed into his chest, feeling his heart as if it were mine, matching his breath, inhaling the earthy scent of good leather and wood.

His voice vibrated through me as he read:

"I seem to have loved you in numberless forms, numberless times…
  In life after life, in age after age, forever.
  My spellbound heart has made and remade the necklace of songs,
  That you take as a gift, wear round your neck in your many forms,
  In life after life, in age after age, forever …"

He loves me. He'll protect me. My breathing deepened.

"You and I have floated here on the stream that brings from the fount.
  At the heart of time, love of one for another.
  We have played alongside millions of lovers, shared in the same
  Shy sweetness of meeting, the same distressful tears of farewell-
  Old love but in shapes that renew and renew forever."

I closed my eyes, hoping against all hope that I could stay here forever, relishing the heavy peace that had finally, finally settled in my chest.

I love you. I allowed sleep to envelop me before I could dare to say it out loud.

THURSDAY, NOVEMBER 26TH

TIMMY SAT on the ground behind a huge tree stump, the only one on the dark, abandoned playground. He ran his finger over initials someone had cut into the wood and peered into the night. The tree shouldn't have been there, surrounded by concrete.

He shouldn't be there either.

He leaned against the trunk while his mother finished her business behind the wall to the side of the old school playground. If only the school behind him was still full of students, with other kids just like him. He would go every day if he could. He pictured walking to school, hair spiked and gelled, backpack slung over one shoulder the way the cool kids did it on television.

Hey, Timmy! they would call, smiling at him as he walked by.

Want to come over tomorrow? they would ask.

He covered his ears in case she made any noises—he always felt dirty for even hearing them. And he wouldn't need to listen for her calling him. She had given him the same old speech: "I'll be right back, honey, okay? Don't talk to anyone and don't move. I'll come back for you when we have enough for groceries."

He crossed his legs on the frozen ground like the good boy he was.

Hey, Tim! Will you play with me at recess?

Hey, Tim, let's swing together!

He took his hands off his head. It was suddenly quiet—too quiet. A chill ran through the puffy coat he wore. He grabbed the blanket his mother had left with him, climbed to his feet and cocked his head, listening.

Nothing but the wind.

"Mom?" he called softly. Maybe she was finished working and was waiting for him. His stomach grumbled. He was ready to go too.

He squinted into the blackness.

"Mom?" he called, a little louder. His heart beat faster as he took a few sneaky steps, knowing he wasn't supposed to bother her while she was working. The wind whistled around him, bit at his numb hands and froze the tip of his nose. The building loomed above him.

She wasn't done, or she would have come to get him. They probably went in to get out of the cold, he thought, congratulating himself on solving the puzzle. He braced himself against the bitter wind and crept toward the old school to warm up while he waited. If he was quiet, they would never even know he was there.

THURSDAY, NOVEMBER 26TH

He had strapped her down on an old cafeteria table. Though convenient this time, it wasn't his favorite type of work surface; the metal grooves in the table collected the gore and made everything slippery. Not that she'd minded. Or even noticed.

He watched the cockroach wriggle inside the sheath of her stomach, its legs twitching as it fought to survive in her meager juices. Even after thirty minutes and twelve seconds, the bug still lived.

These fuckers will outlast us all. He touched it with the point of the scalpel and the bug writhed away from him, perhaps alarmed.

Creak.

He turned around. A blanket dropped to the floor as the boy hiding behind it stared, open-mouthed, brown eyes wide.

"Momma?"

In two strides he was upon the child, slicing through fascia and muscle along the front of the boy's throat. The hole in the child's neck gurgled, a last attempt to suck air though a severed windpipe. A waterfall of life spurted down the child's jacket. Then the eyes closed and the boy collapsed backwards. A tear drop peeked from under one dead lid like a single cell trying to escape demise.

He removed the boy's jacket, tossed it aside and carried him to the table. The cockroach stuck in the woman's body was still struggling, but slower, sluggish. Perhaps the boy's stomach acid would be more robust, paralyzing the bug in moments if he were to place it directly into the child's gut.

He glanced at his watch. *No time.* But there was always another boy, another day.

He arranged the child on top of the woman, snuggling his lower half among her disordered intestines as if she were trying to pull him into the gaping hole.

Back from whence you came.

He positioned the boy's head on her chest, between the two abominable bluebird tattoos near the front of her shoulders. The birds appeared to be flying headlong into the child's hair.

He dropped the bloody scalpel into a plastic bag, an inconvenience but a necessary one. The police would be getting closer now.

The wind howled through the silent building. He dipped a latexed finger into the gore that had settled in the metal grooves on the table top and scrawled bloody calligraphy along the bench.

> In a Wonderland they lie,
> Dreaming as the days go by,
> Dreaming as the summers die:

His work complete, he walked out listening to the wind singing an eerie lullaby to the boy nestled peacefully in his mother's final embrace.

FRIDAY, NOVEMBER 27TH

I CUT another slice of turkey for the women in the shelter dining room and grinned at the plates like a sappy idiot. Apparently, nothing made me giddy like a good night's rest and a morning eating Dominic's leftover turkey, mashed potatoes, and pie.

Pie made everything more awesome. And the way Dominic had woken me up wasn't half bad either.

I flushed and glanced at Ms. LaPorte, who was faring less well. She slumped and shuffled, head hung low as she slopped potatoes on the plates, like someone had sucked all the energy from her bones. Holidays did that to you. I didn't usually make coffee this late in the afternoon, but there might not be a choice if I wanted her to make it through dinner.

"Are you okay?" I set the last plate down and laid my hand on her arm.

She turned to me, her eyes watery and bloodshot.

Oh shit.

"I knew she had some trouble, but that boy ... that poor boy." She wiped a tear with the back of her hand.

My chest, my throat, everything constricted. Another murder? "Ms. LaPorte? What happened?" Please let it be something else. *Anything else.*

Her eyes widened. "Hannah, have you not been watching the news?"

My mouth was too dry to speak. I'd been avoiding the news, avoiding all the sadness and the hurt out there.

"Do you remember Antoinette? Her little boy Tim?"

Ms. LaPorte grabbed my hands as realization sank into my stomach like a knife. I shook my head in disbelief.

"Hannah, I know you've been through a lot lately. If you don't want to know—"

"Please ... what happened?" My voice had gone shrill and my heart was hammering so loudly I worried I might not be able to hear her. I gripped her hands to steady myself but it didn't stop the trembling in my legs.

She leaned close to me. "Someone came here this morning, looking for Tim after he missed a visit with his social worker. They were only here for a few minutes. And then we heard the sirens at the school across the street, and I looked out the window—" she choked back a sob. "It was just horrible. Those black bags ..."

I shivered. Cold. I was so cold.

He's a good kid.

Momma, can I have another hot dog?

I sucked air through my nose, my mouth, but there wasn't enough oxygen in the room.

That poor kid.

I let go of Ms. LaPorte, grabbed the serving dishes from the counter, and retreated to the sink.

Ms. LaPorte followed me. "You look a little pale, dear. Maybe you should take off." She blew her nose on a paper towel.

I shook my head. "No, I want to be here. To help you. I ... just can't believe it."

"Me either, dear. And to think all these killings have something to do with girls from our shelter."

"Did the police say that?" My voice was hoarse. My nerves vibrated.

Dominic will protect me.

"No, but they implied it. Told me to watch out here. Be careful leaving."

This has nothing to do with me. Nothing at all. It's just a terrible coincidence. But—

I couldn't be here. But I had to be here. Maybe I'd take Dominic up on that private bodyguard thing.

"I think we need to shut our doors for a few weeks," Ms. LaPorte said.

"You're sure?" *Thank goodness.*

She held up a hand. "I know; they need us. But if someone is taking these women from here, like the police seem to think, I don't want to put them in harm's way. I already told Brandy she could stay with me for the time being."

Relief. Guilt at the relief. I nodded, mute.

"Will you be okay, Hannah?"

"Yeah, I just need ... I don't know what I need." A baseball bat. A place to hide. Something to whack a killer in the balls.

I need to call Dominic.

PETROSKY GRABBED an antacid from the roll on his desk and chewed it slowly. His hands shook. It was probably from too much coffee. He worried it was from not enough booze.

Another one from the shelter. The scene had been horrific, but the aftermath was making him even more anxious than standing in that empty school cafeteria, the tinny scent of blood and human waste hanging in the air like thick perfume.

And that kid—

He ground his teeth. She had been another hooker, one that fit the victim profile to a T. But this time, there had been two victims. At least this time he had found out about the scene before the bodies were put in bags.

Ms. Montgomery would be frightened; she had been scared the first time. And maybe she should be.

Petrosky slammed his desk drawer closed and walked down the hall to the conference room. Graves stood looking out the window, still apparently waiting for their killer to come to them. Outside, snowflakes melted to slush in the salted parking lot.

"Sir?"

Graves turned.

"I have a bad feeling about this one."

"A bad feeling about a dead woman and her kid, huh? Go figure."

Petrosky could feel the irritation building in the pit of his stomach. "Is there any way to increase the presence around Ms. Montgomery?"

"We've already surveilled her, and she's alibied on the nights in question. We don't have the manpower to keep following a suspect who we know isn't one."

Petrosky frowned. "I'm more concerned that she's a target."

"I doubt that. And anyways"—Graves shook his head—"we've already freaked her out enough."

What the fuck? Petrosky raised his eyebrows.

"One of your officers decided to go rogue and search her car while she was at work. She saw him, but—" Graves sighed. "We don't need the illegal actions of one force member compromising the integrity of the entire case." His eye twitched.

Liar. It had probably been one of Graves's agents who'd broken into her car. Maybe Graves had even put the guy up to it.

"Dammit, we have to do *something*! What about the poems? There's only one more verse."

"We have nothing to indicate that Ms. Montgomery is in danger at all. If anything, she's an unlikely target: employed, no children, no history of drug use or prostitution. Yes, half of the victims happened to spend time at the shelter she volunteers at, but there aren't that many domestic violence shelters around. And the other victims frequented shelters that are completely unconnected to her."

"What about her boyfriend?"

"Maybe Campbell's secret fuck buddy was one of the other victims and he knew something about her killer. We've got men on it now." Graves's jaw was set. "We just can't afford any more bad publicity on this."

"Wouldn't it be worse publicity if she dies?"

Footsteps approached. Graves broke eye contact and nodded to someone behind Petrosky.

Petrosky's phone buzzed in his pocket.

"Paulson, expand the library record searches on that book to cover fifty more miles. It's a stretch, but this guy likes to play. I want every copy back here and checked for markings, notes, anything. Then take a partner and see if you can find any links to other women's shelters."

Graves was grasping at straws. Wasting time. Petrosky's phone buzzed again.

"Yes, sir," Paulson said.

No one acknowledged Petrosky as he walked out and mashed his phone to his ear. "Petrosky," he snapped.

"It's Shannon."

"What are you doing working the day after Thanksgiving?"

"Why, is it a holiday or something?"

"Not around here." Petrosky glanced back toward the conference room door but no one emerged. Graves and Paulson were probably both staring at the parking lot like a couple of fuck sticks. "So what'd I do this time, Taylor?"

"Nothing."

"How'd you get this number?"

"Morrison."

"You calling my rookie in your off hours?"

"That's not your business, Petrosky. What *is* your business is the tip I'm about to give you on your serial."

Petrosky accelerated his pace down the hall. "I'm sure you heard the Feds are on it now, Taylor," he said. "Why'd you call me instead of Graves?"

The phone crackled. "Everyone over here has been pretty pissed about how it was handled. And Graves is a piece of work in his own right. I heard two of his last three cases were solved at the expense of some uncooperative witnesses who turned at the last minute, testifying with information that put them in danger one way or another. Pretty convenient, if you ask me."

Pretty convenient, indeed. Maybe those witnesses had even had someone break into their car.

"Either way, I trust you. I might have to call him eventually but I can plead busy for a few more hours. Actually, fuck it, you tell him if you want him to know."

Petrosky entered the bullpen and yanked a pad of paper from his desk. "Hang on." He ignored Morrison's raised brow across the aisle and dropped into the chair. "Okay, I'm listening."

"Got a colleague prosecuting a Xavier Kroll, K-R-O-L-L, heroin addict, small-time crook. Kroll apparently knew Antoinette and Timothy Michaels. Says he lived with a woman who was friends with Antoinette's mother."

Petrosky scrawled the name. "Interesting."

"Kroll says Antoinette lived at his girlfriend's house with the kid. Off and on, never for longer than a few months, but she was there recently. I doubt you'll see that address on any forms."

"Where's it at?"

"Chapman. 4587." She paused. "The guy might be full of shit, trying to swing a plea, but the prosecutor was going to follow up anyway. I convinced him to wait until after you checked it out."

"Why'd he agree?"

"He's friends with Morrison too."

"California, huh? The boy gets around," Petrosky said as Morrison approached his desk.

"Don't we all?"

"Thanks, Taylor. Give me a few hours."

"No problem. Tell Detective Morrison I said hello. And tell him I saved him some of yesterday's pumpkin pie if he can get free for dinner."

Petrosky glanced at Morrison. Morrison grinned.

"Tell him yourself, Taylor. I'll keep you posted." He pocketed the phone and stood. "Got a lead, ten minutes out. I'll call you with whatever she gives me and get you to run it from here. In the meantime, get me a background on Xavier Kroll."

"On it, Boss." Morrison looked at his watch. "You want a granola bar for the road?"

"I wouldn't want a granola bar if I was fucking starving. By the way, Taylor has some pie for you."

"Really?"

"Yup. And how the hell do you know everyone in the prosecutor's office?"

"They like granola too." Morrison winked.

"Save it for your girlfriend, Surfer Boy."

SATURDAY, NOVEMBER 28TH

SATURDAY DAWNED FRIGID, but clear. I spent the morning alternating between staring through the skylights, working out with Dominic, and scratching behind Duke's ears while Dominic finished some paperwork.

Everything was ... peaceful. Or had been since last night, when Dominic talked me down from my freak out over the shelter. "I'm sure those girls got into all kinds of things they shouldn't have," he had said. "And Jake too. But you're not in danger any more than I'd be in danger of a contact high for knowing other CEOs who snort cocaine. And you don't have to go back until the police sort this out. No use worrying before there's something to worry about."

I had balked. "You know people who snort cocaine?" He'd just laughed, and my anxiety had evaporated.

After lunch, we left to get my dress for the symphony. Dominic drove us around the lake where ice gleamed off the edges of the water and dusted the sparse cattails that had not yet called it quits. They were apparently stubborn bastards, like the cats for which they were named.

We fought traffic for a few miles, then turned off the main drag. The shops were tucked back from the street, off a long, curvy road that wound through fir trees heavy with snow. I hadn't even known this place existed.

His world. I'm in his world. I wanted to press my forehead against the window, relishing the sight of every jewelry store, every suit shop. We parked in front of a large window filled with oil paintings and expensive-looking pottery.

Dominic led me down the walk and through a wooden door carved with a fairy tale scene: a woman in a ball gown singing to a bird. Hokey, but somehow perfect. Inside the dress shop, row upon row of luscious fabrics lined the walls. I fingered an ornate blue gown wrapped in a layer of creamy lace.

From the back room, a woman with thin lines around her eyes approached us, her smile painted in candy-apple red. "Can I help you?" she asked me. I looked at Dominic.

"Tell her what you want. I will take a walk while you decide."

Wait ... what? This isn't my world! My heart pounded in my throat as he handed the woman his credit card, stooped to kiss my cheek and headed out the door.

Everything's fine. He'll be right back.

The woman looked at me expectantly.

What did I want? "Um ... I don't ... it's for the symphony."

She put a finger against her lips, appraising me.

I fought the urge to run.

"Come with me," she said finally. "I have a lovely organza that I think will suit you nicely."

An hour later, I left the shop with a garment bag over my arm and found Dominic on the sidewalk outside.

He took the dress. "How did it go?"

"Pretty good, I think." Salt crunched under our shoes. "Why did you leave me alone in there?"

He kept his eyes on the walk in front of us. "I'm not sure what you mean. They didn't have anything in my size."

"What?" *Just laugh, let it go.* No, I could tell him anything. I cleared my throat, my face hot. "I ... sometimes don't do that well with new people."

"You are stronger than you think." He squeezed my hand.

I snorted.

"You got the dress, didn't you?"

I squeezed his hand back, the warmth draining from my cheeks.

Dominic stopped in front of a set of double glass doors, pulled the handle, and led me inside a room with high ceilings and four separate hallways leading toward the back of the building. Cinnamon and orange peel tickled my nose. I was still taking in the photographs of serene waterfalls when Dominic addressed the woman at the front desk.

"We have a four o'clock appointment with Genevieve."

"Right away, sir." The brunette behind the counter glanced at me, then back at Dominic. "Will you be accompanying our guest today?" A smocked attendant wandered by, grinning cordially with huge white teeth. I tried to smile back but it might have looked like a grimace.

Dominic met my eyes. "Yes," he said.

Thank goodness.

We took the blue-gray corridor on the far right and emerged into a large salon, complete with leather seats and sea green towels that looked plush enough to sleep on.

A tall blonde wearing high heels and a skin-tight black sweater approached and held out her hand. "I'm Genevieve," she said. "Welcome." The corners of her lips turned up and it made her look younger, friendlier. Her hand was warm.

I relaxed into the cushioned back of the chair as she pushed the foot pedal to raise it.

"So, what would you like to do today?" she said.

Dominic smiled down at me. "You need me for this, or shall I leave you to it?"

His eyes showed no irritation, only confident support. I sat taller, suddenly more self-assured. "Go ahead."

My heart raced as it had in the dress shop, but this time I was ready for it. I watched Dominic's broad back in the mirror as he retreated down the hallway.

You're stronger than you think. I glanced up at Genevieve, sure that I would see some sign of contempt at being kept waiting. She smiled kindly.

I can do this. I am in control. I took in the green of my eyes, the milky hue of my skin, the mahogany of my hair. Somehow it all felt wrong. In the lighted vanity, the colors lent themselves to a face that looked far too much like... *him.*

I set my jaw. "You know, I think I may be up for a change."

Genevieve reached for a comb.

I smiled at the mirror. *I'm not his little girl. Not anymore.*

PETROSKY STOOD in the middle of the room and tried not to touch anything. All goddamn day yesterday she had been gone, and now that she was finally here, he hoped he hadn't wasted his time. Not that he had more pressing engagements since Graves had hijacked his fucking case.

Margaret Garner sat on the couch, a maze of tiny blue veins creeping across her nearly translucent chest like spiderwebs. "I just can't believe she's gone," she said over the dry whir of the space heater.

Petrosky studied Garner's face. He saw sorrow there, expected from someone who had been closer to his victim than her own estranged mother. But her eyes were purely sad, no twinge of surprise, no disbelief. Had Garner expected something to happen to Antoinette Michaels? What had she seen in the last three years that Michaels had been her off-and-on roommate?

"And Tim ... oh god." She collapsed into sobs.

There's her surprise. No one ever expected kids to die.

Petrosky watched Garner pick at a plume of stuffing peeking

through the threadbare arm of the couch, her tears leaking onto her pants.

"Tell me about the last few weeks," he said.

Garner sniffed and swiped at her eyes with a tissue. "The usual. She was trying to get back on her feet. She always got clean for a few weeks, then every time, back into the life. She worried constantly about Tim, about how she was going to get him into a good school district or whether she'd have enough money for food."

"Nothing out of the ordinary recently?"

Garner shrugged.

"Then why did she go to the shelter?"

"Oh, *that*." Garner ran a hand through hair slick with grease. "Someone beat her up, and pretty good too. But it's all ... I mean, it happens with what she was doin'."

"Do you know who the guy was?"

She paused for too long.

Suspicion corded Petrosky's neck.

"I—I don't think he was a regular, but I don't know. I haven't done anything like that since I found my boyfriend." Her lips twitched into a half smile, but the corners of her mouth trembled.

She was lying. But was she hiding something relevant to this case? "I'm not here to arrest you. If I were, I'd be packing up that needle on the kitchen counter and hauling you in."

Her mouth dropped open, eyes flicking to the kitchen.

Petrosky stepped closer. "I have no interest in your drug use, your occupation, or anything else besides finding out who killed Antoinette and Tim."

Garner's shoulders slumped, eyes on her lap. "I did ... I mean, I can't get in trouble for taking a message, right?"

Petrosky stared hard at her until she met his gaze.

She licked her lips. "I took a message for her." Her sour breath hung in the air between them.

"When?"

"The night she got beat. Like I said, he wasn't a regular, he just left an address because I told her she could use my car for the evening."

"He left you an address?" That didn't make sense. His killer wouldn't just throw his address to anyone who asked for it. The guy was smarter than that, he could feel it in his bones.

"Well, he left *her* an address." Garner swallowed hard. "When I answered I was hoping it was ... a friend of mine and—"

"You tried to take the job."

She stared at him. "He got the number from one of us. I didn't know if it was her or me. So I just pretended to be who he was looking for."

"But he asked for her?"

Silence.

"Ma'am?"

She sighed. "Yes, he asked for her. But these guys won't leave their information with anyone besides the girl who's coming, and most of the time they don't call back. I was tryin' to help her out. I didn't mean for her to get ... for Tim to get—" Her chest heaved and her eyes slid back to her lap.

"This wasn't your fault. But if you have information, any information, you need to tell me now. Help me catch him, Margaret."

She raised her eyes and her breath was slower, more controlled. "Like I said, I just took a message. Told him I'd be ... I mean, *she'd* be over in a little while."

"Do you still have the address? A name?"

"Course. It's good business to keep 'em if things get slow later." She grinned, then shook her head, her proud smile faltering. "I've got an address for you. They don't leave names, though, not that we need 'em. We ladies never forget a ... face."

PETROSKY CALLED Morrison on his way to the precinct. When he stopped behind the building, Morrison ran out and jumped in the car, his beach-boy face flushed from the winter chill.

"The address belongs to a James Clark," Morrison said, talking so fast his words were almost unintelligible.

Petrosky sucked on a cigarette and furrowed his brows. *James...* He exhaled in a burst and jerked his head backwards. "The guy Montgomery was out with the night after Campbell was snatched?"

Morrison looked like a cat that just ate a fucking canary. "It gets better. Apparently that's not even his real name. James Clark, AKA Robert Fredricks, has a pretty significant record. Did a prison stint for two counts of first degree rape at age eighteen. Got out about five years ago."

Petrosky's muscles shivered with excitement. At least he hoped the shakes were from excitement and not because the bottle of Jack Daniels under the passenger seat was still full. He should have emptied the liquor into his coffee before he got to the precinct.

Morrison opened his window and waved the smoke away from his face. "Should we go in and tell Graves?"

Petrosky took another drag, blew it out violently and crushed the cigarette into the ashtray. "Let's take a drive first."

AN HOUR later they pulled into a small neighborhood near the Everette crime scene and squeezed their car down deeply rutted dirt roads that were barely wide enough for one vehicle. Petrosky could see the shore of a small, tranquil lake within walking distance of the street, but the cottages surrounding it were anything but quaint. Peeling paint was commonplace, some of the homes had shutters swinging from single rusty hinges, and behind one rickety fence, a Doberman snarled at them as they rolled by.

The car bounced over a particularly deep rut in the frozen dirt road. Petrosky hit his head on the roof, swore, and gripped the wheel harder.

"Gotta watch that, Boss. Maybe you should be wearing your seat belt."

Petrosky rubbed his smarting head. "This is it." The difference between this house and the ones around it was remarkable. It was small, but freshly painted, with doors and windows in good repair. The roof looked new. The flower beds, now frozen, contained neatly-trimmed evergreen bushes, and not a single leaf peeked through the snow that covered the lawn.

Well-maintained.

Meticulous.

Careful.

The front porch had been swept clean of snow and salt granules crunched under their feet. Morrison picked up the door knocker and dropped it. Somewhere, water on ice ticked steadily.

The hairs on the back of Petrosky's neck prickled. He knocked with his fist. Nothing. He tried the knob. Locked.

Petrosky pulled his Swiss Army knife from his back pocket and wiggled it into the door jamb. The lock gave way with a click.

"Boss—" Morrison began, but Petrosky was already turning the handle. "We've got one shot, Surfer Boy. They'll be all over the place giving us the run around as soon as we call it in." He nodded to the mat. "Wipe your feet."

Petrosky stepped inside. Morrison followed and closed the door.

The front entryway opened into the kitchen, strong with the scent of lemons. The stainless steel appliances and porcelain floors gleamed in the light streaming through the spotless windows. Framed black and white photographs hung on the walls—copies, but good quality ones. *Expensive.*

Morrison was still standing by the door, shifting his weight from foot to foot like a nervous first grader. Petrosky left him and wandered farther into the house. To the left of the kitchen, an archway opened to a small but nicely furnished living room with a big screen television. He stole past leather sofas into a hallway. The first door opened to a small, tidy bathroom—spotless, like the rest of the house.

From there, he entered a huge bedroom with a king-sized bed. Four poster spindles nearly touched the ceiling, each one painted to appear old or tarnished. Shabby chic bullshit.

No, he thought as he moved closer. *They're actually marked.*

He touched the headboard. The black iron was gouged with slivers of silver. Metal scored by metal? *Did you handcuff them and torture them here first, you sick bastard?*

He opened the nightstand drawer. Toenail clippers, remote control, phone charger. He closed the drawer and turned on the closet light.

Boots creaked on the carpet behind him. Morrison whistled at the wide array of suits and ties.

"Nice of you to show up." Petrosky squinted at the ceiling—smooth. No shelves on the upper walls. "Any wisdom to offer?"

"Well, this dude obviously has money. Why would he be living out in the middle of nowhere in a neighborhood full of thugs and crime?"

Dude? Fucking surfers. Petrosky fingered a silk tie. "In these neighborhoods, people mind their own business." *Which hopefully means they won't notice we're here.* He ran a hand behind the wall of shirts. Nothing. He scanned the floor. A corner of brown peeked from under the shoe rack. Petrosky crouched, grabbed the corner—a shoebox—and pulled it into the light.

Morrison edged around him.

The box was full of photos. The one on top showed a blond woman lying nude on the bed in the same master bedroom. She was handcuffed to the iron posts, her eyes wide with terror, irises colored in with red marker.

Petrosky's heart faltered, then hammered painfully against his ribs.

He pulled out a stack and rifled through them. Here, another blonde was bent over the bed, her right wrist handcuffed to the bedpost, her face turned toward the camera. A piece of duct tape covered her mouth. In another, a woman was cuffed face down on the bed, her back and buttocks slashed with weeping, bloody wounds. From a knife? A whip?

Petrosky's stomach roiled, but he kept flipping, faster and faster. There were other young girls with their legs spread wide on the bed and their arms attached to the posts. In some, the camera had snapped shots from above: girls with male genitalia in their mouths, duct tape still hanging from the sides of their lips. Some were blindfolded but unrestrained. Others had their ankles tied to either side of the bed. In every photo, their eyes had been colored in with red, making them look demonic.

Petrosky flipped another photo.

Morrison gasped.

Antoinette Michaels stared back at them, arms handcuffed above her head, mouth covered in duct tape. The beginnings of fresh bruises on her cheek were obvious in the picture as was the horror etched on her face.

He had no doubt they would find photos of the other victims there.

Petrosky's skin crawled with electricity. He put the pictures back in the box and covered them with the lid. The box shushed as he slid it back under the shoes.

"Boss, what are you—"

Petrosky put his hands on his knees and pushed himself up. "We broke in, California. Without a warrant we can't use them anyway. Right now, we need to get out of here, get a warrant, and stake this place out before he hurts someone else."

They hurried back through the house and out the front door. Petrosky locked it behind them, his heart throbbing in his ears. Outside, the only sounds were the steady drip of melting ice and the wail of the wind.

"Find a good parking place down the road," Petrosky said, sliding into the passenger seat. "Make sure we can see the house."

"Aye aye, Boss." Morrison put the car in gear. Tires crunched over ice and salt and rocks.

Petrosky stared at the phone. He had no choice.

"Graves here."

"Sir, we have some new information." Petrosky explained as Morrison pulled behind an abandoned house a block from Clark's place.

Graves was silent on the other end of the line.

"Sir?"

"You're there now." It was not a question.

"Yes."

"He home?"

"No."

"Take off. Now. We'll get a warrant and retain him for questioning."

Petrosky's heart sank. "But, sir—"

"If we fuck this up, we lose the evidence we need to nail him. We'll put out an APB on his car and watch him if we see him sneaking around another abandoned building tonight. Now, get out of there before you scare him off."

Petrosky hung up the phone and shook a cigarette from his pack, his muscles twitching with the desire to leap from the car and hide in the bushes to wait. "Head back to the station."

Morrison maneuvered out of the neighborhood. Petrosky dragged smoke deep into his lungs and watched the house recede in the rearview mirror.

They had their killer.

Now where the hell was he?

SATURDAY, NOVEMBER 28TH

Thomas lay on the couch, his face drawn and pale.

"You all right?" Robert said. "You haven't moved since we got here." He sat in a chair across from Thomas, head cocked, eyes on Thomas's face.

Thomas shook his head weakly. "I'm not sure. Ever since lunch it's just been ... shit." He leaned over and vomited into the bucket next to the couch.

Robert averted his eyes until Thomas had finished puking.

"I can't go tonight," Thomas said, collapsing back onto the couch. "I feel like death."

"I'm sorry." Robert swallowed a smirk. "I wish I could do something."

Thomas cast his eyes down, defeated. "It took me two weeks and three hundred bucks to get that reservation." He sighed. "Noelle seemed so excited about it too—Hey!" Robert could almost see the light bulb turn on over Thomas's head as he looked back up. "Jim? Is there any way you might do me a favor?"

Robert tried not to smirk. "Anything. Just name it."

Noelle had sounded disappointed on the phone, but she'd insisted on coming over to Thomas's place. Now she knelt next to the couch.

Robert watched from the kitchen.

"Let me take care of you." She put her hand on Thomas's head.

They all think they're fucking nurses. Robert pictured her in a nurse's uniform as she bent to pull up the blanket, and his groin throbbed impatiently.

"No, really, there isn't anything you can do. I just need to get some rest and—" Thomas's eyes bulged. He retched again.

Noelle winced and stood.

"Seriously, honey, I just want to sleep. Let me know if the place is good enough to take you to in another month, okay? I had to bribe the maître-d to get in before February and I'll be pissed if we waste the reservation. I'd rather my two favorite people use it." He smiled thinly. "Just don't go falling for Jim." His eyes closed.

Noelle turned toward the kitchen where Robert stood waiting, keys in hand.

"I'll drive," he said.

She followed him down the stairs. "I hope Thomas feels better soon."

"He will." Robert smiled. *Eye drops only make someone ill for so long.*

I WAS A WHOLE DIFFERENT PERSON. A better person. A person I barely recognized with my long, white-blond hair and a chartreuse gown that brushed my legs with silky fingers. A person who held hands with the love of her life and sniffed through a melancholy symphony, relieved that her current life felt so normal, so damn happy, in comparison to whatever the composer had been going through when he wrote the music. And I couldn't keep my hands off the emerald pendant Dominic had picked out for me as Genevieve worked on my hair. By the time the last note rang out, my eyes were dewy with joy, just from the opportunity to be there, with him.

Holy crap, I was turning into a ball of mush.

We drove back to his house in silence, but not uncomfortable, awkward silence—just the shared I'm-cool-with-you-not-talking silence. I stole fleeting glances at him as he steered the car through the quiet streets. Once, he caught me watching him and smiled and a slow heat rose from my abdomen into my chest. Those eyes. So full of comfort and understanding. Eyes that never seemed to show uncertainty, or anger, or fear. I wondered if he could make me more like that, like him.

Actually, I thought, *he already has.*

When we arrived at the house, he took off his jacket and shoes in the mudroom and walked into the kitchen. "Would you like some water?" he called over his shoulder.

"Yes, thanks." I kicked off my shoes and ducked into the half bath. I unzipped my dress, shimmied out of my nylons, and unhooked my bra, laying everything on the sink.

When only the emerald necklace remained, I padded into the kitchen. Dominic's back was to me. I ran my hands up his back to his shoulders and kissed his arm through his shirt.

He turned, two glasses of sparkling water in his hands.

The edges of his mouth curved into a smile. He abandoned the water and wrapped his left arm around me as I arched into him. He reached between my legs. I was already wet.

I love you, I thought. Maybe tonight I would tell him.

NOELLE HAD ONLY AGREED to go with Jim because Thomas was so bummed out about wasting the reservation. But without Thomas there, the whole restaurant felt a little awkward and business-like. Jim was reserved and kinda boring, a gentlemanly cliché, holding doors and pulling back chairs and talking about appropriately mundane work topics. But it wasn't as bad as she had anticipated, especially after a couple of daiquiris, and the tinkling notes of the in-house pianist filled any gaps in their conversation. With Thomas she wouldn't have needed the piano; he'd surely have been ready with some weird story about his elementary school or a parallel between politicians and Wolverine. The only thing that made Jim's eyes light up was talking about Hannah.

"So how long have you and Hannah known each other?" Jim said over after-dinner coffee.

Noelle washed down molten chocolate cake with a sip of her Kahlua and cream. The booze warmed her insides. "A year or so. She was my first friend when I moved here." Her only friend, really.

"Are you two close?"

She nodded.

"Thomas and I are pretty close friends, too." He lowered his voice. "Plus, I hoped you'd put in a good word ... you know, if she ever drops that other guy."

Poor guy. He really does care for her. But he doesn't stand a chance now that Dominic's in the picture. Noelle smiled and hoped it looked more like kindness than pity. "Will do."

JIM DROVE them out of the restaurant lot, Noelle's after-dinner drinks still sloshing hotly in her stomach.

"Should we go back to Thomas's and check on him?" she asked.

Jim nodded at the clock on his dashboard. "It's a little early yet. Maybe we should find something to do for an hour or two so he can get a little more rest."

She looked at the clock. He was right. They had only been gone for two hours and Thomas had just been dozing off when they left. Not that she couldn't go snuggle up beside him and spend a few hours smelling the sour stench from the bucket on the floor. Eh, later. She shook her head against the fuzziness that was settling in her vision.

Jim kept his eyes on the road. "Want to take a drive? I found a cool overlook not too far from here. One of those scenic view type places. I wanted to bring Hannah up here back when I still had a chance, but..."

Sympathy tugged at Noelle's chest as she imagined how hard it might be for her to lose Thomas. She looked at the clock again and shrugged. "Sure, why not?"

"Great!" Jim squinted at an upcoming red light and turned down a side street. "Faster this way," he said.

The neighborhood homes glowed under bluish-white light from the street lamps. They emerged onto another, dimmer, main street and turned left. "Maybe you can take Thomas up here when he feels better." He grinned, cutting the wheel right onto a sparsely lighted road where the homes were set far back from the street. Above them, the moon shone through a film of murky clouds. "Thomas is always looking for weird, out-of-the-way places. I think they remind him of the lab where they hid the Hulk ... or maybe planet Krypton."

Along the road, the evergreen trees had thickened into a solid wall of iced needles, the ground beneath them heavy and black. She smiled but it felt forced. "You're probably right about that. But you'll have to draw me a map so I can find it again."

Uncertainty pricked at the edge of her subconscious but she brushed it away. *Thomas really would love it out here. Hopefully he'll be feeling better when we get back.*

Noelle took her cell from the purse at her feet. The battery flashed red. One percent. She let it thunk back into the bag.

They emerged from the woods and into a small clearing that ended in a chain link fence at the edge of a cliff. A small lake surrounded by tiny cottages twinkled below the edge of the precipice. The moon tucked itself behind a cloud and winked back again, turning the scene into a sleepy, sparkling town straight out of a children's book.

She leaned forward. "It ... I mean, wow." *If only Thomas were here.*

She didn't register that Jim had moved until she felt his hand on her shoulder. Crystals of fear began at his fingertips and radiated through her, chilling her blood, encasing her lungs in ice. His face, suddenly so close to hers, thrummed with an anxious energy that bounced around her like a thousand bits of hail. His eyes, that just hours ago had been so friendly, glittered darkly with madness or ... evil.

"Jim?"

His hand slithered down her back. His fingers wound tight around her arm, digging into her flesh.

Noelle screamed, the trees and moon her only audience.

SATURDAY, NOVEMBER 28TH

Petrosky knocked before he could change his mind. Biting, midnight wind whistled from the lake and around the monstrous concrete building. There were no sounds coming from inside the house.

Either these walls are really thick, or no one's home.

"Wait for me, Boss!" Morrison ran up the steps.

"I thought you were waiting in the car before you got fired."

"I figured you could use the moral support. Plus, there's always Cali."

"You mean California?"

The door opened. A tall, dark-haired man, presumably Dominic Harwick, looked the detectives up and down. He wore only a pair of silk pajama pants, his bare, washboard abs glinting in the porch light. Another gym rat, like Morrison. Petrosky sighed.

"Can I help you?" Harwick stifled a yawn.

Petrosky showed his badge. "I'm sorry to disturb you at this hour, but we're looking for a man who works for your company."

"Officers, I have thousands of employees. Surely you don't think I can keep track of—"

"We believe Hannah Montgomery knows him personally and this was the forwarding address given at her apartment. Is she available?"

"She's resting." Harwick paused, then opened the door wider. "Come in and I will get her." He glanced down at their shoes, thick with snow.

Petrosky knocked the snow off on the stoop, Morrison followed suit, and they squeaked into the biggest living room Petrosky had ever seen.

"Can I offer you gentlemen something? Coffee perhaps?"

"No thank you, sir."

Harwick gestured to a set of enormous leather couches. "Make yourselves comfortable. I will be right back." He walked to the back of the room and disappeared through an archway at the far corner.

Morrison goggled. "Holy shit, this place is crazy!"

"Looks like Hannah is moving up. A few months ago she was dating our suspect and now—"

Petrosky stopped talking as a striking blond in a blue silk robe emerged from the back hallway. She strode to the couch and sat across from them, posture erect.

"Evening, ma'am," Morrison said.

"Evening."

Petrosky did a double take. "Ms. Montgomery?" Some detective he was. His head swam. Maybe it was the shot of Jack he'd had when Morrison got out of the car to piss, but he didn't think so. This wasn't normal. She wasn't normal. People don't just change, not like that. If there was a magic formula to boost someone's self-esteem and quell anxiety overnight, McCallum would be out of a fucking job.

"Oh, yeah." She touched a blond curl. Her face shone. "I changed my hair." She looked at Petrosky. "What can I do for you?"

"James Clark is wanted for questioning. Do you have any idea where he might be?"

Now her face paled. "Is this about the murders? Jake?"

"Yes, ma'am."

She twisted the hem of her robe in her fist. "I ... oh my god, no, I mean, I haven't seen him. Jesus."

"Is everything okay here?" Harwick marched toward them and Petrosky's hackles rose.

"Yes, sir," Morrison said.

"When was the last time you spoke to him?" Petrosky asked her. "If you have any idea where he might be, any information at all ... it's important that we locate him."

She twisted her robe harder, the fabric tightening against her thigh like a coiled snake. Harwick sat beside her and put his hand on her knee, gently stroking her with his thumb until she dropped the hem of her robe. Her shoulders relaxed. "I have no idea where he is." Her voice was soft, but crisp, without a trace of the anxiety they had just witnessed.

Harwick must be one hell of a goddamn guy. Not that it took much to be more stable than her ex. Montgomery looked at Harwick, expectant, as if waiting for him to make everything all better. Petrosky's eyes narrowed. Then again, being too dependent was how abusive relationships got started. And she was vulnerable to that abusive bullshit, if her relationship with Campbell was any indication.

Petrosky eyed Harwick. Harwick watched Montgomery, hand still on her leg.

Protective, or possessive?

Montgomery shot to her feet and Petrosky reared back on the couch. "Wait! Noelle might know. She was going out with Thomas tonight."

She padded into the kitchen and returned with her cell phone at her ear. "—it's really important. Okay, bye." She sat and leaned against Harwick, phone in hand. "I had to leave a message."

Petrosky held out his business card as he and Morrison stood. "If you think of anything else—"

Harwick took the card. "Detectives, if he shows up for work on Monday, I will have security bring him down and detain him. Do you have any reason to think he would show up here?"

Petrosky hesitated.

"No, sir," Morrison said.

Montgomery put her head against Harwick's shoulder.

It's more than happiness, Petrosky thought. *She knows she's safe.*

If only I could have given Julie that kind of security.

But feeling *safe doesn't actually mean you* are *safe.*

Petrosky's stomach churned, acid rising until it felt like it was burning a hole straight through to his heart.

Harwick led them to the front door. "Thank you for your diligence. I hope you find him soon."

Suave motherfucker. "I hope so too, sir."

The door clicked shut. Petrosky paused on the porch, listening for anything amiss—a scream from inside or a subtle thud. But there was only the wind, howling around his ears. Maybe Harwick really was a decent guy. Maybe she really was secure and content and happy.

Morrison snickered as they climbed into the car. "It really is amazing what a rich guy can do for a woman."

Petrosky jerked his cigarette pack from the console. "No wonder my ex-wife left."

"I thought she married a construction worker."

"Thanks a lot, *dude.*"

SUNDAY, NOVEMBER 29TH

My back was still tingling the next day, as if Dominic's fingers had etched their imprint on my skin. I barely noticed the stiff chair in Tammy's office, or the way her lips were pursed with displeasure. Thus far, we'd covered the usual rigmarole about how I was feeling about Jake's death, how work was going, and what else was new. What was new was that things were generally ... okay. It felt good to say that out loud and actually mean it. I'd been a little worried when I'd gotten Noelle's voicemail again this morning, but Dominic had assured me she was fine. She'd probably just slept over at Thomas's. It was silly to worry before you had something to worry about, he'd told me. Tammy might have said that to me in the past, but when Dominic said it, I believed him.

"Are you sure you've been okay? You missed your last appointment." There was a hint of disapproval in Tammy's voice.

I prepared myself for the guilt. I felt none.

"I feel like things are going a lot better," I said, instead of apologizing. "I've definitely been feeling better overall. More optimistic, I guess."

Tammy made a note in the file in front of her. "How about your sleep?"

"Better, at least sometimes."

"What about the rest of the time?"

I shrugged. "It's hard to say. Some nights I sleep better than I ever have. Some nights I have bad dreams and wake Dominic. He seems to have a calming effect on me, though." *And he actually knows about my past and understands me, unlike you.*

Tammy nodded thoughtfully. If something ever happened to my shrink, someone could make her life-sized bobble head twin and it would be just as effective as she was now.

"It is possible that his presence makes you feel safer. It is also possible that the days you sleep better are the result of less outside stress, maybe fewer work issues. Is this increase in quality sleep usually on the weekends?"

I furrowed my brows. *Was it?* No, some days I showed up to work in the middle of the week, ready to take on the world. And sometimes, I had to sleep in on Sunday because I'd tossed and turned all night long. I shook my head.

Tammy put a finger to her lips. "Before attributing these improvements in sleeping patterns to another person, perhaps you should look in your journal, at your sleep recording exercise. I don't want you giving all the credit to someone else."

Like, someone besides you? "I'll look, but so far, I haven't noticed any patterns. Seems random."

Tammy stood. "Take another look and see what you can find. We will talk about it next week."

Why do shrinks use shock treatment?
To prepare patients for their bills!

"Next Saturday, nine o'clock? I can't do Sunday again."

I nodded, but I was already tuning her out.

I don't need her anymore. I only need him.

I DROVE BACK to Dominic's house and let myself in. *No,* I corrected myself. *Our house.* My heart felt as if it had sprouted wings.

I glanced at the clock on the oven and caught a reflection of my face, grinning like an idiot. It was only ten. Dominic wouldn't be home until eleven-thirty.

What to do?

I could watch TV, but I wasn't really in the mood. I could try Noelle again, but I didn't want to be all stalker-y, especially since she was probably busy with her boyfriend. Even Duke was out at the groomer's.

I frowned and peered across the living room, toward the far archway. After Dominic's twilight poetry reading, the library was fast becoming my favorite room. I could still hear his voice in there if I concentrated: *I seem to have loved you in numberless forms, numberless times ... In life after life, in age after age, forever.*

Maybe I could find something beautiful to read to him.

The library welcomed me with the subtly sweet scent of old books and furniture polish. *I wonder where he stuck that poetry book.* I headed to the back wall of shelves and ran my finger along the spines, each uniform ridge a smooth transition to the next book. *A History of the World. Economics: Past, Present, Future. Global Transactions.*

A little much for light Saturday morning reading, I thought, though picturing him reading the educational stuff made my heart swell. That was the side he showed to the world: the businessman, the intellectual. His softer side he showed only to me.

Thump. My hand stopped at a thick text sticking out further than the rest on the top shelf. I pulled it down. *Poems for the lovestruck, here I come!*

I looked at the cover and frowned.

Through the Looking Glass? That does not sound like poetry. The pages rippled when I leafed through them. Nope, not poetry.

Or maybe it was?

> Tweedledum and Tweedledee
> Agreed to have a battle;
> For Tweedledum said Tweedledee
> Had spoiled his nice new rattle.

Hmm. So some regular story, some poetry, and the occasional photo of chessboards or rabbits or obese children. Weird, but whatever. It had to be better than *Economics* and I could always find a romantic poem later.

I walked to the couch, stretched out with my back against the arm rest, and dove in.

"Any signs of physical harm?" Petrosky asked.

The baby-faced rookie shook his head. "Nah, she just freaked out when he tried to get fresh. Went running into the woods. A group from a nearby house was out there roasting marshmallows and saw her before he even caught up. He did have handcuffs in his trunk though, so who knows what he had planned."

"Thanks for calling Morrison before you called Graves."

"Hey, you guys are dicks less often. Not a *lot* less, but still."

"I'll get you a donut tomorrow."

"Make it a cruller."

"Deal." Petrosky dismissed him with a wave and tapped the file with his thumb. James Clark, born Robert Fredricks, had completed his engineering degree during his five-year prison stint, and had somehow managed to score a respectable position at Harwick Technical Solutions. He had been up here in Michigan for less than two years: plenty of time to get comfortable and to explore out-of-the-way places to dump half a dozen bodies. And it took a cool head to go to work and smile every day with some woman's blood still under your fingernails. *Manipulative. Calculating.* Then there were the photo souvenirs.

Everything fit. Almost too nicely.

Petrosky squinted at his suspect through the one-way mirror.

Fredricks's face was impassive, his fingers laced on the tabletop in front of him. His blue eyes raked the room as if looking for something. Probably someone else's daughter.

Fucking bastard.

Petrosky's fist clenched around the file. He squared his shoulders and marched into the interrogation room, letting the door slam behind him.

"So, Jimmy, I just got back from your place. You live a long way from the office."

Fredricks stared at him. "It's quiet there." His voice was bland, but with an edge, as if he were struggling to keep it even.

"Try again."

A manic rapping sounded under the table. Fredricks's foot. He was nervous, panicked even. How nervous had he been when he was slicing through his victims' bellies, torturing them, until they probably begged for death?

"I couldn't live anywhere else. I was supposed to report my residence and my status as a sex offender. Three neighborhoods petitioned before I gave up and went somewhere where no one would care."

That felt like the truth. He let it go for now. "How'd you manage to score such a ripe gig at Harwick Tech?"

Fredricks looked down at his hands. "I put in an application, I think. They called me and I went."

"Once you got here, you met some nice girls, huh?"

Fredricks's jaw worked furiously. His hands balled into fists on the table.

Here we go.

"How about Hannah Montgomery?" Petrosky's heart quickened at her name, but he snuffed the feeling and kept his eyes on the shithead at the table. "She's pretty, isn't she? Is that how you chose the other women? Did you follow her to the shelter?"

Fredricks's face twisted with rage. "She has *nothing* to do with this." Spittle flew from his mouth and landed on the table.

"We're going to make this easy on each other," Petrosky said. "You are going to tell me what I want to know. I am going to pretend that I didn't see the pictures of all the little girls you have at your house. They don't take kindly to pedophiles in prison, though I suspect you already know that."

The blood drained from Fredricks's face. His body listed unsteadily and he caught himself on the table, knuckles white. "I... I... They all told me they were eighteen!"

Fucking liar. "And the dead girls?"

Fredricks stared at him. "What?"

"You're not fooling anyone. You have photos of each of the murder victims in your closet."

Understanding crept across Fredricks's face. His mouth dropped open. "Wait, hang on! I ... those were just—" He collapsed into sobs. "I just liked the pictures, the excitement. I paid them all. They ... they all went home. Oh, God—" He wheezed.

Maybe Fredricks would pass out and crack his head open on the floor. The thought was comforting.

"You have young women in your past who almost didn't go home. Remember Charlotte Ostick?"

Fredricks paled still more. His lips opened and closed in manic little movements as if his brain was working far too quickly for his mouth.

"She almost died too," Petrosky said savagely. "You didn't bring her inside a building, though. You anally raped her, beat her, and left her in a fucking field to die from internal bleeding. Would she have been your first, Jimmy? Did the fact that a twelve-year-old girl survived make you rethink your locations so a well-meaning farmer wouldn't find your victims before they were beyond saving? Maybe this shit isn't as satisfying if you think they may survive."

Fredricks's tears fell on his clenched, white knuckles. "I tried to stop." It was a whisper. "I ... I couldn't. I hired people. I paid every one of them. They all agreed—"

"Did they agree to die?"

A muffled choking sound.

Choke, fucker.

"I didn't kill anyone!"

"It's all over, Jimmy. Let's work together and I'll make sure your sexual escapades don't get broadcast all over the prison mess hall. Deal?"

"No! I didn't do anything! I mean ... I didn't kill them! You have to believe me!"

"Too late for that, Jimmy. Enjoy prison."

He'd let Fredricks sweat and come back later for his confession.

THE BELL RANG AGAIN. The white shag rug was too soft under Noelle's bare feet, as if toying with her, teasing her with nice comforting things while she waded through the knowledge that she had almost been the next dead girl on the news.

"Noelle, open up!" Hannah's voice. Noelle had called her after Thomas had left this morning because she hadn't wanted to be alone. Now the pine door to her apartment seemed bigger than usual, alien.

The door squealed as Noelle pulled on the knob.

"I'm so glad you're okay!" Hannah threw her arms around her. "I can't believe this."

"Me either. It's just ..." She really didn't want to talk about it. Not now. Noelle stepped back, her jaw dropping when she saw Hannah's face. "What happened to your hair?"

Hannah ran a hand through her blond waves. "Do you like it?" She sounded like she wasn't sure about it, or maybe she was just unsure of Noelle's reaction.

"I love it. Now we can be twins."

Hannah's face lit up. "I don't have the boobs."

"Now that you landed a rich dude, you can inflate those puppies."

Hannah shrugged. "Eh, Dominic likes them the way they are."

They sat on the loveseat bought with her late father's money, the very least he could contribute to her life. Noelle suddenly wondered if things would have been different if he were still alive. Would she have called him to tell him she was okay? What would he have done besides vow litigation and his firm's involvement in a high profile case? At least she had Thomas. He had stayed with her all night, holding her and apologizing for suggesting she go out with Jim. He'd probably never forgive himself. She understood that feeling.

Noelle's stomach knotted. "I still feel like an idiot," she whispered.

"Me too. To think that Jim might have killed Jake, that I might have played a part in that is just …" Hannah leaned back against the couch. "But there's no way we could have known. That guy fooled everybody. I used to get nervous around him and I still didn't suspect that he was … you know … that kind of crazy. And if Dominic hired him he must have been a damn good faker, because Dominic's no fool."

"It's one thing to see someone in a job interview and another to be in the same room over and over again and just not … see it. I'm so … stupid."

Hannah searched Noelle's eyes. "You're smarter than you think. Give yourself some credit, everyone else does. Hell, Dominic was shocked when he found out. Said you had a good head on your shoulders and that Jim must have been a really good faker."

"Yeah, maybe."

Had Dominic really said that?

"Plus, there's the way you strong-armed your way out of there. Like a freaking kick boxer."

Noelle almost smiled. "It was kinda bad ass." Thomas had compared her to Wonder Woman. "Hopefully I never have to do it again, though I think Thomas might be sticking around. So no more serial killer dates for me."

"He's not a no-good murdering psycho, is he?"

Noelle laughed. "I sure as hell hope not. He'd have a hard time explaining his comic book fascination to other inmates. Same with that cat."

"Thomas might have weird hobbies, but at least he was honest about them. He put his weirdness right up front. It's scary how Jim seemed so normal. But he must have just pretended so he could fit in."

Noelle shrugged. "Even psychos need to have a life, I guess."

Hannah squeezed her hand. "Everybody does."

THURSDAY, DECEMBER 3RD

No out, no help, no hope. Robert's will to fight had disappeared the first day he'd begged his attorney to believe him.

"I'm not sure what to tell you," the troll of a man had said. "The evidence is pretty compelling. You don't have one single alibi. Pleading guilty should at least make the process easier on you."

"I didn't do anything!" He'd had to clasp his hands together to avoid grabbing his attorney and shaking the shit out of him.

"You did enough to kill any sympathy a jury might have had." The lawyer had tapped his foot, obviously eager to be dismissed and on to a case he had a chance of winning.

"But I didn't kill anyone! How can that not matter?" It was more critical than a lifelong prison sentence. It was a matter of eternity, of salvation versus writhing on a blistering bed of coals.

If I can't get out soon, I will never see her again.

If I stay in here, I am doomed to Hell.

The lawyer had merely shrugged his meaty shoulders. "Consider pleading guilty. It's your best bet." *Because you're bad, Robert.* His innocence was irrelevant. Any attorney he hired would see his depravity and seek to punish him.

That had been the beginning of the end. Each day his panic was replaced by a hopelessness that wound itself around his chest, growing tighter and tighter as days turned to nights and back to days again. His face itched from the dark hair that crawled across his lower jaw. There was no mirror in his cell, but he knew his eyes looked like hollow orbs, blank and eerily unexpressive as if the life had been sucked right out of him.

And it had.

He left his food tray on the floor of his cell, untouched. He spent his days sitting silently on the cot, searching the cinderblock wall for some answer to his plight, refusing to speak to another soul.

But he listened. He had always listened. And the more he ignored the world that had forsaken him, the louder the voices became.

And into the gates of Hell, the sinners of the world shall pass. A woman from his father's church whispered the words into his ear, her beautiful blond locks shimmering against his cheek, awakening the lust in his belly.

Those whose hearts are pure are temples of the Holy Spirit. He saw Mindy Jacobs writhing underneath him, her eyes vacant, St. Lucy's words crackling from her lips with the hiss of Hellfire.

He stood in the dark and pulled the sheet from his bed.

Only the chaste man and the chaste woman are capable of true love. And it was the girl in the field, her scrawny hip bones sharp under his hands as he threw her over a hay bale and forced himself into her, her insides rupturing, his thighs covered in her blood.

He looped the sheet around the pipe in the ceiling and tied a smaller loop close enough that his feet would not touch the ground when it was time.

And your sins will follow you, casting you down away from those who sought the love of Jesus Christ, your immortal soul to be punished, writhing in agony for all eternity, for the sins of the flesh you cannot escape. Hannah came to him now, his Hannah, smiling as he climbed the bars to the top of the cell. He gripped the pipe with one hand and slid his head through the knotted cotton.

Do not be afraid; our fate cannot be taken from us. All of them chorused in unison, each lustful apparition pleased with his penance as they'd never been pleased before. He deserved this. Always had. He closed his eyes and released himself into the abyss. Tightness seared his throat and he lurched, his feverish fingers clawing at the noose as his feet kicked air. A rush of blood blistered his face as his airway constricted—demons preparing him for the heat of eternity.

He opened his eyes. Below him, his father smiled knowingly as Robert swung from the hanging tree in front of his childhood home, a final sunset blazing red in the distance like the blood that had been spilled there long before his time. The crimson orb sank silently into darkness. Above him, pinpricks of light twinkled into existence and swelled until he was blinded by their brilliance.

Robert raised his sightless eyes to the heavens and smiled.

FRIDAY, DECEMBER 4TH

She lay on the couch, arm extended, palm open to the sky as if she were begging for something. A needle hung from one swollen vein. He wondered if it would eventually rip free. If he stayed there long enough, he might get to watch it happen.

He knelt in front of her. She stared at him, unfocused, unseeing, not really there at all. In a way, she never had been.

A white crust clung to her blue lips, and a slippery trail of vomit ended in a milky puddle on the floor. Her chest rose and fell, again and again. Much too fast, much too shallow.

He touched her hand. Cold.

A single tear trailed a path down her face. He traced it with his finger.

He did not cry. He did not understand the gesture. As if watery eyes made bad things any less terrible. Not that this was bad.

He looked at the Mickey Mouse watch he had found, dropped by some john, the only thing that was just his. Twelve minutes, he guessed; it would take twelve minutes before she stopped breathing altogether. That was seven hundred and twenty seconds. Most five-year-olds did not know their multiplication tables, but he did, from counting out baggies of drugs and figuring out how long it took for her to sleep off a hit. It was safer to be hidden before she woke up.

He pulled a banana from a bag on the table, the latest delivery from the church outreach. They smelled even better now that he would not have to share them. Her breath quickened, then slowed abruptly. He peeled the fruit and counted out the seconds in earnest.

Five hundred and forty-two, five hundred and forty-three—

The life drained from her in a matter of seconds. He watched her eyes, trying to catch a glimpse of ... something. But there was nothing. She was no less dull in death than she had been in life.

He sighed. Off by one hundred and seventy-seven seconds. He hated to be wrong, even if it was not by much. Perhaps eventually, if he practiced enough, he would get better at guessing things like that.

He took a bite of the banana and walked to the bathroom. It would be a few days before anyone noticed her missing. Probably around four days, six hours and forty-six minutes. He calculated the day and time he expected the first knock at the door, and wrote his guess in eyeliner on the bathroom mirror so he would be reminded of his success ... or failure. He dropped the pencil in the sink—

And awoke.

He turned to the clock. *Five oh five.* Thirty-five minutes before the alarm. Too late to go back to sleep. He might as well get up and make coffee.

In the kitchen he scooped grounds into the espresso machine, blinking sleep from his eyes. A pillow of steam escaped with a raspy whisper.

What a strange dream. Or memory. Not that it mattered.

They had shielded his eyes when they removed him from the apartment, though any idiot would know he had already seen it. By then his mother's body had been a nest of ants on the damp, putrid sofa; even the bodily fluids had stopped leaking onto the untreated floor, though he had been surprised by how long that part had taken. *Three days, four hours, six minutes.*

The car ride to the hospital had taken twenty-four minutes. When they arrived, men in white coats tore the watch from his hand and forced him onto a bed. He had fought violently until a sharp prick in his buttocks made him slip away into nothingness.

Three days, twelve hours and thirty-two minutes later, he escaped from his room and fled down the maze of hallways. When the trailing footsteps got too near, he ducked into a room in a dark back corner. The woman in the bed had reached for him, zombie-like. He'd watched, fascinated.

From the chair, a man's voice, not like his, but like his all the same. "That was a hug."

He did not respond, just watched the man with the buzz cut.

"My wife loves to hug. She likes to do a lot of things that never made sense to me. Her face was an open book that I couldn't read. I understand now, though."

He and the man stared at each other, playing a silent game of wits.

"You don't get it either," the man said simply. "We're not like other people."

He looked at the man's shoes. They were the shiniest things he had ever seen.

"You'll learn," the man told him.

THE ORDERLIES DISCOVERED him asleep in the chair next to the woman and took him back to his room. Twenty-six hours and five minutes later the man appeared at his bedside.

"My wife's dying," the man said.

They listened to the beeping of the heart monitor.

"Your mom's already dead." The man pulled a chair to the side of his bed. "You're on your way to foster care. I hear it's a pretty awful place."

Beep ... Beep ... Beep ...

"So what did they do to you when you got here? Strip your clothes? Take your things?"

Beep ... Beep ... Beep ...

The man nodded. "You don't feel a thing, do you?"

Beep ... Beep ... Beep ...

"I understand. It works wonderfully in the military, being numb enough to shoot the enemy in the face or leave your comrade behind. But you need to use it differently out here."

"How?" His own voice sounded foreign after so many days spent in silence, avoiding the questions of the hospital staff.

"You'll learn," the man said again. "People like us always can."

The man sat in the chair for one minute and twenty-two seconds before he spoke again. "Would you like to hear a story to pass the time? It was my wife's favorite." The man opened the small brown book in his lap without waiting for a reply.

"The Walrus and the Carpenter
  Were walking close at hand:
  They wept like anything to see
  Such quantities of sand:"

He closed his eyes and tried to pretend he was free and walking along the beach, or even just along the sidewalk. Anywhere but this place where he had no choice but to bend to the will of those larger and stronger.

"'Oh oysters come and walk with us!'
  The Walrus did beseech.
  'A pleasant walk, a pleasant talk,
  Along a briny beach.'"

Maybe one day he would see sand, ocean, waves.

"'It seems a shame,' the Walrus said

To play them such a trick.'"

The oysters were idiots to follow the walrus in the first place, he had thought. They deserved what they got.

Three days, twelve hours and thirty-two minutes after his hospital admission he had run into Linda Harwick's hospital room. Six days, four hours and eight minutes later, he went home in the custody of Rupert Harwick. That period was the most vital nine days, sixteen hours and forty minutes of his life.

A final belch of steam poured from the espresso maker. Dominic grabbed a cup from the cupboard, poured a steaming mug and finished it with a squeeze of lemon.

His footsteps were nearly soundless on the stairs. The upstairs rugs swallowed the tap of his slippers. In the bedroom, Hannah lay sprawled out on her stomach, the sheets pulled up to the middle of her back, her arms in disarray.

Like a common drunk, he thought. He noted the way her hair lay on her back in disordered waves, rising and falling as she drew breath.

He thought of Linda Harwick, her stiff form, the casket, the guilt-ridden mourners. Unlike his own mother, whose death had been of no consequence to anyone, Linda had apparently been useful to many, including her husband.

Marrying Hannah could work. That might be more useful in the future.

But not nearly as much fun as watching her bleed.

He sipped his espresso and peered through the skylight where the gray was just beginning to show through the freezing winter clouds. It would be so easy, so—

She rolled onto her back and wrinkled her nose. Her arm rested across her breasts now, the outline of her rib cage visible beneath the thin silk sheet. Her cheeks flushed pink, the warm color a beacon of vitality.

She is lovely, he thought. Like an antique vase, or a really nice leather briefcase. He wondered if she would keep that warm, elegant quality, or if it would fade immediately as she expired, her diminishing color turning her just as bland as anyone else. He guessed the latter. Time would tell. Maybe.

He glanced at her pale throat, incandescent in the dimness.

Too easy, he thought. When the time came, if the time came, he would draw it out. He would watch her recoil and thrash and writhe. And he would relish every moment. It wasn't as if he'd miss her.

SATURDAY, DECEMBER 5TH

Snowflakes pelted the skylights and blocked out the sun, like the room was wrapped in a protective blanket.

Dominic was already awake and typing on his laptop, his eyes jumping in concentration. From across the room I took in the curves of his toned body in flannel pants and a white T-shirt. That tiny curl of dark hair that sometimes snuck to his forehead. *Delicious*.

He looked up.

I smiled. "Morning."

"Good morning," he said. "I didn't wake you, did I?"

"No." I rolled onto my side toward him. "Though I wouldn't mind if you had."

He set the computer aside, a touch of a smile at the corner of his mouth. "I have meetings all day, and then this evening there's that new-hire welcome I told you about last week."

"But it's Saturday."

He chuckled, climbed into the bed next to me and leaned close to my ear. "Let's say I wake you up appropriately, then come back home and put you to bed even more nicely?"

I snuggled against him. "Anything you say, sir."

His fingers sank into me and I forgot everything else.

I was still in bed when he emerged from the closet dressed in gray pinstripes and a tailored blue shirt that set off his eyes.

"Hurry back."

He pinched my nipple. "You know I will." Then he was gone.

I stretched my still-throbbing muscles and headed to the weight room, nude.

My workout clothes hung from the hook on the wall, where they belonged. I tugged them on, climbed on the treadmill and appraised my face in the mirror. I looked different, and it wasn't just the hair.

I smiled. My reflection smiled back. Then I turned up the speed, pushing myself harder than usual, testing my limits.

I can do it. I had dealt with trauma and grief, with a crazy father and a crazy boyfriend and a psycho killer colleague. I could deal with running just a little faster.

An hour and a half later I was showered, exhausted and satisfied. I toasted a couple of English muffins and made a beeline for the library. I had a feeling eating in there would be frowned upon, but what he didn't know wouldn't hurt him.

Such a rebel.

I laughed aloud.

I set the plate on the end table and walked to the shelf to grab my book, still tucked into the same place it always had been so Dominic wouldn't know I was reading it. Every time I opened my mouth to tell him, my face got hot and I changed the subject. Maybe I was embarrassed for reading a little kid's book when he was reading about economics. Or maybe it was because every time I touched the leather cover, I had a fit of nostalgia, as if I was rediscovering some missed thing from my childhood.

Maybe it is something I missed. While everyone else was reading stuff like this, I was—

I pushed the thought away. I wasn't that girl anymore. I was here now.

The couch beckoned, soft and warm. Even the frozen chess game seemed comforting, a piece of memory steeped in love that I could almost share by being nearby.

The worn book cover was satiny under my fingertips. I took a bite of my muffin and flipped to the page where I'd left off, wondering what Alice would do next.

The department was still riding the wave of praise for catching Robert Fredricks. Graves spent his time strutting around and grinning like a fool for the cameras, but the continuous press conferences were starting to give Petrosky a headache. He assumed that things would die down once the trial began.

Or maybe not. There was plenty of sensational evidence, more than enough to create a media circus. The search warrant had unearthed the photos plus two sets of leather restraints and a bloody scalpel found underneath the kitchen sink behind some cleaning supplies. DNA tests had confirmed the blood belonged to Antoinette and Timothy Michaels,

Fredericks's final victims. The case would be open and shut. Everyone was expecting a conviction, even the court-appointed attorney who'd reluctantly agreed to represent him.

Petrosky closed his notepad and headed for the front of the building where yet another question-and-answer press conference would be held. Graves had given him the opportunity to address the public this time. Maybe because Morrison had told the chief that they, not Graves, had found the lead on Fredricks. Or maybe Graves didn't want to risk stonewalling them and causing a scene when Petrosky hit him in the mouth. Either way, it was about time he got a little respect, even if he'd have preferred a mention in the paper instead of having to give a speech. Maybe that's why that fucker had offered him the speech.

Petrosky pushed the glass doors leading to the outdoor pavilion and the steady buzz of the journalists swelled in his ears. But there was another noise ... flashbulbs? No. Footsteps.

Petrosky turned and raised an eyebrow as he watched Morrison dash toward him up the hallway, red-faced and panting.

"Petrosky! Wait!"

"Come on, dude! Looks like someone needs to hit the gym."

Morrison grabbed the door handle. "We need to talk."

Petrosky glanced at the throng of reporters. "You earned it, Petrosky," Graves had said. It might have been bullshit, but it felt damn good.

"Right now?" Petrosky asked.

"Yeah, now." Morrison released the door handle. "There's not going to be any trial."

THE PLACE REEKED with the noxious mix of urine and feces that hadn't yet been cleaned from the floor. Directly above the small puddle hung remnants of white cloth, presumably the bed sheet that had been looped around ol' Jimmy's neck before they'd cut him down.

Petrosky took a breath through his mouth. *Not good.* "So where is it?"

Morrison grabbed a single sheet of paper from the now bare mattress and handed it to Petrosky.

> Pity, like a naked newborn babe,
> Striding the blast, or heaven's cherubim, horsed
> Upon the sightless couriers of the air,
> Shall blow the horrid deed in every eye,
> That tears shall drown the wind.

Petrosky rubbed his temple. "What the fuck is it with this guy and the rhymes? Who does he think he is?"

"Shakespeare," Morrison said.

Shakespeare. Not the final bloody verse from the poem he'd left at the crime scenes. An uneasy ache settled in Petrosky's stomach. *What the hell was this guy doing?*

He passed the page back to Morrison. "So, Mr. Big Shot literature major, what the hell does it mean?"

Morrison furrowed his brows. "It's about the death of an innocent."

"Lots of innocent women died at his hands." The tattered bed sheet mocked Petrosky from the ceiling, twisting in the draft from the heating vent. The murky light from the hallway stippled the cotton with glaring yellow eyeballs.

Morrison stared at the poem. "Yeah, they did. It could be a confession, I guess. A way to say, 'Hey I killed a bunch of innocent people.' But I don't think he thought those women were innocent."

If not the girls, then who? The kid? His killer had found the women repugnant; had to in order to tear them apart like that. And from what Petrosky had seen, the killer wasn't sorry, either. There had been no tears to drown the wind. A tourniquet ringed his abdomen, squeezing bile into his throat.

It's not a confession.
It's a warning.

SATURDAY, DECEMBER 5TH

THE HOTEL BALLROOM teemed with three hundred or so local engineers already under the umbrella of Harwick Technical Solutions. They milled around like sheep, jostling one another to get to the hors d'oeuvres. And the drinks. Dominic eyed them disapprovingly, but never long enough for them to notice.

A few came up to shake the hands of the other managers. The more daring employees approached him as well, and were rewarded for their temerity with a handshake and a broad smile that was convincing enough. They'd not recognize his disdain, not while they were half drunk and clambering for his approval. They were all broken, troubled, sick, each with something to prove. And the right level of disturbance paired with the right job ensured he would spend his days watching his bottom line climb ever higher, even as his workers cried themselves to sleep or fucked little kids or beat their wives or sliced through their own skin with razor blades. Some of them were even like … him.

And numbers never lied.

He listened to snippets of conversation as he walked to the bar.

"Did you hear about Jim? I met him at a quality control meeting last year—"

"Yeah, that was crazy. He looked totally normal in his picture—"

Dominic ordered a sparkling water and scanned the room.

Jim had seemed totally normal, but guys like that never changed. Dominic had counted on that when he sought the man out. If Jim had suddenly done a one-eighty, it would have been a statistical anomaly. Dominic had put his money on the math. And on the tracking chip he'd installed on Jim's—Robert's—car.

He took his drink.

"Did you hear that wasn't even his real name?"

"I heard he changed it before he sent in his resume—"

The game had been fun while it had lasted. But there would always be time for another round as long as he examined the opportunities around him. Stayed one step ahead of the rest. His father had shown him that much—that, and how a dismally boring existence could be transformed the first time you held someone's still pulsing organs in your hand.

As Dominic walked back to his table, the sea of people parted for him. A man wearing a dark blue suit jacket and a hopeful expression sidled up to him. Dominic forced himself to look pleased.

Idiots. He shook the man's hand. *Fucking Oysters.*

SOMETHING MOLTEN SCORCHED MY INSIDES, the flick of a lighter before the flame. On the table next to me, the English muffin had long since grown cold. I reached for it blindly, registering the clatter of the plate on wood, but it seemed far away. The book sat open on my lap, the page invisible despite how hard I stared at it.

It isn't possible.

The book closed in slow motion, as if my hand were disconnected from my body. Then the bookcase was before me, the book sliding into its place, though I didn't remember getting up.

Books. So many books.

Anyone could have that book. It's just a coincidence.

I took the plate to the sink, scrubbed it with shaking hands and turned to the dishwasher. The plate slipped and shattered against the marble floor.

The broom. The sweeping. Don't think. I took slow, deliberate breaths into quivering lungs. My chest hurt.

This is ridiculous. Talk about an overreaction.

It's okay. Just go read something else.

Yeah, something not connected to a series of violent killings.

Stop it, Hannah.

I dumped the glass shards in the trash. The kitchen was alive, pulsing in time to my heart. My legs wobbled and I grabbed the counter. I really was crazy.

I staggered into the living room over white marble that suddenly seemed cold and rude and indignant. *It's just a floor, Hannah.* The nearly invisible seam up on the ceiling watched me, waiting to distract me with the hidden television.

I need to rest. Just rest.

I AWOKE to a high-pitched voice talking about a flood in Indonesia. The last thing I remembered, I had been watching some game show.

I pushed myself upright and brushed matted hair from my face.

Note to self: No sleeping on leather.

Why do I feel so strange?

On the screen, a swirling torrent of water crashed into the side of a building, obliterating the foundation and washing it out to sea. The scene shifted to a woman in a newsroom saying something about requests for aid.

There are plenty of people far worse off than you.

Yeah, because nothing is wrong with your life.

I squeezed my eyes shut.

One little coincidence and I almost lost my shit.

"In breaking news," the woman said, "New information has been released on the man responsible for seven deaths in or near the Metro Detroit area. His violent killing spree began on October first with the murder of a prostitute in Ash Park and culminated on November twenty-sixth when another woman and her young child were found brutally murdered in an abandoned school."

November twenty-sixth ...

"Channel Eight is here on the scene where sources say that Robert Fredricks died earlier this afternoon—"

I put my hands over my ears, but the thoughts kept coming. I grabbed my phone off the coffee table and pulled up my web browser.

Don't do this again.

October first, November twenty-sixth ...

I punched in keywords until I found what I was looking for. Dread bloomed in my abdomen. I ran to my purse and yanked out my journal, flipping through scribbled sleeping notes. Here, I slept. There, I didn't.

A coincidence, just a coincidence.

My sleep hadn't changed until I had moved in here. I ran a shaking finger down the pages.

I slept better when other people were dying, and in the days leading up to those times.

Gotta have time to case a victim.

Stop it, Hannah. You're just a little tired today.

Does that mean someone else is dead?

It didn't even make sense. How do you get someone to sleep on demand?

You hold their hand and bring them orange juice. Or make them dinner.

But that would mean he ... what? Drugged me?

No. No way. I dropped the journal and put away my phone.

You're crazy, Hannah.

But I couldn't stop thinking, couldn't stop moving. What if I was wrong? I had been wrong about Jake. Maybe I was wrong about ... everything.

My feet flew through the living room and up the stairs, independent of coherent thought. In the bathroom, I tore through the medicine cabinet like a possessed raccoon, tossing bottles and scattering toothpicks, cotton balls, gauze.

Nothing.

I snatched at the drawers underneath the sink and rummaged through the linen closet. In the bedroom, I searched under the mattress, behind the bed posts, around the night tables.

My heart slowed.

This is crazy. You're crazy. It has to be a coincidence.

But it wasn't. I knew it in my core, somewhere unmentionable and primitive, just as I had known my love for my father was wrong. A nest of weasels in my chest scampered into my brain, into my lungs, until their clawing feet were all I could hear, feel, sense.

Then his voice. *Just don't clean my man cave.*

I ran. The bright light of the workout room assaulted my eyes. I wrenched open the closet door. Bleach, towels, rags, buckets. The buckets were empty. Towels flew over my shoulder, cleaning rags ripped from their resting place. Dull thuds, empty swishes of cloth, and then, the telltale clatter of plastic on rubber. I fell to my knees next to a small, unlabeled, orange bottle and poured a few of the pills into my shaking palm. Small and blue. No telltale markings that made any sense to me.

It's probably just a painkiller for if he overdoes his workout.

Unlabeled in the back of the closet?

I pulled out my phone, fumbled it against my thigh, and called up photos for medicine identification. There were thousands, but you could narrow it by shape and color and type. Blue. Oval. What helped you calm down? Tammy had recommended them once and I'd refused. *Shit.* Narcotics? No. *Benzodiazepines.* I stopped scrolling.

Xanax. Five milligrams.

It was identical.

Maybe he was suffering from anxiety and I had accidentally ingested the pills.

Then why were they in the closet, the one place I had been told not to go?

The bottle went into my pocket. I watched my numb fingers fold the towels and put them back on the shelf.

Run, Hannah! Run!

I folded the rags and put away the buckets.

What the fuck are you doing? Get out now!

When everything was in place, I walked downstairs to the living room, my legs not quite connected to me, but moving, still moving. I opened the flue and started the gas fireplace. Then I retrieved my journal and flung it into the hole.

Oily flames licked the cover and the cardboard crinkled and disintegrated. The urge to reach in and salvage the burning pages tugged at my arm, as if by keeping the journal I could save what was left of my dreams. When the inner pages curled in the heat, I let the tears fall. Fear thrummed through my veins, thick, liquid, and scorching.

No one can ever know.

My lungs cracked and shriveled, wrenched in an iron fist of hopelessness. As much as I tried to wish it away, his secret was mine now, locked forever in the ashes on the fireplace floor. I wiped my tears with the back of my hand. If he was a monster, then I was just as much a monster for loving him so much.

I have failed every man I ever loved.
I cannot fail again.

I sat on the couch to wait for him.

PETROSKY SUCKED smoke deep into his lungs and blew it at the no-smoking sign on the wall next to his desk. He needed a stiff drink—several, actually. But he couldn't bring himself to leave.

Since discovering Fredricks's body, he'd gone over the case again and again. Fredricks had to have been their killer. It was the simplest explanation, the obvious explanation. They had a mountain of evidence.

Just not a confession.

Fredricks's eyes blazed in his memory—and the way he'd turned hostile when Petrosky had mentioned Hannah Montgomery. Hostile but almost … protective. Their guy was supposed to be a sadistic psychopath, removed from all human emotion. But Fredricks had *cared*.

Maybe he was a good faker. Petrosky had seen that before.

Or maybe you're wrong.

He flicked ashes onto the floor. If he was wrong, then the real killer must have followed Fredricks, preying on the women he abused after he was done with them. That left Jacob Campbell—the biggest question mark in this whole ordeal. Fredricks had a motive to kill Campbell, if only to free Montgomery for himself. If he was lonely enough, desperate enough, crazy enough to think no one else would do … Petrosky could see it. And who else had that motive? Certainly not her new guy. That high-horse-riding motherfucker only had to look at her and she would have followed him home, just like most of the women in America.

Petrosky sighed. Something wasn't making sense.

You're losing your shit, Petrosky.
Hannah isn't Julie. Hannah's fine.

Trying to ignore the gnawing in his gut, he shoved the folders into the drawer, slammed it closed, and marched out of the precinct. He would not waste any more time driving himself fucking crazy. He was already close enough.

SATURDAY, DECEMBER 5TH

I STOOD by the wall of windows, veiled in moonlight.

Dominic stepped into the middle of the room, ten feet away, though it felt like a chasm separated us. Even in the dark, the moonlight reflecting off the white marble illuminated him like a figure in a shadow box and I could see nothing else. The howl of the night wind faded. I could sense his very breath sucking the air from the room.

"Hannah?"

His voice was almost enough to undo everything I had been thinking.
He has been so good to me.

He stepped forward, and terror buzzed frantic through my body.

"Hannah, are you—"

"Why?" It came out a choked whisper, like my brain was trying to tell me to just shut the fuck up before I gave away what I knew. But my heart needed to hear his confession, needed to know for sure, so I didn't spend my whole life wondering whether this was nothing but the wild imagination of another fucked-up girl with a fucked-up daddy.

"Why what?"

I tossed him the bottle. He snatched it out of the air.

"You drugged me."

He pocketed the bottle. "I thought you needed more sleep."

He's lying. They all lie.

"Did you ever love me?"

If he loves me, maybe everything is going to be okay.

Hannah, that's crazy.

He's never hurt me.

Just drugged you senseless.

"I needed you," he said.

He needs me. Maybe I can help him. If he knows it was wrong, we can make this better together. No one else has to know. I can fix this.

"I need you too," I whispered, taking a step forward. We had each other. It wasn't too late.

"You may be misunderstanding the situation," he said.

The air in the room changed suddenly, like a draft from an open window freezing my marrow as it crept up my arms and into my chest. But there was no window, no opening to the elements that would have caused such a chill. "I know you did some things that were—" It stuck in my throat. I didn't even know what the words were for something like this. "You're not a bad person. Let me help."

"You did help," he said softly. "You made me normal."

I couldn't breathe. Jesus fucking Christ, I couldn't breathe.

Emotional thinking never leads to anything good.

But ... don't you feel anything about all this?

Not really.

Pretending to be normal is the best way to make people think you are.

"That's why you gave me the pills. So you could ... leave?"

He watched me, silent.

"And I would be your alibi because I didn't know any different."

I waited for him to tell me it wasn't true, but he didn't deny it, just fixed his gaze on me as my heart thrashed in my frozen chest.

"Did Jim help? Did he talk you into it?" Hope sputtered, tried to catch.

"Jim can't keep his dick in his pants. He never could."

"But that doesn't—"

"Jim was predictable in his compulsions and statistically likely to fuck up. Sometimes people don't do what you expect them to, but when they do, there is nothing more rewarding." A corner of his mouth turned up. I couldn't tell if it was a smile or a snarl.

Outside, the frozen moon ducked behind a cloud, casting us into dusky shadow. A shoe clacked on the floor, and another. The moon reemerged and he was nearer now, six feet and closing. His face was clear, as beautiful as a marble sculpture. I fought hysteria. "He could have killed Noelle!"

Dominic crept forward. I slid backwards on my fluffy socks.

"I doubt that."

"What are you—"

"His wasn't that kind of damage."

Hot coals in my chest fanned into flame and singed my lungs. "Did you choose me because I was damaged?"

"Yes."

"But you ... you helped me, helped to fix me—"

But then I knew: helping me had been a side effect, not the goal.

What was the goal? He clearly hadn't fixed those other women. Or Timmy. Or... Jake.

He killed for me. He loves me.

No he doesn't. He's going to kill me.

It wasn't a question. His face mutated into a mask of predatory excitement. Adrenaline zinged from me to him and back again, a ricochet like a wayward bullet.

My muscles coiled in anticipation.

He lunged, impossibly slow, as if the world had stopped spinning. I leaped sideways and pain shot through my skull as he dragged me by the hair, the room sliding past my socks on the marble as if I were walking on ice. I skidded, flailed, kicked, and pain blazed up my leg through my ankle under the distant sound of shattering glass.

The world wobbled. A dream, just a dream.

I clawed at his fist and he tightened his grip on my hair. Bright orange pain pulsed through the top of my head into my vision, dimming the shadowy white plaster of the moonlit ceiling. Then the white ceiling disappeared. A light flickered on, illuminating deep wood, and I could smell leather and books and my own rank sweat. Rugs. Wood.

He stopped at the bookshelf and reached for something. A sound like a slithering snake hissed in my ear, then a thunk as he threw something on the table. I clung to his arms, tears blurring my vision as the room pulsed black and focused again.

On the table, a box full of silver tools glittered sharply on velvet. A scalpel.

Panic screened my senses and tunneled my vision, and there was only him, the box and the scalpel he grasped. Then I was being dragged again, attached to his fist like a doll, flailing, clawing, kicking until my knee connected with something hard and a clatter reverberated through the room. Chess pieces rained off the table from the toppled board.

He stopped and stared, then jerked me toward him, my feet skidding against the hardwood as he raised the scalpel and plunged it into my upper arm.

Pain—hot, white, exquisite—shot through me. My arm weakened and my hand faltered against his.

He tore the scalpel free and the scent of copper thickened the air.

The pain. Endorphins poured into my bloodstream, smooth and warm. My vision opened. Air filled my lungs.

I wondered how long it would take me to die.

He pulled me out of the library and into the living room, and the ceiling swam, painted in bloody moonlight. Glass jangled around our feet as he dragged me through the kitchen toward the mudroom door.

No, no, no, I cannot leave this house with him. My fingernails dug into his skin, slipping in my blood.

"Dominic, please! I won't, I'll never—"

His chuckle told me there was no point. He'd just make it hurt more. Like my father had.

My pulse thundered in my temples. I could see, feel, smell the cold, dark room where sheets of poetry would be scattered over pieces of my body. Here a foot, there my ear, here my entrails shoved into my dead, gaping mouth.

The pain. Focus.

I drove my palms against his hand, every drop of energy pooling in my wrists, pushing away from his grasp on my hair. An audible grinding screamed inside my head as the roots of my hair cleaved a chunk from my scalp. Wetness dripped over my ear. I crashed to the marble, free.

Run! I scrambled toward the living room, glass from the broken sculpture tearing into my feet, my lungs burning, threatening to implode. His shoes crunched closer, closer. I cut around the couch, slipped and fell to my knees. My fingertips closed around a chunk of broken sculpture—sharp, jagged, deadly.

He bared his teeth and lunged, arms extended.

You're stronger than you think.

I lurched upwards with the piece of broken glass and thrust it into his belly. Blood bloomed across his abdomen in a vibrant red stain. *A dream, just a dream.* I plunged the glass into his flesh again, pushing until the hilt disappeared into the wall of his stomach.

He reached for me again but I leapt backwards, sliding on the glass and on blood that was probably mine, but maybe his too. I tumbled onto my left side and my head struck the floor. The world turned in dizzy circles—some nightmarish alternate universe where I had just stabbed the man I loved. He raised his arm above him in a final gesture of hope.

But the blackness didn't care about hope. It was trying to swallow me. Maybe I wanted it to.

Why couldn't he just love me?

I closed my eyes and let the darkness take me.

SATURDAY, DECEMBER 5TH

NOELLE PULLED the blanket up to her neck, wondering if she should try to sleep some more or just give up and watch television. The nightmares had been decreasing, so she probably wouldn't have another tonight. But that didn't mean she felt like risking it.

The curtain whispered in the dark, rippling in the current of the heat vent. She took a deep breath and blew it out slowly. The attack itself was not what was bothering her. No matter what Jim had planned, she was alive. And he wasn't. The news story about him swinging in his jail cell had been oddly comforting.

All men were assholes.

Well, almost all men.

She exhaled, forcing her frustration into the air.

What am I missing?

She had slapped him when he tried to kiss her, then managed to get her knee in between them enough to pop the car door and roll out. Even in heels, she had torn through the woods until she found someone else, someone to help her. "Like a freaking kickboxer," Hannah had said.

That was the problem. Hannah.

Jim had cried when the police slapped the cuffs on his wrists.

"I need her, Noelle. Please, I need your help! I thought if I could make her jealous ... I just love her so much."

As they'd ducked his head into the car he had stared straight at her, straining against the officers.

"I can save her from him! She will save me, too. Please! I can save her!"

Then he was gone.

Noelle rolled over. Her friend didn't need saving from anyone. Now that Jake was gone, Hannah could finally be happy like she deserved to be. With Dominic.

Maybe I should call her.

Noelle looked at the bedside clock. *12:10 a.m.*

She sighed. Hannah was fine. Waking her up wouldn't do anyone any good. Besides, what was she going to say? *That killer dude wanted to save you from ... uh ... not sure who?*

Thomas's scent clung to her pillow. Her stomach flipped.

Thomas had been Jim's best friend. What if—

She shook her head. Jim was a serious whack job who'd fooled everyone, even his boss. And Thomas was the nicest guy she had ever met. The fact that he was charming, and friendly, and super smart didn't hurt either. Besides, he idolized Superman. How twisted could he be?

She fought the urge to get her phone.

None of this shit mattered anyway. That asshole was dead.

Noelle pushed aside the tingling that ran along the back of her neck and wrapped her arm around the pillow. She'd call Hannah first thing in the morning.

I FELT like I was on a bed of hot coals, skin sizzling under me. The wet throb of my heart pulsed sharp, bright pain through my skull, into my arm and down over my ankle.

Asleep. I was just sleeping. Just dreaming. It'd be over soon.

I opened my eyes. Glittering pieces of broken sculpture peppered the living room. I'd have to clean that up later. And someone had spilled something on the marble, dark and shiny in the moonlight. That would stain if I didn't take care of it.

And ... his legs. Unmoving. Still. Understanding crashed through me. I pushed myself to my knees, my injured arm twitching and throbbing—letting myself hope, for one exquisite moment, that he was not dead.

No.

Dizziness tried to pull me to the floor. He was just sleeping. Tired. Everything would be better in the morning, if only he could take this much needed rest.

I should get him a blanket, I thought suddenly.

But the deep, black pool on the pristine marble was a river I could never go back across. A river that separated who I was now from the semblance of sanity I had so briefly enjoyed. The glass in my knees no longer hurt and I longed for the pain. For now, anything felt like pleasure compared to this aching, pulsing dread that had settled into my stomach like a tumor.

Luminescent moonlight bathed the room, a room where I had been happy and in love just hours before.

Happy, because of him.

My scream echoed off the walls as if searching for someone else to hear, to understand that this was a loss so deep I could never truly recover. He had saved me in every possible way. He had proven to me that I was strong, and I had used that strength to cut him down with brutal finality.

I felt it then, a visceral snapping, a break in the rope that had held me to myself, that had bound me to a world where pain meant you were alive, if only you could put up with it. Dizziness pulled. I pushed back.

I inched forward on knees and forearms. Still-warm blood seeped into my pants, glazed my arms, my hands, my legs, until I felt like I was wrapped in a blanket of gore, coating myself in the essence of what he used to be.

I pulled myself onto him and laid my head on his bloody chest. His body felt warm against my cheek, but not warm enough. And he was still. So still. My heart seized. I gripped his shirt with quivering fingers, listening for any murmur within the recesses of his rib cage.

There was only silence.

Voices began as a tingle in the back of my mind and grew to such a violent swell that I feared they might erupt from my fractured brain and alert passersby to this horrible thing that I had done.

Run, Hannah. Run. Save yourself.

There is nothing to live for.

And suddenly he was there, too, a voice from the past resounding through the blackness in my soul.

You're worthless to anyone but me.

Let me show you how good it feels to make me happy.

I was five years old again, his arm around my shoulder.

Do you love me, Hannah?

Yes, Daddy.

Moonlight glinted off something in the coagulating pool near my knee.

The scalpel. I picked it up. In a way, it had ended him, but just as surely, it had ended me, or what I once had been.

I couldn't let everyone know he had done these things. They wouldn't—couldn't—understand.

He had saved me. I had to find some way to save him, even a small part of him, in death.

There was resistance, a rip like paper tearing, as I brought the scalpel across his belly. His insides were warm, so warm, blood and gore and pieces of him oozing around my fingers as if they were still alive. I got hold of something and pulled. A worm, a tube. I was holding his—

Jesus.

I skittered backwards, feet slipping, stomach convulsing. I was halfway to the couch before I realized I was still gripping his intestines.

"I love you," I whispered, half expecting him to answer.

I tried to stand, but my limbs were heavy, like I was dragging myself through cement. I'd never make it upstairs.

Help me, Dominic. I inched through the living room. In the mudroom, I wrenched the doorknob and fell onto the back porch, the frigid air biting at my face and arms. I dragged myself across the porch, panting and choking on tears. The bathroom door came into focus. *Almost there.*

But someone was watching. Someone who knew what I'd done.

I swallowed bile and peered into the blackness. "Hello?"

No response. But I felt the unseen eyes burning into me like hot pokers. Whoever was there was waiting, biding their time to attack.

Move. Now.

I lurched into the bathroom, slammed the door, and clawed the knob, blindly fumbling for the lock. My fingers were weak, but it clicked. I stumbled into the shower and collapsed against the wall, listening, waiting for the watcher to break down the door and take me.

There was nothing except my ragged breath wheezing in my ears. My oozing skin crackled and stung and throbbed. I braced myself against the wall and stripped off my clothes. Blood seeped from my mangled arm, but slower now. I turned on the water and whimpered, biting my lip as my skin shrieked from a thousand fissures. The basin went red.

I choked back a sob and turned under the spray as the cascade of water took some of the smaller shards, pushed others deeper. The basin turned pink. The wall of the shower wavered.

I turned off the water and peered out from the stall. All was quiet. The towel I wrapped around my breasts would be useless against groping fingers or a blade, but it might at least help stop the worst of the bleeding.

I unlocked the door and scanned the porch.

Nothing. But something. My heart surged.

Whether I ran, tripped or floated I wasn't sure, but suddenly my feet were on marble again. I heaved the deadbolt into place.

Don't look. Out the back windows, tree limbs twisted in the wind and I focused on them, let them guide me forward, past the glass, past the blood, to the stairs and up. I left the stained towel on the floor and dressed my deeper wounds with the bathroom first aid kit and a roll of gauze. Some other cuts were still bleeding but they were small, hopefully small enough to stop on their own.

Don't think. Just move.

Jeans and a sweater. Underwear. Shoes. Q-tips. The hazy room twisted as I sucked in a breath.

I watched the trees through the windows on the way back downstairs and retrieved the book from the library. It vibrated against my skin as I picked my way into the living room—or maybe I was shaking. I dropped the book on the couch and flipped to the last page. *If only it were all a dream, Alice.*

I picked up the Q-tip.

Don't look. It's paint. It's just paint.

When I was done, I laid the book and the makeshift pen on the ashes, stoking the embers with a nearby poker until a flame licked the leather cover, the orange and red caressing the pages, as sensual as his hands had been on my body. Greasy black smoke rose and disappeared into the dark void of the chimney.

I will not fail you.

I stood straighter, pulled by the strings of an invisible puppeteer.

You're stronger than you think.

Everything will be okay.

As the last of the leather curled and crumbled into ash, I retrieved my purse from the kitchen, pulled the duffel over my good arm, and unlocked the back door.

SUNDAY, DECEMBER 6TH

Focus, or she's dead.

Petrosky ground his teeth together, but it didn't stop the panic from swelling hot and frantic within him. After the arrest last week, this crime should have been fucking impossible.

He wished it were a copycat. He knew it wasn't.

Anger knotted his chest as he examined the corpse that lay in the middle of the cavernous living room. Dominic Harwick's intestines spilled onto the white marble floor as though someone had tried to run off with them. His eyes were wide, milky at the edges already, so it had been awhile since someone gutted his sorry ass and turned him into a rag doll in a three-thousand-dollar suit.

That rich prick should have been able to protect her.

Petrosky looked at the couch: luxurious, empty, cold. Last week Hannah had sat on that couch, staring at him with wide green eyes that made her seem older than her twenty-three years. She had been happy, like Julie had been before she was stolen from him. He pictured Hannah as she might have been at eight years old, skirt twirling, dark hair flying, face flushed with sun, like one of the photos of Julie he kept tucked in his wallet.

They all started so innocent, so pure, so … *vulnerable.*

The idea that Hannah was the catalyst in the deaths of eight others, the cornerstone of some serial killer's plan, had not occurred to him when they first met. But it had later. It did now.

Petrosky resisted the urge to kick the body and refocused on the couch. Crimson congealed along the white leather as if marking Hannah's departure.

He wondered if the blood was hers.

The click of a doorknob caught Petrosky's attention. He turned to see Bryant Graves entering the room from the garage door, followed by four other agents. Petrosky tried not to think about what might be in the garage. Instead, he watched the four men survey the living room from different angles, their movements practically choreographed.

"Damn, does everyone that girl knows get whacked?" one of the agents asked.

"Pretty much," said another.

A plain-clothed agent stooped to inspect a chunk of scalp on the floor. Whitish-blond hair waved, tentacle-like, from the dead skin, beckoning Petrosky to touch it.

"You know this guy?" one of Graves's cronies asked from the doorway.

"Dominic Harwick." Petrosky nearly spat out the bastard's name.

"No signs of forced entry, so one of them knew the killer," Graves said.

"*She* knew the killer," Petrosky said. "Obsession builds over time. This level of obsession indicates it was probably someone she knew well."

But who?

Petrosky turned back to the floor in front of him, where words scrawled in blood had dried sickly brown in the morning light.

> Ever drifting down the stream—
> Lingering in the golden gleam—
> Life, what is it but a dream?

Petrosky's gut clenched. He forced himself to look at Graves. "And, Han—" *Hannah.* Her name caught in his throat, sharp like a razor blade. "The girl?"

"There are bloody drag marks heading out to the back shower and a pile of bloody clothes," Graves said. "He must have cleaned her up before taking her. We've got the techs on it now, but they're working the perimeter first." Graves bent and used a pencil to lift the edge of the scalp, but it was suctioned to the floor with dried blood.

"Hair? That's new," said another voice. Petrosky didn't bother to find out who had spoken. He stared at the coppery stains on the floor, his muscles twitching with anticipation. Someone could be tearing her apart as the agents roped off the room. How long did she have? He wanted to run, to find her, but he had no idea where to look.

"Bag it," Graves said to the agent examining the scalp, then turned to Petrosky. "It's all been connected from the beginning. Either Hannah Montgomery was his target all along or she's just another random victim. I think the fact that she isn't filleted on the floor like the others points to her being the goal, not an extra."

"He's got something special planned for her," Petrosky whispered. He hung his head, hoping it wasn't already too late.

If it was, it was all his fault.

EPILOGUE

The pre-dawn humidity covered the freeway in frozen mist. I glanced at the clock. *Seven forty-five.* I should be there before nightfall. I set my jaw and fingered the emerald pendant that lay against my clavicle, warmed by the heat of my body.

A whimper rose from the backseat. In the rearview mirror, a massive black head eclipsed the back window.

"It's okay, buddy. Just relax. We'll be there in no time."

Duke slumped onto his belly on the seat and rested his head on his paws. On the dash, the panda bobbled, silly and childish and stupidly innocent. I backhanded it. It toppled to the floor.

I gripped the wheel tighter.

Before me, the brilliant red and yellow glow of sunrise streaked across the road and illuminated the tops of distant evergreen trees, lighting the sky with hope, with promise.

It's not promise. It's power.

I slid my hand underneath the bag on the passenger seat and let my fingers brush the cool metal of the scalpel. I squeezed. The sharp point bit into my finger. I pulled my hand back and watched a tiny crimson drop swell and drip onto the steering wheel. I smeared it with my thumb.

Duke whined, low and hollow.

"It's okay, boy," I said softly. "It won't be long now." The pavement whispered under my tires. I kept my eyes on the bloody dawn.

Baby's coming home.

Join my reader group at MeghanOFlynn.com, and get a FREE SHORT STORY! You'll also be first in line for new release information. No spam, and you can opt out anytime.

CONVICTION

AN ASH PARK NOVEL

*For my mother
who didn't raise no fool and who also managed to
teach me the appropriate use of double negatives.
I am what I am today because of your love and support.
But that won't stop me from kicking your ass in bridge.
You've been warned.
I love you, Mom.*

PROLOGUE

ASHLEY JOHNSON FELT the hatred the moment she stepped inside the courtroom from the door behind the judge's bench. It thickened the air, choked the breath from her lungs, and severed the hope that she'd managed to scrape together while waiting in her cell. There was no hope in this room. Just anger. The cuffs on her wrists jangled obscenely in the condemning hush of the courtroom.

They might as well kill her now. It would be preferable to the slow agony she would suffer imagining every major event in her daughter's life—her birthdays, her college acceptance letters, her wedding—from inside stone walls.

The jury's eyes burned into Ashley from their box on the right side of the room, and her legs tried to buckle. Maybe she deserved some of their judgment. It was true that she'd made some bad choices.

The choice to be with Derek was the worst one of all.

She tried not to look at the front of the courtroom as she passed, tried not to see the stand where Derek's dead body had been turned into a poster, his sightless eyes watching and accusing her even through the film of death. The wall behind him was splattered with the bloody remains of his skull. Every time, she tried not to look, but every time, she failed.

Frank Griffen sat, shoulders square, mouth set, his black-rimmed glasses frozen halfway down his nose. But his pinky fingers twitched like he could feel the energy too. Not that he ever sat perfectly still—his mouth or fingers or eyes, something was always moving. He wouldn't have been her first pick for a defense attorney, but she was broke. And he was good enough. If he got her out of there.

Eyes forward, don't look at the jury. Don't look at the poster. Don't look.

Behind Griffen, Detective Eddie Petrosky frowned, squinting—agitated. Griffen said the detective'd had that look since some serial killer had gotten away on his watch last year, but to Ashley, those lines of irritation on Eddie's forehead showed that he gave a shit. Down the row, Dr. McCallum, the shrink who'd interviewed her before the trial, sat watching, his enormous belly squished against the back of the pew in front of him. He had deemed her depressed, testified that she'd likely been suicidal the night Derek died. He hadn't been wrong. She had often prayed for death though she'd never come close to acting. It was a fantasy, slipping away when things got too hard—but not a fantasy she wanted to embrace.

Her feet seemed stuck to the floor as she scanned the rest of the crowd. Her caseworker, Diamond's caseworker, sat in the back. Some lady in a short skirt sat across the way, maybe a hooker waiting on her own court appearance. The one person who might've offered her hope, or at least a reassuring smile, was nowhere to be found. He'd visit on his own time, he'd said, and if she tried to stir things up without his consent, he'd leave her to die in prison. She couldn't even think his name, for fear it would tumble out of her mouth. The guard behind her coughed, probably annoyed that she'd stopped in the middle of the courtroom, or maybe he was trying to remind her to move.

Then she saw her. Diamond entered the courtroom, her baby girl, already grown bigger in the months since Ashley'd been locked up. And with her, Ashley's dead boyfriend's mother: Lucinda Lewis, Diamond's grandmother, if you believed the birth certificate. Lucinda glared at Ashley.

Ashley resisted the urge to run to her baby, to kiss her and hug her and tell her everything was going to be okay, that her mommy was coming home soon, and they'd be a family again. She wanted just one moment with Diamond. To smell her. To hold her. Instead, she watched her baby pass her by and disappear behind Lucinda as the woman turned to the seats. Ashley's chest constricted.

Derek's idiot brother, Trey, had shown up today too, his red bandana tucked haphazardly into his jeans pocket. Derek's aunts held hands as they followed down the aisle after Lucinda and slid into one of the long benches that held families like church pews—the law's last shot at redemption in a city where there was more blood than holy water.

The guard prodded Ashley forward so hard she stumbled into the table where Griffen sat. He jumped up and helped her to her seat, and she sank into the chair next to his, noting that Griffen's bony nose was leaking again.

He swiped at his forehead and then his nose with an orange handkerchief, then shoved it into his pocket more violently than seemed necessary. He didn't look at her, but she could see the tightness of his mouth. Not a good sign.

Tears burned behind her eyes though she wouldn't give anyone the satisfaction of watching her cry. Not the jury and definitely not the prosecution. She didn't want everyone to head home tonight feeling superior because of her pain. It was bad enough they were all free while she was locked in a cage, especially when she didn't deserve to be there.

She'd made bad choices, that was true. But she wasn't a killer.

Her throat threatened to close on her, and she swallowed over the tightness, trying to remember what Eddie had told her. *We'll figure it out, Ashley. I'll find a way.*

But he hadn't. Neither had the one she'd expected to get her out of this mess; the one who was supposed to care. But maybe he'd been a mistake too.

Where is he?

Like a shotgun blast, the bang of a gavel reverberated through Ashley's shoulder muscles and shivered down her back. Church was in session. She relaxed her fists in her lap and raised her eyes to that fat bastard judge, Clarence Delacour.

"We have already heard from the prosecution. Are you ready for closing arguments, Mr. Griffen?"

Griffen stood and walked around the table, buttoning the front of his suit jacket with twitchy little movements. He was barely taller than Ashley herself, but the set of his shoulders was rigid and determined, and this made him seem much larger. He walked to the jury box and put his hands on the rail, his grip soft like he was polishing the wood with his index finger instead of making a point.

Ashley tuned out after his "Ladies and gentlemen of the jury." She knew there was reasonable doubt, or at least Griffen had told her there was. But she also knew what the prosecution thought: that she'd come home, found her daughter injured, and bludgeoned Derek in the head with a blunt object, probably the hammer she'd used to hang a picture earlier that morning. A hammer that was now missing, which Griffen had assured her, was a good thing. Defendants had been released for less.

Ashley's neck was damp with perspiration by the time Griffen cleared his throat and strutted to the podium for his final statements.

"Ashley Johnson was ambushed," he said. "When she came home, the living room was dark, and she was unable to see what remained of her boyfriend. She walked through the room without turning on a light and into Diamond's bedroom to check on her little girl. And when her back was turned, someone stuck a syringe in Ashley's neck and carried her to the bathtub. She almost died at the hands of the same person who killed Derek Lewis. Our lack of another identifiable suspect does not equate to Ashley Johnson being guilty."

Griffen turned and caught the eye of someone behind her, and Ashley sat straighter. *Is he here? Did he come?* Out of the corner of her eye, she watched Petrosky nod to Griffen, the detective's face softening a fraction before reverting to its usual stoniness.

Griffen turned back to the jury box. "This girl did not kill Derek Lewis. And if you make the mistake of convicting her, you will be allowing a killer to go free."

The silence in the room felt heavy, like it was closing in on Ashley from all sides, until the judge spoke again.

"Is the prosecution ready for rebuttal?" Delacour's eyes were on the clock on the side wall—not on Ashley, not on Griffen—as her lawyer walked back to his seat. Obviously, the judge thought she was expendable. Like trash. Maybe she was. Maybe she had always been.

Shannon Taylor, the prosecuting attorney, rose to her feet, thin and blond and a fucking bitch. "Ready, Your Honor."

Ashley looked down at her hands, and the cuffs glinted like crude bracelets that weighed down her soul instead of her wrists.

Taylor cleared her throat. "At just after five o'clock on the evening of February fifteenth, a noise complaint came into the station, stating that someone was arguing at the apartment Derek Lewis and Ashley Johnson shared."

Ashley's hands trembled. She pressed her palms together and squeezed them between her knees.

"When police arrived at six-thirty, Derek Lewis was alone at the house, alive and in good health, and informed the responding officers that Johnson had gone to the drugstore and then to drop off their daughter at a neighbor's. Both of these statements were later verified. What Derek didn't know is that he had only four hours to live."

In her peripheral vision, Ashley tried to see what the jury was doing, but her vision was blurry. Her face burned.

When Taylor spoke again, her voice was softer, but her words somehow rang throughout the courtroom. Aggressive. Dangerous. "At seven-thirty, Ashley Johnson arrived for a job interview at an all-night garage where she was described as 'distracted' by the owner. After the interview, Johnson disappeared." Taylor cut her eyes at Ashley, and Ashley's stomach twisted.

"No one seems to know what the defendant was doing during this time, but she was gone for long enough that she neglected to pick up her daughter from her babysitter's home. When the sitter had to leave, she dropped young Diamond home with her father, Derek. And at eleven o'clock, when Ashley Johnson finally returned to the apartment, she found her daughter with a fresh bruise on her lower back and another on her leg, marks the sitter testified were not present earlier that day. Indeed, the one on Diamond's hip was a clear imprint of Derek Lewis's belt buckle."

Ashley's breath came hot and fast as she saw Diamond in her mind's eye, saw the bruises on her sweet baby's legs. *She's trying to get to you, trying to make you react.* Her leg muscles shook with anger. She swallowed hard.

"Ashley Johnson may have put up with Derek hitting her. She might have been neglectful herself, not bothering to pick her daughter up on time. But the defendant wasn't about to let her boyfriend get away with hitting her little girl." Taylor paced in front of the jury box. "Johnson found Derek sleeping on the couch. She grabbed a hammer, walked behind the couch, and hit her boyfriend in the head, again and again and again." Taylor mimed each strike, and the jury winced as they visualized Derek's head being smashed to bits.

Ashley could see it too, the blood, the fragments of skull and brain, gooey clumps landing on the wall. She tried to focus on the prosecutor instead. Better to look angry at the false accusation than pissed at her dead boyfriend whose corpse was even now staring back at her from the easel, his face bloody and eerily blank. *Well, ex-boyfriend.*

"Ashley Johnson panicked, got rid of the murder weapon, and wiped down as many surfaces as she could, but she only managed to smear the blood. She did leave one intact handprint on the wall in the hallway, though. Her fingers. Her palm. In Derek Lewis's blood."

Ashley focused on the blond knot at the nape of the prosecutor's neck, trying to ignore the jury. Every frown, every sympathetic look, was horribly wrong. If they were going to let her go, they'd look more hopeful, wouldn't they? Their faces said they'd already decided she'd had a good reason to kill him—and that she had, in fact, done it. She inhaled through her nose to push back the nausea.

"Panic, ladies and gentlemen. Panic, in a severely depressed woman already stressed to her breaking point. And the defendant realized there was nowhere to go. The mess was too big. She had no money. No one to turn to. No options, no way out." The pause was deafening, a ringing silence that hurt Ashley's ears.

"So she prepared a syringe from Derek Lewis's stash with a deadly overdose of heroin, left the front door ajar to ensure that someone would find her daughter, then climbed into a full bathtub and injected the drugs into her own neck."

The jurors' eyes swung to Ashley's table, and she saw pity and an agitation she almost couldn't bear to acknowledge. The air thickened further until the heaviness of it clogged her throat entirely, blocking her breath. *Jesus, help me, please...*

Taylor stilled, placing her hands on the polished wood of the jury box. "Just after midnight, a neighbor happened upon Johnson's open front door and found Derek dead on the couch, Diamond in her crib, wailing, and Ashley Johnson unconscious in the bathtub, the water pink with Derek Lewis's blood."

Ashley prayed silently. Please, God, help me. I'll go to church every Sunday. I'll do anything.

"The defense wants you to believe that she was framed. But Ashley Johnson had both motive and opportunity to commit this crime."

Yes, she'd had both of those things. She'd had the opportunity. And some nights, even now, she lies awake in her cell praying God would send Derek back just so she could fucking kill him again for hurting Diamond. No, she hadn't done it, she knew she hadn't. But the way the police had interrogated her, repeated their questions over and over, every word from their mouths wrapping around her throat like a noose that would eventually strangle her...sometimes she doubted her own innocence. Was it possible she'd lost it on Derek and blocked the whole thing from her mind? Had the memory of the sharp needle sting in her neck as she bent over Diamond's crib been a hallucination, the start of some kind of psychotic break? Why would anyone want to kill her? She was a nobody. Maybe she really *had* killed Derek. But Eddie Petrosky didn't believe that, and if he could trust her, then she could trust herself, too. She clenched her fists, and her face flushed with fresh determination.

Taylor's shoes echoed against the wooden walls as she strode back to the podium and gestured to the photo of Derek's corpse. "We can all sympathize with a mother protecting her child. But this is not the way. If we accept vigilante justice, if we set a precedent suggesting that we can harm those who get in our way, that we can take the law into our own hands, then we fail. Society fails. Derek Lewis wasn't perfect. He should have been punished for his crimes but *in accordance with the law*. This isn't about whether you like the victim or empathize with the aggressor. Even if you think Derek Lewis deserved to be punished for what he allegedly did, Ashley Johnson did not have the legal right to inflict that punishment."

The world was fading around the edges, every sound like the shush of Diamond's breathing when Ashley used to rock her to sleep—hazy and hot and peaceful. Those hours had been a reprieve from planning how they were going to escape from Derek.

Derek did deserve to die. *But I didn't do it.*

Taylor stared pointedly behind Ashley, probably at Diamond.

Don't look, Ashley. Don't.

"Ashley Johnson needs to suffer the consequences of the crime she has committed. She and others like her need to know that one cannot simply take the law into their own hands and kill someone who does them wrong. You must return a verdict of guilty of murder in the second degree."

The quiet seemed alive, squirming around Ashley, and the judge's scrutiny wiggled up her sleeves and down her back. Shannon Taylor walked back to her chair and sat, and Ashley listened to the rustling of shoes on the floor, the sound of jurors preparing for dismissal, the audience collecting their things.

Beside Ashley, Griffen blew his nose, a low, hollow honk. Behind her, Diamond cried out. Ashley watched Shannon Taylor and clenched her fists, her eyes burning with unshed tears.

1

SHANNON TAYLOR LEFT the courtroom with a pit in her stomach. She should have been happy. It had taken less than two hours for the jurors to return a verdict of guilty. Ashley Johnson had buried her face in her hands and sobbed until they took her away while Frank Griffen looked on after her, his face drawn and pale.

I'm right. I have to be. All the evidence had pointed that way, but damn. If only she'd been prosecuting Derek Lewis for abuse, then the tension in her shoulders would have abated with the verdict, not intensified. Being right didn't always feel good. It should, but...

Her stomach growled when she passed someone on a wooden bench in the hallway eating a sub sandwich. Maybe she'd get some sushi. No, Mexican. She glanced at her watch. Maybe fast food, though she'd probably regret it later tonight when she was sweating her way through grease-induced cramps at the gym.

Shannon kept her eyes on the marble floor, where cracks in the once-opulent stone threatened to snag the heels of her shoes. It was freaking depressing, watching Ash Park crumble. You could almost feel it in your bones, pulling at you, like the earth itself might slit you open and shove the bad inside so you could never escape.

She pushed through the front door and hurried down the steps, eyes forward, ignoring a beggar's call for change in favor of keeping her footing as she made her way toward her car.

"Taylor!"

Shit. Shannon turned to see Detective Petrosky approaching, his blue eyes bright with what looked like hatred, but Shannon knew it was just his resting bitch face. Or maybe it *was* hatred. He was good at his job, but damn if he wasn't a dick, especially when it came to his "girls." Sex crime detectives probably all ended up like that eventually—they either cared too much, sensitive to every nuanced attack, or they stopped caring at all.

"You shouldn't be here, Petrosky. You know there's nothing else to say."

"There's plenty more to say, Taylor. Someone else was in the house earlier that day, fighting with Lewis. Someone who got loud enough for the cops to show up. It wasn't her."

"Just because you know her doesn't mean she isn't a killer."

Petrosky ground his teeth. "I don't know her."

"You know her well enough. You set up that job interview for her, and—"

"She needed a leg up."

"And she got one, didn't she, when you threatened the garage manager with a parole violation if he didn't give her the job."

Petrosky stared at her, all ice and daggers. She gave it right back.

"She didn't kill him, Taylor. She was set up. Someone drugged her and tried to kill her too, and just because your ex-husband decided to prosecute—"

"Roger has nothing to do with this, Petrosky."

"He's the head prosecutor, he sure as shit does."

She shook her head. "I went for murder two because she was guilty. We've been over this. She was depressed, Petrosky. Her friends admitted it. Ashley Johnson herself admitted it. Dr. McCallum, your favorite department shrink, testified that even without the depression, years of domestic abuse can cause a person to snap. Add to it that Johnson *saw* her daughter hurt. It doesn't make any sense that a killer would murder Lewis, then sneak up behind Johnson and give her drugs. They'd have smashed her skull in too."

"Not if they wanted to frame her."

For god's sake. Shannon crossed her arms.

"They never found the murder weapon, Taylor. If she was going to kill herself anyway, why would she get rid of evidence?" Petrosky advanced on Shannon close enough that she could smell the sharp tang of booze under his mouthwash.

Who the hell does he think he's fooling? She should turn his alcoholic ass in. "People do strange things when they're in panic mode, Petrosky. Johnson didn't start the day wanting to die. A subsequent suicide once she realized what she'd done makes more sense with her history, and no one else had a motive." Derek Lewis was a small-time drug dealer, and no one had mentioned any bad blood between him and others in the neighborhood. He didn't even owe anyone money. And someone after the drugs themselves sure as hell wouldn't waste them by pumping them into Ashley Johnson's veins. Johnson had killed him. Panicked. And once Johnson knew she was fucked, she'd tried to take her own life. Case closed.

Petrosky's nostrils flared. "Someone else fought with Lewis that evening, Taylor. Ashley might have been scared, angry, but she didn't kill him."

Shannon sighed and edged toward her car. "I know, I know, it was the mystery person at the house."

Petrosky matched her step for step. "What about the later phone call, after Lewis was dead? The call about the supposed gunshot? There was no bullet damage, no powder residue, no other witnesses who heard a shot go off, nothing. We never even found a gun." Petrosky ran one thick paw down his face, sighing like an exasperated bulldog. "And if Lewis did have a gun, if Ashley had access to it, why didn't she use that to kill him? And how'd the caller even hear it? The call originated miles from the apartment."

"Doesn't matter." Shannon reached her car, clicked the unlock button, and slid inside. "Someone else found her before the call even came in."

"But the caller didn't know that. They called to make sure we got her while she was still clinging to life, maybe even wanted to make sure the baby was okay."

"Right, because all cold-blooded killers who meticulously frame someone else end up feeling so guilty that they risk detection to protect the kids in the house."

"Your snot-nosed buddy Griffen agrees with me."

Snot-nosed. Perpetual allergies to dust he'd told her once in college, during their days of pizza and study sessions and sneaking into the courthouse through an unalarmed back window to smoke pot. Back when they used to wear jeans and T-shirts instead of suits, and the plastic bands on their wrists were pink for breast cancer—before they realized that awareness wasn't doing shit for research and tossed them out.

"Of course, Griffen agrees. If you're right, his client really is innocent, unlike the throng of people he usually defends who just pretend to be." Shannon grabbed the door handle, and Petrosky backed up.

"I'm going to figure out who did this, Taylor. Someone has to do their job correctly."

"Fuck you, Petrosky." She slammed the car door and left Petrosky standing by himself in the parking lot with his hands jammed in his pockets.

SHANNON WHITE-KNUCKLED her car from the parking lot onto the freeway, her neck muscles as taut as violin strings. A Styrofoam coffee cup rolling across the pavement tumbled under her tire as she flew by, the crunch not nearly as satisfying as it would have been if it were Petrosky's head. But it helped. To the east, stray orange construction cones, dented and abused, littered the shoulder amidst signs warning of steep fines and imprisonment should you kill a worker. As if there was ever anyone out working on this road. She hit a jagged pothole hard enough to lock her seat belt.

Shannon rotated her neck, Petrosky's voice echoing in her head as she pictured Ashley Johnson's glassy eyes. Then she remembered Lucinda Lewis, her arms around her granddaughter, her eyes swollen with the knowledge that her son was never coming home because of what Johnson had done. She loosened her grip on the wheel and punched the stereo button. Def Leppard.

Shannon cranked the volume and watched apartment buildings grind by along the side of the freeway, their windows ugly and vacant. Metallica came on next, pounding through her speakers as apartments gave way to office buildings, then finally to townhouses and the occasional movie theater or shopping center or grocery store. When at last she pulled off onto the ramp toward the hospital, The Offspring was screaming at her about getting away. *If only I could.*

The hospital was an eighties relic, an appropriately sick-looking building of brown brick with bay windows protruding from the side like giant, water-filled blisters. And the inside was no better. The interior of the hospital always made her nose itch with the smell of antiseptic, made her eyes hurt with its too-bright fluorescents.

The women manning the reception desk did not acknowledge her as she passed, not that she really expected them to—if she worked here, she would have tried to distance herself too. Even as a visitor, she focused on the sights and smells and sounds of this place, forgetting for three glorious minutes of transit why she was there.

Shannon pushed the elevator button, and a curly-haired woman with a nurse's badge—*Sadie*—scurried up beside her, wearing rubbing alcohol like perfume. Sadie pulled her mouth into a grin, but any joy was surely painted on her mouth like the lipstick on the women at the reception desk. Always there—expected, but it couldn't possibly be real.

On the third floor, Shannon gave Sadie the obligatory have-a-nice-day nod, and Sadie returned it, though it was only a polite formality—more a wish that wouldn't likely be granted to those getting off on the oncology floor.

To her left, a long nurse's station beckoned with smiling, sympathetic people in scrubs. Shannon's muscles twitched, one step from dragging her back to the elevators, not because of the smell or her sore eyes or the god-awful way everyone in this place pretended that the grief wasn't about to leap up and bite their faces off—but because *he* was here. Seeing him like this was almost as bad as she imagined his death would be, though she'd not have to wonder about that for much longer.

She walked down the hall and into his room without knocking, sure that this time someone else's brother would be there looking too small under the blue hospital blanket, tubes coming from his arms and nose, gaunt cheeks turning him into a caricature of himself. "We made an error," the ladies at the desk would say. "Your brother was ill from the radiation and the chemo we mistakenly gave him. He's on his way home now."

But of course, he was there, like always, shuffling a deck of cards on his meal tray with bony, yellowed fingers. His gray eyes flashed when he saw her, crinkling at the corners, and he was all teeth, face filled with joy —real joy. For a minute, Shannon forgot to be sad, and she was just Shanny, Derry's sister, twelve years old again and huddled with him on her bed while he taught her how to deal blackjack.

Derry slapped the cards on the plastic tray table, making it jiggle. His real name was Jerry, but she'd always called him Derry, short for Derrière, her childhood nickname for him.

"Shanny! My god, I thought you'd never show up. How'd everything go today?"

Shannon smiled at him and pulled a chair from the side of the room to the bedside. "Got a conviction."

He squinted at her. "You look less happy than you should for someone who just did her job like a fucking boss."

"I had a little run-in with one of the detectives afterward. Someone who thinks the defendant didn't do it."

Derry raised an eyebrow. "He right?"

"No," she said, sharper than she meant to.

He picked up the cards. "Five-card draw, winner gets to tell Mom she's a bitch."

"Mom's dead."

"Oops, looks like I'll be the first one to tell her anyway." Derry stuck his tongue out, and Shannon's stomach heaved like someone had punched her in the gut. "Come on, Shanny, that was funny."

"You wouldn't know funny if it bit you in the ass."

"Let's have Dr. Coleman look at your funny bone for you." Derry winked at the doorway behind her, and Shannon turned to see Dr. Alex Coleman, almost impossibly handsome at six feet tall—dark hair, blue eyes, and straight teeth. He'd been beautiful even when they were children.

"He telling death jokes again?"

Shannon nodded. "You need to get him to knock it off."

The cards shuddered in Derry's hands as he shuffled and flipped them out onto the table. "What's he going to do, Shanny? Kill me?"

Alex sighed and walked around to Derry's bedside, giving Shannon's arm a brief, familiar squeeze, just like he'd done when they were little kid BFFs. Very first best friend, turned first love, turned first rejection, though, at the time, she hadn't understood why he'd refused her advances. At least he'd kept it in the family.

Alex put a hand on Derry's shoulder. "How are you feeling?"

"About as well as you'd expect for someone who's had poison pumped through their veins for hours on end."

"The infection in your leg any better?"

"You know it is. Don't pretend you didn't check the chart. I'm pretty sure poking through my records was the reason you scored me this fancy room at your hospital instead of letting the oncologist send me home."

"It is lovely and convenient for me to be able to see my fiancé on breaks between ER shifts." Alex's gold band glinted in the light from the overheads. They'd started wearing them the day after Derry's diagnosis. Now or never.

Shannon swallowed hard.

"Shut up and come play," Derry said. His ring finger had grown too thin to wear his band. "I'm *dying* for a chance to beat you."

"Asshole." Shannon scooped her cards from the table.

Alex rolled his eyes, sat on the end of the bed, and grabbed his own cards as Derry turned to Shannon. "Whatcha need, Shanny?"

Shannon tried to ignore the dark bags under his eyes and glanced at her hand: two fours, an eight, a queen, and a ten. She tossed an eight and a ten onto the tray.

Derry dealt her two back. "Alex?"

"None."

"None?" Derry shook his head. "You confident bastard. You better not be letting me win again."

"I never let you win," Alex said.

"In that case, I open with two weeks' worth of doing the dishes."

Shannon flipped a five and...a third four. *Three of a kind, suckers.* "I see your dishes and raise you making dinner for a week," she said.

Alex knocked on the tray to call her bet.

Derry snorted, pursing his lips with what looked like disgust. "Oh, Alex is taking the sissy's way out."

"Misogynist," Shannon said.

"Feminist," Derry shot back.

Shannon slapped her cards onto the tray. "That's not an insult."

"Obviously, you're not a Republican." Derry considered his cards for a moment, then slid them onto the tray. He met Shannon's eyes. "I'll see you and raise you my life's savings."

"Your life—"

"Take it or leave it, Shanny."

"I'll take it."

"Will you be getting your inheritance a few weeks early, or did you just make Alex that much richer?"

"Goddammit, Derry," Shannon said.

"Fold," Alex said.

"Sucker." Derry flipped his cards. Pair of jacks.

Shannon shrugged and swept her cards into the pile. "I assumed you didn't have anything."

Alex watched her, his eyes narrowed, but she ignored him.

"Huzzah!" Derry slapped the table knocking his cards to the bed. "If I keep betting like this, I'm going to be living in the lap of luxury right up to the moment I bite the big one." He winked at Alex. "Literally."

Shannon shook her head, but a smile was tugging at the corner of her mouth.

Alex stood. "I better get back down to the ER. Be back later." He kissed Derry on the cheek, squeezed Shannon's shoulder, and left the room.

Derry's eyes darkened as he watched Alex disappear through the door. "He doesn't deserve this."

"He loves you."

"Loves me enough to marry me for my money."

"You're the one who said no to the wedding." Derry had told her that he wasn't hitting the aisle in a wheelchair because it wasn't the memory he wanted Alex to have for his first wedding. Maybe for his second, but definitely not his first. "Love's all that matters, Derry. He wants you to be happy, and so does Abby." Her eyes wandered to the bedside table, where a skinny little girl rocking an AC/DC T-shirt and a blond bob stared into the room from a photograph. "So do I."

"You don't deserve this either."

"None of us deserves this." Tears smarted behind her lids. "How is Abby?"

"She's fine. Hanging in there, I guess. Do me a favor and do something fun when you pick her up tonight. She won't be ready until eight because she's going to Chuck E. Cheese with a friend, but...she needs to get her mind off everything. Pretty sure her little girlfriends don't have a parent dying of metastatic liver cancer. Did I tell you it's in my brain now?"

"I rented *Terminator*," Shannon blurted out.

Derry raised an eyebrow. "Nothing lifts one's spirits like blowing shit up. If only you could avoid blowing this game. I kick your ass every time." The brightness in his eyes was back—there'd be no more heart-to-heart talks, not today. "It really is too bad you guys are stuck with a clearly superior poker player, albeit not for long." He wagged his eyebrows.

"Jesus fucking Christ, Derry."

"I'm going to tell on you when I meet him, all this taking-his-name-in-vain shit."

"Watch it, or you're going to meet him sooner than you think."

Derry put his hands up in mock surprise. "Shanny! Did you just threaten my life? I've got half a mind to toss you out of here."

"Lucky for me, you literally only have half a brain now. You'll probably forget this whole conversation by sundown."

"No doubt." Derry reached over the table and grabbed her hand. "I love you, Shanny."

"Love you too, Derry. But you're still an ass."

"Takes one to know one." Derry released her hand and sat back against his pillows. "Now deal. And this time, don't let me win."

Shannon avoided his eyes and shuffled the cards with shaking hands.

2

WHEN SHANNON LEFT THE HOSPITAL, the sun was sinking low in the western sky, turning the clouds into billowing plumes of fluorescent smoke against the newly budding trees. Her breath fogged in front of her—not quite spring, but it was trying. Though with Derry on his way out, everything would probably look darker soon: more drab, more boring. More dead. The thought of losing him tore holes in her heart until her chest felt like bloody cheesecloth.

She headed south, back into the city. Twilight was in full effect by the time she pulled the car into a strip mall that housed a pizza place and two vacant stores with For Rent signs in the front windows. Behind the strip mall was a nondescript warehouse with a sandwich board sign out front: "CrossFit Ash Park." She locked the car and headed for the entrance, an enormous garage door yawning open like the maw of some carnivorous beast.

The whoosh of air that greeted her inside was as cold as that of the hospital, exposed as the place was to the elements through the open warehouse door. But the air here was alive, not sterile and antiseptic. Warm rubber, salt, and ammonia, a mix of sweat and cleaning products, invaded her nostrils. It was like coming home—if home meant screaming hard work.

Backed by mirrors, the warehouse was filled with every piece of weight-lifting equipment she could imagine, plus kettlebells, acrobatic rings, and pull-up bars: the ultimate in police training. Park Kimball, the right-hand man for the chief of police, had opened the warehouse for tactical training last year. How he'd managed to afford the up-front costs on his salary, Shannon had no idea, but since then, he'd been offering classes three nights a week, weekend personal sessions for those entering the police academy, and free gym access for his friends on the force who needed a place to work out after a day of public servitude.

In the back of the room was an intricate setup of bars that looked more like a kid's jungle gym than weight-training equipment. Kimball stood on a dense gray mat beneath the setup, heaving a bar full of weights onto his shoulders and flipping them back down to his waist. Then up again. Then down. They called Kimball "Jackie Chan," a fitting nickname, especially when the tendons in his neck tightened with exertion. He dropped the bar with a thud and winked at Shannon.

She nodded back, though his gaze made her shoulders tighten. She hated that Kimball was closer friends with her ex-husband than he was with her—Kimball and his wife Amanda had invited Roger to Thanksgiving this past year, before the divorce was even official, while her invite seemed to have been misplaced. Shannon used to think of Kimball as family. But since her divorce, Kimball more closely resembled the misogynistic, xenophobic uncle she avoided at holiday parties.

"Ohh, look out! It's about to get stone cold in here, gentlemen!" Off to Kimball's left, Officer Isaac Valentine smiled at Shannon and hefted a barbell over his shoulders, perspiration shimmering on his forehead like diamonds. She grinned at him. Valentine was on the Ash Park force, a good guy and enthusiastic about his work, maybe overly so. And while Kimball was with Roger's bitch ass, Valentine and his wife Lillian had invited Shannon and her best friend to join them at Thanksgiving, conveniently forgetting to invite Roger. A department divided by divorce, like children in the midst of a custody battle. But here at the gym, any personal or professional strife disappeared in a haze of sweat. Plus, it was the one place Roger never showed up.

Next to Valentine, Detective Curtis Morrison's broad shoulders gleamed as he completed kettlebell thrusters, squatting with the ball, then pressing it overhead and back to a squat. Morrison caught her eye in the mirror and smiled. She tried to smile back, but the sudden image of Morrison's asshole partner—Petrosky, with his fleshy face, his five o'clock shadow—made the anger bubble up in her stomach again. Morrison's face fell. He always knew. She probably looked as irritated as she had last week when someone had cut her off in traffic on their way to lunch. She had called the other driver a goat fucker. Morrison had ordered lamb at the restaurant and asked her over and over whether she thought anyone might like to have their way with his meal.

She ignored the twittering in her chest and turned back to Valentine. "Five minutes before I kick your ass in kettlebell swings."

"Bring it, Taylor." Valentine dropped his barbell. "Nice work on Johnson today, by the way, especially considering you got fucked on jury selection."

So much for leaving her cases outside the gym. "Yeah, seems like Griffen always gets what he wants. Didn't help him this time, though."

"Hey, any of you catch the game last night?" Morrison asked. In the mirror, his face did not change, but she'd spent enough evenings with him to know he didn't watch any sports at all. That didn't stop Valentine from forgetting about the Johnson trial and going on about some pre-season nonsense. A bead of sweat dripped between Morrison's shoulder blades and down his back.

Shannon resisted the urge to mouth *thank you* at Morrison and walked through a doorway into the single bathroom, shivering at the chill in the air. She set her bag on the toilet. Hopefully, one day Kimball'd put in locker rooms.

In shorts, a tank top, and a pair of leather half-gloves to avoid tearing her hands on the metal bars, she yanked her perfectly blow-dried hair into a ragged ponytail and headed back to the main room.

"Let's make this happen!" Kimball called to her from the back of the warehouse, where he was swinging a kettlebell between his legs and up above his head.

Shannon shrugged. "If you really want it, Kimball. I've got all night to make you look like a punk."

Valentine hooted from the floor, where he was doing sit-ups with a kettlebell. "Shannon's going to fuck you up, Kimball!"

Kimball paused with the kettlebell over his head and narrowed his eyes at Valentine. "What's with the gut? You look like a black Chris Farley."

Valentine's abdominals flexed in a perfect washboard with each sit-up. Shannon shook her head. *Men.* Very few women showed up there, limiting her options for female-to-female interaction, but one didn't need a vagina to be a good friend. She'd learned from her mother that women can be far more dangerous, far more hurtful than any man. She stood on her tiptoes and stretched her arms to the ceiling.

"I told you," said Valentine, "my wife is pregnant, and I gained a few pounds to make her feel better. That all right with you, you Jackie Chan-looking motherfucker?"

"Fine with me. I'm not the one who has to look at that fat gut every night."

Shannon looked at Kimball as she leaned over an extended leg, stretching her hamstring. He was huge—easily twice as big as he'd been just six months ago, protein shakes and weight training definitely piling on the bulk. The pressures of gym ownership. Even so, he still didn't have anything on Morrison. Shannon stretched her other leg and watched Morrison's blond hair catch the overhead lights like a halo as he hauled himself up on the rings, paused, and let himself drop in a perfectly controlled movement. His abdominal muscles flexed, and his arms bulged with effort, but his full lips were relaxed, calm, serene. Always so damn chill. She probably looked like a grimacing walrus halfway through her set of bench presses, though he was too good a friend to ever tell her that.

Valentine dropped the ball, sat up, and ran a hand over his stomach. "My wife can't get enough of this."

"Fuck you, Valentine." Kimball dropped the kettlebell and moved to the weight rack. "What're you doing later, California?"

"Don't call him that," Valentine retorted. "It's almost like Petrosky's here when you pull that shit."

Petrosky. Shannon's heart accelerated, and it wasn't from the impending workout. The way he treated his partner was bad enough, always acting like Morrison didn't know what he was doing. But to harass her after she'd done her job? Based on nothing but some crazy hunch?

Such an asshole.

Valentine grabbed a pair of hand weights and hefted them onto his shoulders. "I'm just gonna call Morrison 'Silent but Deadly' until he comes up with something better."

"Sounds like a fucking fart," Kimball said behind her.

Shannon stalked to the bench and began adjusting the weights on the barbell positioned above it.

Morrison dropped from the rings and approached. "Need a spot?"

She nodded and leaned back on the bench, eyes on the bar above her chin. Morrison took his position at the head of the bench, his thick legs above her head but far enough away that his balls weren't in her face, which she very much appreciated.

He put his hands on the middle of the bar. "One, two—"

Gripping the bar in both hands, she inhaled, pushed the bar to remove it from the holder, and lowered it slowly, carefully. The muscles in her arms whined as she pushed it back up. On the way back down, she took a deep breath, her first full one all day. Morrison smelled earthy with just a touch of the lavender soap he used still lingering under the musk.

"Hey, Shannon," Valentine began, "you want to come to the art exhibit with Lillian and me tonight? Starts at six. Morrison might come, too, if I can convince him to blow off the rest of his workout."

Morrison winked at her. She couldn't smile back because the weights were taking all her concentration, but the silent encouragement in his eyes made her push harder.

Kimball snorted. "You're a bunch of fucking fags, going to an art show."

The hair on the back of Shannon's neck stood up. She opened her mouth, ready to replace the bar and launch into a tirade about Kimball's choice of words, but Morrison beat her to it.

"We're cultured." He spoke quietly, but there was no mistaking the challenge in his voice.

"What are you doing tonight anyway, motherfucker?" Valentine chortled. "Playing chauffeur to dance class?"

Shannon suppressed a smile.

"Dana loves dance, asshole," Kimball said. "And I'm not about to deny my baby girl. Besides, Amanda has to work late again."

"Maybe your social-working wife got tired of looking at your flabby ass and found a real man," Valentine said.

Shannon's arms were on fire. She stared at Morrison's face, gritted her teeth, and lowered the bar again.

"So how about it, Shannon? You coming? We'll hit O'Doole's to celebrate your conviction afterward."

"Maybe," she wheezed as Morrison grabbed the bar. He helped her put it back into the holder, then walked around the bench and offered her a hand. Her grip was slick with sweat, but he managed to pull her to seated.

"I can't stay long, though," she said. "I have to get Abby at eight."

Kimball muttered something Shannon couldn't hear, then said, "I'm done for today. Morrison, you'll lock it up for me? Got a long day tomorrow."

Valentine laughed. "Yeah, a long day wiping the chief's ass."

"Fuck off," Kimball spat.

Valentine ignored him. "I gotta head off too, get changed. Morrison, half an hour in front of the art gallery?"

"Not tonight. I need to drop off a file at Petrosky's after I finish up here. But I'm up for O'Doole's." He nodded at Kimball. "I'll clean the bars too. I want to squeeze in one more set of toe touches."

"Petrosky's got you by the nuts." Valentine shook his head, sighing with resignation. "Fine. I'll call you when we're heading to O'Doole's. Hopefully, I can get in and out of that exhibit fast, and we'll be over there in an hour."

"Later," Shannon said. She hated the way her voice was still strained from the presses.

Morrison watched them leave, then turned back to her. "Sorry about Petrosky earlier."

"He told you about that, huh?" She stood, wiping her hands on her shorts.

Morrison nodded. "He gets carried away."

"Your partner is an asshole."

"Maybe."

"That's it? 'Maybe'?" She met his eyes.

"He might be." Morrison's gaze was unwavering. "But that doesn't necessarily make him wrong."

Her chest heated. Morrison couldn't possibly believe that Johnson was innocent. Could he? "A jury found her guilty beyond a reasonable doubt."

Morrison's face remained unlined and still. His chest was just as unmoving—he may not even have been breathing. "I think there's always another side."

She frowned. "You say that about everything, but not all things are relative." He'd once tried to argue that even if Donald Trump was a dick, he probably had a reasonably good side to him underneath somewhere, just because he was human. "Some things just are," she said. She stretched her arms over her head, then locked them behind her.

"Some things. Maybe even this thing." Morrison smiled, but it seemed forced. "Sorry, dude. How about you just enjoy your victory? You can tell me about whatever crappy movie you picked for Abby tonight. And if you have to sit through some princess nonsense, I'll play you in Scrabble again. Just don't let her see you doing it. Last time she whipped my butt, and my ego can't take another hit like that." He lowered his voice. "But seriously, think about Johnson. It might not be so cut-and-dried."

She shook her head. "You're lucky I like you, Morrison." He was probably the only reason she stayed in Ash Park at all after her messy divorce from the head prosecutor. It was hard to leave your best friend. Especially when they were one of your only friends. She didn't attach easily.

"Yeah, I know I'm lucky." He grinned. "So you going with us to O'Doole's? We can grab coffee first."

She dropped her arms. "I don't drink coffee at night. You know that."

"A glass of wine?"

"We're going to a *bar*."

"True enough. Silly me." He stood. Silent. Calm. Waiting.

She couldn't remember when he'd started this nonsense. Maybe he'd been serious the first time. Probably not, though. "Are you going to ask me if I want food so I can tell you I'm not hungry?"

Morrison shook his head. "Not tonight. Gotta keep you on your toes." He smiled and headed for the bars. She watched his back until he leaped to grab the first bar, pulled himself up, and turned his face to the ceiling.

3

O'DOOLE'S CRACKLED with the click of heeled pumps and the energy of forty professionals putting off bedtime for another hour. Valentine waved at Morrison and Shannon from the bar area and gestured to a booth in the corner. On Valentine's arm, his wife Lillian turned and smiled, petite until she turned sideways, then—*bam!*—her belly stuck out like a basketball.

Shannon rested her hand on her own stomach. *Abby*. She'd never regretted the surrogacy, not even when she'd found herself in Dr. McCallum's office feeling like an empty shell while the psychiatrist handed her tissues and a prescription for postpartum antidepressants.

Six years since she'd had Abby. Two since Derry's doctor had said "cancer." How things had changed.

Morrison touched her arm. "I'll grab us drinks. Red wine?" He met her eyes and smiled, and she nodded. At least some things stuck.

They sat in a corner booth far enough from the hubbub of the bar that they could hear one another. Morrison returned with the drinks, plunked the glasses in front of them, and took his seat across from her.

"To the best damn prosecutor I've ever met," Valentine said, raising his glass to Shannon.

Shannon clinked his cup with her own. Valentine had been first on the scene, finding Johnson in the tub and calling for an ambulance. He'd managed to preserve the crime scene too, not an easy task with EMS personnel. All she'd done was finish the job of putting Johnson away.

Valentine leaned across the table and lowered his voice. "Between you and me, though, I wasn't the least bit upset that Johnson took care of Derek. That fucker, beating on his kid, he didn't deserve to—"

"Isaac, enough," Lillian said, touching his elbow. "You're going to get yourself all worked up again."

Valentine shrugged. "You know what I'm saying."

Shannon did. Derek Lewis had hurt Diamond, and society wasn't any worse off after Ashley Johnson killed him. And Johnson *had* killed him, even if Petrosky—and maybe Morrison—didn't agree. She'd have to pick Morrison's brain later. Maybe. For now, she avoided his eyes and sipped her wine as Valentine sat back in his chair.

"Speaking of…" Morrison said, and Shannon swiveled in her seat to see what he was looking at. *Griffen.* Same suit he'd worn in the courtroom, one she'd seen a hundred times before. *Frugal bastard.* At least he'd loosened his tie.

Griffen slid into one of the stools at the bar, his posture erect but not quite as confident as it'd been this morning. He tossed something into his mouth and swallowed it dry. A pill? The strawberry-ash blonde on the stool next to him—familiar, though Shannon couldn't place her—laid a hand on Griffen's arm, her mouth at his ear. Looked like things hadn't worked out with Griffen's last stick-in-her-ass girlfriend, the one who'd said: "It's your friendship with Shannon or your relationship with me." Served him right. Shannon had always been there for Griffen, but there'd never been a romance between them—and no reason for her to be cut off like a gangrenous limb. Though if Griffen hadn't severed their friendship, she'd never have gotten so close to Morrison. And Morrison didn't date much, nor did it seem like he'd respond well to someone telling him to drop his best friend. Then again…she'd never expected Griffen to drop her either. She finished her wine.

The strawberry-haired woman was looking Shannon's way now—prettier than his last girlfriend, thin, with wide eyes, full lips, and a fuller chest. Griffen was following her gaze, though he avoided eye contact with anyone at Shannon's table.

Morrison was already standing. "I'm going to say hi." His eyes were serene but still sharp somehow. "He's a nice guy. Can't blame him for doing his job."

Valentine sighed. "I'll grab another chair."

Griffen said something to the bartender, probably ordering his favorite martini—dry with two olives—and part of Shannon ached with nostalgia because she knew that. She waved Morrison down. "No, I'll go." He glanced at the couple at the bar and back at her and nodded.

Griffen looked up when she approached, but his smile was tight, and he refused to meet her eyes, opting to look over her shoulder at the table, or maybe at the wall. "How are you, Shannon? It's been a while."

"It has. Too long." She raised her glass. "To the trial being over?"

Griffen touched her glass with his own, his eyes on his half-empty drink. His face was still drawn and disappointed. No one likes to lose. Shannon turned to Griffen's date to introduce herself, but the woman beat her to it.

"Shannon Taylor, esquire," the redhead said knowingly. "I watched the trial."

Now Shannon remembered where she'd see her. "You were there this morning." *Behind Petrosky's stupid ass.*

"Had a case right before yours with Delacour." The woman extended her hand. "Where are my manners? I'm Karen. I work over at the rehab center, so I'm at the courthouse to testify occasionally if one of our guys gets into trouble. Though now I have another reason." She gestured to Griffen. "You'll have to excuse him. He's had a headache all day. I'm sure you understand."

Shannon nodded. He'd gotten stress headaches in college too, just like she had.

Griffen had downed his martini and was ordering another, his lips still moving, pursing and relaxing like he was already drinking it. He hadn't even looked at her. *What a dick.* Unless he felt guilty about how they'd parted ways. As he should, but...

Fuck it. She reached over to the bar and squeezed his hand. "Nice job today. Really. I've been hoping you were doing well."

Griffen looked at his arm, at her hand, and then at Karen, who seemed stiff beside her though Shannon didn't really care why. He finally smiled at her—friendly, the way he'd been in college. "Thanks, Shannon. I've hoped all was going well with you too. So things are good?"

Some things. She pushed the flash of Derry's thin fingers from her mind and nodded. The silence stretched. "Anyway, I just wanted to come say, hey." She took her hand back and gestured to the table where Morrison and Valentine were peering over their drinks, Morrison impassive, Valentine almost...pouting. "Want to join us?"

Griffen looked over at the table but shook his head. Karen examined the group, maybe Valentine or maybe Morrison, as if still trying to decide whether they should join the party.

"I really appreciate the offer," Griffen said, "but we just stopped in on the way to my place. I need another ibuprofen and a little rest. Maybe a rain check?"

Karen frowned at the table and drew her eyes back to Shannon.

"Absolutely," Shannon said, trying not to feel too guilty about the way her chest relaxed. "You just let me know when." Shannon headed back to the table. She plopped into her seat and winced, her muscles already starting to ache from her workout.

Valentine sneered. "So how was our good friend, The Defense?"

Shannon rolled her eyes at him. "He's fine."

"Doesn't look fine. He looks pissed."

Shannon glanced over her shoulder in time to see Griffen and Karen heading out the door. Karen threw her a cool backward glance before she disappeared onto the street. *Griffen sure knows how to pick them.* "That's how I look when I lose, too."

"True enough." Valentine threw back the last of his beer.

Morrison was still staring after Griffen. "I swear I know that woman from somewhere."

"She works over at Breckenridge Rehab. You've probably seen her in court."

Morrison frowned, but his face softened when Lillian jumped.

"Sorry. Nothing like a baby kick in the ribs to wake you up."

"Did you decide what you're going to name that baby yet?" Morrison asked.

Valentine set his glass down. "All out of crazy hippie suggestions, are you?"

"For now."

"Thank goodness." Lillian yawned. "We like Mason. It was my grandfather's name."

"I love that." Shannon had considered naming her own theoretical children after her late grandparents: Evelyn and Terrence. They were probably the only reason she was halfway normal.

Valentine put an affectionate hand on Lillian's belly. "You making Mommy tired already, kid?"

Morrison pushed his drink aside. "Probably need to head out too. Long day tomorrow."

Lillian's belly rolled like a puppy under a blanket. Shannon watched it writhe until Morrison tapped her on the hand to leave.

4

WHEN SHANNON AWOKE the next morning, a hazy darkness enveloped her room. Thunderheads had already crept their way across the dawn and blotted out the morning sun. Storms today. She sighed and shoved her feet into her shoes.

Abby was still asleep, her short, straight hair plastered to the side of her head, her kitten Lucky curled against her neck in a way that made it look like he might suffocate her.

Shannon's heart skipped a beat. "Abs?" She touched Abby's shoulder just as Abby squinted through the dusky gray dawn, her slightly upturned nose wrinkling. Even half-asleep, she was adorable.

"Morning, Aunt Shanny." Lucky yawned and stretched his front paws.

Shannon sneezed. "Morning, Ab. Ready to get up and go to school?"

Abby put an arm around Lucky, and the kitten started up like a motor. "Nope."

"Understood. Let's do it anyway."

Abby pushed herself to seated, Lucky scampering onto her lap. "Will you make me pancakes?"

"Of course." Shannon smiled and left the room, easing the door shut behind her. Abby seemed so...happy. Normal. But what was about to happen to her wasn't normal at all. No kid should have to lose a parent. Well, no kid should lose a good parent, anyway.

The griddle was sizzling with blueberry dough when Abby finally entered the kitchen in a knee-length tie-dye shirt and aqua leggings.

Shannon flipped a pancake. "Nice shirt," she said.

"The kids at school think it's ugly."

"They don't know anything about fashion."

"That's what I said." Abby sat at the table, and Lucky leapt onto her lap.

"Oh. Good." What a fucking amazing kid. Shannon slid the pancakes onto plates and topped them with fresh berries, then carried the plates to the table and sat beside Abby.

Lucky pawed Abby's hand as she picked up her fork. She giggled and shoveled a big bite into her mouth, watching as Shannon did the same. "These are good, Aunt Shanny." Three bites. Four. Five. "Daddy always says you're a good cook." Her face fell.

Don't do it, Ab. Don't bring it up. Shannon didn't want to think about her brother dying right now. Didn't want to talk about it now. But if Abby needed to...

Abby put her fork down on her nearly empty plate. "I wish I could make Daddy better. I was looking online, and there was an article about bone marrow transplants and—"

Shannon shook her head. "Abby." The cancer was everywhere: his bones, his liver, his brain. "We can't fix it." No matter how much they wanted to. They were helpless. Hopeless.

"When do you think he'll get to come home?"

"Hopefully, in the next week." Shannon pushed her half-eaten pancake aside and took Abby's hand. "They just wanted to keep an eye on that big infection he's got on his leg."

"That was my fault," Abby whispered. Lucky leapt from her lap and ran between Shannon's feet. "He was trying to fix my bike, and the wrench slipped and—"

"It wasn't your fault, Ab."

Abby's lip quivered, and Lucky clambered back on top of her knees. She released Shannon's hand and stroked his head.

"The chemo for the cancer makes his immune system weak, Abby. It wasn't your fault. He loves you so much that he'd do anything in the world to make you happy, and if you told him he wasn't allowed to touch your bike, he'd probably throw a fit."

Tears pooled in Abby's hazel eyes. "I know."

"Your daddy is a stubborn guy. He'll have a little longer. And then we'll have to be strong, but we'll be together, okay?"

Abby bit her lip, "Will you get cancer?"

"No, I don't think so."

"What about Dad?"

Daddy, Derry. Dad, Alex. Pretty soon, she'd have only one of them. Shannon set her fork down so Abby wouldn't see it shaking. "We'll be fine. Your daddy just had wicked bad luck. We'll do the best we can to enjoy the time we have left." But there'd never be enough time. *Fuck cancer.* Shannon stood. "Did you get enough to eat?"

Abby nodded, her eyes on Lucky's striped fur. The kitten purred like an engine, and Shannon liked the little sneeze machine even more because of Abby's calmness as she stroked his back.

"Get your bag, okay, sweetie? We don't want to be late." Shannon picked up the plates and took them to the sink, her vision blurred by the tears in her eyes.

THE CLOUDS WERE heavy with rain or maybe one last snow, judging by the layer of frost on her windshield. *So much for spring.* Shannon parked in front of the Ash Park precinct and headed for the adjacent brown building where the prosecutor's office waited for her like an old, sullen dog someone had left out in the cold. The side entrance was unlocked, the lobby silent. She trotted up the back stairs. They'd never had the budget for security, and they didn't need it; if they had a crisis, they'd have a barrage of cops here in ten seconds.

In the bland, beige hallway, three framed paintings of watercolor butterflies hung at eye level, probably meant to convey a deeper significance than bugs or flight, but Shannon had never had time to ponder it. In all probability, neither had the three other attorneys who worked there with her, two men and one other woman. Their offices were at the far end of the hall; past hers and far enough away that she never had to see them unless they were brushing elbows at the office mailboxes. They didn't like her. Or maybe they'd just stayed away from her because of whom she'd married. She could hardly blame them.

Brown carpet muted the clacking of her heels as she turned the corner toward her office. Her heart dropped.

"Morning, Shannon." Roger McFadden stood just outside her door, six feet five inches of impeccable Brooks Brothers suit and flawless blond hair, smiling at her with his million teeth. The same smile he gave to every jury that was swinging in his favor. The same shit-eating grin he'd worn on their wedding day.

Bastard. Her chest heated with old hurt and new irritation. "Roger." She squeezed past him more aggressively than probably necessary.

His eyes bored a hole in her back. "Shannon. Nice work yesterday on Johnson."

"Thanks, *boss.*" She shoved the key into the lock, and her keychain banged against the door, echoing down the hall. She needed to chill out, or he'd know his mere presence still got to her.

"You of all people don't have to call me that. Though head prosecutors do get some perks, I suppose." More teeth. He followed her into her office and sat across from her desk in one of the black leather chairs she had taken in their divorce settlement.

She sat reluctantly. *I should get a new job.* "What do you need, Roger?"

His eyes were tight, but it felt fake. "How's Jerry?" he said.

Shannon yanked a file from the top drawer of her desk. "Fine."

"Is he really? I thought he was—"

She slammed the folder on the desk. "He's as fine as he can be, Roger, you know what I meant."

His eyes blazed: angry, not hurt. "Just because we're not together anymore doesn't mean I don't care about your family. About Abby. About you. It's hard to work together when you hate me."

"You should have considered that before."

"I made one stupid mistake."

"Four. That I know of. They were just all the same type of mistake." *Why the hell are we still having this conversation?*

"You were just as guilty of finding comfort outside our marriage. The only reason you aren't attached now is that your rebound likes men."

She squared her shoulders. "Morrison isn't a rebound. He's just a friend, same as he was before we got married." Like she had the time or the desire to date anyway after dealing with Roger's bullshit. She wouldn't be ready for a relationship for a good long time—if ever. "And just because he also happens to be friends with my brother doesn't mean he's gay. Sexuality isn't contagious." *Dumbass.* She bit her lip to keep from saying it.

She should have let Roger think they'd gotten it on just to wipe that smug look off his face. Shannon glanced at the desk. Maybe he'd be humbler if she threw her stapler at him. "I'm not the one who came here to meet with you today, Roger. What do you want?"

Roger shook his head. "I just wanted to help. You're always so suspicious of my intentions. It's hurtful."

I'm not falling for your mind games today, Roger. She jerked the desk drawer open again and retrieved a pen. "If you're done badgering me, I need to get some work done."

"Actually, there is one more thing."

She raised an eyebrow.

"You've got a case there on your desk, a Reverend Jack Wilson, arrested after his six-year-old daughter died of a traumatic brain injury."

Shannon shuffled through the files on her desk, pulled Wilson's free, and flipped it open. "Jesus."

"Cops found the kid on the floor, Wilson holding a towel to her head. Said he dropped her. The cops didn't buy it because of the medical examiner's report that there were fractures in more than one cranial bone, but Wilson claimed she hit a toy on her way down, which could be consistent with the ME's report." Roger ran a hand over a face that was free of wrinkles, hair, and any telltale signs of a conscience. "However, there are...extenuating circumstances. The kid wasn't with his wife, and he'd only just found out about her the month prior."

A month ago. So he'd found out he had an illegitimate kid, realized it might hurt his pious career, and tried to get rid of her. "We've got another first degree? Second degree?" His rap sheet was clean, save for a few parking tickets. She flipped back to the photos.

"This is a tricky one. We're keeping it quiet to protect his mistress. If the press calls, no interviews."

"I don't understand." But she did. *Protecting other cheaters, eh, Roger?* Yet bringing that up would turn the conversation back to their relationship, probably what he wanted, and she wasn't biting. Shannon flipped to the photos of a little girl, snow-white skin, black hair, vibrant red stain from temple to ear. "Looks like Reverend Wilson needs to practice what he preaches."

"Probably so." Roger consulted his watch. "Protecting the privacy of the mother matters. It's the right thing to do, keeping it quiet."

Roger had never given a damn about the right thing. Shannon pursed her lips as she scanned the file. "I'm sure Wilson is glad for that. *Grieving as he is.*"

"Grieving...yeah." Roger shrugged. "Anyway, the police reports are sketchy, and we've got a few days before the arraignment, so I'm thinking we'll drop the charges down, see what we can get easy."

Reduce the charges. Again. "It's not always about easy, Roger. What about justice for this child?" Shannon traced the little girl's cheek in the photo. "Poor kid."

"Shame. I'll let you get to it." His voice was dull, flippant even, and the hairs on her neck rose. "Have a good day, Shannon."

Asshole. Shannon glared at his back until the door clicked shut. She sucked a breath of paper and leather and stale air conditioning and opened the next new file.

Ishantey Webster, nineteen. Rape victim refusing to file charges. She could encourage Webster to testify, but if Shannon tried to force the woman to trial, she ran the risk of re-traumatizing the poor girl and would be accused of trying losing cases based on gut feelings that would never fly in court. Not that it would have been the first time. That was why Roger had the position he did and she was still stuck in the office taking orders from a man she never wanted to be beholden to again.

Somewhere outside, thunder boomed. She tossed the Webster file aside and pulled out Wilson. The reverend who had probably murdered his love child had apparently managed to buy himself a jet by telling parishioners Jesus wanted him to have it, or some such nonsense. Shit, he was worth a ton of money. She ran her finger down the list of witnesses. The girl's mother, the reverend himself, a neighbor who showed up when she heard screaming. The first responders. She rubbed her temples and winced. There had to be someone else—someone he'd confided in about it. Suddenly finding out you had an illegitimate kid wouldn't go down easy.

Shannon pulled her laptop from her briefcase to search for articles on Wilson. Lots on the jet, less on any open transgressions. But one article buried in the search results caught her eye: a blogger named Jason Delaney had written a piece claiming Wilson had been spotted at a local pub on several occasions—a big no-no for a holy man. Delaney's blog had since been shut down, but a larger website on crooked ministers had picked it up and reblogged it. The bar angle could be nothing, but it'd be easier to get a conviction if she had a witness saying he was freaked out about the kid. And nothing loosened the tongue like liquor. *Plead it down, my ass.* Maybe she'd give the detectives a call back, ask them about it. She tried not to look toward Roger's stupid office.

The sky was still threatening to open and drown the world when a loud rap at the door made her squiggle a ragged line across the page she was jotting notes on. *What now?*

"Who is it?"

"Morrison."

The hammering in her head lessened. "Come in."

Morrison let himself into the room and set a cup of coffee on her desk. "Didn't have time to make coffee this morning, so I got you a caramel...something. Oh, and"— he set a paper sack on the table next to the coffee— "kale Caesar salad. I know it's not your favorite, but it was that or Greek."

"I hate Greek. Feta ruins everything."

"I know."

She picked up the coffee and narrowed her eyes at him. "You buttering me up for something?"

He grinned. "Got one for Valentine, too, and Petrosky. I don't see any of us walking over to the deli today in the storm that's coming. Except maybe Petrosky—he doesn't give a crap about the rain or his hair."

"So, just making the coffee rounds then?"

"And I like to see you smile."

"You like to see everyone smile."

"True."

She cocked her head. "Am I smiling?"

"Nope." He grinned, and she stared into his Pacific-blue eyes until the crinkle ironed itself from the corners, and he looked down at his shoes. "Okay, so maybe I found some new information on Johnson."

Oh, for fuck's sake. "I'm not working on Johnson anymore." She sighed. "Did you find this supposed clue, or did Petrosky?"

"I found it."

"Did Petrosky tell you to tell me?"

"He mentioned you might want to know, yes."

Fucking Petrosky. "Hey, you guys are cool," she said in her best gravelly Petrosky voice. "Why don't you go talk to her, Surfer Boy?" But Morrison wasn't a fool, and he knew better than to come at her with bullshit. It must be good.

She crossed her arms over her chest and leaned back in her chair. "So, what is it?"

"A video."

"Of?"

"The pay phone where the anonymous call about the gunshot came from. Looks like a guy covering his face."

On the day of the murder, hours before Lewis was killed, a neighbor had filed a noise complaint about yelling coming from the Lewis place. It was an easily verifiable phone call from the same building, one that fit with the rest of the day's events: argument between Johnson and Lewis, Johnson takes off, lets the anger fester, then she comes home to find Diamond, and there goes his freaking skull. But at midnight, after Derek Lewis's murder, an anonymous tip had come in from a pay phone, blocks from the scene, claiming that gunshots were heard inside Lewis's apartment. Yet, like she'd discussed with Petrosky ad nauseam, they hadn't found gun residue on Johnson or Lewis or anywhere in the apartment.

"Whoever called did it from this pay phone so they wouldn't be seen," Morrison said.

"They hit that phone because there wasn't another pay phone nearby. There's what? Twelve working pay phones in all of Metro Detroit?"

"I don't think that's it. If it was an emergency, if someone had really heard gunshots, there were tons of open gas stations and liquor stores near the scene. And this lot's been closed for the last two months, which is why we couldn't get hold of the owners before now—whoever called probably thought the place was deserted already." His brows knitted together. "Someone else knew that something bad had happened at Lewis's apartment."

Shannon shook her head. "Like I've told Petrosky three thousand damn times, there's no way to prove that. Hell, maybe Ashley Johnson caught a ride down there and called after she killed Lewis to make sure someone found Diamond. She knows how long the cops take to respond from her arguments with Lewis; she could have made the call and still have had at least forty-five minutes to get back and kill herself. She already has enough of her day unaccounted for."

"Unaccounted for?" Morrison squinted at her, confused, and a wave of recognition hit her.

She set down her coffee. *She wasn't depressed that day*, Petrosky had said.

"Was *Petrosky* with her?" Her fists clenched under the table. "Was that where she spent her missing hours after her fight with Lewis and before she cracked his skull?"

Morrison cocked his head. "Petrosky didn't tell you? Maybe it's something he's—"

"Morrison, what the fuck is going on?"

"She met with Petrosky to pick up some clothes. For her interview."

"What time?"

"He picked her up about an hour before the first noise complaint came in. That's how we know she wasn't the one arguing with Lewis."

Are you fucking kidding? "You're telling me that Ashley Johnson's missing hours were spent with *Petrosky?*" she growled. "Why didn't he bring that up before trial?" But Petrosky wasn't responsible for the ache in her gut. She lowered her voice. "Why didn't *you* tell me?"

"He said he told you."

"And you believed that lying asshole?"

Morrison shrugged, but his face didn't change. Sometimes she wanted to slap him just to see if he'd flinch.

She leaned back in her chair, breathing around the block of cement that had settled in her chest. *Why would Petrosky keep this back?* "Was Johnson fucking him?" Not that it mattered; it was too late for Johnson now anyway. And it was definitely too late for Lewis. Either way, screw Morrison's partner.

"Nope, he was just helping her out. She didn't want Lewis to know about it." He frowned. "I don't know, Shannon. Maybe Petrosky figured he'd wait until he had more proof to tie it all up for you. All I know is he took her to the Goodwill on Main and then to dinner at Holly's. There'd be people who saw them, cameras at the Goodwill. The server at the restaurant. His credit card receipt." He shrugged. "Like I said, I thought you knew."

"You really thought he'd told me?" Shannon's heart throbbed in her ears. She glanced at the wall between her office and Roger's and tried to lower her voice again, but it wasn't going to work for long.

"We've been friends a long time, Shannon. I've never lied to you about anything."

The hard edges in her chest softened. "You lied about liking Valentine's pumpkin pie last Thanksgiving."

"I didn't lie to you about it. Just to Lillian."

She sighed. Who had Lewis argued with? Who had called after he died? It really didn't matter, not now, but it would have been nice to know this information weeks ago. *Petrosky. What a fuckhead.*

"Maybe we can talk about this more over dinner?" Morrison said.

"I'm swamped." She put her hands on the desk, shuffled her case files around.

Morrison watched her flip the Webster case to the top of the stack. "Coffee?"

"Never in the afternoon."

"Wine?"

"I don't drink."

He smiled. "Liar." He turned toward the door and paused with his hand on the knob, waiting. "See you at the gym."

She stared at his back but didn't respond.

He sighed, glanced over his shoulder, and nodded almost imperceptibly, mouth tight. Sad.

Good. He knew he'd fucked up. When she said nothing more, he turned back to the exit. "Until we meet under the barbell, Shanny." He eased the door closed behind him.

When she heard the clack of the latch, she grabbed the bag and speared a bite of salad as thunder rolled and rain and sleet attacked the roof like thousands of angry marbles. The kale was bitter but good, and probably healthier than the roast beef sandwich she'd planned on ordering from the deli down the street—not to mention drier.

She stared at the icy rain sheeting down her window and obscuring the world like she was trapped in a filmy bubble. *Fuck*. No wonder Petrosky was so adamant about this Johnson case. And to hide all this for months was just...God, he was an asshole. Maybe even an asshole who obstructed justice. Unless he was just lying to get Shannon to look at the case. Or...did something happen during his time with Johnson that implicated her further? Was there something Johnson said or did that made her look guilty? Something he hadn't wanted to testify about?

That was probably it. Petrosky treated half these women like they were his own fucking daughters. Probably because he'd lost his own so horribly. She poked at a cucumber with her fork. How would "Daddy" react if he found out some asshole was beating on his girl and her child? Shannon blew her hair out of her face, giving her frustration a voice. *Shit, could it have been...*

No way. Petrosky was a dick, but not a murderer.

She speared a final forkful of salad but tossed it, along with the carton, into the trash. Her throat had become too tight with dread to swallow another bite.

5

THE SLEET WARMED to a chaotic rain that had eased to a trickle by the time Shannon got into her car that evening. Wet earth and last season's leaves, their scents awakened by the melting ice, crept in through the closed car windows as she drove down Main Street toward the gym to sweat out the remnants of her agitation. On her right, the original Ash Park loomed from behind a wrought iron gate, its hinges long since rusted beyond use. Shame. In the back, knotty ash trees coiled in on themselves behind what was left of a park bench—all hiding in the shadow of the old elementary school, its windows boarded and forgotten. The year before, a serial killer had used the school to gut a prostitute and her son; left their bodies for the rats. Petrosky had taken it hard. Maybe he'd been close to that girl too, though he'd never said. Sometimes as Shannon drove by, she imagined she could still hear them screaming.

The CrossFit warehouse vibrated with the anticipatory energy of six regulars plus a curly-haired blond woman Shannon didn't recognize, all stretching their legs and doing warm-up exercises at the frantic pace of people trying to catch up after not doing shit all week. Morrison was already there, stretching his hamstrings, watching her wearily. He cocked an eyebrow like he was asking if she was still pissed. The hardness in her chest softened. It wasn't his fault Petrosky was a jerk. And Morrison clearly couldn't be expected to verify what his partner did or didn't tell her. Shannon nodded to him, smiled, and watched him grin back before heading to the bathroom to change.

But something was still gnawing at her insides, irritating the lining of her belly. In the bathroom mirror, her eyes looked sharp and blue, mouth too tight, forehead still crinkled with annoyance. Petrosky. He was a dick, but she *had* been wrong about Johnson arguing with Derek

Lewis. Had she been wrong about Johnson killing him too? She shook her head. No. *Hell no.* She had done her due diligence on that case. Johnson had killed Lewis. The end.

Fuck you, Petrosky. Goddammit. She pulled her workout gear from the bag with enough force to tear the zipper.

When she emerged from the bathroom, Kimball was stepping to the front of the class and clapping his hands in a short staccato burst that meant *it's go time*. "Today we're starting with twenty laps around the warehouse," he said, practically yelling, though there was no other sound in the room save for the gentle patter of the waning raindrops on the roof. "Then suck it up for fifty double unders, hip-shoulder mobility stretches, thirty squats, twenty pass-throughs with a PVC pipe, and thirty overhead squats." Staccato hand clap. "And go!"

Shannon fell into step with Morrison as they took off around the interior perimeter of the warehouse. She took the first corner faster than he did, but he recovered and caught her before the next turn. Around and around and around. Third lap. Fourth. Shannon tuned in to the dull thunk of their shoes, the scrape of rubber against cement, her own aggravated breath that had nothing to do with the run. *Fuck Petrosky. Fuck him in his stupid eye.*

"You okay?" Morrison asked.

He always knew, goddamn him. Ahead of them, the woman with blond corkscrew curls bobbled, righted herself, and swiped an arm across her forehead. She was obviously new—she'd pass out halfway through Kimball's workout if she tried to maintain this pace.

Shannon caught Morrison's eye before refocusing on the path ahead. "I'm fine."

"Want to talk about it?"

"No."

"No?"

"Well...maybe," she panted.

They circled around to the front of the warehouse for the... fifteenth time? Eighteenth time? She had no idea, but Kimball was gesturing for them to come back to the main workout area. As the blond woman in front of her passed him, he ran his fingers over her arm, lightly, suggestively, and Shannon caught the woman giving him a wink. *Huh.*

Kimball didn't smile at Shannon when she passed. Or touch her arm or any other part of her. She would have kicked him in the balls. "Grab your ropes!" he barked, turning on the music: hip-hop.

Shannon headed to the middle of the room, where the jump ropes lay across wooden utility crates, one for each of them. She grabbed hers and got into position.

"Double unders, let me see 'em!"

"Is it about Johnson?" Morrison said beside her, his jump rope whipping through the air. How the fuck was he talking? She could barely catch her breath.

"Keep it going, people. Forty more," Kimball called.

Shannon counted, pushing every thought she had into her laboring muscles, the bounce in the balls of her feet, the rope whistling twice under for each jump.

"Ten more, people."

"Shannon? Is it about Johnson?"

"Lay 'em down, people, we're gonna stretch it out," Kimball yelled, and his voice had an agitated edge. Angry, even. Must have had a bad day, though she'd have thought the pretty blonde he was flirting with earlier might have taken the edge off.

"Yeah. Obviously, it's about Johnson," she said to Morrison. It came out breathy and strained. She sank into a deep lunge, one leg in front of the other, knee almost touching the floor.

Morrison lunged beside her.

"Switch legs." Kimball leveled a hard stare at her, then at Morrison, who was paying him no attention.

Shannon pulled one leg back and lunged with her other. "I—" The room was suddenly too quiet, maybe between songs. At the front of the room, Kimball lunged too, eyeing them with a furrowed brow and tight lips. When he caught her looking, he turned his attention to Bouncy Curls on Shannon's left, and his face softened. "Switch legs. Last set."

Shannon's heart was throbbing in her ears as loudly as the bass line by the time she completed her squats and pass-throughs. Every muscle in her upper body sang. Her arms ached, but she held the pipe and panted through the overhead squats. Shannon thought she felt Morrison's eyes on her as she completed the last ten reps, but when she looked, he was focused straight ahead, breathing hard, sweat glistening at the crook of his elbow and wetting the ocean wave on his T-shirt. *So he's human after all.*

"That's it," Kimball called. "Nice work."

Shannon strode past Morrison to the bathroom, where she wiped herself off and threw her suit back on so she wouldn't freeze in the chilly night air with her soaked gym clothes. When she emerged, wrinkled and exhausted, Morrison had already changed his shirt and was toweling his hair. He shoved the towel into his gym bag.

Valentine walked over to her from the entrance. *When did he get here?* She wracked her brain, trying to remember if he'd been there the whole class...no, she was sure he hadn't. And he didn't have a drop of sweat on him. Maybe he was just coming to do some after-class reps before heading home.

"Missed you in class tonight," she said.

"No worries, I'll see you tomorrow in court. I've got the spot after you with Judge Oliver."

She glanced around the room for the curly-haired lady who was probably halfway to screwing Kimball—there were cheaters everywhere, she would know—but the woman was gone. Must have run out as soon as class was over. Maybe out puking in the parking lot—that happened sometimes with the first-timers. "What are you in court on?" she asked Valentine.

"People contesting parking tickets. The usual shit for a flatfoot." He winked, but his face fell when Kimball cleared his throat from behind him. Kimball gestured to the warehouse door.

"Anyway, see you guys," Valentine said and headed for the bathroom.

Shannon nodded to Valentine and followed Morrison to the exit. As they passed Kimball, he waved goodbye with one terse jerk of the wrist.

"Did he just dismiss us?" Shannon said.

Morrison nodded. "He must have somewhere to go. Like always."

"Not in a hurry to toss Valentine out, though, is he?" And Morrison had a key, why would Kimball give a shit if they stayed?

A crisp breeze sharp enough to cut skin blew through the garage doors, mingling the reek of body odor with asphalt and soggy dirt. Morrison ran a hand through his damp hair.

"Want to get coffee?"

"No caffeine for me, I—" She stopped short at the garage door and stared across the lot. Her car. Something was wrong with her car. The back window had been smashed, bits of glass glistening on the ground. The papers fluttering across the lot looked like the yellow legal pad she used to keep notes. In fact—

Shannon dropped her bag and ran to her car. Her briefcase lay over the broken window, half in and half out of the vehicle, her files tossed on the pavement. She peered at the dash, expecting the stereo to be tampered with—or gone—but it looked intact. She clicked unlock to disable the apparently fucking useless alarm, opened her car door, and reached across to the console where she had tossed her jewelry before going into the warehouse. Her earrings glinted in the overhead lights. What the hell? Not that she wanted to be stolen from, but if they hadn't broken in for valuables…

Morrison bent toward the broken window and peered inside. "You set the alarm?"

The pit in Shannon's stomach twisted. She sat back in the driver's seat. "Yeah, I did, but it only sounds if someone opens the doors."

Morrison's brows furrowed. "What did you have in the briefcase?"

"Just files from work." She closed the glove box. "Nothing identifying, just my notes. All my official files are at the office." She chewed her lip, thinking. She'd had information on a couple of assaults that looked like they'd get off. A child manslaughter case that would be settled with a plea. No paperwork worth taking. Shannon stared through the windshield across the lot. Kimball was approaching from the warehouse, phone in hand. Where was Valentine? This was his kind of thing.

Morrison knelt behind the car, trying to grab the remaining sheets skittering around the lot. "They all in here? Or most of them?" He passed her the papers he'd collected.

Shannon sifted through the paperwork. I...I'm missing a few pages on a sexual assault I got yesterday, though the main fact sheet is still here. And...Johnson's." She flipped. "All of Johnson's notes."

"Johnson? But—"

"I had some stuff left over from the trial, mostly from my final summation." She peeled back page after page. Someone took her notes? *Now?* No, that made no sense; the case was over. The sheets were probably wafting around in the woods that backed the lot or shimmying across the street, ready to disintegrate with the next rainstorm. Had to be. But...what if they weren't?

Goddammit all to hell. She needed a drink. "Let's go get some food."

"I just asked you for coffee. Don't you think you're jumping the gun a little?" His face remained flat, but she could feel the lilt in his voice.

"Oh, fuck off, Morrison. This is not the time."

He put his hands up in acquiescence. "All right, you've convinced me—dinner it is. We can take my car. I'll get a tow and file a report on this later tonight."

Shannon nodded mutely, her heart palpitating, and exited the car while Morrison peered into the night behind her.

RED VELVET CURTAINS straddled every window, but abstract art hanging from wires on the ceiling kept the place from feeling pretentious—local stuff, maybe from the high school, all swirls in obnoxious colors. The waitress directed an irritating thousand-watt smile at Morrison.

Shannon glared at her until she walked away. "How'd you find this place?"

"A phone app. Got tons of great places around here, most of them out of the way."

She stabbed a piece of salmon, trying to ignore the errant creases in her blouse and how completely disgusting she felt. She should have gone home to shower. "Fuck today. I mean, seriously." She stuck the salmon in her mouth and forced herself to swallow, but her stomach flipped. She set her fork down.

"I understand. Sometimes life's tricky."

"Tricky? Jesus, Morrison, you've got all the passion of a paper clip."

Morrison smiled and sipped his water. "I'll let Petrosky know what happened. I'm sure he'll want —"

"Screw Petrosky. What's he going to do, look into it and withhold information again like a royal dick?" She took a gulp of wine and relished the gentle acidic burn as it slid down her throat and calmed her heart. Or maybe she just hoped it would calm her; her glass rattled against the table as she set it down. "You couldn't pay me enough to deal with him on a regular basis."

"He's a good guy. A little rough, but a good guy."

"Why are you so forgiving of him?"

Morrison shrugged. "He kind of reminds me of my dad, that closed-off demeanor. Not easy for everyone to love"—he gestured to her— "case in point." He waited while she grabbed her wine glass again. "Plus, he doesn't have any other family, not since Julie died."

Her heart seized. She hated that she still had a soft spot for Petrosky, but no one deserved to lose a child. "Is that why he helps all the working girls? Because of what happened with his daughter?"

"Petrosky's teenage daughter was not a prostitute."

"No, but she was kidnapped, right? Raped and murdered?"

Morrison nodded, eyes on the wall behind her.

"So is that why he does it? He thinks he's helping the girls?"

"I don't know. He just helps. Gives them food. Money."

"Clothes on the down-low."

Morrison pushed a tomato around on his plate. "A place to stay."

He lets hookers stay at his house? Her jaw dropped. "Why would he let those women stay with him? It's... Isn't he worried they'll steal his stuff? Maybe get in trouble if people think he's soliciting?"

"I think things get a little lonely for him." He took a bite of salad and washed it down with mineral water.

"Nothing like a hooker to make you feel less lonely."

Morrison laughed. "Indeed." He put down his fork, his eyes on her full plate.

"God, I hate this." She didn't have to say "the car"; she could tell he already knew by the way he nodded, knew that even the wine couldn't turn her brain off. She sighed. The break-in wasn't necessarily related to Johnson, but the timing was too perfect—just after Johnson's conviction, and whoever it was hadn't taken any other files. But why now? Why not before, earlier in the trial? It would have made more sense to take her notes then, whether someone was trying to help Johnson or incriminate the woman further. Shannon tucked a stray hair behind her ear.

Morrison watched her closely, his blue eyes locked on her, supportive, questioning. "You know it isn't a coincidence."

Not a coincidence...because he thought she'd prosecuted the wrong person. Was Johnson innocent? No. *But what if she is?* No, she had to stop thinking that way. "Whatever. I know you guys are going to have to investigate, but I don't need Petrosky all over me about it, which is the only reason I haven't confronted him about that information he withheld on Johnson. And I need evidence more conclusive than Derek arguing with a mystery person before you guys come at me on this again. I'm not about to go telling Roger that I convicted the wrong girl based on some random phone call and a smashed window."

"You're not worried about Roger."

She clenched her fist, released it. "Fine. If Johnson really is guilty and I go shedding doubt on her conviction, Griffen could appeal and get it tossed. Doubtful, but possible. I don't want to be responsible for a guilty person going free any more than for an innocent person being locked up." She drummed her fingers on the table. "You can tell Petrosky so long as he keeps it close to the vest. Which apparently he's good at doing if he's letting prostitutes live with him." She forked an asparagus spear but just stared at it. Her car. *Someone trashed my fucking car.* She set the asparagus back on her plate and wiped her fingers on a napkin. Her hand shook.

Morrison leaned forward, appraising her and what was left of her fish. "You need dessert."

Her chest was tight enough that she feared she'd never be able to swallow. "I can't really eat right now."

"Trust me." Morrison summoned the waitress. "The usual, Kim." The girl grinned at him, shot daggers at Shannon, and left.

She raised an eyebrow at the waitress's back. "You come here often?"

"Are you trying to pick me up?"

Shannon stifled a smile. "I mean, come on, 'the usual'? And you're on a first-name basis with the waitress?"

"I've been here a handful of times."

"With who?" Was he seeing someone and hadn't told her? Her stomach tightened. Nah, he'd have mentioned it. They were buddies. Best buddies. Had been for years, since before she'd married Roger, and they'd had enough conversations about his stupid ass.

"I come alone," he said. "Usually at lunch. Been trying to get Petrosky to come too, but the one time he did, he ordered meatballs and bread to make it into a sandwich." Morrison shook his head and smiled affectionately. "I'd have brought you sooner, but you say you're busy half the time. Always eating at your desk."

"I also say I don't drink." Shannon nodded at her glass of wine.

"That's because you're a liar. But I still like you." He winked.

Kim returned with crème brûlée and two spoons, which she deposited in front of Morrison, without so much as a glance in Shannon's direction. *Looks like someone doesn't want a tip.* When the waitress was gone, Shannon reached over and grabbed a utensil, but Morrison stopped her short of actually spooning anything into her mouth.

"Let's play a game."

She furrowed her brows. "You're going to try that Zen bullshit again, aren't you?"

He chuckled. "Zip it and close your eyes. Have I ever steered you wrong before?"

Shannon leaned on her elbows, with her fingers laced together and perched her chin on her knuckles.

"Your eyes aren't closed."

She blew a stray hair out of her face and closed her eyes.

"Now inhale, and describe what you smell."

After a moment, the light scent of sweet cream invaded her sinuses. "Sugar."

"Try again."

"Vanilla?"

"More."

She sniffed again, the heat from his hand on the spoon tingling along her cheekbone as the scent of the food wafted into her nostrils. "Maybe…alcohol?"

"Grand Marnier. Okay, open your mouth."

She opened her mouth, and he laid a teaspoon of the dessert on the tip of her tongue.

"Let it rest there, but don't swallow."

She closed her lips and swirled the custard around the roof of her mouth.

"What do you taste?"

"Besides what I just smelled?"

"Yes."

"Fruity. Orange?"

"Orange peel. Did you notice that before?"

"Nope." She swallowed, easily, and opened her eyes. With her throat finally relaxed, she picked up her fork and finished her salmon. "That's a good trick, dammit. Plus, I bet it makes you eat less. I could probably stand to eat less brownies."

"Eh, you can eat as many brownies as you want, Stone Cold."

She shivered. "Ick. Don't call me that. It's creepy."

"Better than mine, though." He took a bite of the custard and held it in his mouth before swallowing, just as he'd had her do.

"I'll just call you Buddha."

"I can't live up to that." He leaned back in his chair. Shannon met his eyes, and for a moment, she was in the ocean, could almost feel the waves washing over her, her limbs floating in liquid salt. She picked up her wine again as Morrison's phone buzzed.

Morrison looked at his cell. "Looks like Petrosky's headed to the hospital on something," he said. "You want to swing by and see Derry? I told him I'd come say hi this week anyway."

Shannon's face was hot. Why was her face hot? She frowned at the wine glass and nodded.

6

By the time they arrived at the hospital, the crisp evening breeze had cooled Shannon's face. But Petrosky looked as irritated as ever, scowling at the ER doors, his cheeks pink with cold—or rage—a cigarette between his teeth. When Shannon and Morrison stepped onto the curb, Petrosky tossed his cigarette to the ground and headed inside through the automatic doors. "Domestic Violence case turned homicide," Petrosky muttered at the fluorescent hallway in front of them.

"Why'd they call us?" Morrison asked Petrosky's back.

"Abuse history. She called the cops yesterday and had him picked up. Tonight he shot her for her trouble. It'll be routine and over today, if I can grab the evidence." Petrosky pried an antacid from a roll, shoved it into his mouth, and stuck the roll back into his pocket. "I'm trying to get them to pull the bullet for me tonight, but they're giving me shit about it. I hate when they give me shit." He stopped in front of a door and leaned against the wall opposite. "That's why I'll wait here until I have what I need. That, and I want to snag this twat before he heads to Canada."

"Harassing the doctors might not be the best way to get what you want," Shannon said.

Petrosky kept his eyes on the door. "Always worked in the past."

Shannon balked as a thin woman with gray-streaked hair and flowered scrubs exited the room. The nurse smiled at each of them solemnly, though with tired eyes and lips that didn't quite curl up all the way. "They'll do what they can, dear," she said to Petrosky. "But we're backed up tonight, and they need to focus on the living before they get to your… er, request. Even the morgue is behind."

Petrosky nodded and took her hands in his. "Thank you, Frannie, I do appreciate you."

Shannon did a double take. Since when was Petrosky that…considerate?

The nurse nodded like Petrosky's behavior was perfectly normal. Shannon supposed it was, but certainly not for him.

"You go on and do what you have to do," the nurse said. "Find who did this to that poor girl."

"Oh, we will." Petrosky released her hands, and the nurse retreated down the hall.

Shannon watched her go, trying to remain calm by channeling her inner crème-brûlée-eating monk but ended up glaring at Petrosky instead. *Manipulative bastard. Just like Roger.* He didn't deserve a free pass on the material he'd kept from her on Johnson. "So I hear you withheld information on Johnson's whereabouts the day Lewis died."

"It didn't matter—you were still going to convict her." Petrosky twisted his head, and his neck popped, but his eyes stayed with her, defiant. "Easy win for the prosecution."

Shannon's heart rate tripled, and her shoulders went rigid. "I didn't take it because it was easy, you asshole. What the fuck could have been that important to Johnson that she would withhold something like that? That *you* would withhold it?"

"Maybe she didn't feel obliged to tell the person who was going after her."

"Okay, but—"

"I was only with her for a couple hours, well before Lewis's murder. After dinner, she said she wanted to take a walk before her interview. I didn't argue with her."

"So really, she could have been doing anything. Maybe she was high as hell on smack before she even got to the apartment, killed Derek for no reason at all."

"And you wonder why she didn't tell you? Besides, heroin doesn't make people go ape shit and murder folks."

Shannon crossed her arms, the crème brûlée burbling in her stomach. "You're lucky I don't call you out for obstruction."

Petrosky shrugged.

"Shannon?"

She felt a hand on her shoulder and whipped around. *If just one more person fucks with me right now, I swear to god—*

But it was Alex, his face drawn and pale, and her agitation melted into concern and settled heavy at the bottom of her stomach. "I didn't know you were coming up today," he said. His voice was strained.

"I…didn't know I was coming either." The words hung in the air between them, thick with unspoken explanations. *What happened?* Had Derry taken a turn for the worse? The doctors said he could deteriorate fast, but surely not within a day or two. She examined Alex's tense jaw, fighting the urge to run upstairs.

Morrison nodded to Alex, unsmiling, so he must have noticed that something was deeply wrong too. "Good to see you, Alex." Morrison glanced at his partner.

Shannon had almost forgotten Petrosky was there. "Oh, uh, Dr. Coleman, this is Detective Petrosky." Shannon gestured between the two. "Petrosky, Dr. Coleman."

Petrosky shoved his hands in his pockets, jaw tight, eyes narrow and suspicious. *What the fuck is that about?*

Alex ignored the slight and turned to Morrison to take his offered hand. "Good to see you again, Curt. Jerry said you were coming by. I just didn't know it would be tonight."

"Spur of the moment," Morrison admitted, peering into Alex's face. The worry lines around his mouth deepened.

Alex stepped back and addressed Shannon, lowering his voice. "Hey, if you have an extra minute, come on up to Jerry's room. I think it would be good for Abby to see you. She had a rough day."

Rough day. *Shit, not Derry. Please, not Derry.* "What happened?" The words trembled on her tongue but sounded okay in the air.

"Lucky…died." His words were *not* steady in the air—they vibrated from his lips, ragged and hoarse.

Lucky? "He was fine this morning!" If it'd been something at her house that made him sick, she'd never forgive herself.

"It wasn't…natural causes. Someone got to him this afternoon." Alex wiped at his eyes as if trying to unsee it, trying to make it not true. "They ripped him apart."

"Jesus." Shannon covered her mouth with her hands. How was that even possible? Alex and Derry lived in a beautiful lakefront home in a safe, upscale neighborhood. Not that money made people stop being crazy, but… "Did Abby—"

"No, no, I got there first, found him when I stopped there to meet Abby's bus."

"An animal, maybe?" It was a crapshoot, too hopeful. She knew the answer before he said it from the way he refused to meet her eyes.

"Whoever did it left a pile of limbs on the porch, neat, in a row. Couldn't even find his head, probably some dog grabbed it and carted it away. Or they kept it, sick bastards. I'll file a police report as soon as I get a chance." He still wouldn't look at her. "God, there was blood everywhere on the porch, you wouldn't think there'd be so much, he was so…small…"

Shannon's stomach heaved, and she sucked breath through her nose, the rubbing alcohol stench nowhere near enough to cover the tang of bile in her throat. "I'll come up in a little."

"Okay." Alex turned to Morrison. "Good luck with your case, gentlemen," he said and started down the hall toward the elevators. Toward

Derry's room. To help her grieving niece to deal with a dead cat and a soon to be dead—

"Who's Lucky?" Petrosky asked.

"A kitten. My niece's kitten."

Petrosky's eyes stayed on Alex's back, his mouth twitching. "Your brother live near a bunch of psychopaths?"

"Nope. They live right off Square Lake Road." She watched Petrosky's jowls clench and unclench. What was she missing? "Do you and Alex know each other?"

Alex rounded the corner, and Petrosky's glower faded. Without another word, he turned and started off down the hall in the other direction, toward the front doors.

Shannon watched Petrosky's receding back and turned to Morrison. "What the fuck was that about?"

"Not sure. My guess is that Petrosky was here being, as he would say, a twat in the emergency room, and Alex called him out on it. Wouldn't be the first time Petrosky pushed a little too hard." He averted his eyes and looked in the direction Petrosky had gone. "I was going to stop up to see Derry with you, but this…you go ahead. I'll wait in the car for you."

He knew. He always knew. He'd known the night she found out Derry was sick when she'd curled up in the back of his car, and he'd stood watch outside instead of trying to placate her with stupid platitudes and bullshit ideologies about things being God's plan or whatever the fuck else people said. But it wasn't fair to make him sit around and wait tonight. "I can call a cab home."

"Nope. I'll be in the car. Got some paperwork I need to finish on the laptop anyway." His eyes were kind, stoic, but determined.

She pecked him on the cheek. "Thanks."

"Anytime, Shanny."

When she turned the corner toward the elevators, he was still standing there, staring after her.

THE ATMOSPHERE in Derry's room was dank, cold, morose. You could almost smell the despair that some said closed in at the very end of life, though it was probably only the fluids leaking from a body preparing to die. But this room was not only clogged with sorrow from the imminent loss of a loved one. Here there existed a more immediate tragedy—a child, bitterly grieving her murdered pet.

Abby slumped on the bed, her arms around Derry, her face pressed into his scrawny chest. Shannon resisted the urge to cover them both with a blanket. She couldn't stand looking at Derry's emaciated arms sticking from the hospital gown, the bones in his hands like hash marks counting down the days until he lost the fight.

Derry looked up as she walked in, his eyes glassy, his face wet.

"I'm so sorry, honey." Shannon crossed to the bed, sat on the edge, and put her hand on Abby's back.

Abby's muffled sobs wracked her lithe body. Shannon stroked her arm, against the grain, like she used to do when Abby was a baby—hurting for her, with her, but helpless to fix it. Derry kissed Abby's head.

Shannon raised her eyes to her brother's damp face. "Lucky was a good kitten. I think we'll all miss him."

Abby whimpered again, and Derry brushed her hair with his fingertips until her sobs subsided. "He'll be making you sneeze from the afterlife until you wash your sheets," he said.

Abby turned her face to Shannon, keeping her cheek on Derry's shoulder. "Lucky always thought that was funny. You sneezing." Abby sniffed, and Shannon handed her a tissue from the bedside table. "Remember when you sneezed so hard it made him jump half a mile in the air?"

Shannon smiled, but her lip quivered. "I remember." Her throat burned with unshed tears as she met Derry's red-rimmed eyes. She could feel it, the question, the worry, the fear. This was smaller, this loss. Soon his little girl would suffer one far greater—a devastating, heart-wrenching loss, and he would not be there to offer comfort. A tear dripped down Derry's cheek and onto his shirt. He stared at it, brows furrowed.

Shannon stood, straightening her blouse. "I think you guys need some time together. But I'll see you soon, okay, Abby?"

Abby nodded.

Shannon squeezed Derry's hand, so much thinner even than last week, more papery, more cold. She left the room before she could consider what that meant.

7

LUCKY'S FUR still lingered on the comforter in the spare bedroom when Shannon awoke the following morning, tiny white and orange hairs clinging to the yellow fabric. She stood in the doorway, staring at the sheets as if she had expected all evidence of the kitten to disappear the moment he stopped breathing. All night, visions had assailed her: his tiny broken body, limbs torn asunder, intestines spilling onto the porch, no longer whole, just a pile of pieces. When she'd finally drifted off, the dreams had been worse—knives and gore to the soundtrack of Abby sobbing, the coppery tang of blood in her nose.

Everything felt jagged and sharp. In the shower, the water seemed to slice at her skin, and when she stepped out, the chill of the bathroom tile froze her feet. Her silk blouse felt prickly against her flesh as she threaded her arms through the sleeves of her suit jacket.

She'd refused Morrison's offer of a ride to work this morning and called a cab to take her to the rental car place. She'd always had a tendency to isolate when things got hard, though, during her bout with postpartum depression, she'd learned to rethink that strategy. Loss and isolation don't go well together, Dr. McCallum had said. He'd also said she was so afraid things would go wrong that she'd rather destroy something perfectly good on her terms than leave it to chance and risk being hurt. He'd been right. It was probably leftover bullshit from years of convincing herself she didn't need anyone and was surely one of the reasons Roger had cut her so deeply. So...she'd connect with the guys. But later.

The cab reeked of stale cologne and garlic, or maybe that was just the driver. Shannon felt every bump on the freeway. The sun trying to peek through the fog was far too bright, the *shh* of the pavement grated like sandpaper against her eardrums, and though she knew she might only be trying to distract herself from images of torn-apart kittens, anger pulsed every time she considered the Johnson case.

Did it really matter that Petrosky had been with Johnson that day? Probably not. He obviously wasn't with her later that night, at the time of the murder. And just because someone else had fought with Lewis, so what? Johnson going missing hours after she left Petrosky didn't matter to the case unless it was something that implicated her or absolved her—and if it absolved her, she'd have told someone. At the end of the day, all this bullshit was just Petrosky trying to save one of "his girls." He couldn't stand the thought that this girl he'd tried to help had bludgeoned someone to death.

The rental car company was manned by a dour-faced soul with acne-like chicken pox who gave her the keys with barely a glance once her credit card cleared. Shannon thanked him silently; she had no desire to speak to anyone.

As she headed through the lot to her rental, Shannon pictured her car: windows smashed, briefcase torn open. It wasn't right, the missing papers, but she couldn't think of a reason anyone would care about Johnson after the fact. Even if someone else had been there the night Lewis died, they'd have been thrilled that Johnson took the fall. Unless... they thought the cops were looking for an accomplice and wanted to know what they had so far. That would make sense if Petrosky was poking around. Maybe. But an accomplice wouldn't risk alerting anyone to his presence just because he was curious about what they knew.

So, who else might have needed something from her? Shannon didn't have any other cases that were particularly evidence heavy, no other defendants that she could see being desperate to figure out what she had on them...except maybe the reverend. She'd focus harder on him. She'd look around on Johnson too. Worst case, she'd sent the wrong person to prison. Shannon sighed and rubbed her temples like she could squeeze the agitation out of her brain. Best case scenario, she'd affirm that Johnson was guilty and sleep a little better at night.

By the time she pulled up in front of her office building, Shannon had to actively resist the urge to drive home and go back to bed. She'd rather have walked across hot coals than go speak to Roger.

Her shoes clacked through the lot and up the stairs and thudded down the carpeted hallway to the door bearing the placard "Roger McFadden, Esquire." She opened it before he answered the knock.

Roger's eyes widened, but he recovered quickly, smiling into the cell in his hand. "Sounds good, honey," he said into the phone. Syrupy sweet. Must be a new lover—he'd lose that tone soon enough. Roger met Shannon's eyes. "And wear that lace thing I like." He smirked.

Shannon's fist clenched around the handle of her briefcase. *Don't respond, Shannon.*

Roger pocketed the phone and stood behind his desk, which was already piled with files and legal pads. Smug as fuck. Waiting for her to say something.

"I want to look at the Johnson case again."

The leery smile on his face fell. He came around the side of his desk and perched his ass on the edge of it. "You just got Johnson convicted beyond a reasonable doubt."

Shannon looked at the door, her hand still on the knob. She dropped her fist. "Some new information has come up, and I'm not sure if Johnson did it alone. I just want to be thorough."

"Then haul this 'someone else' in and charge them with your new evidence, get everyone put away." He stood and strode back around to his chair. "My god, Shannon, I almost thought you were suggesting she was innocent." He grinned at her, all teeth. Predatory.

She stared at him until his smile disappeared. "I don't know exactly what to think. Someone broke into my car last night."

"So?"

"The only files completely missing were Johnson's."

"Coincidence. Or some whacko wanted to collect original docs on the trial he'd been following for the last month."

True. She hadn't even considered the people who turned murder trials into spectator sports.

Roger sat and slapped open a folder on the desktop. "How's the Lambert case?"

"The—fine. Finished with the preliminary stuff, got an arraignment coming up."

"Good." He made a note on his legal pad. "Simpson?"

"Dropped. She won't testify."

"Good."

She stood, silent, watching him.

Roger scrawled something on a page. "Let your boy toy worry about your car." His eyes remained on his files. "We're not reopening Johnson."

Shannon succeeded in not stomping out of the room, but she closed the door hard enough to rattle the office window. "Fuck you, Roger," she whispered to the empty hallway.

Inside her own office, her files were where she'd left them. She plopped into her chair and glared at them for a minute before diving in and busying herself with motions and appeals and all the paper-pushing bullshit that lawyers do, but no one ever sees. Nothing more glamorous than hours of legal research. She was grateful to drop the pen from her aching hand when her cell phone buzzed on her desk, rattling with a noise like snapping twigs. Alex. *Oh shit.*

Her stomach churned. "Alex...what's... Is Derry—"

"Oh, no, Derry's fine." His voice sounded as tired as she felt. "I mean, he's...same as yesterday. I just wanted to thank you."

She squinted at the wall like it was hiding a secret from her. "Thank me for what?"

"The cop outside the house last night. Abby was really scared after what happened to Lucky, and with everything going on at the hospital, I didn't have time to file a report. Really helped Abby sleep better. And me too, honestly."

"Wait...outside the house?" *What the hell?* Why would anyone stalk her brother's house? Unless...did someone believe Alex and Abby were in danger? But it hadn't been Morrison; Alex would have called him by name.

The silence stretched on the other end of the line. "Didn't you tell him to?" A hint of worry had edged its way into Alex's voice.

Shannon pressed the phone to her ear to stop her hands from shaking. "Yeah, I mean...yeah. Of course. I just... Who ended up staying with you guys?"

"Detective Petrosky. I really thought he hated me from the way he acted yesterday, but now I think he's just a little...intense. Kind of a jerk, but looks out for people he cares about. Now I feel bad about reporting him yesterday afternoon."

"You called on him?" Of course, he had called on him. *Disagreement, my ass.* Now Petrosky's irritability at the hospital made sense.

"He was in the emergency room trying to bully my docs into—wait, did you not know that?"

Shannon was barely listening. Petrosky had stayed with Abby. But there was no way it was just because Abby was scared. He knew something Shannon didn't.

He knew there was reason to be afraid.

8

PETROSKY'S DAYS of having inside information are over.

Shannon crossed the street to the Ash Park Detention Center, where Ashley Johnson was being held. From the corner of her eye, the back side of the courthouse loomed, gray and ugly, but achingly sentimental like a childhood friend. Even the frayed alarm wire in one of the center windows hadn't changed. Had it really been ten years since she and Griffen climbed through and wandered the halls, smoking weed and dreaming of prosecuting, of being big shots, of saving lives? Romantic, this notion, but they'd been just college kids, full of shit and brimming with naïve idealism. Of course, for the guilty, the courthouse was the place where it all ended. It was unfortunate that once you walked through the front door in a suit, the glamour disappeared.

Inside the detention center, Shannon put her briefcase on the belt for inspection and walked through the metal detector toward an officer whose uniform was stretched tight over her ample bosom. "Ms. Taylor." The guard's matronly smile somehow managed not to feel out of place as she took Shannon's briefcase and peeked into it.

"How are you, Beatrice?"

"Good, good. Grandkids are keeping me busy, I'll tell you what." She handed the bag back. "How's your daughter?"

"Niece."

"Right. Sorry."

"No worries." Shannon shifted the case to her other hand, trying to ignore the ache in her chest. "She's getting big."

"Oh lord, they do that too, don't they? Never stop growing!"

Shannon nodded her goodbyes and walked into the reception area, a glorified DMV with extra bars and more bulletproof glass. Behind a Plexiglas window along the far wall, Officer Anton Cook's face lit up as she approached. "Taylor! Who you here for?" He pushed a yellow request form through the metal tray under the glass.

"Johnson. Ashley."

Cook raised a bushy eyebrow that looked like a caterpillar that had crawled onto his face to take a pit stop before making a cocoon.

"Just some follow-up." She pulled the page toward her and grabbed a pen.

"Right on. You're the second one in two days."

Her pen stopped mid-scribble. "Who else was here?"

"Frieda Burke."

Frieda Burke. *Huh.* Johnson's CPS worker and Griffen's ex-girlfriend. The one who had made him choose between Shannon, his completely platonic college friend, and her, his lover. A tinge of disquiet settled between Shannon's shoulder blades like the tingle of someone watching her. Shit happened, and sometimes it sucked, but that wasn't what was bothering her now.

What reason would Burke have to visit Johnson after the trial? Johnson's daughter, Diamond, was no longer in Johnson's care, and social workers were always swamped.

"Hey, you seen Morrison?" Cook's eyes danced. He seemed oblivious to her unease. Hopefully, Johnson wouldn't notice either, though Shannon could play it off as irritability. Not like she was currently a paragon of relaxation. "I haven't seen him since last night at the"—*hospital*—"gym."

"Oh yeah, you guys and your exercise. He put a hand on his gut. "I thought about joining, but Kimball is a little…intense for me lately." He held up a stainless steel coffee cup. "Tell Morrison I got his mug. He'll want it back eventually."

She nodded, still trying to settle her roiling belly. "I will."

Cook retreated through the steel door at the back of his little office box. Shannon leaned against the counter and glanced back at the empty chairs in the waiting area; the vacuum track marks not yet disturbed by visitors. Through the front door, outside, she caught a glimpse of a familiar figure: Petrosky, with his back to her, smoke from a cigarette wafting above his head like his face was on fire. *Stalker bastard.* No wonder she felt unsteady.

"Taylor?" Cook stood at the steel door to the waiting room, holding it open for her.

Shannon followed him through, and the door latched behind them, confining her in a claustrophobic tomb. She wiped her palms on her suit pants as Cook pressed a button, and a clear door of bulletproof glass slid open in front of them. *One more.* She took a deep breath, walked through the door, and waited with Cook in the next little clear box. The door behind them shut, and the entrance to the holding area opened.

"I put her on the end, last in the row." Cook gestured to the rows of halls. Shannon had always thought the place resembled a library, though instead of bookshelves, chest-high cinderblock walls were topped with black metal mesh that reached to the ceiling. "Thanks."

"No worries. I'll wait here."

Ashley Johnson was waiting for her on the other side of the mesh, mouth tight. "They said it was you, but I didn't believe them." Johnson's voice was soft and even, not a hint of anxiety or agitation. *Strange*. The first time Shannon had come, Johnson had cried through the entire interview. Maybe she'd been faking. Or maybe she was so hopeless now that she was numb. Despondent. During the trial, McCallum had said she was depressed. If she wasn't guilty and was locked up anyway, without her child…

Without her child. Shannon pushed thoughts of her own dark postpartum days from her mind and refocused on Johnson's now-trembling lip. There was the sadness. But sad or no, Shannon didn't have time to waste. "I know where you were the night Derek died."

Johnson turned her face away from the mesh, but not before Shannon saw her eyes widen with alarm.

"Why didn't you tell me, Ms. Johnson?"

Johnson shrugged and spoke to the side wall. "I didn't want anyone to get into trouble."

She couldn't really think Petrosky would have gotten into trouble for buying her second-hand clothes, could she? She must have met with someone else. Someone she'd be more nervous about getting caught with. So who would Johnson have to hide? "Why would they get into trouble?"

"I don't know."

The edge on the last word caught Shannon's ear. *Liar*. "Should I go ask them why they'd get into trouble?"

Johnson cleared her throat and stared at Shannon, chewing her lip like the wheels were turning in her brain. "You mean…Detective Petrosky?" she asked tentatively.

Shannon nodded and watched Johnson's eyes go from twitchy to steady and confident. Petrosky was not the big secret Johnson was keeping. So who was?

"Tell me about Detective Petrosky," Shannon said.

"Eddie was the only one who was ever really nice to me, never asked for anything in return. Gave me food, clothes, shoes for my interviews. Even let me sleep at his place a few times. Said if I had to, I could stay there with Diamond while I got myself together…I mean, if I had to because of Derek or whatever. I thanked God for Eddie so many times."

Eddie? Johnson was being pretty forthcoming for someone trying to protect a friend. "Where did you go that day after dinner?"

The alarm flashed in Johnson's eyes again, brief, but clear. She looked down at her wrists. "I just walked around. Stopped at a gas station to change and went to my interview."

"And after the interview?"

Johnson's mouth dropped, but she recovered quickly. The hairs on Shannon's neck stood up. "I wasn't ready to go back," Johnson said. "I just walked."

Bullshit. It had been February, much too cold for an evening stroll. "Who were you with, Ms. Johnson?"

Johnson stared at the wall and said nothing. Perhaps she'd been with someone else, someone who'd brought her home. Someone who'd maybe still been there when she killed Lewis. Someone she was protecting. But Petrosky was wrong. Johnson was a liar and a killer. Whatever she had been doing, it wasn't anything that would absolve her or she'd spill it.

Johnson leaned toward the screen, eyes finally meeting Shannon's. "Are you reopening my case?" Her voice wavered ever so slightly. Hopeful.

"No. Especially since you seem content to stonewall me." Shannon stepped away from the mesh and turned down the aisle.

"Wait."

Here we go. Shannon turned back slowly. "Who?"

"I'm sure there was... I mean, not someone I was with, but someone Derek was with when I was gone. His mom was always fighting with him, maybe that call...maybe it was her at the apartment. Maybe they had an argument."

Whoever had been there had left well before the cops showed up, but his mom? *Right.* "Derek's mother didn't kill him, Ms. Johnson."

"No, but she might have fought with him. She'd been trying to get custody of Diamond, and I think she might have called CPS on us. She had another social worker on us and everything. My friend Angela—the one who watches Diamond—said she saw the other worker at the house earlier that day. A guy."

There was nothing about another social worker anywhere in the files. Shannon stepped back to the mesh window. "You knew this person was at the house, and you kept it to yourself?"

Johnson shrugged. "Derek's mom was trying to take my baby even though I was doing everything right. And Diamond had already been in foster care once. I didn't want to lose her again."

If Derek and his mother had been trying to get Diamond taken away from Johnson, that was motive enough for murder. But if there had been another worker at the house the day of the killing, the fact that this other worker hadn't come forward was very suspicious. Had they seen something or someone that afternoon that they shouldn't have? Maybe Petrosky knew who the other social worker was. Shit, maybe he'd even told Johnson not to say anything if he thought it made her look worse. *Why the fuck am I even here?*

Shannon stepped back from the mesh but paused at a sudden thought about Johnson's visitors. "Your normal caseworker is Frieda Burke, yes?"

Slow nod.

"Did she come to visit you yesterday?"

"Yeah."

"Did she know who this other social worker was?"

"I didn't mention the other worker at all. She just wanted to know how I was holding up, gave me an update on the baby, let me know that Derek's mom was planning to go forward with adoption after they terminate my parental rights next year. Lucinda got exactly what she wanted."

Got what she wanted, my ass. "She lost her son, Ms. Johnson. Because of you."

"It wasn't because of me!" But her eyes radiated uncertainty. "And she *did* want Diamond. She always did." Johnson sniffed. "Ms. Burke said she went over there to check on the baby, make sure she was safe. She said Diamond's trying to walk now. And I'm gonna miss it." Tears welled in her eyes. "I'm gonna miss everything."

9

SHANNON LEFT the detention center as tense as she'd been when she entered. More questions, no answers, and Ashley Johnson was definitely withholding information about what she did after Petrosky left her. So if Johnson wasn't guilty...

She shook her head. No. This was all bullshit. Sometimes the right answer is the simplest one, and no matter how good Johnson was at playing innocent, no one else would have killed Derek over hurting his child. Who else could possibly have benefitted from his death?

Shannon peered into the parking lot, shielding her eyes from the white-hot sun that filtered through the clouds and cast the shadows of still-barren trees on the ground. What had her rental car looked like? Blue? She wiped dew from her forehead.

"Taylor!" Petrosky hustled up behind her, red-faced, smoke wafting from his nose.

If I had a nickel for every time he chased me across this lot... She whirled on him. "Why were you at my brother's house?"

"I was concerned."

"About what?"

Petrosky tossed his cigarette to the pavement and ground it out with his heel. "How's Ashley?"

"Oh, she's hanging in there, *Eddie*." Her fist clenched around her briefcase. "Why were you outside the detention center? You're not tired of stalking my family yet?"

"I saw you leave the office. I had an appointment across the street."

"With McCallum?"

"Yep."

"Good, I'm sure you need it. You better get out of here, you smell like booze."

His eyes narrowed. "No I don't. You just think that. You think a lot of shit that isn't true."

"Fuck you, Petrosky." Every fucking time.

Petrosky pulled his lips into an almost passable smile, pulled his cigarette pack from his breast pocket, and tapped a fresh one into his hand. "So, what's the deal with Ashley? You got anything new?"

"Nope."

"Come on, Taylor. You're a terrible liar when you're angry. And I'm exhausted from staying up all night outside your brother's house and then trying to finish up other cases today."

Shannon crossed her arms, her briefcase swinging against her abdomen. Back and forth, back and forth. "So, are you finally going to tell me what you were doing there last night?"

"Making sure."

"Making sure of what?"

"That they were safe."

Right. "I'm surprised you'd care what happens to Alex after last night."

Petrosky flinched. "We're all just trying to do our jobs, Taylor."

"Staking out the homes of civilians?"

"We look out for our own." He met her eyes, defiant but somehow kind, and Shannon's fists loosened. "Come on, Taylor. Tell me about Ashley. We're on the same side here."

She dropped her arms, and her case banged against her hip. "Fine, but I don't think it means much. Johnson thinks Lewis's mother wanted custody of her kid. Says a neighbor saw another social worker going into their apartment earlier that day. A man."

Petrosky's mouth tensed as he lit another cigarette, tainting her air with nicotine.

"Did you know about that, Petrosky? I swear if I find one more thing you kept from me—"

He blew smoke through his nostrils and shook his head. "I didn't know about the other social worker. And if this guy didn't come forward, didn't file any paperwork..." He puffed again and grimaced at the glowing ash. "Probably someone posing as a social worker. What else?"

Shannon pulled her keys from her briefcase and unlocked the doors on the rental car with a beep. "Not now, Petrosky."

"Did you talk to Roger about reopening Johnson?"

She started toward the car. "Yep. He doesn't want—Hey!"

Petrosky's fingers sank through her sleeve into the flesh of her upper arm.

"What the fuck, Pet—"

"Wait, Taylor, just wait." He dropped her arm and took off for her car, closing the gap in four frantic steps, his hand jerking to his gun. Shannon ran after him, watching the lot, but saw no one. He stooped and peered at her hood. No...not the hood. At a letter-sized manila envelope on the windshield, oily pockets of moisture seeping through the mustard-colored paper.

"What the—"

"Stay there, Taylor."

"Like hell."

Cigarette in his teeth, he grabbed a corner of the envelope from under the wiper and hefted the bulky package over the hood, pulling a Swiss Army knife from his back pocket.

"What are you doing?"

He ignored her, sliced the top of the envelope, and peered inside. His face went still. Frozen. Like her lungs.

She forced a breath, watching Petrosky's haunted gaze and the tremble in his hand that might have been alcohol withdrawal but probably wasn't. "Petrosky, what is it?"

Petrosky pinched the envelope between two fingers and lowered it to his side. "I wouldn't look in there, Taylor."

She reached for the package. Petrosky stepped back, trying to keep it from her.

Oh no you don't. Shannon pivoted and snatched at a corner. The envelope fell to the pavement in slow motion, straight down, hitting way too hard with a sickening thunk. The paper tore along oily lines. And she knew. She knew before it rolled from the lip of the envelope where the seam had given way, a mass of fur and blood, a circle of white bone peeking from the severed neck. And those eyes, dead and milky and bulging, tiny teeth unable to hold back the tongue, which protruded like an emerging slug, purple and rotten and horrid.

Bile rose into Shannon's esophagus.

Petrosky stooped and picked up Lucky's head with a piece of torn envelope, covering the dead eyes, the fat tongue, every lifeless piece. And suddenly it was Derry, going into the ground, never again whole, never again smiling or laughing or playing cards into the wee hours of the morning.

The air had thinned, all the oxygen sucked from the universe like her brother's soul was about to be, and Shannon put her hand on the hood and choked back a noise that sounded oddly like a sob. The noise itself angered her. *Those fucking bastards. Those—*

"You gonna let me keep it this time, Taylor?" Petrosky cradled the envelope in one gnarled paw.

She inhaled through her nose, fighting nausea. *Keep it together, Shannon.* Freaking out wouldn't help her—or her family. "So this is...what? A warning? A threat?"

Petrosky nodded, eyes on the envelope, perhaps hoping it stayed together until he could get it inside.

"You knew it—that this was about me. Us. That's why you were at my brother's."

Petrosky took a drag from his cigarette and watched the smoke curl into a cloud above his head. "I had a hunch." He turned the envelope and held it out to her. Shannon recoiled, but he held it steady until she looked at the pen scratch on the bottom: *It was me.* Block letters in what looked like a child's handwriting, but had probably been written in the non-dominant hand to avoid identification. Because there was no way it was a child who did this. It was not a child who'd murdered Lucky and left him bloody and dismembered. Not a child who had followed her and put a severed head on her car. *It was me.* Johnson might have killed Lewis in a moment of passionate fury, but this was premeditated.

"It was me, huh?" Petrosky's voice was so low she could barely hear him.

Shannon shook her head, but her jaw clenched. "Johnson had something to do with this, Petrosky. I'm not altogether wrong."

"You *are* wrong unless you think Johnson somehow snuck out of jail and tore your niece's pet limb from limb."

"Maybe Johnson knows whoever did this," she stammered. "Wants to punish me for putting her away. She still could have killed Derek Lewis." But the accusation didn't feel right, not anymore.

Petrosky didn't seem to be in the mood for speculating. "It's risky to drop a severed head on a car in broad daylight. Killers like this enjoy the thrill, the rush." He tapped the envelope, and Shannon imagined Lucky's eyeball wobbling in its socket. She inhaled through her nose to avoid vomiting.

"All of this is the work of someone else, Taylor. Not Ashley Johnson. And she doesn't know who the killer is or she'd have told us to save her own ass."

So someone was still out there. Someone dangerous. Her shoulders slumped. "I can't do this."

He eyed her but said nothing.

"My brother is...he's dying, Petrosky. Abby and Alex can't take any more right now. I just... Let me know how it all works out, okay? You can go harass Roger about it if you want. I just can't."

Petrosky sucked hard on his cigarette, the glowing ash nearly touching his fingertips. "That's why they're doing this to you."

"What?"

"No one killed my fucking cat, Taylor."

"You don't have a—"

"No one took Morrison's dog, and he loves that thing like his own flesh and blood. Whoever did this knows you're vulnerable and knows enough about you to figure out exactly where to hit you, so you'll give him what he wants."

"He knows where to hit me, so...what? What does he want?"

"Credit."

Petrosky was a fucking idiot. Credit for killing some low-level drug dealer? She'd be more likely to believe that Reverend Wilson was a kitten-killing psycho than that some random person had murdered Derek Lewis and framed Ashley Johnson and only later decided to get all pissy about it. "I can't do this," she repeated, her abdominal muscles twitching.

Petrosky crushed the cigarette with his heel. "Take care of yourself, Taylor." He turned his back to her and started across the lot, Shannon's throat growing tighter with each step he took.

"Thank you," she called to his back.

He stopped and looked over his shoulder.

"Alex said you were there until he went to bed this morning."

"I just showed up to take the report and hung out for a few hours." Their eyes met. "Morrison stayed the rest of the night, watched the house incognito from up the road. He's on his third cup of coffee already, and you know how California feels about excessive stimulants. You should thank him, too."

She watched Petrosky stride across the lot toward the precinct, the envelope with Lucky's head still clutched precariously in one hand. When he disappeared into the precinct, she finally unclenched her fists, extracting her fingernails from her palms. The bleeding crescents resembled cat scratches.

10

Shannon saw Lucky's tongue twice on the way to the hospital: once in the rearview and once peeking through the leather buckle on her briefcase, the image so vivid that she almost swerved into a truck and went to meet Lucky in the afterlife. The windshield had been scrubbed clean at a gas station, yet every time she glanced at it, there seemed to be a blemish there, some invisible filth that made her anxious to get her own car back. Her car. The one everyone expected her to be driving. Her chest tightened.

Someone had been watching her. Stalking her. There was no other way for Lucky's killer to know she'd driven a different car to the office today.

Shannon parked in the hospital garage, every muscle singing with tension as she exited the car and peered around the dimly-lit lot. Though there was no fetid, sulfuric odor to indicate the presence of a murderous beast, the shadows from every corner felt as if they were reaching toward her like creatures from another world, set to tear her asunder and leave her leaking gore onto the cement.

She hustled into the hospital, ignoring the cold, the smells, the orderlies, the ladies at the reception desk, the buzz of the elevator. It was as if a fog had descended on the hospital, thickening the air around her until she couldn't breathe, let alone use her sanity checklist to tick off all the mundane things around her. None of it mattered. Nothing mattered. They were all dead, sooner or later, every one of them. *Derry. Lucky. Derry. Lucky.*

Derry was leaning back against a pile of pillows, a clear plastic cannula snaking up his nose, blankets drooping around his frail shoulders. Classical music played from an iPhone dock on the end table, piano and cello—or maybe violin. Slow and haunting and melancholic. And he smelled—a ripe, rank, acidic stench. Maybe it had always been there. But today it wrapped around her head and seeped into her brain, forcing her to recognize what that smell actually was.

Disease. Dying. Decay.

Derry opened his eyes as she entered. "Shanny?" His voice had a harshness to it, a whispery quality that did not belong to the vibrant Derry who used to tease her for wearing pigtails. It was the voice of an old man, the raspy whisper of a stooped geriatric talking to ducks at a park. But Derry would never see old age. He wouldn't even see his next birthday.

She sat on the bed before he could register how much her legs were shaking. "How are you feeling? You sound tired."

Derry pulled the cannula from his nose and pushed a button near his hand. The bed hummed him up to a sitting position. "It's all the extra oxygen. Dries out your sinuses." But the bags under his eyes were more pronounced than they'd been yesterday; he hadn't stayed up all night because the oxygen was drying him out.

"Shanny, are you okay?"

Tell him you're fine. But he'd know she was lying, and she couldn't do that, not this close to the end, not when she needed him to know the truth. Or maybe she just needed him to forgive her. Truth and forgiveness. Throughout their dysfunctional childhoods, those elements had rarely come from anywhere but one another. And once he was gone...

She took a deep breath, air wheezing through her nostrils. "Lucky... It was... He died because of me. Because of a case I'm working on."

He gaped at her.

Say something, Derry. She put her hand over his. "It's my fault. I'm so sorry."

His face softened from surprise to concern. He flipped his hand over and squeezed hers, but softer than she wanted him too. Halfhearted? Or was he just that weak?

"It wasn't because of you. People are crazy."

"Yeah, they are. But I just... I can't...*fuck.*" Her chest was heavy, thick; her lungs smashed inside her rib cage. "Derry, I'm so sorry." She wept, wanting to be strong for him but failing with every choked gasp of air. Salt ran into her mouth and covered her shirt as her shoulders convulsed. Derry squeezed her hand again, but it was feeble, Jesus, *he* was feeble, and it made her feel a thousand times worse. She sucked in a breath through her nose and willed her chest to settle.

"Tell me what happened, Shanny."

"The Johnson case, I think. There were some things I didn't know. She might not have done it, or maybe she did it with someone else, I'm not sure. Maybe it's from another case entirely. But someone wants recognition. Someone wants me to... I don't know. Maybe they just want the fame. I don't understand what's happening." She sat and wiped a hand across her face. "But I can't get involved. I can't put you and Abby in danger, have these crazies running around by your house looking for god-knows-what to threaten me with. I just feel so—"

Derry dropped her hand and put his palms on either side of his skeleton—no, his legs. "You need to be involved in this case."

"What?" There was no way. She had no idea how long it would take to catch Lucky's killer and in the meantime…she couldn't risk something else happening to Derry. To Alex. To Abby.

"You need to figure out who did this. And you're going to."

"Derry, this isn't about us. Abby could get hurt. And I don't even know for sure Johnson is innocent. It might just be someone else who wants to get famous, some crackpot who—"

"You're rationalizing." He smiled feebly.

"I'm not rationalizing!"

"You know she's innocent, don't you?" He coughed, wet and heavy.

"I don't know anything." *Except that Johnson's lying.* And that there was someone else out there hurting people. Hurting her family. Hurting Abby. Her nerves jittered with electricity, the urge to run, the need to stay, the overwhelming desire to punch something.

"Come the fuck off it." Derry hacked again, and the tray table rattled like the fluid in his chest. "You wouldn't be digging around at all if you didn't think there was a chance she was innocent. You're trying to find a reason not to get involved here so that your poor, dead-in-a-month brother doesn't have to put up with people coming to his house and killing his pets. We promised Abby a dog, by the way. If we get one big enough, there's no way someone can hack it up."

"Derry, you can't be serious."

"You expect me to be afraid for what little remains of my life? To have you let this asshole go free? You want to let me die knowing that that the person who murdered Abby's fucking kitten is still out there?"

"Derry, just listen to yourself! I'm not just going to—"

"You are. Because it's the right thing to do. I'm not afraid to die, Shannon, but I am afraid to leave my daughter here with some maniac running around targeting us every time your office doesn't do what the fuck he wants! I don't want to die knowing that this asshole can go rip up my daughter at any time."

"But—"

"Goddamn you, Shanny. You know better. Now get the hell out of here until you're ready to make a dying man's wish come true." His voice was stronger now, louder, as if he were using all his energy to make sure she got his point.

"Derry, you're such an—"

"An adorable, brilliant, dead man, I know. Now go find this fucker, or I will kick your ass." He grabbed the cannula and stuck it back under his nose.

"You're not kicking anyone's ass."
"Ghosts are crafty, Shanny. Do not test me."

Shannon trudged back to the office, her stomach twisted in knots, her neck aching with unspent energy. She needed to fix this, but it wasn't like she had some awesome lead here. She had nothing. And Petrosky was handling it—he was just as motivated to figure out what was going on as she was.

Yet Derry's words kept zinging through her brain as she slogged through her case files, reading and rereading the same paragraphs over and over but absorbing none of the words. The briefs might as well have been written in Greek. She didn't hear the doorknob turning, but when she saw the door move out of the corner of her eye, she jumped up from her chair and leapt to the side of the desk, pen fisted in her hand, ready to stab the ballpoint tip into someone's throat.

"Shannon?"

Sweat trickled between her shoulder blades, down her spine, and into the waistband of her suit pants. She straightened and sat back down behind the desk, feigning calm and probably failing. "What do you want, Roger?"

"Progress on the Lambert case?"

"Arraignment in the morning."

"Expected plea?"

"Not sure yet. He's wavering."

"Drop it to felony murder."

Not now, Roger, goddammit. She fit her fingernails into the still-healing crescents in her palms and squeezed. "That asshole beat a little girl to death while her mother was at work. We can get second degree easy, especially with his priors. History of DUIs, the last time with an unregistered forty-five in the backseat, and three prior assault charges. Almost killed a guy in a Walmart on Black Friday."

His face remained bland, bored, as he gazed out the window behind her. "Doesn't matter. We'd spend twice as much time in court, and we don't have the time or the resources. See if he'll plead no contest. If he will, drop it down."

"I had a case last month, almost the same deal. Why didn't we drop that one?"

Roger didn't appear to have heard her. He just stared over her head out the window. "He'll end up put away where he can't hurt anyone else. Isn't that the ultimate goal from your point of view? Protecting the innocent?" He finally met her eyes and shrugged. "No reason to risk some jury actually letting him walk because they think it was an accident—discipline gone wrong."

Shannon balled her fist, then released it. "Okay."

"Excellent." Roger sat in the chair across from her and smirked.

What's he so fucking smug about now?

"I saw the chief this morning after you left." Roger's eyes twinkled. "Did you know Petrosky and Morrison aren't supposed to be anywhere near the Johnson case or Lewis's murder?"

She stared at him. "So you...what? Walked over there and told on them like a third grader?"

Roger's smile faltered. "They were forbidden from looking at it well before I got there. Seems Petrosky made a big stink with Kimball and the chief, got thrown out of her office. And last night, someone over at the hospital actually filed a report against Petrosky for harassing doctors about test results. Different case, but it didn't help their cause."

Alex. She sighed. "Listen, you should know that I'm involved, whether I want to be or not. Someone broke into my car."

"You told me. And that doesn't mean—"

"Someone killed Abby's kitten."

The arrogance in Roger's eyes petered out a little, but he only shrugged. "Sorry about the cat, but—"

"They left his head on my windshield. With a note that said 'It was me.'"

Roger sat, jaw working. Then: "It was me? Who... What was them?"

"I assume it was in reference to the murder of Derek Lewis." She didn't know that, not for certain, but she was glad she'd said it. The stunned look on Roger's face was priceless. "Someone wants us to know that he isn't pleased that someone else is taking credit for his handiwork."

Roger didn't seem to buy it as his shock morphed into aggravation. He rolled his eyes. "You have dozens of cases simmering right now, and none of them involve kind, calm individuals."

"Yeah, but this is the only one where someone else got credit."

"*If* someone else got credit. Two days ago, you were convinced that Johnson did it."

And maybe I was wrong. "It isn't a coincidence that my car got trashed the night after the trial. It isn't a coincidence that I found a severed head on my windshield the day after that." That rang true. None of this made any logical sense, but it wasn't coincidence—she was certain of that.

Roger's smug annoyance finally mellowed into something that almost resembled sympathy. "How's Abby taking everything?"

"She's upset."

"Did she see it? The cat?"

"No, she didn't."

"Well, thank goodness for that." Roger watched her, his face frozen like an ice sculpture, but his eyes were suspiciously disappointed like he'd hoped to hear that Abby had found the cat herself. Shannon thought about the way his face had twisted when she'd shown him her stretch marks, how he'd hated the idea of children as a general rule, hated that someone had once lived in her body. As if it were an intrusion.

She leaned toward him. "You can't leave the Johnson case unopened. If we don't investigate, whoever killed Lucky is still out there. And I'm in danger. So is Abby. So are Derry and Alex."

His face did not change. Roger didn't give a shit about Derry or any of them. The only person Roger cared about was Roger.

"And," she added, "if they happen to think I like you, you might be in danger as well."

Now the wrinkles around his mouth deepened until he almost looked his age. He pulled his lips into a half smile, half grimace. "Guess it's a good thing you don't like me, huh, Shannon?"

"Guess so." She stared daggers at him, wishing they could actually cut. "All we really need to do is open the animal abuse case, prosecute for malicious animal cruelty. Anything found in the course of the investigation on Lucky will be useful in the Johnson case too." *Assuming they're related.*

Roger tapped his fingers on the arm of the chair, his shoulders slumped ever so slightly. Shannon couldn't remember why she had ever found him attractive.

"I'm sure the chief is looking at it now, Roger, approving investigation into *something*. Might as well look like a visionary and call her first, let her know the prosecutor's office won't take the harassment of one of its esteemed attorneys lying down. Let them know that we are reexamining evidence before they send someone else over here to do it for us."

Roger scowled. He pushed himself to standing, his face drawn, and let himself out without another word.

Shannon unwound her fist and stared at the pen in her hand. Sticky. Sweaty. She cracked it in half and threw it at the far wall, watching the blue ink spatter across the beige contractor's paint in a stain that looked like bulging, dead veins.

11

THE DETENTION CENTER across the road was disturbingly still as if no one living resided within its walls. Not vacant. Not empty. Just lifeless. Even the cars in the precinct lot looked forgotten, like they belonged in some apocalyptic movie where everyone had been wiped out by brain-eating zombies. At the moment, it would not have surprised Shannon to find her own brain missing.

She wrapped her coat tightly around her as she raced from the precinct to her car, the only sounds were her heels on the pavement, her own haggard breath, and the continuous thoughts that buzzed through her head like insects. Did Johnson know who had killed Derek? Did she do it herself? Everything that had happened today had only deepened the mystery, only made her more confused, and the damn parking lot wasn't helping matters. With every step, she felt an imaginary stalker's breath on the back of her neck.

Shannon slammed the car door, flipped on the headlights, and shoved the car into drive, rubber squealing. Had Derry been there to hear her thoughts, he would have told her to buck the hell up before someone slapped her. Probably him. Or Jesus. Derry had always insisted that Jesus was surely a slappy fellow. "He'd throw a chair at your ass, Shanny. I saw it in a painting. Probably whip your behind, too." Thoughts of Derry almost made her smile, though any grin would have been tinged with raw and utterly incurable heartbreak.

She eased her foot off the gas and drew her eyes to the rearview, blinded for a moment by the brights from the car behind her. *Asshole.* She peered into the side-view mirror as the brights dimmed to normal, but Shannon remained unsettled. The leathery chemical smell in her car suddenly felt like it was strangling her. The headlights were probably nothing to worry about; just some idiot driving too close. *Hopefully.*

Once she hit the freeway, they'd drop from her tail, and she'd scoff at her own paranoia.

She watched the sign for the freeway creep from the post-twilight haze toward her. One mile. The twin beams cut through the blackness behind her, eerily blue instead of the typical muted yellow, like some formidable blue-eyed wolf tracking her through a herd of yellow-eyed deer. She gunned the engine. The car behind her followed suit, accelerating until she was sure he'd clip the bumper if she tapped the brakes.

Her hands tightened on the wheel. *No way. You can't intimidate me, you sorry motherfucker.*

She cut onto the freeway, shot down the on-ramp, and flew around a green truck that honked angrily in response. *And fuck you too.* Behind her, the blue lights wove around the truck and accelerated toward her side door, trying to come up level. To shoot her? Run her off the road and then dismember her like he'd done to Lucky? Her palms wet the steering wheel as she slammed her foot to the floorboard, cutting over rows of cars, the angry blare of horns almost drowned out by the thunderous beating of her heart.

The car was definitely tailing her. Not overtly, but diligently, letting her put distance between them, then cutting around other vehicles and gaining on her until she had a break in traffic and could shoot ahead again. She groped for her briefcase, trying to get at her phone, but she was going too fast. Gravel and broken asphalt spun beneath the tires. Her heart slammed into her rib cage. She dropped the bag onto the floor of the passenger seat and maneuvered the car back into the lane.

Her exit approached, the green of the sign a beacon of safety, or maybe it was just yelling at her to slam on the gas. She bit her lip, cut into the second lane over, and waited for the car to switch behind her. Half a mile. The blue-eyed wolf gained ground. Quarter mile.

Shannon put on her left blinker. The car behind her closed in. One hundred feet. Then she jerked the wheel to the right and bulleted up the off-ramp, tires screeching all around her.

Her heart throbbed in her ears. She pulled into the left exit lane, stopped at the light at the end of the ramp, and stared into her rearview. Nothing. The light stayed red. Then—

It was there, flying up the ramp behind her. *Fuck you, dickhead.* She gripped the wheel and scanned the street in front of her. Too many cars. She'd cause a wreck if she blew through the light. The red circle glared down at her from above.

The moment it turned green, she squealed into the intersection. The car behind her honked, but she ignored it. One mile up. Two. Eyes on the rearview. No blue headlights. She pried her hands from the steering wheel, shaking one hand then the other, replacing them more loosely, trying to force herself to relax. She looked in the rearview again. Still no headlights from the offending car. Her neck ached from playing lookie-loo.

As she neared her street, she took a final glance in the rearview but saw nothing suspicious. Her eyes were strained, irritated from the constant scanning, but she was almost there. Almost home.

She was stepping from the car with her briefcase on her shoulder when the lights returned, streaming up the road, blinding her. Her throat went dry. She ran for the house.

The car honked. Why would he be calling attention to himself if he had unlawful intentions? She leapt up the porch steps, and the honk came again, two short bursts. A car door slammed. Shannon turned back to the street, blinking hard, every muscle taut and ready to pounce, her keys positioned between her fingers like a weapon. She made a pitiful Freddie Kreuger, but it'd hurt if she drove her fist into some fucker's face.

Her eyes focused. She lowered her hands. "Morrison?" Her back went limp with relief.

He met her on the lawn, stainless steel coffee mug in his fist. "Pretty tricky moves, Shannon, I'll give you that."

"I thought you were... I didn't know it was you."

"Yeah, I figured after that off-ramp maneuver." He rubbed the back of his neck, a move Roger used to pull when he was lying to her. But maybe Morrison was just nervous? Or maybe *she* was just nervous and seeing shit that wasn't there like Roger had always tried to convince her she was guilty of. Maybe she was crazy.

"Why didn't you just call?" Shannon asked, hating that it sounded plaintive.

"I did. You didn't answer. And I can't very well watch for jerks who might be following you unless I follow you too."

Her red brick colonial loomed, empty and quiet and lonely. The white shutters on the upper windows were like eyelashes that she almost expected to blink. Behind Morrison, the street slithered away from them, hushed save for the occasional cricket, empty save for the occasional car in the road. The other houses already glowed from within. Probably lights from dining rooms where residents were eating dessert and doing homework, blissfully unaware of all the dirty bullshit going on out here.

"I'm going to sit outside your place tonight. Petrosky has your brother's."

"You don't need to protect me, Morrison." But her limbs suddenly felt weak and unwieldy. She needed to rest. And the fact that there was police presence at Derry's place...she might actually sleep tonight. "But I'm glad you're here."

The porch light haloed Morrison's hair and glistened against his forehead. Somewhere a night bird called, long and lonely.

Exhaustion settled onto her shoulders and neck like a boulder. "I just want to go to bed. I had an incredibly shitty day."

"Yeah, I know." He blew into the hole in his coffee mug and sipped. Calm. Undisturbed.

Her muscles were suddenly taut again. "How would you know? Where were you all day, anyway?" *Some friend.* She had expected him to be there. To bring her coffee. To...show up. He had to have known about Lucky. Right?

Morrison lowered the mug, a blue peace sign on the back of the cup garish and out of place. "Didn't Roger tell you?"

"Tell me what?"

"I saw him outside the office on my way in. Brought some tea for you, chamomile. To help you calm down. Roger said you were in court and that you would be indisposed until later in the afternoon."

Goddammit, Roger. Her knuckles ached as she balled her fists. "He lied."

"So he stole your tea, that rat bastard."

"He's an ass," she said, but the twinkle in Morrison's eyes almost made her smile.

"He loves you." It wasn't a question.

Like hell he does. "Roger only loves himself."

If Morrison had any thoughts about her statement, he didn't show it. "I did swing by the courthouse, but I didn't see you."

"Why didn't you come back to the office if you knew I wasn't in court?"

"I was trying to get everything together on a few other cases, so we don't all get fired if Johnson is a no-go."

"You mean, so Petrosky doesn't get fired." The heaviness in her neck spread into her back. Morrison was always looking out for this grown-ass man who could surely take care of his damn self. It was about Petrosky, always about Petrosky. She focused the tension into one clenched fist, wanting to drive it into Petrosky's junk. "If Petrosky gets fired, it's his own damn fault."

"I guess." He shrugged. "Will you be in court all day tomorrow?"

"I've got a case before the judge in the morning. Why?"

"Trying to figure out where I need to be."

"Be wherever the hell you want."

He frowned into his coffee mug, and her shoulders softened. "Sorry."

"No need to be. I understand." He nodded toward the house. "I'm going to go in and check out the house to make sure. You wait in the car with the doors locked. Anything seems weird, take off. Otherwise, I'll come out to get you in a few. Code still the same?"

"Yeah. You still have your key?"

He held it up and jangled it.

THE QUIET PRESSED in around her as she waited, the throbbing in her head achingly soft compared to the steady hoof beats in her chest. She peered out the windshield at the hood where the envelope had rested. *Poor, poor Lucky.* And poor, poor Abby. How much loss could one little girl be expected to take? The image of the cat's severed neck smeared across her memory, and she looked away from the hood to see Morrison coming down the front steps, broad shoulders square against the porch light, his silhouette domineering but soft —protective.

Shannon grabbed her briefcase and exited the car. She pulled her suit jacket tight against the bitter breeze that had arisen while she was locked in her vehicle, the gusts of chilly air kicking up dirt and the scent of last season's decomposing leaves. Or maybe she just hadn't noticed the wind before because she'd thought she was running from a killer.

Morrison nodded to her. "Everything looks good inside. I'll wait out here, watch the street."

"You're not staying outside, Morrison."

"If someone's after you, they probably aren't going to walk in. They'll watch first."

"You can see the street from the upstairs bedrooms." She gestured to the windows on the top floor.

His gaze swung from the house to the road. "I won't be able to see all the way down the street, but it might be better to do occasional rounds anyway. Make me look like a...houseguest." His voice was quieter than it should have been as they trudged to the front door. Tired? He had to be exhausted after last night.

"You *are* a houseguest. Not like it's the first time." The knob didn't want to turn. The front door felt as if it was made of lead. "Plus, it'll be nice to have someone to talk to when I can't sleep tonight. I think I need to keep my mind off of...everything."

"Distraction I can do." Morrison followed her into the foyer and pulled cards from his pocket, nodding to the dining room table in the next room. "Gin rummy? I'd guess we have about an hour or two before anyone would dare show up. But I can sit at the window if you believe differently."

"No, no. Sit. I appreciate you being here. And rummy's fine." She dropped her briefcase beside the door and sank into the chair across from him. Pajamas would be nice. Bed would be nicer. But her legs were too tired to scale the steps to her bedroom despite her too-active brain.

"I figured you might need a break from poker." His fingers flew as he shuffled and dealt. "Saw Derry earlier. He said you've been sucking at five-card draw all week."

"Sounds like him," she said, but the cards froze against her fingers.

"I already owe him three lunches and twelve packs of bubble gum, so you're in good company."

She lowered her hands. "He never said anything about that."

"Why would he?"

"No, I mean, I guess he wouldn't." Her brother was allowed to have friends, and he and Morrison had hit it off the moment they'd met. So why did Morrison visiting feel so…secretive? Deceptive? She must be tired. Or maybe she was just overly protective of Derry's last months or weeks or days or—

"He probably doesn't want you to know how much practice he's getting. So you don't feel bad about losing…or should I say, letting him win."

Shannon tapped her pinky against the table, watching Morrison's face as he examined his cards, features placid and still, to avoid giving away his hand. She waited for him to ask her about Lucky's head. About the hospital. Did he already know she had been there? That Derry had talked her into getting involved? Or maybe Morrison had convinced Derry to make sure she stayed on the case. But no, Morrison would never do that. *What the hell is wrong with me?*

Morrison picked a card from the pile, discarded another, and looked at her. She exchanged her own cards, her throat hot and tighter than it should have been. They repeated the pattern in silence, one after another, the constant thrum of the crickets outside spiking the shuffling and the thunk of cards on the table until the knot in her throat melted.

Shannon beat Morrison six times in a row, but he grinned every time she laid down her hand and offered to deal the next.

"You suck at this, Morrison."

"It's all in the cards. Can't control them."

"You say that about a lot of stuff."

"That's because it's true about a lot of stuff."

He was so accepting. Relaxed. "You are relentlessly chill."

His eyes dropped to his cards. "I had a mean streak when I was younger. Angry at life."

She had known Morrison'd had a rough time as a kid, but she hadn't realized he'd been aggressive.

"I guess that's why my folks thought it'd be a good idea to put me in karate." He frowned as if disturbed by a memory, but he didn't look up.

So that was where he got all that martial arts stuff he did with Kimball. Shannon pulled a card from the draw pile. Four. She tossed it into the discards.

"I do less martial arts these days and more yoga," Morrison said. He selected a card and laid it on the pile. "You should try it, Shanny. Very relaxing."

"I guess you need all the help you can get dealing with Petrosky."

He finally met her gaze, and there was sadness there, though he seemed to be trying to hide it behind a smile. "You'll learn to love him."

"Love's a strong word, Morrison."

Morrison shrugged and turned back to his hand. "He's human too."

TEN ROUNDS. Shannon had won eight. She might have been annoyingly self-satisfied if she could have managed to lift her lips into a smile.

Their banter, and the card games themselves, had managed to pull her focus from the stress that had been suffocating her all day. But as they climbed the stairs, the twisting in her gut returned. Lucky. Derry. She had to find a killer. But her entire body was too heavy to go chasing after anyone tonight. Exhaustion pulled at Shannon's eyelids.

Morrison gestured to the unicorn poster staring out at them through the open doorway to the spare room. "How often has Abby been here in the last few weeks?"

"Once a week, at least. Whenever Alex has to work the night shift."

"She always brought the cat, right? Any other pattern that someone watching might have noticed? Was she just here on certain days?"

Shannon shook her head. "Nope. It was usually in the evenings, but no pattern week-to-week unless they happened to know Alex's schedule." *Poor Lucky.* She ignored the tightness in her chest, crossed to the bedroom window and pulled back the curtain. "You can see the backyard from here, and the road behind it." They both looked past the ten-foot cement wall that separated her patch of green lawn from the office buildings beyond.

"I forgot your yard backs up to an office complex. That's where I'd come from if I was trying to sneak up on the place. But I'll watch the front too."

They headed for Shannon's bedroom, decorated in muted blues and greens with a bright-white comforter on the bed. A massive black dresser stood across from the bed, a remnant from Roger's brief stint at playing house. Some nights, a fantasy of burning the dresser out back was the only thing that helped her sleep.

Morrison's footsteps stopped in the center of the room. "Nice."

Men. She sighed, looked at the dresser again and realized Morrison was not admiring it but rather was staring at the art above the bed: an oil painting of three sunflowers twisting toward an azure sky. "Oh. Thanks." She'd won the picture from Derry last month in a particularly intense poker game. She purposefully hadn't won a game since. Part of her suspected that Derry was trying to give his things away, and she wasn't ready to accept the pieces of him that would be left after he was cold and buried.

Morrison peered through the gauzy curtains. "Leave the door unlocked, and I'll rotate through here. I'll be quiet, so I don't wake you."

The thought of him coming in while she was dead to the world made something jerk around inside her belly. *Seriously, what the hell is wrong with me today?* "You can't stay up all night," she said.

"I'll rest in the spare when I need to."

"You think they'll assign anyone else to the case?"

"Not to do this. They're still farting around with exactly what to open. Oh, and that reminds me: Petrosky filed the report for you on... the envelope. Lucky. You need to come in and sign it tomorrow."

Her stomach lurched. "I will."

"I'm going to go scope out the parking lot at the office back there." Morrison dropped the curtain and turned from the window.

She nodded, struck by the set of his jaw, the shadow of stubble creeping across his chin.

"I'll set the alarm," he said. "Let me know if you need me."

When the door closed behind him, Shannon disrobed and pulled on a flannel nightgown. Soft and cozy. Morrison had seen it before, and she'd felt perfectly fine about it then. But this time...

She looked down at it: frumpy material, old and faded, and the plaid made her look ten pounds heavier. Why did she care?

Her face warmed. Nope. *No way, Shannon.* Roger had been enough man trouble for ten lifetimes. *And I'll fuck it up—he's my best friend. I can't lose him right now.* But...it was warmer tonight, definitely getting to be springtime. She didn't want to sweat to death. She pulled the flannel nightgown off and rummaged in her drawer until she found one in silk.

Crickets chirped as she flicked off the light on the night table and slipped under the covers before she could consider her pajama choice further. Outside in the night, a dog barked—someone's not-dead pet. Her skin crawled as she pulled the covers tighter.

Morrison's footsteps sounded from somewhere on the floor below, steady and calm. She listened to him pace the kitchen, the stairs, the spare room. He was on the stairs again when she finally closed her eyes and slept.

12

Shannon wasn't alone. Still bleary and half-immobile with sleep, her breath caught as she registered the rustling and scuffling of an intruder. Close. So close to her that she could almost feel the heat coming off them in waves, tightening her muscles. Every part of her was ready to bolt as she shot to seated and—

Her shoulders relaxed. Morrison stood at the window in an unwrinkled button-down shirt, coffee cup in hand, his frame silhouetted against the outline of the bleak, gray dawn. But why was he... Oh yeah. *Lucky*. She blinked sleep from her eyes.

"Did I wake you?"

Yes. She stretched her legs. "No."

"Good."

She swung her feet to the floor, the chill of the morning, sending goose bumps shivering up her arms. She pulled the blanket back up around her shoulders. "Anything overnight?"

"No one suspicious," he said, shaking his head. "Though I did find a raccoon eating your trash. I lured it across the road with the hamburger Petrosky left on my passenger seat."

"Sounds like you just invited him to come back the next time he wants a burger."

"Yeah, maybe. I'm not very scary."

She yawned. "True enough."

"I made that special coffee," he said.

"The stuff you keep in your trunk?"

He nodded. "Yup. Won't make you jittery. It's got mushrooms in it, you know, more antioxidants. Supposed to be good for cholesterol."

"Chol—" She cocked her head. "That's what I've been drinking for the last three years?"

He grinned like a schoolboy. "You've always said you liked the taste."

He's got me there. She dropped the blanket and stood, the air kissing her legs and sending a fresh prickle of goose bumps from toes to thighs. She wrapped her arms around her chest. "I've never seen you jittery in my life. And how did I not know this about your coffee?"

"Gotta have a few secrets," he said hurriedly. "Okay, well, there's more downstairs." He lowered his eyes and headed for the door. "I'll let you get ready." It wasn't until the door closed that she remembered she was wearing her silk nightgown. Not that it mattered.

When she came downstairs all showered and dressed, Morrison was at the kitchen table, shoveling food into his mouth. He swallowed and held up his spoon. "Oatmeal?"

She sat across from him where a place was already set for her and moved the porridge around with her spoon. Red and black peppered the beige mush. "Goji berries and chia seed again?"

"You know it. And hemp."

If only the hemp were enough to get her stoned. She could use a little high right now. Shannon had dressed too quickly to think about anything unpleasant, but now memories of the day before were trickling back into her consciousness. Derry's thin face. Poor little Lucky. The tears on Abby's cheeks as she clung to her father's skeletal frame. *Make a dying man's wish come true, Shanny.* She needed to figure this case out and fast.

Morrison picked up his spoon again. "Your arraignment is at what time?"

"Nine." She spooned a bite to her lips and chewed. Good. Bland but good.

"After that?"

"Just paperwork. Got a few things to file."

"I'll drive us." He put up a hand when he saw her face. "I'm supposed to be watching you."

"Like I need a babysitter."

"Like you wouldn't be hanging out with me anyway." He winked, and she couldn't help smiling back.

"Anyway, I'll drop you at the courthouse. You can get your filing completed, and I'll meet you back there after I visit Ms. Lewis."

Derek's mother. A spoon of mush froze halfway to her lips. "What makes you think you're going over there alone?"

"You don't need to be there, Shannon. If Derek's killing really is related to her—"

"It isn't."

"I kinda thought you wanted out of this."

Of course he thought that—she had been pretty clear on the point with Petrosky. And from the look on his face and the way he was encouraging her to stay home, he obviously hadn't told Derry to convince her otherwise. But...she *had* been convinced. She needed to find this fucker. She needed to see Derry's eyes when she told him, "It's over now, Derry, Abby'll be fine, just worry about getting better." Except...he wasn't ever getting better. She dropped her spoon into the bowl. "I interviewed Lucinda Lewis three times before Johnson's court case began, and I just put away the person she thinks hurt her son. Maybe I can help make things go more smoothly."

Morrison chewed silently and sipped his coffee. "Okay. After court, we'll go to Lewis's. I'll clear it with Petrosky."

"You don't have to clear it with him."

"I know I don't have to, but I'm sure he'd appreciate it. And asking him won't hurt anything. Win-win."

"And if he says no?" She crossed her arms. "What then, smart guy?"

Morrison stood and took one last bite on the way to the sink. "If he says no, we'll do it anyway."

She approached to set her dish beside his, and the scent of his lavender soap and shaving foam overpowered the oats.

Morrison glanced at her bowl, still mostly full. "I thought you liked oatmeal."

She shrugged.

"You'll get used to it. You want to grab some workout clothes? We can hit Kimball's class tonight if we have time." *We.* He took the bowl from her, brushing her fingers, and a jolt of electricity shimmered up her arm and into her chest.

Shannon stared at his fingers. *Nope. Not happening. I am not losing my best friend to some hormonal whim.* She wouldn't make it through Derry's death without his support, and shit had a way of falling apart once you played pants-off dance-off.

"Shanny? Hey, you all right?"

She nodded. *I just need to get out more. Maybe fuck a stranger. Win-win.* "Yep, fine. I'll get my gym bag."

IKE LAMBERT WAS ALREADY SEATED in the defendant's chair when she entered, his brows furrowed, glasses askew. His snub nostrils flared and settled as she sat across the aisle. Beside him, Griffen tapped the desk, adjusting his own glasses and ruffling papers with the twitchy dexterity of a rabbit. No one sat behind Lambert, no friend or family member to offer an affectionate gaze or a pat on the shoulder. *Good.* Lambert was a piece of shit. The pews behind Shannon were empty as well—not even the girl's mother had shown up to watch this bastard enter a plea.

Shannon stood to the rustle of fabric around her and faced the front. The judge had a shock of white hair and cheekbones that looked like they'd cut anyone who touched them. His voice was just as sharp, as were the punishments he doled out. He sat and picked up the gavel.

"Come to order, court is now in session, the Honorable Judge Klein presiding." The gavel sounded, and fabric rustled again as everyone sat.

"Is the prosecution ready to proceed?" he barked.

Shannon stood. "Yes, Your Honor."

"The defense?"

Griffen winced and rolled himself to standing until his shoulders were square. "Yes, Your Honor."

"Ike Lambert, a complaint has been filed against you, case number 43277901A that alleges in count one, the felony homicide of Cindy Waters, age seven, committed on the fourth of March…"

Shannon turned to Lambert as Klein rattled off the list of crimes, the numbers, the dates. Lambert locked eyes with her. Not a twitch of the mouth, not a quiver of the lip. Only his nose betrayed his true emotions, nostrils flaring with anger and malice. No remorse, just like the killer she was still looking for. Lambert was probably proud of murdering another human being. Someone like him would be just as proud of killing a cat. Icicles tore up her back and raced along her arms.

"How does the defense plead?"

Griffen's fingertips danced on the table in front of him. "No contest, Your Honor."

Lambert ran his tongue over his lips. Like a reptile.

Shannon responded to the judge when prompted and spent the rest of the time grinding her teeth together, the sound of them creaking in her ears as Griffen and the judge spoke back and forth, back and forth. Even in profile, Griffen looked tired, blue tinting the skin under his eyes. He hadn't been sleeping. Though the bags might have been guilt—he couldn't be happy about getting a better deal for this murdering asshole. Griffen was too good a guy for that. Which was the problem with defense; even when you won, sometimes you felt like you were failing humanity. It was the reason she'd flipped over to prosecution.

Not that it was all that much better on her side.

Griffen finally nodded at the judge and ran a jerky finger over his watch—the face looked like it was made of wood—and then the band on his wrist—red was for…AIDS awareness, right? Definitely not for justice, that was for damn sure. Lambert smiled, self-assured and heartless. *What a fucking psycho.*

The gavel sounded over her creaking teeth and the whoosh of blood in her ears. She grabbed her briefcase and was turning to stride from the courtroom when Griffen stepped in front of her. "Oh…hey, Griffen."

"Hey." He glanced back over his shoulder at his client, who was being escorted from the room in handcuffs. Lambert was still grinning. Her skin bristled.

"You have a moment?" he asked.

She looked longingly at the door and dragged her eyes back, hoping he'd take the hint. When he just stood there waiting for her answer, she sighed. "Sure. What's up?"

His mouth opened and closed like he was trying to figure out what exactly to say to her. He still hadn't met her gaze. "Well…there's been some talk, Shannon. Are you okay?"

Talk? Probably about Lucky. "Yeah, I'm okay. What exactly did you hear?"

"You know how I feel about Roger." His eyes flicked to her and away again. "How I've always felt about Roger since the day you started dating him."

Shannon said nothing, just waited while Griffen's face reddened.

"He's had a lot to say, as of late. He seems to… It's about you; that you may be…in a precarious situation." He was trying to be judicious, diplomatic. What he meant was that Roger was talking a bunch of shit, trying to play the martyr who wanted to save her from herself. Some things never changed.

"I thought it was ridiculous, of course, but then it came up again, this time from someone out of the chief's office and—"

"You know you can't believe everything Roger says." Or everything out of the chief's office if it came from Kimball, Roger's BFF. But her throat tightened anyway. If Griffen had heard about Lucky, everyone else probably had too.

"But is it true? About the cat?" He finally looked at her, and his face was drawn, his eyes searching. He really was worried.

She sighed and peeked behind them at the pews. Everyone else had gone, but still she lowered her voice just above a whisper. "Listen, between you and me, off the record…"

"Of…course." But his face was pained like it would fucking kill him to keep it to himself. Jesus, he really had changed. Or maybe he was just different to her because she no longer gave him her secrets to keep.

"There've been some…issues," Shannon said. "Someone is none too happy about the fact that Johnson got put away. And now I'm scrambling, trying to make sure I got everything right."

Griffen's mouth dropped open, and he closed it again, but his eyes flicked to the wall, and back to her like someone behind her was telling him it wasn't true. "You believe it now? That she's innocent?"

"I don't know what I believe. But I could use anything you have." She shifted her briefcase to her other hand. Roger was going to be pissed as hell when he discovered she'd thrown doubt on their conviction, and to the defense attorney at that. "Did you know about a second social worker going to Johnson's house the day Lewis was murdered? Seems he was there earlier that afternoon."

"What? No!" His eyes widened. "This could be—perhaps they saw something or someone or maybe—"

"Between you and me, *counsel*, I'm doing what I can. And I'll keep you posted. We'll attack this together, okay?"

"Yes, of course. Here...let me give you my new cell number." His face was bright with excitement, though the corners of his eyes remained tight. "Shannon, this could be amazing. I mean—"

Amazing that she'd convicted an innocent person? She silenced him with a look, happy her ability to do that hadn't changed over the last few years.

"Okay," he said more subdued. "Just let me know what else you find. Petrosky already has copies of all my files." Griffen adjusted his pocket square; the material red and faded. She wondered if it was the one she'd given him half a dozen years ago for Christmas. It wouldn't have surprised her, and the familiarity of him, of them, tugged at her.

"Listen, I told Karen about what happened between us," he said, seemingly reading her mind. "About how our friendship...ended." He winced like it hurt to say, and maybe it did—guilt at walking away? Or maybe he was wincing because Karen had reacted the same as his ex. Her cold eyes at the bar sure hadn't looked very understanding.

"Karen thinks I miss you. And I believe...that she's right. We did make great friends, Shan."

Shannon balked; recovered. "Yeah, we did." She forced a smile, but hearing his nickname for her on his lips felt wrong after so much time had passed. And now her memories of hanging out at the bar with him and working long hours prepping for court together were bittersweet— tinged with the pain he'd caused when he severed their friendship. When he'd proven to her, yet again, that people are not to be trusted, even in a platonic capacity.

"Maybe we can all get together some night," he began slowly. "You and me and Karen and Morrison?"

Her heart slammed against her breastbone, drowning out the background noise of a courtroom door closing somewhere in the hallway. "Morrison and I aren't a couple." Morrison hadn't even glanced at her in that silk. Not that it would have mattered if he had.

He frowned. "Oh. Well, bring whoever you want then. Friend, boyfriend, whatever. Anyone but Valentine. I think he hates me. He always looks at me like he wants to kick my ass."

That was true enough. Life got tricky when one friend was content to beat the snot out of another. Not that Valentine was particularly violent, but he had no time for those who defended criminals and made law enforcement's job harder. If she'd known Valentine back when she was on the defense side, maybe he would have hated her just as much.

13

Shannon's back was still tense when she exited the courtroom and headed into the hall. Around her, other attorneys scuttled their clients through the halls like rats in a maze, urgent whispers of what to do—and what not to do—in court echoing off the walls. She kept her eyes downcast, avoiding the clamor. Trying to think. Trying to figure this case out while Derry could still high five her and offer her a medal, or keys to his vast fortune, or whatever thing he'd presume to be funny when she told him he no longer had to worry about cat-killing assholes running around his neighborhood.

Think, Shannon.

Lucinda Lewis wouldn't know much, but it was critical that Shannon go today with an open mind. Last time she'd spoken to Lucinda, both women had been convinced Ashley Johnson was guilty. Maybe Shannon had heard what she wanted to hear. But this time, she wasn't going to make any errors in judgment.

Shannon skirted a man in a pinstriped suit, yanked open the heavy wooden front door, and winced against the damp, biting wind. The parking lot was thick with dreary mist. She stepped over the threshold, eyes on her shoes and the cracked cement, and plowed directly into someone: Dr. McCallum.

Fucking hell. Shannon managed to keep hold of her briefcase, but his fell to the pavement. *Seriously, I'm spending the rest of the day locked up somewhere.* "I'm so sorry, Doctor."

"No worries, Ms. Taylor." McCallum's cheeks were rouged with the effort of walking across the lot, or maybe from embarrassment. The buttons on his jacket strained against a girth larger than Lillian Valentine's baby bump. He bent and grabbed the handle on his case.

"How are you?" she asked. "Haven't seen you around for a few weeks."

"Oh, you know how it is. Clients all day long, don't get out much." McCallum met her eyes, and she flinched under his stare: that I-see-into-your-soul look that all shrinks seemed to have. "How have you been? And Abby?"

"She's…big."

He appraised her as if looking for a chink in her armor. She averted her gaze. Under her shoes, the pock-marked cement threatened to swallow her heels.

Shannon drew her eyes back to McCallum. "Who are you here on? You testifying?"

"Stanley case." McCallum glanced over her shoulder at the parking lot. Twitchy. Nervous? Or was it just her? "Did a psychological evaluation to determine whether the girl could consent to the relationship and on the implications of the trauma."

"Ah." More information than she needed. Though she'd offered little in response, his eyes were alight as if the conversation was the best thing he had experienced all day. She tried to recall ever seeing McCallum with anyone else—a friend, a colleague at a lunch meeting—but came up empty. Shame for him to be so lonely. He was always so kind to her. Though the fact that he knew her darkest secrets didn't make her feel entirely comfortable with him outside the confines of his office.

She glanced at the lot, looking for Morrison's car. "I'd better run."

McCallum looked into the lot and back at her, raising a brow in question.

"I'm meeting Morrison on a case." Now who was giving away too much information?

McCallum's pudgy face broke into a smile. "Ah, well, tell him I said hello. And send my salutations to his partner as well. I haven't seen them around in weeks either."

Weeks? Hadn't Petrosky told her he'd been with McCallum just the other day?

Alarm must have registered on her face because McCallum patted her arm, kindly, almost fatherly. "Come down and visit sometime. My services are always covered for those on the force. Perk of the job." He stepped toward the door.

"Alas, I'm not on the force."

"Close enough." He grabbed the door handle.

No, she had paid him out of pocket after Abby was born, when the raging postpartum depression had tried to eat her alive. Though, he had come to the hospital to see her after the birth, free of charge. He'd probably just forgotten.

"I'll see you around, Doctor."

"Until we meet again, Ms. Taylor."

Something about the exchange was off; she felt it in her gut, but could not place it. Why had McCallum been so fidgety? That wasn't like him—at least the him she knew from her time as a patient. And what the hell was Petrosky trying to pull?

The lot was silent as a graveyard, not a car on the road, not even a rustle from the single tree that perched precariously at the curb near the precinct. She found Morrison's Fusion behind a truck, Morrison in the driver's seat writing in a notebook propped against the steering wheel. When he saw her, he flipped the book closed and leaned over to push open the passenger door. She tossed her briefcase into the back and climbed in beside him, unease gnawing at her chest.

Morrison raised an eyebrow but turned to the windshield and put the car in drive. She watched the precinct roll by, then the courthouse, then her office, as he pulled onto the main road.

"So...you going to tell me what's wrong?"

She drummed her fingers on the console. "Petrosky lied to me. About going to see McCallum."

He kept his eyes on the road, but not a muscle twitched with surprise. "Huh." He stopped at a light.

"That's it? Just 'huh'?" She wanted him to be just as irritated as she was by Petrosky's behavior. Anger heated her chest. It was bad enough to know that Petrosky was a lush—worse, that she was impotent to do anything about it. If she turned him in, Morrison would never speak to her again. "Petrosky needs to see McCallum. You're enabling him. In the parking lot the other day, he reeked of liquor."

"You can't force these things." The light changed, and Morrison gunned it through the intersection. The softness in his voice was betrayed by the hardness in his jaw. "He's been a little messed up since the Hannah Montgomery case, but he's still doing everything he needs to do at work."

Hannah Montgomery was a girl taken by a serial killer a few years back, after her boyfriend, prominent businessman Dominic Harwick, was brutally murdered along with seven others. They'd never found a body, only her blood on the steering wheel of an empty car three states over, any trace of the killer gone. Petrosky had taken leave, but judging by his boozy breath, not for long enough.

"He always has other people's best interests at heart."

"Not an excuse."

Silence fell over them as buildings rushed by outside the windows—gas stations, fast food, strip malls. But the silence wasn't necessarily uncomfortable, just strange. Different. Like they were slowly becoming something besides what they'd always been. She hoped she wasn't losing her best friend over this case, though if it came down to it, maybe Morrison would choose Petrosky over her anyway. Not that she'd give him an ultimatum like Griffen's ex-girlfriend had done. But eventually,

Petrosky might do something worse than simply withholding evidence or telling little white lies, something that she'd not be able to ignore, especially if he kept drinking, and then—

Morrison's voice pulled her out of her head and back into the car. "He takes it all real hard, you know? He doesn't like to see people suffer. It eats at him."

"I'm sure it does. But he's got issues, Morrison. He's okay with harassing doctors and lab techs to get what he wants. And he lied to me about Johnson for no reason I can figure except that it didn't suit his version of the truth. Obstruction isn't nothing. If you really care about him, get him some help."

Morrison didn't respond. She turned away.

And then: "Petrosky's not a dick to everyone." He hooked a left and coasted down a side street where neatly trimmed bushes sat in square rows. "And some people deserve it, like the assholes who do stupid shit but won't ever see the inside of a courtroom. He has a knack for getting jerks to back off even if they haven't officially committed a prosecutable crime."

"What? Who?" Probably the boyfriends of his "girls."

Morrison pulled into a lot and parked near the door. Lucinda Lewis's apartment building was five stories of red brick and stone with a heavy wooden door that looked like it belonged on a storybook mansion—or maybe the courthouse—instead of an apartment building. Somewhere nearby, a dog howled. "I'm just saying, there are people who shouldn't be out there hurting people. Then there's everyone else that we need to protect. Petrosky does what he has to."

Shannon searched his eyes. "That's why you like him, isn't it? It's that whole hero complex. Vigilante justice." Maybe that was why he liked Johnson too: even if she'd been guilty, he might not have thought she'd been wrong either. Just like Valentine. *I wasn't the least bit upset that Johnson took care of Derek. That fucker, beating on his kid...* She pushed the thought away.

Morrison grabbed the door handle. "I just think Petrosky's a good guy. One of the nicest people I know, actually." He kept the focus off himself, she noticed. No response to her amateur psychological analysis.

"It's sad you don't know nicer people," she said.

"I don't think so."

The door to the building's main entrance creaked open ominously, but the inside looked undisturbed, normal, if not ostentatious—thick red carpets, gilded picture frames, and an entry table holding a potted plant beside a wall of copper-colored mailboxes. And yet, the niggling inside her chest remained, a sensation far too common in the last few days. Worry about Derry? But that ache was more poignant, always present in the pit of her stomach, sometimes stabbing at her heart in quiet moments. No, probably from just talking about Petrosky. *Goddamn that man.*

They ascended the stairs to the third floor and started down the hallway toward Lucinda Lewis's apartment. Paisley wallpaper, in reds and golds, shimmered under the glow of bronze fixtures, and every brass door knocker seemed to watch them, the one on Lewis's door especially—the head of a lion perched to snarl and spring. The harsh report of brass on brass drew a threatening growl from behind a neighboring door. Shannon eyed the door beside Lewis's warily, as if the animal could claw its way through the scarred wood and wrench her head from her body. What the hell was her deal? This was routine stuff. She even knew the lady for fuck's sake.

The door in front of them opened a crack. "Yes?"

"Ms. Lewis? Police, ma'am."

The heavy-lidded eyeball in the crack shifted to Shannon. "Oh, it's you." The dog next door growled again. Lewis's door shut, and the rattle of the security chain being disengaged clanked from the other side. From next door came muffled human shouts, then something thunked against the door. The dog yelped and fell silent.

Lewis opened the door and stood back so Morrison and Shannon could enter. The overpowering smell of potpourri followed them down the hallway and into the living room, harsh and thick as cigar smoke in the back of Shannon's throat.

"Diamond is asleep. The worker always sees her when she comes, though, so you can ask her if you're worried." Her eyes radiated haughty determination, a warning that she was not one to be trifled with. Ms. Lewis sat in a wingback chair striped in white and black like old prison garb and gestured to the flowered love seat across from her. Morrison and Shannon sat, thighs touching, his deodorant sharp and crisp like menthol. On the wall behind Lewis, a framed image of Jesus holding a lamb looked down on them condescendingly, his grip on the animal appearing less nurturing and more corrupt. Shannon blinked at the picture, and Jesus loosened his grip. Nope, nothing sinister about it. Just her mood.

"Has your CPS caseworker been here to see you lately?" Morrison's phone buzzed in his pocket, and he reached a finger inside to turn it off.

"Ms. Burke? She was here yesterday. Been checking to make sure everything is all right with Diamond. Even set me up with some services to get help with meals and diapers and whatnot." She nodded. "Real nice girl."

"Have you ever had another worker stop by here?"

"Ms. Burke asked me about that too." She folded her hands in her lap and studied them. "Never seen anyone but her. There something I need to know?"

Shannon and Morrison exchanged a look.

"Did Derek ever mention another worker?" Shannon asked.

"He didn't talk to me about that stuff. Thought I was the one who called."

"Weren't you?" Morrison said.

Lewis glowered at Morrison and pursed her lips.

"Ma'am?"

She crossed her arms, defiant. "That baby deserves better. Every time I stopped by, those two were arguing. Yellin' and carrying on. Any good grandmother woulda done the same." Her lip quivered, grief melting the confidence. "And now...now Diamond's all I have left of him. I did the best I could after Derek's father ran, but the street just...took him from me. All that fear, none of the good. What he saw was his friends dying and the drugs taking the pain away. I kept believing he'd get back one day, but—" Lewis shrugged one fleshy shoulder, and her pressed blouse whispered crisply with starch.

"I'm so sorry for your loss, Ms. Lewis," Morrison said. "I wish there was more I could do."

"Yeah, the social worker said that too." She nodded. "You're good people."

From the next room, a screech split the air, and Shannon jumped.

"That'll be her." Lewis leveled a hard gaze at Shannon. "You find out who hurt my boy."

Unease fluttered in Shannon's chest, just a notch below panic. Find out? She'd just tossed someone in jail. But maybe Ashley Johnson hadn't killed Derek, and Lucinda Lewis knew it. Maybe she'd known it all along. Shannon swallowed hard. "What do you mean, Ms.—"

Lewis stood. "Ashley's fine where she is. Won't get a chance to hurt Diamond with her...lifestyle. But something else is going on, or you wouldn't be here. Besides, Ashley never seemed the type to—" Her eyes glazed, and Shannon heard the words she couldn't say: *To kill my son. To smash my boy's skull in.*

Lewis leaned toward her and aimed a finger at Shannon's chest. "But you mark my words, Ashley knows who killed Derek. She ain't innocent." She straightened up and gestured to the door.

The sickly sweet of Lewis's apartment was still messing with Shannon's sinuses as she and Morrison descended the stairs. Morrison was looking at his phone, which was buzzing again.

"What's up, boss?" His voice echoed in the stairwell.

Boss. Shannon sighed, and Morrison winked at her.

"Yeah, we're leaving now. Said her worker had mentioned another... Oh, good. Okay. We'll meet you there."

Morrison pocketed the phone as they escaped the confines of the stairwell and entered the lobby. "Petrosky's got an appointment with infamous social worker Frieda Burke. He wants us to swing by in thirty minutes. Hopefully, we can get a lead on who else was at the house that day, figure out if there actually was another worker from their office poking around over there like Ashley Johnson seems to think." He opened the door to the outside, and the air, slightly rotten with exhaust from the nearby road, was almost refreshing after the thick perfume inside the building.

"You have time to run over there, or do you need to get back to the office?"

Shannon could feel eyes on her back as she walked away from the building. *It's this place. This situation. This...life.* She had a full day's worth of reports on her desk, but half of them would be pleas. And this case was the only one with the potential to protect the people she loved. Maybe. Not that she was psyched about dealing with Burke—her temples were already throbbing.

She nodded. "I've got time."

14

FRIEDA BURKE MET them under the awning outside the social work building just as the rain began to spit on the overhang. Her curly hair poofed around her head in a Little Orphan Annie way, except it was brown, not red, and fell over tense eyes—eyes that seemed to embed her frustration into her face. Or maybe it was residual jealousy toward Shannon. She wondered if Burke knew about the flowers Griffen had sent, the constant apologies that came for months after Shannon had officially stopped speaking to him. He'd felt guilty about screwing up their friendship. Shannon hoped Burke had felt bad too. She searched Burke's face for the slightest hint of contrition but saw only agitation on her lipless mouth.

Petrosky clumped up behind them, raindrops splattering his jacket, and Shannon coughed at the tobacco-mint thing he had going on. Cigarettes. Booze. And the stereotypical mouthwash cover-up. She wondered if Burke might recognize Petrosky's shenanigans from her work with other alcoholics. Shannon hoped not—she wanted Petrosky to get help, but not at Burke's discretion. And the woman already despised Shannon. Morrison was their only hope of getting the information they needed unless Petrosky bullied it out of her.

Burke buzzed them into the building with her key card and led them into the lobby, then to an office dominated by a poster of smiley face sketches with "How Do You Feel Today?" emblazoned across the top. Petrosky sat in the only chair in front of Burke's desk. Shannon leaned against the back wall with Morrison and watched Burke, who currently looked like the little cartoon face labeled "Irritable." Just as she had at Ashley Johnson's hearing. Though Shannon knew she hadn't been there to testify. Hadn't needed to go visit Johnson in jail either.

"I saw you at the hearing," Shannon said. "Ashley Johnson's closing arguments."

Burke's eyes flashed alarm and settled, but not before Petrosky shifted in his chair. "I wanted to see Lucinda Lewis under pressure and watch the verdict," she said carefully.

Petrosky leaned toward her. "Do you go to the trials of everyone on your caseload? I imagine that's rather time consuming."

Her mouth tensed. She stared back. "I was called in for questioning before that trial, so I suppose it's only natural that I'd want to see it play out in court." Her tone was dangerous. Defensive. Shannon's shoulders went rigid.

"What about your visit to Johnson this week?" Petrosky said.

"Updating her on her daughter. A closing session essentially. I know it wasn't necessary, but...none of us wants to lose a child. No matter what Ashley did, that's a horrible thing to go through." Color had crept into Burke's cheeks like a bad rouge job. "You think that's wrong too?"

"Just being thorough," Petrosky said. "It seemed odd that someone so busy would take the time to visit. Even more odd that you'd spend an afternoon watching a trial when you could do absolutely nothing except gawk. I don't like odd."

Burke's jaw dropped. She crossed her arms. "It isn't odd. There was no other family available. If Lucinda proved unable to care for Diamond or seemed unstable, I would have needed to change my plans and look at fosters. I try to keep them with family as much as possible, but it doesn't always work that way, for obvious reasons. A clean house and cooked meals are more than enough if you ask half the kids in this godforsaken city." Her eyes narrowed at Shannon, perhaps to avoid Petrosky's glare, or maybe for another reason altogether. Griffen had said that Burke wanted to adopt but had been unsuccessful, that Shannon's easy surrogacy had made Burke uncomfortable, distressed. As if it were up to Shannon to shoulder this woman's burdens.

Shannon purposefully loosened her balled fists, but the rigidity in her chest remained. *This is all wrong.* Burke would have known whether Lucinda Lewis was stable before the trial. And breaking down at a trial would certainly not be cause to remove a grandchild from her care. So what was Burke really doing at the hearing? The nagging itch in Shannon's brain intensified.

"Sounds like you don't like your job much, Ms. Burke," Petrosky said.

"Seeing this...stuff every day—it's sad." But her eyes were hard, not sad, as they flicked around the room and finally landed on Shannon. Shannon held her gaze until Petrosky spoke again.

"Did you know another worker went to visit Derek Lewis?"

"No," Burke said and broke eye contact. Shannon leaned forward, off the wall, as if lying had a scent she could catch.

Morrison straightened beside her and laid a hand on Petrosky's shoulder. "No?" Morrison said to Burke, his voice soft but accusing. "You told Lucinda Lewis that if anyone else showed up, she should call you."

Burke dragged her eyes to Morrison but didn't seem especially intimidated. "Oh, that." She waved her hand dismissively. "I believe I heard something about that from Ashley when I went in to meet with her the one day." It rang false, and Shannon knew why: Ashley Johnson had insisted she'd said nothing of this other worker to Burke. Was Johnson lying? Or was Burke?

Petrosky cleared his throat.

Burke's eyes narrowed. "I was worried it was some weirdo trying to get in on the fame after a murder trial. I told Lucinda to let me know if anyone came posing as a worker."

"You think it's a faker?" Petrosky asked, but Shannon already knew he believed that—he'd said as much the day they'd found Lucky's head.

Morrison stepped back to take his place next to Shannon on the wall.

"I'm not really sure, but it happens. On normal cases, we occasionally get some overlap, an accidental second call put through to the wrong worker, and paperwork gets screwed up. But we almost always catch those double-ups quick and make a note in the chart. Worst case, Lucinda calls me if they show up, and it's just someone with a duplicate file. But if it's someone who shouldn't be there, it's that much more important to find out who it is. I work with other care providers all over the city, and things do occasionally slip through. Communication isn't perfect." She smiled, but it was strained. "Is there anything else I can do for you?" She was being dismissive; she clearly didn't want to help them. Or Ashley Johnson.

"We'd like to talk to your boss," Petrosky said. Shannon's chest loosened a touch. Maybe they'd actually manage to get what they needed from someone else.

"My boss?"

"Where's his office?"

"*Her* office is at the end of the hall. She's usually out on cases, but she got back a little bit ago."

"The boss is out getting her hands dirty, too, huh?"

"The lead social worker is still a social worker, detectives, and a damn good one at that." Her eyes were fiery, a little too upset for the occasion.

Petrosky's index finger twitched against his knee as he stared Burke down.

"She might be able to spare a few minutes, but our time is stretched thin these days," Burke said. "All of us are scrambling to pick up Benjamin's caseload since he left." She shook her head. "I'll call her first to make sure it's okay."

"Benjamin who? And when did he quit?" Shannon blurted out, and Burke's hand froze over the phone. If it was a month ago, when Derek was killed—

"Just in the last few days. And he had a helluva caseload. Like we all do, I guess."

The last few days. After the trial. Around the time her car got ransacked, and Lucky was crushed underfoot. Not that it necessarily meant anything, but—

"He been here long?" Petrosky asked.

"A year or so."

"Anything weird about him leaving?"

Burke glanced at the ceiling—considering, not guilty. "I don't know. You'll have to ask Amanda."

Fuck. Amanda Kimball, Park Kimball's wife. How had she forgotten? Amanda was another friend Roger had stolen in the divorce, but Shannon hadn't been shocked by that—she'd never really trusted Amanda. And now Roger would know within hours that they'd been at the social work office, and Shannon would hear about it this afternoon. A knot between her shoulder blades throbbed.

Petrosky stood. "Thank you, Ms. Burke."

She smiled, but her eyes remained guarded. "If you need anything else, just call." She pulled a card from her desk and handed it over, but the look on her face said that she hoped they would never use it.

Burke led them down the hall and rapped on the door to Amanda Kimball's office. The easy grin Amanda gave Burke faltered when she saw who Burke had brought with her.

"Nice to see you again, Mrs. Kimball," Petrosky said.

"Likewise," she said through clenched teeth.

Was there anyone in the free world who didn't want to kick Petrosky's ass?

Three chairs in Amanda Kimball's office, not just one. *Fancy.* Amanda's keys twinkled from a nail in the wall behind her desk, and Shannon wondered how many times she had to lose her keys in a disordered purse or drawer to make slamming a nail into plaster seem like the only solution to keep track of them.

"Nice computer," Morrison said, gesturing at Amanda's shiny laptop in the corner of the desk. "MacBook?"

Amanda's expression warmed when she looked at Morrison. "Park gave it to me. But you helped him pick it out, didn't you?"

Morrison smiled in response and pulled out his notepad.

"Thanks for seeing us on short notice," Petrosky said. Amanda didn't acknowledge him. Or Shannon. That stung more than she wanted to admit, but she couldn't dwell on it—they didn't have time for personal nonsense. Or maybe they did because the tension wasn't going to subside on its own.

Shannon cleared her throat. "Amanda, I know it's been a while and that things have been...difficult in recent months." *Ever since you and your husband decided you'd rather be buddies with my cheating ex.* "But, we need your help with this."

Amanda sighed, finally meeting Shannon's eyes. "I wanted to call."

Sure you did. Shannon bit her tongue and waited.

"With the hours I work these days, I can barely squeeze in grocery shopping, let alone anything else."

Find common ground; then I can get what I'm after. "Yeah, I know. It's hard for me too. And juggling work and everything else...at least Park can pick up a little of the slack with stuff around the house or running Dana to dance, right?"

Amanda's eyes dropped to the desktop. "Dana doesn't have much going on these days." Brusque. Dismissive? Maybe even angry. Mad at her husband? Or at Shannon? Maybe Roger had given Amanda reason to be pissed—he wasn't above spreading rumors about his exes, she knew that all too well.

Amanda side-eyed Petrosky and leaned back in her chair, her shoulders slumped—defeated. "No matter what's happened outside the office, I have no interest in hindering a police investigation. Just tell me what you need."

No matter what's happened? From the way Amanda continued to avoid Shannon's gaze, Roger must have told some fantastic lies. Shannon's stomach twisted. Maybe he'd tried to make Shannon look crazy—or hateful. It wouldn't have been the first time. Roger had once told Morrison that she had spoken badly of him at home, made jokes at her best friend's expense. Morrison had ignored him, thank god, but...

That fucker. It wasn't enough for Roger to just cut her out of their old friends' lives—he wanted them to hate her.

Petrosky cleared his throat. "Do you have any idea which social worker might have gone to Derek Lewis's house on February fifteenth?"

"The Lewis case again?" Amanda shook her head. "You already did quite a number on Frieda, and all she did was her job."

Petrosky must have harassed the crap out of Burke during the trial, but he didn't look sorry. "We got some new evidence, Mrs. Kimball. A witness who indicates there was someone else at the house the day Derek Lewis was murdered. Someone who identified themselves as Lewis's social worker."

Her eyes widened. "You think someone in this office—"

"We'll need to talk to anyone who had reason to be in the area that day. They might be a witness but not be aware of it." He lowered his voice and leaned toward the desk. "Or maybe whoever it was thought they'd get in trouble for fighting with Lewis just before he mysteriously ended up dead."

The blood drained from Amanda's cheeks. "We have incredible people here. Truly amazing. Half of them would offer you the shirt off their backs. Did you know that Frieda even fosters sometimes when kids have no one to stay with? She fostered Diamond twice: once last year, and again while we vetted Lucinda. She's...incredible."

Back to Burke again. Those two definitely had a close work relationship. Shannon opened her mouth to ask, but Petrosky did it for her.

"You guys seem pretty chummy."

"Frieda and I have been friends for years."

Amanda had never mentioned her friendship with Burke to Shannon, even six months ago, when they were still friends. Not that this was necessarily an issue, but—

"That aside," Amanda said, "no one who works here would do anything that would hurt these children, and that includes withholding information that could be...questionable." The fire burning in her eyes indicated that she believed that. But that didn't mean she wasn't wrong.

Petrosky rubbed his chin. "I'm not saying that someone in your department committed a crime, Mrs. Kimball, merely that if they happened to be at the scene on the day of the murder, they might have been concerned about the implications of their presence."

Amanda clamped her mouth shut and crossed her arms.

"You have a lot of male social workers?" Petrosky asked.

The only noise for a moment was Morrison's pen scratching on his notepad as Amanda paused.

"I mean...no, we don't have a lot of male workers. Just one. Or we *had* one."

That narrowed it down.

"Benjamin?" Petrosky asked.

She nodded warily. "Benjamin Wheatley."

"Tell me about Benjamin," Petrosky said, probably trying not to sound demanding but failing. He needed to take it down a notch, or he'd lose Amanda's tentative cooperation.

"He been here long?" Petrosky continued.

"Longer than some."

Vaguely confrontational. *Hmm*.

"When was the last time you saw him?"

"Um, Thursday morning? He didn't come back to close his day out online. Didn't even send his resignation. I've called four times but no answer."

He had disappeared two days after the trial. Morrison shifted in his seat and flipped another page in his notebook. "Does that happen often?" Morrison asked without looking up. "People just taking off like that?"

Amanda looked at him and nodded, her face softening ever so slightly. "We lose social workers all the time. We have one of the highest rates of burnout as a profession—low pay, lots of work, tons of emotional strain. Sometimes they just...ghost." She shrugged. "But the fact that he hasn't stopped by is weird. I still have his last paycheck because we can't release it until he gives back his badge."

"So Mr. Wheatley still has access to the building?"

"He'll lose his privileges on Monday when he's officially fired. Would have done it before, but he's damn good, and we don't have a replacement yet." She shook her head. "Every time someone takes off, I'm surprised. You'd think I'd be used to it by now."

"What about records?"

"Frieda is taking some, and I—"

"Not records for social work cases. Records for his security badge." Petrosky put his hands on his knees. "Can you tell when it was last used? If he's been back here in the past few days since he…ghosted?"

"Yes, we can tell when people use their badges." She lowered her voice as if worried an employee would hear, despite the fact they'd seen no one except Burke. Wouldn't Burke already know about the badges given how close she and Amanda were? Looked like Amanda didn't have a problem hiding things from her best buddy. *Serves Frieda right.*

"But we don't advertise that we track entrances and exits," Amanda said. "It helps us verify whether workers are keeping appointments. If someone says they met with a client and they were logged in as being here, we know something's up."

"Does that happen often?"

"Not here. But there have been cases of overworked individuals just charting the notes without doing the required visits. Sometimes the kids fall through the cracks and end up injured or…worse."

"And no one here knows about this tracking system?"

"No."

Not even your good buddy next door? Maybe the issues here were worse than Amanda was letting on if she was worried about Burke lying to her. And Shannon knew all too well how manipulative Burke could be.

Amanda pulled her laptop in front of her and tapped on the keyboard, squinting at the screen. "Okay, here it is. Benjamin was—" Her eyes widened.

"Mrs. Kimball?"

"He was here at two-fifteen this morning."

Petrosky glanced at Morrison, whose pen was scratching furiously on the notepad. "Mrs. Kimball, are there cameras on the door?"

She shook her head. "Just on the parking lot."

"We'll need access to that."

Amanda turned back to the screen, the clack of her fingers on the keys hard and frantic. "The camera system is all online, videos, reports, everything. They oversee it from the security office upstate, but we only use them for maintenance."

"You're expected to monitor this too?"

"Not unless there's a concern, which has only happened once with someone getting a purse snatched. And then we just called you guys."

She hit another key and turned the laptop toward them. A grainy image of the empty parking lot filled the screen.

"One o'clock," she said. She hit a key, and the video fast-forwarded. A bird flitted in and out of frame. A piece of paper appeared and vanished. "Two o'clock."

"Did Benjamin have a car?" Morrison asked.

"Yes, he did. It's one of the requirements for the job because we do house calls."

But the car wasn't on the recording. The lot stayed empty.

"Three o'clock." Amanda hit a key, and the video paused, a sparrow or some other bird in mid-flight over the lot.

"So he walked it," Petrosky muttered. He leaned back in his chair. "I'll need access to his desk, any personal effects as well. And a photo, so I can match him with the person seen entering Lewis's apartment the day he died."

Finally, a lead. They had a direction, a plan...on a case none of them were supposed to be touching. Roger was going to be pissed.

Amanda chewed her lip. "His license is in his personnel file, though his desk looked rather...sparse when I went in earlier to check for charts." Her eyebrows rose, face suddenly hopeful. "Maybe that's what he came back for? The stuff in his office?"

Right, because normal people suddenly feel the need to grab all their stuff at two in the morning.

"Are your workers aware of the cameras?" Petrosky said.

"Like with the cards, we don't advertise that we're watching the lot, but the cameras are pretty obvious out there."

So Benjamin Wheatley probably knew someone would see his car, but didn't know Amanda was monitoring his badge. Which meant he didn't want anyone to see him. They'd check his office, but if Wheatley had been there this morning, he'd surely have taken anything incriminating with him.

"I'll pull his privileges immediately." Amanda turned the computer screen back to herself, shaking her head. "I can't believe this."

Shannon glanced at the wall in the direction of Burke's office. Burke might have misremembered where she'd heard about the other worker at Derek Lewis's house, but she hadn't been secretive in inquiring about it. She hadn't been worried about someone finding out. But Wheatley...

Wheatley definitely had a secret to hide.

15

Shannon was inappropriately jealous of Petrosky and Morrison's freedom when they dropped her at the office and set out to locate Benjamin Wheatley. Her day was a predictable whirlwind of paperwork and Roger dropping in to harass her about her other cases while she tried not to punch him for talking shit to Amanda Kimball. That was all he wanted—a rise. A fight. She wasn't fucking giving it to him. When dusk, at last, crept in, she locked up her office and met Morrison downstairs so he could give her a ride over to Kimball's warehouse.

Her chest tightened as they passed the spot where she'd found her vandalized car. Shards of windshield glass still glittered on the asphalt, some edged with white from the shatterproof coating, making the whole mess resemble broken teeth. Shannon shot Morrison a thank-you glance when he parked at the other end of the lot.

Inside, the warehouse was bright, cool, and already smelled of sweat...and bleach. Kimball waved as they entered. "Stone Cold and Silent. Welcome back." He marched from under the weight machine, nodded to Morrison, and touched Shannon's elbow. She tried not to flinch.

"I'm really sorry about your car. I ordered some extra floodlights and a set of security cameras for the perimeter. They'll be here next week."

She pulled her arm away. "You didn't have to do that, Kimball."

"I should have from the get-go. I just didn't think..." He looked at the back wall as if expecting someone to sneak in through the door to the alley. Had Kimball talked to his wife? Did Kimball know Amanda had possibly spent the last year in charge of a very crazy person? Maybe not since Shannon hadn't heard a word about it from Roger. And Shannon sure as hell wasn't going to be the one to bring up Wheatley and the fact that she'd spent half the day skipping work and prying into a case her boss had specifically told her to avoid.

Kimball pulled his gaze from the wall. "How's Abby doing?"

Shannon faltered, and the lingering knots in her shoulders tightened like her spine was in a vise. "She's...okay. As well as can be expected, I guess." No wonder he was being weird and awkward. There was no good way to ask about a disemboweled cat.

"They don't think that cat thing was connected to your car break-in, do they?"

Of course they're connected. Someone had threatened her with a decapitated head two days after the trial, right after someone had smashed their way into her car. During that same time frame, Wheatley just happened to be doing weirdo stuff in the same office that dispatched workers to Derek Lewis's house. Now Wheatley was gone. Scared or guilty?

Morrison stiffened beside her.

"The cat...is a hell of a coincidence," Shannon said.

Kimball nodded. "Now, I'm really glad I got those new lights." He scanned the room again, and looked back at Shannon, his eyes too narrowed, mouth too drawn like his words and his thoughts were fighting for control of his face. "Well, go get ready. I've got a doozy of a workout for us tonight, then I've gotta run to get Dana from dance class."

Something about the way he said it struck Shannon as strange, but she had no time to consider it because Valentine had shown up and was clapping Kimball on the back. "Sure, sure. You know you're teaching that dance class, you fancy ass—"

Shannon left them and headed for the bathroom. As soon as she slipped into her shorts and tank top, she felt like she could breathe for the first time all day. Maybe her bun was just too tight all the time. *I need to try a fucking braid.* But the gnawing in her stomach remained as she gathered her things and shoved them into her bag.

Outside the room, Morrison was leaning against the wall. He swept past her into the restroom in a haze of lavender and a smell distinctly musky, masculine. She stared at the door for a beat after he passed through it, then grabbed her weights from the back, and took her place behind one of the eight crates Kimball had set up. Five were already full.

"Today, we've got dumbbell swings, elevators, Turkish get-ups, then power deck squats with weights, and inchworms to grasshoppers." Kimball's voice rose with each exercise he named, and Shannon's pulse quickened with anticipation, or maybe with defensiveness at the posture Kimball had taken like he'd beat the crap out of anyone who tried to tell him they weren't doing his bullshit workout. Maybe he did know about her visit with Amanda and was pissed that neither she nor Morrison had volunteered the information.

Bring it, Kimball. Shannon shook out her legs and arms as Morrison returned from the bathroom and took his place at the crate next to her. The woman beside Shannon groaned quietly.

"Let's do this." Kimball pressed a button on the stereo behind him, and the room filled with Kid Rock yelling over a deep bass beat that vibrated Shannon's marrow. "Twenty. Make it happen."

Shannon bent her knees and hinged forward at the hips, swinging the weight between her legs and back up over her head as if the act would extinguish the disquiet spreading through her like poison from a needle, from her neck, down into the veins in her chest, then to her stomach. Innocent people locked up. Guilty people going free sooner than they should. On the second set, she pushed the weight faster, harder, and her thoughts solidified. She envisioned punishing people from her caseload—smashing baby-killing Ike Lambert's teeth, crushing the reverend's nose—as she brought the weight down again and again and again. Then she envisioned Wheatley standing over Derek Lewis's body and Ashley Johnson staring at her with red-rimmed eyes: *Why did you do this to me, Shannon?* Shannon punched the weights higher, harder, every muscle screaming, and the image splintered and fell apart like a broken mirror.

"Keep it up!"

She panted, punched, lunged. Sweat stung her eyes, and she blinked to clear it. Her mouth tasted like salt. But so help her, she'd sweat this shit out.

"Elevators!"

"Get-ups!"

"Power decks!"

Roll, squat, leap, sit, roll, squat, leap, sit, and it all became one fluid motion; just breath and an aching cramp in her chest.

"Modified inchworms! I want five mock lunges on each side before inching down to plank."

She stood, gasping at too-thin air, then hinged forward before dropping to plank. *You can't fall, Shanny. Everybody needs you.* And, suddenly, there was Lucky, his sweet, tiny face rubbing against Abby's chin, a motorboat engine rumbling contentment under the kitchen table. A lump swelled in her throat, and she wheezed over it, bringing one leg under her body from a down dog-ish position, then back, then the other leg, pretending she was kneeing the asshole in the balls, the person who had killed Derek Lewis, framed Ashley Johnson. The dickwad who had suddenly decided he wanted some fucking credit and sucked Shannon into this nonsense. The person who had made her niece cry by killing Lucky, who had made Abby's life worse than it already was because Derry was leaving them, he was going to die, and no one could fucking stop it. She jumped to a squat, stood, and started over, every movement of her leg more violent until she was kicking at the air beneath her. Her heart throbbed, but she wasn't sure it was from the workout. She wanted it to be, wanted it to be from the pushing, from the testing of her endurance and not fear and pain. Her hands slipped on the mat beneath her, and she righted herself and tried again, harder this time, her own labored panting mingling with hard rock and bass for a soundtrack born of human suffering.

"Let it go and stretch it out," Kimball called. She stood, shirt stuck to her skin, tears and sweat covering her face, her legs wet and sticky. Beside her, the woman in blue was spread-eagled on the floor like she was about to make a snow angel. Around them, the panting echoed over Kimball's muscle-stretching music—something classical—and she tried to focus on the stringed instruments. But every muscle felt like it was tightened to the point of splitting, as though one more reach would tear her muscles and cause her to crumple like a marionette whose ropes had been severed.

Morrison touched Shannon's arm. His fingers left searing hot imprints on her skin. "Shannon?"

She jerked her arm from his grasp. People were dispersing, toweling off, collecting their things. She could hear the warehouse door opening, the grinding of metal, the crisp splatter of the rain outside growing louder and louder. Morrison sat on his crate off to the side. Still. Quiet.

"You staying?" Kimball called from his spot near the door. He already had his gym bag slung over his shoulder, so she must have been stretching for at least ten minutes. But time seemed to have stopped. If only it would—she'd have Derry with her forever.

"Gotta get Dana from dance," Kimball said, a trace of impatience in his voice.

She barely heard him. She wanted to fucking punch him. For having a normal life. For not having to think about any of this stupid bullshit. For only having to worry about some stupid dance class when she had to worry about very real monsters killing family pets and diseases that could wipe those closest to her from the face of the fucking earth.

"I want to hit the rings for a few," Morrison said to Kimball. "Go on. I'll clean up."

"Sounds good. I'll lock the door on my way out." Kimball's shoes thwacked over the floors toward the exit. "See ya, Shannon," Kimball called, and she wondered at the use of her name, at the lilt in his voice that you used with little kids. Maybe he thought she was fragile. She'd show him fucking fragile. She'd show everyone.

Everyone's counting on you, Shanny...

There was an agitated squeal, an angry clang of metal on ground from the warehouse door, and then silence, stretching around her until she could almost feel a vindictive puppeteer rising above her, scissors poised to cut. The muscles in her back screamed as she pushed herself to standing.

"Want to talk about it?" Morrison's gaze bored into her side, as palpable as if he were physically touching her. "Shanny—"

She whirled to face him. "What?"

He said nothing, but she could read the question in his gaze.

"Fine! No, I don't want to fucking talk about it! Anytime I talk about it, it's like everything just…falls…apart." She put her hands on her knees, her mouth dry, full of ashes. Ash Park: sucking the life out of everything, slowly, methodically, inevitably. But some of them would die sooner than others. Gone forever, and soon. Too fucking soon.

She was weeping when he pulled her to him, her every muscle heaving with the force of her tears. His arms, slick with sweat, slid over her back, marrying with the dew on her skin. She clutched his shoulders. Her legs threatened to buckle.

"Relax. I've got you."

Relax? She shoved him away. "You can't fix this, Morrison. You can't just make everything better by pretending things will be okay. Forget your Zen bullshit for once. No matter how much you meditate, you can't bring people back from the dead." She was yelling at him, her voice echoing over the equipment with a metallic twang.

"I know how much it hurts to lose someone you love. I know there's no fixing it."

She wiped her nose on her hand. "My brother's dying." There. They were out. The words that she had shoved down, choked back, bitten from her own tongue, now hung in the air, sharp and vicious and utterly devastating.

He met her eyes and nodded. "I know, Shanny. And I love him too. I've only known him three years, but he's a great guy."

"You think everyone's a great guy." A shuddering sob wracked her body as the world spun, and then she was in his arms again, her face pressed into his shirt, her fists clenched. He was always so goddamn calm.

When she was steady, she pulled away. "Were you really going to do rings?"

He shrugged. "I will if you want to. Or we can hit the bags. You looked like you wanted to punch something earlier." The bags behind him swung slightly as if taunting her. "Or, you can hit me."

Her hands remained balled in tight fists. She couldn't seem to release them. "Will you hit me back?"

He glanced at his shoes, and his fingers twitched. "No."

"Then what's the point?"

In response, Morrison walked toward the back of the room and tossed her a pair of gloves from the floor. The first one slid on, but she grappled with the second, its enormous padding thwarting her efforts like a dog trying to put on goddamn pants. She blew damp hair off her forehead, grinding her teeth until her jaw ached.

"Here." Morrison took the glove and held it. She wanted to shove him away, but instead, she slid her hand into the mitt and let him Velcro it closed. He was watching her.

She ignored him, and the moment he walked behind the punching bag, she attacked it. The bag was Lambert. It was Roger. It was Wheatley. It was some masked intruder killing Lucky. It was cancer. It was all of them.

Morrison wasn't sweating, wasn't straining, was just standing, holding the bag steady. "Arms higher."

She lifted her elbows, attacking the bag with her fists, her knees.

"Careful with your wrists. Sometimes restraint is just as important as accuracy."

Restraint. She had heard Kimball say that too, but she suspected he didn't believe it either, with his widening shoulders, his ever more irritable attitude. *Fuck restraint.* She envisioned Lambert's nose beneath her glove, splintering, blood flying. Roger's perfect teeth reduced to a row of shattered piano keys beneath her fist. The cowardly shadow who was making Derry's death into a race to find the person who had gone after Abby's kitten—someone she had to find soon so that Derry could die peacefully knowing his little girl was safe. This killer…he was making it into a fucking game. Toying with her. With her brother.

The fury was building, creeping through her veins like a virus. Cancer had a name but nothing tangible for her to annihilate, but their killer, goddamn him, she'd find him and fuck his shit up. Someone had to pay for the shithole that had become her life.

The leather thunked under the force of her gloves, her face heated, her shirt soaked through with sweat, and through it all Morrison stood still, his face quiet and peaceful and accepting. She hated him for being able to turn his emotions off. For being able to hold it together when her life was falling apart. He wasn't supposed to be okay when she wasn't. He was her best fucking friend, goddamn him. *Break down with me. Let me break.* Her breath echoed in her ears, fast as the throbbing in her hollow chest.

She staggered back, her arms already sore. He stepped from behind the bag, and his face was still calm, serene, a paragon of fucking relaxation when every shred of her control had disintegrated. She raised her quaking arms and shoved him hard with her gloved hands.

He stumbled but didn't fall, and when he locked eyes with her, she shoved him again, hands against his chest. This time he didn't even stagger. Just stood like he was made of granite.

"Hit me back."

He shook his head slowly.

She pushed him again, then again, and he stepped back with his right foot to avoid falling backward.

"Hit me!"

He didn't move. She socked him in the stomach, and he gritted his teeth as air escaped him with an *oomph*. He winced. Finally, a reaction.

"I'll miss him too, Shanny. I know it hurts, but—"

"You don't know *anything*. You always think you do, but you don't know shit. Not about this." She struck out again, but this time he dodged the punch and pivoted around her.

"I lost my mom," he said. "My dad. More close friends than I want to think about. I know, Shannon. I know."

"Do you? Have you ever had to watch it for months and months, knowing it's coming, seeing someone you love suffer? *Smelling* them fucking dying every time you enter the room? Knowing it will be on you to pull things back together when it's impossible because there is no way to fix that kind of broken?" She didn't wait for an answer, just went at him again, socking him in the arm, pivoting and striking at his lower back. He danced around her on tiptoes as she punched again and again, the wet thwack of gloves on skin the only sound over her heavy breathing. Sweat dripped down her back, into her eyes, down her legs. "You don't know, Morrison. It's just not the same for you."

"It isn't."

"You don't love him like I do."

But he did care. Deeply. And his eyes held such sorrow that she regretted the words the moment they tumbled from her lips. What was she doing? She lowered her arms and put her forehead against his chest, gloved hands slack at her sides. "I'm sorry," she whispered as tears trickled through the sweat on her cheeks.

He wrapped his arms around her and rested his chin on the top of her head. "Me too."

16

THE SILENCE on the ride back to the house was so heavy and thick that Shannon half believed she could take it in her hand and watch it ooze through her fingers. Morrison kept his eyes on the road. She was grateful for that. She didn't want to see the look on his face, didn't want to have to say she was sorry again. She was in too much pain to feel sorry for anyone but herself.

And he knew that. He'd known it in the gym too, known she'd wanted—no, needed—to hit him. Her head was sticky on the seat back as she listened to his steady breath and the whir of tires, wondering if she'd ever be able to see into his head the way he did into hers.

Morrison parked in the driveway and waited by the side of the car until she got out and followed him up the steps. Somewhere a crow cawed, and Shannon jumped, but she saw nothing but the infinite blackness of night. No killer. *I'll find you, motherfucker. For Derry.*

She pointed Morrison to the downstairs bath and dragged her smarting legs upstairs to shower. Her pulse was steady now, and the anger, so furious and blistering an hour before, had drained from her during the car ride. By the time she stepped under the water, she felt as though her insides had been sucked out with a straw.

When the last of the soap had disappeared down the drain, she threw on a T-shirt with a picture of The Doors, the one that always made Morrison grin and say, "I was the brother Jim Morrison never knew he wanted." But this time when Morrison saw her in the shirt, he just nodded, a few droplets of water still clinging to his clean forehead.

"Turmeric milk," he said, offering her a steaming mug. "It'll calm you down."

Turmeric? She took the cup, sipped, and grimaced. "Strong."

"That'll be the vodka." He picked up his own cup off the counter. His mouth was drawn, and he was looking at her now with one eyebrow just a little higher than the other as if trying to figure out the right thing to say. Or to do.

She didn't need help. And she sure as fuck didn't need his pity. But when she searched his eyes, she saw no pity, only frustration—probably at the case—mingling with the gut-crushing sadness they shared, though he was infinitely better at handling it. She wanted to be him, calm like him, just for a minute. Just for one minute, she wanted that kind of peace.

"Just know I'm here, okay, Shanny?"

She set the mug on the counter and wrapped her arms around his waist. He stilled, inhaled sharply, then he set his cup down and held her. He'd always been there for her. More than anyone else, even during the hellish two years she was married to Roger. Hell, even before she'd gotten married. And then during the divorce. Now she'd been divorced for four months, and through it all, Morrison had been the one she could talk to. Morrison had been the one she and Derry had gone out with on the weekends when her husband refused. And when Derry's illness had begun to overtake him... God, had they really only been friends for three years? It seemed like forever. "You're always here," she said.

"Yep. And I always will be."

"Always is a long time."

"Time we have." There was something in the way he said it that sent tingles of electricity down her back as if the words themselves had climbed from his lips over her head and run down her spine on feathered feet.

Don't do it, Shannon. But she couldn't help it. When she raised her lips to his, her insides melted, every inch of her liquid and hot and waiting to be flooded with him—his touch, his scent, his calm. But he made no move to pull her closer, just stood, arms frozen—rigid. The warmth in her belly cooled to ice. She pulled back and looked at him—his eyes were wide, lips open in shock.

Oh my god. She had been reading him wrong. He felt only friendship, nothing more. Shit, maybe Roger was right. Was he gay? No, but she'd have known that, for sure. Had he ever talked about anyone? Dated anyone? *I can't believe I just did that. I ruined everything. No, no, no.* She dropped her arms. "Morrison, I'm—"

But then his lips were on hers, warm and pliable and so soft compared to the hardness of his chest as he pulled her against him, his arms encircling her waist. When he released her mouth, she sought his lips again, but he raised his face out of her reach and lowered his chin to the top of her head. "I don't want to be a distraction," he muttered into her hair.

She nuzzled her face into the crook of his neck, the soft throb of his heart palpable against her lips. His posture was stiff, too stiff. "You could never be only that."

But she had been only that, hadn't she? Friends. Buddies. And she couldn't lose that. *I can't do this.* But she had no time to think; she barely registered that he had moved until his lips were on hers again, the taste of his mouth sweet on her tongue. Her breasts flattened against his chest as his hardness pressed into her groin, and she opened her mouth wider, the gentle caress of his tongue on hers, sending a rush of heat pulsing through her abdomen.

He pulled back, rolled her T-shirt from the bottom, and up over her head, and then they were tugging, groping, stumbling up the steps toward her bedroom. When she tripped midway up, he rolled her over to face him and ran his hands over the roadmap of post-pregnancy stretch marks on her belly, kissing the skin between her breasts until she moaned and arched toward him.

What am I thinking? He's my best friend. But when he slid her shorts and panties down over her ankles, his fingers leaving a trail of brilliant electricity in their wake, she no longer cared about what she wasn't supposed to do. Everything in her life was about what she was supposed to do; what she was supposed to be. *Everything but this.*

He lowered his mouth to tongue the apex of her thighs, searching her, exploring her as she leaned back against the steps, gripping the railing for support. Every nerve vibrated with his energy. She clawed at his shoulders with her free hand, gnarled her fingers in his hair and pulled, daring him to take her—begging him.

But he just smiled, just fucking smiled, and slid a finger inside her, barely out of breath while she fought the aching heat that throbbed painfully between her legs and in every stinging muscle in her thighs. *Oh god. This.* How had they gone for so long without this?

She pulled herself up one stair and then another, and he came after her, followed her with his hands, caressing her, pursuing her. Four more stairs up, and his tongue was in her mouth again, his fingers at her rib cage, on her abdomen. She sought him with her hips. When he moved his hand to her nipple, she hooked her fingers under his waistband, pushed down his shorts and stroked him—he was solid and perfect and ready. He scooted around her and stood, trying to escape up the last stair to the landing. But she rose to her knees and took him in her mouth— salty and sweet—and as he sighed her name, she ignored the ache in her body, ignored everything but pulling him to the brink and letting him go, over and over again, until he was panting above her. He reached for her, and she let him draw her up into his arms.

"Shanny—"

"Don't let me go." She wrapped her legs around his waist, locking herself against his hardness, their bodies wet and slippery and warm. She ground against him as he carried her to the bedroom. He laid her on the comforter, and she tried to pull him to her, but he climbed off the bed, leaving her lonely and aching.

"Morrison," She arched her pelvis toward him, but he shook his head and knelt on the floor at the foot of the bed.

"Close your eyes."

She hesitated at first, then did as he'd asked—letting him take over. She embraced the blackness, succumbed to feeling as he took her foot in his hand and rubbed the arch, massaged her calf, her thigh, following his deft fingers with his lips and tongue from ankle to knee as she sighed the tension from her bones. When he reached the apex of her thighs, he put her knees over his shoulders and put his face to her sex, his breath hot, his tongue meandering over her slowly, deliberately, always just shy of where she needed him.

Then he stopped. He lowered her knees to the bed. The pulsing ache at her center took over, seeking release as he climbed toward her, running his fingers lightly over her belly. She widened her legs, but he lay beside her, not on top of her, not where she needed him.

"Goddammit, Morrison, just...god." She was going to lose her fucking mind.

His mouth was at her ear. "Breathe with me."

She squeezed her eyelids together. Her body throbbed painfully. She felt him moving down the mattress again, lower and lower until he was back on the floor. He picked up her foot from the bed, massaging the pad, rotating her ankle, his breath hot on her shin. She followed each of his exhales, matching his breath to her own. He worked her shin, lips at her knee. Then her thigh. He matched his massage to their breathing, every movement a dance they were doing together, the pressure building inside her as he approached the top of her thigh, and finally, he exhaled softly, sweetly, against her most tender part. He held her hips and inhaled deeply, exhaling as she moaned, almost there, one touch, and she was—

His breath on her sent her spiraling over the edge, and then he was tonguing her open, kissing her there the way he'd kissed her mouth, stroking her internally with his finger as she bucked her hips against his hand. Pressure and release, it became a cycle, his breath, her breath, his tongue, her moans.

"Curt." She opened her eyes and met his gaze, his eyes glittering, blue and deep, and she was lost there, lost with him. They'd never be the same. She didn't want them to ever be the same. All this time, every platonic outing, every dinner, every heart-to-heart conversation. It could have been this. "Curt, please."

She was still shivering with desire when he rose over her and pressed himself against her opening, softly, then harder, sinking into her to the hilt. He stilled then, their eyes still locked, his gaze calm, but there was an intensity there, a need, something feral. He touched her cheek. She matched his breath again as he began to move, slowly, his rhythm matching the pulse in her abdomen as they ebbed and flowed together like the ocean tide, his eyes the sea, their breath the waves, washing over them slowly, then harder and faster as she quivered in his arms, still lost in his eyes. This was what she'd been missing. This.

He pulled himself from her depths, lifted her to the pillow, and crawled up behind her, laying his lips against the back of her head. Her insides were still quaking as he stroked her hair and moved lower with his hand, kneading each tender knot around her spine. Lower. His fingers trailed over her hip and then between her legs for one fleeting moment as he wrapped his arms around her and pressed his chest against her back, the heat of him stoking the warmth in her belly. Then his hand was on her hip, lifting her thigh ever so slightly as he eased himself inside her again, slowly, agonizingly slowly, every aftershock in her pelvis tightening around him. She watched his hands—*Morrison's hands*—as he touched her nipple and stroked between her legs. The low burn in her belly spread until all of her was aflame. Her breathing quickened. Then—

Electricity slammed through her body, every inch of her pulsing and shuddering. She clawed at his arms, and he held her tighter against him, fingers dancing on her clit until she couldn't breathe, couldn't move, couldn't think.

"Curt," she whispered. No more air. He bit her shoulder, forcefully enough to draw blood, and the tenuous hold she had on reality snapped. She screamed his name as the whole world throbbed and broke apart, and he went over with her, grasping her hips so hard it hurt, growling unintelligible words into her hair.

17

They slept curled around one another, skin to skin, limbs and arms and hair haphazard like a puzzle she didn't want to solve. Every so often, he would rise from the bed and creep downstairs to check, listen, watch, and then he would climb back in beside her and cling to her as if he were frightened she'd float away if he let go.

Dawn broke dismally gray, but there was a peaceful quiet about it, like the mist that remains after a storm. Shannon watched it, breathing in the haze as if she could keep the morning forever. Once day broke, it was all over, but now—now she relished Morrison's arms around her, his fingertips lightly stroking her back, one of his legs over her hip, keeping her close to him. Connected. She blinked hard, taking a mental picture of the moment, of the sound of his gentle breath, of the way her body felt: exhilarated, alive, and deliciously used.

But. There was always a but. The deliciousness faded as the sun rose higher, and anxiety took its place, a nagging in her belly that grew more insistent with every inhale she took. He hadn't wanted to be a distraction. And he hadn't been—he'd been so much more. He had awakened quiet pieces inside her that had lain dormant, tarnished from disuse, and he'd made them shiny again. For a few blissful moments, she'd been complete.

But in the light of day...she couldn't allow herself to be this vulnerable. She had too much to lose. She had *him* to lose. His friendship. Panic was wrapping itself tighter and tighter around her throat with every beat of her heart, every exhaled whisper of his breath. Partly because she wanted this. Partly because she couldn't have it. Partly because of how much this would hurt him—unless she was thinking too highly of herself, though that might have been rationalization too. Dr. McCallum had taught her all about that word. If only he could have taught her how to avoid fucking up her life.

"About last night," she said into his chest.

He kissed the top of her head and ran a hand over her hip. "It was perfect."

It had been perfect. But a mistake. She wasn't ready. She had Derry to think of and Abby. This case. And she couldn't take any more complications, the potential for hurt, for more pain, when she was already stretched to her limit. Just because he was perfect now didn't mean it would last. A few days? A few months? Roger had seemed perfect too when they'd first started dating. But she and Morrison had been perfect before—they'd had the perfect friendship. Jesus, how badly had she fucked things up?

"It was...amazing. You were amazing. But it...it probably shouldn't happen again. I've got a lot going on, and I just... I don't know what to do here."

His hand stilled on her thigh. "You're scared."

She wanted to deny it, but how could she ignore the way her stomach tightened imagining opening herself up to him, actually being with him, loving him with all of her for longer than a night? She let out a breath. *Yes. I'm terrified.* "No, I'm just...confused."

"Okay."

Her stomach clamped down at the whispered hurt in his voice. "We can still be friends."

He ran a finger down her backbone. "Of course, Shannon. We'll always be friends. And I'll always be here for you. I'll always take care of you."

He took care of everyone. "You'll be there because I'm human, right?"

"If you say so."

"Is that a dig at my humanity?"

He let go of her and rolled toward the window, away from her. "It was a dig at your reasoning."

She stared past him out the window, willing the burning in her belly to subside. When it didn't, she slid from the bed and headed for the door, scanning the room for a towel, a robe. Friends wore robes in front of each other, right?

His phone buzzed on the bedside table as she put her hand on the knob. He sat and stared at her, mouth opening once, then closing.

Please don't make this harder, Curt...Morrison. Morrison.

The phone buzzed again, and he picked it up and turned it over. "Petrosky," he said to the screen and put the cell to his ear. "Hey, boss." He raised his gaze to the ceiling—listening, thinking. Or maybe avoiding looking at her.

She stared at his back, at the angry, red fingernail gouges from shoulder blade to hip. She'd already injured him. Shannon averted her eyes, hoping the wounds would heal.

"Be right there." His voice was tight. Morrison swung his feet off the bed and laid the phone on the table, still facing the window.

Shannon stepped toward him, no longer concerned about her nakedness. "What happened?"

He kept his eyes on the window and the morning fog. "They found Wheatley's car."

THROUGH THE WINDSHIELD, the bleary sky loomed ominous and heavy, though the temperature teased them with the promise of spring. The ride was silent, tense, but every muscle in her body was still warm and pliable from last night's gentle caresses. Everything today was a contradiction.

Petrosky was waiting for Morrison and Shannon outside the precinct, a halo of smoke following him as he climbed into the backseat. At least he hadn't changed overnight. Morrison handed him a granola bar from the console, and Petrosky glanced at it for a second, then shoved it into his pocket with a grunt. Morrison closed the console without offering Shannon one. She turned to face the window, the sting of tears hot behind her eyes. *This is why I don't need a relationship—bullshit like this.* She didn't need anyone. She just needed to concentrate on the case.

Ash Park passed by the window in an insectile buzz of tires—here a burned-out building with a graffitied smiley face, there a vacant lot where empty plastic bags skittered with the breeze over chunks of broken asphalt. By the time they reached the city limits, the deep ruts in the road were encouraging Shannon's coffee to make a comeback.

The case. *Think.* They'd found no prints or other identifying forensic evidence on Lucky's body or the envelope, save for soil ground into Lucky's fur, common fertilized dirt that might have been there before he was killed. Someone had been careful. Okay, so…Wheatley's car. Had he abandoned it once he found out that they were looking for him? Petrosky had already said they'd had no luck tracking him down yesterday, but maybe someone had tipped him off. Maybe Wheatley was still in contact with his coworkers at the social work office. Amanda had seemed genuinely worried about Wheatley's late-night entry, and Burke…well, she seemed a little off, but then again, she would; she and Shannon had a history.

Still, try as she might, Shannon could think of no possible reason for Wheatley or anyone in the social work department to hurt Derek Lewis. He was a royal dick who beat women and children, but social workers saw that every day. If they felt compelled to kill people over shitty parenting or domestic violence, there'd be a hell of a lot more bodies.

But one of the social workers *had* been there, according to Johnson's friend Angela Perez, the witness they were still trying to locate. If the tip was legit, it had to have been Wheatley. And Wheatley must have seen something; why else would he avoid coming forward and then suddenly disappear once their killer decided he wanted more attention than he'd gotten? Was Wheatley trying to figure out if what he'd seen was important? Or was someone scaring him into silence? He couldn't be the killer, could he? These clues were not adding up.

She rolled her window down, but the stagnant air of the river did little to quell the angry burbling in her stomach. Morrison's silence wasn't helping, either. He wouldn't even look at her. Fine, she'd stop looking at him too.

Shannon breathed through her mouth as Morrison took a left behind what looked like an abandoned factory, all steel and bars and broken glass. And there was the car—a green import of some kind, the rear wheel wells grown over with rust, a spiderweb crack spanning the front windshield. They pulled up beside it and got out.

The air was heady with the stink of moldering vegetation or brackish water, and maybe dead fish. She could almost taste the decay. Petrosky walked to the side door and peered through the glass into the backseat.

"Who called it in?" Shannon walked around to the other side and looked through the driver's window at a seat littered with fast-food bags and an empty two-liter of Red Pop.

"Uniform," Petrosky said. "Came down here because someone was screaming."

"Screaming?"

"Some schizo." Petrosky frowned at a smudge on the window, though Shannon couldn't figure out why that of all things would bother him.

"Isn't 'schizo' a little politically incorrect?" she said.

Petrosky squinted at the door handles. "Not if it's true. Cop took the guy to the ER. Got him some meds and a bed for the night."

Shannon straightened and looked at him over the top of the car. "But, they didn't pull the car to the impound?"

"I told them not to."

Shannon cocked an eyebrow.

Petrosky walked to the hood and stooped over the headlights. "He said it smelled." He bent to examine the tires, then walked to the back and put his face close to the exhaust pipe. Then up to the trunk. He sniffed, grimaced, and reared back.

He said it smelled. Horror washed through her, and her already agitated stomach flipped. "Is that smell...not from the river?" She chanced a look at the front of the car, where Morrison was examining the grille.

Morrison met her eye and shook his head grimly. *Not the river.* They all stared at the trunk.

Petrosky pulled gloves and a knife from his back pocket, and with latexed fingers, he jimmied the trunk lock open. Shannon held her breath. Petrosky gagged but leaned his head over the open trunk cavity. From the look on his face, whatever was in there, was disgusting. Morrison edged closer to him, leaned over too, and turned away.

Shannon released her breath and took another, the horrid, rotting stink stronger than it had been moments before. She swallowed hard and approached anyway. "Is it Wheatley?"

"You sure you want to see this, Taylor?"

"I've seen enough crime scene photos. I can handle it." But she didn't want to look.

"I wouldn't have involved you to begin with if I didn't think you could handle it. But that doesn't mean you need to see more than necessary." Petrosky pulled his head out of the trunk and started for the river. "Get a breath first," he called over his shoulder.

Shannon turned her head and inhaled sharply but couldn't shake the stench of rotten meat and sulfur. She squared her shoulders and stepped toward the car, arms crossed as if that might protect her from whatever was in there. Or whoever was in there. She peered inside.

Not Wheatley, not even parts of Wheatley, but the sight was almost as grotesque.

At the bottom of the trunk, lay a mass of gnarled towels, black and heavy with what looked like semi-congealed blood and writhing with enough maggots that the entire crumpled bundle was almost a living, breathing organism, the squirming brain of some alien creature. Gravel crunched as Petrosky returned. Shannon stepped away and turned her head from the wet mess to get a breath of air while Petrosky poked at the bloody towels with a stick he must have picked up by the water. Maggots suctioned to the wood. He set the stick aside and reached through the wriggling creatures, smearing dark stains across his gloved knuckles.

Maggots didn't just appear. Blowflies needed to find blood and lay eggs before the maggots could hatch. That meant the car had been abandoned long before they'd visited the social work office, probably just after the trial. Wednesday—maybe as late as Thursday. If the blood in the trunk was someone else's, another victim's, Wheatley might be running; but if it belonged to a new victim, then who? And if it was Wheatley's blood, then someone else—the killer—was tying up loose ends. And she was no closer to finding their murderer.

Shannon stepped farther from the trunk, from the mess, from Petrosky, who was leaning into it, face inches from the wiggling pile. Neither he nor Morrison said a thing, but she knew they could feel it too, the dark omen in the air. A whisper that this was a beginning rather than an ending, that bloody towels would be the least of the horrors they encountered. At the horizon line, the sun sat, pale and white, barely illuminating the fog that rose from the river like disturbed ashes.

18

PETROSKY STAYED to wait for the tow truck and the crime techs. Morrison drove Shannon back to the office, the air thick with things they couldn't say, maybe about the bloody scene they had witnessed that morning, maybe about death, maybe about Derry. Maybe about the two of them. Shannon stared hard out the window.

Morrison parked out front and touched her arm. "You okay?" The first words he had uttered since they left the river.

She nodded. "Yeah, I just... I feel like I'm drowning in death lately." Too much. Too vulnerable. These were feelings she could confess to a friend, but...Morrison wasn't just a friend anymore. She gritted her teeth. They had to go back to being just that—just friends. She'd never survive the next few months without his support.

Morrison averted his eyes. "I know the feeling."

She looked at her hands and back at his profile. His jaw was hard. Angry, maybe. He should be furious with her—she'd just fucked everything up for both of them. But at least they were alive. And she had to make sure they all stayed that way. "Do you think Abby needs someone with her at school?"

"Valentine is already over there."

Valentine. She visualized the tight line of his mouth when he talked about Derek Lewis, his gentleness with Lillian's belly. Yeah, he'd watch out for Abby. He wouldn't let anyone near her.

They stared up at her office building together, and her eyes dropped to Dr. McCallum's window on the ground floor. Maybe she'd take him up on his therapy offer—again. But watching the curtains in McCallum's office gave her a sinking feeling like her life was going backward. She looked away.

"Can I walk you up?" Morrison said.

"No, I'll be fine."

"I know. Maybe I'll follow you anyway, just to make sure."

They were silent in the hallway, their footsteps covered by the bustle of other lawyers in the offices nearby. Odd—she rarely noticed the sound of printers and agitated attorneys on the phone with their clients, and on Saturday the bustle was usually even more subdued. Perhaps it was her senses that were heightened, as if the bloody rags in Benjamin Wheatley's car had made the rest of the world stand out if only for its normalcy. Or perhaps she'd woken up different, her nerves still on fire from the night before. She wondered if the sensations would dull in a day or two, hiding themselves forevermore in some deep, internal cave. Numb but safe. And without someone there to wake them up again...

Not now, Shannon. Her heart ached as she nodded goodbye to Morrison and escaped into her office. Three new folders had arrived on her desk while she'd been down at the river. Shannon stowed her briefcase next to her chair and opened the top one. Maggie Batsom, age four, beaten within an inch of her life, multiple lacerations and seventeen fractures including neck, arms, legs—some injuries old, some new. Two other children in the house, CPS involved. Stephanie Batsom, the mother, was arrested when she took the girl to the hospital, claiming she'd fallen down the stairs, which didn't explain the fingerprints around Maggie's throat. Mom claimed it was a boyfriend who was out of state at the time of the hospitalization. *Bullshit.*

Shannon flipped through the police report to the photos. A girl with a round baby face lay on a bed, eyes closed, a white bandage seeping blood wrapping her forehead. Every limb was encased in a different plaster cast.

Her stomach turned. *Attempted fucking murder.* She frowned toward Roger's office, made a note on the top page, and slapped the file shut. The next file contained more of the same: neglect, bodily injury, bloody bandages, unconfirmed presence of someone else in the home.

She spent three more hours researching and making phone calls and trying to ignore the heaviness in her belly, the tightness in her chest that might have been fear or, somehow, more horrible, loneliness. Shit was going down, and she'd lost the one person she could have talked to. Maybe she did need more girlfriends. Or maybe she needed to not fuck her friends like a goddamn idiot. Mistakes, everyone made them, but she was most upset that she couldn't decide whether sleeping with Morrison actually *had* been a mistake. And she didn't have time to really consider it—or a head clear enough to do the thinking part justice.

Shannon flipped another folder closed and hauled out the files in her briefcase, reviewing her to-do list and scribbling notes. So many people to talk to and not enough time. One lead seemed promising on Reverend Wilson: according to the detective on the case, Wilson had told another bar patron that he was going to "take care of the girl." Leave it to alcohol to loosen one's tongue. It was always the alcohol or a partner that did you in.

She was making final notes in his file when someone tapped on her open door.

Petrosky. "Still looking for Angela Perez," he said, "the girl who told Johnson about the other social worker. But today wasn't a total waste: blood type in Wheatley's trunk matches Wheatley, though they can't tell definitively if the amount that was there would have been enough to kill him. Probably, though." Petrosky leaned his bulk against the doorframe, Morrison's granola bar in his hand. He tore it open, and a hot pang of jealousy ripped through Shannon's chest, even as she grimaced at the thought of eating while discussing Wheatley's bloody remains.

Oh my god, I can get my own granola. She put her pen aside.

"And Wheatley isn't at home. Not that I expected him to be; he's probably buried in a shallow grave." Petrosky swallowed his food. "I went into his place anyway, poked around a bit."

"Poked around?"

Petrosky grunted and took another bite.

She closed the file and pushed it aside. "You're going to get arrested, Petrosky." Not for this, she knew. He had cause after finding the bloody towels in the car, though she doubted he'd followed protocol even there.

"No one's hauling me in over looking in his closets. Which are full, by the way, undisturbed, and with a complete set of luggage sitting there empty. He didn't leave the social work office high and dry."

"You think he was…taken? Against his will?"

Petrosky shrugged one shoulder. "Just because his card went back to the office doesn't mean he did."

Of course. She'd known it didn't make sense for Wheatley to have gone back, especially not in the middle of the night. Even if he had been planning on running away, he still could've gone in earlier without arousing a bit of suspicion. In for a few, get what he needed, and out again, on the road. How had she missed something so simple? "Okay, so someone used his card to gain access in the middle of the night. What do you think they were looking for?"

"Don't know. Something Wheatley had, or something they thought he had. Maybe notes, like in your car, trying to figure out exactly what he knew. Same reason they hit you." He stepped inside her office, put a hand on her desk. and lowered his voice. "Also found a buddy of Wheatley's. Theodore Ruskin over in Grosse Pointe. Only caller on Wheatley's cell records outside of business calls. Lonely guy." Petrosky took the last bite of the granola bar, and crumbs fell from the wrapper to her desktop.

She glared at them. "Does Cur—Morrison know you're actually eating that?" She nodded at the empty granola package.

He crumpled the wrapper in his palm and shrugged.

Her heart rate picked up. She avoided Petrosky's eyes and tried to look nonchalant. "Where is Morrison?"

"California's busy running down Wheatley's credit cards, knocking on the doors of offices around the social work building, and interviewing anyone and everyone around Wheatley's place. That's why I'm here to give you this." Petrosky pulled another granola bar out of his pocket and dropped it onto her desk. Cranberry white chocolate.

"He said you liked caramel," Petrosky said. "Yelled at me for eating that one. He'll be even more pissed that I ate the blueberry one too. But no one likes cranberries."

Shannon cocked an eyebrow. "He *yelled* at you?" She'd never once seen Morrison yell. Maybe she didn't know him as well as she'd thought. After all, she'd only just learned that he had a "mean streak."

"He frowned at me. Which is as close to yelling as California gets."

"Maybe he frowned at you because you gave him the busywork. He's a good detective, Petrosky."

"Good detectives do busywork. Hell, almost all of it's busywork, just like this lawyer gig. You oughta know that." Petrosky tossed his wrapper into her trash can. "Plus, California takes better notes than I do—says it helps him get his thoughts together. Man's a born writer. Might as well let him put that fancy English degree to use." He kicked the door closed and sat, leveling his eyes at Shannon. "Got some shit on your husband too."

She grimaced. *Roger is not my husband anymore.* She bit her tongue and waited for him to go on.

"There are four on his caseload now that have had sudden changes in charges or even full drops. And more overlap with cases Wheatley was working on than you'd expect based on random chance."

"You think Wheatley and Roger were—"

"Ike Lambert's case was one of Wheatley's. I met with his ex about an hour ago. Lambert's a bad, bad guy. Druggie. Almost killed another little boy a few years back while under the influence of cocaine. Roger dropped him to a drug charge and misdemeanor assault." His eyes glittered in her overhead lights. He was a hair away from outright smirking. "And Lambert had cash. Ex thought he might have paid for his freedom."

Paid for his freedom? Was Petrosky kidding? "Have you found any evidence that Roger's taking bribes?"

Petrosky's face soured. "Not yet."

"There are tons of reasons to plead down, Petrosky. With Lambert, it made sense. It's a judgment call, really." Though that wasn't entirely true—she'd been pissed as hell over the Lambert case. He'd gotten off too easy.

"That one might have made sense, but some of his charges are being dropped way below what could reasonably have been prosecuted. He's a sneaky fucker; I'll give you that, Taylor. He does a good job making it not look too obvious."

What is he getting at? "But Roger never asked me to reduce charges on Johnson. Not once."

"Of course he didn't. Roger never had a relationship with Johnson. But Derek Lewis used Roger as a defense attorney about ten years back, before he was a prosecutor. Roger got Lewis off clean on a drug charge. Funny that he went full throttle on the murder charge when half the people your office prosecutes end up with reductions."

"Maybe he liked Lewis. Wanted to see his killer put away."

"Or maybe Lewis knew that Roger was getting bribed by defendants to reduce their charges and Roger offed him for it. And he was happy to put Ashley Johnson away instead."

What the fuck? "You can't seriously think Roger played a part in Lewis's death."

"Not necessarily." But the hardness in his eyes said maybe.

"That's insane, Petrosky." Her head spun.

"Is it? We both know he's lowering those charges. I don't know how Lewis would have found out, but I'm working on it. And if Roger was using Wheatley to somehow flush out who might have the resources to pay for their freedom, we've got a link there too."

Petrosky had lost his goddamn mind. "Roger would have just paid people off. He wouldn't kill anyone." She never thought he'd cheat either. But still, murder was extreme. And the fact that Petrosky was pushing something so ridiculous, shutting out dialogue where they might explore other valid options... Was there something he was trying to ignore? Something he wanted to hide?

"Fine, okay? Fine. I don't have a good reason for motive, not yet." Petrosky glowered out the window behind her. "But there's something there. And he is a sneaky fucker."

She shook her head. "Jesus Christ, Petrosky, you just want it to be Roger."

"He's got issues, Taylor. McCallum says he's a narcissist, though I suspect you already know that. But he might actually be a full-on psycho. Neither personality gets emotional for shit unless you piss them off. And they're gifted liars."

You haven't seen McCallum in weeks. Roger wasn't the only liar here. Her teeth hurt, and she loosened her jaw. "Roger's just an asshole. Not a killer." He was reducing charges, but only to up their percentage of convictions without going to court—not for pay. And no one was complaining except her. "I just can't—"

"With all due respect, Shannon, Roger has a history of hiding things. From you especially." He glanced at the door as if expecting Roger to appear. "Did he know where you were going to be, Shannon?"

"What? When?"

"When you were at the gym. When your car got vandalized."

"Petrosky, he could have just looked in my briefcase. Hell, he didn't even have to sneak anything. All he had to do was ask."

"Not if you weren't supposed to be on that case. Or maybe he wanted to throw suspicion elsewhere—no one would believe that the lead prosecutor is out smashing car windows." Petrosky touched his shirt pocket as if to make sure his smokes were still there.

"Whoever left Lucky's head on my car wasn't worried about being found out, Petrosky. They *wanted* us to pay attention. They wanted to scare me."

"And whoever did it, knew just how to get to you. Knew what would bother you. Who your family was." Petrosky met her eyes. "Maybe you should hit the training sessions without the classes for a little while. Be less predictable."

Maybe she should skip the workouts altogether since she just fucked her gym buddy.

Petrosky's phone buzzed, and he glanced at it, then back at the granola bar on the desk. "If you don't eat that, you'll hurt California's feelings."

"Since when are you worried about anyone's feelings?"

The corner of Petrosky's mouth turned up, but he said nothing.

"I'll save it for later. Thanks for bringing it by, though."

"Least I can do for California's girlfriend." He pulled a cigarette from his pack, stuck it between his teeth, and stepped toward the door.

"I'm not his girlfriend," she called after him.

He turned back to her, his face a mask of incredulity.

Does he…know?

"Come off it, Taylor. You know better, and so do I. He yelled at me over food."

"He frowned." But her abdomen tightened like someone had punched her in the gut.

"Just don't fuck with him. Whatever hippie bullshit California might be into, he's a good man."

"What?"

"I'm not repeating that shit, not to you or anyone else." Petrosky pulled a lighter from his coat. "Ever." He cut his eyes to the hall and back to her, lip curling as if he had smelled something bad. Her neck tensed.

Sure enough, Roger's stupid face appeared in her office, a fake and completely inappropriate smile plastered across his maw. "What's going on in here?"

"Consultation," Petrosky said.

"On what, may I ask?"

Petrosky smiled and lit his cigarette. "Nope, you may not." He turned and pushed past Roger into the hallway.

Roger staggered against the doorframe and scowled at Petrosky's back until the stairwell door slammed. "Not a good idea, Shannon."

She fingered the granola bar on her desk, but all she could see was a bloody mass of towels teeming with bugs. She took a deep breath. "I can be friends with whomever I want."

"Petrosky and Morrison are no one's friends. Unless you're a prostitute."

She squeezed the bar, and the wrapper crinkled as if it were trying to scream. "Kiss my ass, Roger." The phone on her desk rang.

He smiled at her, but it looked like a snarl. "Not if you paid me." Roger turned to leave, hand on the doorknob.

There's the man I walked away from. She opened her mouth to tell him to fuck off, but the phone buzzed again. She ignored Roger instead and pressed the receiver to her ear, knuckles white.

"Sorry to call you at the office, but I've been trying to get ahold of you all morning." Alex's voice shook.

She straightened, the sound of Roger slamming her door almost mute under the pounding in her ears and Alex's heavy breathing. "What's happened?"

"I'm taking him home in an hour," Alex said. "I—" His voice caught, and Shannon's heart seized. "His liver's failing, kidneys too, and his lungs...fuck. They can't tell me exactly how long but...they're done treating any of it or the wound on his leg. Maybe the infection even contributed, but they don't... Shit, I'm a doctor, and I knew it was coming, and I just can't..." There was a sharp intake of breath on the line. "He begged them to let him go home, *begged* them, and it looks like he's going fast. They're discharging him into home hospice care. Nurse once a day, a...priest or some shit. I refused that part." Alex sniffed. "I don't know how to tell Abby."

"I'll be there in twenty minutes." She hung up the phone and yanked her suit jacket from the back of the chair. Then she was in the hall, somehow on the stairs, the hollow echo of her footsteps following her as she ran down, every step clanging like a bell that was ticking off minutes until eternity caught up with her. She was running toward doom. Derry's end. Racing toward the last look, the last hug, the last everything. Twice she paused, hand gripping the railing, her body a magnet, her office the North Pole. If she went back, she wouldn't have to face this. Wouldn't have to watch Derry go home to die. And then it would be almost like he never died at all, and for the rest of her life, she could live in a state of delusional bliss, convinced that he was still alive and well but just...somewhere else. She stepped forward, again and again and again, the dread weighting her feet like cement boots, every nerve in her body screaming at her to stop. But there was no stopping the inevitable. And the fire behind her eyes, the panic buzzing through her chest, even her heavy feet knew that tragedy was coming whether she stood still or not.

She was in the parking lot before she remembered that she didn't have her car. A cab would take an hour to arrive. She grabbed her cell and scrolled through the contact list, past Morrison's number, flinching when she realized there was no one but him she could call, no one but him she could trust to come running. Her finger hovered over the call button. Petrosky? Maybe Petrosky. He'd still be close by, and probably perfectly willing to take her anywhere she needed to go. But...she didn't just need a ride. Tears stung her eyes. Her chest hurt. She needed her best friend. She needed Morrison.

He answered on the first ring. "Hey, Shannon." But his voice lacked its usual friendliness; his tone laced with something thick and tired and sad.

She stared at the courthouse, at the single ash tree at the far corner, barren despite the impending spring. She'd screwed up. She'd screwed everything up. *Breathe.* But she couldn't catch her breath any more than she could force the tree into a sudden full bloom. "Sorry to bother you, but...are you around?" She was whispering, wheezing. She laid a hand on her knee.

"Shanny—what's wrong? I'm here at the precinct."

"Can you give me a ride to the hospital?" Her voice wavered, and she fought to control it. The phone was silent in her hand. "Morrison?"

Then the shriek of a squeaky door sounded in the phone and from across the lot, and when she looked up toward the noise, she saw him emerge through the front door of the precinct.

He ran. "Shanny."

Her steps were leaden, her feet numb. When she stumbled, he grabbed her elbow and led her to the passenger seat of his car. "It sucks, Shanny," he whispered. "But you've got this." No bullshit. No banality. "I'm here, okay?"

He knew. He always knew. She watched through the windshield as he raced around the car and jumped in, shoving the keys into the ignition. She forced a cough over the lump in her throat, trying to find her breath. "Thanks, Morrison. I appreciate it." But her voice cracked on the last word.

He leaned over the console and put his arms around her shoulders.

She laid her head against his neck and sobbed.

19

The ladies at the desk were morose, or seemed to be, staring at their computers and tapping furiously on their keyboards. Wanting to be somewhere else, like she did, somewhere death didn't hang in the air like a cheap perfume.

Derry's things were already packed in a duffel bag by the door. He sat in a wheelchair parallel to the bed, his sweatshirt hanging off his bony shoulders. The skin on his face sagged in a way that made him look thirty years older. She went to him and squeezed his hand. "Derry."

"It's really not a bad weight loss plan," he said, gesturing feebly to his chest. His voice was raspy and strange and grotesque. "I lost thirty pounds in thirty days!"

She blinked back tears. "Where's Alex?"

"Finishing the last of the paperwork. He's going to take me home, then go get Abby."

Shannon's heart throbbed, viscous and sluggish as if the muscle was swimming in glue. "They give you oxygen to take home?"

Beside her, Derry's chest rose and fell, his breath crinkling like paper. "Alex is getting that too."

"Good." She stared at the back wall, avoiding his face.

Derry coughed. "He here for you?"

Right. Morrison. She turned. He'd been standing in the corridor, but he approached when he saw her looking. "Yes. I mean, for you too, but he drove me here and—"

Morrison poked his head into the room. "What's up, old man?"

"Ahh, nothing better than old man end-of-life references at vulnerable times."

"You sure as hell weren't vulnerable last week when you took all my money."

Derry grinned, but the corner of his mouth twitched with pain.

Morrison winced and nodded to Shannon.

She patted Derry's hand. "Be right back." They took a few steps away from the room, far enough so Derry couldn't hear them. The hospital swam by around her, busy with the effort of hustling death.

"You can head out if you want," Shannon said, though her chest tightened at the thought of being alone with Derry and Alex. "I'll ride back with them."

"Your brother has a Prius. There's no way they'll get him and the wheelchair and you in that car." Morrison glanced back into the hospital room. "Plus the supplies. I'll wait downstairs in the lot."

He knew what she needed. What Derry needed. And the flush in his cheeks had never been more alive, more vital, than now when everything else felt so...dead. She tried to ignore the image of Derry's chalky pallor that had crept into her brain and stuck like a parasite—sucking the life out of her too.

Her arms tingled with the desire to hug Morrison, to draw from his strength, to brush her lips against his warm neck, but she clenched her fists at her sides. "Thank you."

He nodded and headed down the hallway as Shannon crossed back to Derry's room. Her body felt as though it weighed a thousand pounds, every step an almost Herculean feat.

Derry peered at her through narrowed eyes. "Are you guys...a thing? God, please tell me you're a thing. Right from the beginning, I hoped you'd date him instead of Roger, but..." He coughed wetly and struggled to catch his breath, gasping as he inhaled. "So?"

"He's just helping me out."

Derry studied her face. "Spill it, girlfriend. I saw how you looked at him." His voice was higher, inflated with mock flamboyance, but its unusual hoarseness grated over her eardrums.

Shit, Derry, I can't, I... She sighed. "Okay, fine, we *might* be a thing. A little bit of a thing. I'm not sure." *A little bit of a thing?* Out loud, the words sounded trite, dismissive, and nowhere near reflective of what had transpired between her and Morrison.

Derry wheezed in a breath. "Oh, honey, it's not worth wasting your time on a little thing." He leaned toward her, but he groaned with the effort, wincing in pain, and her stomach twisted at the misery in his eyes. "So, is he good?" He smiled, and for one glorious second, they were almost themselves again, the hospital and death and the hissing oxygen tank fading away.

She wanted to stay like that forever, just talking, teasing each other—not dying. "Yes, he's good." *God yes.*

He nodded at the door and slumped back into the wheelchair. "About damn time. I've always liked him."

"You'd like anyone who wasn't Roger."

"Maybe so. But I loved Curt from that first day you brought him out to dinner with us and Abs." He coughed, swallowed phlegm. "He's got...a kindness about him, you know?"

She nodded. She knew. "But we've been friends for so long, and I don't want to lose that. I..."

He shook his head feebly. "You sound just like Mom."

"I'm not like her at all!"

"You are, Shanny. Angry. Stubborn. Pessimistic about relationships because you can't see the potential unless some narcissistic asshole hammers how great they are into your fucking head." He coughed, wheezing air through his nose. "And seriously? You can't be friends with your lover? What the hell is wrong with you?" He closed his eyes for a moment, pain etched on his face.

Everything was wrong with her. She was being ridiculous. But... "I just don't have time."

"Don't have time?" Derry opened his eyes. "Time for what exactly?"

"For a relationship."

"Make time."

"It isn't that easy."

"Bullshit, Shanny. Time is what you have. I'd love to have more." And they were back in the hospital, circling the drain. Her eyes filled with tears.

"Be happy, Shanny. Be with people who make you happy. That's what Alex does for me. Even with all this,"—he gestured to his ruined body—" he still makes me smile." His mouth tightened, and he hissed a breath through clenched teeth. "I'll leave this world knowing someone loves me and always will."

"Abby loves you too." Shannon put her hand on his shoulder, and the bones were sharp under her palm. "And I love you. Always."

Derry put his hand over hers. "I love you too, Shanny. Now stop fucking around and letting your long-ass life pass you by. God knows you wasted enough time on your asshole ex." He squeezed her hand, his knuckles whitening. "And grab the nurse."

THE NEXT FEW hours were a blur. Morrison clutched her hand on the center console but stayed blessedly silent as he drove back to Derry's house. Shannon watched the sky, the vibrant blue finally peeking through the storm clouds, and it seemed too hot, too bright, too...happy. She let the tears fill her eyes and watched the city pass through a watery film, pretending that she was drowning. If she couldn't breathe, she couldn't hurt.

When they got to Derry's, Shannon and Morrison unloaded Alex's car while Alex settled Derry into the office on the first floor where a hospital bed dwarfed Derry's antique desk in the corner. When the car was empty, Shannon sat in a folding chair beside her brother's bed, her head resting on the duvet near Derry's emaciated calf. Alex squeezed her hand, said something about groceries and picking up Abby, and left. Derry snored quietly through it all, presumably because of the drugs the nurse had given him before they left the hospital. Morphine. Ativan. Every four hours, to keep him comfortable.

But not to save him.

A car door clanged outside, and Shannon raised her head to look out the window as Petrosky stepped out of his car in the circular drive. Roger's Mercedes pulled in behind him.

Fuck. The folding chair clattered to the floor behind her as she left Derry wheezing softly in the office and walked out onto the crowded front porch. Morrison was already out there, facing Roger. Petrosky stood behind them, leaning against the house.

Roger turned to Shannon as the front door swung shut behind her. "What the fuck are these guys doing here? You take off from work, don't tell anyone where you're going—"

"No, Roger, I just didn't tell *you*, which is the reason you're upset."

"This isn't about us, Shannon. I shouldn't have to call back the last known number on your office phone to find out where you went."

Narcissistic. Maybe psychopathic. Anger seared through her, boiling her blood, turning her bones to ash. "You shouldn't be doing that at all."

Roger's face twisted into one of concern, and he stepped toward her and reached out to touch her arm. "I'm sorry about Jerry."

Shannon slapped his hand away, and Morrison stiffened.

The hurt in Roger's eyes hardened into rage. "You need to take some time off." His voice was soft, measured, dangerous. "Before you let your instability get the better of you."

I promised Derry. I'm going to find this fucker. She glowered at Roger. "I don't need time off. I need to figure out what's going on with this case."

"Figuring out this case isn't in the scope of your job. Stick to your job."

"The right thing, that's the scope of my job. Finding the truth, that's my job. Putting the right people away, that's my job." Her voice was rising, higher and louder, and she didn't care. A breeze sweetened with spring and new life whipped her words away, and she could feel the vestiges of winter underneath it—the cold, the death. "Don't you dare try to tell me what I need to do. It's not like you have any frame of right or wrong, anyway. You do whatever it takes to get an easy win."

Roger's eyes flicked to Petrosky, to Morrison, and back to her. "You're wrong on that."

"Am I? What about Sandusky? Easily second-degree murder, but we pleaded down despite no shortage of evidence."

"It was easier to—"

"And Lambert. He should have been put away forever."

"We didn't have enough to guarantee he would." Roger shrugged. "Everything isn't always cut-and-dried."

"Some things are." Morrison's voice was low, almost a whisper.

Roger sneered, his jaw working. "This isn't your business, asshole."

Petrosky pulled a cigarette from his pack. "Derek Lewis dead in a lonely apartment, though, that is our business. Decapitated pets, that's our business. Ditto on a trunk full of bloody towels."

Roger turned on him. "What the fuck are you talking about?"

"Oh, I'm sure you'll hear all about it on Monday, Roger." Petrosky lit his cigarette. "By the way, how well did you know Benjamin Wheatley?"

"Who?"

Petrosky smiled at him, but it wasn't a friendly grin.

Shannon glanced down the street. "Alex and Abby will be back soon. You need to be gone before they get here."

Roger's mouth tightened. "All of us?"

"Just you."

Roger's nostrils flared. He shook his head. "You always were a fucking whore."

There was a flash of activity, Roger smirking, Petrosky straightening, and then Morrison's arm shot out, his fist connecting with Roger's face.

Roger grunted, hands over his nose, blood spurting through his fingers. "You fucking—" He looked at his hands, bared his teeth, and lunged. Morrison sidestepped him, grabbed his wrist, and flipped him over the porch railing and into the flower bed. Roger groaned but didn't stand. Morrison stood above him, hands twitching and ready at his sides.

Petrosky blew smoke rings toward the roof and peered into the flower bed. "You okay there, Rog? You seem a little unsteady on your feet."

Roger clambered out of the bushes, grasping his nose, and shook a finger at Morrison. "You'll regret that." He pointed at Shannon. "You too."

Morrison didn't move.

Roger stumbled back to his car, and they watched him squeal down the drive and out onto the street.

Petrosky balanced his cigarette between his teeth. "You need to watch yourself around him, Taylor."

"What could he possibly do to me now that he didn't already do in our four years together?"

"I'm just saying; he might have more to lose now. And you're no longer married—he's lost his leverage."

She glanced toward the house, her chest tightening.

Petrosky squinted through the smoke. "You should go inside, get some rest." He met her eyes once more then strode down the porch steps toward his car.

"I don't need rest," she called after him. But every muscle in her body pulsed with a dull ache as if she'd just run a marathon. Her brain felt like it was encased in sludge.

Morrison kept his eyes on the road until Petrosky was out of sight. Then he reached over and squeezed Shannon's hand, sending currents of warm liquid up her arm. Roger's blood was still streaked across his knuckles like an exclamation point. He'd hit Roger. Maybe risked his career. And he was still here, helping her, supporting her.

She was turning to wrap herself in his arms when Alex's Prius turned into the drive.

"I'll be in the car if you need me, Shanny." Morrison released her and stepped off the porch.

She stared after him, her hand burning.

ABBY WAS in Shannon's arms before Alex got out of the car. Shannon knelt and held Abby's quaking body, her blouse soaking through with tears.

"I didn't get the groceries," Alex said, his voice an octave higher than usual as if he were forcing each word through a lake of unshed tears. "I just... couldn't. We went to the park, the one where I...proposed."

Shannon looked into his bloodshot eyes and kissed Abby's head. "I'll take care of it."

"I want to see Daddy." Abby's voice quavered. She let go of Shannon and took Alex's hand.

"Of course, honey," Alex said. "I'll go with you. He might be sleeping, but we can sit with him and just talk awhile, okay?" He kissed her knuckles, and Abby sniffed.

Keep it together. Don't let everyone down now. She straightened. "Alex, can I take your car?" Her rental was still at her house.

"Yeah, thanks, Shanny." Alex handed her his keys, and she squeezed his arm and stepped off the porch, barely registering Morrison's footsteps as she popped the lock. He was at the door before she got it closed.

"Where are you going?"

"Grocery store." *And no one's going to tell me I can't, not now.*

"You need to—"

So much for fucking support. "What, Morrison? What do I need to do right now?"

"Petrosky can grab some stuff."

"Why? You think Roger's staking out the grocery store, so he can off me? That Wheatley's going to miraculously show up and murder me in the fucking frozen food aisle?" *And even if someone did come up behind her and slit her throat, would that be the worst thing that could happen?*

She shook away the dark thought. *Yes. Yes, it would.* Abby needed her. Alex needed her.

Morrison shook his head almost imperceptibly. "No, I—"

"I don't need a babysitter, Morrison. I'll be fine."

"Shannon—"

"Stop." She buckled her seat belt and shoved the key into the ignition. "It's three blocks from here. Just watch them. I'll be back in a few minutes."

Morrison jumped back as she slammed the car door, the edge of it barely missing his already bloodied hand. Her heart hammered in her temples. She put the car in gear and took off, the houses a blur, every passing car shoving her heart into overdrive, every stop sign shrinking the car until it was as confining as a coffin.

Roger. He was an ass. But he wasn't a killer. Petrosky was an idiot. And Morrison with his stupid granola and his fucking shroom coffee and the way he always looked at her like he could fix everything—

Shannon slammed her palms against the steering wheel and turned onto the main road. Why couldn't Roger be the one with cancer? Or Ike Lambert or Benjamin fucking Wheatley? Anyone but Derry. Not her Derry. Alex's Derry. Abby's Derry. The only thing she could do was make his last days as peaceful and pain-free as possible. And find the asshole who slunk up to his daughter's porch and murdered her cat. *I'm not afraid to die, Shannon, but I am afraid to leave my daughter here with some maniac running around...*

I'll find him, Derry. Goddammit, I will fucking find him for you.

Shannon parked in the back of the lot and yanked the keys from the ignition, frustration bubbling inside her chest and thickening near her throat like molten rock, depriving her lungs of oxygen. She checked the windows and locked the doors, and then she screamed, beating her fists against the steering wheel and kicking at the useless pedals. Her hands ached and throbbed as she punched again and again, every impact a welcome pain that brought her back to herself and away from what was happening tomorrow or the next day or the next. The day very soon when Derry would die. Whether he died peacefully...that was up to her.

When her knuckles were throbbing and cracked open with the weight of injustice, she shook out her fists, exited the car, and went into the store to buy groceries. And bandages.

20

Morrison was asleep on the couch when she crept downstairs the next morning. His chest rose and fell with his breath, a tendril of blond hair stuck to his forehead like he was a little kid. She resisted the urge to brush it away.

"Sleep well?" Petrosky walked in from the dining room, coffee in hand. Shannon jumped and banged her elbow against the wall.

Morrison stirred.

She rubbed her sore arm. "I didn't know you were here."

"I came to relieve California. Much as he'll deny it, he needs sleep like anyone else."

Shannon peered past him into the dining room. "Where is everyone?" The stillness of the house was unnerving like someone had died. But that hadn't happened. Not yet. *Had it?* Her stomach turned.

"Alex went to the twenty-four-hour pharmacy to pick up a prescription. Abby's asleep. California will be up to look after them when I leave."

Leave? Shannon raised an eyebrow.

"I've got an appointment in half an hour with Wheatley's best friend, Theodore Ruskin."

Ruskin. Fine. Good.

"You want in?"

She realized her eyes were still on Morrison. She glanced back at the staircase, then at Petrosky. "Yeah. I'm thinking Alex and Abby could use some time alone."

Petrosky sipped his coffee and glanced at her bandaged knuckles. "Good."

He actually wanted her to come? "You could just go yourself," she said slowly.

"So, I could. But it might be nice to have a witness."

"A witness? For what?"

"The chief likes it when I do. Might as well make her happy." He winked a craggy eye.

The chief. She was ballsy, didn't take shit from anyone, especially Petrosky. If she wanted someone to keep an eye on him, she had a reason. Maybe over the hospital complaint? "Did she threaten to suspend you?" Shannon asked.

"Nope. She threatened to suspend Surfer Boy. Even called me on my cell." The corner of his mouth curved up. "It was very special."

Shannon looked again at Morrison's face: unlined and peaceful. "Because he punched Roger?" she hissed at Petrosky. "I can't believe that asshole."

"I prefer 'douche canoe,' but sure."

"What the fuck are you—"

"I got it from a blog. I like it." He downed the rest of his coffee. "Anyway, California has a squeaky-clean record and near-perfect attendance. And he brings coffee and donuts to the staff, does shit to keep morale up. They might riot if she lets him go." He waved to the door. "You need breakfast or…?"

She dragged her eyes from Morrison's snoozing profile. "Let's do it."

Theodore Ruskin lived in a one-story box of gray brick. A triangle of white siding stretched to the A-line roof over a shuttered front window. Shannon and Petrosky exited the car and stepped across the muddy front lawn to a postage-stamp cement porch. Petrosky rapped twice.

Ruskin opened the door blinking like a mole who hadn't seen daylight in months. Acne erupted over his pasty, sallow chin. He shoved enormous green-rimmed eighties glasses into place on his nose and looked from Shannon to Petrosky.

"Mr. Ruskin?" Petrosky said.

He nodded, and his glasses slipped down his nose. "Yes?"

Petrosky pulled his badge. "Detective Petrosky with the Ash Park PD. We have a few questions about a friend of yours."

"Friend?" Ruskin's eyes widened.

Petrosky peered past him into the house. "Are you alone, sir?"

Ruskin cocked his head as if no one would ever assume anything else. "Sir?"

"Yes, I'm alone."

"We're looking for a Benjamin Wheatley." Petrosky replaced his badge. "May we come in?"

Ruskin held the door open and pointed to a room directly to the left of the entry. A high-definition television screen hung from one wall, the cords to a variety of gaming systems snaking from the back of it and down to the consoles on a sofa table below. Individual leather theater seats sat within arm's reach of the controllers. On the far wall, a bookshelf bumped up against a wooden L-shaped desk that ran from the corner by the books to below the front window.

Ruskin looked around the room as if pondering where to sit.

"Interesting setup you have here, Ruskin," Petrosky said as he eased himself into one of the gaming chairs. He gestured to the desk. Ruskin took the desk chair and turned it to face the room while Petrosky swiveled both gamer's chairs to face Ruskin. Shannon sat tentatively in one, tensing her legs to keep the rocker from pitching to the floor.

"Thanks. I think," Ruskin said, the question apparent in his voice.

Petrosky put his hands on his knees, feigning calm. "Tell me about Benjamin Wheatley."

"Ben and I have known each other a long time."

"You see him often?"

"No, he didn't go out too much." Ruskin shifted in his seat. "And my wife didn't really like him. Probably why we didn't talk that much anymore."

I'm obviously not the only one who knows how romance screws up friendships.

Ruskin gestured to the desk where a set of framed pictures grinned back at them. In one photo, Ruskin had his arm around a beautiful Jessica Rabbit redhead in a tight white dress.

"That's your wife, Mr. Ruskin?" Petrosky said, sounding far less surprised than she was.

Ruskin smiled. "I know. I don't know what she sees in me." Shannon appraised his doughy body. Ruskin must be a hell of a smart guy. Maybe he was super funny. She pictured her own wedding photos. Superficial attraction only went so far anyway.

Petrosky pulled his eyes from the pictures. "So, Wheatley. Not real outgoing, but you were friends?"

Ruskin shrugged. "Dunno...I guess. We've known each other since middle school. We both wanted to be writers." He looked at his bookshelf and back at Petrosky. "Plus, we were both kinda geeky." Back at the bookshelf again, the clock, the front window. He was avoiding looking Petrosky in the eye. "You think something happened to him?"

"Why would you think that, Mr. Ruskin?"

Ruskin picked at an invisible spot on his pants.

Shannon sat straighter, her muscles taut.

"Do *you* think something happened to him, Mr. Ruskin?"

"No...I mean, I don't think so."

Petrosky stood suddenly enough that Shannon jumped. He stepped between Ruskin and the window and bent so close his breath fogged Ruskin's glasses. The man's eyes widened.

"You're not telling me the truth, Mr. Ruskin, and I can't say I like it."

"I am! I don't know where he is."

"But you know *something*, don't you?"

Shannon stared at Ruskin, who was chewing the inside of his cheek like it was bubble gum.

"Mr. Ruskin, your friend may be responsible for the murders of two people."

Shannon stared at Petrosky in surprise. Did he really think Wheatley'd killed Lewis? Or...two, so Lewis and Lucky? Unless he was just fucking with Ruskin to get him to spill what he knew.

"Wait, wait! You think that Benjamin—"

Petrosky slammed his fist on the arm of Ruskin's chair, and Ruskin's jaw clamped shut. "What do you know, Mr. Ruskin? Either you tell us now, or we take you in and find out the hard way. And if you pick door number two—"

Shannon stood, and Petrosky backed from Ruskin's desk.

"Okay, all right?" Ruskin raised his hands in surrender. "Okay. I mean, I don't even know if it's anything, you know? It might be nothing."

"We'll decide that, Mr. Ruskin."

"Okay, so the only thing I can think of is this thing he told me about at work—like a bust."

"A bust? He was a social worker, Mr. Ruskin, not a cop."

"I know, I know, that's why it was like...secret. He said he saw some guy over at one of the places he visits, maybe buying dope, and the guy was like...important. But he said he wanted to make sure he was right before he turned him in, so he was going to go over there and find out."

Wheatley had seen someone buying drugs. Someone prominent in the community. Someone with a lot to lose if it came out. But that could be a lot of people, right? She couldn't let Petrosky's wild imagination get into her head and snuff logical thought.

Petrosky paced in front of the window. "Did he? Go over there?"

"I don't know."

"How long ago was that, Mr. Ruskin?"

"Maybe... I dunno, a few months?" He chewed harder on his cheek. Shannon was certain he was drawing blood.

"We're going to need you to be more specific on the time."

"I... Shit. Okay. It was before my last book came out. *The Yeti Returns* —I published February twentieth. So maybe...beginning or middle of January?"

"That's almost four months, Mr. Ruskin. Have you talked to him since?"

"Yeah, a few times. Just a quick lunch here and there to catch up. He didn't mention this again, and I didn't ask about it because I pretty much thought he was full of shit."

Shannon and Petrosky exchanged a look. If Wheatley had waited until February to go have that chat with Lewis, he could have been the one arguing with Lewis the day he died.

"Okay, so Wheatley tells you he's going to see some guy to verify that some other guy is buying drugs from him." Petrosky leaned close to Ruskin again. "What was Wheatley planning to do once he got there? Threaten the guy into telling him what he knew?"

"Well, I'm not really sure. He didn't say. But if I know Benjamin, he just planned on talking."

"Did he ever mention a girl? An Ashley Johnson?"

Ruskin's jaw dropped as the name sank in. "Wait...that girl who killed her boyfriend? This is about that? Holy shit." A drop of sweat from his forehead slid through the grease and down onto the side of his nose. "I don't know anything about that. He just said he was going to talk to a guy to make sure of what he saw before he contacted the police. Maybe he'd even be okay with me telling you that part. He was going to call anyway."

"I don't think you have to worry about what Wheatley thinks is okay at this point, Mr. Ruskin. I'd be more worried about going to jail."

Jail? Ruskin hadn't done anything to warrant an arrest. Shannon cleared her throat, preparing to tell Petrosky to lay off before they were the ones in trouble for badgering this twerky idiot.

"But I told you everything! I don't—"

"Obstructing justice is a very serious offense, Mr. Ruskin." Obstruction. Petrosky would know about that. "You know what else is serious? Accessory to murder. And we found Wheatley's car last night with a ton of bloody towels in the trunk."

"Take it easy, Petrosky..." Shannon began.

Ruskin shot her a pleading look. "Bloody...what? I swear I don't—"

Petrosky leaned closer to Ruskin. "If this was such a secret, Mr. Ruskin, why would Benjamin tell you? Were you going to help him?"

Ruskin reared back, his eyes wide.

Petrosky stayed with him, practically nose to nose. "And by the way, I read your book, the one about the little girls on spring break from middle school, written under a pen name, right? Through some shitty indie press for perverts? *Travis.*"

"What? No, that isn't me! You've got the wrong guy! Listen, I—"

"Why would Wheatley tell you, anyway? Did you have an extra set of towels to help him clean himself off after he killed Derek Lewis? After he used a hammer to blast a man's skull clean out? Level with us, or you're going away right along with him."

What the fuck is Petrosky doing? He didn't really think Wheatley was the one who killed Lewis, did he? Wheatley had run the day she'd found Lucky's head—without his clothes. Even if he'd done it, he sure wouldn't draw attention to himself with the note and then panic and disappear.

Ruskin leaned back so far the chair tipped. "No! He just told me because he thought I might like the whole vigilante government worker going after drug lord thing as an idea for another book. Said he knew about someone getting all hopped up who shouldn't have been. That's it."

Enough. Shannon paused halfway to Petrosky, trying to decide the best way to intervene.

"Who?" Petrosky growled.

"I'm not sure; he didn't—"

"Who was it, Ruskin?"

"He didn't tell me any names or anything, oh my god, I swear he didn't, and I don't know who Travis is!" Ruskin was panting, his pockmarked face pink and shiny with sweat and oil.

"I'll be calling you, Ruskin. And I'm going to need you to keep in touch. If Wheatley shows up here, if anyone shows up here asking questions, you need to call me, or I will make sure they throw you in jail with the guys who will settle for flabby computer geek tits since they can't get anything else. You got it?"

Ruskin reeled forward and reached for a drawer in his desk. Petrosky leapt forward, snatched Ruskin's hand, and stepped behind the chair, jerking Ruskin's wrist behind his back.

Ruskin's eyes were wide, his mouth gaping like a fish out of water. "In...haler," he croaked.

"Petrosky!" Shannon grabbed Petrosky's arm, and Ruskin collapsed back into the chair, face red, fleshy lips going purple. She reached into the drawer and yanked out a rescue inhaler. Ruskin uncapped it and puffed hungrily, the whoosh like the sound of the air through Derry's oxygen machine. But this guy would live. Probably.

"They don't like guys like you in prison, Ruskin. You call if you see your buddy." Petrosky tossed his card on the desk and walked out, Shannon at his heels.

As soon as the front door closed behind them, Shannon turned on Petrosky. "What the fuck was that?"

"Interrogation." He stepped off the porch and onto the walk.

She hustled after him. "Threats are not interrogation."

Petrosky shrugged. "Well, now we know he probably didn't do anything except keep a secret for Wheatley. And Ruskin was scared enough that he would have told us if he knew more. He'll definitely call us if Wheatley shows up here." Petrosky stomped off the sidewalk and through the lawn, mud splattering his jeans.

What had Wheatley gotten himself involved in? What had he done? He couldn't be their murderer; their killer was after notoriety. "It was me," the note had said. It was a bid for attention, and not a subtle one—definitely not the words of the type of guy who ran away, who hinted to his friends about knowing things but wouldn't spill his secrets. Who kept confidentiality agreements as part of his job as a social worker, just as she did as a lawyer. Hell, maybe he'd heard a confession during a session that had tipped him off, and he hadn't been able to call the police for help because of confidentiality constraints.

Shannon's heel caught in the mushy grass. She hauled it out, squished to the car, and got in, slamming the door hard enough to jar her shoulder. "All that was bullshit, Petrosky. That stuff you said, implying Wheatley was the murderer."

"I don't know yet, Taylor. Just batting around theories. Could still be Roger. If I were a guy like Roger, maybe I'd do a little smack in a place I knew I wouldn't get caught. And maybe I'd kill both the dealer and any potential tattletales to make sure no one ever found out. Maybe I'd even frame the girlfriend since I'd know what it would take for a jury to convict."

"And then you'd leave a note on my car to alert everyone that the wrong person had been put away? Bullshit."

"I'm still working on that part." Petrosky started the engine.

Shannon leaned back against the headrest. "If Wheatley saw something, someone...why wouldn't he have come forward after Lewis was killed?"

"He could have figured that Johnson really had killed Lewis. Not that far out of line, really, since he'd have been privy to her files and would have known about Lewis's history of domestic violence. But if Wheatley's anything like his chickenshit friend in there, maybe he was scared. Scared of the killer, or scared of the fact that snooping around right before a murder makes him look suspicious as fuck."

Had Wheatley thought Johnson guilty? Or was he just scared like Petrosky was saying? Maybe he'd run to avoid being accused of something, but it was more likely he was afraid for his own life. If the blood in the trunk was any indication, he was probably already dead.

Shannon listened to the rumble of the car engine and Petrosky's labored breathing, obviously still recovering from the tongue lashing he'd given Ruskin. "Is Ruskin really an undercover indie author named Travis?"

"Nope. I made that up, trying to throw him off balance, so he'd let his guard down."

She watched Ruskin's house grow smaller in her side-view mirror then turned to Petrosky with narrowed eyes. "You didn't need a witness. You needed a good cop."

Petrosky tapped the steering wheel. "California couldn't be here, and he's usually the good one."

"I'm telling him you said that."

"Don't even think about it, or I'll tell him you think he's hung like a horse."

Shannon's jaw dropped. "He...he *told* you?"

Petrosky's brows hit his hairline, eyes wide. "Told me what?"

"Fuck you, Petrosky." She turned back to the window. "Seriously, fuck you."

21

The courtroom was alive, breathing ghastly, frosty breaths down the back of Shannon's blouse. She wished she were out with Petrosky and Morrison, investigating other individuals on Wheatley's caseload, running credit cards, and searching for who knew what else. Instead, she was stuck here with...them. The pews were full today: middle-aged men, young men, and a dozen or so women, all solemn and watchful. Assessing the room. Assessing...her. The gaze of three dozen sets of eyes bored into her back as she stared at the empty judge's chair. She shook her head. They were probably students from some criminal justice class. There was no reason for her to be so rattled.

Her breath caught when the door banged open, and Roger entered the courtroom, his nose splinted and taped with a white bandage from cheekbone to cheekbone. What the hell was he doing there? Roger winked at one of the young women in the pews in true smarmy player style. The thin, pretty woman smiled at his attention until he rearranged his face into "super dickhead" and approached Shannon up the aisle. The woman's eyes followed with thinly veiled contempt as if Shannon were ruining her chances of landing him. If she only knew.

"Ms. Taylor." Roger sat beside her, and the skin on her arms squirmed. Shannon followed his gaze to the defendant's chair where Reverend Jack Wilson reclined in the seat, eyes more curious than frightened. Three attorneys in expensive suits flanked him, haughty and smug, Rolexes glinting from their wrists. Maybe Wilson would buy them all jets if they got him off.

She turned to Roger. "What are you doing here?" she whispered.

"You've been out of the office so often lately that I've had no time to advise you on this case."

"There's no need for advice, Roger."

"Ah, but there is. You're going too hard here, and the department is concerned you have some personal vendetta that's marring your judgment."

The department? You mean you? "You're out of your mind."

Roger slapped his briefcase on the desk and withdrew a sheaf of papers. "We're charging him with reckless endangerment."

"Reckless endangerment? Roger, what the hell is—"

"Reverend Wilson is an upstanding member of the community at large and—"

"Mr. Wilson murdered his child," she hissed. "He was overheard telling a friend that night that he would take care of the kid before it ruined his family."

"I hardly think saying you're going to care for a child is evidence of intent to harm," Roger said.

"The injuries—"

"Are consistent with dropping the kid on the floor while they were playing, just as Reverend Wilson said, Ms. Taylor. He now admits he threw her into the air during a game. And he called the police right after it happened."

"Because he wanted to be able to play it off as a mistake."

"Because it was an accident."

"If it was an accident, why is he here at all?" No one with Wilson's resources would take a plea deal unless they really thought they'd be convicted.

"He has made it publicly clear that he wishes to atone for his sins, whether committed with malice or otherwise."

"And…he has a book deal already, doesn't he? About his persecution as a holy man." A misdemeanor charge and a slap on the wrist, and he would gain notoriety as a martyr. Shannon glared at Roger, and he shrugged. She looked into the courtroom behind her, avoiding the eyes that were now less solemn and more interested like they were watching *The* mother fucking *Bachelor*. "This isn't right. We should be pushing for his conviction, for the victim's sake, for her mother's sake."

Roger set the papers on the desk and snapped his case closed.

"What'd you tell the victim's mother, Roger, to convince her not to go public fighting the decision to let his ass go? That a jury would find him not guilty? That there was no point in taking it to civil court? What?" He'd manipulated that poor woman. All in the name of less paperwork and easy wins and maybe…

Her eyes flicked once more to the Rolexes.

Roger put the case on the ground and nodded to Wilson, who raised one corner of his chicken-lipped mouth and turned to the bench. "You'd know more if you'd bothered to speak to her after the discovery phase."

Ouch. Shannon's heart rate climbed. But everything she'd needed was in the file. What more could she have gleaned from badgering a grieving mother? Evidently something. Roger's eyes were so cool, so confident, so knowing. Maybe she really was losing her touch. Getting sloppy. Then she registered the familiar twitch of his mouth, the one that always told her he thought he was winning. *Not this time, you manipulative bastard.*

She squared her shoulders as the courtroom shrank around the two of them until it seemed there was no one else in the room. Her leg muscles tingled with a repressed desire to kick him in the junk. "He offered her cash." It wasn't a question. She could feel it in the air, the tainted damp of sweaty money on moldering justice.

"Reverend Wilson has agreed to provide restitution as a part of his sentence, in an amount the family has deemed more than fair."

The woman had lost her child. There was no restitution for that. "Why are you trying to protect him?"

Roger opened his mouth to speak just as the door behind the judge's station opened, and Judge Miller entered, swiping a long black braid over her shoulder. She sat behind the bench and banged the gavel, and the courtroom hushed as everyone found their seats. Roger's leg brushed Shannon's. She scooted away, her chair squealing loud enough that the entirety of the defendant's table looked over, eyebrows raised in question, identical smirks plastered on their faces.

Her chest heated. *Fuck them all.*

Judge Miller pushed her glasses up her straight Grecian nose and studied the paperwork in front of her.

"Case number 3834022Z, Reverend Jack Wilson." Shannon watched her rattle off the numbers, the case specifics, everything for the transcription, nothing that mattered for life or death, nothing that mattered at all. None of this mattered—not her presence, not the courtroom, not the judge, certainly not the lawyers sworn to uphold the laws. This fucker had murdered his own daughter and was going to get away with it. He'd serve a few months, and then he'd be free to kill some other little girl who didn't fit into his life plans.

"Ms. Taylor?" Miller peered over her glasses at Shannon. "Again, I understand there have been some changes to the case. Is the prosecution ready to proceed?"

Shannon put her hands on the desk, preparing to push herself upright, but Roger beat her to it, almost leaping to standing beside her in a whoosh of starch and cologne that might have made her gag had she been less shocked.

"Yes, Your Honor," Roger said.

Shannon froze, staring up at him, and removed her hands from the desk, the dampness from her palms streaking the wood. Her mouth was pasty. She could leave now. She could run the fuck out of here, and it wouldn't make any difference. But maybe it would make a point to the judge. She eyed the bench as Miller said: "The charges?"

"Reckless endangerment," Roger said.

Miller's eyes narrowed, and Shannon's heart skipped a beat. The judge didn't seem to like this any more than she did, though that might have been wishful thinking. Maybe the judge would deny the plea.

"Reckless endangerment?" Miller said.

"Yes, Your Honor."

Miller met Shannon's eyes, and Shannon tried to hold back the sick sense of culpability she felt standing on this side of the table with Roger. Her ex was a leech, taking what he wanted while ignoring ethical responsibilities, ignoring anything besides making his own life easier.

Miller's mouth remained grim; the mask judges wore, the one they all had to wear. She turned to Wilson. "How do you wish to plead?"

Wilson licked his lips and glanced at Roger, then back to Miller. "No contest."

Miller's eyebrow cocked, her mouth still tense. The air in the courtroom thinned. Sweat dampened Shannon's underarms, and she tried to recall whether she had put on deodorant that morning. Had she even brought it from her house to Alex's?

"Very well," Miller said, her voice pensive. "Bail is set at five hundred thousand dollars. We'll reconvene for sentencing in two weeks after I review this case in its entirety." The gavel rang through the room, and Roger grabbed his case. Wilson stood, cuffs clanking on his wrists, but not for long, that bastard. He'd have no problem coming up with half a million dollars. He could probably just trade in his watch.

SHANNON KEPT her thoughts about Miller and Roger to herself on the way home. Petrosky was driving, face agitated, already brooding, and getting him all worked up over Roger again wouldn't do anyone any good. She wanted the killer to be Roger too, if only because she wanted it to be simple and easy and almost over. But it didn't feel right. It didn't make sense. Still, she entertained the thoughts; they were preferable to considering that these were probably her last weeks with Derry. When she thought of sitting in the house, holding Derry's hand, watching him creep slowly toward his inevitable demise, her breath quickened, and she feared she might pass out. It wasn't until Petrosky parked in front of Alex's house, and she'd gotten out of the car that she realized they'd ridden the entire way in silence.

Abby tackled Shannon at the front door.

"Holy cow, what's—" Shannon gaped as a massive gray pit bull skidded to a stop on the wood floor behind Abby. "Roxy!" Shannon kicked the door closed and knelt to greet the animal. "What are you doing here, girl?"

"Easy, Rox," Morrison called as he entered from the kitchen. Roxy put her butt on the floor, her tail thumping the wood, and licked Shannon's face.

Abby threw her arms around the dog's neck. "Mr. Morrison brought his dog, and he said that she can stay with us while he's hanging out here." The dog abandoned Shannon and turned her attention to Abby, licking her ears, her hair, her chin. Abby giggled maniacally. "Isn't she great?"

Morrison usually left the dog at Valentine's while he worked. Doggie playdates or some such thing.

Morrison knelt and scratched Roxy's ears, talking like a goofball cartoon character. "And she's so excited about it. Aren't you, girl? Who's excited? Who's an excited girl?"

Roxy licked his face and turned herself in a few excited circles, then made a beeline for Shannon and flopped to the ground on her back.

Abby laughed. "Mr. Morrison taught me karate too."

Shannon cocked an eyebrow at him, and he shrugged. "Martial arts and a dog? You've been busy." She sat on the floor to scratch Roxy's belly. "Alex was okay with this?"

Morrison opened his mouth, but Abby beat him to it. Her grin was infectious. "Daddy said she was awesome and that he wanted to get one just like her one day."

Morrison's eyes sparkled. "Did he now?"

Abby nodded, her eyes on Roxy. "Can she come play out back again? I'll watch her." Roxy leapt up and pushed her huge head into Abby's palm, begging for love, and Abby kissed her nose.

Happy. Content. But something else in the house pulled at Shannon, tugged at a place behind her stomach until she could no longer ignore the discomfort. *Don't look at the office door. Just let Abby enjoy this.*

"You remember what to say?" Morrison asked.

"Funtime, Roxy!" Abby's face lit up with a grin, and Shannon's heart surged as her niece bounded out of the room, Roxy at her heels.

"Funtime? I'd almost forgotten about that."

Morrison shrugged. "It's a good command to let her know it's time to play and not to work."

"She still works?"

"You know, dog stuff. Sniffing shit. Chasing cats." His voice was light, friendly, but he didn't meet her eyes.

"Some job."

"Someone's got to do it." Then his smile was gone, his eyes on Derry's door. Her chest vibrated with a painful thudding. She was going to end up having a fucking heart attack.

"Alex is with him now," Morrison said. "Been about the same today as yesterday, though he is sleeping more. The painkillers, probably." He finally pulled his gaze from Derry's room to the front door behind Shannon. "Where's Petrosky?"

"Parking." But it had been a while. They both looked at the front door. Petrosky was probably hitting a bottle he had stored under a seat. For his sake, she hoped he was just smoking a cigarette.

Morrison leaned toward her and touched her arm. "How are you, Shanny?"

Her heart raced and slowed, a speedball of emotion. "I'm...dealing. Roger was a real ass today. Switched up another set of charges last minute. Totally took over in court. I wasn't prepared for it."

"He showed up unexpected?" he asked, and he finally met her gaze, concern in his narrowed eyes.

"Yeah. Said he hadn't had time to advise me. Made a deal with the defense on the sly."

"That seems...impulsive." Morrison peered at the ceiling. "Aggressive, even. He ever done that before, in court like that?"

She shook her head.

"He ever show signs of instability before? When you were together?"

"Instability?"

"Or impulsivity. You know what I mean."

She breathed through her nose. Morrison smelled like lemon dishwashing detergent. He still had a cluster of stray bubbles on his sleeve near his elbow. "I guess. He used to buy things we didn't need. He came home with a boat once, without talking to me about it, but it wasn't like we didn't have the money."

"Oh, I remember that." He shook his head. "I can take a look at the case tomorrow. Which one was it?"

"Wilson."

"The reverend?"

"That's the one. Roger got the mother some money."

"Maybe he took a little for himself, too. You know...legal fees." He almost spit the words out; his mouth contorted in what might have been rage. Shannon's eyes widened. Roger didn't need to take cash for offering lighter charges—he had an inheritance from his family that would keep him comfortable even if he never worked again. And yet...

From the backyard, Abby's giggling drifted over them like notes on a piano, and Morrison's face molded itself back into the mask she was used to, calm and peaceful and quiet.

She pulled her eyes from him as the office door clicked. Alex emerged, wiping his cheeks on his sleeve. Alex caught Shannon's eye, and she saw her own grief mirrored there, the agonizing knowledge that time was short, a bomb ticking down to inescapable nothingness.

"He's sleeping," Alex said. "Again." He looked down the hall toward the sound of Abby's happy laughter as if confused by it.

Shannon turned as Morrison stepped past her to peer through the window beside the door. As he slid the curtain aside, a shriek of tires cut the muted din of evening. Petrosky's receding headlights bisected the street like lasers, illuminating a row of garbage cans across the street, and then disappeared around the corner.

Morrison stared after the car, his jaw tight. "Petrosky wouldn't have just left like that unless something was up."

She watched the now silent street. "I know."

Abby giggled again from the backyard, and the sound was so full of joy and hope that Shannon wished they could bottle it and keep it on hand for later this week or next month when they'd really need it. When Abby would need it. She drew her eyes from the office door and to the empty space where their garbage should have been, the missing bags of trash a needle in the back of her brain reminding her that the curb was vacant because Derry couldn't do it. Derry had always done it. She could almost see Derry and herself as children, ten and twelve, dragging bags to the curb while their mother yelled drunken obscenities from the house. Derry would stick out his tongue or pretend to gag on the stench of the kitchen trash, and they'd laugh their way back inside. He'd had the same response the night their father had left them in the driveway and taken off for good. And at Mom's funeral, he'd busied himself sticking his tongue out at her every time those around them had looked away. He was her younger brother, but a much older soul.

Morrison's phone buzzed, and he fished it out of his pocket, every muscle in his face rigid. "Hey." Pause. "Really." Not a question. Shannon watched the street as the back door slammed, and a moment later, Alex appeared through the front window, hauling the can up the drive. He set it at the curb and wiped his eyes again. She swallowed over the lump in her throat.

"Shannon."

It took her a moment to realize Morrison was touching her shoulder. She turned.

"They found Wheatley."

22

ALL NIGHT LONG—as she added drugs, as she watched her brother die—Shannon forced her brain to the case, hoping that Wheatley's death would lead them to the killer. She couldn't bear the thought that she hadn't set Derry's mind at ease—that she might not before he...went. "I'll get him, Derry," she whispered to the darkened room.

She stroked Derry's hand. Derry snored and wheezed and dreamed feverishly, eyes rolling behind his lids, lower lip quivering every few minutes as if in pain, or maybe he was trying to cry. But each inhale seemed more shallow than the last. She held his hand tighter as if that could keep him anchored to their world.

A jostling woke her, a voice growling in her ear. "Get me some of the good shit." The voice was so hoarse that, for a moment, she wasn't sure if some sinister demon had entered the room to take Derry for good. She jolted upright in the chair, blinking sleep from her eyes.

"Jumpy, aren't you?" Then Derry's raspy laugh.

"No, just...the what?"

"The good shit. Drugs. For someone who's seen their share of junkie clients, you're not too down on the lingo." He was nearly invisible in the dim room, but his breathing was fast, his voice tight. He was hurting.

Had she missed a dose? She looked at the clock. Five after three. No, he wasn't due for ten minutes. She reached for the bottle on the nightstand and dumped a few into his palm.

"One more can't hurt, Shanny."

"It's Oxycodone. I don't—"

"I've been on it too long. The lower dose isn't doing it anymore."

"No wonder you know the junkie lingo," she said, trying to keep her voice light. She dropped another pill into his hand and grabbed the water for him.

"Totally. I'm a regular addict." He swallowed the pills and lay back on the bed with a sigh. "This sucks, Shanny."

Her eyes filled. "I know it does." *And I hate this.* "But I'm glad I can be here with you."

He squeezed her hand. "Yeah. Me too." He closed his eyes. For a while his breathing remained pressured and quick, but it evened as the drugs kicked in. And when he finally slept, she did too.

THE NEXT MORNING, she awoke with an aching neck. Derry was groaning—long and deep—but he slept, and she drew her eyes from her brother to the window. In the dawn light that filtered down through the branches of the oak tree, a lone robin scratched at the first shoots of grass. He was searching for something too.

She looked away, trying to think, trying to solve the case before Derry's time ran out. So Wheatley had information about one of Derek Lewis's buyers, someone he knew wouldn't want to get caught. Wheatley had planned to confront Lewis, so he was probably the person arguing with Derek Lewis the day he died—they'd get confirmation on that from their witness, Angela Perez. After the argument, Derek Lewis must have told the killer about Wheatley's visit, maybe even threatened to expose the killer's drug use, which is why he ended up taking a hammer to his skull.

But if it was all over avoiding reprisal for drugs, why didn't this person kill Wheatley right away? And why try to take credit for Derek's death so long after the fact, with the envelope on her car? Saying, "Hey, look at me! I did it!" wasn't the mark of someone who would frame an innocent girl to buy their freedom. And she doubted he was just fucking with their heads. No, their killer had to be someone so obsessed with himself that he simply couldn't stand the thought of another person taking credit for something he'd done. Someone like...Fine, Roger was a narcissist, self-obsessed, but Petrosky's theory about Roger was just crazy. Illogical. Roger didn't fit. Did he? Goddammit all to hell, Petrosky was getting into her head. She laid her face against Derry's bed and closed her eyes, listening to the life leak out of him one breath at a time.

PETROSKY ARRIVED at the house around eight with his his hair spiked up on one side of his head. His waxy pallor of the day before had been replaced with bright spots of pink high on his cheekbones and bags of sleeplessness under his eyes. She didn't even want to consider how her face looked. Shannon met him at the front door in sweatpants; her T-shirt rank from her overnight restlessness and fevered checking of

Derry's medications. The fact that her brother was able to sleep should have been a good thing, but she knew it probably wasn't.

"Found Wheatley in an old warehouse near the river," Petrosky began as he stepped over the threshold. "Waiting on the autopsy for specifics, but it looks like he died from blunt force trauma to the head, just like Lewis." He toed the door shut behind him. "They dug a bullet out of his abdomen, probably a torture thing or to incapacitate him, because the ME says he lived for some time afterward. Severely beaten, ligature marks over two broken wrists. Some kind of chalky powder on his shoes. No weapons found as of yet."

Abused. Tortured. So Wheatley did have a secret, and someone needed to know whom else he'd told. And if Wheatley had been killed to keep something hidden, then anyone Wheatley had talked to was in danger. So...who else was in trouble? Maybe nerdy, asthmatic, book-writing Ruskin—but Morrison said someone was already watching his place intermittently. And Petrosky had freaked him out enough that Ruskin surely would have told them if Wheatley had given up names or any other secret worth killing over. Ruskin had nothing to tell. Hopefully, the killer knew that too.

Petrosky swiped a sleeve across his face. "His hands smelled strange too. Like motor oil but sweeter, though it was hard to differentiate between that and the pile of garbage we found him in."

"Maybe he tried to use some kind of lubricant to get out of the restraints? Could have broken his wrists himself, trying to get them off."

"Maybe, but I doubt it." Petrosky coughed wetly, and they both turned as Morrison emerged from the back hallway amidst frantic yelps and the thunk of a tail hitting the wall.

"Easy, Rox."

The dog sat at Morrison's feet and stared adoringly at him, her tail beating a steady rhythm on the baseboard. Shannon looked behind the pair—no Abby, no Alex. Sleeping, still. Hopefully. Suddenly aware of the chill in the air, Shannon hugged her arms around herself.

"The medical examiner's going to call later on Wheatley," Petrosky said.

Shannon dropped her arms. "Today?"

"Maybe. If I harass him enough."

Shannon shook her head. "Give him time, look at other stuff before someone else calls and complains." As soon as she said it, she wished she could suck the words back into her mouth. Just when Petrosky had finally started looking like he didn't want to slap the shit out of Alex... Plus, they needed to do everything they could to expedite the process. They were running out of time.

Petrosky's face darkened as he glanced at the stairway. "Morrison, you've got what you need to investigate remotely from here?"

Morrison nodded and scratched Roxy behind the ears.

"Good." Petrosky turned to Shannon. "And I found Angela Perez yesterday afternoon, the babysitter who told Ashley Johnson that she saw a social worker going into Derek Lewis's apartment the day he was killed. Told her I was coming by. Might as well verify Wheatley was present at Lewis's house. Maybe Perez will even recognize Roger."

Shannon's face heated. Back to Roger again. "Petrosky, Roger doesn't have a motive. He doesn't need to take cash for pleas. He doesn't have any reason—"

"He has some extravagant spending. Some debt you probably don't know about. And he was there last night. At the river."

Roger had gone out on a police call? She wracked her brain but couldn't think of a single other time he'd done that.

"He's all over this case, probably already claimed it for when it filters over to your offices. And he doesn't have alibis for the nights in question. If we're naming him as a suspect, we'll have to do it sooner rather than later."

Her ex, a suspect. Shannon took a deep breath. "I'll go with you."

"You don't have to, Taylor. Stay here with your brother."

Her brother. All she wanted was five minutes to speak to him, but he might not even wake up while she was gone. And if he did, what would she say to him if he asked about Lucky's killer? "I need to move. I can't just sit here all day and…wait for him to…to…" The fire in her cheeks, in her chest, burned hotter than ever. "Look, I made my brother a promise. I need to keep it."

SHANNON WAS ALREADY EXHAUSTED when she and Petrosky set out for Perez's at nine o'clock, both with mugs of Morrison's coffee.

Petrosky sipped from his mug. "Who'd have thought? Fucking fungus."

Shannon watched the city roll by, the sky far too blue and optimistic, and took another bite of the chia-berry oatmeal Morrison had insisted she take with her. It tasted like sawdust. As they neared the river, traffic thinned, and the air grew damper, dejected almost, with the dusty industrial haze blurring their view of the opposite bank. Shannon wondered whether they were close to the place Wheatley's body had been found, but she didn't ask. She didn't really want to know.

They exited the car behind an apartment building ripe with the rotten stink of an overflowing dumpster. Bags and cardboard and food littered the ground outside the container. *Gross.* But at least there was someone to take it out in the first place.

Perez was already outside smoking near the back door, her curly black hair blowing behind her with every gust of breeze. Curvy. Pretty. Perez crushed the cigarette underfoot as they approached.

"Ms. Perez?" Petrosky said.

She nodded, brown eyes cautious. Shannon waited for him to yank out his badge, but instead, he extended his hand, and Perez shook it.

"Nice to meet you, ma'am."

Perez squinted at Shannon. "You're the one who got Ashley locked up."

Guilt swelled in her chest. *I am.*

"She didn't kill anybody."

"That's part of what we're trying to straighten out, Ms. Perez. Will you help us?" Petrosky's tone was soft and gentle, patient even, the same one he'd used with the nurse at the hospital. It was like he had split personalities: Dick and Not a Dick.

"Yeah, I'll help. I want to do what's right by her, you know? We were always friends."

"I know you were." Petrosky pulled out his cigarettes and offered her one. She frowned at the one on the ground, looked back up at Petrosky, and took a cigarette from the pack.

He lit her smoke and pocketed the pack and the lighter. "Tell me about who you saw at Ashley's house. The day Lewis died."

"Well, it was earlier in the day, you know, because I had just gotten back from school."

"Where do you go to school?"

Why did that matter? He probably intended to check her class schedule to verify the time.

"Over at the community college. I was going to transfer to Wayne State in the fall with Ashley, but—" She looked down. "I've been doing well, but it's real hard. So many classes and tests, and I don't remember learning half this stuff in high school."

She was offering them irrelevant information they hadn't asked about, like witnesses on the stand trying to pad the lies they were about to tell you. Shannon watched Perez's eyes, her hands, her posture as she hit the cigarette, but nothing else wavered. Only her words seemed suspect.

"Tell me about that day," Petrosky said.

"Ashley dropped Diamond off, so she could go to that interview. We played inside for a bit, then I took Diamond up to the roof, so I could have a cigarette. Needed to keep the smoke away from her, or Ashley would have killed me." Her eyes widened. "No, I mean, not really *killed* me, but she didn't want anyone smoking around her baby." She grimaced at the cigarette, puffed again. "Really wish I could quit."

"What time was that?"

"Maybe seven? Eight?"

Eight. After Derek's argument, but before his death. Perez hadn't seen the person who had fought with Derek. She'd seen the killer.

Petrosky leaned against the wall of the building, feigning mellow nonchalance. But she could tell by the twitch in his lip, the subtle tension in his shoulders, that he'd made the connection too.

"So, you were on the roof when you saw someone approach the building?"

"Not the building. Derek was standing outside near the curb, and then this car pulled up, and the social worker got out and walked right up to him. They looked kinda tense like they didn't like each other, but Derek took him inside. I remember thinking that he didn't seem the type who was usually in with Derek."

"He didn't look like a druggie."

She bit her lip. "Yeah. He was in a suit, I think."

A suit? That didn't sound like Wheatley or any other social worker, certainly not at that hour. Shannon scanned the street. A few cars in various states of disrepair lined the abandoned road. Not another soul was out. It was as though the neighborhood had been deserted in the wake of some terrible tragedy.

"What made you think he was a social worker, Ms. Perez?"

"Derek said he was. I had to go to work, and Ashley still wasn't home, so I...dropped Diamond off." She lowered her eyes. "I didn't think he'd hurt her. I mean...he still used. Ashley denied that, but I could see it on his face, you know? But I..."

"It's not your fault, and we can't do anything about that now, okay?"

Perez's jaw dropped. She averted her eyes.

If only guilt could be assuaged with a few words.

Petrosky pulled a file folder from under his arm but didn't extend it to Perez. "So, you went to drop Diamond off..."

"Yeah, and I asked him who that guy was because I knew Ashley'd want to know."

"And Derek knew who you were talking about? Just volunteered this information?"

"Well, I asked him if he had a social worker up earlier, and he said yeah. Though he might have answered just so I'd drop it and leave."

Shannon watched Perez's face, the way the girl bit her lip. How would Perez have known to ask if the visitor was a worker?

"I'm still not sure why you'd ask if the guy was a social worker," Petrosky said, reading her mind. "It's a pretty good guess out of nowhere."

"Ashley was always worried about it, you know? Said Derek's mom kept calling, that she thought she'd lose Diamond. So I always kept a lookout for stuff like that, even though she was doing all the right things. Especially since Derek *wasn't* doing the right things—still sold drugs, didn't want to get a job."

Petrosky's brows furrowed. "Tell me about the guy you saw. What can you remember about his physical appearance?"

"I mean, I didn't get a great look at him because I was above them, and it was kinda dark. And he had on a hat, so I couldn't see his face or his hair or anything."

A hat with a suit? He'd gone incognito on purpose, but had he planned to kill Derek that night? Or was he just making sure he wouldn't be recognized? *Who the hell is this guy?*

"Any idea how tall?"

Perez examined the sky. Thinking up a lie or just thinking?

"Not sure on height," Perez said. "I only caught them together for a second, and perspective can make everything seem different, you know? Smaller, bigger. Sometimes you don't even see things that are right there."

Ain't that the truth.

"You studying psychology in school, Ms. Perez?"

"Yeah. How did you know?"

Petrosky opened the file folder and handed her the first picture, a shot of Benjamin Wheatley. "Is this the guy you saw that day with Derek?"

She glanced at it. "No. But I've seen him in the building before."

"When?"

"Not sure, I just know he looks familiar. Probably a few weeks before all…this."

According to his files, Wheatley hadn't had any families in Johnson's building for a good two months before the killing. If Wheatley had been there, he'd been watching for someone, like a private eye. Too bad Petrosky hadn't found any photos or other documentation at Wheatley's place. Unauthorized search or no, anything could be useful right about now. Maybe they should go back, crawl through the window, and…Holy shit. She was turning into Petrosky.

Petrosky exchanged Wheatley's picture for a photo of Roger; one Shannon had taken on their honeymoon in France. He was in a rare T-shirt instead of his usual button-down, but the same brilliant smile was aimed right at her. Shannon's heart raced.

"Ms. Perez, look closely." So intense. Just because you want it to be Roger doesn't mean it is, Petrosky.

Perez shook her head again. "I couldn't really see his face from four stories up, but…this guy doesn't seem right. I'm not real sure why. Just a gut feeling."

Shannon realized she was holding her breath and released it slowly.

"Anything else you recall about the person in question, Ms. Perez?" Petrosky asked.

Perez shook her head.

Fuck. They were so close. They just needed one good lead. One good—

"You said you noticed the car first?"

The car. Why didn't she think of that? Maybe she really did need to take a vacation, though she'd never tell Roger that he was right. Her body suddenly felt heavy as if the iron in her blood had thickened and was slowly pulling her down toward the earth.

"Yeah, I hadn't seen it before." She broke eye contact, and Shannon's hackles rose. *Liar.*

"What did it look like?"

Pause. "Black, I think. Or dark blue."

"What kind of car was it?"

"I'm not... I'm bad at cars, and I wasn't really paying attention." Perez studied the ground. "I don't want any trouble."

Perez knew something, that much was clear. Maybe it was why she had moved—afraid of retribution for knowing more than she was supposed to. She should be scared after what had happened to Wheatley.

"Ms. Perez...Angela. I'm here to help. To find Derek Lewis's killer. To help you if you need helping."

Perez raised her eyes to his, but the suspicion remained.

"Please, Angela. Ashley is your best friend, right? You can save her, and I can help you, but I've got to know what you saw."

Perez leaned back against the wall and looked around the lot, finally swinging her eyes back to Petrosky. "I think it was...well..." She sighed. "A cop car. I remember being surprised that a social worker would drive one, but I figured they do work with the police a lot."

Shannon froze. Police cars were pretty recognizable—not like you could mistake the lights on top.

"You *think* it was a cop car?" Petrosky asked.

"Well, the lights were gone off the top, but it had those big antennae things off the back. And one of those huge spotlights over the side-view mirror."

An unmarked? No social worker drove one of those. Neither did Roger. Petrosky's jaw worked overtime. He looked at Shannon, and her stomach twisted.

Even if Wheatley had been arguing with Derek earlier, his green car could never be mistaken for what Perez saw. Neither could Roger's Mercedes.

The killer was one of them.

Their killer was a cop.

23

Roger's phone slammed into the cradle as Shannon scuttled past his office. He was literally breathing down her neck before she even got her office door unlocked.

"Where have you been, Shannon?"

"Working." *On a case I'm supposed to be ignoring. And you were wrong about there being no connection, Roger.* Her keys shook and scraped against the lock but didn't slide home. *We were both wrong. Maybe about everything.*

"Working on what?"

She steadfastly refused to face him, just focused on the doorknob, and listened to the metal clank of keys against the lock. "I was out doing my job. Like it's any of your concern."

"I just got off the phone with your brother."

The latch popped, and relief flooded through her, but it was short-lived, replaced with anger before she'd even gotten the knob turned. The thud of Roger's shoes on the carpet followed her inside. She walked around to her chair and slammed her briefcase between them on the desk. "Why the fuck would you be calling Jerry?"

"I was—"

She put her hand up. "I don't even care why. Don't call my brother, Roger."

"Well, it isn't like he can answer the phone himself, Shannon."

So he was mad she'd blown him off and was trying to upset her. He wanted her to lose her shit, just like he had during their marriage, wanted to push her until she cracked in front of their families, their friends, their colleagues. He had wanted to make her look crazy. But why today? So he could fire her? *No way, Roger.* She would not give him the satisfaction.

Shannon leaned toward him. The bandage on his nose was bright against the bruising under his eyes. She hoped it hurt like hell. "What do you want, Roger?" She kept her voice low and deliberate. *Give me shit, Roger, you'll get it back.*

Roger stared at her, his lip twitching.

"You here to make me sorry like you promised the other night? Threatening your ex-wife is rather unbecoming of a lead prosecutor."

His shoulders relaxed first, then his chest, then his mouth, a choreographed transformation she had seen time and time again at dinner parties when someone said something he didn't like. During their arguments when he was trying to convince her that "No really, you're crazy, I never touched her." Then later at the divorce proceedings. From asshole to martyr in three seconds flat. Good time to pull it out, now that he saw she wasn't going to give him what he wanted. *Manipulative prick.*

He sat in the chair across from her, smug smile intact, hands loose on the armrests like he hadn't a care in the world. "I'm sorry about that, Shannon. I was just angry; you know that. And I've been worried about you."

Bullshit. She sank into the chair with enough force that it shuddered backward on its wheels. She hauled herself up to the desk and glared at him. "Nothing for you to be worried about."

"You have crazy people at your brother's house, Shanny. With your niece. That should concern you."

She opened her briefcase, a barrier between herself and Roger's fake concern, and took her time pulling out her files. When she moved the case aside, his eyes bored into her skull. *Don't let him see you sweat, Shannon. That's what he wants.* "I told you not to call me that, Roger. And they aren't crazy."

"Are you kidding?" Roger aimed a finger at his nose, and Shannon stifled a smirk. "He's unstable. Both of them are."

"I feel safer when they're around." She folded her hands over the files on the desktop and said nothing else. He'd see her nonresponse as defiant. Maybe she was being defiant—and it was about fucking time.

He crossed his arms. "Well, I don't feel better about your safety when they're around. About Abby's safety."

"You don't get to make that call."

"So I don't." He leveled his gaze at her. "But one day you'll see, Shannon."

Again, the threat, and a cliché one at that. "You're not the fucking Godfather, Roger," she said.

A smile touched the corner of his lip. "Even at a time like this, you remember my favorite movie."

The only thing she remembered about that movie was a severed horse's head on someone's pillow. Kinda like...Lucky. She shook it off.

He leaned toward her desk, close enough that she could hear the wet sucking sound of air through his mangled nose. "What are you working on?"

"Bartleby."

"How's it going?"

"Why?"

"I'm the head prosecutor, remember? Just trying to stay abreast of your cases, since you've been out of the office so often lately." His tone was condescending and quiet like she was a fucking idiot. "You sure you don't want to take leave? I'll approve it to start now before Jerry's officially gone."

Gone. He's fucking with me. She cleared her throat, pulled Bartleby's folder from the stack, and flipped it open, hoping Roger couldn't see the way her hands trembled. "Bartleby is being charged with felony child endangerment, and his ex-wife is poised to get full custody of all of their children. You have an issue with that?"

"Hey, I'm all about punishing the guilty. It's our job."

It was her job, but not his. Not anymore. Her anxiety bubbled into a cauldron of fury as she watched him shrug, superior and self-satisfied. "Ike Lambert was guilty. Reverend Wilson was too. But Bartleby's poor, so who cares, right?"

Roger leaned back in the chair and laced his fingers over his knee. "They were charged," he said with the careful patience of one speaking to a tantrumming child.

"Not with what they should have been, and you know it. Even Judge Miller seemed surprised at Wilson's arraignment. You saw how she looked at you."

The arrogant glitter in his eye sharpened. "Enough about me, Shanny. Let's talk about what you've been doing lately. Spending a lot of time with your new boyfriend?"

"He isn't my boyfriend, Roger."

"Not what I heard, Shannon. He's not who you think he is."

"Neither were you."

Fire flashed in Roger's eyes but disappeared into a sneer.

She opened the folder on her desk. "Why exactly are you here, Roger?"

"I'll be prosecuting the Wheatley case once it shows up at this office."

Just like Petrosky had warned. She'd love to think Roger was trying to take charge out of concern for her wellbeing, but she didn't believe that he cared about her or about Abby or Alex or Derry, not for one second. "We'll have to look at Johnson too, and that one's mine," she said. "You know they're related, Roger."

"I talked to the chief. Someone other than your boyfriend has been assigned to both cases, so you don't need to worry about them anymore. You need to focus on your own work, the cases that have been specifically assigned to you. We can't run an office with people prosecuting whoever the hell they want."

And once word got out that Lewis's killer might be a cop, Internal Affairs would step in and she and Morrison and Petrosky would be even more out of the loop than they were now. They'd wait to open that box of bullshit until they had something. Until she knew who she needed to protect her family from.

"I'm focusing on my other cases, Roger. Haven't missed a single court date."

"Doing a lot more interviews by phone, also, I see."

"People come in to sign their statements when necessary."

"Didn't I tell you pleas are less work?" Roger sat straighter, but he kept his ankle crossed over one knee. "Spend more time with your brother, Ms. Taylor. Spend some time with Abby too. She needs you now more than ever." Roger's face was impassive, but Shannon's lungs clamped shut. She hated the way Abby's name rolled off his tongue. As if he fucking cared about Abby. He'd scowled at her stretch marks every time she disrobed and had played with Abby a grand total of three times while they were dating. Probably less than that once they were married. Each time, Abby had cried.

Roger released his hands and stood. "I'll be checking on you tomorrow morning, Ms. Taylor. Make sure you're here before nine."

He didn't care about her workload or her family. He wanted to scare her off, just like whoever had left Lucky's severed head on her windshield. Maybe. Then again, he'd always hated cats. Her chest lightened at the thought of watching Roger led away in handcuffs, smirk permanently erased.

PETROSKY KEPT his eyes on the road on the way to the gym, popping antacid after antacid. He'd convinced Shannon to let him drive her. Again. She'd told him she didn't need a babysitter. He didn't agree, but she was too overwhelmed with life and death and work and men to argue the point. Besides, he was probably already pissed that the chief had pulled him off the Wheatley case after Roger's phone call.

She stared out the side window, clutching the door handle, hoping they wouldn't have to talk about it. She didn't need talk—she needed to punch something. Hopefully, this time, she'd avoid hitting Morrison.

Shannon warmed at the thought of him, at the memory of beating his ass and taking him home to...make up for it. Her stomach sank. Sleeping with him had been a mistake—an incredible, beautiful, amazing mistake, but a mistake nonetheless. And even after all that, he was there for her and she for him. They were friends, best friends. Always? *Always is a long time.* But they could pull it off. It'd just be a little...awkward for a while.

Petrosky pulled up in front of the converted warehouse, and she opened the car door before he'd fully stopped. The woman who passed out last time was there already, working the rings, her blond curls hidden beneath a bandana and a look of such grim determination on her face that she might as well have had "I've fucking got this" tattooed across her forehead. Kimball was helping her, hoisting her up as she gritted her teeth and shook. He nodded, and she dropped. There was no way she'd make it through class if Kimball was giving her a private lesson now.

Shannon changed, then took a few minutes to stretch out her arms and legs, neck muscles singing with tension all the way up and around to her forehead when she tried to rotate her shoulders. She exhaled violently enough that Kimball turned her way as she strode past him to grab a crate. The blonde was setting up her own crate near the middle of the room.

"You all right?" Kimball asked Shannon.

"Long day."

"I hear that." But his face looked more alert than ever, eyes bright, cheeks pink. He left her and made his way around the room, saying hello to people who looked appropriately anxious about the evening's workout. One man—all burl and muscle—grimaced as Kimball mimed an exercise. Another furrowed his brows as Kimball pointed out weights. When he reached the blonde again, he touched her lower back, and she smiled at him in a way that was more than friendly. Kimball gave it right back to her and winked, then nodded to the bars in the back.

Fucking cheater. No wonder he and Roger got along so well.

Shannon carried her crate to the middle of the room and set it up near the one belonging to Kimball's new squeeze, trying not to think about his wife, Amanda. Trying not to watch them flirt, as if that would make it better. The punching bag in the back corner swung back and forth, back and forth. She looked away from that too. The bag felt far too intimate now, but it'd pass—a week or two, and she'd be over there attacking it again without feeling guilty. The rings swung of their own accord as if in a nonexistent breeze, or maybe it was the tumultuous energy in the air around her disrupting their rest.

She looked away and stared straight ahead at the gymnast bars, squinting at the metal glistening in the fluorescents. Toe touches. She'd need a little extra workout tonight. But…something was different. It took her a moment to realize what it was, but finally it clicked that the thick mats beneath the bars had been removed, leaving the cement bare. Maybe Kimball had fucked his girlfriend at the gym and made a mess. *Gross.* Now she was starting to sound like Derry. But way less hilarious.

Someone touched her shoulder, and she jumped as Morrison nudged his crate into place beside hers. "Whoa, Shanny, you okay?" His brows were furrowed, but his forehead relaxed when she nodded.

"Yeah, just...tired, maybe. Glad you made it. Petrosky said you'd be here, but I wondered when I didn't see you."

"You know he wouldn't have left you here alone."

"I'm not alone."

"You know what I mean. He likes being needed. And if you got hurt, neither of us would forgive ourselves." He leaned close enough that she could feel his breath on her ear, and electricity shimmered from her neck down to her toes. "I walked around the warehouse, just checking it out," he said. "No sign of anything weird, and the new lights really do make a difference in the lot." He straightened and positioned himself in front of his crate, pulling an arm across himself to stretch.

"How's everything at the house?" Shannon bent over to fiddle with her already tied shoe, afraid of what she'd see in Morrison's eyes. She was asking how fast her brother was dying, wasn't she? Then there were Roger's words: *Abby needs you now more than ever*. Guilt writhed in her belly. "And how's Abby?"

"The house is fine, no changes. Derry's just tired. Abby seems okay—Roxy's her new favorite thing."

She stood and forced herself to look at Morrison. "Thanks for bringing her over."

"Alex said they were going to get one. I said they could keep her."

"What? You did?" He'd had that dog for years. She belonged with him. "Why would you do that?"

He was watching the rings, jaw tight. "They need her more than I do. And maybe you'll sleep better, knowing that she's there with them. She wouldn't let anyone hurt your family." Morrison bent at the waist and stretched his hamstrings then fingered his own tied laces. Avoiding her eyes.

He was replacing himself. Making his presence unnecessary. So, he could...leave them. *Leave me.* Shit, what was she thinking? They weren't even together. But her chest felt too small.

"I can't let you do this."

"It's done," he said, head still at his knees.

Roxy had gone everywhere with him: jogging, hiking, even vacation. That dog was family. Her lip quivered, and the tightness around her ribs intensified so that it felt like someone was trying to snap her in two. Morrison loved Roxy. *But he loves me more.* And she couldn't for the life of her figure out a way to make the pain ease, not for any of them.

Down in front, the blonde walked to the bars with Kimball. Shannon looked at the clock. Two minutes until class. *I need to get it together.* But her eyes stung, and the longer she watched Curt's bent form, the more she felt compelled to wrap her arms around him, and that thought was more terrifying than anything else because she knew she'd never come back from it. After that, she'd be his. Right now, she couldn't even handle being hers.

The blond woman ran her hands over the chalk ball next to the bars and slapped her palms together, making a puff of dust. Shannon watched the particles fall to the cement floor... The bare cement floor, lighter than the area around it, but it wasn't from spilled chalk. It wasn't...dusty. The floor was always dusty. She squinted. Bleached?

Kimball's hand lingered on the woman's hip as he half lifted her to the bar. She swung her legs up, touched her toes to the bar, and Kimball smiled at her, though she was clearly preoccupied. What the hell was he doing? Class was already late getting started. Kimball touched the lower bar, frowned at his fingers and touched them to the chalk, probably to avoid staining her fancy workout gear with the oily residue from the stuff they used to clean the equipment.

Her heart raced. The oil. They cleaned the bars with...what? Some industrial cleaner—she'd seen Morrison do it before. And every week they wiped them with...WD-40.

He patted the blonde on the shoulder, glanced at the front door, and made another remark. She laughed again and dropped to the cement floor. Still smiling at him.

Charismatic. Weren't psychos always charismatic? Or was that just narcissists? Roger had charisma—it was how he'd gotten her to marry him. Shannon watched them walk toward her, or maybe it was toward the dumbbells that Kimball had been hitting so hard lately. Kimball's obsession with his body surely bordered on narcissism, didn't it? But then, everyone at this gym had a little of that. Was his more severe, more noteworthy? More violent? Narcissists got angry, sometimes inexplicably so, but—maybe that was the type of killer that couldn't handle anyone else taking credit for their crimes.

Kimball looked at the door then walked toward the center of the room, near where Shannon stood. Morrison nodded to him.

Shannon licked her parched lips. Had the mats been gone the last time she was here? She hadn't noticed. She'd been too busy socking Morrison in the gut. "What happened to the mats under the bars, Kimball?" *He'll say he doesn't know. That they were stolen or damaged.*

"Someone spilled something on them." He shrugged. "Good opportunity to get a few new ones anyway. Those ones had too much potential for slippage, so I ordered a few with better traction. Should be here by next week." He winked at her. Flirty? No. *Manipulative.* Like Roger.

She looked back at the bar, picturing Wheatley, hanging from broken wrists, his essence shimmering from a bullet wound in his gut. Gore slithering onto the mats. Her blood ran cold.

Kimball squinted at her, and her heart pounded against her rib cage. "Shannon, you okay?"

She could hear Morrison's sneakered footsteps approaching from the side, but she didn't look at him. She was frozen, rooted to the floor. "I'm just a little... I don't feel well."

Kimball walked over to her and every muscle in her body tensed, preparing to flee. "Take a breather before class, okay? I don't want our star prosecutor suing me because she passed out and hit her head." He patted her on the shoulder, and her skin crawled.

Had Kimball known they were looking at Wheatley? He worked for the chief of police, so he'd have access to the case files. And even if there hadn't been any paperwork mentioning the social worker, Amanda might have mentioned Wheatley in passing to her husband—perhaps a snarky remark from Wheatley had made Kimball suspicious without Amanda even realizing it.

She needed to call Petrosky. He could drive over with Luminol, and they could show that there had been blood under the bars. Then they could arrest Kimball. Then she could go home and wait for Derry to wake up, so she could tell him that everything was going to be okay from now on, that he could rest easy. That he could go, and Abby would be safe.

Kimball tossed her a towel, and she jumped—almost fell.

"Hey, Kimball?" Her voice was shaking, but she didn't even try to control it. "I need to sit for a second, but I don't want to miss tonight's workout. Would you mind if I stayed a little later? Maybe I can do some work after class instead?"

"Man, even sick, you're brutal." He looked at the door then grinned at her, and Shannon's throat clamped shut. "But look, if you aren't feeling well, you need to go home. It's a liability."

"I'm fine. It's just stress, and I didn't eat enough. I'm going to grab a snack and come right back."

Kimball squinted at her, sighed, and glanced at the open warehouse door again. Ready to run? Did he know she'd figured him out?

She finally met Morrison's eyes. His face was impassive, but she could see the subtle twitch of his nostrils. He knew something was very wrong. *Don't ask me what it is, not in front of Kimball.*

"Sounds good. But Shannon, seriously, I don't want you to—" Kimball turned to the warehouse door.

She heard the tires then, shrieking through the warehouse and echoing off the walls. In the lot, someone yelled.

Shannon stared toward the entrance as three officers rushed inside, guns holstered but prominent. She didn't recognize any of them—had to be Internal Affairs. But they shot looks of contrition at Kimball, which meant they knew about him. Petrosky knew. It was over. *We got him, Derry.* Shannon's heart soared.

But why didn't Kimball look more...shocked? She backed away from Kimball as he took another step toward the officers. The sweat on her back froze. They weren't looking at Kimball. They were looking at—

"Detective Curtis Morrison. You need to come with us."

Her jaw dropped. She didn't understand.

One officer strode forward more quickly, shoulders tight, eyes narrowed, watching as if he expected Morrison to make a break for the door. Morrison didn't move, just stood. The others inched closer, their hands on their weapons, waiting for a reason to use them. "Hands behind your head!" one of the inchers called. Morrison didn't move, didn't comply. One officer glanced at Kimball and almost smirked. Shannon hated the guy instantly, but her hatred was tempered with confusion. Did she need to put her hands behind her head? After all, if they were taking Morrison, they'd want her too, right? But no, that didn't make sense: investigating a case you weren't assigned to wasn't a crime. Her head felt like it was stuffed with cotton, fuzzy and dense.

The officer drew his eyes from Kimball back to Morrison's stiff profile and pulled his weapon. "On the ground!"

Morrison put his hands behind his head but did not drop. Then officers seemed to be everywhere, only three, but their energy was fierce, hungry, like a pack of wolves circling them, ready to attack. Morrison dropped to his knees beside her and lay on the floor face down. Her stomach heaved.

She stared at Morrison's back, still not understanding. Did she need to lie down too? Then, through the front door, she saw him: Roger, standing in the lot behind the cars with another officer, peering into the warehouse. *He* had done this. And he'd come to watch the carnage.

Behind her, someone was talking about arrest, and then she was being pulled away to the clinking sound of metal on metal, but the cuffs weren't on her, they were on Morrison. They were doing it wrong, but no one would care, no one would listen because whatever Roger had convinced them of, he had done a thorough job. He had manipulated them all.

Morrison was still belly-down on the mat, hands cuffed behind him. She met his eyes for an instant—saw fear but not surprise—before she was dragged outside to the parking lot by one of the officers.

"Get the hell off me," she said and twisted from the man's grasp.

He went for her arm again, and she tensed, ready to read him his fucking rights, or maybe to sock him in the jaw, but then Roger's voice sounded from across the lot: "Not her. She's good." The officer put both his hands up, stepped away from Shannon, and headed for the warehouse.

She met Roger in front of the cars. "What the fuck is going on, Roger? You know he would have come with you peacefully if you had questions for him."

"I told you he was dangerous, Shannon, but I had no idea how dangerous." He shook his head. "You really know how to pick them."

"I picked you, dumbass."

His smugness tightened into anger. "We have more than questions."

But they didn't have proof. Roger was wrong, just like he was wrong about everything else. But Roger could be incredibly convincing when he wanted to be, and the guys who didn't know Morrison...

Her blood boiled. "You told them he'd resist, didn't you?"

"You never know, Shanny."

She ignored the nickname and his idiotic grin. "It was Kimball"—Roger raised an eyebrow and shook his head—" the mats, underneath the bars, Roger. They're missing. And Wheatley had oil on his hands, just like the stuff they use to clean the equipment."

Roger's jaw dropped, and he looked past her, crooking a finger at an officer stationed by the warehouse door. "Kimball has an alibi," he said without meeting her gaze.

Her heartbeat thundered in her ears. "Maybe someone's covering for him, or..." Maybe Roger was covering for him. No wonder Kimball had been staring at the door all night—he'd known they were coming.

"He was at a fundraising banquet with the chief of police the night we suspect Wheatley was killed. I'll bet he's got alibis for the other days too. The beauty of family." He absentmindedly touched his bare ring finger.

Beauty? *Right*. As if keeping someone's lying ass out of jail was clearly the only reason to have a family. Not that Roger was capable of understanding that.

"Morrison has been at my brother's."

The officer Roger had summoned appeared at his side, and Roger whispered something in his ear. The cop took off across the lot. Shannon watched his retreat until Roger spoke again.

"I called your brother's, Shannon. And you know what Alex told me? That he's been having trouble sleeping and has been taking Ativan. That Jerry, the only one sleeping in the room next to Morrison's spot on the couch, is so full of morphine you could run a truck through there without waking him. That Abby sleeps like the dead. That he occasionally heard the door open and close because Morrison routinely leaves the house to pace around outside."

That's why Roger had called her brother's house this morning while she was talking to Perez. Not to check up on her—to fuck Morrison over. He'd known this whole time. Rage burned Shannon's face and spread through her chest and down into her already clenched fists. Roger had finally gone too far.

Across the lot, Kimball's face turned red then blue then red in the flashing police lights. "Did Kimball know you were investigating Morrison?" But if Roger knew, if they'd called in Internal Affairs, Kimball had to know too.

"So what if he did?" Roger said. "It doesn't matter. Your boyfriend has a very big problem."

"You're wrong, Roger. You'll regret this."

"Now who's making threats, Ms. Taylor?" Roger puffed out his chest and turned to walk away.

Shannon grabbed his arm. "What you're saying...it's impossible. I was with Morrison the night someone trashed my car."

"You have no evidence that your car is related to this case. None."

"We have evidence that Wheatley was investigating something he shouldn't have been."

"Maybe he found some nasty surprises about your boyfriend."

"Roger, listen to me! Someone else was there the day Derek Lewis died. A cop."

"And now we've got a cop in custody. How convenient."

"Morrison doesn't drive an unmarked. It was someone else, someone who had—"

"Morrison could easily get access to an unmarked if he needed one. So could most everyone in the precinct. They have a bunch just sitting in the lot to take out anytime someone has a vehicle in the shop. All you need to do is sign it out. You could probably even forget to put your name down."

"Sign it out? Where?"

"The chief's office, I'm guessing."

The chief's office. Where Kimball worked.

Roger was grinning, and she wanted to smash her fist into his nose. Or maybe his balls. *Godfuckingdammit, just give me a reason.*

"And anyway," he sneered, "why wasn't this alleged unmarked brought up at trial?"

"The girl who saw it didn't recognize what she'd seen." She needed to go back to Angela Perez's apartment. They'd already looked for cameras, other witnesses, but—nothing. Maybe she'd go back to Ruskin's too. "We're getting there, Roger, just—"

Roger straightened his tie. "You're welcome to go home, Ms. Taylor." Arrogant. Incredulous. "If we have any questions for you, we'll call."

Either Roger didn't believe her about the unmarked, or he didn't give a shit. Probably the latter—he wasn't going to let Morrison go without a fight whether he was guilty or not. *Not.* Definitely not. She stood in the middle of the lot, watching Roger walk to his car. If only it were legal to run him over.

Shannon jerked around when movement at the entrance of the warehouse caught her eye. *Morrison.* Two officers held either elbow, one of the cops the dickhead who'd tried to manhandle her earlier. He avoided her glare. Morrison's face was impassive, eyes tense and glassy, as they walked him to the squad car.

An officer, with a solemn mouth and eyes the color of Roxy's fur, approached her. "Do you have things inside?"

"What?"

He nodded gently in Morrison's direction. "He was worried about you, wanted me to give you his keys, but we're impounding his car. Do you have someone you can call?"

"Who was worried?"

"Mor—uh, the suspect."

She met his eyes.

"He's a nice guy. Helped me out once." His shoulders slumped. "Just… where's your stuff? I'll get it for you."

"Next to the bathroom. Black gym bag."

"That it?"

"Yeah."

"Okay."

Shannon turned back to the squad car. The back door was open now, and Morrison's eyes flicked around the lot, his head jerking this way and that. The officer at Morrison's left shoulder tensed and tightened his grip. Then Morrison's eyes found Shannon, and he stood there a moment, alternating blue and red in the lights of the squad cars. She held his gaze until he ducked into the car and disappeared.

When the taillights receded from sight, she walked to the corner of the lot behind the trees and vomited into the brush.

24

Petrosky was out of the car and at her side before she had a chance to approach him. "Where the fuck is he?" His jowly face was hard, shoulders tight with rage.

"Gone. I assume they took him to the precinct."

"What about your fuckweasel of an ex-husband?"

"Gone, Petrosky, they're all gone. Just some crime scene techs—"

"What've they got on him?"

"They..." She had no idea. Roger had twisted it and turned it and avoided telling her jack shit. And she'd fallen for it. But they had *something*, or there was no way they could have arrested him. "I don't know."

Petrosky ran a hand over his flaming cheeks. "Fuck."

"I know." She touched his arm, and his bicep was rigid as stone. He didn't seem to notice her hand, just stared at the lot, at the warehouse.

"There's nothing to do here, Petrosky," she said gently, though all she wanted to do was scream. "And I'm sure the guys at the door have specific instructions not to let you through."

"Like hell they—"

"You can't help Morrison if you're in jail too. And you sure as hell can't help me. Or Abby."

Petrosky glanced back at the car, and she followed his gaze. Abby's nose was smashed against the back window, her eyes wide and shining under Kimball's brand-new floodlights. Roxy was licking the window beside her head. "You brought Abby?"

"I brought everyone"—*except Derry*— "because we have a murderer running around who seems to have it in for you, and no one's looking out for your family anymore because they're too busy fucking with the wrong guy. And since I can't be in two places at once..." He turned to her. "You get sick?"

She looked at her shirt, at the wet stain between her breasts. "A little."

"California says peppermint tea works. You have that at home, or should we stop and get some?"

She gaped at him.

"Let's go."

She followed him to the car on legs that felt like they belonged to somebody else.

In the backseat, Abby threw her arms around Shannon, either oblivious to the smell of puke or blessedly detached. Roxy licked her face over Abby's shoulder. "Aunt Shanny! Are you okay? Eddie said you were at the gym and that you were okay, but I was super scared because we had to go so fast and everything."

Eddie? Shannon squeezed her eyes closed to avoid dog saliva in the eyeball and hugged Abby to her, careful her niece's face wasn't being smashed into the vomit on her shirt.

"Roxy, chill," Alex said. Roxy stopped slobbering all over the place and lay on the backseat. Shannon peered at Alex from beneath slimy lids. "Thanks."

He reached over the seat and squeezed her shoulder in that familiar way he'd always done when they were kids. *Everything's okay, Shanny. Friends to the end.* She had never been so grateful for his presence as she was now when she otherwise felt so painfully alone.

ALEX AND ABBY and Roxy settled into what used to be Derry and Alex's room but was now only Alex's. Shannon crept upstairs to the spare, leaving Petrosky on the downstairs couch. Sweat and salt plastered her clothes to her back despite the cool night, and she could still taste the putrid remnants of vomit on her tongue even after she'd brushed her teeth.

And then there was her brain. Images of Morrison's eyes seared through her consciousness every time she let her guard down. His look as they pushed him into the police car—helpless, hopeless. Afraid. Then the eyes belonged to Roger, smiling at her on their honeymoon, deadly angry when she disagreed with him—or full of grim satisfaction like in the parking lot of the CrossFit gym. Then Kimball's eyes, crinkling at the corners as he tried to convince her that he was going to get his daughter, but really he was creeping down to the riverbank with Wheatley's body, his wife yelling "Our daughter doesn't do much dance anymore! My husband just likes to fuck other women!" Then Morrison was there again, eyes calm and blue as ever as he slapped Kimball a high five over Wheatley's corpse. When Morrison began dismembering Wheatley and tossing his body parts into the trunk of a car like enormous bloody branches, she jerked to sitting, soaked in sweat.

Giving up on rest, she left the bed and slunk downstairs past where Petrosky was snoring lightly on the couch and let herself into the office. The heavy wheeze of Derry's breathing croaked through air that reeked of piss and decay. The drainage bag attached to the side of the bed was too dark to be healthy urine, obvious even by the muted light filtering in from outside. She sat in the chair beside the bed and leaned her face against the comforter near his hip, grateful it was dark enough that the yellow of his skin at least could be written off as shadow.

"I don't know what to do, Derry," she whispered.

He didn't stir. He hadn't stirred all day. Had they already spoken their last words? Was it possible that things could go just that quick? If she'd missed her chance... She slipped her hand into his, and it was like touching chicken wrapped in deli paper from the fridge: dry and cold and lifeless.

She'd thought she'd gotten it all figured out. But she hadn't. Now... was she wrong now? About everything? About Morrison? She had definitely been wrong about Roger. But Derry hadn't been wrong—and he had always loved Morrison. That thought lit the tiniest spark of hope in her chest, though any flames were stifled by grief.

She squeezed Derry's hand, gingerly. "You knew from the beginning, Derry. You knew Roger was an asshole. You begged me not to marry him. And he might be even worse than you thought." Her brother didn't respond, but his presence bade her to keep going, to keep talking, as if his shallow breath might suddenly whisper the answer she needed. "Or maybe it's Kimball... I think he lied about taking his daughter to dance, but I just... I don't know. I feel like I don't know anything anymore."

Even about Curt...Morrison. Maybe he was just like Roger, manipulative and conniving, sweet until he got what he wanted, concealing the dark parts of himself until it was too late. But she couldn't put that into words, not even here with Derry. She didn't want to be mistaken about Morrison. Tears slid over her cheeks and onto the bed. "I need your help, Derry. I'm failing."

Derry's breath gurgled through the room, but he did not respond. Not that she expected him to. When had she lost hope? She watched her thumb stroking his fingers, but she couldn't feel him, only the cold. "I'll find this guy, Derry. If they're wrong"— *of course they're wrong—*" I'll find him. Abby will be okay."

Shannon gritted her teeth, buried her face in the bed, and shuddered as the tears came, first a slow trickle then a gushing wound that wet the sheets. Derry's icy hand tethered her to the room, like the fist of a zombie clutching at the heroine's ankle in an old movie she and Roger had once seen. Maybe Roger had always been that zombie. Maybe she had always been the girl handcuffed to the earth by some jerk. She had chosen to marry someone who was very likely a psychopath. She'd put an innocent girl in prison. She pictured Morrison's stoic face in her mind. Maybe this time was no different.

It would not be the first time she had been grievously wrong.

25

Morrison stretched his arms above his head in warrior pose though he felt less like a warrior and more like a battered piece of meat. His head throbbed with memories of the drug, whispers in the back of his mind telling him to give in, to let go, to forget for just a little while.

He deserved to be here. Maybe he had always deserved it. It was cathartic in a way, an external manifestation of the prison he'd already created for himself. He was, and always would be, a slave, no matter how long he was clean. Now, trapped behind bars of steel, he felt no less a prisoner than when he was roaming free.

Sweat beaded on his forehead as he brought his elbow to the inside of his knee, still deep in a lunge, hands in prayer pose but acknowledging that this was as close as he ever got to praying. Narcotics Anonymous would have frowned on that, but it was no matter. He hadn't been to a meeting in years.

His breath filled the room, and he focused on it, willed himself to sink into it, stay with it, but the chill in the air brought him back to the jail cell again and again. It was a cold that had nothing to do with temperature—it was the panicked realization that he would soon succumb.

He could feel the drug's presence as surely as if he were cloaked in a robe of needles, the prickling of promise at once terrifying and euphoric. One stick and you could soar, above the world, beyond your pain, free of everything. But he knew he'd have to crash back to earth, and then the pain would follow. And this roller coaster, of desire and disgust, pleasure and pain...it wouldn't stop until he was dead.

Was Petrosky clean? Did it matter? Morrison had long pretended it was so, for in Petrosky's sobriety he saw his own, a bit of success held up like a mirror of triumph. But it was a fragile balance—mirrors could crack and falter, shatter into thousands of pieces that sliced at your skin until you were left bleeding hope onto the bedroom floor. Stress always made sober living harder, and lately, it had been a struggle. Now, here, there was no triumph, only vaguely shrouded opportunity to use, potential dealers whispering to him from every corner of steel and stone. And once he was arraigned, he'd be locked up with them.

In jail, there was nothing but the drugs, the cackling of sweet relief. He knew the others in their cells had access. He knew they had needles. He knew heroin was but a rightly placed question away, a look, a nudge in the lunch hall. He could smell it on their sallow skin, see it in their dull, bloodshot eyes, the lids at half-mast—the lonely euphoria of a simple need met. But it was a need met now and only now, because for those men, now was all that existed. Tomorrow would be but a half-intoxicated nightmare. Tomorrow would be a race to resupply before plunging into hell.

And yet, still, he loved it.

Even after years of sobriety, he could not deny the adoration that coexisted with loathing like interwoven threads of lace—though maybe that was how love always was. But not his love for *her*. They'd met three years ago, blistered autumn leaves from the tree next to the courthouse swirling at their feet. Shannon's presence had been a rope, tethering him, sustaining him. Watching her sleep in his arms had been the most blissful thing he'd done in years. She was becoming his drug. Not that she'd love him back if she knew. She couldn't love him, she'd made that plain, though he couldn't let go of this hope that she would come around. But even if she did, how long would she stay? She didn't know what he was—and if he had any say in the matter, she'd never find out.

No one knew everything. Not even Petrosky, and his respect seemed precarious at best. Even on the days Morrison was most certain of their bond, he feared it would soon fray and tear under the weight of the unforgivable things he had done. He wished he didn't have to bear his secrets alone, but what other choice did he have? No one in their right mind would be that understanding, that tolerant.

He could almost smell the blood on his hands, taste it in his mouth. He could still see the body when he closed his eyes, broken and blue, the tops of his shoes speckled with gore.

He deserved to be here in this cell, caged and alone.

He'd committed atrocities no man should get away with. And he still couldn't remember why.

26

THE NAUSEA from the night before made a comeback before she opened her eyes. She leapt from Derry's bedside and raced into the hall bathroom. Bile, thick and yellow, splattered into the toilet, but she could not purge the vile bullshit that was sloshing around in her brain.

Had she been wrong about Ashley Johnson? Probably. But did that mean Kimball was a killer? And what about Morrison? Her doubts about Morrison twisted her insides until she could barely breathe.

He was stoic to be sure. Calm in situations where any other man would lose his shit. She had never seen him cry, never seen him worry, not really. Was that the Zen thing, or did he just not feel anything at all? Emotionless. *Like a psychopath.* She rinsed her mouth and left the bathroom.

The commotion had apparently roused Petrosky, who stood peering at the street, his fingers drumming on the window. *Tap-tap-tap. Tap-tap-tap.* "Got ballistics back on the bullet from Wheatley's belly," he said to the curtain.

"And?"

"Gun was Kimball's." He turned from the window. "Bought it at a police auction four years ago."

She hadn't been wrong. The fist that held her stomach loosened its grip. "So they're arresting him?"

"Nope. He kept it in his glovebox, reported it missing last month, admits he had the car doors unlocked at the gym. With the break-in on your car, Kimball's not looking suspicious to Internal Affairs, and he's definitely not looking suspicious to Roger."

Not suspicious to the rest of the police force, but the look in Petrosky's eyes told her that he thought Kimball looked suspicious as hell. It didn't take a genius or even a fucking detective to know that there was something very, very wrong with Wheatley being shot with a bullet from Kimball's gun, even if Kimball had a solid alibi.

"I think he lied about having to take his daughter to dance," Shannon said.

"I'll look into it." Petrosky frowned at her tank top, the same one she'd been wearing at the gym yesterday, still crusted with dried vomit. He averted his eyes. "You need to eat. Low blood sugar will make you nauseous."

She squinted at him. "Oh...thanks."

Petrosky jerked his chin to the office door. "How is he?"

He. Her brother. Her almost dead brother.

"Not great."

"I had a friend die like that." His mouth was impassive, but his eyes shone dark and deep as he finally looked at her. "We were best buds in the academy. Never smoked a day in his life, yet there it was, lung cancer at thirty. His wife didn't take it well, killed herself the next year, left two little kids to fend for themselves."

Hell of a sad story, but why was he telling her this? Surely Petrosky didn't think Alex would kill himself.

If Petrosky noticed the quiver in her hands, he didn't show it. "It hurts, Shannon. It hurts like a fucking bitch, but it can't own you unless you let it. And you won't let it. No matter how shitty it is, you won't give up."

"That's a little melodramatic." But his words rang through to her very core, hot and sharp as a spear.

"You've thought it, though. We all do, if only for a heartbeat. How the hell am I going to get through this? How am I going to do it without him? But we do." He stepped toward her until she could smell the tobacco stench that clung to his clothes. "We find what we need. And until we get Morrison back out here, you tell *me* what you need." He squeezed her arm, dropped his eyes. "I'm going to walk the perimeter before everyone else gets up. You better get ready for work, Taylor, or we'll be late." He released her and headed for the back hallway, shoulders sagging, leaving her staring after him.

EVERY MUSCLE in Shannon's body felt like rubber as she struggled through her case files, making stacks of things to file, people to call, dates to set. *Derry's sleeping. Just do your job.* The beige walls of her office glared at her, pale and sickly, but still a healthier tone than her brother's skin. The blue stain from her cracked pen looked like a bruise.

Her knuckles were white around her new pen when the knocking started, timid rapping, then harder, swelling to an aggravated pounding: one, two, three, four distinct hits. Shannon knew that knock. She frowned at the door, pulled a sheet from the stack, and wrote a note at the top. Roger had gotten the wrong person thrown in jail last night. He could fucking wait.

He knocked again, four hard raps, but not unreasonably hard, and she could almost see his face melting from anger to faux indifference on the other side.

She laid her latest batch of legal research aside with a sigh and unlocked the door. If she hadn't needed to know what was going on with Morrison's case, she would have let him wait forever.

Roger leaned against the doorframe as if content to stay all day and harass the shit out of her. The purple bruising under his eyes was fading to a sickly yellow-green. Like alien flesh. Inhuman.

"What do you want?"

"Just to talk." His jaw tightened. Bad news?

Bad news for Roger would mean… Her heart leapt. Had they questioned and released Morrison already? No, she'd have heard from Petrosky if that were the case. And Roger wouldn't be here to tell her she had been right—he'd have let her suffer.

Roger pushed past her and sat, folding his hands over his crossed knee. "You working on Anderson?" His face gave away nothing.

Anderson? He hadn't come to talk about Anderson. Fire worked its way into her face as she walked back to her chair, trying to avoid stomping, or he'd know how much his presence got to her. Her back was rigid in her seat. "The asshole who shot his three-year-old in front of two other kids while cleaning his loaded gun?"

"That's the one. What are you charging with?"

She didn't realize her knee was bouncing until the chair chirped underneath her. She stilled her leg. "Involuntary manslaughter."

"Drop the charges, Shannon."

"Every day innocent kids are killed with firearms, Roger. Eventually we have to start holding adults accountable for—"

"Not today, Shannon. It's a hot-button topic. We'll never get a conviction."

"It doesn't mean we shouldn't try." She leveled her stare at him, hating his calm, still face. Why the fuck were they discussing Anderson? Was he purposefully avoiding questions about Morrison? Teasing her? Getting ready to rub her face in some perceived victory? "Confuse, deflect, destroy" was pretty much Roger's motto.

"Maybe you just want to avoid all gun-related issues," she said. "After all, Kimball's gun sure as shit pumped a bullet into someone, and you're not even bothering with that." *Because he's your best friend, Roger? Or is he your partner in crime?*

"Your politics are showing, Shannon. Try looking at things objectively, and we'll all be better off."

"Fine." She slapped the file shut. *Enough with this shit.* "What about Morrison? Are you dropping the charges on him?"

"I've already talked to the judge. There're more than enough to keep him."

Shannon's jaw dropped. "On what grounds?" Roger was insane. Morrison had no motive for killing anyone—not Derek Lewis, not Benjamin Wheatley. Definitely not Lucky. No judge in their right mind would keep him.

He chuckled. "Well, we both know how chummy Morrison's partner was with that family. Those types of people. Maybe he got involved with Johnson, killed Derek out of spite. Killed Wheatley for finding out." His grin fell, eyes sharpening into daggers. "Morrison's not as good and pure as you think he is, Shannon. He's got a history. Aggression, especially after his mother was killed—ironically, brains bashed in by a boyfriend. Sounds like he's replaying her death to me."

His mom's death. Ten years after his dad was killed in a robbery, Morrison's mother had been murdered by an abusive boyfriend. Morrison had many reasons to be angry, but so did she. So did a lot of people. She shook her head. "He isn't—"

"Then there's his drug history, including heroin, which he admitted to. And that's just what we have so far."

"Half the people in helping professions have histories, Roger. That's why they want to give back." But her stomach rolled. An addict? That's something she definitely should have known. *I had a mean streak as a kid.* Wasn't that what Morrison had said? "You have no evidence. You can't hold him forever."

"Kimball reported the gun missing weeks ago. And those towels in Wheatley's trunk? A couple of the ones hidden near the bottom had a recognizable image on them—some logo that looks like a mushroom. Morrison identified the towels himself. They're from his gym bag."

"Anyone at the gym could have gotten hold of them, Roger. Same with the gun. It's all circumstantial."

"You were right about the bars. We found traces of Wheatley's blood in the grooves around the base. He was definitely killed at the gym. And Kimball has an alibi. Your buddy has the only other key."

"No, Roger. This isn't right." They had to have a spare key. She pictured Amanda Kimball's office, the keys on the hook, in plain view. "Anyone could have—"

"We got other stuff from his place too, Shannon." Roger crossed his fingers over his knee. "His writing is especially interesting."

The air left her like she'd been stabbed in the chest. "Who gave you a warrant so fast?"

"He gave us permission to look. And we found a rather interesting piece in his garage: a hammer tucked away in the bottom of a Rubbermaid bin. A hammer that someone had taken the time to scrub clean. No other tools nearby. Odd, don't you think? Equally odd that we never found the weapon used to bash in Derek Lewis's skull."

Roger sat back and smiled. "We've got forensics working on it now. Looks like there's still a trace of something in the wood on the hammer. Preliminaries say it's blood. My guess is it belongs to Lewis."

Her mouth felt like it was stuffed with cotton. *Roxy.* Wouldn't the dog have lost her shit in the garage, smelling blood every time she walked by the door? But no—she was at Derry's now. Was that the real reason he'd brought her to Derry's?

"Roger." She tried to keep her voice light. Patient. "If he really killed Lewis and Wheatley, why would he give you permission to go through his stuff?"

"Maybe he wanted to get caught." Roger shrugged, and Shannon ground her teeth together.

It was me. They'd thought the killer had been bragging with the letter, but what if he'd wanted someone to stop him?

Roger gripped his knee harder, the tendons in his hand straining. "There's also an entire spiral notebook full of what look like poems. Songs. Drawings. Disturbing shit. We saw enough to think he might be unstable."

No way. *There is no fucking way.* "So, what, did he write a song about killing Derek Lewis?" *The hammer.* Morrison had the hammer. The knife in her chest twisted.

Roger released his knee and examined his fingernails. "Found a few other things too. About lovers."

Lovers. She felt naked. Exposed. What the hell had he written? But so help her, she wanted to read it, wanted to know what went on inside Morrison's head. She watched Roger release his knee, his eyes dead and cold and as angry as she'd ever seen them.

"I knew you were fucking him." He stared at her like he wanted her to justify it. To deny it. Maybe to assure him he was a better screw.

Her face blistered with rage. This part of her wasn't Roger's to pry into, not anymore. He had no right. And she hated the way he was looking at her now, leering like he could see clear through her clothes. Depending on what Morrison had written, maybe he could.

"From a marriage to the head prosecutor to shacking up with a killer cop. Quite the nosedive." Roger smiled.

I'll show you nosedive, motherfucker. Her fists clenched, every muscle in her neck screaming with tension. Petrosky was right: Roger was a lying, cheating, douche canoe. Roger was the one who should be in jail.

"Maybe Morrison will pay you to drop it, Roger," she hissed. "Like all the others."

"What did you just say?" In a heartbeat, all traces of amusement were gone. His eyes were icy; his lips pulled into a sneer. She wanted to punch him in the goddamn mouth.

"You heard me. You're fucking dirty, Roger."

"I haven't done anything wrong, Shannon. You might not like the charges, but we're getting through more cases than ever. The whole department is running more smoothly. The other attorneys are less stressed about their caseloads." He flipped his palms to the sky, a magician's ta-da. "And bad guys are still going away."

"Not for as long as they should."

"That's a matter of opinion. Luckily, yours no longer matters to me." A corner of his mouth turned up in a half smile, half sneer. "I think the stress of your brother's death is starting to get to you. If you want to keep your job..." Roger stood and backed toward the door, and she followed suit, advancing on him around the desk.

"You can't fire me, Roger. It'll never stick."

He pursed his lips and dropped his gaze like he felt sorry for her. "You're not a great judge of character these days, Shanny. Why don't you leave the important decisions to me?"

She slammed the door on him, her body thrumming with repressed rage. If someone had told her four years ago that she'd want to stab Roger in the eye, she'd have laughed in their face. Now, Roger was lucky she didn't have a letter opener in her desk.

She laid her palms against the closed door and willed the coolness of it to pull the hot rage from her body. Sanity was fleeting, fragile. Anyone could be a killer.

Anyone.

27

Even through her office window, the afternoon sun was so bright that it hurt her soul. The sounds of spring made her want to kick something. How dare the birds chirp when her life was falling the fuck apart. Petrosky had called to tell her about Morrison's preliminary trial—after the fact. Roger had been right. Morrison was staying in jail—a flight risk due to the nature of the charges—though his new attorney, the illustrious Frank Griffen, had done his damnedest to get him released. It had only been a day, and already the loneliness was eating at her so fiercely that she'd picked the cuticle around her nail down to the meat, bloodying it every time she thought of him. Morrison. Not Curt. Maybe if she kept it friendly, professional even, her heart wouldn't hurt so badly.

It already hurt enough. Derry had barely woken in days. It was as if the moment they'd gotten him, home he'd given up. And with his constant, raspy wheezing... it wouldn't be long. She needed to solve this, today. While she could still tell Derry about it. While she could put his mind at ease before—

She shook her head, trying to clear the bullshit. *The case. Think about the case.*

They had interviewed Kimball and cleared him of wrongdoing, or more specifically, Roger's handpicked detectives had cleared Kimball and turned the information over to Internal Affairs, who hadn't challenged their conclusions thus far. But...the gun. The gym. His daughter's nonexistent dance classes. The irritability that had only increased in the last month. But Kimball had been with her when her car was trashed, which meant...he must have a partner. Someone she hadn't seen in the gym that night. Valentine's face flashed in her brain, but he wouldn't hurt a fly... Well, unless you hurt a child...like Lewis had. She shook her head again. *Stop, Shannon, regroup.* Kimball and Roger? No one had a concrete motive. Nothing made sense. *Nothing.*

Especially not Morrison standing under the bars, kicking Wheatley, watching him bleed. No way. No fucking way. Kimball was the one being sneaky. Kimball was the one lying, the one cheating, the one getting more and more aggressive by the day. Kimball was the one—

The telephone rang, and she stared at it like it was a grotesque, hairy mole. Caller ID was someone in Detroit. *Nope, not now.* She waited until it stopped ringing then took it off the hook. If Alex needed her, he'd call her cell. For now, she needed to get her mind off Derry, off Morrison, and into work mode. Not like she could concentrate on the case right now anyway.

She stretched her arms over her head and rolled her neck. *Anderson.* She'd finish the Anderson case. And that bastard wasn't getting off on this one. One of her law professors used to say that regardless of how it happened, whether a premeditated act or an impulsive act of vengeance, everyone needs a reason to stop, a reason to avoid committing the same crime again. She was going to give every one of these dickheads on her caseload a reason. And then, once her head was clear, she was going to figure out who had killed Wheatley and nail them to the fucking wall. For Derry. For Morrison. For Abby. For all of them.

She researched, scrawled notes, typed reports, and signed forms so viciously that she tore a hole in one of her files. No thinking. No more thinking. She needed to step away from the constant analysis. She could almost feel the answer hiding there like a sliver beneath the surface, the kind that pushed a little deeper every time you tried to scratch it up. Maybe time would allow the sliver to work its way to the surface.

Half an hour later, the Anderson file was ready, and her stomach was grumbling. She shoved her folders into her briefcase and left the office, still trying to get a handle on her whirling thoughts. Maybe lunch would help. But the thought of food made her stomach clench as if her gut would reject anything she tried to swallow. She'd go anyway. She started from the office, glanced back at her briefcase, and returned to take it with her.

Petrosky's car was at the curb outside the office. *Has he been out here all day?* He was supposed to be investigating how to get Morrison the fuck out of jail. Petrosky waved her over, and she slid into the passenger seat.

"Why are you here, Petrosky?"

"I was just coming to get you." He put the car in gear, and they drove from the lot. "You could have told me you were leaving."

Like she had to answer to him. She'd spent years answering to Roger. Shit, she still had to answer to Roger at work. Once this case was over, she'd move. Find a new job in a place that wasn't full of old baggage. She shrugged. "I needed some time to think."

"This isn't a game, Shannon."

Shannon tightened her grip on the door handle. "You think I don't know that?" Derry needed her to figure this out. She would figure this out. A sandwich, and then she'd be able to focus. "How's Valentine?"

"Good. Following Abby around like a bloodhound." She wanted to ask about Morrison but couldn't bring her mouth to form the words. Maybe she was letting her emotions get the better of her. She'd definitely said too much to Roger earlier.

Petrosky turned toward the freeway. "Taylor—"

"Listen, I fucked up. I was arguing with Roger this morning, and I might've accused him of taking bribes. I kind of...exploded."

"He'll probably think you're just angry, throwing accusations around," Petrosky said, but his eyes were tight, and spots of pink rouged his cheeks.

"It was pretty specific for throwing things around." She looked out the window at the trees, at the brilliant blue sky. But the sunlight didn't feel warm or happy—it was hot, scorching, menacing.

"Won't matter. If anything, he'll get flustered and fuck himself up. That's what usually happens." He took a deep, phlegmy breath and coughed.

"Find out anything about Kimball's daughter's dance classes?"

"His daughter hasn't taken dance in six months."

I knew it. So, what had Wheatley seen that had given Kimball justification to off him? Was Kimball on drugs? Had to be drugs. Ruskin had said—

"I'll look into it more, Taylor, find out what he's been doing. We need to focus on other things."

Right. There was probably tons to do, especially since Morrison was out of commission. Knowing she'd been right about Kimball, even if it was just about dance class, was reviving her brain. Shannon pushed her hair out of her face. "I'll help. I just need some coffee, and then I can start—"

"You need to go home, Taylor." His tone held no demand, just bone-crushing sadness.

Her chest collapsed against her heart. *Derry.* "That's why you were trying to find me. It wasn't about the case?" She'd been so focused on finding the killer for Derry that she'd forgotten to actually be there for him. And now it was too late.

Petrosky stared out the windshield. Shannon blinked back tears and held onto the door handle, the hardness of it grounding her in the moment. But she couldn't hold onto the door—or Derry—forever.

THERE WAS a new guy in the corner of Derry's office-turned-bedroom, a balding man with a hospital ID badge around his throat like a noose. A nurse? Another doctor? Who the fuck had called him?

He nodded solemnly as she entered. "I'm Raj. A colleague of Alex's."

She ignored him and looked at the bed.

Alex sat at Derry's bedside, his eyes glassy. Abby lay next to Derry, her head on his chest, Alex's hand on her back. *Derry*. Her baby brother. Under his yellowed skin, something dull and gray had seeped in, blotting out any remnants of the peach and pink of his youth.

Derry's eyes were half-open, his jaw slack.

"Is he awake?" She touched his head, as bald as he'd been when their parents brought him home from the hospital. She had slapped him that first meeting, though she couldn't remember doing it; she only knew because of the story her mom had told her. But she vaguely remembered that he'd been warm then, and now he was cold, or colder than he should be. She swallowed hard.

Alex wiped his eyes with his palm. "Coma. But he's lost the ability to close his eyes due to the wasting in the muscles." His words were clotted with sorrow. "He's close. I knew it the moment I walked in here. And when Raj stopped by—I could barely talk. And I didn't want to be here alone in case it happened...fast." He glanced at the door. "Is Petrosky here? Raj said your line was busy."

"Outside."

Alex sniffed. "I'm glad you made it."

She nodded and sat beside the bed next to Alex, where someone had added an extra folding chair. A shuffling from the back corner caught her attention, then the bedroom door closed, maybe Raj leaving, but she couldn't take her eyes from Derry's body. *So still.*

Abby's face rested on Derry's chest, rising and falling with each of his shallow, ragged gurgles. Every time his breath caught and stopped for a beat too long, Abby's chin quivered, but she did not cry, just stared out past them all with a blank gaze like she could see straight into the afterlife and was watching for the reaper.

Shannon tried to breathe, but the room was suffocating her, the air like molasses. She was drowning. Tears ran freely down Alex's face, his eyes red and raw and helpless. She wrapped her arms around him and let his tears wet her blouse, much like she'd done with her mother when her father had left.

"The blood's pooling and everything is settling," Alex whispered in her ear. "I see people die every day, but he's...cold, my god, he feels so much colder than they do."

They sat. Listened to Derry's ragged breath. Listened to the silence when his body forgot to breathe. Abby was still and silent on his chest, her eyes closed as if she were asleep, but no one could sleep with that rattle in their ear.

Shannon did not know how much time had passed when Alex disentangled himself from her and laid a finger on Derry's jugular. His eyes filled, but he bent to Derry's ear, whispering words she couldn't discern. Alex's chest heaved. He choked back a sob and kissed Derry's forehead, pressing his lips so hard against her brother's face that Shannon expected the skin to split. It didn't, and Alex sat back, his entire body trembling.

Time. They were out of time. And yet it kept passing, achingly slowly. The jangle of air moving through his lungs became a constant, lingering sound even when his body paused, and the silence stretched before them like a road to nowhere. Outside, the sky slowly darkened to a bloody red, then to black. At some point, before the stars emerged, Abby fell asleep.

And still, he breathed. But less. And less.

What time Alex laid his head on Derry's pillow and fell asleep too, Shannon wasn't quite sure. Nor was she certain when Abby moved from Derry's chest to the pillow beside him. But there they all were as dawn broke and birds chirped and early morning commuters went about their normal, boring lives. A new day and all she wanted to do was reverse the clock.

Shannon's neck ached from resting her head on her chest. She stood and put her lips at Derry's ear, whispering low so that Abby couldn't hear her. "Growing up, you always made me better than I was. I'm so grateful that I got to have you as a brother." Tightness wrapped her throat. "I love you, Derry." She blinked hard, willing herself to keep her shit together, to show Abby strength like the strength Derry had shown throughout their entire childhood. She caught a glimpse of Abby's face in her peripheral vision, eyes closed, mouth open in sleep.

She put her hand on one side of Derry's face, the skin cold and dry and horrible. "I'll take care of them, Derry. I won't fail you." She released him and collapsed back into her chair beside Alex as Abby opened her eyes. Looked at her daddy. Laid her hand on his chest. Frowned.

It took Shannon a moment to realize the rattling had stopped. Alex lifted his head from the pillow and touched Derry's neck again. This time he pulled his hand back quickly and picked up Derry's wrist, searching, searching. Then he set Derry's hand back on the bed, patted it gently, and shook his head. Shannon choked back all the stinging tears she wouldn't—couldn't—let fall. *Be strong. For Derry.*

A single tear escaped Abby's eye. "I'll miss you, Daddy. So, so much," Abby touched Derry's face. "And I love you so much too." She kissed Derry's sunken cheek, crawled off the far side of the bed, and ran around to Alex's lap. Shannon's chest felt like it was going to implode, and she forced a breath to inflate it. They huddled there, Shannon's arms around them both, listening to the silence.

28

Derry had never been a fan of funerals or churches, so they skipped the wake and held a memorial at Alex's house the following Wednesday. They had needed at least that long to complete the cremation and to plan what Derry had always called his going-away party. "You fuckers should party all night just to give yourselves an excuse to skip work," he'd said. But the gathering felt anything but festive. The food looked good, though Shannon tasted none of it. Sushi. Mexican. Take out from all his favorite places. They played the songs he'd chosen. She'd never listen to the Grateful Dead again.

All she could do was yearn for her brother as people she knew and people she didn't trudged through offering condolences and cake and lasagna and cards and empty consolations that he was in a better place—as if that was what she needed to accept. As if Derry would have been happier somewhere without them. As if having had him for a brief time rather than not at all somehow made it all okay that he'd died way too early. As if she should be fucking *thankful*.

She'd always hated that flowery bullshit, and she hated it now more than ever. Pretty words wouldn't give her back her brother, wouldn't allow her to hear his voice again. Wouldn't give Abby back her father. Morrison would have known what to say. He would have known when to shut up and just hold her hand too. But he wasn't there. He was gone. *Gone*.

She should have taken time in the past week to visit Morrison in jail. But she couldn't, couldn't face him, knowing she wasn't doing shit to help him get out. There was nothing she could do—not for anyone. The case didn't make sense; her life didn't make sense. Even her own body had betrayed her by completely forgetting how to sleep—in the mornings, she could barely get out of bed. And after the first three days had gone by in a fog of grief and loss, she'd felt guiltier than ever about her absence, and it was even harder to consider Morrison, wrongfully imprisoned in the detention center.

When she couldn't stand the trite condolences any longer, she hid in the office, sitting on the hospital bed that the medical supply place had yet to pick up, watching through the front window as the visitors came, stayed a socially acceptable amount of time, and left. Watching Valentine, who never moved from his spot at the street except to accompany Lillian to the door when she arrived with a bouquet of flowers.

Shannon left the office to meet her. Lillian smelled like talcum powder already, well ahead of her delivery date. Valentine smelled like his car and fast food and Morrison's special coffee, which made her heart ache that much more. But she couldn't think about it, couldn't really think about anything except the hole that seemed to grow in her chest every time she saw the hollow look in Abby's eyes. Shannon offered hugs, but Abby felt wooden, just like the stiff, brittle arms of everyone else today. Eventually, the stream of visitors slowed to a trickle, and she was grateful for the moments of solitude in between the empty apologies.

Griffen showed up as twilight fell, his beanie cap pulled over his ears, bringing a coffee cake on a plate she recognized from his house. The same dishes after all these years. For some reason, that struck her as horribly sad. She saw him coming and met him on the porch.

"Thanks, Griffen. Did you make that?"

"Alas, I did not. But I shall send along your regards to Karen. When I see her." His eyes were watery, mouth tight. Like he was in pain. And he looked thin.

God, not again. In college, he'd had a girlfriend: Natasha...something. Ugly as sin, and equally irritable. But he was down for a month when she left him, barely slept, barely ate. Shannon had been so pissed at him for letting that girl have such an effect. Come to think of it, Shannon had probably been the only woman he'd ever met who hadn't taken advantage of him somehow. Even Burke had given him most of the bills when they'd moved in together, and she'd surely controlled all their social activities. No wonder he missed Shannon. Everyone needs one trustworthy person—someone steady, someone who will just...be there, without demands or expectations. Morrison was her person, though it turned out she was shitty at reciprocation. Then she pictured Alex's bloodshot eyes as he watched his fiancé leave the house for the last time —on a gurney. Her chest lit on fire. She couldn't breathe.

Think about something else, anything else. Fucking hell. She glanced at the flower bed where Roger had landed after Morrison punched him. *Morrison.* Nope, not helping.

"How are things with Karen?" she asked.

Griffen shook his head. "Shan, you were always too worried about other people even when you were the one in need of assistance."

She wrapped her coat tighter around her body. "Look who's talking. You had mono, and you still defended that dude with the bum leg who killed his mother."

He smiled, but it looked forced. "Allegedly."

"Yeah, right." She sighed. "It's not like there's anything anyone can do for me. Might as well hear about you." And she could definitely use some distraction from the hole in her heart. "Come on, Griffen. I know something's wrong."

"Ah. Well, it's no big deal, really. I'm…just considering whether Karen and I are meant to be." Griffen shook his head, opened his mouth, and closed it again.

This is new. Something bad must have happened—she'd never known him to break up with anyone. He was usually the one who got left. But he gave her no time to comment on it.

"Perhaps I don't deserve her anyway. I couldn't even keep an innocent girl out of jail. A really, truly, innocent girl. If I'm honest, it's been eating me up. I barely sleep anymore." And there was the Griffen she knew. He kicked at a smudge of mud on the porch, left behind by some well-wisher. Derry would have hosed it off.

She met Griffen's glassy eyes. "I was the one who put her away. If you're feeling shitty about your role, mine was a thousand times more terrible."

He broke eye contact and stared off into the night behind her, his mouth working again. His nerves must have gotten worse over the last few years. How had she not noticed?

"I'm sorry, Shan, I—"

She waved away his apology. "I didn't take it that way. I'm just saying…we all do our best, right? It's like Professor Moore used to say: the truth prevails eventually. That's why we have appeals."

"And where the accused began their trial, so shall it end righteously if the court is just," he recited, rubbing his temple. "I just hope this one ends well."

"Yeah." Her chest tightened. "Endings are always the hardest." She blinked rapidly but was unable to stop the tears from spilling down her cheeks.

"They certainly are." Griffen wrapped his arms around her. He was shaking. Maybe from the cold, she couldn't quite feel. Every part of her was numb.

"I'm so sorry, Shan. For not being here for you. For…everything."

She said nothing, just leaned into him, and watched the sky blacken to ash.

. . .

Petrosky arrived a little after nine, the orange glow from his cigarette preceding him in the driveway. He stumbled off the sidewalk, righted himself, and stared into the flower bed as he finished his smoke. Drunk? Or clumsy? *Who cares?* If Shannon didn't have to look out for Abby and Alex, she'd have been completely wasted hours ago.

He turned when she stepped onto the lawn. "Taylor. How are you?" He smelled intensely minty, the reek of mouthwash over tobacco over who knew what else.

How am I? She ignored the question rather than trying to describe the gaping, pulsing wound in her chest. "Valentine took me to pick up my car up today," she said instead, and her voice was lower than she remembered. "I thought I'd go home tonight."

Petrosky shook his head, and she fought the urge to slap him. *Don't fucking tell me no, you asshole.* But it wasn't him she was mad at. She had failed her brother. Shannon could almost hear Derry's voice whispering from the walls: *Why can't you find who did this?* But Derry was no longer around to care, and it was no longer their case. Petrosky would take care of Morrison. She had to get out—she was just so…tired. Tired of smelling death and coffee cake, tired of seeing that office every time she walked into the house, tired of feeling like she was trapped in her brother's crypt. Tired of being alone while Alex and Abby slept in Alex's room, suffering, but together, sharing the burden of grief so that it was less…stifling.

"I was here to be with Derry, but now, I—"

"Taylor, I know, okay? You want to be alone to heal. But there's someone out there who has it out for you."

"No one's looking for me."

He sighed. "Someone *might* be looking for you, Taylor. You need to be worried about your family."

"I can't just sit here and look at his ashes, Petrosky. Alex and Abby are moving on, grieving, but they're together. And here I am, just…sitting. Waiting for something else to happen. I can't spend the rest of my life sitting. You of all people should understand that." *You're the one who threw yourself into your work instead of grieving for your daughter. You're the one who never let it go, who never healed.* Maybe she'd be like that too, consumed by the dead, glaring at the living because no matter how awesome they were, they'd never be the one person she wanted them to be.

Petrosky tossed his cigarette into the barely-there grass, and she had the irrational urge to leap down and grab it. Derry had loved his lawn, though he'd adored ruining it with bounce houses for Abby's birthday. Wait…hadn't he? Or had his eye twitched ever so slightly every time another kid leapt to the ground and exposed the mud? Was she already forgetting him? How much more would she forget? The thought stabbed hot and sharp into her chest, and she breathed over it until the pain lessened.

Petrosky followed her gaze and bent to retrieve the cigarette butt. "Roger held a press conference today with the chief of police. Made it clear there's still another player after they got a different set of latent prints off one of Wheatley's shoes. Got a dark hair too, again, not Morrison's. Male, but not much else. They're claiming it's from the addict that Morrison was coercing because the hair tested positive for heroin, but it's probably from someone Wheatley saw that day. Young's ruling out people on Wheatley's caseload now."

"What? They can't hold him—"

"Roger also said he's got a statement from someone at the rehab center, corroborating that Morrison has a history of preying on addicts, getting drugs or sex in exchange for not arresting them."

Preying on addicts? Taking drugs? Had she really been that blind? "That's—that's fucking—"

"It's obviously not true, Taylor. It's bullshit lies. And Roger's not releasing his source, though he'll have to tell Internal Affairs if he hasn't already. My guess is someone Morrison put away is screwing with him, and Roger made it nice and easy for them to lie, probably asked leading questions." Petrosky grimaced, nostrils flaring. "Unless Roger's lying altogether, which I wouldn't put past him."

The rehab center. "Griffen's girlfriend works at the rehab center—Karen, remember her? I wonder if she knows who said that…if there is someone."

"I asked Griffen. He said she had no idea."

Of course Petrosky had thought of that. "What about Kimball?"

"They printed him to rule out his marks on the equipment. Wasn't his prints on Wheatley either, and with his alibi, they aren't pushing it. And Roger's got a hard-on for California. He's got the chief breathing down my neck to stay away from it, conflict of interest or some bullshit —they don't even want me to see him."

Roger. He was orchestrating everything, from the evidence, to the arrest, to Morrison's confinement. Cutting Morrison off from the people who were trying to help him.

"The detectives are saying Morrison bought drugs from Derek Lewis, Wheatley found out about it accidentally, and Morrison offed them both, though he had assistance on Wheatley from someone at the rehab center, someone who's now missing. I think they're speculating that Morrison killed his junkie partner too and dumped the body."

Insanity. "What about Lucky? What's their opinion on that?"

Petrosky grunted. "That Morrison's a fucking psycho. Unstable. Wants the fame. Maybe a drug-induced moment of insanity. The usual."

"But Morrison doesn't do drugs, right?" *Anymore.* "Didn't they test him?"

"I'm sure they did. Not that they'd let me see the file. But Roger isn't rubbing it in my face, so it's a fair bet the test was negative."

A fair bet, but not certain.

Petrosky's face was cloaked in the shadow of the awning, but she could feel the tension. The heaviness of whatever he was holding back.

"What else?" she asked, not sure she wanted to know. But there had to be more, or they'd have let Morrison go once they found someone else's DNA. The night breathed around them, fast and sharp, almost panting with the tense energy of revelation.

"They got the forensics back on the towels in Wheatley's trunk—Morrison's DNA all over them, though that isn't a surprise. But the hammer found in Morrison's garage..." Petrosky averted his eyes and stared into the night. "There was some hair, Taylor. And blood. Stuck in the groove between the handle and the top. DNA matched Derek Lewis."

Her pulse went into overdrive, beating a frantic rhythm in her temples.

"He never should have let them search," Petrosky said.

Because he's guilty? But she knew what he meant: with someone on the force implicated in the crimes, Morrison should have known it'd have been easy for them to plant something at his house, especially now that Roxy wasn't there.

"California's not an idiot—he'd have gotten rid of the hammer and the towels. But it doesn't look good from the outside. Morrison's a loner, quiet unless he's being charming in that goofy beach boy way of his. He doesn't show much emotion. All marks of a psychopath if you spin it right."

A psychopath. She'd sometimes thought Morrison's incessant calm was strange, but in a passing way: a little too relaxed here, oddly unaffected there. After four years with Roger, she was sensitive to people who didn't respond normally—almost too sensitive. But wasn't calm good?

"Plus, he has a little bit of a...history that doesn't bode well for him right now." Petrosky jerked his cigarettes from his pocket, a tremor in his fingers.

A history. Same thing Roger had said. So maybe it wasn't just schoolyard shenanigans, but still... "What exactly does that mean?" *Besides the drugs*, she wanted to add.

"He did some things that Roger will argue are markings of antisocial personality disorder, psychopathy, you know? Minor legal infringements. Drugs, mostly, when he was a kid. Juvenile detention after beating the shit out of a bully at school."

Drugs. Juvenile detention. Turned born again yogi? Best friends and he'd kept it all from her, hiding his secrets behind his placid facade. Though...he *had* hinted at a past, and she hadn't asked him for details. And she hadn't exactly spilled her elementary school secrets either.

Because they aren't relevant anymore. The present was what mattered. The future. She could almost feel Morrison's hand stroking her back, but she brushed the thought away before it could take root. "Did he tell you all this?" If he'd told Petrosky and not her, maybe they weren't as close as she'd thought.

Petrosky shook his head. "He's a quiet guy, Taylor. I don't push him. But I always know who I'm working with."

He'd investigated Morrison. "Now you're the one who sounds like a psycho," she said, but his words loosened the knot that had formed in her chest.

"Married to Roger, you can probably pick them out of a lineup."

She clenched her fists. He was right—she had often thought the same —but the words felt different coming out of someone else's mouth.

"Sorry, below the belt."

Her shoulders stayed high and tight, but her balled fists released. "What are you going to do tonight?" The house behind her suddenly loomed like a prison, cold and unforgiving.

"Poke around. Our best bet at getting California out is giving them the person who actually did it. But stick around here, don't let your guard down. And take care of yourself. I know how easy it is to stop giving a shit after something like this."

"I'll be fine, Petrosky. Maybe I'll take a run around the lake, get some of this energy out. No one's coming for me." *No one.* She was…alone.

"I don't know how you can be so sure. Unless you think California's guilty." His voice was low, dangerous, but pained. Challenging her to say she thought Morrison was responsible.

"I don't think Morrison did it. You know that." But did she really believe it? She wasn't sure. He had the hammer, for god's sake. Maybe she was just afraid. Afraid that he was guilty. Afraid that the one person she thought she could rely on had turned out to be worse than the rest. Or was she afraid he was innocent and would come home, ready to…be with her? She really was fucked up if she couldn't decide. Not that it was a good time in her life to be deciding anything, but—

"Good. Then stay here for him, Taylor."

Her heart was beating too fast, her lungs too tight. *I can't stay here. I'll suffocate.*

"I'm going to get him out, but I can't do that if you're running all over the place like—"

You can't make me stay. "Like what?" Shannon's heart was in her throat. "Like some fucking idiot who doesn't know what's good for them? Like your partner's plaything?" Petrosky stared at her, eyes widening with surprise. But she couldn't stop. "I don't need your permission. I'm not a fucking prisoner."

"I was going to say like you don't care someone might be following you," Petrosky said slowly. "And I never wanted to make you feel like a prisoner, Taylor. I just need to know you're safe."

"You don't need to know shit. I'm not your fucking daughter." Her chest was on fire, all her grief channeling into fury.

Petrosky froze, his eyes locked on her face. "So you're not." He lumbered off across the lawn to his car as Shannon stalked into the house and slammed the door behind her.

Ten minutes later, Shannon emerged wearing one of Derry's old sweat suits and a pair of her own sneakers. Petrosky's car was gone. *Good.* Though her heart was already aching over what she'd said to him. If only she could take it back; she of all people knew what it was like to lose someone—and to want to protect those you had left.

Valentine got out of the car, his gaze swinging from one side of the road to the other. "Taylor? You're not leaving, are you?"

Goddammit, not you too. She bristled. "I can do anything I please, Valentine."

"Hey, I'm not here to manhandle you like Petrosky. I'm just your friend, you know? We've known each other a long time."

Since before she'd had Abby. Since before she'd gotten married. Since before Derry got sick. But they'd never been close. Even when he'd come to see her in the hospital, he'd only stayed long enough to drop off flowers and hold the baby before disappearing. He hadn't known what she needed. No one had; even Derry was too wrapped up in his new daughter to worry about Shannon, and rightly so. But the thick, suffocating aloneness she'd felt then was much like the ache she felt now, even in Valentine's presence.

The space left by Morrison's absence gaped like a black hole in her chest, already hollowed out by Derry's loss. She wanted to scream. To cry. The panic that her best friend might be gone for good thrummed in her veins, far hotter than any worry about what he might expect of her once—*if*—he got out.

Valentine knowing her "a long time" hadn't translated into knowing shit about her. Without Morrison, having company was superficial—pointless. She needed to be alone. She needed to get away. Or...she needed her fucking brother back. Her shoulders sagged.

Valentine put a hand on her arm. "Hey, Taylor, why don't you go inside, eh?"

She pulled her arm away. "Just watch the house. I'll be back."

"Where are you going?"

I don't have to answer to you either. But she didn't feel like arguing, didn't have the energy. "I'm just going to run around the neighborhood. I might circle the lake."

"At least—hey, Taylor, wait!"

She ignored him and took off down the road. Fuck Petrosky. Fuck Valentine too, and his fake concern. And Morrison. And Roger. And cancer. Fuck them all. She could run all night, and she'd be perfectly safe. And if she wasn't—hell, maybe if someone bludgeoned her with a hammer too, she'd finally get a little sleep.

Her feet were a blunt metronome on the sidewalk. Living room lights and the blue glare of televisions glowed behind curtained windows in happy houses where people were alive and intact and unburdened by death. People who had brothers and fathers they probably didn't even appreciate. *Fuck them too.* She ran faster, channeling all her worry, all her rage, all her grief, into her legs.

Her thighs were aching by the time she turned onto the side street that led to the lake. No asphalt here, just dirt and rocks that crunched underfoot as she made her way down to the water where the surface sparkled under the light of a half-moon. To her other side, the houses were more scattered, separated by patches of scrubby woods. She wheezed in the acrid air from someone's wood-burning fireplace and kept going. Her shirt stuck to her back. Her exhales fogged in front of her, and then the glistening houses stopped entirely, and it was just her and the water kissing the shore and the raccoons shuffling through the brush on the other side. The breeze whipped against her back, angry, stinging, then went still.

The rustling grew louder. A stray dog? A coyote?

Shannon was turning to peer into the trees when movement behind her caught her eye. *What the—*

It was too late. The dull thunk of wood on bone rang through the night. Hot, white pain shot through her leg as she tumbled and went down, and a fist—a knee maybe—smashed into the back of her skull. Stars exploded behind her eyes. Then an arm was around her throat, closing off her airway—

No, fuck, no. She slashed at the arm around her neck with her nails, listening to her assailant's breathing, the sound loud and ragged in her ears. In front of her, the lake was placid and still. Derry would have liked it. Her vision wavered. And there was Abby's face, tear-stained, mouth open in a silent wail.

No. Abby could not lose anyone else, not now.

Shannon heaved herself up on one foot, driving her attacker backward. The grip on her throat lessened, and she sucked in a frenzied breath of something spicy-sweet. Then the fingers on her throat clamped down again, harder, tighter, and her sweaty palms slipped and slid as she tried to tear the gloved fingers from her throat. Black tugged at the corners of her vision. She drove an elbow into her attacker's chest and felt a pop, maybe the snap of a clavicle, and a sharp exhale hit the back of her neck. But no sound from the person behind her, nothing but the water on the shore and the throbbing of her pulse. The pressure on her windpipe remained.

She closed her eyes and heaved backward, toppling herself and her attacker to the dirt. The pressure on her neck disappeared, and she surged to her feet and hurtled backward along the road. Her shin screamed. Her attacker leapt up—short, wearing a ski mask, wrapped in a puffy jacket, or maybe that was bulk. Behind the mask, eyes shone black and beady in the gloom.

Shannon ran forward, intending to drive a shoulder into her attacker's gut, but the asshole stumbled back and fled. She watched them go, gasping air into her burning lungs, coughing blood from a split lip.

Headlights shot around the corner and cut through the night, exposing her and blinding her at the same time. She hurtled toward the woods, scrambling over dead leaves and brush, frantically feeling for trees to hide behind—not that a tree would help much if the car jumped the curb to mow her down. Her heel caught in a rut. She stumbled and hit her knees and tears sprang into her eyes, but she did not stop—Shannon ripped at the underbrush, groping for a branch, anything that she could use as a weapon if they got out of the car.

The car screeched to a halt, its headlights sending a cone of light around her. *Not like this. Not tonight.* She missed Derry, but she was not ready to meet him again just yet. She scrambled for the trees and slung herself behind a fir, grabbing a branch to use like a baseball bat. Her throat felt hot and swollen. Dizziness pulled at her.

"Shannon?" Shoes crunched from the car. *Petrosky. Petrosky?* "Jesus Christ, Taylor."

She dropped the branch and slumped against the tree, the world already hazy and fading around her. The last thing she remembered was Petrosky scooping her into his arms.

29

SHE WAS WALKING with Derry along the shore, hand in hand, watching Abby scamper ahead of them at the edge of the surf. "Wait," Shannon yelled, but Abby was gone, leaping into the ocean, disappearing under the waves. Shannon ran, screaming into the sea, but she could not hear Abby's cries. There was only the steady pulse of the ocean. Then a wave, high and white-crested, swelled in front of her, and Morrison rose above her on a surfboard, his hair flying like King Triton. "Help me!" she yelled to him. He threw his head back and vomited water tinged red with blood.

"Ms. Taylor?" A soft female voice, tense but confident, cut into the remnants of her dreams. Then: "I don't think she can see you now, sir."

"It's important for an investigation." *Petrosky.*

Shannon tried to force her eyes open, but her lids felt as if they were weighted down. "I'm... He's okay."

"You've had quite a scare, Ms. Taylor. You need rest."

I can't let him leave. "I need to talk to him." Her tongue felt twice its normal size, and her voice crackled like the rasp of Derry's final breaths. And it reminded her of the sounds, the whispers in the woods, the crunch of gravel beneath her shoes, the snapping twigs she'd assumed were coyotes. She could practically feel the pressure on her neck. Could almost see those eyes, beady in the dark, and the puffy, thick shoulders. The scent of herbs and sweat still clung to the back of her throat. The gloves, she realized, had been to protect his skin—he had been watching her. Waiting for her to be alone. He'd been ready to kill her.

She coughed, and the pain in her throat caused her to clench her eyelids together more tightly.

"We need some water," Petrosky said.

"On the table, sir." The nurse's voice had lost its edge. Then the sound of plastic on plastic, the wet whoosh of liquid, and the cup was pressed against her lower lip, carrying with it the scent of cigarettes from Petrosky's hand.

She let the liquid rush into her mouth and swallowed. "Thanks." Her eyelids still didn't want to open, but she dragged them into a squint, trying to focus on Petrosky's face as her vision adjusted. The light was blinding. "How long have I been out?"

"Six hours." He grabbed the remote and pushed a button to incline the bed.

Her shoulders tightened. "Oh, shit. Abby. And Alex."

"They're sleeping, and Valentine is still posted outside, watching them. I'll let them know in the morning."

She relaxed against the pillow. The back of her head throbbed. "What happened? I mean...what's wrong with me?"

"To start with, you're crazy." His eyes twinkled then dimmed.

She almost smiled, but everything hurt too much. "Physically, Petrosky. I think we both know I made an error in judgment. Is anything broken?" She tested one leg, then the other. Sore. Bruised, certainly, but she'd know the sharp agony of a fracture.

"No breaks. Blunt force trauma to the head, probably a concussion. Lots of bumps and bruises. Nothing too major."

"They go over everything in my chart with you?"

"Nope. Swiped it from the nurses' station. I also took swabs from under your fingernails. Looks like you got cloth, no skin, so if you scratched anyone, their DNA is still inside their jacket." Petrosky sank into the chair beside the bed. "I never should have left. I'm sorry."

"I told you to."

"No excuse. And Valentine is a fucking pushover."

"And you're a fucking asshole." She sighed. "I'm sorry too."

He squinted at her as if trying to remember what she'd done. Finally, he shrugged. "No worries, Taylor. Let's just find the fucker who attacked you. Then we can both be pissed at them."

"Deal." She almost smiled then closed her eyes, trying to think. There had to be something. Why hadn't she heard anyone? "No one followed me running, and there was no car...until you. I don't know where they came from."

"There's a back road there, runs behind the lake houses. Anyone who saw you leave, and had a vague idea of where you were headed, could have pulled up there and waited in the woods until you ran by." He drew something out of his coat, a bottle barely bigger than his hand. Jack Daniels.

"They're going to throw you out, Petrosky."

"Can't throw me out. I'm the *law*." He unscrewed the top and put the bottle to his lips.

"How much have you had already?"

"Not enough."

"Morrison's going to kick your ass."

"Ohh, too bad Morrison's not here."

She looked down at her hands, the backs scraped and raw. All her thoughts felt fuzzy around the edges. "I know."

Petrosky rested the bottle in his lap. "What do you remember about the person who attacked you?"

Gloves. And a mask. And they were strong, but it might have just felt that way because they'd gotten her from behind. "They were on the shorter side, shorter than me."

"Could it have been Roger?"

She shook her head, and pain shot from the back of her skull down into her neck. "Roger's not short." Nausea rolled through her abdomen and upset the water sloshing around in her belly.

"You sure, Taylor? I could use something on him. I've been watching his bank accounts, his credit cards, his computers, for evidence of bribes. Nothing. You'd think after your outburst he'd have panicked, done something, but…"

She pushed herself up, straighter on the bed. "How do you know that, about his accounts, and his computers?"

"Morrison set up a tracking device on his computer before he got put away."

What? "That'll never be admissible, Petrosky. Even if you did find solid evidence, he'd get away with all of it. And Roger didn't do this to me."

His eyes darkened. "You didn't get a good look at his face."

Petrosky wanted it to be Roger as much as Roger wanted it to be Morrison. "I would know his hands."

"Maybe not if he never hit you before."

Roger almost had, the week before she left him. And she'd been just as ready to punch him back. "The person who grabbed me was short," she repeated, thinking. "About my height, because their chin was digging into my shoulder."

"Kimball's height?"

She stared at him. "Maybe."

"A few witnesses say Kimball's had a temper on him lately."

She pictured Kimball frothing at the mouth, how angry his eyes had been at the gym. But…it couldn't be him, could it? Internal Affairs would have found something. "If there was a real problem, they'd have suspended him by now."

"Not everyone notices real problems, Taylor. Look at Columbine."

"That's completely different," Shannon said. She pushed hair out of her face and winced as she brushed a tender spot near her temple.

Petrosky raised the bottle again and took a long swallow. "Maybe. Or maybe in both cases, we're talking about psychos. And power." He reached a file folder off the end table and set it on her lap. "Got these too. Interesting, I think."

Pain throbbed through her forehead and splintered down across her cheeks to her ears, but she blinked rapidly to force her eyes to focus on what he'd put in front of her. Papers. Photos. The first picture was of Kimball and his wife, her in a blue dress, Kimball smiling and dapper in a suit.

"Mrs. Amanda Kimball was a product of the system herself. Broken home, tossed from one foster home to another. The Kimballs even tried to adopt a few years back—guess they wanted to add a little boy to their clan. But it never happened, and they never had another one of her own." His voice was lower, gruffer. Maybe drunker. "Know what causes infertility, Taylor? Steroids. And they mess with your brain. Mania, depression, instability, aggression, impulsiveness—all things he's been tagged for in the last few months."

Infertility. The Kimballs had talked about it once at a dinner party. Later, Roger had said it was Amanda, but maybe he'd lied about that too. And Kimball had bulked up so quickly. Were they looking at roid rage?

Petrosky belched and wiped his mouth. "Derek Lewis wasn't known for selling steroids, but who knows? Maybe Kimball went to buy and, due to some overreaction to an argument, Lewis ended up dead. The rest was cover-up, trying to get rid of anyone else who knew anything that could lead back to him."

Was steroid use big enough to risk murdering someone over? It wasn't like Kimball was using cocaine—he probably wouldn't have even gone to jail. Might have lost the gym, but...

The bottle clanked against the arm of the chair as Petrosky shifted in the seat. "Found some interesting financial statements too. Seems Kimball's been hurting since he opened the gym—nearly forty thousand in the hole. Maybe he and Roger had some kind of agreement going on. They both could have been in on that plea deal thing."

This again? She fought a wave of dizziness. "Kimball wouldn't have known anything about the cases, would have had no contact with the families." Roger wouldn't have needed him.

"But his wife knew all about the cases—she would have been perfect to vet who might pay for a reduction in charges."

And Roger wouldn't have had to do anything but change the plea.

"Plus, the social work department works close with the rehab center —if they want Morrison to stay put away"—he took another drink—" they've got people who will say whatever it takes to keep out of jail themselves. Hell, half of them would give a false statement for one clean drug test."

Shannon flipped to the next photo, which showed Frieda Burke in a ball gown laughing at a grinning Kimball. Same tux. Same party. "Where'd you get these, Petrosky?"

"The photographer always takes some candids at the policeman's ball after he does the posed ones. For the website. 'Look at us! Cops are just like you!'" Petrosky's jazz hands were unnerving. He lowered them before she had to say anything.

"Social workers always go to these parties?" Her voice came out a half groan, and she immediately wanted to take the words back. She sounded weak.

"Nope. Not sure why Burke was there."

Pain sliced through her brain. She dropped the photos back into the file, put her hands to her head, and inhaled through her nostrils.

"You okay?" Petrosky leaned toward the bed, hands on his knees.

"I'm okay. A little...nauseous."

"A concussion will do that." Petrosky settled back into the chair and took another slug from the bottle. His eyes looked...worried, sad even, but that might have been a trick of her wavering vision. "Does Morrison know, Taylor?"

"Know what?" She put her hands at her sides, every movement painfully sharp.

"About the baby."

"I..." Dizziness unfocused her eyes. "Whose baby?"

"I didn't think so." He lifted the bottle again.

The room around Shannon pulsed, and nausea pulled at her, harder this time, her stomach slithering around, trying to creep up into her throat. *No. I can't be pregnant.* "I'm gonna be sick."

Petrosky reached from the end table and thrust a plastic kidney under her face. He held her hair as she vomited bile and the water she'd just sipped. When she was done, he handed her a towel and set the kidney back on the table, all nonchalant, like it wasn't full of puke.

"Water?"

"Not now." *The baby.* She stared at him. "I'm pregnant?"

"You didn't know?"

"No!" She watched him squint at her. *Is he fucking with me?* "How did you—"

"Read your chart, remember?" He raised the bottle again. "And listened in on the residents discussing your condition during shift change."

She put a hand on her stomach. *A baby.* A baby? What had she done? She wasn't ready for this, was she? "Is it...okay?"

"Yep. But it's real early. Probably wouldn't have shown on a home test for a couple weeks." Petrosky collapsed back into the chair. "Morrison's a good man, Taylor. You should tell him. He's not even pissed that you haven't been over there, just keeps asking if you're okay."

"I just found out, Petrosky. Give me a minute to process before we discuss who I need to tell." And it wasn't true anyway. Couldn't be. Could it? She tried to recall her last period, the date that she and

Morrison had... Shit. And he was in jail, accused of murder. She thought he was innocent, but that was no guarantee—Roger had held himself in check too, calm for years before the bullshit started. She couldn't risk being wrong again. She'd do this baby thing herself if she decided to do it at all.

"I don't need a good man."

"Enough with the feminist bullshit."

"Excuse me?"

Petrosky waved a hand in the air like he was waving away a bad smell. "I know, I know, you don't need him. He doesn't need you either. But you want each other. Not all of us tell our friends that we want them around. Morrison? Hell, he told me years ago he was going to marry you."

"Sounds like he only confides in you." *Instead of me.* The thought made her already sensitive stomach burble, but she couldn't tell if it was from the pain of hearing Morrison's secrets from someone else or the...*pregnancy*.

"You know he doesn't just say it out like that. He said you were his kind of awesome. Which seems like Surfer Boy speak for, 'I want to fuck her,' except that California has never said anything like that about anyone."

"Or maybe you're reading too much into it."

Petrosky appraised the bottle, picked at the label with a fingernail. "He doesn't trust that relationship shit, much, Taylor. Doesn't get involved easy." He met her gaze, eyes clear and focused and earnest. "But he'd marry you in a second."

Bile rose in her throat again, and she swallowed it back. "I'm never getting remarried," she spat. And if it turned out that Morrison really had... She couldn't finish the thought. Her limbs felt like they were sinking into the bed. "So, you've been to see him?"

Petrosky scowled at the wall like he wanted to shove his fist through it. "Once. Cook said I was on a list—he had to escort me back, and Morrison and I didn't really get to chat. Cook said Roger cited some Supreme Court bullshit about restricting non-family visitors for drug users, but I assume he mostly told them I'd be a troublemaker if they let us alone." The alcohol had thickened Petrosky's voice. "I don't necessarily disagree."

"Am I on the list?"

"Don't know. Probably. Roger's convinced that we're covering for Morrison. That Morrison's been buying drugs from Lewis for a long time. Roger'll probably be over at the detention center himself tomorrow, trying to convince Ashley Johnson to testify that it's true in exchange for her freedom. As it is, he probably won't be able to hold her much longer."

Ashley Johnson was going to go free. The weight on Shannon's chest grew heavier. She'd put Johnson in jail for a crime that she hadn't committed, and if Johnson was innocent, someone else was guilty. And Morrison was a druggie. Maybe he did do it. Maybe he'd been so high he didn't even remember doing it. Maybe this baby was doomed to be a totally emotionless psychotic freak too. But...no. Jesus, what was she thinking?

"I was going to write a strongly-worded letter to the warden, but now I think I'll just throw eggs at Roger's house. Maybe a Molotov cocktail." Petrosky pulled at the bottle. "I fucked up, Taylor. I'm sorry. I shouldn't have left." His words were definitely slurred.

"Lie down and rest, Petrosky. We've got a big day tomorrow."

He leaned back in the chair and stuck the half-empty bottle under his shirt. "I was afraid you'd say that."

30

They let her out the next morning, shaky and disoriented, but with a furious fire in her belly that wouldn't relent. Someone had tried to kill her. Someone had fucked with the wrong girl.

Petrosky appeared unfazed by his night in the rigid hospital chair or by the now empty bottle of whiskey hidden in the hospital trash. He dropped her at her house—her own house—and waited in the kitchen while she showered and dressed, eating leftover cookies from the wake. She tried to choke down a bite of chocolate chunk, but it stuck in her throat. What she wanted was chia-berry oatmeal.

Petrosky brushed crumbs from his shirt. "Morrison leave any of that mushroom coffee over here?"

"I don't think so." She could almost taste the coffee, almost smell it, almost smell…him. And it wasn't enough.

Petrosky was watching her like he knew exactly what she was thinking. "How you feeling, Taylor?"

"Tired. Weak." She shook her head to clear her thoughts and winced at the pain radiating from the back of her head down into her neck. *I need to go see Morrison.* "I thought… Can you drive me to the detention center? I should go, you know? Talk to Morrison."

Petrosky glanced at her stomach.

"Not about that. About the case." But guilt tingled in the back of her brain. *You can't tell him, Shannon. Not until you decide what you want to do about it. About…her. Or him.* "Maybe I'll visit Ashley Johnson, too. See if Roger got to her yet."

"California's had a lot of time to think. Maybe he came up with something." Petrosky wiped chocolate from his lips with the back of his hand. "I'll drive you to the detention center and wait outside."

Shannon grabbed her jacket. "You don't need to go with me."

"I know. But need is a funny thing, Taylor." He opened her front door, and chill air stung her face. "Lots of shit you don't need to do," he said to the driveway. "But you do it anyway."

AT THE DETENTION CENTER, Cook gave her a sideways look but admitted her into the holding area and stepped back to the entrance with a whispered, "Sorry, Shannon." She ignored him and headed for the stalls, for the mesh, for her best friend.

She gasped when she saw Morrison. He looked ten pounds lighter, shrunken as if the cell walls had sucked the meat from his bones. Stubble crawled along his jawline, ragged and angry.

"Hey," he said. The word hung in the air between them, burgeoning with the possibility of things that needed to be said but couldn't be, not right then. Or maybe ever. If he was guilty, if she decided to get rid of the baby... She cleared her throat. "We need to get you out of here."

"Give it time. They'll figure it out." His eyes were bloodshot, but his shoulders stayed square.

She gripped the ledge so hard her fingers ached. "Roger doesn't want to figure it out. He wants to lock you up forever."

"I'd imagine so." The corner of his mouth turned up, and her heart quickened. *Not normal.* Not a normal response at all and his eyes weren't as downcast as she'd thought they would be. He looked almost... *What the fuck?* Did he want to be here? Did he really not care? But he did, she knew he cared. Just as she knew she wanted to curl up in his arms and shut out the world. The worst fucking week of her life and she had needed him to be there. Wanted him to hold her and tell her things were going to be okay—even if they weren't.

"I'm sorry about Derry," he said. "I hate that I wasn't there, Shanny."

"Me too." Heartache blistered her insides. *The case; focus on the case.* "Morrison, someone at the rehab center is telling Roger that you... coerced them into doing things they didn't want to do."

They stared at one another through the mesh, his breathing harsh but even, hers shallow so she didn't puke again.

"I've never taken advantage of anyone. I've put a lot of people away, though, so..." He shrugged. Same thing Petrosky had said, almost as if Petrosky had coached him. One addict enabling another? And if that were true, what did that make her? After all, she was in love with a druggie. Maybe a psycho.

But she was in love, and when he met her eyes, she didn't doubt her feelings. She needed help. A therapist. She put a hand on her stomach. Love wasn't enough to justify rash, life-altering decisions. She had a month to make up her mind, maybe two, but she couldn't wait that long to decide—the thought of dragging everything out made the throbbing in her head begin anew.

Talk, Shannon, say something. "Had any epiphanies while you've been in here?" Her voice was strained, and she cleared her throat instead of dwelling on why that was.

"More just...wonderings. Wonderings that I can't do anything about." He leaned toward the mesh. "Months before Lewis's death, Wheatley was doing Google searches on drugs, on charges for drug crimes, probably trying to ascertain how bad things would be for the person he saw at Lewis's apartment. Eventually, Wheatley must have talked to Lewis about what he'd seen, maybe even warned him against dealing. But our killer saw Wheatley leaving, or else Lewis mentioned Wheatley to the killer. Then panic, and goodbye, Derek."

Other than the Google searches, it was nothing she didn't already know. But there was still something that didn't make sense about any of these alternative killer scenarios. How had she not seen it before? Maybe she hadn't wanted to. "But Johnson didn't just wander in, say, 'Oh look, he's dead,' and go attempt suicide in the bathtub. Framing someone like that requires premeditation."

"I don't think the killer intended to frame her. I think he planned to kill her too. She might even have been the target."

"You think Ashley and not Derek was the... That doesn't make sense, Morrison."

"Just hear me out, okay?" His voice was strained, pressured, any hint of his earlier smile extinguished. "If Lewis was the target, the killer was probably someone who'd been to the house before—someone Ashley knew. She'd have been able to pick him out. Maybe the killer snuck up and stuck her in the neck, then carried her to the bathroom, not to frame her, but to kill her to make sure any traces of himself were gone. Then, later on, he realized the scene looked like Ashley could have done it and called it in from the pay phone, thinking she'd be dead by the time anyone got there."

The coffee Shannon had forced down in the car, bubbled up in her esophagus. It was a stretch and a big one at that. "Why not just wait? If he wanted her to die, why risk calling and saving her life?"

"Maybe he was worried about the baby."

The baby. Her heart shuddered, and she inhaled sharply through her nose, then forced out the air along with any lingering thoughts about her situation. "Morrison, this guy murders two people in cold blood and has a soft spot for their child?"

Morrison scratched at his stubble. "So let's pretend Ashley Johnson was the target. That Lewis and Wheatley died because they saw someone with *her*. What if that someone was Kimball?"

They had just cleared Kimball...again. Shannon shook her head. "I don't follow."

"I mean...you know he's a little flirty. But I think he had other women on the side."

Wow, Morrison's a regular rocket scientist. She couldn't decide why she was so angry at him, but she could feel the rage sizzling in her belly, mingling with the coffee, trying to escape.

"Specifically, I think Kimball had Ashley Johnson on the side."

The rage mellowed to agitated curiosity. He knew better. Unless he was trying to throw her off on purpose. Or...maybe, he was right. But he sure as hell needed more than just a gut feeling. "Kimball wasn't screwing Johnson in the apartment she shared with her boyfriend, Morrison. Derek Lewis hardly ever left the house because of his business, and when he did, he had friends in the apartment complex who would surely have noticed a guy like Kimball sauntering in there to keep Ashley company. We'd have more bodies if he was covering that up."

In another row, someone coughed, maybe Cook, and she jerked toward the sound and back to the mesh. Morrison looked like he wanted to say more.

"Time's up," Cook called through the room, but he sounded apologetic.

Morrison's gaze locked with hers, and the corner of his eye twitched. There was more, another secret he wasn't telling her. "Morrison?"

He peered past her and into the hall behind her.

"Morrison, what?"

He leaned so close his face almost touched the mesh. "There were some strange cash withdrawals," he whispered, and his scent was unfamiliar, no coffee, no oats, no lavender, just the harsh tang of mint and laundry soap. "From Kimball's bank accounts. Stopped the week Johnson went away."

That's it? She shook her head. "Those withdrawals could have been for anything. There's no way to trace that, Morrison."

"There is. Because when Ashley Johnson had funds, she called Petrosky. He didn't connect it, but I recalled a few of the dates on the month prior. Dates we picked her up and dropped her at the bank. Or days she asked to stay at Petrosky's house, saying she was scared. Maybe she was just scared Lewis would find the money and take it."

But the cash flow wasn't a definite connection, and it certainly wouldn't pass the standard of reasonable doubt. Plus, it was all inadmissible. There was no way he'd gotten a warrant to look at Kimball's stuff, which meant... "You hacked into Kimball's accounts, didn't you?" Shannon watched as he nodded, almost imperceptibly. Hacking into the bank's server was illegal. *And impressively tricky.* But still illegal. "Petrosky doesn't know this yet?" He'd probably jump right on board with this crazy theory.

Morrison shook his head. "I got put away before I could tell him. And I didn't really connect it in my head until this morning, sitting here alone."

Alone. Her gut clenched.

"And I know Kimball wasn't giving Johnson money for drugs. It was hundreds of dollars at a time, always the same amount, like a payoff. Not even close to a junkie's pattern."

He'd know about a junkie's pattern, right? She pushed the thought aside. If Kimball was paying Johnson for something, and that was a big if, Derek and Wheatley could have found out. Then Kimball would have had motive to kill both of them. But still not the opportunity if he was at the policeman's ball. Not that he couldn't have snuck out for half an hour, especially if someone else—their mystery heroin-addict-hair-donor—was watching Wheatley for him.

"Kimball's a cheat," Morrison said. "But he's charismatic. I think Johnson fell for him. I think Diamond's his."

She sucked in a breath, and the dry air burned the inside of her nose. That would explain the call to the precinct to make sure the baby was taken care of. "But even a narcissistic asshole like Kimball is too smart to leave a note on my car." Though he'd certainly have been able to—he worked right there at the precinct so no one would think it strange for him to be in the lot with an envelope. "Even if you're right, he could have made Wheatley look like an accident, let Johnson rot. Why on earth would he have thrown doubt that we had the right person by leaving that envelope?" It was illogical. Morrison was losing his shit.

Morrison slapped his hands onto either side of his head, peering through the mesh, his eyes darting around like a caged animal. "I just can't think. I can't get my head around all this. I…"

Shannon's stomach turned, watching his face contort as if, inside him, something was coming unhinged.

The first set of bulletproof doors buzzed closed behind her, and with everything silenced, the world felt stiff and unwieldy, the pressure of the mere air humming in her ears as loudly as if someone were screaming.

If Morrison was right…could Kimball really be Diamond's father? And who else knew about it that might need protection? Perez had moved out of the building—so maybe she'd been frightened of Kimball too. But no…she'd met them in broad daylight in front of her building. And Perez would have mentioned a secret like the paternity of Ashley's baby. She wanted to get Ashley out of jail. No, any bribes from Kimball, any information about Diamond's father, Johnson had kept to herself.

The door in front of her opened. She walked into the next chamber and waited. *Whoosh.* She was trapped between the walls of bulletproof glass, trapped inside her head. And no matter how insane Morrison's ideas were, he had been right about Ashley Johnson from the beginning. She owed it to him to look. And she owed it to herself—if there was any truth to this theory, she could get Morrison out of there. And home. With her.

At the front desk, Shannon headed to the bulletproof window, where Cook was already seated. He shrugged at her. "Sorry, Taylor."

"No worries." She lowered her voice. "Can I see the list of people who have been in to see Ashley Johnson since her arrest?"

"Aw, hell, Taylor, you know I'm not supposed to give you that."

"What? Why? I've taken those before."

"I wasn't even supposed to let you back, but I figured it couldn't hurt. But this isn't your case, and from what I understand, Internal Affairs wants all you guys separated while they investigate."

All of them separated? "Who told you that?"

"Roger."

"Fuck Roger."

His caterpillar brows lifted into his thinning hairline.

Shannon leaned toward the window. "You think Morrison's a murderer, Cook?"

His face fell. He shook his head.

"Help me out. I won't say a word. Maybe you can just happen to leave it on the desk for a minute." Like they were in some cheesy murder mystery.

"You know, I am due for a bathroom break," he said slowly and disappeared into a back room. Shannon paced and stared out the front window into the gray drizzle, half expecting Petrosky to be standing outside smoking a soggy cigarette. She was a little disappointed that he wasn't, but she had little time to ponder that; a door closed, Cook's footsteps receded, and she stepped to the window and peered down at the piece of paper left on the desk.

The visitor list for Ashley Johnson was short. Her. Petrosky. Burke.

And Park Kimball.

She waited, pacing, until Cook returned. "I need to see one more person," she said.

Cook nodded. "I thought you might."

31

Ashley Johnson had stared. She'd cried. She'd avoided the questions about Kimball. But in the end, Shannon had blown up and told Ashley they were going public with Kimball's bank records and that the money Kimball had given her would be seized. That had done it.

Kimball and Johnson had met innocuously enough, at a bar. One broken condom later, and they both had a secret to keep. Kimball had offered Johnson an allowance, four hundred, paid every other week, but told her it would end if she opened her mouth about Diamond. The night Derek died, Johnson met Kimball at a hotel to pick up the money. The pocketful of cash was one reason she'd snuck past Derek that night, hoping he'd stay asleep until the morning when she could get to the bank before he discovered her secret.

Shannon didn't tell Ashley that Kimball had more to lose. She didn't mention that child support was a legal obligation once paternity was verified. She left the detention center, head pounding, and ran for Petrosky's car.

It wasn't Kimball who had attacked her last night: Petrosky had already verified his alibi, and he was too strong for her to fight off anyway. But someone had attacked her. Someone who might be concerned about their progress on the case. Someone who would have wanted to punish Ashley Johnson.

Amanda Kimball smiled at Shannon—self-assured, almost haughty—a far cry from the awkward guilt of the other day. But the look she gave Petrosky was the same as before. He could have been an insect she wanted to smash under her heel. "Back again?" she asked, eyes on her computer screen.

Shannon peered at Amanda's throat, but little was visible behind the collar of her sweater. Had she worn her hair down the last time they'd seen her? Or ever? Maybe she was hiding a bruise from Shannon's elbow beneath her waves.

"Just following up on a few things about your former employee," Petrosky said.

Amanda raised an eyebrow. "Mm-hmm. I actually thought you guys had been removed from that case." Half smile. Definitely haughty. *Smug bitch.*

Petrosky didn't appear to have heard her. "We're looking into the Johnson case too."

Amanda chewed the inside of her cheek, probably torn between telling them to leave and the desire to find out what they knew. Surely her husband had told her that Shannon and Petrosky had been booted off Johnson as well.

Amanda sighed. "What can I do for you?"

Never underestimate curiosity. Unless she was trying to figure out whether to leave the country.

"Mrs. Kimball, I'm having a little trouble remembering...can you tell us again where you were on the evening of February fifteenth?"

Amanda cocked her head. "I'm sorry?"

"We're just trying to figure out if any workers in the area might have seen something that would help us. I gotta admit, this case is a doozy." He ran a hand over his forehead, and Shannon squinted at him. "Makes me feel like a real idiot," he said and cut his eyes at Shannon until she turned away.

The hard lines around Amanda's mouth softened. Less anxious now. "Sounds like you're reaching, but I'm not sure I can help. You already have my statement about that day."

"Maybe you can tell me again. Who from your office was scheduled to be in the area around Derek Lewis's apartment that evening?"

Amanda paused, her shoulders tense again, and she pulled her keyboard closer to her and resumed tapping. "We've been over this. I visited a family on Vista Marie about four. Frieda was three streets up, with a family on Dover at five-thirty, but she would have been there at least an hour or so. And Wheatley was scheduled to see someone up the road on Henrietta at three-thirty, but I don't have anything for him after that." She pushed the keyboard aside. "That all?"

Petrosky splayed his fingers on the desk. "And where did you go after your appointment?"

Her expression hardened. "Not sure what you're getting at with that question. I'd feel better if I talked to my husband about this."

"Why, does he know where you were the night Derek Lewis gasped his final breath?"

Amanda's jaw dropped.

"Does he know where you were last night? Funny, he has an alibi with the department, but no one seems to know where you were."

"What's this all—"

"It's a little warm in here, isn't it?" Petrosky nodded to Amanda's arms, thoroughly encased in navy cotton. "Can you roll up your sleeves, Mrs. Kimball?"

The hard line of her mouth whitened as she pressed her lips together. She crossed her arms. "Please leave."

Petrosky touched Amanda's elbow, and she glowered at him but didn't move. "Where were you last night, Mrs. Kimball?"

"At home. Not that it's any of your business."

"Anyone else there?"

"No, just me." She jerked her arm away.

Petrosky's eyes darted around the room. "Where's your coat, Ms. Kimball?" *The coat.* If they could match the fibers from under Shannon's nails—

Amanda reached for her phone, touching buttons rapid-fire.

Petrosky smiled. "You calling your husband? Make sure you ask him what he was really doing on the nights he was supposedly picking up your daughter from her nonexistent ballet practices. Maybe getting into drugs? Or maybe he was busy screwing someone else? Before he got her tossed in jail, maybe he was hanging out with his baby's mother and their year-old daughter?"

Amanda's fingers froze over the buttons.

"You can't possibly tell me you didn't know." Petrosky leaned his bulldog face over the desk. "You never wondered where all that money was going?"

Amanda dropped the phone and shot to her feet, her hands planted on the desk as if she needed the furniture to bear the weight of her rage. Her lips pulled into a snarl like a rabid dog. But Shannon was not looking at the curl of her lip—her eyes were trained on the gap in Amanda's sweater, now hanging slightly open. No bruise on her neck. Nothing on her upper chest. Even if Shannon hadn't broken Amanda's clavicle, there would be a mark.

"Get out," Amanda hissed.

"Touchy, touchy." Petrosky backed toward the door. "We'll be back, Mrs. Kimball."

Petrosky slammed Amanda's office door behind them, the sound reverberating through the hallway like growling thunder. In the back of Shannon's brain, something snapped, the sound of the rolling hall morphing into the pop she had felt under her elbow, and suddenly she could smell the lake air and the spicy stink of the person who had their fingers around her throat. Shannon's head throbbed dully. *I have to get out of here.* She didn't realize Petrosky's hand was on her elbow until his fingers tightened.

"Wait," he said.

The door to Frieda Burke's office opened, and Burke hurried into the hall, turning toward Amanda's office. She stopped short when she saw them. Shannon's heart thundered in her ears like the slamming door had moments before.

"She came running fast, didn't she?" Petrosky muttered. He advanced on Burke, and she backed toward her office, snagging her heel on the carpet. He caught her by the arm of her turtleneck sweater before she could fall.

"Everything okay, Ms. Burke?"

She righted herself and leaned against the doorframe. "I heard the door. I thought maybe Amanda had an unruly client." Burke scanned the hallway, avoiding Petrosky's icy glare. Avoiding Shannon too. "I was just...surprised because I didn't know she had anyone coming in."

"You always keep tabs on her?" Petrosky asked.

"I... Not really. I don't know."

Petrosky cocked his head at her, his eyes roving over her sleeved arms. "What happened to your wrist?"

Burke shrugged. "Nothing."

"Looked like it hurt to touch. You winced pretty good there," he said wryly.

She shook her head. "No, just surprised. You grabbed me hard."

Burke was small. Thin. What did her clavicle look like? Adrenaline thrummed through Shannon's bloodstream. She trained her eyes on Burke, who was still frozen against the doorframe and staring at Petrosky with unconcealed hatred. Petrosky gave it back. Burke had been involved, in some capacity, with every person who had been murdered. She was Lewis and Johnson's caseworker. Wheatley's coworker. And Lucky...well, she had a history of hating Shannon, and she'd been living with Griffen after Abby's birth. Burke would have known where to hit to scare Shannon. But why?

Petrosky stared at Burke as she pushed past them, curls bobbing in time with her steps as she approached Amanda's door. Shannon stared after her, trying to ignore the rage blistering her abdomen. *Something isn't right.* Whoever was after Shannon had hurt Lucky. Whoever had hurt Lucky—*It was me*—had hurt others. Lewis. Wheatley. She could hate Burke all she wanted, but the woman wasn't a killer. Burke had no motive.

But Park and Amanda Kimball, they had motive for killing Ashley Johnson and Derek Lewis too, if they thought he knew about Diamond's paternity. Ditto on Benjamin Wheatley. And Lucky's murder, Shannon's attack, everything had to be connected. It wasn't coincidental—couldn't be.

"Feisty, isn't she?" Petrosky said as they walked down the hall and out the front doors to the parking lot. "Wonder what's under her sweater."

Outside, the air was muddy with tension and an impending storm. Shannon followed Petrosky to the car, massaging her aching neck. "If anyone but you had said that, Petrosky, I would have thought it was a come on."

He didn't smile. Derry would have smiled. She suddenly missed her brother so terribly it felt like the world was collapsing around her. She could almost hear his voice in the deep gray sky above, but there was no hint of her brother's warmth, only streaks of a deeper black, a storm ready to unleash hell on earth. Someone needed to pay. For killing Derek Lewis. For murdering Lucky. For the fact that Derry had died without knowing his daughter was safe. For everything.

But...there was more, she knew it. There was something she was missing. Something she'd been told.

"Mrs. Kimball seemed a little shocked to hear about her husband's love child, didn't she?" Petrosky said, too quietly, like he was trying to avoid waking a child in the backseat.

Amanda had seemed surprised. Shocked, even. Either she really hadn't known her husband was cheating or she was a damn good liar. "I'm not buying Amanda Kimball as a killer. She had no marks on her, and I hit my attacker pretty hard...or I thought I did."

"We still have our mystery person. With the prints and the hair. Maybe they hired out."

She rubbed her still smarting head, thoughts solidifying at the pressure on her temples. "Wait." She put a hand on Petrosky's arm. "Burke lied to me. To us."

Petrosky raised an eyebrow, but he stopped. "About what?"

"The first time I spoke to Ashley Johnson after the trial, she told me she didn't say anything to Burke about the other social worker being there. But Lucinda Lewis said that Burke knew about it, mentioned it. And last time we met with Burke, she herself admitted to knowing another worker had been there." At the time, it hadn't seemed like much, a misunderstanding. But now...it might be something.

Petrosky pulled a cigarette from his pack, looked at Shannon's still-flat belly, and replaced it in his pocket.

"How'd she know, Petrosky? How'd she know about the other worker? It wasn't in the file, or I would have known. The police didn't know. Even Griffen, Johnson's own defense attorney, didn't know another social worker had been to Lewis's apartment that day."

"Good enough for me." Petrosky cut his eyes at the building behind them and turned toward the car. "Can I drop you at home?"

Her head throbbed, and every step she took felt like slogging through quicksand. But nothing waited for her at home except utter silence and her dead brother's picture on the mantel, reminding her that things had once been happy. "I'm coming with you." *For Derry.* For Morrison. She put a hand on her stomach. *For all of us.*

"Suit yourself."

A whoosh of dank spring air still laced with the chill of winter kicked up around Shannon's feet, and she shivered involuntarily. "Where are we going?"

"We'll check out Burke's place." He unlocked the car and climbed inside as Shannon scrambled into the passenger seat. "We'll get Roxy too. In case."

In case Burke's a fucking psycho? Shannon squinted out the windshield. Could Burke have been as jealous of Ashley Johnson as she had been of Shannon, everyone having babies when she couldn't? That would mean Wheatley and Lewis were just collateral damage, which made no sense. Shannon turned to Petrosky, examined the set of his jaw, the twitch in his temple that screamed determination—or wrath.

"We getting a warrant?" she asked. They didn't have enough for a warrant. And they couldn't just go through her stuff. Above, the clouds loomed lower, and the air thickened with soggy humidity.

"I don't need it to be admissible." Petrosky started the car and pulled out of the lot. "I just need to know."

SHANNON LEANED her head against the seat back and watched the sky through the car windshield. The headache she'd been fighting all morning clawed at her brain. *If the rain starts before we get inside, we're fucked—she'll know we were there. We shouldn't be doing this at all.* "Are you sure this is a good idea?"

Petrosky's fingers beat a frantic rhythm against the console. "I never said it was a good idea. But we need more than what we've got right now." He popped his neck and turned into a neighborhood near the gym full of cookie-cutter houses and the occasional tire swing.

She gestured behind her, where Roxy was panting out the back window. "I'm still not sold on bringing her."

"Roxy's a good girl, aren't you Roxy?" *Tick tick tick*, fingers on leather. From the backseat, Roxy yipped.

Shannon raised an eyebrow, and a sharp pain shot into her forehead. "Good girl, my ass. You know she used to be a police dog. You want her to search." *Tick tick tick.* "But you know we need a warrant, and if she ruins something—"

"She won't ruin anything. We need to see if there's anything worthwhile to find first. If we need to, we'll figure out probable cause after." *Tick tick tick tick.*

"Not the way it's supposed to work, Petrosky."

"Sue me, Taylor."

Eventually, someone will. She straightened and put her hand over his vibrating fingers to still the racket before her head exploded. "What's up with you, Petrosky?"

Roxy put her bull head over the console and licked Shannon's arm.

Petrosky shrugged and put his hand back on the steering wheel, muscles still taut with nervous energy. If Petrosky was this jittery, he had a reason to be. And it wasn't about the search—he did stuff like this all the time. Did he know something she didn't? Her hand tensed over Roxy's head, and the dog's ears pricked forward. They were there.

Burke's house was a red brick colonial, complete with picket fence and hyacinths in the garden just barely shooting green sprouts through the dirt, electric in the gloom. Two, maybe three blocks from the gym. Walking distance. Petrosky parked four houses up.

Shannon hesitated with her hand on the door handle. She wanted to tell Petrosky yet again that they needed to get out of there, that they should get a warrant, that getting arrested themselves wouldn't help Morrison. But doing things the right way hadn't helped them at all so far. They were dealing with someone who had framed the man she... loved. *Loved.* She cleared her throat. "You really think Burke's involved?"

"She knows all the victims. And she's got quite a vendetta against people who hurt kids. Spends her life trying to make things better, right? It's gotta be frustrating."

True. Burke had also— "And you know what? She fostered Diamond too. Maybe she has a vested interest in punishing anyone who injured that little girl—Derek for hitting her; Ashley for not protecting her." Shannon relaxed her grip on the door, but the rigidity in her arm remained. "But why would Wheatley have been scoping the place out for months before Derek's murder? It can't just be unconnected." Unless... Burke was one of Derek's customers. Beat Wheatley to make sure he hadn't told anyone. And Burke could easily have taken Amanda Kimball's gym keys, though there was no way in hell Burke dragged Wheatley into the warehouse by herself.

"We'll find out more soon enough." He held up two silver keys and a gold one, all dangling from a keychain that read "Hug a Social Worker."

"Where did you—"

"I took them out of her pocket when she rammed into me."

"You mean when you grabbed her."

"Whatever." He shrugged. "Now come on, Taylor, I need a smoke." He popped open the car door and nodded to Roxy, who leapt from the backseat and onto the sidewalk.

Since when doesn't he smoke in his car? No wonder he'd been jittery on the way over.

"You coming, Taylor?" he said, smoke already thick around his face. "You can always stay here, claim innocence, if you don't want to get your hands dirty."

Fuck that. She followed him around the car as he started up the walk, scanning the neighborhood and flicking the ash from his cigarette on the muddy spring lawns as they passed. But there was not a soul to interrupt the subtle melody of still-bare branches rustling in the breeze. Any other time, the rustling might have been calming, mere white noise, but today, the hushed rippling sounded crass, almost dangerous, the whisper of a nightmare you couldn't shake. Roxy turned her face to the sky as if she too could feel the unsettled hum of the very air they breathed.

They turned up Burke's driveway and headed through the gate and around to the back. The back door opened into a blue and yellow kitchen straight out of a fifties home decor magazine. They'd barely stepped inside when Petrosky patted the dog on the head. Roxy's nostrils quivered.

"Seek, Roxy," Petrosky said.

Roxy took off, her nose at the cupboards, along the baseboards, poking into the next room. Petrosky opened the kitchen drawers, peered inside, and closed them again.

"What are you looking for?"

"Anything unusual. Maybe a bloody glove. It didn't help convict OJ, but..." He left the kitchen and strode into a cozy living room with traditional furniture—heavy wood. The air was thick with the smell of cinnamon, just like at the office. Shannon's stomach roiled. Spicy. Sweet. Potpourri? Was that what she'd smelled on her attacker?

Petrosky peered at the fireplace mantel. "Lots of pictures of her and Amanda."

On the mantel? That was prime real estate, not the place you'd expect to see a shrine to someone's coworker.

Shannon joined him at the photos. In the first one, Amanda and Burke were holding hands on a beach...or rather, Burke was holding onto Amanda's wrist, eyes on her friend, while Amanda smiled into the camera clutching some fruity drink. On either side of the vacation picture were more photos: Amanda and Burke at a fundraiser, Amanda with a child Shannon didn't recognize. In some of them, Amanda's face was turned away from the lens. Had she known those photos were being snapped?

"Wonder if we have a single white female situation. An obsession with Amanda and Burke's screwing Kimball on the side? We already know he's a cad who will fuck anything that moves."

"A...cad?"

"Trying to watch my mouth."

Shannon narrowed her eyes at him, then turned her attention back to the mantel. "Burke does seem awfully protective of Amanda. Maybe she found out that Kimball was Diamond's father and decided to get rid of the evidence before Amanda found out. Took out Lewis and tried to take out Johnson. Then Wheatley for knowing about it." Shannon shook her head. "But Burke couldn't hurt the baby, so she made that midnight call to the station to make sure someone took care of Diamond." Shannon peered at another photo on a nearby built-in bookcase: Amanda and Burke at some marathon, numbers pinned to their shirts, faces pink and shiny with a post-race glow. Again, Burke ignored the camera in favor of looking at Amanda.

Petrosky snorted from the desk and held up a torn photo of Burke sitting on a boulder. At some point, there had been someone else in the picture, but now all that was left of them was half a severed arm, two orange bracelets on their wrist. Burke held the bracelet-clad hand with her own. "Looks like trouble in paradise."

Disquiet settled in Shannon's bones. "That's—I think that's Griffen's hand. The bands. On his wrist."

Petrosky cocked an eyebrow. But the torn picture wasn't really that unexpected—Griffen and Burke had gone through a dramatic breakup. Although...why would anyone keep half a photo? Why not just throw the whole thing away?

They combed through Burke's bedroom and the spare and found nothing unusual. Shannon headed to the bathroom to peek through the medicine cabinet—a few pain relievers, Q-tips, cotton balls, makeup. Normal. *What did I expect, a severed limb?* Shannon was rummaging through a cabinet drawer when Petrosky called her from the office, and she went to meet him.

"These pictures of Griffen too?" He turned a computer monitor her way and scrolled. "Can't see his face."

A dozen shots of Griffen and Karen: Karen on her own, here standing in a garden, there walking into an aluminum-sided colonial. Griffen coming out of his office, getting into his car, going to the grocery. Facing away from the camera in every picture. Burke couldn't very well snap them with Griffen or Karen looking at her—it was clear the couple didn't know the photos were being taken. "Yeah, that's Griffen. I recognize his hat. And Karen."

"Creepy."

"Yeah."

"Where's Griffen live, Taylor?"

"Used to have a place a few blocks up. Close to work so he could ride his bike. I think he lived here with Burke for a little while, but I'm not really sure when he moved out."

Roxy's howl split the silence and pain splintered the back of Shannon's skull. Petrosky was through the living room and gone before she could swallow back the grossness creeping up her throat. She followed his staccato footsteps into a small but tidy mudroom, where Roxy sat rigid in front of a door, barking—thin and high and acute.

Petrosky yanked the knob. Just outside the door, a chest freezer hummed like the monotonous drone of sitting monks. But like the twittering leaves, there was nothing calming or meditative about it—Shannon's brain buzzed with pain and the harsh sound of Roxy's toenails scraping the cement as the dog skidded to a halt and sat, nose against the mat by the door that led to the outside.

Petrosky patted Roxy on the head. "Good girl, Roxy. Off." He peered at the mat. Shannon approached, stepping lightly to avoid jarring her already throbbing skull. Goddamn concussion. Unless that was the... baby. But no, it was too early for symptoms. She pushed her thoughts aside and squinted at the dark stains littering the mat. Looked like dirt. Or...

Petrosky put his thumb next to a tiny brown drip smeared into the grime.

"Blood?"

"Maybe." He snapped on a pair of latex gloves and pulled a vial from his jacket.

Shannon stepped back and hit her elbow on the wall as Roxy whined. Petrosky scraped some of the stain into the tube with an enclosed plastic scraper and dropped it into his coat pocket. Then he walked to the window, squinted at the pane, and hoisted the window open. The shrill screech of an alarm split the air.

"Petrosky, what the—"

"I was out walking the dog, Shannon. And Roxy just couldn't wait to get in here, with this window being open and all..."

"You're going to get arrested." The alarm. *Shit.* She pressed her fingers to her temple.

"Nah. Might not be admissible, might get sued, but..." He headed for the front door. "I'll finish up here and make some calls to find your buddy Griffen and his new girlfriend. Make sure they're okay. You go back to the car and wait for Valentine. You're pale as hell."

Shannon wanted to fight him on it, to stay there to see what happened. God knows she would have, but the dizziness rolling over her soured her stomach and pulled the room out of focus. "I'll wait across the street. Tell him to hurry."

Valentine drove Shannon home while Petrosky headed back to the station. Her head was pounding so violently that she had a hard time responding to Valentine's questions, and eventually, he gave up, leaving her to her pain and her thoughts. *Illegal search and seizure.* Petrosky was an idiot. Nothing they'd found would be admissible. Though maybe he was looking for something bigger—probably figured he'd get a confession. For Morrison's sake, she hoped he was right.

The nausea had crept up and stuck. She had thrown up twice on her way across the road, and again as Valentine pulled up. Her head throbbed more forcibly every time she retched. But even now, with her stomach empty and Valentine silent beside her, Shannon's brain ran wild. So many questions, so few answers. Revelations struggling toward realization but collapsing, frustratingly flat, before coming to fruition. Every pulse of pain from the lump on her head brought a new, disturbing idea. Yet each grisly scenario was preferable to the thought that Morrison was a murderer.

Shannon could see Burke going after Lewis and Johnson for hurting Diamond. She could see her going after them for Amanda's sake, too, regardless of whether Amanda had known about the affair before. Either way, Wheatley had been in the wrong place at the wrong time. And either way, whoever was after Shannon knew where to hit her to make it hurt—and they had.

But not everything fit. The note on her car was a broken spoke, jamming the cogwheel of every theory she produced. *It was me.* Would Burke have wanted to get caught, or wanted the credit? She didn't strike Shannon that way. Burke was insecure, needy even, if her response to Shannon's friendship with Griffen was any indication. Obsessive. But if Burke was that unhinged, why hadn't she attacked Karen? Brutal enough to kill to hide a secret for her best friend, or to protect a child, but she didn't go after the girlfriend of the dude she's obsessed with? And if Burke was obsessed with Amanda, she'd have gone after Kimball, right? It didn't add up. Then there was the car. As a social worker, Burke would have had no access to the police car Perez had seen outside Lewis's apartment—nor would Perez have mistaken Burke for the man she'd seen. Maybe Burke had a new boyfriend who'd helped her move Wheatley's body. That would explain their hair donor, and also why Burke might have left Karen alone. But there was no evidence of a boyfriend at Burke's house. So who had helped her, and why?

Valentine parked in her driveway, cut the engine, and took an enormous bite of the donut he held in wax paper. Morrison would have frowned and offered her a parfait or a granola bar or some coffee. *Mushroom coffee.* The thought made her heart hurt. As she approached the house, the rustling tree branches sighed a mournful ballad of grief and loss and sorrow. Somewhere above, a bird screamed. It sounded like the animal was crying.

She paced the silent hallways of her house, trying not to collapse. Everything felt empty. Cold. Lonely. As hollow as her chest. She tried to find solace in her office, but Derry's photo smiled at her, and she didn't deserve that grin—she hadn't been able to figure this case out, the one thing Derry had asked her for. And Morrison was still locked up, taken from her because she couldn't prove he was innocent. Karma for falsely imprisoning Ashley Johnson, maybe. Or for not being able to…save her brother.

The grief crashed over her like a ton of stone. They were closing in on their killer. Derry would have been so proud. But Derry wasn't here to tell. Even Alex and Abby were gone, off to his mother's in Georgia.

She was alone. Utterly alone.

She headed for the bedroom, but the bed loomed silent and huge, and she could almost smell Morrison's skin—lavender and musk and salt. *Almost.* She grabbed one of Derry's T-shirts she had brought from Alex's house and slipped into it on her way across the hall to Abby's room. The unicorn poster on the wall stared down at her, its horn more deadly than mythical. She lay down on the bed and buried her face in the comforter, curled up among Abby's pillows, and slept. She dreamed of a smiling Frieda Burke, half of someone else's arm wrapped around her body, sitting on a rock that looked suspiciously like Lucky's severed head.

32

Petrosky was sitting at Shannon's dining table when she awoke an hour and a half later. She raised an eyebrow but found she didn't give a flying fuck about the fact that he'd walked in and made himself at home. He passed her a cup of coffee. She sipped it, willing the pain in her head to subside. At least the nausea had passed.

"You get ahold of Griffen?" she asked.

He watched her with that bitchy-but-concerned look on his face. "Not yet. He's not at the office. No answer at home either."

Dammit. Couldn't just one thing go smoothly? And where was he? She felt like she was on the verge of understanding, but there was some bit of information a touch beyond her reach. Maybe it was just leftovers from her dreams. Or from her life. "You try his cell?"

"I was looking Karen's up when the chief told me to go the fuck home before Detective Young—the dickwad who's supposed to be handling the Wheatley case—beat my ass. I figured I might as well listen, stay on her good side."

"You care about being on the chief's good side?"

"I do if it makes it easier to get Surfer Boy out."

"Yeah, right." She stared at the coffee cup, wishing it was Morrison's stainless steel mug.

"Shannon?" His voice was soft, concerned.

She swallowed hard. There was a twinge in her stomach, and it wasn't the baby or the caffeine or the concussion. It was deeper, murkier, some abstract thing hiding in her gut waiting to burst free.

"You okay?"

"Yeah, I just… I feel like we should know the answers here."

"You and me both." Petrosky pulled out his cell. "I guess I can shoot

Griffen an email so he'll get it whenever he shows up at work...or home." He grimaced. "I fucking hate email, but we don't have much choice since he got rid of his cell. Said he was simplifying his life or some shit. But now, with those pictures at Burke's...maybe she was harassing him."

"No." She rubbed her temples and put the coffee down. "He just gave me his number the other day. Hang on." She rummaged in her briefcase on the countertop. "When did Griffen get rid of his cell, anyway?" Maybe the number she had was no good. After all, a lot had changed in the last couple weeks; when he'd given it to her, she still had a brother.

Petrosky's cough stopped her throat from clamping shut. "Hasn't been long. I met with him the day we found...the envelope, the day you talked to Johnson, to see if he knew anything about the social worker she mentioned. I asked if I could call him to follow-up, and he told me to use the office line because he'd canceled his cell."

"Weird." Shannon pulled out a Post-It and reached for her cell phone. *Wait*...Griffen had seemed shocked when Shannon mentioned the social worker to him in court, but if Petrosky had told him about Wheatley earlier...A female voice answered on the second ring.

"Hey...oh, uh, Karen?"

"Yes. Who is this?" Polite, friendly, nothing more, not the least bit concerned. Burke's polar opposite.

Shannon relaxed just a touch, though Petrosky's eyebrows hit his hairline. "Hey, it's Shannon."

"Oh, hey! Frank said you might be calling me because he canceled his phone. Men, right?" She had a laugh like the peal of a bell.

Did men do shit like that? Roger would never have given someone her number if he'd lost his phone—but then again, Roger was a lying, cheating bastard. Just like Kimball. And...well, if Karen suspected Burke was still into Griffen, *she* might have told him to cancel his phone. Knowing him, he'd have done it. "Right. Men," Shannon said slowly. "So, is he there?"

"Oh, sorry, I'm not with him. I'm out running errands while he picks up a *friend* from the precinct." Her voice was suddenly tight.

Shannon's heart rate climbed. "Is he picking up Frieda Burke?" Why would he be picking her up? She didn't think Griffen was still involved with Burke...and if he was, he wouldn't have told Karen, would he? There had to be more, a connection she wasn't seeing.

"Yes—how did you...how did you know?"

And finally, like pieces snapping together, everything fell into place. Griffen in his knit cap, the one he always wore. Perez saying, "He had on a hat so I couldn't see his face or his hair or anything." Not a disguise, just him. His worry about Johnson, his insistence on her innocence. His sleeplessness over her being put away. Even the note: *It was me*. It hadn't been someone trying to steal the glory—Lucky had been about guilt, a dramatic cry for help, a plea to be discovered. A cry to *her*, the person who'd stuck it out with him through college and their early working days. But...why hurt Lucky? She couldn't quite see it, and yet—

Her heartbeat was thumping in her ears, in her head, but she could barely feel it. He'd seemed so thin lately. Sickly. In pain, probably more than usual, twitchy with it, even. Maybe Griffen's addiction had started honestly, something stronger for his headaches, and then...he'd needed more. He'd found Derek. Maybe Derek Lewis had told Griffen someone was over there asking questions, but not who. The moment Petrosky had asked Griffen about a social worker at the apartment—the only male social worker in Ash Park—he'd signed Wheatley's death certificate.

No. There was no way. Griffen was passive, quiet. He couldn't even break up with a woman. Shannon's disbelief must have shown on her face because Petrosky stood abruptly, the chair scraping across the floor behind him as he came around the kitchen table to the opposite side of the counter.

Karen was still waiting for a response. *Frieda Burke...* Shannon knew he was picking her up, but not why, at least not enough to explain to Karen. Were Burke and Griffen in this together? Maybe Burke was manipulating him. *No way.* Burke could convince Griffen to drop his friends, but to murder someone? She hadn't even been able to get him to leave Karen. "Lucky guess," Shannon croaked.

Karen paused, sniffed. "You know, between you and me, she doesn't really seem stable. Sad, really, calling him all the time." She lowered her voice. "I hope Frank can talk her into getting some help."

Griffen. It couldn't be, just couldn't. The idea that Griffen was a killer —it meant Griffen had tried to kill *her*. Her friend had tried to murder her in cold blood. And he could try to murder his girlfriend just as easily if he thought she suspected something. Which Karen might after this phone call.

"Karen, he isn't bringing her back there, is he?" She tried to keep her voice even, but the words came out rushed.

"He said he was just going to drive her home..." She trailed off, each word more tense than the last. "What's wrong? You sound weird."

"Karen, listen." Shannon grabbed the countertop as the room spun. "Tell me where you are, and I can send someone to you."

"I don't understand. What's—"

"I'll explain later. Trust me here, okay?"

"Okay, okay. Where am I supposed to go?"

"Just tell me where you are. I'll send Officer Valentine to get you."

"I'm near the precinct. Should I—"

"Yes. Go inside and tell them who you are and that you're waiting for Officer Valentine. I'll be there soon."

"Shannon..." Her voice was higher, tighter. Afraid. "Should I be worried?"

This poor woman. She at least deserved the truth. "Yes. You should be worried."

Shannon shoved the phone into her pocket, Petrosky's eyes boring a hole in her head. "It's Griffen."

33

"That pasty fuck?" Petrosky jerked out his phone and stalked to the other side of the room with it plastered to his ear, barking something about searching for a car. *Griffen.* Could it really be Griffen? Across the room, Petrosky clenched the phone so hard his knuckles were white.

Maybe she should have known. Would have known if she'd rekindled their friendship after he broke up with Burke, but she had been far too upset and far too afraid that he'd hurt her again. Though at the time, she'd only been concerned about her feelings—not that he wanted to put her in a pine box.

Petrosky yanked the phone from his ear, tapped the screen again, and put it back to his face. "Guess who picked up an unmarked police car at the auction last year?" he snapped over his shoulder.

Of course. Of course Griffen fucking had an old police car. And unless she'd watched him get in, she'd never have noticed it in the lot, not amidst the sea of other cop cars.

"Yeah, need to talk to Detective Young..." Petrosky barked into the phone. "I don't give a fuck what he's doing—" Every word vibrated in Shannon's temples until it felt like her head might explode. She was right; she had to be right this time. But if she wasn't, oh god, if she was wrong again—

They're all counting on you, Shanny. Don't fuck it up.

Petrosky's voice rose with each word. "When? How long? Fuck." He shoved his phone into his pocket. "Griffen already picked Burke up—half an hour ago."

"Petrosky—"

"Stay here." He started for the door.

"Fuck you."

"Shannon—"

"Fuck you, Petrosky. Goddammit."

He held the door for her. "No wonder California likes you."

EVERY MUSCLE in Shannon's body was wound like a spring as they drove through town toward Burke's house, though her head throbbed less thanks to the stash of ibuprofen Petrosky kept in his glovebox. She had pretended not to notice the airplane bottles of Jack Daniels, nearly all of them empty.

There was no car in Burke's driveway, unmarked or otherwise. Shannon squinted at the dark windows. "You think they came here? Maybe he took her to his place."

Petrosky stepped onto the front porch and peered through the window beside the door. The air around them hummed with energy. Birds chirped, telling them to turn around. Tree branches clacked together, angry. A van full of yelling children passed, a soccer ball sticker affixed to its rear bumper. Petrosky tried the doorknob. It turned.

Is she here? "Did you leave it open earlier?" Shannon asked.

He shook his head. "Young showed up quick, said we'd bring her in for questioning, and closed the place up again. Didn't even take samples of his own."

If the door was open...someone had been here.

"Come on, Taylor, and stay low."

The moment the door closed behind them, taking with it the rushing cars and the twitter of birds, Shannon's heart went into overdrive. Something was very wrong inside this house. She could feel it in her bones, not so much a presence, but a lack of essence. No noise. No life. The house didn't just feel empty—it felt abandoned.

Like a tomb.

Burke's boots sat in the entry hallway, still-wet mud dribbling onto the linoleum. Had Griffen just dropped her off? Or maybe they'd swung by here to grab a bag so they could run off together.

Petrosky obviously didn't think so—he'd pulled out his gun. They crept down the hall to an alcove. "Stay here, back against the wall, Taylor," he whispered, and she did as he asked. "Now call her," he said.

"Ms. Burke?" Shannon's voice trembled through the house. Petrosky set his sights on the kitchen doorway. Not a sound. Not a swish of a door, a creak of a floorboard, or a whisper of breath from any direction. Shannon jumped when Petrosky threw himself through the kitchen doorway, gun in front of him. He skidded to a halt before she got there too and tried to push her back but wasn't fast enough.

Burke lay on the floor, knees bent as if she'd been standing, and just keeled over backward. But she hadn't fainted. She wasn't sleeping. Her chest was covered with ugly, weeping holes that had only recently stopped bleeding, the blood soaking her shirt and pooling around her head—gelatinous and shiny. Her dead eyes stared at the wall, and her head lolled awkwardly, nearly sawed clean off so that her spine was visible through her neck, all of it gaping like a ghoulish smile.

Shannon's heart was in her throat. She felt suddenly alone and exposed—deserted in the doorway, waiting to be slashed apart by a predator. By Griffen. By her…friend. Where was Petrosky? Why wasn't he at the body?

She dragged her eyes from Burke's mangled corpse, her breath coming erratically, too fast, too hard. Petrosky was bent over something on the counter—a notebook?—peeling back one page after another with his pocket knife. Shannon couldn't remember him taking it out, and his weapon suddenly seemed more violent and sinister than it should have. She wanted to flee, screaming, into the street.

Petrosky was speaking, but Shannon couldn't hear him. Her mind was deathly silent. The birds had quieted, frightened and hiding. Even the tree branches outside had ceased to move. Then he was next to her, his arm on her elbow.

"Taylor? Did you hear me?"

She shook her head.

"Read it. Last entry. You know him better than I do."

Shannon tiptoed around the body to meet Petrosky at the counter, trying not to smell the death that lingered in the air, but she couldn't help it; the tang of metal, a musk that might have been urine, and the smooth, hot cinnamon underneath it all from a candle still burning on the kitchen counter.

The journal page was speckled with blood, but the words on the page Petrosky had chosen were readable:

> *I am possessed by a demon. Not a demon in the traditional sense of the word, the kind who rises from hell and has fingers long as knitting needles and teeth like knives. It is inside me, as if my brain hates me, like it's turned dark and alien, and I have become a mere host for its lunacy.*

Shannon breathed through her mouth, trying to avoid the stench. Her friend. Once, her best friend. He was as foreign to himself as he was to her.

> *Rage eats at me night and day, piercing the center of my forehead like a steel rivet and sending sparks of incoherent fury through my mind. I no longer try to calm myself, for the harder I struggle against the thoughts, the more insistent they become. And when they scream at me to act, particularly her voice, I do not feel entirely in possession of myself. I know this explanation is irrational, but I cannot explain it any other way.*

Her voice? Hallucinations? She tried to picture Griffen in court, the way he'd look off into space. She'd always thought he'd been thinking. Had he been listening to more than just his own internal ramblings?

> *I tried to tell her to let me turn myself in and be done with it. But she will not allow it. Her voice attacks me at all hours, insisting I do more. It is a thorn in the core of my being, a barb scraping and tearing and gouging until there is nothing left but a gaping hole. I have this idea that I can fill the empty hole with blood, and that my pain will stop. It is a strange dichotomy, the way the vision of this battlefield horrifies and pleases me at the same time. It strikes me as a valid sentiment even as I register its illogical nature. These fascinations are a thing of repugnant beauty, oxymoronic only in the nature of how I feel about them: confused, disgusted, exhilarated.*
>
> *Today will end in bloody warfare. Destruction. Ruin. Misery. I am not brave. I am only sorry.*
>
> *Back where it begins, where it ends, where all hope dies, so shall they. So shall she.*
>
> *And so shall I.*
>
> *I am so sorry, Shannon.*

Griffen. But not the Griffen she'd once called a friend. Sanity was fragile...fleeting...and apparently, he thought she should have known. Maybe she should have. *Back where it begins, where it ends, where all hope dies, so shall they. And so shall I.*

She turned to Petrosky. *Where all hope dies.* She could almost smell the weed that had clung to them freshman year, could almost hear Griffen talking as they explored the darkened courthouse in the dead of night. And because of the faulty wiring around the back window, they'd always had a way in. Now Griffen could still get in through that same window —then he'd find a place to sit and wait until morning when he could inflict the most damage.

She ran from the house without a word, Petrosky at her heels.

34

Petrosky waited until they were in the courthouse parking lot before he called for backup, something about other officers distracting him or not letting him do his job. Not that it would take long for them to arrive —cops in the precinct would be over in minutes from the building next door, and officers patrolling the area would race in here moments later, sirens blaring. Petrosky just wanted a head start. And he'd get it.

But Shannon had stopped caring about his reasons. Griffen had tried to kill her. He'd threatened her and her family, murdered Lucky and taken the one thing that had given Abby joy. They'd been friends once— until Burke. And now there was no more sweetened regret when she considered him, only fury. She wanted him alone for just three minutes.

A courtroom. He'd be in a courtroom. *Where it all started.*

Johnson's case? Was that the beginning of the end for him? "Room seven," Shannon said as they opened the car doors.

"Wait. Floorboard."

She leaned down and felt around beneath the seat. "A vest?"

"Either put it on or stay here. But it won't help you if he shoots you in the head, so stay fucking low, or California will have my ass."

She slid it on and stepped out of the car. Petrosky nodded and pulled a gun from his ankle holster and handed it to her, its cold weight at once disconcerting and exhilarating. She wasn't a marksman, or so Morrison had told her the one time they'd gone to the range—she'd need to be close. She clicked the safety into place and shoved the weapon into her waistband.

Sweat popped out on her forehead as she and Petrosky tore along the side of the building to the back. Their footsteps were hollow, the breeze electric, the world muted with dusk as if the skyline had been drawn with charcoal. She blinked salt from her eyes and squinted at the back facade. Then she saw it—the third window in was open, the thin, severed wire hanging from the corner like a tiny forgotten noose, as it always had been, invisible unless you were looking. Ten years, and it was still there.

Petrosky pulled himself through first and reached to haul her in after him. Their footsteps against the marble floors resounded into the still air, hitting her eardrum like firecrackers, and she switched to running on her toes. But there was no way to escape the sound echoing on the empty walls that had once held a promise of justice and now seemed more like a prison.

They stopped at the door with a brass #7 bolted to the right of the doorframe, Shannon on one side and Petrosky on the other. Yellow light glowed from the base of the jamb.

Petrosky bent to his knees and put his ear against the bottom of the door, probably trying to avoid getting his head blown off. No sound from inside. The door was oak—thick, heavy, substantial. Like it was conspiring to hide Griffen from them.

Petrosky put up his hand. One finger. *Two*. On three, Petrosky shoved the door open, and they went in low, ducking behind the first row of pews like Shannon had seen in movies but had never actually done. She peeked around the side, her heart hammering in her ears as her eyes adjusted to the light.

Griffen stood at the podium, unmoving, as if addressing a nonexistent jury. An assault rifle hung against his back. Shannon straightened.

Petrosky tried to pull her back down, but she shook him off and trained her weapon on the back of Griffen's head.

"Goddammit, Taylor," Petrosky hissed.

Shannon ignored him. "Griffen?"

He turned, and she saw a second assault rifle swinging at his belly. Petrosky leapt to standing beside her. Griffen made no move to raise either weapon. He smiled, though his eyes remained dull. "You came."

She tensed, training her weapon on his face. Petrosky left her side and slid around the pew to the left aisle. Griffen didn't acknowledge him, just kept his gaze focused on Shannon, so intently she felt like he was using his eyes to peel off her skin.

"Wouldn't miss it," she said, her voice far more steady and sure than she felt.

His hands stayed at his side as she approached, but his eye twitched as Petrosky sidled closer. Then his wrist shifted, just barely, but enough that Shannon tightened her grip on the trigger. Griffen looked at the wall, one eyebrow raised as if he was listening to a voice no one else could hear.

"They think... I mean, I think you'll lose this one. I don't want this, but—"

"You're wrong."

"She promised you'd lose."

She. Frieda Burke? Had she really been fucking with him because he'd left her? Manipulating him, knowing he was sick?

"She told me it would all be okay," he said.

I'm sure she did. She probably told you it was also fine if you guys killed me and tossed me in the fucking lake. "She's a cunt." The thought of Burke's body no longer turned her stomach. She was glad Griffen had killed Burke first.

He stepped from the podium into the aisle, and Petrosky shuttled down the pew toward him. Griffen's eyes did not leave hers.

"I didn't want to do it. She *made* me." His speech was pressured and seemed to consume the air around them. "I had hoped you'd find me sooner. I wanted you to. I thought maybe you could feel the…wrongness in me. But I suppose that was my imagination." He swallowed hard. "I wanted to stop."

He was so sick. Could she have helped him if she'd found out earlier? If she had noticed the strangeness when they were together? But she *had*. She'd seen the eccentricities, the oddities—him staring into space, his constantly moving mouth, and she'd thought it was just…him. He'd always been a little twitchy. But this…*this* was not the man she'd known.

Her gun hand wavered, and he snapped his eyes to the gun, then back up to her. Their eyes met. His gaze was unfocused, maybe confused, but there was no doubting the fury that burned beyond his irises; he was like a rabid animal, unknown to her, but who'd not hesitate to bite. The friend she'd once loved had been snuffed out. All that remained was this wild-eyed lunatic who had tried to murder her like he'd murdered Derek Lewis, Frieda Burke, Benjamin Wheatley. He'd tried to ruin Morrison, tried to take his life as surely as if he'd slit his throat. And Abby…my god—

Her hands no longer shook. *Say you tried to kill me, asshole. That you killed Lucky. That you're a murderer.* She wanted to hear him say it, say he loved the thrill of it. Then she could release her grief and her guilt and embrace the fury that was threatening to explode from her chest.

Petrosky crept down the pew in front of her, headed right for Griffen, but Griffen still didn't look at him. He seemed to see only her.

"Kimball's gun was a nice touch," she said, her voice rising along with her blood pressure.

Griffen's face darkened. "I see now that using Kimball's gun was too vague to link back to me. I should have left another note, perhaps done something more…flagrant. But I didn't really know… I mean…I'm not a criminal."

You are a goddamn criminal. And instead of turning himself in, he'd chosen Morrison as a scapegoat. "And Morrison? He was always nice to you."

"*She* hated him. And you deserved better." Griffen's mouth was moving like a fish gasping its final breath on shore. His nostrils flared, and his eyes darted to the far corners of the room as if an assailant was hiding beyond the drywall.

Nice didn't matter. Not when you had completely lost your mind. But still...not a confession. And the more he watched the room behind her, the more he responded to things that weren't here with them, the more her resolve crumbled. And she needed to do this. She needed to focus and take him down so Petrosky could lock him up for good.

Say it, goddammit. Say you're a fucking killer. "What kind of an asshole murders a kitten?"

He dragged his eyes from the back wall and looked down at his shoes —clean white sneakers. He'd probably stashed his bloody kicks in a closet somewhere after killing Burke. "She *made* me. And it was...regrettable. But I did it quickly. He didn't feel much; I can promise you that."

Close enough. Her blood boiled, thudded in her temples. "'Regrettable?' Seems like an understatement, Griffen." Her voice sounded foreign to her, too soft, too calm, at odds with the storm raging inside her.

"They were all regrettable, but I was blinded by rage. I couldn't even remember picking up the hammer, but then...there it was. There he was." His voice was soft, almost wistful.

She shook her head but kept her eyes fixed on him, on his hands. On the weapons. "Wheatley wasn't an impulsive act of violence. You tortured him."

He looked to the corner again and back to her. "I wish I had never found out who Lewis meant when he asked if I had sent 'that guy' there." Griffen turned his head toward Petrosky so quickly she almost jumped for cover behind a pew, but Griffen's hands did not shift to the weapons. "Even then, I had no desire to harm Wheatley, but I was convinced his death was necessary. She told me..." He lowered his eyes, and when he spoke again, it was a whisper. "She told me I had to. She's stronger than I am. And she's the only one who understands."

"Who, Griffen? Burke? Is that why you killed her?"

Griffen cocked his head, his eyes narrowed. "What?" But he gave her no time to respond. He jerked his head to the back corner of the room. "No. No!" He wasn't talking to them—to her. He was talking to someone she couldn't see. Fighting. Maybe fighting on her behalf. And the aggression, the hatred, singed into her belly, mingling with the heavy grief of their lost friendship. He'd been normal once. Happy. She raked her eyes over his stubbly jaw—his mouth still moving, his lips almost forming words. She'd spent this entire time trying to work logically on the case. But there was no logic here. Only madness.

"I can't make the voices stop. They are horrible, senseless. And more persistent even than our strictest law school instructor." His face softened suddenly, almost nostalgic, and he took a step toward her, then another, ten feet and closing. Petrosky was a dozen feet from Griffen's right side. "Back in those days, I was free. I yearn for that again, the peace of it." His eyes filled. "Every night, I pray that I will go to sleep and never awaken."

He was close enough that she could smell his stink, the dank, ripe scent of perspiration. He'd killed Lucky, made Abby cry during the worst month of her life. Maybe the stress had killed Derry faster too. And all the while, he'd fucking smiled to her face, asked her how she was, watched her in court, brought her a goddamn coffee cake, and held her in his arms without the slightest bit of remorse. Now...what, crocodile tears? He wasn't sorry. He was just fucking sad it was over. Fire blazed through Shannon's arms and down to her fists. Her muscles tensed.

Griffen bared his teeth, though his eyes remained glassy. "Shan—" He lunged toward her.

Shannon didn't hear the first shot or the second, just a wild ringing in her ears and the stench of gunpowder in her nose as Petrosky took him down. Griffen slammed into the endcap of the pew, writhing and spitting, blood seeping from his thigh and more from his knee. He collapsed into the seat. She stepped toward him and rounded the pew so she could see his face.

Petrosky was yelling, a low growly rumble, but Shannon ignored him—couldn't hear him anyway over the buzzing in her head.

Griffen smiled at her, peaceful. "I'm glad you're here." She intuited the words from the movements of his mouth rather than hearing them, so focused on his lips that she almost didn't see him shift in the seat. But she did. He raised the assault rifle.

Shannon pushed her gun into his eye, pulled the trigger, and watched the back of his head explode against the pew behind him.

Petrosky grabbed her arm, and she looked at him, watching his mouth form unintelligible words. The ringing in her ears intensified.

She looked back to the podium, where Petrosky was pointing at the metal bullets littering the floor.

Bullets. Scattered like they'd been ejected from a gun. She looked back at Griffen's gun, her ears still ringing but not as bad as before.

Petrosky squeezed her arm. "You made the right call," he said, his voice tinny and strained.

She stepped back, with her hand protectively against her belly and watched Griffen's brain matter drip onto the floor.

35

Shannon raised her palm like a visor against the midmorning sun and tried to see the courthouse through the glare. The world felt too bright, too brittle. As it was, she could barely make out Petrosky's bulk a few steps up as he paced back and forth and smoked his seventeenth cigarette of the day. She almost wanted one too. Or a drink. Something to take the edge off, though hearing that Judge Miller had rejected Reverend Wilson's no contest plea helped a little. Knowing Roger was under the microscope helped a little more. Though there was no evidence of wrongdoing so far, it would be a wake-up call; Roger wouldn't be dumb enough to break the law again—if he ever had.

But all was not well. Her hands were clean now, but she could still feel Griffen's blood speckled across her skin like burning oil. Every day, she tried to forget. Forget that he'd raised an empty gun. Forget that she'd shot him, that she'd helped a man who'd once been her best friend commit suicide. The anger at Griffen had persisted, hot and achy in the middle of the night, but...maybe that was grief. It was hard to tell one emotion from another anymore.

Karen had frozen when they'd told her about her boyfriend's murderous rampage. Her shock had made Shannon feel a little better about not seeing Griffen's insanity before, though Karen's tears had turned her stomach. Even if Griffen had been criminally insane, Karen had lost someone she cared about that day. And Shannon didn't wish that ache on anyone.

Though they were still wrapping things up, it appeared that Griffen had acted alone. Except for a note at Derek Lewis's house informing Ashley Johnson of parenting class times—probably from an earlier home visit—no trace evidence of Burke's presence was found at any of the crime scenes. The single drop of blood on Burke's welcome mat belonged to Derek Lewis, but it was smashed into the mat along with fertilized earth consistent with the soil in front of the house. And since Karen admitted that Griffen had gone to Burke's home in the days after the Lewis murder, it was likely that Griffen had just tracked in a speck of dried blood on his shoes.

And it made sense that Griffen had visited Burke—Burke and Griffen had remained in contact, and the journal entries indicated that Lewis had told Griffen someone had come to the house asking about him, but not who it was. Maybe Griffen had decided to pick Burke's brain under the guise of helping his newest client. Burke had probably asked around a little just to help him out. Her conversation with Lucinda Lewis didn't necessarily show that she knew there had been another social worker out there—Shannon had just assumed as much because of what Angela Perez had seen. And Burke, though jealous and more than a little stalkery, didn't seem capable of murdering anyone or cleaning up crime scenes, even for Griffen's sake. The illustrious Dr. McCallum concurred based on the psychological screenings Burke had completed prior to becoming a foster mom.

Even Griffen's references to "her voice" could be explained without Burke's involvement: hallucinations due to opiate withdrawal. Griffen had filled no fewer than three dozen painkiller prescriptions from various doctors in the last six months—it seemed that once the doctors had stopped prescribing, he had moved on to heroin. Enter Derek Lewis. And it turned out Griffen had another reason to hear things: the pathologist had found a tumor the size of a dime near his amygdala, amidst central brain tissue. A tumor in that location could easily trigger hallucinations, rage, and impulsivity, the doctor said. Griffen had tried to stop—he just couldn't. Shannon tried not to think about that either, how quickly your mind could snap and take all of you with it.

Petrosky rejoined her on the sidewalk in front of the courthouse, and together they watched women and men milling around, some in suits, some in baseball caps with ponytails pulled through the backs. Shannon could feel their eyes on her, and it made her skin crawl. But that might have been the stains that she couldn't wash away, at least not yet. Maybe one day she'd feel clean again.

"How's Ashley Johnson?" she asked Petrosky as they started toward the street and the detention center. Morrison would be getting out soon, and the thought made her insides flutter with anxiety, or maybe excitement. Or maybe that was the kid making her stomach act up.

"She's hanging in there. I got her an apartment over by Perez. Figured they could start school together in the fall."

"Did you foot the bill for that?" Now that Kimball had been abruptly —but quietly—fired, Ashley Johnson didn't have much outside support.

Petrosky avoided her eyes.

She suppressed a smile. "What about Diamond?"

"A few social work visits and Johnson will be in the clear. Without Lewis around, I doubt she'll have an issue maintaining custody so long as she keeps herself straight. Which she will."

Shannon looked over her shoulder at the courthouse. How could she go back there, practice law in the very room where she'd killed a man? "I still think we should tell them who really killed Griffen."

"He's dead, Taylor. It was my gun, a weapon you should never have touched. If I'd had my way, you wouldn't have been in there at all. Plus, I had residue from the same gun on my hands." They reached the road and Petrosky threw his arm out to stop her as if she was going to walk right into oncoming traffic.

"You had residue on your hands because you shot my gun into the wall." She stared at his hand until he dropped it. "After Griffen was dead."

They crossed the road and into the shadow of the detention center. "Prove it," Petrosky said.

She put her hand on his arm.

He glanced at her fingers as if confused and raised his eyes to the detention center's front entrance. "There's your boy."

She looked up as Morrison walked outside, golden hair glistening in the sun, smile brighter than the hair. His clothes were wrinkled, but they surely felt better than an inmate's jumpsuit. Morrison...or Curt? But no, he'd been Morrison when she'd fallen in love with him. It had happened a long time before she'd been able to admit it.

Petrosky stepped back as Morrison approached. "Good to see you, Surfer Boy. Meet anyone nice in prison?"

Morrison grinned, but it only accentuated the bags under his eyes. "A few guys."

"Made a bunch of friends, eh? Must have stock in Vaseline. Guess that's how they do it in California."

"Yep, that's how we do it," Morrison said, but his eyes were locked on Shannon's. He offered his hand.

She threw her arms around him, and the heat of him melted the rigidity from her back. "I'm so glad you're out."

He said nothing, just held her.

"I missed you," she whispered.

"I missed you too. Hard to be without your friends in jail."

Friends. Were they only that in his mind? She pulled back to look him in the eye, and the warmth in his gaze, the longing she saw mirrored there—it wasn't a glance you'd give a buddy. They were so much more than that, so much...

Morrison released her, and she looked back at Petrosky, but he was already halfway across the parking lot. "Catch you later, boss!"

Petrosky waved, backhanded, without turning around, and opened his car door.

"So," Shannon said, turning back to Morrison. "What do you want to do?"

He raised one arm and put his nose in his armpit. "Shower."

She smiled. "I'll get you home so you can get cleaned up. You want to grab some food afterward?"

"Only if you're going with me."

She squeezed his hand. "I'll be there." They did have a few things to discuss, not the least of which was why she'd questioned their relationship the morning after they'd slept together. She'd make it up to him—after all, she had helped get him out of jail. There were worse ways to start the reconciliation process.

"We can start with coffee," he said.

"I don't know. Maybe one cup."

He cocked his head. "How about a drink?"

She put her hand on her belly, still taut from the CrossFit workouts, though the button on her pants seemed to press a little harder into her abdomen this morning. Probably her imagination. Though she had heard the second pregnancy always gets bigger faster. "I don't drink."

He nodded in mock chagrin. "One day, maybe."

She smiled again. "Maybe." *Maybe on our kid's first birthday.*

"I'll have to run to the bank first." His gaze traveled across the road to the courthouse. Probably thinking about the day some judge had told him he was going to jail, the day she'd almost lost him.

She wouldn't lose him again. Shannon put her hand on his cheek and drew his mouth to hers, and the guilt that had been eating her insides disappeared in a wave of warmth. She wasn't dirty because of what she'd done. She'd saved the people she loved from ever having to think about the monster who had hurt them. Shannon imagined the cerulean sky was draping them in a protective blanket, the world outside fading into a tranquil haze. Spring, finally in the air, kissed her bare arms.

Their tongues entwined. He slid an arm around her lower back, gentle, so gentle. Tenuous. Maybe he was worried it wouldn't last. Maybe he was as scared as she was.

When their lips parted, they remained nose to nose, wrapped in one another, her hair tickling their cheeks. "I'm so sorry," she whispered. "For not being here. For... I didn't even give us a chance. I won't make that mistake again."

He brushed the hair off her face and tucked it behind her ear. "There's no sorry here, Shanny. You were trying to protect yourself. One day, if I'm very, very lucky, you'll trust me enough to let me help protect you too."

"And exactly what do I need protection from? I just saved your ass, buddy."

He shrugged. "Eh, you know. Killers, though you seem to be doing fine with those pickledicks too."

"Pickle—"

"I learned it on the inside."

She narrowed her eyes.

"Kidding. I heard it from Petrosky."

She had to laugh. "So, you'll protect me from pickledicks."

"That's right. Your ex-husband, too. I've got a mean right hook to help with that." But she could also read what he didn't say. He'd protect her feelings. He'd worry about her. Take care of her. And she'd take care of him right back.

She grabbed him and pulled him to her again, and something hard pressed into her leg from his front pocket. "Hey now, at least wait until we get out of here. Hell, maybe you should just shower at my house." She winked to show she was kidding. Though she wasn't exactly sure she *was* kidding.

"Oh." He reached into his pocket and pulled out a velvet box. "Sorry." He stared at it a moment and shrugged, then went to put it back into his pocket.

She laid her hand over his. "No secrets among friends, right?" She fiddled with the lid. "Especially ones who saved your—" Her jaw dropped at the diamond and emerald ring inside.

He took it out of the box and held it up to the sunlight. "It was my mother's. I've been carrying it since the day we—" He looked down and stuck the ring back into the box. "I figured I'd just have it, wait for the right time. You never know."

"It looks like an…engagement ring."

"It is."

This was crazy. Too sudden. Had Petrosky brought the ring for him from the house along with his change of clothes? *Shit, he knows about the pregnancy.* She furrowed her brows. "Did Petrosky tell you?"

He squinted at her, earnest confusion in his eyes. "Tell me what?"

"Nothing." She ran her finger over the emeralds. "But you're going to have to slow it down a little bit."

He closed the ring box and put it back in his pocket. "I'll wait. We've got time."

"That we do, Morrison. That we do."

EPILOGUE

THE WAVES BROKE behind Morrison's back as if they were trying to be careful with the earth, the gentle swoosh of salt on sand more a meander than a race. It was the easy pull of love, not the torrid rush of lust. Though the lust was there; it always was. Shannon moved slowly toward him up the aisle, his love, his life, the wind kissing her hair like a thousand breezy fingers. White lace danced around her ankles. Petrosky's arm was linked with hers, protective and fatherly as he marched beside her.

On Morrison's chest, Evelyn nuzzled her perfect face into him, her breath hot and fast and soft against the Hawaiian print shirt that Shannon had said was perfect for the wedding. He would have worn anything she'd wanted. He'd have dressed Evie in anything Shannon wanted too, but Shannon had insisted Evie wear the onesie Morrison had made for her, the one that said: "Will you marry my daddy?"

"I've got you, baby girl, I've got you," he whispered, and Evie settled, this angel, his angel, her trust a balm against all evil, a warm tide cocooning them from all the wrongness in the world.

Morrison smiled down at her, and the love within him multiplied itself ten times over, welling in his chest until he felt he might burst. He looked at Shannon, close now, nearing him. This. Forever and ever. Behind him, the waves sighed their relief.

But then he heard it, that familiar, throaty murmur like a gremlin in the back of his brain trying to convince him that things would never stick. He knew the voice was like the cloud that ensnares the moon, only to release it; it would pass. Behind him, the waves tried to assuage his uneasiness by caressing the shore with salt and sea, but still, the addiction pulled at him, wrapping his mind in gauzy promises. *Come,* it said, *I'll take you back, you'll be happier than you've ever been. Even she can't give you this bliss.* He had almost succumbed when Shannon turned him down the first time. He'd almost run from the fear that she'd never say yes, never want him the way he wanted her. But he had stayed. Waited. And eventually, she had loved him back.

Shannon drew closer. Petrosky's eyes were clear, blue, no hint of irritation or late nights or whiskey in his morning coffee—just him, and Morrison was glad of it. The wind whipped Shannon's hair around her face, and the old needle scars near the crook of Morrison's thigh throbbed once and stilled. Behind him, the waves whispered *no, no, no,* but then Evie gurgled, and the burgeoning panic that had been rising in his throat subsided. Shannon's eyes glistened with love and joy and hope. He'd take this kind of happy. This happy would sustain him.

It won't, the voice whispered and was gone. But it'd be back. The voice always came back, no matter how long Morrison ignored it. It ate at him like a cancer, day after day, a gnawing in his gut that said that life wasn't really getting better, that the ones he loved would eventually leave, that he could never be worthy of such happiness.

That only the drug would do what it promised.

He wanted to believe the drug was a liar, but life was fickle, a twisted roller coaster of pain and loss. Given a long enough period of time, the voice was always proven right.

Nothing lasted forever.

YOUR NEXT BOOK IS WAITING!
Sign up for the newsletter at MEGHANOFLYNN.COM
and get a FREE SHORT STORY!
No spam, and you can opt out anytime.

"VISCERAL, FEARLESS, AND ADDICTIVE, *REPRESSED* WILL KEEP YOU
ON THE EDGE OF YOUR SEAT."
~AWARD-WINNING AUTHOR MANDI CASTLE

REPRESSED

AN ASH PARK NOVEL

For my husband
who would probably try to get me back if I went missing.
But don't pay the kidnappers too much, honey. I can gnaw my arm off or something. So really just offer them half the price of a new arm, and if they let me go, we'll come out ahead. And we can spend the other half of the "arm money" making decisions at least two thirds as questionable as bartering with a kidnapper.
Incidentally, my decision to marry you
was one of my best.
I love you, babe.

There is a demon in my head,
No angel to confront him;
With whispers sharp as razor wire,
His voice becomes my anthem.
He never sleeps, just watches…and waits for me to break.

On bloodied knees, I scream,
To loose the monster within;
But no wail of anguish can erase,
Teeth like glass in shredded skin.
And they listen to me scream, waiting for me to break.

And when my cries have faded,
He is still, no use to plead;
And I alone try to recall,
Why I watch him bleed.
There I stand, forever alone, waiting for my soul to break.

> "Deep into that darkness, peering, long I stood there wondering, fearing, doubting, dreaming dreams no mortal ever dared to dream before."
> ~Edgar Allan Poe, "The Raven"

1

THE HOUSE WAS HUSHED, steeped in the steely gray of dawn as he made his way to the kitchen and flipped on the lights: the white tile floors, the white cabinets, the light-green soapstone, all of it at once harsh and as vital as the pulse in his veins. Each morning it was that split second of jarring blindness that finally connected him to his body. But that connection wouldn't last. Detective Curtis Morrison was not so much a stranger to his home or to himself—it was his mere existence, the world of men and earth, that seemed utterly foreign.

Around him the noises of morning murmured to him, less sharp than the light, but just as poignant: the click of the heater, the agitated tapping of a backyard woodpecker, the cat's gentle mewl, and, as he moved about his morning routine, the hiss of the coffee pot, rising like an ocean wave and cresting over his eardrum. In these quiet moments, before the present caught up with him, he felt he was on the brink of a precipice, a place where if he concentrated hard enough, he might hear hushed voices from another dimension—from the world where he really, truly belonged.

Telling him how to get home.

From the cabinet, he pulled down Shannon's coffee mug, the one that read "Arguing with a lawyer may prove ineffective," and set it on the counter hard enough that the clatter sent the cat skittering from the room. He stilled, staring at the mug. It was his job to be in control. Thinking like a detective was a skill comprising fire and ice—the passionate pursuit of justice and the cool logic of calculated deliberation, all centered on the *now*. Which was good. The past was hazy at best, and he couldn't bear to consider what it might have been at worst. The ugliness that lurked in his soul was like a malignant blister begging to burst at the first irritation. Common for cops, maybe; guns and violence and blood were a part of the daily routine. Few remained unscathed.

Breathe. Connect. Center.

Morrison padded upstairs to the bedroom where Shannon sat against the upholstered headboard with their daughter, Evie, both wrapped in the blue comforter to ward off the late spring chill. The entire room felt as if it were swaddled—cozy. Shannon said the colors reminded her of the sea. And if the room was the sea, she was a siren, waiting for him as the first rays of sunlight filtered through the curtains and bathed her blond hair in reddish-gold. She raised her hand to block Evie's face from the glare, and he set Shannon's mug on the wooden end table next to her, squinting briefly at his own hands. He knew they were his, yet he'd not have been surprised to learn they'd belonged to someone else all along. Perhaps common for other cops. Perhaps not.

He sat beside Shannon and ran a hand over her thigh, over her leg trapped inside the cotton shell of the comforter.

"What's up, Iron Man?" Shannon's voice was still hoarse with sleep. She put her hand over his fingers, still resting on her shrouded knee. "Ready to go catch some bad guys?"

Nope, not ready. He released her and pulled his guitar onto his knee, relishing the cool of the strings—more familiar than any part of his body. Shannon squeezed his bicep, Evie smiled at him, and suddenly all was right with the world, whether he truly belonged to it or not. They couldn't see the sorrow through his smile, and there was a pleasure in that—not in the hiding, but in the knowledge that they were safe from the pain he carried, the secrets that remained etched on his gut like scars from a jagged blade. Here, with Shannon and Evie, he was just Daddy. Some days he could almost convince himself that he had never been anything else.

While Evie gurgled at him, he strummed and sang: "I loved you from the first, baby, baby girl..." By the time he rode into the second chorus, Evie was squealing with delight, and Shannon was laughing, stroking Evie's head like they were actors in a sappy holiday commercial. But that peaceful tranquility hadn't been easy for her, not lately.

He strummed the final notes of the song and set the guitar beside the bed, then walked downstairs with Shannon to the living room past the white and gray couch Shannon had insisted they buy because it didn't remind them of her ex-husband or of Morrison's bachelor years. He hadn't argued—his pre-detective days were fraught with a wildness he had worried he'd never tame. These days he felt more domestic, but that didn't make him less of a liar.

Or less of an addict.

Shannon touched his shoulder. "You okay?"

"Yeah." He wasn't worried about himself. The bottle of antidepressants on the dresser was some comfort, a safeguard against him coming home to Shannon crying in the kitchen with her hands over her ears, Evie in her crib wailing. "I can't do this," she'd said that night. "I want to drop her at the fire station."

Maybe they should have expected it—she'd had some depression after her surrogacy with her brother's child. Morrison had assumed that episode was related to Shannon going home from the hospital alone while baby Abby went to live with her fathers.

He'd been wrong.

Morrison tried to force the memory from his brain, busying himself by pouring fresh grounds into the coffee maker—one more pot, enough to top Shannon off and keep Petrosky alert and focused for whatever the day had in store.

"You ready to deal with your partner all day long?" Shannon asked from behind him as if reading his mind.

He turned and made a silly face at Evie, and her cherub cheeks grew wider as she grinned back at him. He tickled her foot and met Shannon's eyes: ice blue and collected...but concerned. About him. "As ready as I'll ever be," he said, forcing a smile.

"Good. You need to get back to work. A month off is long enough."

"Tired of me harassing you, eh?"

"I didn't mean it that way." She shook her head. "Sorry."

"No sorries here, Shanny. Just love." He kissed her cheek. "I'll be back around lunchtime so that I can meet the candidates." He poured the coffee into two stainless-steel mugs and refilled Shannon's when she held her cup out to him, the inscription already marred with a streak of drying coffee.

"Really, I can handle nanny interviews. I've only got two this afternoon." She sipped, then set the cup down when Evie kicked and almost spilled it.

"You didn't let me in on the last ones. You met them at a coffee shop."

"I didn't want you to scare them off."

"I'm not scary!" He stuck his tongue out at Evie to prove his point. Evie tried to kick him too.

She rolled her eyes. "You know what I mean. When it comes to your daughter, you get this 'don't you dare fuck with her' look."

Morrison frowned, but he pulled Shannon close and put his other hand on Evie's back. She was right. He'd have spent all his time cross-examining the potential candidates and scared the good ones off. Interrogating them. Petrosky would have been proud. Shannon would have been pissed.

"I love that you love her, Morrison."

She had never called him "Curt"—he'd been "Morrison" when she'd fallen in love with him. "I love you too, you know," he said.

"I do." She kissed his neck, the highest she could reach. He brushed his lips against her cheek, then over Evie's downy head, inhaling talcum and milk and something sour and ripe that he should maybe take care of before he left. But even if he offered, Shannon would yell at him to get out anyway. And no one in their right mind started the day fighting with a lawyer.

"Go to work," Shannon said. "I've got shit to take care of." She pulled herself from his arms and peeked at Evie's bottom. "Literally. Besides, you know you miss Petrosky. Might as well stop and grab him some donuts. He's going to make you go later anyway."

"Already got him a granola bar."

Shannon smirked. "Oh, he'll love that." She glanced at the clock. "I have to get ready too. Meeting Lillian at the park for an hour early this morning since she's going to meet Isaac for lunch." Isaac Valentine was a good cop and an even better friend with more goofy jokes than Morrison and a brand-new scar on his cheekbone after a run-in with an agitated burglary suspect. Valentine was also married to Shannon's friend Lillian. Even their kids were besties—Valentine was convinced Evie and his son Mason were going to get married one day and officially make them "one big milk chocolate family."

Morrison grabbed the stainless-steel coffee cups off the counter before he could convince himself to call in sick. "Whether he loves the granola or not, Petrosky will eat it. He's probably too swamped at the precinct to get any food at all." He opened the front door, and the still-damp air from last night's storm stuck to his skin.

"Yeah, right. He's probably busy shoving all the paperwork to the side for you." Shannon slapped his ass. "Now stop stalling and get out."

He forced himself not to look back as he headed to his Fusion, struggling with the coffee cups and his keys and the pressure in his chest that was urging him to stay home.

2

The bullpen smelled like old coffee, older paperwork, and dry perspiration, same as it always had. It felt the same, too, the dynamic energy of cops running on caffeine and sugar and a rage that always simmered just under the surface. It was anger at the bad guys, probably, or maybe indignation at the cases they hadn't managed to solve. For every arrest, there was at least one cold case—some douchebag walking free. He gripped the stainless-steel coffee mugs tighter like they were the wrists of an elusive, and definitely guilty, perp.

Morrison cut down the center of the room, a dozen desks on either side of him, a giant post in the middle, making the usable sitting space more L-shaped. He nodded to a pair of plainclothes in suits and ties, one of whom looked familiar—*homicide detective*—the other with the nervous eyes of a cornered opossum. *New guy.* Morrison smiled at him, and the guy smiled back, though his eye twitched.

As Morrison approached his desk, someone clapped him on the shoulder, and he turned to see Detective Oliver Decantor—broad face, broader smile.

"Heard you were coming back today!" Decantor's smile was infectious, though Morrison's chest remained tight, a subtle pressure, but persistent. "I knew you'd eventually get sick of sitting around watching people drool." He crossed his arms over his barrel chest and winked.

Morrison snorted, glancing across the room at Decantor's desk, where he kept his files and his celebrity crush of the week. "You're right; I can always come watch you guys drool over Jennifer Lopez." But he let the grin creep onto his face. "You're not nearly as cute as Evelyn, though."

Decantor rubbed his chin. "Can't argue with that."

They both turned at Petrosky's cough, more of a bark. Petrosky didn't turn toward them, but the set of his shoulders was stiff like he was listening to their conversation. He was probably just anxious to get his hands on Morrison's coffee—the precinct coffee was shit.

"Catch you later, Morrison," Decantor said, his smile suddenly at half-mast. He stared across the bullpen at Petrosky.

Morrison nodded to Decantor's back, then headed for their desks, smack in the middle of the bullpen at the crook of the L. "What's up, Boss?"

"Who you yammering with over there?" Petrosky looked like he'd gained a few pounds in the months since he'd walked Shannon down the aisle in place of her absent father. The zipper on his jacket strained over his belly, and his jowly face had filled out. Morrison hadn't noticed it when Petrosky had visited the house, but at work, everything came into sharper focus. Life: constructed of the details you paid attention to.

"Decantor just stopped by to say hi," Morrison said.

Petrosky raised an eyebrow. "Decantor?"

"I know what you're thinking. Decantor, like the thing you put mimosas in for brunch. But he spells it differently."

"Decant...what the fuck are you talking about? I just thought he was on vacation this week." Petrosky shook his head. "Brunch. I don't know what you've been doing this month, but I don't want to hear any more shit about mimosas."

"You got it, Boss." Morrison suppressed a smile, tossed the cereal bar onto the desktop, and peered into Petrosky's empty Styrofoam cup. The coffee dregs were thick and oily. Typical. "Looks like I got back here just in time."

Petrosky side-eyed the granola bar. "You trying to get me back on your hippie diet?" He rubbed a hand over his belly. "Don't need it. I've just got a little winter padding."

That's what happens when you replace whiskey and beer with cookies and jelly beans. Hopefully, Petrosky's heart was holding out along with his sobriety. Morrison set one of the cups on the desk. "It's not winter, Boss, it's May. You been to a doc lately?"

"Fuck off, California," Petrosky said, but his eyes crinkled, and his mouth turned up at the corners. He grabbed the mug.

"Miss me, did you?"

"With every bullet so far. Not that I'm aiming too hard."

It was more than Petrosky would say for most people.

"We've got a lot to catch up on." Petrosky gestured to the three stacks of file folders on his desk. The police department was perpetually overworked and understaffed, though probably more so in recent years. No surprise. Ash Park itself shared the police department's undercurrent of agitation—a quiet but desperate despondence that seemed to permeate the air, the water, the citizens who would leave—if they had the means.

But understaffed or no, it didn't look like Petrosky had filed a single report since Morrison left.

"Your paperwork skills are atrocious," Morrison said.

"You're the English Lit major—thought your guys loved that paperwork bullshit as much as your fancy-ass words." He snorted and shook his head, muttering: "Atrocious."

"Figured if I confused you, you'd forget about making me write the reports." Morrison pulled up a chair from his own adjacent desk and gestured to the shortest stack of file folders. "So, what've we got?"

Petrosky grunted and pulled the manila stack closer. "The usual. One missing persons, thirteen-year-old girl, turned homicide. Davis thinks sex trafficking, which is why we ended up with it."

Morrison squinted at Petrosky, watching for signs of distress. Petrosky's daughter, Julie, had been raped and murdered before her fifteenth birthday, and his marriage had dissolved soon after.

Petrosky's eyes betrayed nothing. "We've also got two domestic violence cases, one with a stabbing, the other with sexual assault history, both almost wrapped except for the paperwork. Valentine's got one guy in holding now, picked him up on a routine traffic stop. Though you might already know that."

Petrosky peered at the side tabs, slid a folder from the center of the pile, and laid it in front of Morrison. "Then, we have this one."

Morrison opened the folder to the crime scene photos. A dark-haired man, burly, face down in a storm drain. Messy tribal tattoos covered his shoulders, though the stains might just as easily have been grease—or maybe they *were* grease. No pants. Blood pooled under his groin.

"Rape?"

"Nope. Someone took his dick as a souvenir."

Morrison winced, trying not to imagine the searing pain of amputation. He crossed his legs.

"Keep it in check, California," Petrosky said, but his voice had lost the hard edge of condescension.

Morrison passed the folder back. "Any promising leads?"

"Ex-girlfriend. Melanie Shiffer, got a place over on Wildshire. She's probably home now."

Morrison's mouth dropped open. "You know who she is? Why haven't you gotten her yet?"

"Waiting for you."

Morrison stared until Petrosky sighed.

"Fine. I picked the victim up several years back for molesting Shiffer's two-year-old daughter. He took a deal for seventy months, only served four years. Got out last week." He stood. "Maybe we can convince the prosecutor's office to plead her down on the murder the way they did on his charges."

"Not sure the prosecution will go for it unless this guy went after

mother or daughter," Morrison said. "She intentionally severed his junk."
And I probably would have done the same.

"Maybe she didn't mean to kill him." But the look on Petrosky's face told Morrison he didn't believe that either. "They can plea molestation down, might as well see if they'll plea vengeance."

Morrison nodded, but he didn't believe it'd happen, even though Roger McFadden—lead prosecutor and Shannon's dick of an ex-husband—did have a rather impressive history of dreaming up plea deals. In the past, Roger had taken cash for it, too—or so Morrison believed. He'd never had enough evidence to do anything about it, and an internal investigation the year before hadn't turned up a thing.

"What time do you have to be home to pick out nannies?"

"Around noon." Morrison raised the coffee mug but stopped it halfway to his lips. "How'd you know about that?"

"Fucking detective, remember? Like you used to be." Petrosky grabbed the folder and stood. "Let's get Shiffer squared away so you can get back to your own manhood—Shannon keeps it on the kitchen counter, right?"

"In the bathroom next to the mouthwash."

Petrosky half grinned. "Good to have you back, Surfer Boy."

MELANIE SHIFFER LIVED in a whitewashed townhouse with a tattered broom leaning in a corner on the front porch and a doormat that read "Beware of Attack Cat." No one answered the first knock, but the front curtain flipped—a finger, nothing more—and went still. Petrosky put his hand on his gun.

Morrison's mind flashed to the man in the storm drain, and he squared his shoulders, hand on his own gun, as an edgy heat rose into his chest. He'd nearly forgotten that feeling—dirty diapers were slightly less stressful than approaching the home of a killer. "She got weapons registered?"

"Nope." Petrosky tried the handle. It turned. "Ma'am?" No answer from inside, just a subtle shuffling to the left of the foyer, like a rat scuttling through tissue paper. Petrosky disappeared into the hazy dimness of the house, and Morrison followed, alert for the source of the sound. He saw her as they emerged into the next room.

Shiffer sat on a green rocking chair in the front room, her hair disheveled, staring down at a photo album in her lap. She did not look up as they entered, just flipped a page, then another—a family vacation somewhere, a little girl playing in the water, another picture of the girl on Shiffer's shoulders.

Morrison's gaze darted around the room, looking for any other person, the little girl, signs of disturbance…or a weapon. But everything was orderly, almost inexplicably so. There were fresh vacuum tracks on the beige carpet.

Petrosky stepped closer to the chair. "Ms. Shiffer?"

She looked up slowly, as if awakening from a dream or perhaps a nightmare, her glassy eyes punctuated by starbursts of broken blood vessels. "I remember you," she said to Petrosky. Her voice was barely a whisper as if she was trying not to wake a sleeping child. Morrison might as well have been invisible.

Petrosky said nothing.

"She still cries at night, you know," she said. A single tear trailed down her cheek.

Morrison approached her and laid a hand on her shoulder, half for comfort, half to prevent her from reaching for a weapon, though nothing in her manner suggested aggression. Just bone-crushing sadness. His own heart ached for the little girl, abused, still fearful of the man who had hurt her, and for a moment, his ears filled with Evie's cries. Something hot and vile bloomed in his gut. He pictured the heat draining from his chest, and his body cooled accordingly. "Is she home now, ma'am?"

She shook her head. "At school." She looked at Morrison, set the album aside, and stood. "I'll never regret it. Not for one second." Her eyes were dull.

Neither of them reached for their cuffs. She came willingly to the car, the crisp, blue sky overhead heavy and oppressive as if they were all bearing the weight of injustice on their backs.

3

MORRISON LEFT the precinct in a haze of discontent. Reading the details in the reports had drained him. Sex crimes had been bad enough before he'd become a father, but now it was like every kid was Evie—with every story of an injured, raped, murdered child, he could almost see her face staring at him from the files.

As he crossed the lot to his car, Morrison turned to the courthouse steps to see someone watching him. Karen...something. Her red hair seemed darker than it used to be, and her belt was cinched tight around a barely-there waist. Karen waved, one quick, nervous jerk of the wrist, then averted her eyes and bounded up the courthouse steps, probably late for a case.

She worked at the local rehab center and had been the girlfriend of Frank Griffen, an old college buddy of Shannon's. Morrison's fist clenched involuntarily. Last year, Griffen had suddenly gone off the deep end and bludgeoned two people to death. He'd killed Shannon's niece's kitten, too, then framed an innocent woman along with Morrison himself for the murders. Then he'd attacked Shannon, murdered his own ex-girlfriend, and headed to the courthouse to blow more people away. Petrosky had put a bullet in Griffen's very fucked-up brain, maybe right through the tumor that had caused the hallucinations and aggression, though Morrison hadn't asked. Petrosky and Shannon never spoke of The Incident. But afterward, Karen seemed to be around all the more.

Poor girl. Had to be hard watching someone you love unravel.

Morrison waved back, but she was already gone, leaving him with an uneasy feeling in his belly. Griffen's journal entries were full of references to voices, and the way they'd plagued the man was all too familiar. Morrison had his own mysterious voices, some memories, some surely imagined, and even for him, the line between imagination and reality was hazy at best. Was it the far reaches of his past still whispering as he awoke, or a simple trick of the mind, mere remnants of a dream? And what happened if the ramblings in his head became like Griffen's—sinister and murderous and barbaric? Not that a mere voice could get you to act, but…

Morrison got into his car and headed out, mindful of the steering wheel, the pressure of his foot on the gas, the leather against his back as he sped home, each green light surely the universe's way of telling him he should be with his family instead of at work. He turned into his neighborhood. On either side, two-story brick houses passed along with the occasional stone ranch, some with pools, though he'd be damned if Evie played at any of those houses before she knew how to swim. He'd gotten called on a child drowning case last year. Though the child had been injured and unconscious before being thrown into the water, every whiff of chlorine recalled the memory of that baby's purple face.

He pushed the thoughts aside, forced a smile, and waved to his neighbor, Mr. Hensen, an eighty-two-year-old chatterbox who still wore his purple heart on Veteran's Day.

Shannon met Morrison at the door. "Hey! Welcome home!" Her smile faltered when she saw his face. "Bad first day?"

He put his hand against the small of her back and leaned over to kiss her on the mouth. She tasted like Cheetos and coffee—probably skipped lunch caring for Evie. He'd make her something to eat before he left.

"Not a bad day, really. Just the usual." He followed her into the kitchen. The usual was brutal and distressing, but Petrosky would have slapped the shit out of him if he'd said those thoughts out loud. *You can't let it get to you. Go in and do your job and fuck everything else.* Morrison hoped he would never see the day where he wasn't affected by someone abusing children. Killing children. That ache in his gut was the least he could do for a tiny life so violently snuffed out.

"You can call me if you need to, you know," she said.

"I know." But they'd never been that couple, the kind who chitchatted about nothing over the phone. Shannon had always stared at a ringing phone like it was a boil on the ass of humanity, and after the baby, their phone communication all but ceased. She'd said she was busy. He'd worried she was lonely.

He kissed the top of her head, happy that her hair smelled like lemon shampoo and that Dr. McCallum had given her the shrinky go-ahead to go back to work after she returned from visiting her brother-in-law and niece in Atlanta. He knew the loss of her brother, Jerry, to cancer last year still weighed on her, but the look on her face when she talked about the trip—excited and resolute—showed him that his take-no-prisoners wife was back. Though he still wasn't sure how he'd sleep without the constant hum of the baby monitor at night. Even now, the silence of the house wrapped around them like a fog, muffling everything but Shannon's breath. Was Evie asleep? Must be.

"So…" Shannon drew close to him. "We had one scheduling conflict, Alyson Kennedy had to come earlier."

"What? But I wanted to meet—"

"Shh. We've got twenty minutes before anyone else gets here…wanna get me out of these pants?"

He pulled back from her and ran a finger over her cheek, down the front of her throat. Her mouth was warm, her tongue fervent against his own. She pressed herself against him, her soft skin a stark contrast to the determined grasp of her fingertips against his belt.

He lifted her onto the counter, and she leaned back so he could undo the button on her jeans, every movement a frenzied dance of need. He pulled her face to his with one hand, the other at the waistband of her panties. Then his thumb was on her clit, his fingers inside her and she was already wet, ready for him, and she moaned into his mouth—

Evie's wail sliced through the sound of their heavy breathing.

Every time. He released his wife, pulling his fingers from her, and she arched against him, then let him go.

"Fuck." She jumped from the counter, buttoning her pants. "Maybe tonight," she called over her shoulder as she padded through the kitchen and toward Evie's bedroom. He stared after her, betting she'd be too exhausted later on. With the way his morning was going, maybe they'd both be ready to fall asleep come nightfall.

From the driveway came the whisper of tires on cement. Their first nanny candidate was early. Sometimes Evie got it right. Not usually but…sometimes.

Morrison washed his hands and thought about baseball. Paperwork. Then he pictured the guy in the sewer drain, blood pouring from his crotch, and Morrison's body wilted like a flower in frost.

NANNY NUMBER ONE, Patricia Weeks, was old as time and stocky as a bull. She had cold eyes that reminded him of a thousand mug shots. Her square jaw and bulbous nose didn't help either, though he knew it was superficial to think that way—what wasn't superficial was the white hair and the musty smell that clung to her. *How old is she?* This woman could die while watching Evie, and neither he nor Shannon would know until after they got off work. And she was so stern. He tickled Evie's chin, watching for the slightest glimmer of warmth in Weeks's eyes, something that would hint at grandmotherly affection, but the woman just answered curtly as Shannon rattled off the questions they'd written up and only smiled halfheartedly when Evie let out a fart that sounded like it might rip straight through her onesie.

"You're doing it again," Shannon told Morrison after Weeks had disappeared down the drive.

"What?"

"That stare."

"She didn't seem bothered," Morrison said, harsher than he'd intended. He took a breath and tried to lighten his tone. "Not that she'd be bothered by much other than the grim reaper and kids playing on her damn lawn."

"She's not that old—"

"She's got at least twenty years on Alice from *The Brady Bunch*."

"She's younger than Petrosky. And he can still chase bad guys."

"If they're running slowly."

She cocked an eyebrow.

"I mean..." He exhaled the tension from his body. "Really, she just didn't seem that interested."

"She might have been bored—I asked her the same questions on the phone last week. And she came highly recommended. I've called every reference on her list."

"Like she'd give references for people who'd say she has all the personality of a dead fish."

Shannon pressed her lips to his, then stepped back. "Morrison, you're pouting."

Between them, Evie farted again.

4

HE LOOKED LIKE A BOY. But he was no boy. And someday he'd show them all.

His heart hammered as she pulled up in front of the house, the sun heating the still-damp walk under his feet and turning the metal of his bicycle into a scalding implement of torture against his bare leg. But he did not shift his calf away from the bar—he could withstand far worse.

Happy, happy, happy.

The red streaks in her hair blew in the breeze like every finger of wind desired her, wanted to touch her, the air itself crackling with the tense energy of unrequited possession. She knew it too, knew she was desirable, powerful, just like every bitch he'd ever met. They all thought they were better. Too good for the likes of him, no matter how many times he did their homework, carried their bags, told them jokes. Just once, he'd wanted to show them the man he was on the inside. He'd wanted to parade one of those girls on his arm. Show the jocks, those self-proclaimed masters of the universe, that he was one of them. To prove he was better. Just once.

But they'd never given him a chance. He knew he deserved more from them, and yet, as the woman raised her eyes to him and nodded, his mouth went dry. That old familiar itch began on the side of his face, on the back of his neck, and he pulled the visor of his ball cap down. The stance he'd taken to hold the bike upright faltered, and he almost crashed to the pavement.

The girl looked up and down the road. Opened her car door to retrieve something—a purse.

He watched. That was what he was supposed to do, though here he was too vulnerable, too exposed. Then again, Frank Griffen had been hiding in plain sight, buddying up to Petrosky, talking to Shannon, all the while planning to kill her. But Griffen had failed. *Weak.*

He was more of a man than Griffen ever was. He was definitely stronger than his so-called buddy from this morning who'd wept like a little cunt just because that stupid kid was dead. He had hoped he could learn from the fucker, but things hadn't quite turned out that way. But he would learn nonetheless.

He was the bigger man. The better man. And someday everyone would know it.

The red-haired bitch finally reached the front door, and as she rang the doorbell, he lowered his gaze to the sidewalk, pushed off from the road, and pedaled up the street, an unassuming streak of metal and gangly limbs.

But his boot left a bloody smear on the pavement, delicious and dark and unquestionably masculine.

5

THE DOORBELL RANG. Morrison tried to beat Shannon to it, but she sidestepped around him, shoved him back, laughing, and opened the front door to reveal a tiny woman who might've been there selling Girl Scout cookies if it weren't for the fine lines around her eyes. She was right around thirty, maybe—sparkling brown eyes and platinum blond hair with red streaks underneath that were too light to be punk. A smiling mouth full of bright, white teeth, too exuberant to be genuine. Across the street, a lanky high school boy on a bicycle had stopped, probably watching her from under his ball cap, though when Morrison approached the door, the boy lowered his gaze to the sidewalk and hit the bricks. *Move it along, son.*

"Natalie Bell." The woman offered her hand. "So nice to meet you in person." Her hand was cold, thin, breakable, and Morrison felt like a bear trying to capture a bird as they shook. She would be no assistance against an intruder—any eighteen-year-old tweaker like the kid out front could throw her into a wall and barge right on in. They'd need to get a dog. A big one. He should have gotten one already.

Bell bent to Evie as Shannon closed the door. "Well, good afternoon, Miss Evie. How are you today?"

Evie kicked her feet and whined. Bell tickled her toes.

Shannon led them to the couch and settled Evie to nurse. Morrison sank onto the sofa next to her, making his face placid and blank, trying to save his intimidation for suspects instead of aiming it at potential caregivers. But despite his efforts, Bell shifted uneasily on the chair across from them, her plastered smile faltering.

"So tell me, Ms. Bell, how long have you been in this business?" he asked. "You were a nanny previously, yes?"

She straightened, her smile returning. "I started when I was eighteen, officially, though I babysat before that."

Evie farted again. Bell laughed. "Sounds like someone ate too many beans."

"And the ages of the children in your charge?" It came out of him more bark than question. Like Petrosky. He was turning into the old man.

Shannon elbowed him and drew a finger across her throat. He shrugged at her, and they both turned back to see Bell staring at them, her eyes wide.

"Um...all ages," she said. "The last family, the Harrises, I started out with one six-week-old, a two-year-old, and a five-year-old. I was there for three years until they moved." She grinned. All teeth. All smiles. But her gaze remained worried, almost...sad. "Now, I work mostly with infants at the gym daycare."

"You said that your previous employer moved out of state?" Shannon asked her.

"Out of the country," she said, fingers laced over one knee. "I think they're in Europe now." She locked eyes with Morrison, and his stomach soured at a twitch in the corner of her still-smiling mouth.

"And you don't have their contact information?" he asked.

Her face fell. "Well, no, I'm so sorry. I have the parents at the gym who can vouch for me, but I've only been there a short time. After the Harrises, I worked odd jobs. Got too attached to the kids, you know? It was hard when they left." Her eyes went glassy. She had all the right responses, but everything felt somehow disconnected, like a poor stage actor reading lines in a play.

Shannon glanced at the sheet. "I'll call the references you listed, Ms. Bell. I'm sure we can figure it out."

"The Harris family," Morrison began, peeking over Shannon's shoulder. "I'll need first names."

Bell's jaw dropped, but she recovered. Evie, still nursing, kicked her legs and tried to turn her head, yanking at Shannon's breast in the process. Shannon kicked him in the shin.

"Sam and uh...Fletcher," Bell said, and he had to lean toward her over the coffee table to hear her properly.

"Two men?"

"No, the mom was Sam. Samantha."

Morrison nodded. He was being a royal dick, as Petrosky would say. But why the hell would she put "the Harris Family" like it was a corporation instead of a person? What kind of psycho nonsense was that?

He'd been working the beat for too long.

Shannon passed him the baby, eyes narrowed in his direction, and walked Bell out. By the time his wife returned to the couch and sat down next to him, his distrust had mellowed, and it shrank further at the tightness around her mouth.

"I know you don't want to leave Evie, Morrison; I don't want to either. But I head to Alex's in two days, and we need the nanny ready to start when I get back. Not like we can keep asking Petrosky to help out so we can go to dinner."

"He doesn't mind. And he—"

"I know, Morrison, okay? But he's got his own issues."

But Evie helped Petrosky. Hell, just being needed helped Petrosky.

"We can't put it off anymore," she said, and her face was suddenly rebuilt in stone. *Don't argue with a lawyer.* "It's time. This girl is a good candidate. Name one thing wrong with her."

He touched Shannon's marble cheek, almost surprised by her warmth, a reminder that she was not hard and unmovable—she was his wife, she loved him, and she was here. Real. "Just let me check the candidates out first, Shanny. Okay?"

She crossed her arms. "You could have done that while you were off."

"I was busy." *I was stalling.*

"You were stalling."

He sighed. "You're right. I'm still not ready to leave her with a stranger. But I know we need to do it."

Her face softened, a chink in the wall of her stoicism. "Fine. I'll give you my top three to look up, but I knew this was coming. Which is why you've already met two of them."

"Weeks and Bell? But they—"

"No buts. They're my favorites based on their résumés, and their interviews didn't change that. Then there's Alyson Kennedy, the one who just beat you here this morning, recently out of Oaklawn."

"The hospital?"

"She used to be a nurse. Super sweet. Played with Evie on the floor throughout the whole interview this morning."

I should have been here. "She was a nurse?" He frowned, back muscles twitching as he leaned forward in the seat. "Why's she leaving the profession? She get caught doing something unscrupulous?"

Shannon rolled her eyes. "You'll find that out soon enough. Research away." She stuck her tongue out at him. He almost returned the gesture until he realized she was looking at Evie. Instead, he sank back in the chair and tickled Shannon's side. She shoved at his shoulders, and he cupped her chin and put his mouth on hers. Cheetos. Definitely Cheetos.

Evie kicked Shannon's arm from her perch on his leg.

Shannon pulled back, her face suddenly serious. "If you really want to know, Kennedy said she needed a change of pace, and I can't say I blame her. It's gotta be hard dealing with sick or dying kids all day. You of all people should know…"

A hook squirmed in his belly and caught the soft spot under his heart. She was right—seeing children in pain was horrible "Fine. But she better be good."

"Oh, she'll be good. Nurses always are. And if I come home and catch her in my nurse's uniform, you're in trouble." She winked and headed for the kitchen. "Just don't take too long to decide," she called over her shoulder. "If we lose all three because you're busy screwing around—"

"I'll look today, Shanny. Promise." He stood as she disappeared around the corner. "Wait, you really have a nurse's uniform?"

She poked her head back into the living room "I do if you can make this nanny thing happen."

He was opening his mouth to respond when his cell rang with the theme from *Miami Vice*. Shannon disappeared into the kitchen as Morrison pulled it from his pocket. "Hey, Boss."

"Fortieth and Shell. The middle school."

Hell. He looked at Evie, flapping her arms like an adorable, and extremely chubby, bird. Maybe he wasn't cut out for detective work anymore. "On my way."

Please don't let it be a kid.

6

It shouldn't have bothered her, but the sound of his car starting up in the drive started Shannon's own heart revving louder than his eco-friendly engine; the car door slamming was the muted thud of goodbye. *Alone.* The first full day in months that she'd been completely on her own. Not that Morrison had helped much when he was home today: the man was being irritating as all hell with this nanny thing, but she knew it was just because he loved her. Because he loved their daughter. But she would have been okay with any of these women...did that mean she didn't love Evie as much?

He deserves better than this. Evie deserves better than me. They deserved better than a wife and mother who would settle for any of the top three instead of fighting for the one perfect nanny for her little girl. Who was so damn fragile that she was terrified by the prospect of her own thoughts—of being alone with herself.

No, that was the depression talking; she was certain of that now. Most days, she squashed those thoughts like she was bringing a boulder down onto them, smashing them into useless pieces. It was a visual that she'd used to demolish negativity from her mother, her father, her ex-husband, every shitty bullshit defendant she'd put away. But every once in a while, these new thoughts bubbled up and reminded her that she wasn't quite...right yet.

Not that she was totally nuts, not like before. Just...stressed. This trip was wearing on her, the mere thought of it rendering her almost unable to think about anything else. Was she going to be okay for so many hours, alone in the car with Evie? Of course, she was. Could she even be trusted to be alone? Of course, she could. Dr. McCallum believed in her. Morrison believed in her—that's why he'd left her alone now. And goddammit, she knew she could do this. Alone? *Alone.* She'd never needed anyone else to hold her up. Why the fuck would she start now?

She squared her shoulders and turned from the door, toward the pack-n-play where Evie was gurgling happily, kicking at the empty air. Shannon's heart swelled at the sight of her. She was a good mother. This bullshit depression would not eat her alive. She would not give in.

But she *was* becoming too dependent on everyone else to keep her steady. Morrison had been back to work for a fucking day, and already, she felt like she might lose her shit. And every time she explained to him why they needed to hire a sitter *now,* she was really justifying it to herself. She'd never thought she'd be one of those women who wanted to stay home raising babies, but…she didn't want to go back to work. Or she did—she just didn't want to leave Evie.

Is that why Morrison was hesitant to hire the nanny? Because he thought she wasn't ready? She could feel it in every worried look he gave her, every concerned hug. Hear it in his voice each time he asked how her day was going. Even on the phone, it was like his concern was bubbling through her ear and into her brain, reminding her that maybe she was sick.

He didn't mean it that way. Her husband loved her. He worried. Fine. But she was going to kick depression in the balls. She could do this trip without his help—without anyone's help. And then she'd be back to kicking ass in the courtroom where she'd always belonged.

Without her daughter.

Below her, Evie gurgled, and Shannon blinked back tears.

7

THE SCHOOL WAS RED BRICK, scarred from continual sandblasting to remove graffiti, but still standing—more than Morrison could say for most of the other schools in Ash Park. Unlike the drab exterior, the signs on the doors were bright, and finger paintings lined the windows. Here and there, a tiny face grinned at him through the glass, little pockets of innocence, probably drawn to the flashing lights of the police cars or the news vans that were now parking in the lot. But the raw trust on those children's faces reminded him that someone on these grounds now understood how unsafe and cruel the world could be.

The earth, still wet from last night's rainstorm, sucked at his shoes. The grass pulsed with a vibrant energy that shuddered through the soles of his feet and up his legs, warning him to turn back toward the car before he had to see whatever waited for him behind the building. He strained his ears, but there was no wail of an ambulance siren, no shouts from an EMT pulling someone back into this world—just the ominous silence of a playground turned graveyard.

Beyond the trembling fingers of grass, swings moved back and forth as if of their own volition—touched, perhaps, by a murderous palm and now terrified of whatever evil lay hidden near the playground. He'd have the techs check for prints. On the far side of the swings, a low wooden fence marked the edge of the school property, and just past that, a few dozen ash and poplar trees waved in the breeze over low-hanging firs. Petrosky stood at the tree line, watching a man in white coveralls string crime tape between two birches. He glanced over as Morrison approached.

"What've we got, Boss?"

"Dylan Acosta. Eleven. Raped and murdered sometime during morning recess—about three hours ago."

A kid. Morrison followed Petrosky's gaze to the earth beneath the nearest fir boughs. Feet, socks. Sneakers, half the size of Morrison's own, heels to the sky.

Fuck. Morrison inhaled through his nose, trying to force the cool air into his burning lungs, trying to ignore the stink of gore and mud and what had to be feces. Trying to forget the fact that this pile of parts used to be a little boy. *Be placid. Cool. Ignore the heat.*

Morrison approached around the perimeter, staying out of the way of the techs who were scouring the ground for prints or bits of hair. His fingers felt numb, or maybe just cold, or maybe they weren't his at all—a collection of cold, random limbs like in the scene before him. He flexed his fingers, balled his hands into fists, and forced himself to look at the body.

Dylan Acosta. Skinny, shoulder blades prominent, face down in the dirt. Holes that looked like a series of small-caliber gunshot wounds marred the boy's bare back and buttocks. A T-shirt that the kid had probably been strangled with lay crumpled and limp above his shoulders like blue wings—a child turned to a broken angel. Morrison hissed in a breath through his teeth. The kid's pants were around his knees, his underwear...missing. If his clothing had been removed and replaced while the child was alive, the act was indicative of prolonged suffering. He hoped the killer had taken the undergarments as a souvenir after the boy was dead.

"Found his underwear in the bushes," Petrosky said, and Morrison swore he could feel the watchful eyes of the boy's spirit on his back. "All torn up. Ditto on his jacket."

So the killer had left the clothing, tossed it like rags. Probably still warm. Probably still smelled like boy.

Morrison let his eyes drift to where techs were bagging debris and cloth. The earth surrounding the dumping ground was muddy and creased in filthy waves. A struggle? He peered at the boy's feet, but the mud didn't cover his shoes as you'd expect if he'd been digging in his heels trying to escape. Instead, the dirt was speckled over the kid's skin, over his sneakered feet, over his legs and buttocks as if it had splashed up from the killer's heels only after the child had been incapacitated. But...there was more than one set of tracks. One appeared to be the shallow treads of a tennis shoe, small, but definitely bigger than the kid's. The other treads were deep, thick rectangles that looked like they'd been left by boots. One set from the killer and another from the person who'd found the kid or—

"We dealing with more than one suspect?"

Petrosky was still frowning at the techs in the bushes. "Appears that way. The teacher who found him came around from the other side—heels don't match these either." Petrosky dragged his gaze from the techs to the impressions in the mud. "From the size of the shoes and the depth of these depressions, the guy in the boots is probably five-nine, and slight—around a hundred and fifty, hundred and sixty tops. The other guy's shorter but heavier: five-eight-ish, a hundred and seventy pounds. Looks like they got into a scuffle."

A scuffle? What would make a couple of raping murderers go after one another? Unless...one of them wasn't a killer at all. Pedophiles didn't usually kill their victims—many genuinely believed that they adored children, that sexual abuse was an expression of love. So had the shorter perp tried to keep the other from murdering the kid? Had someone else been here trying to stop the rape to begin with? But if that were the case, they'd probably have another body.

Morrison followed Petrosky's gaze to the holes in the child's back. His stomach turned. He'd been wrong—the holes were round, but they weren't from a gun. Probably not from a blade, either. Unlike a routine stabbing, where the wounds varied in size and distance from one another, here, each set of round punctures on the boy's back was a uniform distance apart.

Between one set of punctures, four muddy rectangles, smeared and bloody, ran between the round holes. Morrison swallowed hard and held his shudder in check. *Treads from the boot.* "The holes are from a sharp object," he began slowly. "But look at the patterns around the wounds. All the same. Like he strapped...spikes to his boot and..."

"Stomped him to death," Petrosky said. "This fucker didn't want to get his hands dirty."

Morrison could almost feel the sharp prick of a spike in his chest, and he inhaled over the pain until it subsided.

Petrosky walked around him and knelt beside the kid, lifting the boy's head with gloved fingers. When had he put on gloves?

"Lots of blood around the mouth," he said, quietly, almost as reverent as the hush that had fallen over the woods, as if every animal, including the techs working the grounds, felt the solemn emptiness in the air and were hiding from the evil that had caused it. "Punctured lungs, one or both. But we'll have to wait for the medical examiner to confirm."

Morrison avoided looking at the kid's face and squinted at the wounds instead. Middle back, either side of the spine—the kid had probably drowned in his own blood. He'd have been terrified. In agony. Strangulation would have been more humane.

Petrosky laid the boy's head—*Dylan's head, Dylan Acosta's head*—back into the dirt as gently as one might touch a butterfly's wing.

Morrison's eyes were still glued to Acosta's back, to a spot on the kid's side that he'd noticed when Petrosky had moved him. Scratches or maybe another stab wound. He could hear the kid's heartbeat—deep and fast—and was ready to crouch, check for a pulse when he felt the throb in his temples and realized the beat was his own. Morrison wiped his forehead on his sleeve and pointed. "What's there?"

Petrosky pulled the kid toward him, just a little onto his side. Along his rib cage, a few hash marks scored the skin to the left of one long, angry slice—like a crooked number one.

Morrison clenched his fist and released it before Petrosky saw. "You think the killer is saying this is the first?" It had been a few years since a serial killer had terrorized Ash Park, but Morrison could still practically smell the blood from the crime scenes, see the dripping poems that sadistic asshole had left for the cops. They'd never found him. But this wasn't that killer's MO.

"There's no way this is his first," Petrosky said. "No one starts with this level of brutality." He gestured to the school, well within sight of the trees if one were to stand just a foot beyond the body. "Or this level of exposure."

"We'll look for others." Morrison stared at the school, tried to picture Acosta running, leaping for a football. He turned back to Petrosky to erase the image. "But how'd the killer get the"—*Dylan Acosta*—"victim to come back here?" It would have been hard to haul a kid away while he was playing with his friends unless the attacker was someone he knew.

Of course, those closest to a person were often the ones responsible for hurting them—Morrison knew that from experience, and not just his days with the Ash Park PD. Even years after the fact, a female voice from his past whispered in his ear late at night: *My turn! No, me next.* He could not recall who had said it or who was even there, only that he'd been alone when he'd awoken, blood covering his knuckles like he'd been in a brawl. And near the bed, his best friend, Danny, head gashed open, blood pooling on the floor, ants crawling over his face. *Crawling.* He scratched at his arm, the tickle of imaginary insects as real as the hint of blood in the air around him.

Morrison still didn't know if he'd killed Danny—he couldn't remember much of anything from that night—but he'd stopped using drugs after that day, tried to make his life right again. Still, the wrongness of that evening lurked in his memory like a malevolent fog. Sometimes he lay awake at night, trying to force his vision to clear, to let him *see* just once. During the day, he felt hunted, as if the memory had teeth that could eat him alive. Maybe better if he didn't let those images creep into his consciousness.

Behind Morrison, the clank of a gurney brought with it the sounds around him: the medical examiner giving orders, Petrosky's shoes, squelching as he backed up out of the way. And the boy was there—face down. Here, then gone. Just like Danny.

In the back of his brain, electricity crackled, bright and hot. *Me first. No, me.* Blood poured down the walls. *Come back. You can shoot it once; no one will ever know.* He forced himself to listen to the rustle of the body bag, the rattle of the metal gurney, the sharp hiss of the zipper, the keening squall of an obstinate bird overhead, and the gory walls disappeared along with the whispers. The boy in the bag receded across the playground. Morrison tensed his toes, trying to focus on the self-inflicted cramp in his foot, but he could still feel the incessant vibration of insanity, ready to drag him to hell.

8

THE NEXT MORNING started eerily white, the sun burning hot but unseen behind clouds like swollen mushroom caps. Morrison settled into the extra chair at Petrosky's desk.

The precinct hadn't missed him, and the feeling was mutual. By the time he had finished another stack of paperwork the night before, Shannon had been asleep. This morning she had slept through his alarm. But he hadn't missed the "Nannies" folder on her bedside table. On a Post-it note stuck to the top of the folder, she'd scribbled "Things to Do Before Alex's," and a list which included errands like grabbing her niece, Abby, a birthday present. Maybe he'd surprise her and take care of that at lunch.

Petrosky's mood had been as cloudy as the sky all morning as he pecked angrily at his keyboard—not that he was generally a ray of sunshine, but today felt especially bleak. Dylan Acosta's mother'd had to be sedated yesterday and would be in to see them this afternoon, but there was little else to go on until the medical examiner or the crime scene techs came back with some DNA or...something. They needed any little bit of evidence they could find.

Acosta was last seen playing on the swings. No one at the school had noticed him with anyone or seen him go into the woods. Had he been singled out purposefully? Had someone he'd known waved him over, or had Acosta gone back to the trees to play and become the victim of an opportunistic killer? Judging by the cigarettes and empty bottles the techs had found back there, the tree line was a popular place to get hammered, and two men fighting one another at the scene didn't scream premeditation. But there'd been no database matches on the fingerprints from the bottles, save a couple high schoolers previously arrested for burglary. And though the size of their suspects suggested they could be high school kids, both those boys had been in school at the time of the Acosta killing.

Morrison tilted his chair back and listened to Petrosky's agitated typing. At least they'd determined the brand of shoes and boots, though it hadn't helped much: middle price range, both readily available at several local shoe stores. The spikes on the boots—too far apart to be aeration shoes or cleats—had probably been added by the wearer. But Petrosky was looking into any place that might be in the business of altering footwear: shoe repair services and the like.

They'd already confirmed that the cause of death was punctured lungs. Morrison had really wanted to be wrong about that. The punctures were so clean, so resolute—the killer had stomped on the boy, then stood back and watched him choke. Enjoying the child's suffering. What kind of a sick fuck drowns a kid in their own blood?

He jumped at a cough near his ear. "What the fuck, Surfer Boy?" Petrosky's jowly face glowered down at him. "You got a bug in your ass? Probably from those cricket bars you eat."

Morrison forced a smile. "They're full of protein. You'd like them if you tried them, Boss."

"I don't give a fuck about protein unless it's bacon, and if you try to feed me a bug bar, I swear to god I'll shove it up your nose."

"Up my...nose?"

"Better than saying 'up your ass.' I'm cleaning shit up. You're a dad now." Petrosky flipped open a file and slapped it on the desk, and this time, Morrison managed to avoid startling. "I've found three other cases in the last two years that fit the pattern," Petrosky said. "Rapes in schools or the surrounding, victims left under trees or bushes, a couple with signs of strangulation. No stomping, though. No deaths, either. Trying to get the kids to review their statements, but apparently, teenage boys are reluctant to face their childhood attackers."

I can imagine. "Maybe at least one will come down, if only to see justice served."

"They don't give a fuck about justice. They just don't want to relive it."

Morrison closed the folder and slid it next to his final stack of paperwork. "We'll figure it out. Truth always comes out. Has to." But even as he said it, he hoped that wasn't true. Some secrets were best hidden lest they destroy you.

Petrosky stood. "Maybe you can do some of that fancy computer bullshit, see if there are any more vics. I'll go follow up with the ones I've got already."

"Want me to come with?"

"Nah, you see if you can find more." Petrosky hauled his coat over one fleshy shoulder. "I'll be back by noon."

The bustle of the precinct drowned out the images of Acosta's bloody back, and by lunchtime, Morrison had two more potential connections on the middle school rape-homicide, both cold cases fitting the same pattern: clothing around the neck to subdue, attacks occurring in or around the woods. Though in these files, the perp—or perps—had stopped short of the stomping and subsequent murder. The cases he'd found had children who were strangled to unconsciousness and had awoken traumatized—but they did wake up.

At lunch, Morrison hit up the toy store to grab a board game for Abby as well as a stuffed teddy for Evie—just because. The whir of the tires on his way to the park near the precinct was significantly brighter and calmer than it had been before he'd had a stuffed animal riding shotgun. But his peace wavered when he got out of the car. One dead tree stump in the middle of the park. A barren metal skeleton of a swing set to his right, not a single chain left to hint that it had once held swings. But such was the nature of socioeconomic decay—children, and those things that brought them happiness, always deteriorated first. Their voices were smaller, which made them more expendable to the powers that be.

It also made them more vulnerable.

He sat on the broken park bench—two boards missing, but still enough to hold his ass—with a sub sandwich and a folder full of horrible. Maybe Petrosky was already back at the precinct reading through the copy of the file Morrison had left on his desk. That'd save him from having to describe the brutality out loud.

Zachary Reynolds had been taken from his school five years ago, and, like Acosta, had been discovered in the woods that bordered the grounds. His mother had even been volunteering at the school that day. She'd been by the window, someone asked her a question, and *poof* little Zach was gone. Later he was found unconscious with a T-shirt still tied around his neck. Two years later, a seven-year-old girl, Kylie Miller, was taken during a field trip to the firehouse. The girl had been found in the wooded area behind the lot, brutalized and trembling. Not the same as the playground, and nothing around the neck, but she'd said someone had used her shirt to cover her face. Close enough.

Morrison had been in this job long enough to know that pedophiles weren't always choosy. Some male pedophiles even had normal relationships with women: marriage, kids, the works. Some exclusively targeted children. For others, gender was irrelevant, and the attraction was the innocence or the inability of a child to hurt them, common after sexual trauma in the perpetrator's childhood. He and Petrosky would talk to the department shrink, Dr. McCallum, to work up a suspect profile later this week. Or maybe tomorrow, since their perp in the firehouse abduction case was out already, probably roaming the streets for his next victim.

Fucking figured. If they waited long enough, maybe they'd find that guy in a sewer drain with his balls in his mouth.

Petrosky didn't look up from the file as Morrison sat across from him. "How was your break, Cali?"

Morrison raised an eyebrow. "Cali?"

"Less letters, less effort."

Morrison eyed Petrosky's empty coffee cup. "You get comfortable with that lingo, and you'll be quoting rap lyrics before you know it."

Petrosky flipped a page. "I do that, and you need to take me to the hospital."

"To hide you away before someone younger and hipper slaps you?"

"No, because I've obviously had a fucking stroke, Surfer Boy." Petrosky shoved the open file across the desk, brows furrowed, a half-eaten granola bar in his other hand. "I checked out the cases you referenced," Petrosky said. "Got us an appointment with Dr. McCallum on Thursday, once we have little more for him."

Good. They were on the same page with the shrink.

"Also, the guy convicted on the Miller case...Nick Nolte–looking motherfucker, isn't he?"

"You say that about everyone."

"Give 'em enough crank, and everyone looks like Nolte. Best antidrug campaign there is."

Morrison peered at the mug shot. Pale, with flyaway blond hair and eyes so light they were almost purple. "Okay, so he's a little Nick Nolte. That should help us if anyone saw him around. I figured maybe we could haul him in for questioning. He doesn't have any housing registered, a definite no-no with his sex offender conviction."

Petrosky said nothing, just flipped a few more pages and grunted, his shoulders tight. Something had happened. Morrison opened his mouth to ask, but Petrosky cut him off.

"It was a good find, California. But this twat isn't our guy. Neither are the potentials I pulled this morning."

Morrison's cheeks heated, and he envisioned ice on his face, pushing the flush from his head. His skin cooled. "Twat? So much for cleaning up your language, Boss."

"Sometimes, you need the appropriate verbiage," Petrosky said.

Morrison cocked an eyebrow, and Petrosky shrugged.

"You're not the only one who knows words." He handed Morrison a sheet. "I spent lunch in the lab. Got Echols to rush the DNA."

Of course he had. Heather Echols had just started three weeks ago and couldn't seem to say no to Petrosky—or so Petrosky said. She was probably still scared of the old man, but that wouldn't last long.

"And?" Morrison prompted him.

"She told me this was the last time she was rushing shit for me, so it'd better be worth it."

That had taken less time than he'd thought.

"Found blood from one male suspect and semen from another man at the crime scene, but neither sample belongs to that Nolte-looking fuck from the Kylie Miller case. And there's no doubt that the scuffle happened after the murder and not beforehand: they found Acosta's blood and slivers of bone in the boot tracks. The killer stomped him hard enough to crack ribs." Petrosky grimaced. "Far as I can tell, the boot-wearing guy watched while his buddy raped the kid, then stomped Acosta to death. When the killer stepped back, the rapist went at him—or our killer tried to hurt the rapist too. And while they were scuffling, Acosta was gagging on his own blood."

"Jesus." Hearing it like that...

"That water-to-wine motherfucker abandoned us a long time ago, Surfer Boy. But you were right about Zachary Reynolds." He turned back to the paperwork. "DNA from the Reynolds case is a match to the guy who raped Dylan Acosta yesterday. If only they'd fucking caught him five years ago."

The sub sandwich rose in Morrison's esophagus.

Petrosky flipped the folder closed. "We'll head over to the Reynolds place after school. He'd be...what? Fifteen now?"

Morrison nodded, mute. He must have looked as ill as he felt because Petrosky squinted at him. "You think you can handle the trip, or you want research duty until you can pull your shit together?"

"I'm together, Boss."

Petrosky leaned toward him, his blue eyes softer now with just a hint of irritation—the closest he got to genuine concern. "See that you stay that way, California. And for fuck's sake, figure out this nanny bullshit before you worry yourself into a goddamn heart attack."

"Not sure I'm the one in danger of a heart attack, Boss." The pile of crumbs near the granola bar wrapper on Petrosky's desk looked suspiciously like powdered sugar.

Petrosky grunted. "Not everyone wants to live to be a hundred, California. Some of us are happy just to make it through the day."

Wasn't that the truth.

PETROSKY MADE the phone calls about the case while Morrison pounded keys and called nanny references. Half the references on his list weren't home, though the background checks were coming up clean. *Progress.* He even checked the ones who weren't on Shannon's short list. Ms. Ackerman, whom he'd not met, was a former nanny for three families and a current psychology student, but Shannon had an x by her name with a note—*funny bone broken*—which made him smile. He did a check anyway, set her folder aside, and finally looked at one he'd met: Ms. Weeks, the grocery clerk who turned nanny after her children grew up and left home. Background check fine, lots of experience, but she was so...grouchy. And old. And he didn't like her. But she apparently had more clout with Shannon, who had not crossed her name off the list despite her humorless scowl.

Natalie Bell also checked out. No complaints. No weird social media activity, no one bitching on her Facebook wall about holding a grudge. No suggestion of an abusive boyfriend who'd show up at his house to grab her in front of his kid. Her life appeared perfectly normal—boring, even. He liked that in a nanny.

That left one more candidate, the nurse Shannon had tried to sell him on. Alyson Kennedy's boss at the hospital said all the right things, noting that Alyson had been a perfectly-perfect employee, but his voice grated on Morrison's ear as if the words themselves were made of sandpaper. He didn't like it. He also didn't like that he couldn't locate Natalie Bell's last employer, though there was something endearing about her. He'd rather have someone he'd met. Morrison didn't realize he was tapping his foot until Petrosky glared at him. He stilled.

Shannon was obviously having an easier time keeping her head straight about all this. He called her cell. "If you had to pick one—"

"Bell."

He smiled into the phone. "Fine."

"I'll call her. Love you."

It was much like the conversation they'd had about their wedding. Best friends for nearly four years, living together for almost one, and she'd just had his baby—he'd still been terrified when he proposed in the hospital with a onesie that said: "Will you marry my daddy?"

A month later, Shannon had chosen a dress and a spot on the beach for the ceremony.

"When should we do it?" he'd asked.

"Tomorrow," she'd said. "Call Petrosky."

And he'd responded with, "Love you," his heart as full as it had ever been, unaware of the demons she was fighting when he went off to work that first month. She was his lifeline. For the last four years, she'd been his everything. But if she could have it to do over, after the PPD had passed...would she still have married him? Would she do it again now? Unease twisted in his belly, deep but insistent as a writhing serpent. Yet another thing he really didn't want to know.

Dylan Acosta's mother, Tara Lancaster, didn't look up when they entered the interrogation room. Her brown hair was still wet, damp strands plastered to her cheek under bloodshot brown eyes. Water speckled her gray blouse. The sight of those errant drops tightened Morrison's chest as if each one had purposefully escaped from her head, running from the heartbreak, the pain. She kept her blank gaze fixed on the double-sided mirror as if waiting for someone to leap through it and tell her they'd made a mistake, that it was some other woman's child they'd found dead in the woods.

Shock did that to you, or maybe whatever the doc had prescribed her; the medications were the main reason they hadn't been able to see her earlier. A sedated witness, especially one numbed to the point of sleep, belonged in bed and not answering critical questions. Or perhaps her vacant look was denial. Her eye twitched, and Morrison wondered if she could already feel it trying to break through her composed façade: the thick heaviness of sorrow, the impending doom of a life where every day was just another in a new reality where a piece of you would forever be rubbed raw by grief.

Petrosky sat across from her at the metal table. When his chair squawked against the cement floor, she finally turned to face him and sniffed.

Morrison brought his notepad to the corner and stood behind Petrosky, suddenly too antsy to sit across from Lancaster, or maybe he didn't want to look too deeply into her eyes, which surely held a glimpse of her future misery. His heart hurt enough already.

"I was at work," Lancaster said, closing her eyes a beat longer than a blink. "They told me to come to the station right away. I thought...I thought maybe his dad had taken him." She shuddered, though the temperature in the room was always a good five degrees warmer than was comfortable. Then again, Morrison's insides felt cold too.

"Is his father your ex-husband, ma'am?" Petrosky asked.

Slow nod. Then: "But he didn't do this."

Morrison flipped to a clean page and wrote, *ex-husband.*

"We'll need his address." Petrosky's voice was soft, but Morrison recognized the set of his shoulders—they'd investigate the ex. Most victims were abused by someone familiar to them, and it would have been easy for a father to get his son to walk off the playground.

He wasn't sure Lancaster had heard Petrosky until she nodded slowly.

"Any issues with your ex lately?" Petrosky shifted in his seat.

"Arguments about custody. He wanted more time with Dylan. I said no."

"How'd he take that?"

"Terribly. But—"

"What did he say?"

She lowered her gaze to her shaking hands. "That he'd see me in court. And he said he'd make sure Dylan knew what a bitch I was. That he'd drag me through the mud."

The mud. Literally what had happened to Dylan Acosta. But this didn't feel like an angry ex seeking revenge. The crimes committed against Acosta were vicious. And their killer hadn't started with Acosta—this type of rape-homicide was usually carried out by a sexual predator, escalating when the mere act of assault no longer thrilled him.

"How was your ex with Dylan?" Petrosky said. "Any changes in their relationship or Dylan's behavior?"

Morrison touched his pen to the notepad. He'd been in enough interrogations with Petrosky to know what he was getting at—whether her ex had been inappropriate.

"Once we divorced, Glen really started spending more time with Dylan."

Morrison wrote *Glen Acosta* next to *ex-husband* and waited.

"Dylan...loved him," she said to the table. "He never complained, ever." She looked up at Petrosky and blinked rapidly to clear the water from her eyes. "That actually pissed me off a little, that my ex was always the good guy."

"Inappropriate behavior toward Dylan or other boys?"

Her glassy eyes squinted at the ceiling, then settled on Petrosky. "Never. He even coaches Dylan's little league team. Coached." Her voice cracked, and Morrison could almost hear her heart breaking. "Glen's an asshole to me, but you're wasting your time. You find the bastard that did this."

"We'll do our best, ma'am." Petrosky leaned toward her, voice softer now. "Did your ex have any nicknames for Dylan? Maybe his number one kid, anything like that?"

The bloody *#1* carved into the child's side was seared on Morrison's brain too. He could almost feel the blade against his skin. He tightened his grip on his pen, hoping Acosta's mother knew something about the number—if she did, the killer probably knew the boy or his family.

"Nothing like that. My ex isn't very...creative."

Petrosky leaned back, hands clasped on the desktop. "What about other people who spent time with your son? Pastors, coaches, teachers? Anyone Dylan seemed uncomfortable around?"

"You think Dylan...knew the person who did this?"

In the other case they'd found—Zachary Reynolds—the victim hadn't known his attacker. But here there were two suspects instead of just one, and Acosta's killer would have a different pattern from the pedophile who'd raped the boys. Acosta probably knew at least one of them if the suspects lured him off the playground instead of waiting for him to wander into the woods of his own accord.

"We don't know, but those who hurt children often groom them for a period of time."

Petrosky didn't correct her assumption about "the person" who'd done this, and Morrison was thankful for that. She didn't need to find out today that a pair of men had brutalized her child.

"I always told him not to talk to strangers. I thought that'd be enough."

Kids were rarely attacked by strangers. Again, neither of them said a word to correct her.

"Does your son have a computer?" Petrosky asked.

"Of course. They need it for school." Her chest puffed up just slightly like her guilt was boiling over into defensiveness.

"We'll need access to it in case he was communicating with someone online."

"He wasn't communicating with anyone," she said. "I would have known."

"What about online gaming?" Morrison's own voice sounded oddly hollow against the cement walls. Not every interaction would be saved as an email or readily available on a laptop or iPad, but if Acosta'd been using the web to communicate with the men who'd attacked him, Morrison would find it.

Petrosky glanced back, nodded, and turned back to Lancaster.

"No."

"None? At all?" Petrosky cocked his head.

"We don't let him play those grown-up games. There are kids in his class who were getting into trouble with that."

"Trouble like how?" Petrosky asked. "Strangers contacting them or—"

"No, just…there are some vile games out there."

Morrison leaned back against the wall and focused on the pad as Petrosky nodded his agreement about the video games, probably building rapport—he doubted Petrosky had ever actually played one.

When Petrosky stilled, she continued: "All he does is some block building game, but….well, he said you do have to be online. For some of it. And I guess…he did talk to his friends on there. But just his friends, I made sure."

Morrison made a note.

"We'll need those passwords too," Petrosky said. "Whatever user names he has."

"But it's just… I've read articles. Those games are good for his brain. *Were* good for…" Her breath came out rapidly, and the walls reflected it back like a shockwave of regret.

"Did you read about the six-year-old child who was lured from her home and kidnapped after playing a game like that?" Petrosky had obviously decided that Tara Lancaster wasn't providing him with answers fast enough—or that she was stonewalling him, even if she was in denial.

Probably the latter, based on the harshness in his voice and the set of his shoulders.

Lancaster's jaw dropped, and she made no effort to close it.

Petrosky leaned across the table. "It's not the game itself," he said more softly. "The people who victimize children—these guys know how to find kids. They usually pretend to be other kids. There's no way you'd know. It's not your fault." Petrosky pulled out a photo from Zachary Reynolds's case file, a composite sketch of the guy who'd raped Reynolds. The guy whose semen was also found in Lancaster's son. "You ever seen him before?"

She squinted at it and shook her head. "I don't think so."

"Are you certain?"

"As certain as I can be about anything right now."

Petrosky shifted in the seat, grunting faintly with the effort. "Do you have a boyfriend? Babysitters? Anyone who had regular contact with Dylan?"

She shook her head again. "No boyfriend and no sitter. I work at the bank—I drop him off for school and pick him up after. No one else is around, usually. Just at baseball, but you'd have to ask Glen about that."

True, there wouldn't have been a lot of time for a predator to take Acosta aside during a game—let alone actually abuse him between innings. But to groom Acosta, to connect with him, a ballgame was prime abuser territory. Maybe an assistant coach. Another father. A man who wouldn't stick out at a little boy's baseball practice.

"Dylan does...did...spend time with friends. Sleepovers or mall trips with his friends' older siblings, that kind of thing. He was small, but he was almost twelve, so I guess he was...pulling away a little bit. Didn't tell me as much anymore." Her eyes filled, then dripped down her face onto the table. She sniffed.

"I'll need those names also, ma'am," Petrosky said.

"They wouldn't have hurt Dylan. They have kids too."

Half of their solved cases ended with the arrest of a family friend, one with children themselves. Morrison pressed his lips together. No reason to point it out—any correction would be taken as an accusation right now, and she'd already go home wracked with guilt. And if the agony that still tinted Petrosky's eyes like sorrowful watercolors was any indication, the heartbreak would never leave.

MORRISON AND PETROSKY left the interrogation room with a list of contacts from Tara Lancaster. Five stops to start with. Five times they'd have to see the anguish in Acosta's friends, in other parents who were overcome by horror thinking that it could just as easily have been their child. Though maybe in one, they'd see the twinkle of remorse or feel the niggling of guilt like gooseflesh on exposed legs. That'd be good—but it was hard to say whether it was likely. Not only did they have two perps, not typical for this type of case, but they had one rapist and one murderer—maybe. Acosta may have known one and not the other, or they both might have been strangers to the boy.

Outside the precinct, the sky was bright and blue and still, not even the hint of a breeze. Petrosky's car stunk of old grease and cigarettes. Gross, but somehow welcome, like coming home to a dirty house that was still comfortable because it belonged to you. Morrison rolled the window down anyway—even home needed to be aired out, especially since Petrosky was already pulling a smoke from the pack on the dash as he put the car in gear.

They'd start with Dylan's father. Petrosky had called him from the interrogation room after Lancaster left and agreed to meet him in a bar after work. Morrison's heart rate climbed at the prospect—Petrosky and liquor, addicts in their place of addiction. But when Petrosky caught Morrison's stare, he'd leveled a glare so fierce Morrison felt like an ass for even considering it.

Sobriety was a daily battle, but not necessarily a difficult one, at least not every day. Maybe Petrosky'd found a way to make his days easier while Morrison had been changing dirty diapers. He seemed fine, or as fine as he'd ever been. Petrosky had always worn his grouchiness like a badge of honor, possibly because he hated most people but more likely because he was protecting some soft spot inside from harm. God knew the man had been through enough.

They were halfway to the lot exit when a figure crossed the road from the neighboring prosecutor's office. As tall as Morrison himself at well over six feet, with broad shoulders and a blond crew cut, Roger McFadden—Shannon's ex-husband and lead prosecutor and incredible asshole—had a nose that would always be a touch crooked after connecting with Morrison's fist. Too bad his ego still wouldn't accept that he was less than perfect. Roger walked directly toward them, and Petrosky didn't slow—a game of douchebag chicken. Roger's suit was as impeccable as was his gold watch, probably the one Shannon had given him for their second anniversary. They hadn't made it to three. It shouldn't have annoyed him, but every hair on Morrison's arms stood up at the sight of the gold glinting in the morning sun.

Petrosky slammed on his brakes at the last possible moment, the front bumper practically kissing Roger's pants. A part of Morrison was disappointed that Petrosky hadn't mowed him down.

"Well, well, you're back," Roger said. His eyes bored through the windshield as he leaned toward them, hands on the hood, and Morrison immediately regretted rolling down the window. The corner of Roger's mouth turned up. "And how's my lovely wife?"

Roger would spend a lifetime seeking reinforcement, burning for

Shannon to say: "I was wrong. You're worth it; you're better." And yet if that were ever to actually happen, he'd reject her as he had when he'd been married to her. Winning was all that mattered to Roger.

"Shannon's doing just fine." Morrison said, working to keep his voice even.

Petrosky puffed on his cigarette and grinned. "Better watch it, Rog, before he breaks your nose again."

The smug smile slid from Roger's face. "Not if he wants to keep providing for his lovely little family. Even if he is sloppy seconds."

Morrison's fists clenched, but he forced his face to remain placid. He could almost hear the ocean in his head, settling with each breath he took: stormy waves of rage and anger calming to a tumultuous lapping, easing to a gentle whoosh of salt on sand. Peaceful. He smiled and chuckled, making sure Roger saw it.

Roger's face twisted with anger—the man hated nothing more than to be the butt of someone's joke.

Petrosky stuck his head out the window. "Move, fuckhead!"

Roger squared his shoulders and held his ground.

Petrosky jerked the wheel to the right, and Roger leapt out of the way as Petrosky swung around him and sprayed his suit with gravel and dust. Morrison kept his eyes on the side-view mirror, watching Roger frantically brushing at his suit and muttering what were probably curse words under the squeal of the tires as Petrosky turned onto the main road.

"Once a dick, always a dick," Petrosky said.

Morrison dragged his eyes back to the front windshield, his smile still frozen on his lips. He itched with the desire to smash his knuckles into Roger's stupid face. Again.

"He's just pissed that Shannon's always loved you." Petrosky ashed his cigarette out the window and shoved it between his teeth again. "Even when she was married to him."

"I'm not sure that's true," Morrison said, but he felt suddenly lighter.

9

THE REYNOLDS FAMILY lived in Rochester, a forty-five-minute drive from Detroit, in a two-story colonial in a neighborhood where children still rode bikes without looking over their shoulders, and the stray dog wandering in your yard belonged to someone you knew so there was no need to be cautious about approaching it. Ironic that they were going to visit a kid who knew just how easily the illusion of safety could be shattered. It had been five years since Zachary Reynolds's attack, but hopefully, they'd get something they could use.

Mrs. Reynolds answered the door wearing a white turtleneck and a gold treble clef on a chain over her heart. Brown hair, brown eyes, brown freckles over the bridge of her nose. The living room was warm, with worn leather sofas and oak end tables, but there was nothing to indicate people actually lived here. No toys. No books. Just baubles and vases on the shelves flanking the fireplace.

She gestured to the couch. "So how can I help? You said you might have some new information about my son's...attack?" She smoothed down her pencil skirt and sat across from them. Feigning composure. But the subtle quiver in her hands gave her away. "I didn't know they were still looking at his case."

"We may have a related crime," Petrosky said, his face still and watchful as a lion sizing up prey.

"This is about that boy. The one they found...murdered behind the school playground." Not a question. Her mouth tightened—it could have been her kid dead on the ground. Almost had been. She wrung her hands.

Morrison set the case file in his lap and pulled his notebook from his back pocket: *Reynolds, mother*. The mere process of scratching ink on the pad relaxed his shoulders, though he had no real reason to be tense to begin with. Roger must have gotten to him more than he'd thought.

"Why do you think the cases are related, Detective? Because of the… rape at school thing?" She dropped her eyes.

"Yes."

And because of the DNA at the scene. Then there was the T-shirt around Acosta's neck, tied just like the one that had strangled Reynolds. But Petrosky didn't elaborate.

She clutched her necklace, stopping short of touching her throat. "You think he tried to kill my Zach, too?"

"I think he wanted Zach to be quiet," Petrosky said. "Or he managed to stop himself." But it wasn't the shirt around the throat that had killed Acosta. Leaping from rape to stomping a kid to death—or allowing it—was a stretch. And from the struggle at the scene…it didn't seem like this rapist had been ready to take that step. So who had? Morrison tried not to picture the gaping holes in Acosta's back, tried not to imagine the sound of his last breaths as they were reduced to a bloody gurgle.

"You think he's escalating?" she said.

Petrosky raised an eyebrow. "Ma'am?"

"My shrink, he tells me about this stuff. I mean, I ask, and he answers." She reached for a box of tissues on the end table, thought better of it, and smoothed her skirt again. "I read a lot too. Real crime. Books on these…pedophiles. Trying to understand what Zach went through. What he's still going through." She wrung her hands again, then looked Petrosky in the eye. "Ask your questions. It'll be easier for me before he gets here."

"Walk me through the day it happened."

She did, her eyes filling and overflowing. It had been a typical morning. They'd eaten breakfast and headed to the school like every other day. She'd even been working with Zach's homeroom teacher, putting together folders and supervising a class project on Abraham Lincoln.

"Do most parents volunteer like that?" Morrison asked, and Reynolds's eyes widened as if she'd forgotten he was there.

She recovered quickly and shook her head. "Not usually that much. Maybe an hour or two every quarter."

Morrison tapped the notepad with his pen, stopping when she frowned. "But you'd been there that whole week."

"Zach had just gotten out of the hospital, and I wanted to make sure he was…okay." She shuddered. "Leukemia. We almost lost him. And even now…I mean, the risk is there." She was trembling. "And he just keeps tempting fate."

Morrison made a note on his pad—*Acting out?*—while she grabbed a tissue and wiped her eyes like it was the fault of the Kleenex that her son's health had been shitty. He understood. Sometimes there was no one to blame.

"So after the homeroom project…" Petrosky said.

"I went to the office to make copies. The printer is right in front of the window that looks out to the playground. I never should have taken my eyes off him."

"Why did you?" Petrosky asked.

"This wasn't my fault!"

But she'd remember it every day for the rest of her life, that one moment of looking away from her child. And tomorrow, Evie would be gone for a week, away from his own watchful gaze. Morrison's gut clenched.

"Absolutely not your fault, ma'am," Petrosky said. "But the report said that someone asked you a question?"

Her shoulders relaxed. She nodded.

"Someone who worked there?"

"No. It was…just a guy. Came into the office." She furrowed her brows. "He asked whether there was school on President's Day, which I thought was weird because it was over a month away, but it wasn't really that strange of a question, I guess."

Same answer she'd given to the police five years ago—Morrison had looked through the witness statements. But he had yet to scour the atrociously-written and horribly-sorted police notes to see if the cops had actually located the question asker. They'd get on that next.

She glanced from Petrosky to Morrison and his pen and back again. "You think it was on purpose? That this guy asked me something just to get me to look away?"

"Probably not, ma'am. Just covering the bases."

"Then, did someone distract this new boy's teacher while they lured him off the playground?"

"Not that we know of."

"But you think he did it to…wait, was there more than one guy? With this new boy? Is that why you're asking about someone in the office?"

She was quick. Petrosky met her gaze and said nothing, but Morrison could see the wheels working behind her eyes. Petrosky inhaled to speak again, but she beat him to it.

"He was blond. Probably younger than I was then, but not by much. A few wrinkles around the eyes, you know."

"Eye color?"

She considered, then shook her head. "I used to think that every detail of that morning would be imprinted on my brain forever. But this…"

She hadn't known back when Zachary had been attacked—either Petrosky hadn't read the case file, or he was trying to catch her in a lie.

"Short or long hair?"

"Long. Ponytail, actually. I remember thinking that he looked like a hippie. The police must have interviewed him—they interviewed everyone in the school. But this guy was so...different looking. Definitely wasn't the one who attacked Zach—he looked nothing like the guy from the police sketch they did afterward."

"Any distinguishing marks? Scars?"

"No, I don't think." She swallowed hard. "I can't really remember. But like I said, I'm sure they talked to him. They talked to everyone."

"Is there anything else you recall from that day, anything you neglected to tell the officers?"

"I called every week for over a year. Everything I knew, they knew. Now it's been so long...I'm starting to forget details, I guess." Her eyes remained drawn, but there was a hopeful edge to her voice beneath the regret. It had to be rather promising that one *could* forget even small pieces of a day so awful. Perhaps one day, the other memories would fade as the good in life oozed in to crowd out the tragedy. Though the horror never fully disappeared.

"Does the number one mean anything to you? Even the symbol, the pound sign followed by the numeral?"

She shook her head, but the door interrupted her, a hearty slam punctuated by the throbbing beat of heavy soles approaching the doorway.

Zachary Reynolds had a dog collar around his neck and silver rings through his septum and eyebrow. He glared at Morrison and Petrosky, then at his mother. "I told you I didn't want to do this."

"It will just take a moment, honey and—"

"Fuck this." He pointed to Petrosky. "And fuck them."

"He did it to someone else." Petrosky stood abruptly, his eyes on the boy's boots. "Nice kicks. Where'd you get them?"

Kicks? Looked like someone had swapped the old man for a newer, hipper version. Morrison resisted the urge to tell Petrosky that the word might not mean what he thought it did.

The kid glared.

"I gave him the boots," Mrs. Reynolds said from the couch.

"You have more of 'em?" Petrosky asked, though why it mattered was beyond Morrison. It wasn't like Zachary Reynolds had teamed up with his rapist to attack and murder another child. And the boots didn't appear to have treads like those at the Acosta scene—too flat, and no sign of anything that would puncture the skin.

Zach squinted, and his mother answered again. "Just the one pair. For his birthday. Why are you—"

"I said I didn't want to do this," Zach repeated.

Petrosky stepped forward. "You may not give a fuck about this other kid—"

Mrs. Reynolds stood too, her eyes wide. "Detective—"

"It's my job to try to find this asshole," he said to Zach. "I'd like to fry the ever-loving shit out of the guy who hurt you. And if it's the same fellow, all the better when I hook his nipples to a car battery."

Mrs. Reynolds's mouth dropped in shock. "Maybe if you leave your questions, I can ask him later or…"

Zach appraised his mother, lips tight, then returned to Petrosky. "Let's talk outside."

Mrs. Reynolds reached out to touch the boy's arm, but he pulled away and stalked back out the front door. Petrosky followed, Mrs. Reynolds gasping objections behind them. Her cheeks flamed.

Morrison touched her elbow, expecting her to shove him off, but she stopped in the foyer and turned back slowly, her mouth drawn in acquiescence.

"Detective Petrosky might seem a little rough around the edges, but he knows what he's doing," he said quietly.

Her foot was tapping—like she was trying to decide whether to go tearing off after them. But from what he'd just witnessed, her presence would be enough to make the boy stop speaking altogether.

"Do we still have your consent, ma'am? To speak to your son?"

Her yes was barely audible through her heavy sigh.

ZACHARY REYNOLDS and Petrosky were already halfway down the street, twin trails of smoke wafting toward the sky above them. *Mommy would love that.* From down the block, Morrison heard a string of curse words erupt from the teen's mouth. *She'll love that too.*

Morrison caught up with them in time to hear Petrosky say: "—tone of voice? How about anything specific that he said?"

"No, he was kinda quiet. Smiled though, and he seemed so…nice. Gave me candy. Fucking cliché. I know it was stupid, following him, but…" Reynolds looked down. "He did look familiar, but I don't know where we'd met before. I tried for years to figure that out." He shook his head and pulled on the cigarette.

"You don't recall anyone else out there? Even just standing around?"

"Nope, no one."

"I read the report, Zach. Frizzy brownish hair. Scraggly, right?"

Slow nod.

"The report said you weren't sure on the eye color. Remember anything afterward? Not just on the eyes but on his appearance?"

Scars, facial hair, or acne could help them identify a suspect, but even recent eyewitness reports were often inaccurate. Five years ago? Petrosky was really reaching now.

Reynolds shook his head. "Seriously, I don't know. He was shorter than most adults, I guess, but he was old. Like…thirtysomething. And he was strong, and I couldn't…stop him."

Huh. It sounded like the pedophile who'd raped Reynolds five years ago had committed a crime of opportunity—if Reynolds had been groomed, he'd know where he'd met the guy. Would the rapist have stuck to that pattern? Had the *killer* known Dylan Acosta?

"Of course you couldn't stop him, Zach. No one doubts that. Right now, I'm just trying to find something we can use for identification. Stains on his jeans: paint or grease? Some other sign of where he worked? A name tag? The exact pattern on his T-shirt, an extra logo maybe?"

"He wasn't wearing a T-shirt. It was a button-down kinda thing, like a short-sleeved dress shirt. There wasn't anything on it...I don't think."

Petrosky stopped walking. "In the initial report, you told the officers he was wearing a clown shirt."

Reynolds's eyes narrowed as if he were trying to protect them from the smoke wafting from his nostrils. "Clown shirt?"

"That's what was in the file. A picture of a clown on his—"

"It wasn't on his shirt. It was on his stomach."

The pen in Morrison's hand jittered over the page more than he wanted it to. He pressed the tip harder against the paper before Petrosky could notice.

"A tattoo?" Petrosky said it slowly as if worried he'd heard the boy incorrectly.

"I mean, maybe I said it weird. I was tired and scared and...confused. Or I might not have known the name for a tattoo back then." He fingered his eyebrow ring, and the metal glinted in the sun. "Maybe I told them he was wearing a picture? I was all fucked up in the head. I really can't remember what I said, but I know the picture was on his fucking gut, and I only saw it once I tore the buttons off his shirt, trying to get away. It moved when he—" Reynolds's lip quivered, and he covered it by jamming the cigarette between his teeth.

"Sounds like you remember it pretty well."

The kid's face disappeared behind an acrid cloud.

"Can you describe it?"

"Well...a clown, like I said. On a horse. But it was creepy, had fangs and stuff."

"Could you draw it?" Petrosky asked, his voice even. "Doesn't have to be perfect, just what you remember."

Reynolds took the notepad and sketched, his cigarette dangling from his lips. Ash dropped onto his boot, and he paused to shake it off before completing the sketch.

Morrison and Petrosky peered at the drawing: a vampire clown, carrying a rifle and riding a vampire horse, the animal's mouth full of foam and blood.

"You're a good artist," Morrison said.

Reynolds dragged at the smoke. "For all the good it'll do me." He turned to Petrosky. "You think he killed that other kid? My mom told me about it."

"Not sure yet."

"He probably should have killed me too," Reynolds whispered, his eyes on his boots as he toed the dirt. Silent. Probably waiting for them to challenge such a notion.

Petrosky shrugged. "Maybe he should have." Morrison balked, but Petrosky wasn't done. "Because if we get him based on what you said, he's going to be sorry as fuck that he left you alive." He inhaled sharply on the cigarette. "You know what they do to pedophiles in prison, Zach?"

The kid met Petrosky's eyes.

Smoke curled toward the pewter sky. "Use your imagination, before your mother files charges against me for corrupting you. But let's just say, he'll wish he was dead every goddamn day. And he'll never look at a broom the same way again."

Reynolds tossed his cigarette butt on the sidewalk, blew smoke at his shoes, and smiled.

> "But as in ethics, evil is a consequence of good, so in fact, out of joy is sorrow born."
> ~Edgar Allan Poe, *Berenice*

10

THE WORLD WHIPPED by the passenger window, but Morrison barely noticed. A search for scary-ass clowns had given him more results than he would have thought. On his smartphone screen, two men in clown costumes—more Stephen King's *It* than Bozo—screamed about slicing up their girlfriends and impaling them on fence posts outside a circus tent, all over the twang of a banjo. Clown Alley Freaks, a local band that appeared to be a combination of gangster rap and backwoods hillbilly. *Who listens to this stuff?* But he already knew the answer—he wished he knew less about all the sickness in the—

Morrison stopped scrolling through album covers on his cell and tapped one to enlarge.

The cover was purple and yellow, with a torn circus tent as the backdrop. In the foreground, a grisly clown atop a horse sneered at him over the top of a hunting rifle, blood dripping from its mouth, a severed leg in one hand like a club. A single arm was clamped between the horse's teeth, useless tendons stringing toward the ground like ghastly spaghetti. *Sick.* And these people were out there, walking around like normal folks, grocery shopping and hanging out at the park. With his wife. With his daughter. His stomach soured.

"Has to have something to do with these guys," he said, glancing up as Petrosky maneuvered into the precinct parking lot.

Petrosky put the car in park. "Fucking hell. Kid's got a good memory."

"Guess some things you never forget." Morrison pocketed the phone. "Should we start with the east side tattoo parlors? I can pull up a list—"

"Go home."

"But we just got a break—"

"It's Tuesday night. They're not open now, California."

"How do you know?"

"You're worried."

Morrison balked. "What?"

"About Shannon. I can smell it on you." Petrosky chewed on the butt of the cigarette. "She's okay. A few scary post-pregnancy thoughts a few months back, but she's okay now. If thinking about suicide a few times made it happen, we'd all be dead."

"I don't think she's...unstable." Though anyone else she came across might be.

"Of course you don't. But I know you're thinking about how she was with Evie those first few weeks—how she struggled. And it's the first time she's been alone all day since then."

"Well, in just a few days, she'll be with Alex and Abby." But Petrosky was right. The nagging in Morrison's gut wasn't about how many crazy assholes Shannon might encounter on her way to Atlanta.

"If you're not home for dinner, Shannon is going to have your ass. And mine."

She'd still be up in a couple hours. "Nah, she'll—"

"This isn't a trial run where you get to check how she reacts when you stand her up." Petrosky yanked the keys from the ignition and pushed open the car door. "Catch you in the morning, California. And if I see you inside, I'm the one you'll need to worry about, not Shannon."

Morrison nodded, relieved, and pulled his car keys from his pocket. "Got it, Boss."

"I'VE CALLED Natalie Bell three times, but I can't get through." Shannon speared a bite of salad and frowned at the fork. "Maybe she already took another job."

Morrison glanced at Evie, who was nursing at Shannon's breast, dressing from Shannon's salad in her hair. He waited for a twinge of disappointment over the fact that they still hadn't hired a nanny, but felt no such irritation. Maybe he really wasn't ready to have a stranger caring for his daughter. "She got another position that fast?"

"I told you, the good ones get snapped up quickly."

"It's been a day."

"But a week from the first interview I did." She shoved a handful of blond hair off her face. Her curls fell right back down in a messy tangle.

Morrison suppressed a grin. "Maybe she just had something to do today. I'll try her after dinner."

"Oh, because you can make a phone call better than I can?"

"They call me The Master Dialer."

Shannon laughed and put her free hand up in mock surrender. Evie wiggled on her lap, only the top of her head visible under the table and one tiny, fleshy fist punching at Shannon's clothing as if Evie was personally oppressed by her mother's shirt. "Call away."

Movement at Morrison's ankle made him jump. The cat mewed at him, its dark fur glassy as an oil slick. "We need to get another dog."

"You love Slash."

"He hates me. Wakes me up at least four times a week to go outside." Already the cat had moved on to Shannon's side of the table, where his wife was dropping bits of salmon onto the tile floor.

"Install a cat door. And he doesn't hate you." Her eyes were on the animal. Evie's fist swung up again and almost connected with Shannon's chin.

"You tell her, Evie. Tell her Slash is a buttface."

"He's just an outside cat, Morrison. They're a little more...particular."

"He's a jerk."

"So's Petrosky, and we keep him around."

Morrison peered under the table and glowered at the cat, and Slash mewed back. Damn if he wasn't adorable. Morrison pursed his lips. "Don't look at me like that, you little furball."

"What's wrong?" Shannon sat the baby up and wiped salmon from Evie's forehead. Evie babbled in protest and scrunched up her face.

"Nothing."

"Stressed about work? Or the nannies?"

He pushed his own salmon around on his plate. "No. That took some figuring out today, but no." There was the case, but that was just the job. But Shannon was leaving tomorrow. With Evie. They'd be gone for a week and if Shannon started to have those dark thoughts again... No, he was probably just stressed. Or upset about...Roger's gold watch. Yes, just remembering the glint of sun on the watch's face, like Shannon's gift was happy to be on Roger's wrist, stoked an irrational fury deep in Morrison's gut. "I saw Roger today."

"Ah, that'll do it." She searched his face. "How did he seem?"

Why does she care? "Like himself."

"So, like a dickhead?"

Morrison's chest loosened a little, and the sudden lack of tension made him lean back in his chair. Had he really been holding onto that all day? "He was definitely a dickhead."

"I'm not looking forward to going back to work with him. Maybe one day you and I will just move away altogether. Start fresh."

"Yeah."

She furrowed her brows. "But?"

"You know I don't want to—"

"—leave Petrosky." She grabbed her fork. "He'll be okay, Morrison. I promise. We don't have to go far, just...far enough that I don't have to deal with Roger." She ran her fingers through her hair and blew out an exasperated breath. "Sorry. I'm a little stressed too. I've been thinking about getting a position in another city. I don't want to work too far from home, but I can't find much else in Southfield or anywhere within thirty minutes. I'm stuck."

Stuck. With him? *With the job.* The fork handle was digging into his palm, and he released his grip.

"I guess it's good. I can...heal a little more before making big changes. Get back to what I know. But it's been on my mind lately, and even Dr. McCallum seems to think it'd be a good move."

"You talked to McCallum before me?" Of course she'd talked to her shrink. Why wouldn't she? That was his job. But still, he was her best friend, her husband and—

"Well, no." Shannon switched Evie to the other breast, and the kid kicked her in the gut so hard that Shannon winced. "I mean, yeah, I talked to him, but I didn't want to bother you with it until I had it figured out in my own head."

God, he was a hypocrite. Dr. McCallum was the only person who knew—*really knew*—about Morrison's addiction and his missing memories. Now that Morrison was sober, McCallum thought the missing pieces would never come to light. "State-dependent memory requires you to be in a similar state for recall to the one you were in when the memory was formed," the shrink had said. So if you'd repressed a memory of an event that had happened, say, while drinking, you were more likely to retrieve that memory from your brain during an intoxicated state.

The gist, as Morrison understood it, was that he'd need to shoot up to fill in the gaps in his memory. And that wasn't worth one morning of traumatized reminiscing—withdrawal had been a beast. Though not as much of a beast as his emotions had been without the drug. He had never gotten to the sell-your-soul-to-the-devil stage of addiction, but heroin had been like a lover, the only thing that made him feel something besides the bitter emptiness from the deaths of his parents: his dad shot dead in a robbery when Morrison was still in primary school and his mother, beaten to death with a baseball bat by an abusive boyfriend Morrison's freshman year of college. And his best friend Danny, his glazed eyes, the blood on Morrison's hands... Maybe the lack of memory was for the best. Most days, he sincerely didn't want to know what he'd forgotten.

Morrison watched Slash leap onto the extra chair at the dining table and curl into a purring ball. Shannon was right. If she'd asked him earlier about changing jobs, he probably would have asked if she thought big changes were a good idea while transitioning back into the working world. And he should trust her. He *needed* to trust her. Shannon was strong, intelligent—she wasn't one to tolerate being treated like an invalid. It was bad enough that she had doubted herself, but if she hadn't told him...she doubted his faith in her, too.

He touched her hand. "Whatever you want to do, Shanny, you know I'll support you." If they needed to move a little farther out, they would. The market wasn't great, but they'd figure it out. They'd—

Slash picked his head up as Morrison's cell rang. Probably Petrosky—maybe with a lead. Morrison dropped his fork and had raised the phone to his ear before he recognized that the ringtone itself was just the standard buzz and not Petrosky's *Miami Vice* jingle or the ringtone belonging to Valentine or the chief. Telemarketer? "Morrison."

"Hey, this is Natalie Bell." Her voice was hoarse, low. A cold?

"Ms. Bell. Good to hear from you." Across from him, Shannon straightened, and Evie fussed at the movement.

"I know you called about the job, but I took something else." Not sick. *Whispering.* Muffled like she was talking through a cloth or had a hand wrapped over the receiver.

"Oh, okay, thanks for letting us know." The line went dead before Morrison could say goodbye.

Shannon stared at him expectantly, eyebrows at her hairline. "So?"

"No-go on Bell. She found something else."

"Dammit! We should have just offered it to her when she was here. I know it's better to be thorough, but—" She frowned. "Why'd she call you? I left my number earlier."

"I gave her my business card yesterday. Besides, I told you, I'm The Master Dialer." He picked up his fork again.

"You didn't even have a chance to dial." Shannon looked at Slash. "Fuck."

"Indeed."

Shannon put her napkin on the table and stood, tugging her shirt down and shifting Evie to her hip. "You want to call Alyson Kennedy with your magical phone fingers while I take a bath?" She walked around the table and put Evie in his lap, then brushed his ear with her lips. "And if she says no, don't tell me until you've secured us another nanny, okay?"

He put his hand on the small of her back. "You sure Alyson is the one you—"

Her look stopped him. No arguing with lawyers.

"You'll love her," she said. "Trust me." Shannon kissed him again, on the lips this time, and her smell lingered in his nostrils like all that was right with the world was concentrated there in her scent.

"You got it, Shanny."

She headed for the door. "I just nursed Evie, so if you manage to get her down before I get out of the tub, join me. We're leaving for Alex's in the morning, and we won't see you for a week."

Morrison stared down at Evie's round face, at her wide eyes as blue as the sea, her Cupid bow lips grinning at him. "You're not going to let that happen, are you, beautiful?"

Evie just gurgled.

EVIE DIDN'T FALL asleep in his arms until well after Shannon had emerged from the bathtub, but the smell of Shannon's skin was all it took. Their lovemaking was patient, though faster than it had been in the days before Evie, when he used to spend hours stroking Shannon's skin, watching her writhe. Now she'd rather sleep—not that he could blame her. Parenthood was draining in a way he'd not expected—in a way he'd never have known about if he hadn't stayed home this last month. Afterward, he lay beside her and watched the moon cast shadows on her bare back, every familiar plane of her skin hazy beneath the soft glow. Somewhere in the night, a dog howled, loud and long, perhaps seeking another to share the moonlight with him. Seeking what Morrison had already found. The baby monitor crackled from the end table.

Morrison rolled toward the wall where the darkness was deep and quiet—a pleasant break from the harsh glare of day. He drifted off to sleep with his heart full and peaceful, the phantom voices of a repressed memory for once blissfully silent.

11

By the time Morrison woke up Wednesday morning, he'd almost acquiesced to the idea that Alyson Kennedy would make a damn fine nanny for Evie. When he'd called her the night before, she'd practically squealed with excitement. "I'm thrilled. I can't wait to meet you, Mr. Morrison. And I can't wait to care for Evie. She's a doll." Even Evie had seemed extra happy this morning, her pudgy cheeks shining, milk dribbling down her chin as he bounced her in one arm. But Evie didn't know that she and Shannon were leaving for a week.

Morrison's stomach was twisted in knots. He hefted Shannon's suitcase into the trunk alongside the pack-n-play she'd brought for Evie to sleep in, then grabbed the cooler and positioned it in the front seat so Shannon would have easy access when she got hungry. "Say hi to Roxy for me," he said lightly. He still missed the dog he'd given to Shannon's niece, though he wouldn't admit it. Nor would he admit how badly he wished the dog was there now—he'd have felt better knowing Roxy was riding shotgun, protecting his family in his absence.

He tried to smile, but his whole face felt tight, like the muscles in his cheeks were rubber bands stretched to a hair from snapping. "And say hi to Abby and Alex, of course."

"You know I will." Shannon slammed the trunk.

He kissed Evie's soft, downy head. "I'll miss you guys."

"I wish you could come. I wish you hadn't used up all your time off after Evie was born, but...I really needed you then." She wrapped her arms around him and squeezed. The spring air sent the branches crackling above them as if the atmosphere itself was irritated by the thought of their separation.

"And I'm fine now, Morrison. Really. I'm fine, and Evie will be fine." Her voice was tight, rushed, like she was trying to convince herself.

He pulled back. "I know you're fine. I didn't think for one moment you weren't." That might have been a lie, but he couldn't dwell on it. Some of the things she'd told him…

"I can do this. I've got this." He almost winced at the furious intensity in her gaze. Did she resent the mere idea that she'd needed him? He shook off the thought. Postpartum depression can mess with a person's head. But that was over now.

Evie snuggled her face against his chest, and he could almost feel half his own heart in her pulse. "It was my fault, too, running around trying to solve cases while you were here struggling with a new baby. I was…" He should never have gone back to work right after Evie's birth. He hadn't even taken the week off when they'd gotten married. Though the way she was looking at him now…

Her eyes bored into his.

"What?"

Her face softened. "This is the first time we've ever really talked about it. I mean, after it was over."

"I thought you didn't want to." He hadn't wanted to either. Just hearing that she'd fantasized about dropping Evie from an upper-floor window had been enough to keep him awake for weeks. He'd taken immediate vacation time until things had settled.

"I didn't. I just wanted to put it behind us." She reached for Evie, and he laid the baby in her arms. "But I'm glad we did, you know? It feels better, knowing that you don't think I'm nuts."

He ran his thumb over her cheek, memorizing the contours as he'd done so many times before. "I never thought you were nuts, and I don't think it now." *No more than the rest of us, anyway.* "If I was worried, I'd fight you about leaving."

"Instead, you'll just badger me with texts."

"Because I love you."

A subtle question remained in her eyes—was she worried about his thoughts on her craziness?—but she kissed him hard and turned to the car to strap Evie into her car seat. "When we get home, I'll be back to work, and we'll both be struggling to get on track. Enjoy this little reprieve from diapers and making dinner."

"I won't miss the diapers."

She hugged him again, her breath faster than usual. "Screw the diapers," she said, but there was a tremor in her voice he didn't like.

"Shannon?"

She met his eyes.

"I know you're nervous," he said, quietly enough that the breeze around them might have drowned out his voice.

Her gaze slid to her shoes and back up to him. "It's just hard, you know? After…how bad things got, sometimes I just feel…weird I guess."

Her eyes were hard, determined, but her lip quivered almost imperceptibly.

"You're going to be fine, Shanny. You haven't had any of those thoughts in a long time." At least he hoped that was true. Then again, she had kept her desire to move from him—what else might she be hiding?

She nodded, but her silence unnerved him.

Don't beg her to stay. She'll think you don't trust her. McCallum was clear the last time they'd spoken—she needed to know she had his support, his trust. "I know how much this means to you to see Abby this weekend." Why wouldn't she be nervous about her first trip with a baby? He might have wished they were going somewhere else—there was still a part of Morrison that resented Dr. Alex Coleman. He had no logical reason for this disdain, only the image of Shannon's tear-stained face the day she found out Alex was leaving with Abby, her surrogate daughter. As if losing her brother to liver cancer hadn't been bad enough.

"I knew you'd understand." Shannon smiled, but her eyes stayed tight. "I'm nervous, but I *need* to do it. Maybe just to prove to myself that I can. I was always so headstrong, and to think that I needed a crutch, even if that crutch was just having you home with me—it's ridiculous, right?"

Shannon had called the medications a crutch too, but thankfully she'd taken the pills anyway. And she was damn right about being headstrong. Even at work, she had never met a defense attorney she couldn't take to the mat.

"You've got this, Shanny. You don't need the house to feel safe. You don't even need me. But I'll be here whenever you call."

One more hug and she was in the car, buckling her seatbelt, adjusting the rearview so she could see Evie. "I'll call when I get settled into the hotel."

"I'll be waiting by the phone."

She side-eyed him. "Maybe I'll wait until I get to Alex's to call, just to prove that I can make it there without sobbing on your shoulder." She smiled like she was joking. *Was* she kidding? Morrison appraised her as Shannon opened her mouth like she was going to say something else, then closed it.

"Drive safe, Shanny." He slammed the car door for her.

"I will. I love you."

He watched the taillights disappear down the drive and headed back inside to get ready for work. Every room felt empty, the silence stretching before him as though he'd lost them forever, but he knew that wasn't his real fear. It was what the absence of sound meant—the stinging blank in his eardrums screaming at him. *Idle time.* He'd never used it well. But this time, he had a case to work, so it shouldn't be too hard to find something to do.

He climbed into the shower, the rushing water filling his head with white noise. Better. Today would be a good day. Today he'd make

Repressed 551

headway on the Acosta case. Besides the reliable chaos of his family, there was nothing that silenced the whispers in his brain more effectively than catching a killer. And a killer this depraved would demand that much more of his energy.

He lathered his hair with shampoo and considered their most recent lead, the hideous clown tattoo. The image made his stomach turn, not because of the free tendons dangling from the horse's teeth, resembling bloody strands of yarn, but from what the pictures represented for someone who tattooed them onto their abdomen. Did this pedophile like fringe music, the sadism of the group? Or was he more into the images of creepy clowns, a child's nightmare come to fruition? Fear of clowns was pretty common, and if the guy liked scaring people, it would fit with the sadism. Or maybe…maybe he was into the circus shit because kids liked clowns—not that most kids would be impressed with the demonic variety. Would he have used friendlier clowns to get closer to Acosta? To any child? To have a whole clown tattooed on your body, you'd have to be pretty into them, right? Unless you were a clown yourself. Or maybe the clowns had nothing to do with anything. Maybe it was just a stupid tattoo.

By the time Morrison shut the shower off, the silence was bearable. He whistled his way through toweling and dressing and shaving and shoes, shrugged on his jacket, and reached for his gun. He froze.

The dresser was clean except for a bottle of antidepressants—Shannon's name on the label.

SHANNON DIDN'T ANSWER the phone. Maybe she was trying to avoid using him as a crutch like she'd said, but more likely, she was just driving and couldn't hear it over some little kid nursery rhyme CD she'd put on for Evie. He tried again. Voice mail. Morrison resisted the urge to hit redial. She'd think he was stalking her, or worse, that he didn't trust her.

He slipped the phone into his pocket, got into his own car, and headed to the precinct. The neighborhood was still hushed, the birdsong muted in the morning fog. Morrison squinted through the haze, trying to see the creatures, but they were hidden in the gloom. He inhaled deeply and maneuvered onto the main road, then exhaled with such force he was half certain the birds would hear it and disappear for good.

This is ridiculous. He stopped at a light and sent a text.

"Just wanted to let you know you left your pills at home. But don't worry, I'm sure McCallum will call them in. Miss you already."

She'd call when she got free. And there was no point in having her turn back an hour into the trip since McCallum could call in a prescription for her to pick up near Alex's. He climbed the stairs to the bullpen, finding his calm, picturing ocean waves and practically tasting salt. Shannon would be fine. Evie would be fine. He arranged and rearranged his current files, ignoring the stack of delinquent paperwork in the corner.

Morrison had just opened the Acosta file for the second time when Petrosky appeared, pulling a fast-food sandwich from a paper bag.

"The guy at Zachary Reynolds's school was a dad of one of the other kids," Petrosky said. "Found it in the file. Ran him just in case, but he and the family left town last year for his job as a tech executive. Living in China now. He's clean as a goddamn whale fart."

Morrison paused, hand over the files. *Reynolds. Executive.* "Clean as a...what?"

"Also, that fuckstick clown group was popular in the early nineties. Now they all live up on the east coast. Two of them own some fucking auto-body repair shop. They all have alibis for Acosta and Reynolds, no clown tattoos on anyone's stomach, and none of them remember any particularly crazy letters or renegade fans. Nice enough people if you can believe that shit."

"You've been busy." Morrison watched the sandwich disappear incrementally. "Now, about the whales—"

"You got the nanny thing figured out?" Petrosky said around a bite of egg muffin. "When does Bell start?"

"How'd you—"

Petrosky set the paper sack on the desk, and Morrison eyed the grease stains seeping through the bag like blood through a gurney sheet. "Looked at your files," Petrosky said, digging into the sack and producing a hash brown patty.

"Bell was unavailable." Morrison watched Petrosky's face, but nothing changed.

"Alyson Kennedy's a good second."

No way Petrosky could know that one—Morrison hadn't marked it down anywhere. "You talked to Shannon."

"Shannon called a week ago just after she got Kennedy's application. Asked if I knew her from the hospital since I'm often over there harassing the shit out of people. Her words, not mine." Petrosky eyed his potatoes like they owed him money. "Before she switched to pediatrics, Kennedy worked in the morgue for a little bit. I remember her from that."

Autopsy nurse turned nanny. Interesting choices. Not that it was more interesting than his own life decisions. "And the verdict?"

"Met her a few times. Good at her job. Thorough. I'm sure she'll be good with Evie too."

So, Shannon had vetted her choices before she even gave them to him. Knowing he'd recheck. No wonder she had been so confident—not that he should have expected less. *Lawyers.* She really was back to her old self. The tension in Morrison's shoulders eased just a little.

"She left already?" Petrosky shoved the packet of fried hash browns into his mouth.

"Yeah."

Petrosky raised an eyebrow.

"I'm all right." But the pit in his chest told him that wasn't completely true. It would be about time for Evie to eat. If they were home, Shannon would be nursing her, and then he'd burp Evie and change her diaper, and she'd giggle and look at him with those excited baby blues like he was the most awesome person on earth.

Morrison nodded to the remains of the breakfast burger. "Those things will kill you."

"I've lived long enough."

"Give us a few more years, eh? Let Evie get old enough to call you Gramps."

Petrosky shoved the rest of the egg muffin into his mouth and wiped his greasy fingers on a takeout napkin. He was aiming at nonchalant, but the twinkle in his eye gave him away. "You want to drive in case my heart gives out on the way there? I hear you even get free leave if your partner bites it." Petrosky's keys jangled as he held them up. "But I'll see if I can hold out until we find this fucker. I want to be the one to leak his list of charges to his prison mates."

12

THE COLORFUL PICTURES that had been in the windows of Acosta's school the day of the murder had been replaced with children's art projects: crayon crosses and construction paper cutouts with "Dylan" scrawled across the top. A shrine to the dead boy. Inside, the halls were still buzzing with the same nervous energy as the day they'd interviewed Acosta's classmates. But now, the gut-wrenching sadness in the air was stronger still, wrapping him like a mournful blanket.

Petrosky sat across from the principal's desk, Morrison next to him. They'd already spoken to Acosta's father and the families of those the boy hung out with on a regular basis. All of them were devastated. All of them were shocked. None of them had a thing to tell them outside of Mr. Acosta, who apparently thought that Dylan's mother should bear the blame for letting the kid play video games. Petrosky figured the funeral would be a fucking combat zone for Acosta's parents even after they found that the online gaming accounts Acosta interacted with were registered to his school buddies. Careful parents. But if his killer was an older brother of one of those kids or another dad...

They'd look at everyone, like always: parents, teachers, siblings, coaches. But that wasn't feeling right, not with the manner of the killing, not with the rapist's DNA match on Reynolds, and especially not with the place they'd chosen to attack Acosta. If the attackers had known the kid, they'd have brought him somewhere more private, unless the exhibitionism was part of the draw. More likely, the killer had watched Acosta and attacked opportunistically as he'd done with Reynolds. A stranger, or close to. And to find him, they needed all the help they could get.

The principal answered Petrosky's questions with a drawn mouth. Her suit was pressed, her makeup neat, and her black hair was slicked back in a tight bun, but her eyes were bloodshot. Lack of sleep? Probably. Someone had just raped and murdered a little boy on her watch. She wasn't to blame, but it was better for media ratings to sensationalize the event and the media had done just that, thanks to a leak from one of the parents. They'd also leaked the fact that the boy had been sexually assaulted, something responsible news outlets generally didn't disclose. Morrison bristled. At least they'd managed to keep the stomping a secret. So far.

"You said one of your students saw a bike from the classroom window?" Petrosky said. "An adult bike not belonging to staff?"

The melancholy on her face hardened into resolve. "None of our staff bike to school, so it doesn't belong to any of us. And only one boy saw it. I've talked to every teacher here, students who were with Dylan earlier in the day, even the janitor. We are not taking this lightly, detectives, I can assure you." Her words were tight, defensive, but after the news reports claiming that the school allowed Acosta off the property to be attacked by a child killer... She had every right to be.

"No one suspects you're doing anything less than your due diligence, Dr. Goldstein," Petrosky said, and her shoulders relaxed some at the words. The media had definitely been getting to her unless it was just her own guilt. Morrison made a note.

She nodded. "Good. Hopefully, he'll be able to tell you something. I want to see this bastard brought to justice."

Before he does it again, Morrison thought, but no one had to say it. Behind Principal Goldstein, a child's squeal split the room, along with the muffled thunk of balls on pavement. Morrison peered out the window into the brilliant sun and watched a little girl run after a ball. Teachers paced the grounds, their heads jerking this way and that, watching for a monster in the shadows ready to claim someone else's baby. The girl just grabbed the ball and laughed. Probably around ten years old. But give Evie five years, and she'd be in school too, no more nanny, no more days at home, just his little girl flying off on her own to a place where any terrible thing could happen to her and there would be nothing he could do to stop it. Morrison touched his phone, felt the familiar weight in his pocket. Shannon couldn't magically transport herself from Detroit to Atlanta—it'd take her at least five or six hours to reach her halfway-point hotel in Kentucky. She'd call when she stopped for the night.

Petrosky opened the file folder, and Goldstein's eyes widened when she saw the glossy prints. He held out the composite drawn after the Zachary Reynolds attack. "Does he look familiar?"

"You have a mug shot? A suspect already?" She leaned toward them, squinting at the image, and her face fell. "No, I've never seen him."

Of course Goldstein wouldn't know him. No one had seen the suspect around Zachary Reynolds's school, either.

She glanced back into the folder as Petrosky flipped half a dozen pages from the file. He tapped the top sheet. "I've also got some pictures to help us identify the bike your student saw. Did he say where he noticed it?"

"The rack."

Morrison thought back to his initial trek around the school. He hadn't seen a bike when he'd arrived on the scene, and it wasn't in any of the crime scene photos. Their killer must have ridden off on it, maybe while Acosta lay dying. But they had two suspects—so had the men agreed to meet? Or had their bike-riding boot-wearing murderer happened upon Acosta's attack and decided to join the fun, much to the pedophile's chagrin? But no... what were the odds that some psycho would just accidentally come upon another crime, happen to have the tools in hand—or on his feet—and decide to kill someone? Impossible. Morrison shook the idea from his head as Petrosky tapped the bike photos and looked at Goldstein pointedly.

"You need Dimitri," Goldstein said. "I'll send the aide to get him out of class."

FOUR BICYCLE SHOPS all had the same thing to say about the blue ten-speed bike Dimitri had identified: common, found everywhere from toy stores to big box stores to specialty shops. No way to track it, especially since he could have purchased it anytime. Unless the suspect decided to just brazenly ride by the school, it was another dead end.

Petrosky and Morrison spent lunch at a Thai restaurant, poring over the case files and calling professional and amateur clowns in the metro Detroit area. Neither Acosta's mother nor Mrs. Reynolds had been aware of clowns at any birthday parties that their children had attended, but the classified ads had given them a few hits and a list for follow-up, as had the party rental places.

Two dozen clowns later, and they were no closer to anything pertinent. Almost all of the clowns had alibis—turned out most worked day jobs, so their whereabouts could be easily verified.

Petrosky set the phone aside and shoveled spicy chicken into his mouth. "Goofy red-nosed motherfuckers."

At least they could say they'd been thorough. Past cases had been closed with crazier theories, but the birthday clown angle didn't feel right to him anyway—not that his gut had never been wrong. Morrison picked at his noodles and prawns and tried not to worry too much that Shannon still had not called him back.

13

THE FIRST TATTOO shop smelled like rubbing alcohol and reefer and someone's flop sweat. The reek was probably the skinny dude already sitting in the chair, wincing as another tattooed man ran a buzzing needle over his rib cage. The tattoo artists had nothing to share: no knowledge of the tattoo itself or the demonic clown group that had inspired the images. Morrison thought more highly of them for it. The second tattoo shop yielded more blank stares.

On the way to the third parlor, Morrison turned up his phone so that they could listen to the lyrics of *The Lion Tamer*, a song which glorified the dismemberment of a goat—tuneless rapping over a background of tinny circus bells and whistles. Morrison frowned, imagining the type of person who would listen to this garbage and be inspired. But had it inspired him to kill?

Petrosky flicked it off. "Shit's gross, but nothing on the kid angle. The murder thing, though...that's something."

Something, but not a direct link, not that he'd expected to find a song about stomping children to death. He winced, turning his face to the window so Petrosky couldn't see. "It's all like that—mostly just circus nonsense. Clowns as executioners, heavy on the violence. I printed the lyrics for the file, but this was the closest it got to the sexual assault angle because in verse two, they...uh..."

"They fuck the goat."

"Yeah." Morrison stared at Petrosky. "You listen to it, Boss?"

"Guessing. Probably the only way they get any ass. Kill it and take it. Force it. Fucking pussies."

Shannon hated the word pussy and would have flipped him off. *Fuck you, Petrosky.* Morrison coughed but held his tongue.

Petrosky kept his eyes on the windshield. "So call me a misogynist, Morrison. Go right ahead. I can already hear your wife in my brain."

"Glad I'm not the only one." But Morrison finally smiled.

"Tell her to get me a better word for shit like this, and I'll stop saying it."

"No way I'm getting in the middle of that. Tell her yourself."

Petrosky squinted out his side window and swung into a strip mall lot. "Fucking pussy," he muttered.

THE THIRD TATTOO shop had a door so white it looked like someone bleached it daily. Inside, the parlor was one large room with a cream-colored microsuede sofa near the door, the couch flanked by end tables made of clear glass. Along the right wall ran a long counter with a six-foot curtain of beads behind it, covering what was probably the back room or office. In the main area, half a dozen stations with black leather reclining chairs waited for clients, almost like a hair salon. Clean. Modern. Comfortable.

They sifted through the books on the glass coffee table: realistic drawings, pop art, some images that looked like watercolor paintings, everything in between. Lots of real art, too, not just cartoon knockoffs. Some of the pieces were utterly tragic, though he tried not to consider the circumstances that had led to their creation. Morrison was staring at a photographic memorial tattoo of a little girl when Petrosky grabbed the book, slammed it closed, and tossed it back onto the table with the others.

The beaded curtain rustled with a sound like a rain stick, and Morrison looked up to see a bald man covered neck to wrist in ink. "Can I help you guys?" He eyed the closed binders, then looked at each of them in turn, as if trying to guess who he'd be tattooing. "I can sketch you something original if you've got an idea."

"Nothing for us today." Petrosky flipped open his badge and approached the counter. The man appraised the shield with eyes as green as the dragon that snaked from wrist to forearm.

"What can I help you with, officers?"

"You are?"

"Randy. The hired help." His lip ring glinted when he smiled.

Petrosky pocketed his badge. "Looking for a guy with a tattoo."

"Well, that narrows it down."

Petrosky dealt him a withering glare. Randy's smile fell.

"He's a bad, bad man." Petrosky pulled out Zachary Reynolds's drawing of the tattoo and slid it across the counter, along with a copy of the album cover. Morrison looked away from the gory image.

"You seen a tat like this?"

Randy glanced at it, and his eyes lit up, hot and wild. "Hey, Drake!" he called to the curtain. A burly man with a dark ponytail and intelligent brown eyes sauntered out toward them. T-shirt, but no ink on his arms. Or neck. Or anywhere else Morrison could see. Odd. Maybe he was new.

Drake studied the photo. "That guy. Been years though." He shook his head. "That fucking guy."

"Want to tell us about that fucking guy?" Petrosky said.

Drake shrugged. "Not a lot to tell. He was kinda quiet, didn't talk much to me. He liked Jenny's work over mine. She said that he was nice —used to tell her jokes and shit."

"So he's a regular," Petrosky said.

"Was." Drake nodded along with Randy, the dragon boy, and Petrosky put the pictures away.

"Any distinguishing characteristics outside of the tat?"

"Not really." Drake shrugged a shoulder, and the muscles in his arm coiled, then stilled. "Skinny. Kinda dorky, but in a way that seemed like he didn't really know it. More awkward—bland. Not really someone you'd notice walking down the street."

Awkward. Unassuming. Bland. They'd said almost the same about Jeffery Dahmer, and that guy kept his victim's severed body parts in his freezer in case he got hungry.

"Eye color?" Petrosky said.

"Can't recall."

"Hair?"

"Brown? Lighter than mine, though, and kinda scraggly. Over the ears but above the shoulders."

That might be useful if he hadn't dyed it. Or shaved it. Across the counter, Randy's head shone in the fluorescents.

"How tall was he?"

"Shorter than me for sure. Just a few inches taller than Jenny."

Petrosky's eyes narrowed for a beat, then relaxed. Drake's description was confirmation that their shorter, sneakered suspect, the man who had raped Zachary Reynolds and Dylan Acosta, had always been a scraggly, weird-looking dude. But why the rapist was fighting with the killer at the scene—that was eating at Morrison. Unrest between the suspects meant the killer could just as easily have murdered the rapist too. Maybe he already had.

Petrosky produced the composite sketch of Zachary Reynolds's attacker, and Drake nodded.

"Yep, that's him." He studied the ceiling. "Been a while. Two, three years, maybe."

If their rapist was still alive, they could flip him on the murderer, but... They could be searching for another corpse. Not that dead rapists were a bad thing. Morrison noted Drake's statement, and the pen tore a hole in the sheet. He flipped to a new page.

Petrosky nodded to the credit card machine on the counter. "How'd he pay?"

"Cash, I think." Drake squinted. "We just really started taking cards in the last year or so."

"Keep records? Consent forms? Maybe a copy of a driver's license?"

"No consent forms from that far back. And we just check their license to make sure they're over eighteen."

"You get his name from the license?"

"Sorry, man, can't remember his real name. We called him Mr. Magoo, on account of he couldn't look me in the face, stared everywhere else. Seemed to see Jenny just fine, though." He bristled on the last sentence.

Petrosky leaned an elbow against the counter. "Jenny your girl, Drake?"

"She's a girl who married me, yeah." Drake's chest puffed up as he straightened his shoulders. Proud. Morrison pushed an image of Shannon's face from his mind—she'd surely call soon.

"I hear you." Petrosky pulled a photo of the bike from the folder. "Any idea who this belongs to? What'd your Magoo drive?"

Randy shook his head.

Drake gestured to the door, where little of the street was visible beyond the sidewalk immediately in front. "Never saw a car or bike, but that doesn't mean much. Unless we went outside or took a break, we wouldn't have seen a bike or a car anyway, and even then, we wouldn't necessarily know whose it was. Lots of traffic out there." He tapped the photo and leaned toward Petrosky. "So, what'd he do?"

"Not at liberty to say."

"Shit, that's bad, ain't it?" Drake straightened. "He was here, in my shop every couple months. Four times or so, total. If he was a bad guy, really bad, talking to Jenny…"

"I'm going to need a list of his tattoos. Anything you recall."

Drake bent behind the counter, pulled out a few sheets of white paper, and started sketching. "The last one Jenny did was a three-D piece on his back. A hand clawing out of his skin. He said it was for his kid. I figured it was a euphemism, you know? Flesh of my flesh kinda thing, a part of him escaping?"

"So it was a child's hand." Though Petrosky's face didn't change, Morrison could feel the tension radiating from his corded muscles.

A kid's hand. Morrison's stomach turned. Sick bastard wanted a child's fingertips touching him at all times.

"How about a number one?"

Drake stopped sketching. "No, don't recall that. I do remember a few other clowns. And a tent, yellow and purple. Kinda in the background here on his chest." His pencil scratched away. "I know this here still needed more work, but I can't really remember—"

"He had that weird Mr. Ed one too, right?" Randy interjected.

"Oh, yeah." He sketched another line, then another. A horse appeared in front of the tent, and in a moment, it was clear it was dead, blood leaking from its eyes. Macabre. Sadistic. Maybe the rapist *had* taken part in Acosta's killing, even if he'd just encouraged it. But if he was on board, why fight with his murderous spiked boot-wearing partner?

"Creepy," Petrosky said. The dead horse glared at them, bloody eyes dilated and aggressive as if ready to pull any passerby with him to the depths of hell.

"Totally. But some people like that. The...dark stuff. And honestly, Jenny does it better, probably remembers more about his ink than I can." He shook his head. "She won't be back from Florida until Friday morning—down there for a friend's funeral. Damn shame."

"We'll come back."

It wouldn't stand up in court, a composite so many years after the fact, but maybe Jenny would recall something that Zachary Reynolds hadn't. What they really needed from Jenny was a closer copy of artwork she'd needled onto his gut in case there was an image even more telling than the clowns. Another picture that might give them a hint as to where he'd spend his time. Maybe he'd told Jenny something that would help. Maybe Jenny even had some insight into why he hadn't finished his tattoos here—had something happened to spook him? Did he have a weakness they could exploit?

Petrosky peered at the corner of the ceiling, then at another corner. "You guys have security tapes?"

"Nothing like that. Sorry." Drake passed Petrosky the page he'd been working on, and Petrosky slipped it into the folder. "Should I be worried? About Jenny?"

Petrosky shook his head. "I think she's a little old for him."

"She's only..." Drake's eyes widened. "Oh fuck. My daughter, she... You think—"

"How old?"

"Seven."

So she would have been four or five back when their suspect was frequenting this place.

"He show interest in her?" Petrosky asked with a subtle, aggravated twitch of his eye.

"I..." Drake grimaced, almost snarled. "She came up after preschool one day when Jenny was inking him. Sat behind the counter with me. He looked a little too long, got me all upset. But I thought I was just overreacting, that he probably was trying to forget the pain and the needle. If I'd thought he was...well, looking like *that*, I would have fucking killed him myself." He swallowed hard, face reddening to a shade deeper than the rose on Randy's neck. "Not literally... You know what I mean."

Common. Ignore what you don't expect—or what you fear the most. Morrison touched the cell in his pocket.

"I would have felt the same," Petrosky said. "Just watch your daughter close, sir, and enjoy her while you can. Time flies."

Morrison pictured Evie's chubby cheeks, her smiling eyes. He should call Shannon again.

Petrosky turned to head out but stopped short at the door and gestured to Drake's nude arms. "Where're your tattoos?"

"I've always been afraid of needles."

"Interesting career choice."

Drake looked down. "I guess I thought it would help."

They canvassed the street and interviewed other business owners, but none had been there longer than two years. Dead end—just like the other four tattoo parlors nearby. Reynolds's rapist had gotten his tattoos finished somewhere else—if he finished them at all.

By the time Petrosky pulled into the precinct parking lot, Morrison's head was throbbing. He massaged his aching temple. "Want to grab dinner? We can come back here and—"

"You go home, California. I'll pull the names and addresses of the folks who were in that strip mall around the time Mr. Magoo was getting his work done. Maybe one of them will recall something. Tomorrow we'll see what other places one might go to get inked since that dickhead probably got the work done somewhere else."

"Like the slang, Petrosky."

"You would." Petrosky shut off the car. "And with the sheer number of tats, the tattoo shit itself might have become an addiction, the pain, the endorphins. And I think we've established that he has a hard time controlling his drives."

True enough. They'd talk to McCallum about it. "We've got time with the shrink tomorrow, right?" Maybe Morrison could even sneak in a few minutes, if he got there early, to ask about Shannon. Or get McCallum to call in a prescription for Shannon if she hadn't called the doctor already. Hell, she probably had—she might flake on a phone call, but not on her medications.

"We've got McCallum's four-thirty. Plenty of time to run around beforehand. Maybe we'll have more leads by the time we get there."

"Maybe." Morrison leaned his head against the seat.

"Get out," Petrosky barked so harshly that Morrison nearly jumped.

"What?"

"Go home, Cali." Petrosky nodded to Morrison's car next to them in the parking lot. Had Petrosky parked next to his Fusion on purpose?

Morrison reached for the door handle. Petrosky of all people should understand what it was like to just be…alone. Alone with your demons, the pain in your head, the kind that consumes you. The kind that takes bites out of you just when you thought you had a moment's reprieve.

"I don't need—"

"Go home and take a goddamn nap and just be happy you can sleep." Petrosky pulled out his cigarettes and a lighter but paused with his finger on the flint. "Everyone needs time to recharge, even do-gooders." His eyes were far away, flickering with agitation and pain and a grief so intense it tore at Morrison's gut, not the sharpness of a sudden stabbing, but a dull, old wound healed over but not gone. A wound as poignant as his own.

Morrison drove home, preoccupied with the haunted look in Petrosky's eyes. He'd hoped things were getting better—that Petrosky had found some new meaning in his life. God knows having Shannon and Evie had helped Morrison, and now with them away…

Morrison inhaled and blew the breath out sharply as if to clear the thoughts. They would be fine—they *were* fine. But was Petrosky? There remained a nagging in the back of Morrison's head that he was looking at someone just shy of relapse when he saw his partner, just shy of self-abuse, despite the fact that he'd surely deny it—addicts didn't share easily. Morrison never shared at all.

Morrison shut the car off in his driveway and let himself into the kitchen, the silence thick with foreboding. The cat was probably asleep somewhere. They should get another dog—a year already, and he still missed that old girl. And though it hadn't even been a day, he definitely missed his family.

14

THE FIRST THREE hours at home crawled by doing laundry, installing a cat door for Slash, taking a bath. And reading Edgar Allan Poe. He'd read hundreds of books, maybe thousands over the course of his studies as an English major, but there was something about Poe that filled some empty place inside him with an almost tangible serenity. The darkness on those pages made him feel almost normal, not alone, like another soul was there in his head with him. When he got to *The Tell-Tale Heart,* he relished the obsession—the madness. At least he could reasonably tell himself, "Hey, I'm not *that* crazy" when he worried about his wife for the umpteenth time.

But by the time the bathwater had cooled, the apprehensive whispers in his mind had grown to a dull roar. Why hadn't she called back yet? It was well past time for her to have settled into a hotel.

I can do this, Morrison. And to think that I needed a crutch, even if that crutch was just having you home with me, is ridiculous...

She didn't need him checking up on her, didn't want his help. He should have taken her at her word. But goddammit, she could call just to ease his mind, just to squash the thoughts running through his brain.

Has she been in an accident?

Have the meds worn off and left her with horrible fantasies on a dark road somewhere?

No, antidepressants can't wear off that quickly.

Maybe she'd taken Evie and leapt from an overpass.

His heart frantic, he tried her cell again. Again, no answer. He tossed the phone on the bed and closed his eyes.

She's showing herself that she doesn't need me.

He moved on to distraction. It should have been easier, but playing the guitar without Evie on his lap or on the bed beside him made the experience feel empty—like he'd never played before her birth as if every song he'd ever strummed had always been meant for her. He tried to embrace this and accept his preoccupation—turn it into a new song—but his heart was still jerking around in his chest, choking his voice. Sit-ups, pull-ups, nothing took away his agitation. And when he closed his eyes to meditate, he saw the memorial tattoo at Drake's shop, and it suddenly looked like Evie. He saw himself getting her face needled into his forearm, like Petrosky might want to do for Julie, and his stomach turned so that he almost wanted to vomit the idea—and the quinoa he'd eaten. Evie wasn't a memorial. She was fine. Shannon was fine.

And then Shannon came to him, shaky but louder, the panicked tears evident in her voice: *Sometimes I just want to drop her to see what will happen. Or toss her out the car window. I went to the pediatrician this week, and I crossed an overpass and thought for too long about what it might be like to drive over the guardrail.*

He felt half fucking insane. And more than that, he was being obsessive, more so with every hour that passed.

In the tumultuous quiet, the whispers began: *They're not home. No one will ever know. Just this once. You'll be happy.*

The habit was latent but not silent. It would never be completely gone.

He checked his phone again. No missed calls. No texts. No Shannon. No Evie. He dropped the phone onto the bed before he could dial. He trusted her; she had to know that. And she should be at the hotel any minute. Maybe it was taking extra long because she had to stop and nurse the baby. He wouldn't know. He wasn't there.

Just like he hadn't been there when she was considering tossing their child from the second-story window.

A vein in the crook of his leg throbbed wetly, remembering. *It will make you forget about her. It will take away the worry. And no one will ever find out.*

I'll know. I'll never forget.

He pulled out his journal and scribbled everything down: every thought, every whisper, every concern. Every desire, regret. Half an hour later, he was sweating, and his hand was shaking, but it was better. He ripped the pages from the notebook, walked to the kitchen, and shoved them into the garbage disposal. This was not about his family. This was about him looking for an excuse to use.

The motor in the bottom of the sink choked and sputtered like the heart of a man waking up the day after a bender with no spoon, no needle, and no drug. Morrison turned his back on the sink and stared at his shoes by the front door.

Never too late to literally run away.

The neighborhood streets pulsed with the reticent energy of an impending storm, though that surely was just him—the stars above shimmered clear and white, untainted by the murk of amorphous clouds. His breath echoed in his ears, hissing through his chest and into his lungs, and a discarded napkin skittered across his path, reminding him that even perfect things—like a moonlit run—were imperfect. Life was a struggle, perfect in its imperfection. It was a thought that Shannon would have called "zen bullshit," but it helped.

The tightness in his stomach eased along with his thoughts of Shannon, and the case came into clearer focus. *The case.* What were they missing? The punctures, possibly from boots—nothing like that existed in the rape case they knew to be related, and they hadn't found other murders with similar MOs. The rapist seemed to have a pattern—same type of victim, same T-shirt around the neck—but where the hell did this other guy come from? Was he a pedophile too? Or just a voyeur who got off on watching? They'd ask McCallum about that too—a profile should help.

McCallum. Shannon. Morrison's heart beat faster, and he didn't think it was from his pace. He checked his phone again as he ran, then again. Oily sweat from his finger streaked the glass.

Nothing.

A breeze chilled the dew on his brow and rustled through the leaves like the whisper of waves against a shore. He inhaled and exhaled to the rhythm of the wind. His chest cooled, and the film of concern cleared from his mind.

The case. *Think.* He focused on his feet thumping against the pavement.

The clowns were definitely weird. Savage shit. A guy who enjoyed feeling pain? Causing pain? That would explain the punctures, but the killer was a different guy. A night bird startled by his footfalls fluttered through the branches, and something bigger leapt from one tree to another with the crackle of snapping twigs.

He checked his phone again.

Nothing.

Sweat ran down his back and soaked his T-shirt. He ran harder over sidewalk and grass and pavement and tried to ignore the silent cell by listening to the treads of his shoes thumping against the earth. Rhythmic, measured. Grounded. By the time he circled the last block, he'd managed to brush aside the urge to check the phone.

She was fine. She was okay. And everything was as it should be.

As he rounded the final corner to his house, his breath caught in his throat. Headlights flashed in the drive—his drive—and the porch lights caught the reds and blues, turning the front lawn into a lewd and gruesome display, like the reflections of fireworks on a corpse.

She was dead. They were both dead.

He ran.

15

He met Decantor halfway up the drive—Decantor's arm out in front, a proverbial *whoa boy*. Morrison's heart did not slow, but he brought his feet to a halt.

"Is it Shannon? Evie?" He almost vomited the words onto Decantor's shoes.

"Shannon?" Decantor's eyes widened. "Dear god, man, of course not. I wondered why you were tearing up here like someone was chasing you."

She was okay. They were okay. She probably would have slapped him for the horrible thoughts he was having. He gulped in a breath.

The tightness in his chest remained.

Decantor lowered his hand, slower than seemed natural. Was Decantor trying to calm him down? Police training at its finest, maybe, but Morrison was unnerved by it, and he tensed and released his toes to make sure the digits were still there, that he was still there.

"Got a homicide out at Row and Luther, need to chat with you about her."

"Consultation?" Morrison and Petrosky primarily worked special cases—sex crimes and the like—but sometimes he talked through profiles with other detectives. But Decantor's posture was hardly the relaxed shoulders of the guy he'd spoken to earlier that week, someone just interested in a chat. And Decantor had never come to the house about a case. Not once.

"Not exactly a consultation," Decantor said. "Can we go inside? It's fucking cold tonight."

Morrison flexed his fingers. The spring breeze hadn't seemed all that cold, but his hands were tingly and numb. "Yeah, of course. I'll make coffee."

Decantor said nothing, just followed Morrison in through the unlocked front door, and Morrison suddenly regretted leaving the house open. *Had* he left the house open? Must have. He grabbed a dry dish towel from the drawer, green—Shannon's favorite—and mopped the sweat from his face. Decantor didn't move from his spot next to the counter.

"So, what's the deal?" Morrison asked as he poured grounds into a filter, fighting to keep his voice low and steady.

"Got a few questions about Natalie Bell."

Morrison paused, finger over the start button. *The nanny? Fuck.* Had Decantor said…homicide? Bell was dead?

"You knew her, right?"

"She interviewed here. We were looking for a nanny." Morrison punched the button on the coffeepot and turned away from the counter.

"When did you interview her?"

"Two days ago. Monday at lunchtime."

"You and Shannon were both here?"

"Yeah, you can give Shannon a call if you need a statement for the report." *Not that she'll answer her phone.* "She'll be in Atlanta until next Wednesday."

Decantor scribbled on his notepad, and Morrison eyed the book. He hadn't realized Decantor was taking notes. Was he being interrogated? Sweat popped out on the back of his already wet neck as he masked his face with nonchalance. "What have you got so far?" *They're going to lock me up. Again.*

"Found her in her apartment, chain lock cut. It wasn't a robbery—Bell had a gold bracelet lying on her dresser. Looks like the perp snuck in while she was sleeping. Shirt in her mouth, probably to keep her quiet. Some visible tearing in the genital region, and on her lower belly, all of it done with a round, sharp object like an ice pick, but bigger. Raped with the implement used to stab her. She bled out."

What the hell? Just like the wounds on Acosta's back. A couple attacks on little boys didn't fit with this case, and Acosta hadn't had any puncture wounds in the genital region. But that round shape was unusual, and they'd held that information back from the press. Then there was the shirt. Acosta's and Reynolds's shirts had been wrapped around their throats, but shoving it in the victim's mouth wouldn't be much of a stretch. "Sounds like a sex crimes case," he said slowly.

"Yeah, it does. But the chief said you guys were overloaded, and we didn't need specialized training to deal with a homicide—no living victim to assist. And there was no semen, no trace of spermicide, so the medical examiner doesn't think there was penetration by anything other than the spiked object."

Spiked object. It had to be related. Morrison jerked toward a sharp scratching sound just in time to see Slash poke his head through the cat door. The cat peered at Decantor, then yanked his face back through the hole to the outside.

"A jilted lover might fit," Decantor was saying. "Maybe she was out to get revenge on her boyfriend's other woman. Raped her with the knife or whatever for taking what she saw as hers. We did think about Acosta, with the size and shape of the holes, but—"

"How'd you know about the punctures? On Acosta?" Had the stabbing pattern gotten leaked too? Morrison ground his teeth.

"The ME. But he did say the rest didn't match—no rape in Bell's case, not enough force behind the wounds to be a stomping, different locations, vastly different victim. But he's double-checking as a precautionary measure because it is a weird weapon." He stopped writing and leaned against the counter. "Outside of Acosta, what other cases are you guys working on right now?"

Morrison kept his face blank. "Most were reassigned when we got Acosta, but the few remaining are about what you'd expect: some domestic violence, a few sexual assault cases. But they're all wrapped, just finishing up the final paperwork. Why?"

"Just curious because…well, you knew Bell. And"—Decantor tapped the tip of his pen in the book—"someone went through her purse. Left the wallet, but pulled out a bunch of other shit, including your card. I thought maybe you were investigating her for something. Domestic violence incident, thought maybe she was an ex-hooker since that's Petrosky's specialty." He raised his eyebrow in Morrison's direction, maybe asking him to deny it.

"Nope, I just wanted to hire her as a nanny for Evie. But she turned down the job, said she took another position." The final hiss of the coffeepot drew Morrison's attention, but he didn't turn, just watched Decantor process the information.

Decantor's eyebrow sank to its usual position. Acceptance. "Did she say where she took that other job?"

Morrison turned to pour the coffee, swallowing hard over the knot that had taken root behind his Adam's apple. Some coffee splashed over the rim of the first cup, and he wiped it up with his face towel, then passed Decantor a mug. He left his own on the counter.

Decantor stilled—he must have noticed the panic on Morrison's face. "I'm just trying to track her movements," he said gently. "You know how it is. Not a single credit card hit, no ATM stops, nothing. You saw her Monday, so you're the last to see her alive. No one thinks it was…you know…you." Decantor, and the whole Ash Park PD, had seen Morrison's imprisonment last spring, had watched as the incident unfolded in court: the false arrest for Griffen's crimes, the way Shannon's ex-husband had gone after him tooth and nail, trying to keep him locked up, the evidence planted at Morrison's house that would have convicted him if Shannon and Petrosky hadn't uncovered the real killer. Thinking about it still made Morrison nauseous, and he'd only been locked up a week before Shannon and Petrosky had managed to clear him. "It was just an interview," Morrison said. "I'll get you her résumé, but we didn't cover anything except her job history." He went to retrieve Bell's file from the stack still on Shannon's night table and returned to Decantor, who squinted at the fat folder in surprise.

"Really checked the babysitters out, didn't you?"

More than he should have. He probably looked guilty as hell, even though he couldn't imagine another cop who wouldn't do that for his kid. Valentine sure as shit would. Decantor just didn't understand; he was still a bachelor.

"Just background checks." Morrison passed him the folder with a tightness in his throat that he covered with a smile. "Just do me a favor and pretend you did the research yourself, all right?"

Decantor nodded and tucked the folder under his arm. "Absolutely. And I'll give Shannon a call for follow-up, just to have her statement on record."

Morrison recited her cell, and Decantor's pen flew over the page, jotting other notes apparently, maybe about Shannon being out of town. Maybe not.

Morrison cleared his throat. "Seems like there'd be someone else at her apartment building who would have seen her after she came here."

"Yep, and nothing. Doesn't look like anyone noticed her missing."

"Then how'd you—"

"Fluke. Building superintendent went to see her because her car was getting towed—she'd parked in a reserved spot. He got worried when she didn't answer the door because she had a diabetic seizure in the lobby last year—he figured better safe than sorry."

Bell hadn't mentioned anything about being diabetic when she was interviewing for the nanny position. *She should have told us.* And if Bell had withheld something so critical, how could he know whether the nanny they'd actually hired had been forthcoming?

Decantor was still talking, and Morrison had to force himself to tune back in: "—closet full of books, no heels or going-out clothes like you'd expect. Lucky we got the call before she started to smell. Or before a friend or family member found her."

"Lucky."

Decantor nodded. "So you interviewed her on Monday. What time did you call to offer her the position?"

"Shannon called her Tuesday, earlier in the day. She rang me back that night, around...seven or so."

Decantor stopped writing. "Tuesday night?" Worry etched itself into the lines around his tight mouth. "She was dead by then, Morrison. The medical examiner says she died on Monday."

Morrison froze. *Impossible.* The ME had to be wrong. Morrison pulled his phone from his pocket, handed it to Decantor. "The number she called from matched the number on her résumé." He paused. "Though it was weird that she called me and not Shannon—Bell had my card, but Shannon was the one who had called her. Shannon interviewed her initially, too. And the voice on the phone was...a little off, deeper, but I thought she had a cold."

"No cell found at the scene."

Someone had taken it. *And they called me.* It was just a phone call, but he felt almost...violated. His stomach churned, and he turned to the kitchen window, half expecting to see someone watching them. His fist clenched. He stared hard at it until it went slack.

"Why kill someone and call back random numbers the next day?" Decantor said, frowning. "You think he was trying to make it look like she was still alive?"

"Maybe. But why bother to do that?" He met Decantor's eyes. No one would have found her for days without that tow truck, he'd said.

"Maybe he wanted to make sure no one got worried so that he could have his...way. After she was dead and cold." Decantor grimaced. "He probably creamed his pants before he could take it out the first time."

Who the hell called me?

"Gotta be someone she knows," Morrison said. "Someone who stalked her at least, and knew how to get in and out of her apartment. Who knew she'd interviewed with us." The implication tugged at a soft spot in his stomach. "And the voice on the phone was female, so you're looking for a woman, too. Or someone with one of those electronic voice changers." What the fuck was going on? Had they badgered Bell about why she had a cop's card in her wallet? Were they fucking with him? But...the weapon. So similar to the one used on Acosta.

Then again, it wasn't hard to get hold of an ice pick. The press leaks were probably behind this bullshit, too, someone who knew more than they should. Later this week, there'd surely be a big story out about the weapon and the stomping, and everyone and their mother would be wasting the department's time with nonsense tips.

"Maybe Shannon will have some insight since she interviewed Bell initially. You think she'll be up now?"

"Not sure. Haven't talked to her today." She was trying to prove to herself that she could do this alone. That she didn't need him as a crutch. She was driving and trying to be safe. *But she forgot her medication.* "I'll call her now."

HE GOT Shannon's voice mail three times in a row, and in that time, Decantor finished his coffee and moved into the living room, stepping on Shannon's favorite rug with his heavy boots. Though Decantor left no mark, Morrison winced at the intrusion.

"I'm sure she's driving." The phone echoed with the last line of her voice mail, Shannon's voice, and his stomach twisted and turned, the knot in his throat expanding, trying to cut off his air supply. And the needle of panic in the back of his brain wriggling its way free, struggling against his self-restraint and Decantor's worried stare. She'd planned to stop halfway to Atlanta, stay in a hotel, but if Evie was sleeping, she might have kept driving. And there was no telling whether she'd be in a good cell zone, right? Or maybe her phone battery had died.

He forced a smile. "When she calls back, I'll have her call you, okay?" His chest was hot and sweaty, and it had nothing to do with his run. "I'll write out a statement about what happened on Tuesday, too, what the caller said and all that. And I'll email you my phone records so that you can follow-up on the Bell case."

"Okay, man, sounds good. I appreciate it." Decantor nodded. "And I'm sure whoever called was fucking with you. Found a cop's number at the scene, wanted to be an asshole."

With a voice changer?

"I'll walk you out," Morrison said to the dead screen, willing it to ring.

WHEN THE TAILLIGHTS from Decantor's car finally receded, panic wrapped around Morrison's heart like a skeletal hand and crushed the last remnants of calm. She was okay. Had to be. But why wouldn't she call him, dammit? It had been...what? A day? No, not even. Twelve hours. No, fifteen. They could surely go a few hours without talking—she fucking hated talking on the phone. He was being paranoid. He was freaked about being away from them.

But something weird was going on here.

He grabbed his keys to go back to the precinct. He'd run down her credit cards and goddammit he'd drive out to Alex's himself if he had to, just to put his nerves to rest. And to tell her he missed her. That he missed Evie. That this really wasn't about her—it was just his own need for them and nothing more. She'd surely be able to see that. *Hopefully.*

His cell rang. No, not rang—text. Shannon. *Oh, thank fucking god.*

"Sorry, horrible reception. I'll call tomorrow, ok?"

He responded:

"Ok. Love you."

He waited for a response, but none came, and finally, he pocketed the cell.

Of course the reception is bad. Of course it was. Had he really thought the miles of freeway were replete with cell towers? But the silent phone seemed to amplify the quiet of the house—too quiet—and every nerve in his body sang with anxiety and agitation and acute panic. He would have felt so much better just hearing her voice.

Then suddenly, every shadow was an invitation to go back, every creak of the house settling a whisper to return to a life he'd left behind. *I can make the pain stop,* the voice whispered. And it could. Just one hit would soothe his frayed nerves, make sleep come fast and hard, and he could start again tomorrow, refreshed. It was the drug, an emotion more than actual words, but he could feel each syllable echoing in his head, through his chest, and prying into those tiny glorious places of exquisite loveliness that could only be reached with the needle. He hadn't touched those quiet places in years.

Stress. It was always the stress that tried to drag him back. But if Shannon could be strong, avoid her own crutches, then goddammit, he could too. And if he couldn't…he'd never tell her.

No.

He yanked at the doorknob, and his hand slipped, slick with his own sweat. He tried again, felt the click of the latch giving way, and escaped into the night.

16

PETROSKY'S WINDOWS glowed yellow with murky lamplight. There were no other cars in the driveway, but the tinkle of female laughter wafted through the open window and over the porch. Petrosky had picked someone up. Probably someone he shouldn't have, like always. Never for sex, he didn't think, just for company—and because Petrosky wanted to get them off the street, if only for the night.

When Petrosky let him in the front door, the women at the table eyed Morrison suspiciously. One dark, one light; one tall, one short; both thin as rails. One wore shorts so brief only the fringe was visible underneath the hem of a sweatshirt reading "Ash Park PD."

"Am I interrupting something?" Morrison asked.

Petrosky ignored the question and turned to the women, raising his voice so that they could hear him across the room. "Ladies, this is Detective Morrison. Morrison, June and Rita."

Morrison raised a hand in greeting, not trusting his voice enough to speak, and Petrosky gestured to the table. "Now that we have four players...how about some spades? You in, California?"

Anything to distract him from Shannon and her terrible reception. Anything to distract him from the case and the fact that a killer had possibly called him, though surely it was a sick prank or they'd have made some type of demand, right? He should bring up Decantor's visit, almost wanted to, but the thought of having to rehash it right now while the drug was still whispering softly at the back of his mind no matter how he tried to forget—he needed to be distracted from that, too. He needed to forget all of it before he lost his shit. "Yeah, I'll play." He leaned close to Petrosky's ear and lowered his voice. "Did you pull them off the street tonight?"

"Mind your business, California. Nothing illegal about this. Just a couple of people playing cards."

"Yeah, okay, I know." He tried to keep his voice even, hiding his anxiety, his addiction, his past, beneath a grin. "Wouldn't be fair to avoid people based on profession anyway."

"Well fuck, you think they want to avoid us because we're cops? I hadn't even considered that." Petrosky headed for the table and plopped into a chair.

Morrison took the seat across from Rita and her hazel eyes shifted to Petrosky, who grinned at her. She smiled back with teeth so white and clean they could have been featured in a toothpaste commercial. Morrison peered into the plastic cups on the table.

Please don't let him be off the wagon.

Of course he's off. No point even trying to stay clean. We all fall eventually. We'll go down together.

He resisted the urge to smell the cup.

Petrosky saw him looking and frowned. "Shirley Temples." Almost defensive. "Want one?"

Morrison glanced at the counter—bottles of 7up and orange juice sat with a jar of cherries in the glow of the pink princess night-light that had belonged to Petrosky's daughter. No liquor, at least not out in the open.

"You can just make OJ too, straight up," Petrosky said.

"Too bad you got nothing to go with it." June's voice was raspy as sandpaper. She pouted as she dealt the cards, and Petrosky shot her a narrow "stop giving me shit" look, but he lost his scowl when she winked at him. Then she smiled. There was no way these girls were here for free, which was sketchy at best, but at least Petrosky was sober.

"Shirley Temples sound great," Morrison said. Rita stood, but he waved her back down. "No, I'll make it."

"She's been playing bartender all night," Petrosky said. "Rita makes a damn fine drink—she's a professional now, too. I called in a favor over at The Lounge."

"The place Crazy Mark runs? I thought we arrested him."

"We did. He's on probation. Good deeds will help him stay that way." Petrosky winked at Rita, and she beamed.

June picked up her cards. "Eddie got me an interview tomorrow too," she said, not to be outdone. She smiled at Petrosky, then down at her hand while she arranged her cards. "Three."

Morrison exchanged his own cards and waited while June and Petrosky made their plays. They were halfway through the hand before Morrison realized his heart had slowed, and the back of his neck was dry.

The needle in his brain was gone.

> "It was night, and the rain fell; and falling, it was rain, but, having fallen, it was blood."
> Edgar Allan Poe, *Silence - A Fable*

17

There was no light, only the blackness of fear that pulsed in time to her throbbing head. Her breath came in heavy gasps, thick and muffled, echoing in her ears like she had a hood over her face. But there was no hood, only the dark—the cloudy thunderstorm gray of a tomb. Stifling. And all was silent. How long had she been here?

Shannon raised her head, and pain shot through her neck and down to where her shoulder connected with the floor.

The *floor*. Cold, hard. Cement? No, it was smoother than that, but she couldn't tell much more through the coat she had on. Wood floors? Was she inside a house? And...she hadn't had a jacket on when she left the house, but she was certain she did now.

And Evie. She'd had Evie. Her breath quickened to a frenzied panting in the dark. She flexed her legs, and pain shot from her knee to her hip, white and hot, but nothing moved. Her ankles and shins were bound together, her toes numb. How had she gotten here? She gritted her teeth until the pain settled, but the thick numbness in her limbs remained.

She had tried to kick him; she remembered that. She'd stopped to feed Evie, parked in the back of the gas station lot, and he'd come down fast and hard with something, maybe brass knuckles, against her temple. She winked tentatively—felt the tightness of what was probably dried blood on her cheek. At least the gash had stopped oozing.

Would Morrison know she was gone yet? If he didn't, he'd know soon when she didn't call. Though she had specifically told him she was going to avoid him—to prove she was fucking *strong* as if you could prove such a thing by ignoring the people you loved. The panic rose, and she let it in, let it build into a fire stoked by fury and indignation. This motherfucker would pay. But then fear wrapped around her throat like a noose. She didn't believe in God, didn't believe in much of anything outside of hard work and grit, but she prayed now:

God, please don't let him hurt Evie.

She tried to move her arms, but they were also bound, or rather, stuck in front of her in the coat. Not a coat—a straitjacket, and stiff, much harder than cotton. The rough stitches rubbed her arms raw as she struggled. Leather? She flexed her wrists, but her bonds stuck fast, and her fingers cramped from the position of her palms, each held flat against the opposite hip.

She heard her then, a tiny whimper. *Evie.* The noise wasn't a cry, yet it sounded more ominous, more urgent, than the subtle giggles or mewls that trickled through the baby monitor every night. And even the grainy black and white of the monitor was less distorted than the profound darkness around her now.

Where are you, baby? Shannon held her breath, trying to locate her daughter, but her right ear was muffled, probably thick with her own blood unless he'd hit her hard enough to deafen her. *Come on, sweetheart, just a little louder.* Her abdominals cried out as she heaved her head off the floor, wrenching her neck and—

Electricity zapped through her, from one ear to the other, and she caught herself on her elbow. Concussion? But the stinging sensation wasn't coming from the side where she'd been struck. And she wasn't lying on a power grid...she didn't think.

More muffled whimpering came to her through the gloom, and she tried again, throwing herself forward, ignoring the rigidity in her neck, her stomach, her wrists. And saw her. To her right, about six feet from the bottom of Shannon's toes, Evie lay on the floor, her legs already kicking air, her fists balled and working in the manufactured dusk. Evie —healthy and vibrant and *furious.* But deep within Shannon's chest, dread blossomed and grew teeth and gnashed at her lungs.

Shh, honey, shh. She didn't dare say it aloud. She wormed her way toward the sound of Evie's breath, the sound crescendoing with each passing second—here another whimper, there a whine. She squirmed more quickly, the floor bruising her elbows, her hips. Then Evie cried out, long and high, and Shannon's heart skipped a beat. Her breasts tingled, heavy with milk.

Please, baby, hush.

Her abdominals trembled in the half-sit-up position, every muscle screaming with exertion until she collapsed against the floor. Evie could not understand the danger, could not feel the horror in the room around them. Or perhaps she did and knew only to beg her mother to save her.

But Shannon couldn't save her. She was failing. Her worst fear: that she'd hurt Evie, that she'd leave Evie to be hurt, all coming to fruition, and she couldn't do anything to stop it.

Don't think about that. It isn't true. I'm going to get her and get the fuck out of here.

Evie squalled, but softly, the way she sometimes did when she was putting herself back to sleep, and Shannon wrenched her body toward the sound of Evie's shuffling, toward the soft whisper of her cotton footie pajamas, until she could see her daughter, face to face. Four feet away, but it might have been light-years. An impassable void. Shannon whispered across the expanse: "Shh, honey, it's okay." Shannon strained against the shirt, yanking one way, then the other. She'd be out of this contraption before Evie fully awoke.

Then footsteps—heavy and slow, deliberate, somewhere behind her. No squeal of door hinges or clack of a latch. He'd been there the whole time, watching her struggle. *Oh, fuck.* Her heart shuddered, then froze.

Shannon moved faster away from him, her ribs aching, her wrists and knuckles grinding painfully against the floor. She couldn't roll toward the intruder—it would be like leaving Evie alone.

"Now, now, girl, that won't do at all." His voice cracked on the "girl," but the tone was low and hollow, reverberating in her ears like the heady thrum of a plucked cello string. Yet there was nothing melodic about it: each syllable drove icicles of fear into her throat until she feared she'd faint, leaving her limp and powerless to help Evie. Or herself.

Another thunk of foot on floor, then a shuffle, then a stomp as he stepped over her body, his foot next to her ear. The clank of something metal rang from his shoe, which was strange—unless her hearing was off. Her head throbbed. He took one more step over to Evie. *Definitely metal.* And close, too close to her daughter's face like he was moments from smashing her head with his boot. Then he was at the wall, but not far enough from Evie—one step backward, and he'd crush her. He flicked on the light, reducing the room to him, only him, and the contrast of his back against the sudden blinding glare.

Adjust. See. I need to use this shit.

As he retreated, she rolled onto her back to track his movement. In front of her, a wall. White paint, but not clean—scuffed and dirty, and a single window, or what used to be a window if the unused curtain hooks on the ceiling were any indication. The rest of the wall was covered by insulation and thick black plastic—an exterior wall, then. *Escape.* And the plastic itself could be a weapon if she could get a piece over this asshole's face. Above them, metal spines from a small, iron chandelier cast agitated shadows on the walls. Actual metal or just painted to look like iron? Either way, it would hurt if it connected with his fucking skull.

Evie whined again, softly as if she were still dreaming, and the tightness in Shannon's breasts intensified as her milk let down. She turned her head toward Evie, and it hurt—*God, my head*—and her temple felt damp like it might be bleeding again. Evie, so close, on her back. One arm moved, reaching, looking for her momma. "It's okay, baby, Mommy's here. It's okay." Evie's legs kicked the air futilely, then stopped.

Shannon's chest tingled with fear and rage and oily hatred. Milk soaked her shirt. She wrested her face to where he stood hidden in shadow in a corner where the light of the barbed chandelier did not reach. Average-sized, even smaller than, judging from the position of the ceiling, but he seemed huge, and she had to force breath into her lungs. *Fix this, Mommy. Get yourself together.*

Evie fussed again, not yet fully awake, but getting there. Soon she'd be wailing.

"Let me feed her." *Be nice to the big bad asshole, Shannon.* "Please let me feed her, sir." *Give him what he wants.* But what was that? "I don't know what you want, but if it's money, I'll get it."

He stepped forward, the overhead light glinting against something in his hand—a long and pointed thing, metal, with a spear at the top covered with spiky protrusions like thorns and a thick hook glinting on one side. An ax on the other side. Shannon's heart stopped. Evie squalled again, and Shannon's brain, her nerves, her heart, everything went into hyperdrive, panic racing like electrical currents over her chest and into her legs. Her baby's front was exposed, her soft underbelly vulnerable to the hooked blade, but on her side, Shannon couldn't see them both at once, and his face...

The whole front of his head was covered by a mask, leathery like the straitjacket she wore and with heavy stitching on either side of an enormous beak-like nose, as thick as a toucan's. The eyes were covered with what looked like round aviator glasses. From the top of the mask, additional triangles of red metal protruded in different directions, like a bloody porcupine. The entire thing was painted: large red joker's lips, smiling and sinister, and a firework of black around each aviator eye. A circle of garish red stained each cheekbone.

Below the mask, his neck was white, as if he hadn't seen the sun all year, and his collarbone, visible at the neck of his black tunic, was sunken, everything sunken, wasting but in a sharp-featured way. He was skinny, gangly, too awkward like a child trying to get used to his growing limbs. Was he very young? Or maybe sick? He had a sore on his neck, no...several of them, but the shadow under the mask made them hard to see. Measles? Lesions? AIDS? Her eyes flicked to the weapon again. *Please, not that. Focus, find something I can use.* Maybe the marks were burns. Or abscesses from drug use. She never could tell that kind of stuff the way Morrison could—he had a sixth sense from working with the Ash Park PD. She had never missed him so much as in this moment. Hell, it was probably just a shaving cut or an infected fucking pimple. *Stop looking at it and think, Shannon!*

Tears burned behind her lids, but she blinked before they could fill her eyes. *Don't give him the satisfaction. One thing at a time.* "Please."

Shannon glanced at the bed against one wall, black sheets shimmering like they were wet. On the end table sat a heavy-looking lamp, cord severed halfway to the plug. "Just let me take care of her before we draw attention to you. Then you can tell me what it is you want, and I'll—"

The rap of his boots silenced her as the sound echoed through her head: the thunk of rubber soles but something else, a click of... It *was* metal. Orange tinged with green, copper formed in spiked ridges along the back of his shoe, longer than the actual boot treads, making him taller—high heels on crack. But he wasn't stomping; his steps were tentative. Quiet. Almost...secretive. He took a step over to Evie, and the metal tool seemed to shudder in his hand, though it might have been her vision blurring. Every cell in her body vibrated with the desire to tear her child away from the weapon, from this maniac.

"We already have what I want," he said. "Happy, happy, happy."

We, who's we? Her gaze darted around the room again, but there were only walls, yellowed by the light. Then he was moving away from Evie—*thank you, God*—but instead of retreating to his shadowed corner, he marched toward Shannon again. The scrape of metal on wood ground through her eardrums until he stopped just beyond her toes. A breath of air whooshed by her legs as a sound like the squeal of hinges cut the silence—but she would have noticed an exterior door. A closet?

She couldn't breathe, every beat of her heart, forcing the oxygen from her lungs. Sweat-soaked hair matted itself to her cheek as she craned her neck toward her feet, toward the man in the mask, but she could only make out the top of the door: thickly padded. Soundproofed. *Oh, Jesus, he's going to lock me in the closet...* Though it wasn't a closet, but a bleak, black room, an enormous beam across the middle. *A dungeon.* She coughed, choked, as vomit rose in her throat and cut off her air with acid.

He turned back to her. *Get out, run! Run!* She strained again and finally looked down at her own body, at her jacket: mismatched cowhide pieces roughly sewn with upholstery thread. And at the base of one of her wrists, an evil-looking metal lock, rusty and thick, attached to a metal hook sewn into the leather jacket itself. No escape.

Get him talking. Or she was dead, Evie was dead.

"Do we know each other?"

He snorted in response. "You'd never know someone like me." No cracking in his baritone this time, just rage. Had he been snubbed? Humiliated?

"I'm sure I would." She hated that her voice was shaking, but it felt like her bones were trying to vibrate their way out of her body. "You don't need the mask."

"I don't want to smell your stink." As she watched, the air from each breath he took broadened his back, inflating him, steadying him until he was tall, straight—emboldened. He was composing himself. But for what?

Evie screamed, and his shoulders tensed. The tip of the beaked nose caught the light—metal too. Everything so sharp. Shannon's chest dampened her shirt to her belly, still soft from childbirth.

Shh, Evie. She heaved herself over, floundering like a beached whale.

She could feel his eyes on the back of her neck, but she lay still, staring at Evie, wanting to pick her up, desperate to pick her up. She was failing. *No, I am not.* "Please," she whispered, aiming for hopeless, helpless, but in that moment, the fire in her belly burned stronger than her terror, flaming into her face, blistering her insides with incredulous fury. *Just let my arms go. Give me an inch, motherfucker, and I will destroy you.*

He stepped in front of her, away from the padded closet, one heavy boot so close to her face that she could see the mud on the copper spines on the bottom. But no—the hue was far too crimson, not nearly the right shade of brown to be dirt. And the smell: not only the copper of the metal but the cloying wet of a wound not yet healed. Blood? On his boots? She squinted at his feet, at the spikes that could only be weapons —sharp enough to kill.

Her breath caught again as the other boot fell heavy in front of her, close enough to her belly that it snagged the straitjacket. He pulled it free, cursing under his breath, and bent to her, leaning his beaked mask so close she could smell his sweat, setting the metal hook of his bladed tool hard against her shoulder, the coolness of it reaching her skin even through the leather straitjacket. This time, the blade did not shake. He leaned closer, closer, until his breath echoed in her ears louder than her own, amplified by the hollow mask and her own sheer terror.

He peered at her through the mask, with eyes hard and dark and emotionless behind the strange bubble lenses. Looking for something. *He wants to see my fear.* She allowed her lower lip to tremble. Allowed the tears to spring into her eyes.

Please let that be enough.

He cocked his head.

Evie was still wailing, but Shannon could barely hear—like he was sucking the sound waves from the room and swallowing them with his beaked mouth.

Then he straightened, stepped heavily over her, and she hauled herself back to look toward Evie, following his steps. When one taloned boot narrowly missed Evie's head, Shannon cried out, shrill and harsh against the hiss of his breath, jerking so hard against the straitjacket that he turned back to her. His sharp, metal beak was aimed right at her as if he might use it to impale her.

"Please," she whispered. He held the tool out in front of him, the points, the barbs, the hooked, spiked top glinting darkly, consuming her attention, every sliver of the instrument standing out in ominous detail.

"Happy, happy, happy," he growled. And still, he watched her. Showed the weapon to her. She bit her lip.

He bent to one knee in front of Evie.

Shannon screamed.

The man in the mask tipped his face toward the ceiling and laughed.

18

SHE'D BE ANGRY, maybe. But by the next morning, Morrison didn't care. He'd dialed Shannon's number again—twice—and she still wasn't answering. But she had surely hit the road early to take advantage of Evie's happy time; she had to be somewhere with reception by now. So he'd run their credit cards. Last used yesterday near Toledo, only an hour from Ash Park, but she'd get a good six hours of drive time out of that one tank of gas. And she hadn't needed to stop for food—she'd brought a cooler with her because eating out with an infant was a pain in the ass. He'd tried to check on the hotel, too, but she had planned to use their points to book it from the lot, and it would still be another day before it showed on the credit card statement—the company could tell him nothing. *Nothing*. He put a hold on their credit and debit cards. Regardless of her determination to make it to Alex's without his support, she was being selfish, and that fucking pissed him off. But the anger sat on his chest, on the surface, while deeper, more primal fears lurked in his gut, and if he breathed too hard, he felt them swell up and try to consume him.

I've lost them. They're never coming home. The worst was that he was alone—if Morrison called on his fellow officers to look for his wife it made this...real. His girls might be gone. His life might be over. And if Shannon really was gone, Roger would wrongfully throw him in jail again, and he'd be helpless to save his family.

Goddammit, Shannon.

He dialed again—no answer, not then, and not on the five more attempts on his way to work. And all the while, his fears fought with the logical part of his brain, the one that reminded him that Shannon had flat-out told him she was going to wait to call him. That she didn't want him to be her crutch. That this was only the second day—she wouldn't even be at Alex's yet, not when she had to stop to feed Evie every couple hours. And she had texted him. If he waited a little longer, she might call.

By the time lunch rolled around, his agitation had morphed into relentless anxiety; panic seized his innards every time a new thought seared through his brain. He tried to tell himself it was the case. They'd spent the morning ascertaining that none of the prior occupants of the strip mall had seen the bike or Mr. Magoo.

"Not even coffee today?" Petrosky asked him.

Morrison shook his head, his stomach tying itself in knots at the mere scent of food.

"Worried about Shannon?"

"Yeah. But she did text me." His voice was almost defensive. Forcing himself to believe it was okay. Morrison looked away, trying to avoid Petrosky's piercing stare.

"So, what's the problem?"

Morrison sipped at his water but set it down when his stomach rebelled. "Decantor came by last night."

"After my house?"

"Before."

Petrosky narrowed his eyes and dipped a fry in ketchup. Said nothing. But he just glared at the fry instead of eating it.

"I didn't want to say anything in front of your friends." Morrison looked at him pointedly. "And because I was...thinking." *No, I was trying not to think.* He cleared his throat. "Our first-choice nanny, Natalie Bell, was found murdered in her apartment, stabbed in the abdomen and groin."

Petrosky tossed the fry onto his plate, where it landed in a pool of ketchup. "What the fuck, Surfer Boy? Why the hell wouldn't you tell me?"

"Like I said, I was trying—"

"How'd Decantor catch that, anyway?" He drummed his fingers on the table. "Sounds like more than a standard homicide. Should have come through us."

"They figured we had enough to do?"

Petrosky stared at the fry like he wanted to slap the shit out of it. "What else, California?"

Morrison looked at his water glass and grimaced. "Bell died on Monday of wounds just like those on Acosta's back. And the killer took my card from her wallet and used Bell's phone to call me Tuesday night to tell me she wasn't taking the job." *They'd used Bell's phone.* Maybe they'd also used Shannon's to text him. Was she dead too? Morrison tried to shake the thought from his head, but it stuck.

Petrosky's fingertips beat frantically against the table. Morrison half expected the spoon to start vibrating and work its way to the floor where the clatter would surely alert everyone to his predicament—his sanity was hanging by a thread as thin as spider silk.

"You're certain they called you after she was dead?" Petrosky asked.

"I'm sure...or rather Decantor is. He thinks they were just fucking with me." The question was *why*.

"How the hell would they know about Bell's job offer? You think that just randomly came up while she was being stabbed to death?" Petrosky pulled his hands from the tabletop, and the silence was more nerve-racking than his incessant tapping. "Maybe they're coming after you because you're investigating the Acosta case. Hence the similar wounds."

The thought had occurred to Morrison, and he'd pushed it from his head before it had eaten him alive. "But if they wanted to threaten me, they would have. They didn't ask for anything. Just said Bell wouldn't be in to work. Either they didn't want people looking for her because they planned to come back and...mess with the body, or it's a prank." *Even though it doesn't feel like one.*

"Mm-hmm." Petrosky picked up the fry again and shoved it into his mouth. "How many times did Shannon call her?"

"Two. I think. No one answered."

Petrosky shook his head. "She probably called at least three or four times; she's persistent as fuck. Maybe they just called back because they wanted the phone to stop ringing."

They could have turned it off. Petrosky still hated his smartphone—one day, he'd probably put it through the wall before he found the ignore button.

Maybe Shannon's pushing ignore on my calls. His finger twitched with the desire to hit redial, but if she hadn't picked up by now, she wasn't going to. And there was surely a logical reason. Had to be.

Petrosky was drumming on the tabletop again, his pork sandwich getting cold and soggy with coleslaw. "I know there's more, Surfer Boy."

Morrison pushed his water glass away. Someone had called him and pretended to be Bell, and they'd had enough information to know what to say to him. He should have recognized that the voice was disguised—that it hadn't been Bell at all. Some fucking detective he was. "I don't like it, Boss. I can't figure out any reason for them to call me at all. And the way Decantor described the wounds... I mean, there are clearly differences in the crimes, but this isn't right." He ran a hand through his hair.

"And?"

And I need to find her. Now. We need backup. "It's driving me crazy that I can't get ahold of Shannon. I put a block on our credit cards. She's texted me but—"

"I'll call Valentine, put out an APB on her car." Petrosky gestured for the check, practically ripping his wallet from his pocket.

He's worried. And if Petrosky was worried—

"You call Alex first, just to make sure she didn't drive all night and then pass out when she got there. Then we'll keep on this case because if it's the same person who did Acosta, we need to follow what leads we have."

"We don't know that Bell and Acosta are connected. And Shannon doesn't have enough gas to make it there; she hasn't filled up since—"

"Unless she paid cash at some rinky-dink station. Just fucking call Alex." Alex. The man who'd moved away and made Shannon's postpartum period with Evie that much more horrible, like she'd lost everything important to her all at once.

She still had me.

I wasn't enough to make her happy. Morrison followed Petrosky out to the car, tapping his phone. The car felt like a prison cell.

She won't even call me back.

Alex answered on the first ring, and Morrison tried to keep his voice even as Petrosky pulled from the lot and headed toward the home of their last potential contact—a guy who had owned a nail studio next to the tattoo place back during the time their rapist had been there. "Hey, Alex. I was just wondering...did Shannon make it there yet?"

"Not yet, but I wasn't expecting her until later this evening. Figured she'd need lots of breaks with the baby." Alex was quiet a beat, then said, "Why, did she leave earlier or something?"

She's not there. But he'd known it would be a long shot. "Nah, I've just been trying to get through on her cell. Figured I'd ask if she'd called."

Another pause. A sound like a crinkling candy bar wrapper. "Something wrong?"

Morrison didn't answer. He didn't want to lie. Petrosky pulled down a side street.

"Should I be worried?" Alex asked, his voice a touch higher than usual.

Yes. "No, of course not. I just got some bad news on one of the nannies we were considering hiring. Thought she'd want to know."

"Hope you had a backup choice." His voice was back to normal, though Morrison's heart rate climbed with every word. He fought for control.

"Yeah, we have a backup—I just wanted to tell her. But if you talk to her first, maybe leave out the part about it being bad news. You know she'll want all the details, and she'll have a laundry list of questions all set before she even calls back." He tried to force a laugh, but it came out strangled.

"Yeah, she sure will." Alex said, and Morrison could hear his smile over the phone. "I'll have her call as soon as I see her, okay?"

"Deal."

Petrosky pulled out his phone, keeping one eye on the road. His jaw was tight. "Calling in the APB. I'll take the fall on it. She won't think it was you."

"Because it wasn't me." But he didn't care if she thought it was him, not anymore. His heart was beating a thousand times faster than it should, almost whirring at the speed of the tires on the road.

She's dead.
She just left yesterday.
Evie's dead.
Shannon texted me.
Someone took them, stomped them to death in a field.
Shannon told me she wasn't going to use me as a crutch.

His heart slowed, but the thoughts remained, fighting, screaming at one another in his brain.

"Valentine will tell her it was me anyway. Or his wife will." Petrosky stopped at a light and pushed a button on the phone. "And I don't give a fuck if she hates me."

"Yes you do," Morrison muttered as Petrosky put the phone to his ear.

"Valentine. Need an APB on a white Enclave. Yes. Shannon Morrison."

Valentine's exclamation of surprise emanated from the phone, but Petrosky shut him down. "Just do it, Valentine. And call me back." Morrison listened numbly to Petrosky's side of the conversation, trying to focus on something else. Anything else. Anything but the nausea in his gut and the knot throbbing between his shoulder blades. He raised his hand to massage the knot, but his limbs felt weak—shaky. He lowered his arm.

Petrosky shoved his phone into the console and sighed, the sound raising Morrison's hackles more than anything his partner could have said. "Let's toss the Acosta case at Detective Young, maybe even Decantor—if they are connected, he'll solve them both at once. Then we'll drive down to Alex's place to visit your niece. See Roxy. You know you miss that mutt, and she is kinda cute."

"You hate that dog." Morrison still couldn't believe he'd given Roxy away last year, but Abby had felt unsafe after Griffen had stomped her kitten to death. *Stomped.* An image of Dylan Acosta's body sprouted in his brain, and he shoved it away before it could take root.

"How do you know I hate Roxy?" Petrosky half grinned, but it looked forced.

Stop changing the subject. "We can't just leave now—Acosta's murderer is still out there, and we don't know these cases are connected in the first place. And our best shot at finding who did Bell, and who called me, is to follow these leads." The APB was probably a better way to go about finding Shannon anyway. If she had made it to Alex's fine, she'd be pissed when Morrison showed up, and if she was in trouble, he wasn't going to find out just by going Alex's; he'd still have no idea where to look for her, and in Atlanta, he might be a lot farther from Shannon and from his little girl. Which meant he might as well stay here, which meant he needed...a distraction.

"I bet she calls soon. She's probably just trying to prove to herself that she can handle the trip all on her own."

"Sounds like her." Petrosky didn't turn from the windshield, but the muscles in his jaw were working overtime in his fleshy face. "We'll wait on the APB before we head out there."

"Plus, she always says I'm overprotective."

"That's a dad's job, California," Petrosky said, and the pain was apparent in the creases around his eyes, the tightening of his jowls. He pulled into a drive, checked the address, and shut the car off. "Let's meet Mr. Xu."

THE OWNER of the nail salon had answered their questions with frantic little hand movements that belonged to a twittering sparrow, not a grown man. But they didn't come away empty-handed. Xu swore that he'd seen their rape suspect with another man—skinny with a buzz cut—exchanging a large paper sack for an envelope. But whether it had a bearing on the case remained to be seen. Despite Xu's vehemence about what he'd witnessed, this many years after the fact and the distance from the tattoo parlor to the nail salon made it just as likely that he'd seen another man with scraggly hair selling something to a friend. All the same, they'd look on local buying and selling websites, but it was doubtful they'd find anything of value.

By the time they left Xu's, Morrison was actively listening for Petrosky's phone, a buzzing to tell them where Shannon's car might be. But if she was on her way to Alex's, and already out of state, no one would have seen her yet. Not like she'd be likely to get pulled over.

Petrosky slammed his car door and lit a cigarette. "Let's pretend Xu did see our guy. Thoughts on the exchange?"

"Not sure. Something worth cash, if that's what was in the envelope."

"Right. And they wouldn't be so careless if it was porn." Petrosky checked his phone. Watching for Shannon too? For information to come back on her car?

Morrison's scalp itched, but he balled his fist instead of picking at it. *Focus on Xu. The package.* He couldn't make the APB go faster by fucking up his case. "The boots?" He squinted out his window, hating the tightness in his voice. Whatever these men had exchanged in the daytime had to be something less overtly threatening—less illegal—but still something they didn't want others to see. "But that'd mean our tattooed suspect made the boots for the man he eventually tried to stop from using them. And if these guys got together that long ago, you'd think we'd have seen other victims pop up well before now."

"You'd think so, but—"

Morrison's phone buzzed, and he ripped it from his pocket with enough force that he nearly tossed it through the front windshield. *Shannon.*

No, not Shannon. His heart rate quickened, liquefying his insides, pulsing faster and hotter within his chest.

That number—he'd seen it just yesterday when Decantor had come by his house.

Natalie Bell's cell.

He put the phone to his ear, the world around him slowing to a crawl, even the persistent whisper of the tires disappearing into some imperceptible void. "Morrison."

"How's the pig, Curt? Not the food, your partner." Female voice, alto, same as before. Breathy, but clear now and laced with venom.

Bolts of panic slithered up Morrison's back. "Miss Bell?" The world around him returned, and he eased his notepad from his pants pocket, positioning the pen so that he wouldn't miss some crucial bit of information. She wanted something. From him? Or was he merely convenient because they had his private number?

Petrosky jerked his face to Morrison, eyes wide, then back to the street, unable to stop the car as he merged onto the freeway.

"You know very well this isn't Natalie. I hear she was a pretty girl, Curt. Were you going to hire her, get a little strange on the side?"

Petrosky hit the gas, glancing at Morrison out of the corner of his eye. From the phone, there was a rumble like laughter, but not of the amusement variety—this was more like a ripple of madness.

Morrison's mouth was too dry to speak, not that he would have said anything anyway. You don't push crazy.

"I bet you were," the voice said. "You always were a whore."

That was a new one. "If you're not Natalie, then who am I talking to?"

"Tsk tsk, Curt. Don't ask, don't tell."

Curt. She knew his name. It wasn't on his business card—even Shannon didn't call him that.

"I rather think you might enjoy this, Curt. It has to do with everyone's favorite prosecutor."

Shannon. No, not—

"Roger McFadden." Tires squealed as Petrosky skidded past the right-hand lane onto the shoulder and slammed the car into park.

Morrison's heart descended from his throat back into his chest, where it fluttered weakly, trying to pulse within the tightness of his ribs.

"Roger's been a very bad boy. Which I suspect you know already."

Roger. This was about Roger? Probably someone he'd prosecuted, pissed off—career criminal, angry at Roger for putting him away? A criminal's lover? But why kill Bell? Why harass Morrison? Unless… they'd just seen Morrison's card in Bell's wallet, did a little research, and only later decided to bring him into the game. But that seemed too haphazard, too coincidental.

"Roger is an asshole; I'll give you that," Morrison said.

"He's dirty too. How would you like to take down your wife's ex? Cathartic, yes?"

His chest constricted. This woman knew a lot about him. But then, Shannon's former marriage to Roger was public record; the caller didn't need much to find out that information. Just motivation enough to mess with the police.

"I'd love to put Roger away. But I need a reason. Evidence." Too bad—anything he got from this woman was probably moot or a flat-out lie. "I'm more interested in Natalie Bell."

"I'm sure you are." That laugh again. Almost manic. "Roger's got a book in his safe deposit box. A log. Bribes. He needs to go to jail, Curt. And you need to get him locked up in the next twenty-four hours."

Morrison had long suspected Roger of taking bribes, of dropping reasonable charges for a price—though, he'd never been able to prove it. But this… How would this woman know about Roger's safe deposit box? Lucky guess? Either she was full of shit, or she actually knew Roger. Or…he knew Roger; the higher register could still be the trick of a voice-over contraption if this caller really was the same person who'd killed Dylan Acosta.

"Investigations like this take time," Morrison said slowly. "Weeks to uncover evidence, scour bank accounts. I can't exactly walk into a bank and get into his deposit box without hard evidence. Sounds like you've done your homework, so surely you know that."

"He'll give you the book. Then you can go to your chief."

"There's no way—"

"Be persuasive and arrest him. Or kill him. It doesn't matter to me. One way or another, he needs to be punished."

Kill him. The silence stretched on as Morrison jotted notes on the pad: *Natalie Bell's relationship to Roger? Bribery? Notes in safe? Or bullshit?* The buzz of other motorists on the freeway approaching, and then whipping by with the hiss of tires, made him suddenly claustrophobic. He circled "bullshit." The caller was fucking with him because she could. Opportunity, right? Sociopaths took what they could get. Unless she was just a normal—albeit impulsive—person who was really fucking pissed at Roger. He could see that happening too.

But this person wasn't normal. Whoever had Bell's cell had murdered her, tortured her—or at least knew about it. At least the caller wasn't after Shannon. He hadn't even recognized how worried he'd been until he felt the relief at the absence of a ransom demand. Shannon was just driving. Busy. And okay.

"So...what does Natalie Bell's murder have to do with Roger?" he asked.

Silence. "We've got a lot to work through, you and I." The woman's voice was hard, angry, and the words sounded personal—and not at all about Roger.

"I'm not sure I follow." Something about the voice suddenly nagged at him, the lilt of it tugging a memory from somewhere, a memory he couldn't quite retrieve. "Why don't you tell me how we know each other, so I can make sure I don't mess up again?"

"You still don't get it, do you? You see me, but you don't. But you'll figure it out—you'll remember me. And once you do, you'll know exactly how to find me." Her words felt less like a promise and more like a threat. Was she stalking him? He tried to place her voice, but the timbre did not call to mind anyone he knew.

"I'll call back when you're alone. But keep this to yourself, Curt. Keep your appointments. Work your cases. Wouldn't want your boss to get suspicious. And don't fuck it up."

The line went dead.

"What the hell was that about?"

Morrison stared at the phone like it was going to wake up and bite his hand. *Damn crackpots.* Had to be. Right? "Roger."

"What the fuck does that dickbrain have to do with anything?" Petrosky put the car into drive and eased back onto the freeway.

"Long story." Morrison related the details as best he could, starting with the cell call the day after Bell's murder and ending with the caller's suspicions that Roger was taking bribes for pleading cases out. But Bell...the caller hadn't seemed concerned with her at all. Was she just collateral damage, or was she connected to Roger somehow?

"Nothing that fucker does would surprise me. But the call...interesting." Petrosky tapped his knuckles against the console. "When we get back to the precinct, we'll look into it," he said finally. "We've got a few minutes before we need to see the doc, so we can do a trace on the call with that triangulation bullshit, yeah?"

Morrison nodded, but an urgent disquiet rose in his belly. He was just a bystander here, his number stolen and used in a killer's game of intimidation, probably against Roger, the prosecutor who'd done... something to this asshole. So what kind of person were they looking for? If the caller had benefitted from a plea deal with Roger—if the accusations about bribes were even true—they wouldn't be trying to expose Roger now. So maybe Roger had fucked this killer over, maybe jailed her —or him—despite a bribe, or...had Roger refused to take a bribe altogether? Then the killer gets out of jail, finds Roger, and kills someone to make sure the cops pay attention. But...

Morrison sucked air into his lungs as Petrosky pulled off the freeway and stopped at a red light that suddenly looked like an evil eye. *You still don't get it, do you? You see me, but you don't. But you'll figure it out—you'll remember me. And once you do, you'll know exactly how to find me.* Trusting his memory was dubious at best, and for the life of him, he could think of no one who would threaten Roger like this, who would kill an innocent girl. No one who would know the intimate details of Roger's life, well, no one except...

But Shannon had nothing to do with this—the only thing that was keeping Morrison sane. The killer wanted Roger. Why, he wasn't sure, but who didn't want to fuck Roger up?

Petrosky pulled into the precinct parking lot, but Morrison couldn't shake the uneasy feeling in his gut, or the flicker of electricity running over his spine.

19

TRIANGULATION WASN'T DIFFICULT. He clicked the mouse, entered Bell's number, listened to the clack of the keyboard. *Click click click.* There was a time when the focus would have helped—mindfulness quieted voices and memories and cravings far more effectively than talking about those things, dwelling on a jaded past. But today, his thoughts pressed in on him, loud and insistent over the sound of the keyboard. Why was he being dragged into this, and what did Roger have to do with Bell? Was the Acosta case connected? And, at the back of his mind, eclipsing all other thought like the remnants of a disturbing dream you were desperate to forget: *Where the fuck is Shannon?*

He pulled his fingers from the keyboard and tried Shannon's cell. Voice mail. He tried again, each buzz of the ringer more ominous than the last. Voice mail. He slammed the phone onto the desk, checked that it hadn't broken, and opened another computer screen to check her cell records. Why hadn't he thought of that yesterday? He was a fucking idiot. Morrison was hovering over the *locate* button when his cell pinged with a text, and he flipped it over, heart hammering.

Shannon:

"Sorry, just got your message. Love you too."

Morrison:

"Call me."

The phone stayed silent. On the screen, the towers blinked. He clicked back and forth, from Bell's cell to Shannon's and back again, drumming his fingers on the desk as the first, and then the second, cell tower blinked onto Bell's screen and stayed steady. If only they had better department funding and more up-to-date location equipment. Even 9-1-1 operators had a hard time locating callers with their outdated tracking systems.

The third tower blinked once more and solidified.

"Petrosky..."

The caller using Bell's cell was...there. Within a block of the precinct.

Petrosky wheeled over from his desk and peered at the screen.

"What do you make of that?" The disquiet in Morrison's belly was spreading, wrapping around his chest. They'd called *from* the precinct. Was the caller watching him? Or Roger?

"Fucking insider bullshit," Petrosky said. "I don't like it." He grimaced, and Morrison's fist clenched.

Insider bullshit—probably a reference to Shannon's old buddy Griffen. But he was dead. "Griffen was delusional," Morrison said. "Not likely it'd happen again, not like that."

Petrosky stood and shoved his chair toward his desk. It banged into the side, and Morrison jumped, his pulse hammering in his chest so violently he might as well have been running a marathon.

Petrosky raised an eyebrow, then lowered it. "Come on, kid, it's time to visit McCallum."

"Hang on..." On Shannon's screen, the second tower blinked. "Shannon texted me a minute ago." *If it is Shannon.* He turned to Petrosky, trying to keep his voice slow and even. "Any news on the APB?"

No reply.

"Petrosky?"

The boss's eyes were glued to the screen. Morrison turned back to the computer. The last tower was blinking, and like the droning of every ring on Shannon's unanswered cell, each pulse brought with it a sharper, fiercer pang of dread. Then it was up.

Her cell was at the precinct too.

20

MAYBE THE SYSTEM wasn't working—it wouldn't be the first time. Once it had traced all the anonymous 9-1-1 calls to an apartment on the east side, and the residents had almost sued the city for harassment when the cops kept showing up. But the cramp in Morrison's belly crept higher through his chest, into his shoulders, into his neck.

His entire body was stiff by the time Morrison emerged in the parking lot, Petrosky at his heels. *Come on, Shannon, call.* The air outside was electric with an impending storm, and Morrison had to concentrate on the breath in his lungs to make sure they inflated. In, out. In, out. The sky had darkened, and the thick, gray clouds had turned the lot into an apocalyptic sea of ash, stark against the neon green of the grass. Every car in the parking lot was empty, as was the lot itself, save for one wrinkled woman with a shock of white curls, creeping slowly toward the courthouse on a metal cane, wind plastering her hair to one withered cheek.

The breeze scattered leaves and the occasional plastic bottle in an ominous soundtrack. Morrison whipped out his cell as they strode across the lot. Shannon was fine—had to be fine. Evie too. But he didn't feel fine, every gust of wind from the heavens a whisper that his life was about to collapse. *We're looking for her. We'll find her.* And in the meantime... Morrison followed Petrosky's gaze around the lot, up to the windows of the courthouse. No prying eyes watching to see if he went to visit Roger's office.

Fucking Roger. But he'd have to go up there and at least let Roger know someone was trying to get his stupid ass arrested.

"Who you calling, Cali?"

"Decantor. Figured I'd let him know about the call on Roger. Maybe by the time we get out of our meeting with McCallum, he'll have something else on the caller." *Or maybe he'll have something on the APB.*

Voice mail. Morrison clicked off. The muted thuds of their shoes on pavement vibrated through his body, a steady metronome to the frantic beat of his heart as they approached the door to Dr. McCallum's office.

"Morrison!"

He turned to see Valentine running from the precinct, waving one beefy hand over his head. With every step he took, the apprehension in Valentine's eyes became more apparent—even the scar on his cheek seemed agitated.

Petrosky's breathing had increased. He shouldn't be winded. He shouldn't be. Was it his heart, or was it…

"I just ran into Decantor." Valentine had reached them, panting. "He's looking for you."

Stay calm. Morrison nodded, the muscles in his neck corded with nervous energy "I just tried to call him. I'll run over after McCallum… unless it's urgent?"

Valentine didn't respond, just stared at him with the hollow look of a Holocaust survivor. "Decantor said you guys have the same killer. For sure."

Petrosky stilled beside him.

"He just came from the ME's office." Valentine averted his eyes, looking almost guilty, but of course, he couldn't feel guilty—there was nothing to feel bad about. No, not guilt. His friend felt awful. *Distressed.*

Morrison's heart seized.

Valentine looked back up and met Morrison's gaze. "Found a single hair at the Bell scene—blond at the root, black at the tip. Got a DNA match to the blood at the Acosta scene. And that spike thing…uh…that she was…penetrated with? Lab results concluded that it was the same object in both cases, or at least from the same batch of metal—there were patina fragments." He wrung his hands. "And he scraped a number one on Bell too…on that spot between…you know. The taint." He winced. "Before she died."

Morrison swallowed hard, trying to keep his breath even. It was about their case. Not about his wife. *The case.* Dylan Acosta. Natalie Bell. "We've got a few leads on ours too. We'll be heading back to the east side after profiling with McCallum. Tell Decantor we can reconvene afterward, go over everything."

"Oh, okay, yeah, sure that sounds good." But Valentine's eyes were on the building, on his shoes, glancing back at the precinct—everywhere but Petrosky and Morrison. He looked like he wanted to run.

Petrosky coughed and moved to Morrison's side. "Spit it out, Valentine."

Valentine stared at them, his mouth working. Morrison couldn't feel his chest. His legs were numb.

Petrosky clapped twice in front of the man's face. "Valentine!"

"You need to talk to Decantor."

"You said that already," Morrison said, softly, almost whispering because his throat was too tight to do more.

"Goddammit, just—"

"We found Shannon's car."

He said you guys have the same killer. And the killer had called him. Bile rose in his throat, blocking his airway. What if...

"An hour ago. Gas station near Toledo, just over the Ohio border."

She'd barely made it out of state—an hour from the house, two tops. She'd been missing for all of yesterday. He glanced at the sky, the low-hanging clouds, the weak hint of late afternoon illumination. Nearly all of today too.

Missing. But without a struggle? She'd have fought a kidnapper. Maybe she'd leapt from an overpass, thrown Evie into the river. No. *What the hell am I thinking?* No way. She had just texted him—she was fine. She had to be fine. She was fine, completely fine, and probably pissed at him for not trusting her.

Texted him from the precinct. And he hadn't heard her voice.

A glance at Petrosky's face turned his insides to water, the apprehension he saw reaching for him with panicked fingers as tangible as his own. Petrosky had probably told himself it would be fine all the way to identify his daughter's body. And then it wasn't fine. Nothing had ever been fine again.

If their killer had taken Shannon, she was in for a lot worse than a leap off a bridge. And his little girl—no. *No.* He faced Valentine. "You found her car. Did you find my wife?"

Valentine's eyes were glassy. He shook his head.

Dylan Acosta and Natalie Bell—they'd been killed by the same sadistic fuck. The same sadistic fuck who had called Morrison. The vicious monster who had killed both his victims within an hour of first attacking them.

A murderer had his family, and he had no idea where they were.

Or if they were already dead.

21

Petrosky lit a cigarette with quick, jerky movements as Valentine headed back into the precinct under the guise of getting the file. "They probably followed her until she stopped for gas, or to feed Evelyn, then grabbed her."

Morrison watched Petrosky's acrid cloud appear and fly sharply away in the breeze like his own happiness—here, then gone. And again. Every time the wind whipped the cloud away, he saw it taking pieces of his tenuous grasp on sanity.

Petrosky coughed. "We're heading over to—"

"What? They were here! She's here!"

"She's not, Morrison. You think this guy's hiding Shannon at the courthouse? A screaming baby at the prosecutor's office?"

Screaming. God, they'd make her scream. Until they killed her. "I don't know where the fuck he's hiding her, goddammit!"

Petrosky did not respond to his outburst, just said, "And that text you got...anything weird about it?"

The smoke above Petrosky's head was the embodiment of Morrison's own boiling insides—fear, pain, bubbling in his belly and rising through his throat and escaping out his nostrils. But when Morrison exhaled, he saw no plume to indicate the existence of his terror.

"You're the tech genius. Couldn't they just be shooting the signal around? Saying the phone is here when really it's in butt-fuck Egypt?" Petrosky squinted at the sky as if the answer might be written in the indignant clouds.

"I... Maybe. Yeah." They could be scrambling the signal, or they might have used one of those cards that puts any number on a caller ID. Which meant Shannon's actual phone could be anywhere. Fuck.

Petrosky cocked an eyebrow and blew smoke at the sky. "Our best leads are on the Reynolds case—we have a DNA match on the semen, so we know we're looking for the same rapist. And that sick pedophile knows who the killer is. The object used to stab Acosta and Bell is unique—there has to be a way to trace it. I'll talk to the ME, see if he can trace the metal itself."

"When's the DNA back? The rest of the crime scene labs?" Morrison's heart felt like it had stopped beating, but it was beating—had to be.

"Ours is due by tomorrow." Petrosky grimaced. "I'll make it fucking sooner on both ours and Bell's."

Morrison scanned the lot. Along the back, the upper boughs of the ash trees twisted in the wind, though he felt no breeze. In one corner, a maroon Suburban pulled into a parking spot, and a twentysomething white guy in a backward cap leaped out and started toward the sidewalk, hitching up his pants. The man gave them a cursory glance as he removed his ball cap, then disappeared up the stairs and into the courthouse next door.

The world was starkly focused, but Morrison could not seem to attach his thoughts to his body—his brain felt disconnected and fuzzy and wrong. The wind howled and silenced itself just as abruptly, leaving him with the emptiness ringing in his ears. Where did he need to go? What could he do?

"We should talk to Roger." Morrison turned to the building and glanced up at the third floor. Because the caller had threatened Roger. Because whoever had Shannon had a vendetta against Roger. Was Roger the reason Shannon had been taken in the first place? They were aware that Shannon wasn't married to Roger any longer, but no one could mistake the way Roger had lusted after her from the moment she'd left him. If they were watching him, maybe they'd know that. So did Shannon know them too, get out of her vehicle willingly? Know them through Roger? From the prosecutor's office? Shannon was stronger than she looked, though Evie would have slowed her down if she'd been forced from the car.

Morrison's chest burned. Evie. Shannon. *Fuck.* He couldn't breathe. Maybe it was a misunderstanding: someone had swapped her plates in a parking lot, and any moment now, she'd call from Alex's. But he felt the wrongness of that deep in his belly. And if Valentine was right and it was Shannon's car at that gas station—there might be something in the vehicle to help them find her. "We'll go look at the car first." He pulled out his phone to text Decantor.

"Heading to Toledo. Meet back on the cases in a couple hours."

Petrosky ground the cigarette under the heel of his shoe, and they walked across the lot, the ash trees leering at them. Maybe someone *was* watching, lurking behind a pine or a clump of brush. He could feel the rain spitting on his skin, but distantly, each drop merely a subtle pressure devoid of cold or wet. His shoes made a sickly squashing sound, like sucking a brain through a straw.

Someone was trying to scare him. Probably used software like Trickster to fake a caller ID number. Maybe they'd done that to Bell's phone too.

Maybe they didn't have Shannon after all.

He felt the tug of denial and the hope it provided, but hope could be a sickness just as much as a godsend.

If they had her... The world wavered, disappeared, returned, but this time he could no longer feel the thumping in his chest.

They'd start with her car. If they drove fast, they could get there before the coming storm obliterated the evidence.

PETROSKY'S CAR smelled the same as it always did, but everything felt heavier, dank, gluey in the back of his throat like the stale stench of cigarettes was going to drown him in a river of tobacco and confusion.

He couldn't call the police. He *was* the fucking police.

It's up to you, Curt, old boy.

A shock, an electric buzzing jolted through his right hip. Morrison jumped and hit his head on the car window, and his phone buzzed again in his back pocket. He jerked it out. Text message from Shannon. Or Shannon's number.

"Don't miss your appointment. And keep your mouth shut."

Petrosky was staring at him, keys in hand, car still in park. Morrison looked frantically around the lot, but there was no one, only the silvery threads of rain on the window and the thunderheads obscuring his view of the sun. How did they know he was leaving? Petrosky was staring at him, but he couldn't speak, couldn't answer the question written in the lines on Petrosky's forehead.

Breathe. He felt the rain as if it were thrumming through his veins. *Breathe.* But he was drowning in the downpour, every drop that hit the windshield trying to wash away his family and send everything that mattered out to sea. He typed:

"I need to talk to her."

The phone buzzed:

"No."

Nothing else, no instructions, no ransom demands, nothing. Just "no": the severing of hope.

They had her. She was dead. Evie was dead. They were dead already.

Morrison:

"Please."

Shannon:

"You'll do what you're told, or I'll take it out on her. I'll save your baby girl for when you get here if she doesn't starve to death first. Be the same selfish asshole you've always been, and I'll take pleasure in watching them bleed."

Evie. *Starving.* They weren't feeding her? Panic and fury and helplessness roiled in his abdomen.

Morrison:

"Please don't hurt them."

Shannon:

"Fuck off, Curt. Let me know when Roger's taken care of. Then you can talk to your lovely wife. I'll call tomorrow night for a progress report."

Morrison:

"Give me time. Please let them go, and I'll help you with whatever you want."

He stared at the phone, waiting for another reply, another answer, but none came. How'd they know he had decided to skip McCallum's to head to Toledo? He had texted Decantor, but...they must have tapped Morrison's phone. Or bugged the car.

Petrosky was frozen, keys in his palm. "What's up?"

Keep your mouth shut. Morrison felt the weight of the phone in his palm. "Nothing." But he rested his cell on the console and turned it so Petrosky could see.

"You're a fucking liar." But there was no anger in Petrosky's voice as he read the texts, just the whisper of helpless apology and a panic that mirrored Morrison's own.

"We should go see McCallum." Morrison's voice wavered. They wanted him here, so this was the last place he should be. Yet without any idea where Shannon and Evie were, he was helpless to get to them. He needed time. Needed to buy that time by doing what these fuckers wanted... But killing Roger? He pictured Natalie Bell, her smile when she played with Evie, then later, nude, bloody, disfigured by something sharp, the same object used to kill Acosta. They'd done that to her. They'd do that to his wife. *To his child.*

Everything vibrated, and Morrison flung the door wide and vomited bile onto the pavement. When his stomach was empty, he hauled himself onto the seat again and leaned back against the headrest. *They took my family.* Shannon might be dying, carved up like Acosta, like Bell. Evie might be—

"Buy that tiger for Evie yet?" Petrosky snapped, the harshness in his voice betraying his fear. "She'll be happy to see it when they get back."

Morrison balked, but when he met Petrosky's eyes, he saw the earnest question. *Tiger. Tiger.* Then it clicked. Tiger kidnapping: an abduction carried out to coerce another into committing a crime on the kidnapper's behalf. While putting Roger away wasn't illegal, killing him most certainly would be, and there was no way Roger was going down for anything as long as he had a breath in his body.

Morrison's breath shivered through his lungs. "Yeah, she'll like the tiger."

"Shouldn't take too long here with the doc. Ten to thirteen minutes? What do you think?"

McCallum liked to talk—they'd never been there less than half an hour. *Focus. Think.* The way Petrosky was talking now, he seemed to think his car was bugged. So...ten-thirteen, that meant civilians were present and listening. Were they, or was it a ruse? Their suspect had been aware how they'd spent the morning, and they'd known Morrison was planning on canceling the appointment with McCallum even before McCallum did. Morrison nodded again, trying to think, but every thought seemed to run through his brain like sand through a sieve.

His baby.

His wife.

These monsters had his whole world.

Petrosky pulled out his cigarettes, glared into the rearview, mouthed *fuck,* and lit up.

Morrison wiped his lips on the back of his hand, inhaled through his nose, and climbed from the car on shaky legs. He started for the building, the echo of someone else's footfalls in his ears though each thunk matched the beat of his own shoes—marching to his own execution. Maybe he was. If he lost his family, he might as well be dead.

> "The boundaries which divide Life from Death are at best shadowy and vague. Who shall say where the one ends, and where the other begins?"
> ~Edgar Allan Poe, *The Premature Burial*

22

Find Bell's killer. Acosta's killer. Find their killer, and he'd find his family.

This was how you solved cases, caught the bad guys. But every fiber of his being wanted him to tear out of the building, leap into his car, head to Toledo and blast through the streets, gun drawn, until he found his wife and baby girl. Here he was impotent, helpless, and he was well aware of the fact that most kids are murdered within three hours of the abduction. Was Evie dead already? Was Shannon? Even if he got them back, they'd know—for the rest of their lives—that he couldn't keep them safe.

He'd known safety was tenuous at best—even an illusion. But he hadn't wanted Evie to know.

Please let them come home.

Dr. Stephen McCallum met them in the outer office. He led them to the back room where he squeezed his three hundred pounds of shrink and sweater vest behind the desk and watched them with the penetrating eyes of one used to uncovering secrets. Morrison's already turbulent belly squeezed like a sponge, forcing bile up his esophagus so that he had to gulp it back down. His throat burned from the acid he'd vomited onto the parking lot.

Petrosky nodded at him, almost imperceptibly. *Act normal. Do the job. Work this case.*

But he couldn't speak. He couldn't breathe. If McCallum figured out what was going on and alerted anyone, Shannon would die. Right? And Evie...he couldn't even consider it. *No.* He inhaled harsh, stale office air through his nostrils and tried not to retch again.

Petrosky cleared his throat. "Let's get right into it. Looking for two attackers."

"I read the reports," McCallum said. "You have one definite rapist, a pedophile with a distinct pattern—from his previous attack on Zachary Reynolds, he rapes, he strangles, he leaves. That attack was carried out alone. Here, he followed the same pattern: rape, strangulation with the T-shirt, and leaving the boy alive. But you have another man at the Acosta scene—most likely the one who killed the child. If Acosta had died of strangulation, I'd say it was an accident or escalation of your pedophile's normal MO. But you have a totally different pattern here." McCallum tapped a pen against the desktop, and Morrison struggled to remember the doctor picking up the ballpoint. "Combined with the indications of struggle at the scene, I'd say your murderer is the other man, the one with the spiked boots and a penchant for stomping or stabbing, though how or why he was there is another question."

Petrosky had the notepad. When had he taken the notepad? Suddenly unsure what to do with his hands, Morrison dug his fists into the chair on either side of his hips.

"We thought as much," Petrosky said. "And now we have an additional killing: Natalie Bell, twenty-nine, stabbed in the lower belly and groin, penetrated vaginally with the same object. Bled to death. The weapon was distinct—likely of the same batch of metal as the one used on Acosta. Might even be homemade." Petrosky's voice did not waver. How could he sound so normal? Nothing was normal. Nothing would ever be normal again.

McCallum furrowed his brows. "I suspect you have one standard pedophile, and one with piquerism, a fetish that involves penetration. They tend to be sexually sadistic, brutal, and often stab areas of the body related to sex, like what happened to Natalie Bell. In these cases, the stabbing object essentially becomes an extension of his body and the source of sexual excitement. Many notorious serial killers like Albert Fish and Jack the Ripper are thought to have had piqueristic tendencies."

Jack the Ripper. Shit. His lungs were too small. Morrison sucked in a ragged breath, trying not to imagine what it had been like for Acosta as the air left him, trying not to think that his baby girl was wheezing her last, face down in the dirt somewhere.

McCallum's eyes swung to Morrison's. "You okay, son?"

"He's fine. Bad sushi." Petrosky's leg bounced a steady rhythm, but his knuckles were white around his knee—the only indication that something was amiss, different, horrible.

McCallum cleared his throat and glanced at the file. Nodded as if this wasn't the worst fucking thing he'd ever seen, as if Shannon and Evie were just hanging out at home. "Your murder suspect went after Bell right away. The scuffle with the other suspect at the Acosta scene might have dampened the excitement of the killing itself, leading your murderer to attack soon afterward to release that frustrated energy."

"Our pedophile is sick too—has some creepy clown tattoos. Sadistic stuff even if he wasn't the one who killed Acosta."

McCallum nodded knowingly.

Petrosky scribbled a note on the pad. "We might have a woman present as well or someone with a higher voice. Could be using something to alter their voices, though."

A woman. A woman who hated Roger. But there had been no trace of a woman anywhere at either crime scene... Where did she fit into all this? Morrison's stomach lurched, but McCallum was already answering: "It's also possible that either of your suspects is effeminate. If this is the case, he's likely triggered by any challenges to his masculinity—maybe afraid of women if he believes they'll reject him—and that may beget rage. If it's your piquerist, he might be expressing his masculinity through the stabbing. Enough sexual rejection for being effeminate, and he might have begun to enjoy punishing those who reject him; he might even enjoy it more than penetrating them with his penis." McCallum leaned toward them. "He's clearly still angry. He wants to punish someone for perceived slights and rejections."

Morrison could hear the words but was having trouble sorting them—as if each sentence crumbled apart as it hit his ear, rearranging itself like the nonsensical ramblings of a schizophrenic. *Focus.* Who had Shannon? The killer who had gone after Bell, stolen Bell's phone? As McCallum said, their suspects had widely different patterns—and this was definitely more in line with that of the killer. But what if both killer and pedophile were a part of this? Maybe they'd rape Shannon too. They'd rape her and rape Evie. Maybe they'd even taken Shannon for the killer and Evie for the pedophile, and his whole fucking world was already gone.

Petrosky wrote something on the notepad, but his scrawl was unreadable, or maybe it was just Morrison's eyes—everything seemed blurry and unfocused, even Petrosky's hand.

"Individuals with this fetish tend to have a type, just like other rapists. Do you have other female victims or just Bell?"

"Nothing yet."

"What's her type, physically? Small? Vulnerable?"

Morrison nodded, picturing Natalie Bell: her hand had been tiny in his own, and the tension in her eyes could be perceived as vulnerability. She'd worn clothes that could probably have fit a fifteen-year-old. Was she chosen because she looked like a kid? If so, Shannon wouldn't do it for this guy. She was thin, but no one would mistake the gleam in her eyes for that of a child.

"You mentioned our suspect having to kill again to release energy." Petrosky shifted in the chair. "This guy—our stabby bastard, the killer—must have watched his buddy rape the kid. Why would he watch if he's only in it for the stabbing?"

"He might have gotten excited and surprised them both by killing the child. I'm more concerned that he was watching because they're feeding off one another. Your pedophile got off on the voyeuristic elements of being watched, and your killer enjoyed the pain of the child so much he couldn't restrain himself. Or your killer might be...learning, especially if he has a strong history of rejection and emotional shutdown."

Rejection. Had the killer been slighted by Roger specifically? Maybe he'd been pushed aside by a woman who preferred the affections of Shannon's ex over some maniac.

"Your killer might be thinking, watching, considering why people are attracted to his friend. Trying to figure out how to attract meaningful others and avoid rejection, or how to lure them in, specifically to cause pain." He shrugged. "It's just a theory, mind you, but an interesting one."

Interesting, his ass. Was McCallum some kind of psycho? How could he not see that the world was collapsing around them? *Because we didn't tell him.*

Morrison was wasting time. But he had to listen. Work the case. Ask something. Shannon wasn't a target for pedophiles or an opportunistic abduction. She'd had been taken because... Why the fuck did they take her? All the caller had demanded was Roger's suffering—retribution.

But Roger wouldn't get that close to another guy—Shannon had said Roger kept his friends at arm's length. It had to be someone Roger knew intimately. Forget McCallum—they weren't looking for an effeminate man unless he'd tucked his dick back and tricked Roger too. And transsexuals were almost never perpetrators in sex crime cases—victims, yes, perpetrators, no.

Morrison cleared his throat. "If there is a woman involved...what would we be looking for?"

Petrosky was staring at him. McCallum was staring at him. Morrison dropped his eyes to his knuckles.

"Opportunity is the biggest precursor to abuse. Women often have an easier time gaining access to kids, and it is common to see female pedophiles in positions of power over children. Teachers, babysitters, nannies, and the like. But your crimes don't fit what we typically see in those cases."

Teachers. Someone at Acosta's school? Morrison'd had a whole bunch of babysitters and nannies cycling through his own house in the last month, but that didn't mesh. If a sitter were seeking an opportunity, she'd have waited until she was hired and alone with Evie. She'd have waited until—

"Obviously, a profile is tricky because you have more than one suspect; you may have a mastermind and one along for the ride. But one of them is cunning. They staked out the playground beforehand so that they would know exactly where to take the child to avoid being seen from the school itself." McCallum cleared his throat. "Now, I didn't see much evidence that

Acosta was singled out ahead of time, but the number one scored into Acosta's skin, carved along his rib cage—it feels intimate. If he'd been chosen earlier, you'd expect grooming for weeks or months: gifts, kindnesses."

Acosta's parents and friends had denied any such attention being paid to the child, and it hadn't been present in the Reynolds case either.

"The T-shirt could indicate a need for silence, a fear of being caught, or perhaps even not wanting to hurt the boy, maybe letting him sleep through the attack itself if your pedophile convinced himself that he loved the child, as many do. He might even see it as part of the romance."

"Romance?" The word was out of Morrison's mouth before he could stop it, and more words kept tumbling, louder and faster. "It's fucking rape, not dinner and a goddamn movie."

McCallum's eyes widened, and he stilled, though his training was probably preventing him from expressing much surprise at the outburst. More than that—he was fucking *calm*. They all were.

They were liars.

"Some see it as seduction," McCallum began, his voice slow and even as if talking to a rabid dog he feared might bite. "You know that. Some believe they're in love. Some convince themselves of this because they don't want to accept the guilt that they did something horribly, atrociously wrong."

"What the hell kind of delusional—"

Petrosky stiffened too. "Easy, Morrison. We're dealing with tigers."

Tigers. Morrison's shirt had adhered to his back with sweat. The woman on the phone had told him...*he'd remember her*. That he'd know where to find her. Was she going to tell him where his family was if he did as she asked and locked Roger up—or killed him? He'd trade Roger's life for the safety of his family in a heartbeat.

McCallum was watching him, fingers laced on the desk, eyebrow cocked. Waiting. *Or...examining.* Morrison wiped away the sweat beading on his forehead. He had to go. Had to leave. Every muscle screamed with the need to act, to save the people he loved.

But there was nowhere to go. Not yet. The killer had texted him about going to this meeting.

How could he just sit here?

Did he have any other choice?

"Delusional might not be far off," McCallum said, and Morrison scoured his brain trying to recall what question the doctor was responding to. "Some even manage to convince themselves that everyone has these same fantasies, though at first, most are genuinely upset that they are sexually attracted to children. Of course, with the advent of online communities and chatrooms, camaraderie spreads, and eventually, it becomes normalized, acceptable, even just within the group. And that in and of itself can trigger escalation."

Escalation. Murder was sometimes intentional, sometimes accidental; he knew that much. But Shannon and Evie's kidnapping was purposeful—premeditated. Stealing a cop's kid and his prosecutor wife meant you knew what you were doing—had to if you thought you were going to get away with it. Right? And killing Acosta...was that purposeful too, or was it a fetish that got out of control? A tornado waged war inside his brain, tearing snippets of thought from their foundations and mixing them up until all he could make out were disjointed words as they were carried away on the wind.

Escalation. They were killing his wife and his baby *right now*.

Romance. Did they romance Acosta?

No one romanced Reynolds.

Rape.

Kidnapping.

Stabbing.

Murder.

But with Acosta and Bell, it wasn't just escalation or an attack gone wrong in the moment. They'd brought an *object* with them, an object that was used to stab the victims. That required forethought—planning. At least one of the perps had always intended to kill.

McCallum was still speaking, but his voice was far away as if Morrison were listening through a tunnel. "It's safe to say these men have done it before, probably more than just the few times you've found out about. It's unlikely that they'd go right to murder after five years of silence."

Silence. Did they want Roger silenced? They did want Roger locked up, but why? To get to the point where you would kidnap a woman and her child, you had to be desperate.

There was no air. He tried to feel the chair on his back, his feet on the floor, the hot wheezing of the heat vent. Why did McCallum have the heat on?

McCallum must have been talking, probably still about the cases, but now they were all standing, and the walk to the front door took five times as long as usual—his world hyper-focused, every air molecule biting his skin. At the outer exit, he hung back and let Petrosky head through, then leaned toward McCallum's ear, a new, separate concern bubbling to the top of his consciousness.

Shannon was the only one Evie could count on at this moment. She might be incapacitated, but if missing her medications made her more helpless, more hopeless...

"Are there side effects to the medication Shannon's on if she suddenly stopped taking it?"

The worry lines around McCallum's mouth deepened. "There would be some side effects. Though I'd be more concerned about the depression returning. Postpartum depression needs longer-term assistance, and I think in her case—"

"What would happen?"

"She might have some irritability. Brain zaps, like little electric currents in her head. Nausea, too. And of course, anxiety and what we call rebound depression, which can be significantly worse than the original episode." He narrowed his eyes at Morrison. "I strongly advise that she come in before stopping the meds, even if she feels okay."

From outside the door, Petrosky peeked in, appraised Morrison, and left again.

"Morrison?"

"I was just worried that she left her medications on the dresser when she headed off to her brother-in-law's. How hard is it to call in a prescription somewhere out of state?"

McCallum's Santa Claus face softened, and a hint of a smile touched his face. "That's why you're upset, son?"

Morrison nodded, and McCallum patted his shoulder. "I know how much she's struggled, but she'll be fine. Just get me a pharmacy number, and I'll call a script over. She should be able to pick them up within a few hours, and missing one dose won't trigger any unwanted symptoms. I'd advise her to find a pharmacy soon, though. Don't want her to miss more than a couple doses."

It was going on two days. She'd already missed four.

23

You can't fucking go. Petrosky's scrawl on the notepad was barely legible. Shaky. Maybe because Petrosky was writing on the steering wheel. Maybe because one or both of them was shaking—not that Morrison could tell anything about Petrosky's state. His own insides were quaking so violently a roller coaster would have seemed stable.

They hadn't needed to discuss whether Morrison's cell was being tapped. Had their suspects hacked the cell, or added a listening device to the car itself? That was another question, but if the suspects were watching, they'd be pissed if Morrison went out to see Shannon's car instead of speaking to Roger. Hostage takers didn't respond well to being ignored.

Morrison's jaw was clenched so hard his teeth hurt.

Get the fuck up to Roger's office, Petrosky wrote.

You might miss something, Morrison scrawled, not because Petrosky was inept by any stretch but because she was his wife, goddammit, his baby, and he knew what they had with them, what they might have dropped. If one of their toys, a bottle, *a bobby pin,* were left in the lot, he'd find it. He knew their smell so vividly he could almost taste it.

Petrosky was still writing: *I'll take pictures. Tell you everything. We don't know what's going on here. Don't have time to wait on Roger.*

Divide and conquer. It was logical. But it felt wrong.

Can't risk her, Petrosky wrote.

If they'd threatened Petrosky, the old man would have walked into the lot with a bunch of officers, guns blazing, "fuck it, kill me" stamped on his face. But...

Can't risk her.

Petrosky had walked Shannon down the aisle. He'd been there with her after the birth when Morrison went to the nursery with Evie.

Though Petrosky could be a crotchety bastard—with everyone—he truly loved Shannon. And he wouldn't take any chances—he'd already lost a daughter once. If there were evidence to find, Petrosky would find it.

Roger was the one the caller had been after. There had to be a reason the killer hated the prosecutor, just like there had to be a reason Morrison had been chosen to go after Roger in the first place.

He pushed aside the desire to run, to drive, to find her car and touch the last place she had been, to feel her energy as if it would convince him she was still alive and calm the thundering in his chest. He grabbed the case file and threw the car door open.

Petrosky squeezed his shoulder once and let him go.

MORRISON RUSHED into the stairwell leading to the prosecutor's office, trying to focus, trying to avoid thinking about anything but the task before him. He'd taken this trip numerous times to see Shannon—to bring her lunch. Coffee. Just to see her face. And, later, flowers or personalized stationery or little baby shoes that made her smile through her tears as her belly grew and her depression worsened.

Now she was gone.

So was the secretary, her desk empty as the hole in his gut. The butterfly photographs along the tawny walls felt less like they were fluttering and more like they were trying to escape their glass prison. If panic had a voice, it would be his breath against the walls, his shoes against the carpet, and his heart, muted but frantic and heavy and pressured like an elephant stampeding toward a hunter—a battle from which one or the other would not emerge.

What was he going to do? Ask Roger to turn himself in? Morrison had had no proof of wrongdoing, and no guarantees that his actions here would get Shannon back. But he had no choice, either, just the stinging, frenzied horror, the prospect of a life lived without... He couldn't even think it. Couldn't think at all. Every time he blinked, he saw red behind his eyelids.

This is why we don't let the hostage's family make decisions.

Behind Roger's door, Shannon's asshole ex laughed, low and long and...eerily gleeful. Morrison glanced down the hall at the door that had always been Shannon's. His chest pinched, and his breath came faster. He cleared his throat and knocked.

There was some scuttling in the room, and Roger opened the door, his cell phone to his ear. His eyes narrowed when he saw Morrison, and he touched his nose, as if by reflex, like he couldn't help but recall the time they'd come to blows. Morrison had never regretted the way Roger's nose had felt under his fist—the way it had crunched.

Until now.

"I'll call you back." Roger pocketed the phone and glared at Morrison. "What do you want? I swear if Shannon's not back by—"

"This isn't about her maternity leave." Morrison put his shoe against the doorframe before Roger could slam the door in his face. "We need to talk. It's about a case." *A case. My family.* "It's about you."

Roger appraised him, his mouth a smirk that made Morrison want to hit him again, but he wouldn't—couldn't. "You have two minutes. I'm busy."

Morrison closed the door behind them and sat across from Roger in a short wooden chair, not nearly as plush as the leather one Roger eased himself into. A power play—typical for Shannon's ex. But equal seating was a trivial concern compared to what he needed from Roger now.

"I—" The words stuck in his mouth. *Someone kidnapped Shannon and Evie.* It still felt unreal, a dream he'd awaken from. And Roger might not care, even if he did still love Shannon as a conquest—the one who escaped. Escaped to Morrison, who had failed to keep her safe while Roger had kept her intact.

Intact. Emotionally scarred, perhaps, but alive. And Evie, his poor, sweet baby girl...

Roger cocked his head. "What the fuck's wrong with you?"

Keep it on him. Let Roger be the hero. "I need your help."

An arrogant smile plastered itself across Roger's face. "I don't see why I should do you any fucking favors."

Strike one. "It's not a favor, Roger. I got a call this morning. You're taking bribes, and someone knows it."

"Someone who?"

Shit. Morrison swallowed his hatred, his fear. *Be a cop.* "If you turn everything over, I can help you. We can—"

Roger crossed his arms, haughty and indignant. "I haven't done anything wrong."

"You have, Roger." *Please let that be true.* There had to be a way out of this—had to be.

"There's no evidence of that." No change in his face.

"Roger, think. Who knew about it?"

Recognition flashed in Roger's eyes and disappeared into the mask again. "No one." Another flash of white teeth, almost a snarl.

Morrison's heart leapt. "Someone," he said. "Please."

"Get out."

"Roger, listen to me, if you tell me who knows, I can find them." He inhaled sharply. "They called this morning, they—"

"There's nothing to know." Roger touched the head of a glass figurine on the desk, Lady Justice holding scales half as large as herself. But Morrison knew just how easily those scales could be persuaded to tip to one side or the other—they all knew.

Justice was rarely the point.

"They have Shannon," Morrison said. "Someone took her."

"Sure they did."

He stared back, stunned. Of all the possible outcomes, Roger disbelieving the situation had not occurred to him. Roger was erring on the side that put Shannon and Evie in danger. "Roger—"

"And they'll let her go if I just destroy my career? My life? Seems rather convenient. If you wanted to get rid of me, I'd have thought you'd be more creative. At least make it less obvious that you want me locked up the way you think I did to you."

He didn't think it—Morrison *knew* his arrest had been intentional, and that Roger had been behind the whole thing. But Roger was right—he'd never gotten over it.

He never would.

Rage burned in his chest, mingling with white-hot desperation. What was he going to do?

Kill him.

Can't. If he was locked up and the killer decided to keep his family...

"They're not going to stop here, Roger. If someone... If you can just tell me who might want to hurt you, who might want to see you locked up, I'll have a place to start. Better if they have reason to believe that you did something...wrong."

"Every perp I've put away in the last fifteen years wants me gone."

Morrison glanced at the file in his hands. *Every perp.* He'd forgotten about the composite from the Reynolds case. "This guy look familiar?" He flipped open the folder and thrust it at Roger.

"He looks like a fucking goon. And no."

"He's got a partner, around five-nine, thin, blond hair, black at the tips."

Roger snorted, shaking his head like he felt sorry for Morrison now.

"What about someone personally connected to you, someone you've been in a relationship with? Anyone who might want to hurt you?"

"Your wife, maybe. You."

"Roger—"

"Exes always go away a little pissy, don't they? This isn't about me."

Yes it is. The only thing the caller had asked him for was Roger's fucking head.

"Whoever has Shannon already killed someone else. Natalie Bell, found raped and murd—"

"The Bell case, huh? So now Shannon's been gone all week?" He raised his eyebrows as if he'd caught Morrison in a lie.

"No, Shannon was still here when—" Morrison stopped. "How do you know about the Bell case?"

"Maybe you told your good friend Decantor that if he acted like the Bell case had something to do with me that you'd get me fired. Decantor and I have gone toe to toe three times in the last six months over stupid shit. He hasn't won once." Roger sneered again. Predatory.

Morrison rubbed his temples where the rage and fear mingled, whirring painfully through his brain. "Roger, whoever's doing this, whoever knows about what you've done, won't keep it secret. All that will happen is...Shannon will die. Evie will..." His voice cracked on the last word, and he didn't fucking care, not now.

Roger paused, keeping his eyes on the figurine. "And why should I care what happens to my ex-wife? You're the one who has her now. You're the one who's supposed to be taking care of her, not me. Hell, you probably took care of her while we were married."

While they were— "Goddammit, this isn't about you and me, Roger!"

"Ah, but it is. You can't ask a man a favor after you've stolen his wife." He chuckled. "Besides, if you're involved in a kidnapping situation, you know as well as I do that giving them what they want isn't all that likely to help you. Do your job and find out who did it and stop coming in here fucking with me."

"Who knows about your safe deposit box?"

The crinkle at the corners of Roger's eyes died, but his mouth stayed even, his shoulders back. "No one."

"Roger, someone does."

"So some ex-girlfriend or a one-night stand went through my drawers and assumed something that wasn't true. Did they give you the name of the bank?"

They hadn't. He shook his head.

Roger's face relaxed. "Well, there you go. They don't know anything. It's just someone trying to get even."

"You think one of your exes would murder another woman to get back at you?"

"What can I say?" The smile was back.

"This isn't a fucking joke!"

"You're full of shit, Morrison. I know Shannon was going to Alex's this week because she told me when she called with her work-return date. And you know about the box because Shannon knows about it. Even kept her wedding ring there until she sold it." He flattened his palms against the desk and pushed himself to standing. "Convenient that they grabbed her just before she was supposed to be coming back to work. Maybe you're threatened, knowing she'll be here every day with me. That was how you got her in the first place, right? Pulled her away little by little, a CrossFit class here, a dinner after work there."

"This isn't about us, goddammit!"

Roger leaned across the desk, his crooked nose, all the more sinister from above, like a deadly, hooked beak. "Then why are you here, Morrison? Why aren't you out there trying to find who did this?"

Hatred burned in Morrison's chest, a thick, scalding rage. And *fear*.

"They have Evie. Please, Roger. I need time to find them. I need your help to buy that time."

"Fuck you, Morrison."

"Roger—"

"Get the hell out of my office."

The Lady Justice figurine was the last thing Morrison saw before he backed from the office and took the stairs two at a time. He'd find another way to expose Roger. He'd find out what Roger had done, and why the kidnapper wanted Roger dead. He'd get his family back before the killer took them away from him—from this world. *No.* He'd get them back, or he'd die trying. And if Roger got them hurt, he was a fucking dead man.

Morrison's phone buzzed, and he ripped it from his back pocket in time to see Shannon's name. She was back. She was fine. Just texting to tell him that it had all been a bad practical joke, that her phone had been stolen and—

"You know what your asshole partner's doing right now?"

He didn't. But he had a feeling his family was going to be punished for it.

24

As the nighttime hours went on, a fuzzy warmth overtook him, and at some point before dawn, Morrison almost felt a cooling breath against the back of his neck as his nerve endings quieted to a painless hush. He wasn't there. None of them were. A dream, only a dream. He sat at his desk and stared at his fingers. They were someone else's, surely. But with the numbness, the logic seeped back in. And the logic was all he had.

Morrison had responded to the kidnapper's text, insisting that he wasn't sure what Petrosky was doing, but there had been no reply. When he'd triangulated the location, the system claimed the texts coming from Shannon's number were originating somewhere in Nevada—no way could they have traveled that distance in half a day. Whoever had his wife was scrambling the cell signals, maybe had even uploaded a virus into one of the cell companies' databases to assign the numbers to random towers. Maybe. Or maybe he was wrong. Decantor was already researching IT guys and spyware places since their phone scrambler and possible voice-over artist clearly had a penchant for electronics. It was possible—and easy—to get your phone to show one number on a caller ID regardless of where you actually called from. There was no guarantee that the phone was even Shannon's to begin with. That was the cold logic severed from the frenzied heat of terror, and it sustained him for a moment.

But the terror knew the phone was Shannon's. The panic knew they'd taken his baby, his wife. The frenzied energy in the air knew he was helpless to save them.

His muscles twitched involuntarily, first a leg, then an arm, electricity with nowhere to go. He stood and paced the bullpen, empty this time of night—back and forth, back and forth. He knew what would make the cool stay.

He knew what would make him remember.

You see me, but you don't. But you'll figure it out—you'll remember me. And once you do, you'll know exactly how to find me.

He should have known who she was. But where—how? McCallum's words echoed through his head: "Maybe it's for the best that you can't remember everything. Not all memories are useful." But this woman, the memory of her, that was the key to finding Shannon and Evie; he could feel it, and yet he could think of no specific person with a vendetta against him outside of an angry perp or the family member of someone he'd arrested. He didn't have a history of sordid love affairs, hadn't even dated for years before he met Shannon—too much trouble. Too many triggers. Anything questionable he'd left behind him in California. And the caller had a vendetta against Roger, so was it someone local: someone he'd arrested and Roger had put away? But that'd be hundreds of cases. He had no time.

You'll do what you're told, or I'll take it out on her. I'll save your baby girl for when you get here if she doesn't starve to death first.

Daddy's coming, Evie. He needed to figure out how to get to Roger. Fast.

Morrison ran a hand through his hair, ignoring the blond that stuck to his fingers, ignoring an old track mark that throbbed and stilled and pulsed again. *Heroin will make it worse.*

Heroin is bliss—euphoria. The purest love I've ever known.

But that wasn't true, not anymore. Shannon's love was real. And when he looked at Evie…was there anything more pure than the adoration in her eyes? And now they were starving her. *Starving.*

He sat, letting someone else's fingers type for him on the keyboard. Letting his mind wander to the case, to the logic, to the things that would help. Hacking, working around the number blocks, the scrambled signals…a plan. He needed a plan. He kept typing, code after code after code, but he didn't know what the kidnapper had used, where they were scrambling the signals from. He had no idea where to look.

Solve the case. Catch the killer. Find his wife.

You'll remember me. And once you do, you'll know exactly how to find me.

The case files on his desk whispered to him, and he ripped the top one from the stack and devoured the words as if he could tear out the throat of the kidnapper by attacking the page. Decantor's file on the Bell case—there wasn't much to it. Decantor had interviewed a dozen people at her apartment building, none of whom had seen anything suspicious. He tried to ignore the fire building inside him as he squinted at the notes in the margins: *Stabbed in lower abdomen/genitals with rounded object, spike-like, same as Acosta case, ME says copper.* Unusual for a weapon. Then came the reports from people who knew Bell personally. But this wasn't a date rape or an acquaintance killing. If someone had killed her purposefully to get at Roger—and he had to assume so based on the phone call—they had taken Shannon with the same goal in mind: get Roger put away by forcing Morrison's hand. But why did Bell have to die? Why her specifically? Just because she'd interviewed for the nanny position? What was he missing?

Petrosky would be back soon. He'd have something from Shannon's car—a fingerprint from their perp, maybe. But Morrison couldn't sit there and do nothing until Petrosky got back. Already it felt like his brain was sizzling, every rational thought boiling and escaping like steam before it could fully form. He flipped open the Acosta file and scanned the crime scene notes, the teacher interviews, the bike information. He paused on the sheets about the tattoo parlor, the demon horse staring at him, bloodthirsty and horrid. *The psychopathic circus.* He'd research the band.

Morrison pulled the keyboard closer and started with the tattoo. Websites full of Clown Alley Freaks song lyrics, fringe groups claiming to be fan clubs, and chat rooms catering to people steeped in all manner of depravity. On one message board, he found a convoluted discussion of what the "artists" really meant when they sang about disemboweling a circus elephant. "It's clearly a renouncement of the establishment, specifically of the republican right that makes things so difficult for the working class," proclaimed one man identified as Goober15. But eating raw, bloody elephant tripe seemed far less poetic and far more aggressive than any of these individuals could see. He compared IP addresses, hoping to find a clown-loving pedophile living near Acosta's school, but none of the commenters showed up on the sex offender database in any state, and even fewer had addresses within six hundred miles. Not that this meant much—sex offenders often ran to avoid having to register and tell the neighbors that they were sick fucks, and Morrison knew from the DNA that their guy wasn't in the system. But that didn't mean some other pedophile wouldn't know him, especially if they'd met over a mutual love of clowns and carnage.

Facebook pages and Instagram stalking gave him some photos of the commenters on the Clown Alley Freaks websites, and he pulled the ones with tattoos and printed the likenesses—most so damn normal looking. He pulled the fans with dyed hair too—blond at the root, black at the tip. He'd take them back to the tattoo parlor in case one of them had made a trip to visit their pedophile at Drake's shop, maybe to swoon over his clown ink. If they got lucky, one of these guys would be their killer.

Through the side window, a stormy dawn was creeping through the room. He abandoned the clowns and pulled up a chat room for pedophiles. Then another. Three. Looking for clown references, mentions of spiked boots, discussions about Acosta, or the *#1* symbol that had been carved into Acosta's and Bell's skin. But was this even what he wanted? If one of their suspects wasn't a pedophile at all, they wouldn't have met in a pedophile chat room. Maybe...fringe sexual interests? Fetishes?

A hand on his shoulder made Morrison jump. "Anything?" Petrosky's eyes were heavy with lost sleep and...anguish.

"No, Boss." The world shifted, tilted, and his bodily sensations crashed back to him with the force of being hit by a truck. His stomach, painfully clenched, forced bile into his mouth. His bladder spasmed—he had to pee. His neck was as wet as the storm-drenched window. But his thoughts were suddenly stilled, frozen, as though every ounce of logic had been consumed by terror. He sucked in a shuddering breath and held onto the side of the desk. "What did the scene look like?"

"Like a gas station." Petrosky ran a hand over his face, and Morrison could see the dew at his hairline, a subtle darkening. "Got there before the rain. Collected every fucking thing."

"What about her car?" It came out more like a wheeze than a question, and he pulled the chill air into his lungs and held it there, imagining the waves against the shore, the shush of the ocean in his ears, the taste of salt instead of vomit.

"A bunch of prints on the car itself, but they'll have to sort out which are hers, which are yours and which are from friends whose prints are supposed to be there. I've got the lab putting a rush on it now."

Morrison nodded, mute. Petrosky's eyes were drawn, his jowly face sagging as if he'd aged ten years since he went out there last night.

"What else?" Morrison said slowly, prolonging the moment when he'd have to hear whatever was making Petrosky's mouth so tight. But he could feel his composure slipping away with every terrified beat of his heart, every moment one step closer to insanity.

Petrosky met his eyes. "Blood."

His vision tunneled, and tingling began in his fingertips—crept up his arm. *Calm. Cool. Pacific.* A wave of electricity passed through him, and he didn't respond to it, just let it go like the tide going out to sea. His vision opened again, but the tingling remained. "How much?"

"Not much. Some spatter on the headrest. Probably hit her with something to subdue her."

Fuck.

"Not enough to really hurt her."

"Doesn't take much with a head injury." And she'd already had a concussion last year from Griffen, and there was always a chance for a brain bleed or—

"Shannon's tough as nails, kid. And there was nothing in the back—no blood, no signs of struggle around the car seat."

No, because they weren't bleeding Evie. Their pedophile strangled his victims with a T-shirt. And they were...starving her. Were they really? Or had they just told him that to fuck with him? He inhaled low and long imagining the ocean, blue as Evie's eyes, and the air stabbed at his lungs, his belly as if he were imbibing shards of glass.

Petrosky peered at the screen. "Show me what you found. Then we'll swing by to see Jenny at the tattoo shop and get another composite sketch out. Got nothing on the first."

Morrison ran Petrosky through the websites and the utter lack of useful information he'd discovered while Petrosky had been staring at his wife's blood.

"It's something," Petrosky said finally.

"It's nothing."

"Simmer, California."

"Is that all you did, Petrosky? Just look at the car?"

Petrosky cocked his head.

"They texted again." As the words came out, he immediately wished he could take them back. Maybe the killers had heard him. But Petrosky didn't seem bothered, didn't seem upset, and the heat crept into Morrison's cheeks.

"Let's take a look, and we'll—"

"How can you be so *fucking calm?*" Morrison hissed.

Petrosky punched the desk, and across the room, another cop stood—when had he even gotten there?— but the guy turned away again because it was Petrosky, and of course, he was pissed: Petrosky was always pissed about something. But not like this. The tension in Petrosky's jowls was more than agitation. *Fear.* And if Petrosky was scared, Morrison sure as hell better be.

"We need to...work the Acosta case," Petrosky said, almost panting.

Morrison cleared his throat, fighting to keep his voice steady—to keep his heart steady.

"There was a print in the grass just behind her car," Petrosky whispered. "Just one, but enough."

Prints? But they hadn't found fingerprints at the other crime scenes, so why—

Realization dawned, slow and painful in his chest as if his heart were only now awakening to the idea that Shannon had truly been taken by a killer. "Prints from the boots." *Like Acosta.* But they had killed Acosta. They'd killed Bell. And they were saving Evie for when he got there. The words rolled around in his head and settled like marbles in a dish.

Petrosky nodded.

Work your case. They wanted him looking. The kidnapper wanted him to remember something. And if he did, he'd find his family—the caller had said that, right? But she'd given him no other clues. Unless... the kidnapper wanted him to fail, so they'd have an excuse to hurt Shannon. An excuse to take Evie and stab her and watch her bleed.

Morrison swallowed hard, pushing down the warm ooze, trying to creep up his throat. *This is about Roger. All they want is Roger.*

Petrosky glanced at the screen. "This is your call, California. Your family. We can call in the chief. The Feds."

And Shannon's blood would be on his hands. Evie's. He pictured Dylan Acosta's body, the punctures still wet and seeping, and Shannon, begging for her life, for Evie's life. He didn't know what to do. Nothing felt right. His gut instincts were betraying him—he couldn't even trust himself.

"They'll kill her," he whispered. "We need to buy time."

"Drake's wife should be home now, so I'll have them meet us at his tattoo shop this morning," Petrosky said, his voice louder than it needed to be, though perhaps that wasn't for Morrison's benefit—the room was filling now, all officers with families at home. Safe.

Morrison nodded, still numb, wishing he was at home with Shannon, with Evie. He'd never leave them alone again. But he *had* left them alone. He'd not been there when they needed him most, and there was no fixing that. His only consolation would be to see the kidnappers' fucking faces. Look into their eyes. Breathe their foulness, their insanity, right before he ripped them apart.

25

MAYBE THE TATTOO parlor was the same, but it could have been the first time he'd ever seen it. The white door that had seemed so clean yesterday was now blank and dead, the pale face of a corpse when the blood pooled on the underside of the body. The bright and cheery pictures of potential tattoos now seemed sullen and morose, offended at his gaze. Even the yin-yang, white and black surrounded in vibrant blues and greens, burst forth with such rage that Morrison half expected it to leap from the wall, teeth bared.

Drake paced behind the counter, his hands clasped behind his back. From the couch inside the door, a woman with green hair and arms sleeved in wildflower tattoos appraised them. When Petrosky flashed his badge, she stood and extended her hand.

"I'm Jenny."

"Detective Petrosky." She looked at Morrison, but he couldn't find his tongue—he was watching a freckle-faced little girl coming through the back curtain to stand next to Drake, rubbing her eyes. Bib overalls. Blond hair, maybe what Jenny's hair would look like without the dye.

"I've got some things for you to look at," Jenny said and moved with the light steps of a dancer to stand beside her husband and the girl. "Go finish your homework, baby," she said and patted the girl's shoulder, so kind. The girl scampered off.

Morrison watched her go, heart wrenching, and when he pictured Evie as she might look at that age, the wound in his heart expanded like a black hole, widening as if each and every breath he took enhanced its emptiness.

Jenny reached beneath the front counter and produced a folder, manila like jaundiced skin, containing a photograph-quality sketch: a man with scraggly brown hair and a thin mouth. Squirrelly. Despite the light hue of his beady eyes, the man's gaze was blank—dead, vile. Zachary Reynolds's attacker. Their pedophile. But Drake was right—it was far better quality than the composite.

Petrosky pulled the sheet closer to him, and Morrison laid his folder on the counter, showing her the photos of the Clown Alley Freaks fans. Drake and Jenny both leaned close to examine them, eyebrows furrowed. Petrosky did too, glancing back and forth from the mug shots to the picture Jenny had drawn. Heads shook. They flipped through the entire stack.

"Nothing?" Morrison asked.

"Sorry, I don't see anyone familiar," Jenny said. Drake nodded agreement, shrugging his shoulders like it was no big fucking deal that Morrison was no closer to finding his starving baby girl while Drake's own daughter was happy and safe in the back room.

Morrison tossed the sheets back into the folder, stepped back, and dumped the whole mess into the trash can with enough force that the wire basket shook, stuttering and rocking, before settling with a clang. He clenched his fist, trying not to kick the thing over.

"Sorry, man," Drake said, and Morrison could hear the tension in his voice. Petrosky stood like a bulldog, ready to block the path to the counter if Morrison should prove to be unstable.

He *was* unstable.

"Do you recall anything about his voice?" Petrosky asked the couple over his shoulder. "Anything strange? Higher than normal?"

Petrosky was asking whether their suspect sounded like a little bitch.

"Nope, just…normal." *Normal.* Their perp fit in, walking among them, raping children, kidnapping families, starving babies. And passersby never saw the evil in his stare.

"What about badges, name tags, anything he said about interests, or how he spent his time?"

She pursed her lips, then shook her head. "No, nothing about himself. Sometimes he told stories about his…daughter."

Daughter? This guy had a *daughter*? If he did, she was in trouble.

"What'd he say about her, ma'am?" Petrosky said quickly, his shoulders high and rigid.

"Oh, well, I think it was his stepdaughter, actually. And it was nothing strange—just that she was really smart, that he was planning on having her take up the flute. Asked if I ever took music lessons—you know, normal things parents say. I remember thinking it was nice that he was taking such an interest in her." She winced.

"He give a name? An age?"

She shook her head again. "He played everything close to the vest. I guess now I know why, but I wish…"

A daughter. Morrison took out his phone and held it over Jenny's sketch on the counter. They needed to get the photo out on the streets, on the news, find this fuck. But Petrosky's hand on his wrist stopped him just shy of snapping the picture. Petrosky shook his head and pointed to the phone.

Right. Someone might have his phone tapped, and they didn't want the kidnappers to know that they had this asshole's picture until absolutely necessary—or to know they'd connected the Zachary Reynolds case. Morrison would have just fucked them all, maybe killed the people he loved. But...they'd asked him to keep investigating, right? *Do your job.*

And that was why Petrosky hadn't called him from Toledo; he must have thought Morrison's phone was tapped too. But if Morrison shut it down, maybe tried to track the bug inside it...they probably had a safeguard. They'd know. He was good at cracking codes, but not perfect, and the stakes were too high.

"They want an excuse," Petrosky whispered. An excuse—to hurt Shannon and Evie.

"Do you have a fax machine?" Petrosky said to Drake, but he dug his fingers into Morrison's wrist until Morrison registered the pressure, took his hand back, and dropped the phone into his pocket.

"Of course." Jenny gestured to the picture. "Does this help?"

Petrosky nodded. "Yes, ma'am. Better than our sketch artist did."

She smiled. "Well, if you're ever in the market for some ink..."

Petrosky's left eye twitched. Ashes and ink—*in memoriam.* Morrison grabbed the counter and held on as the room wavered, and his breath hitched and stopped.

"If I'm ever in the market, I'll be back here," Petrosky said, and Morrison straightened at the sudden gruffness in Petrosky's voice. "Now...the fax?"

The machine was modern and had more features than the one at the precinct. They faxed the photos to Decantor and used the email feature on the fax machine itself to send it to the contacts they had made when they'd scoured the neighborhood—those who had owned a place in the strip mall back when their suspect was getting his ink. But follow-up calls from Drake's landline yielded a series of "Sorry" and "Nope, never seen him" and "Wish I could help." Only one man was unaccounted for, Mr. Xu, the guy who had owned the nail shop across the road. And he'd already admitted seeing the guy—he'd just never gotten close enough to be more helpful.

Petrosky drove back to the precinct while Morrison held onto the door handle like it was a life preserver in a stormy sea. They'd find their killer. They would. And he'd get Evie back. He'd get them both back.

He took rapid breaths through his nose and stared at the ash trees, at the few leafy branches clawing the clouds—half barren even in the height of spring. Ash Park. Where everything went to die.

Everything. *Everyone.*

Petrosky pulled up at the precinct and opened his door. "You coming,

California?" Voice tight. Strained. Morrison nodded. Petrosky appraised him for a moment, then slammed the door and headed across the lot, his back receding, then going fuzzy as he left Morrison's line of focus.

Disappearing. Where did one find a person who didn't want to be found? If there'd been victims before Zachary Reynolds...maybe he'd done it to his own daughter. But his DNA wasn't in the system; if he'd abused his daughter, it hadn't been reported. Had they missed something at the school? Bell's apartment building? Zachary Reynolds's neighborhood? But they'd already taken the composite of Reynolds's attacker to those places—nothing. Jenny's drawing was better but not so much better that it'd get them a different answer from the same people, and they'd proven as much asking the neighbors around the tattoo shop. It'd be a waste of time—and Shannon and Evie didn't have time to spare. So what else did he know? Decantor had already ruled out connections between Bell and the other victims, outside of the person who'd killed them. No common acquaintances, no similar hangouts, no foreseeable opportunities for them to have met the same person—not that he'd expect a twenty-nine-year-old woman to chill at the park with a bunch of ten-year-olds. In fact, Decantor hadn't found any activities for Bell at all in the days before her death outside of her interview for the nanny position. Morrison's house had been her last known outing.

He'd been the last one to see her alive.

Morrison sat straighter in the seat. Had their killer seen Bell at his house and followed her home? Thus far, he'd assumed that someone was after Roger alone, that he and Shannon had become pawns in a game. But someone had to have known when Shannon left Ash Park. Someone had been watching his house. Watching Shannon. Was Bell dead because she'd been there? Were the other nanny candidates in danger? Then, suddenly, it clicked—the kid on the bike, the one he'd seen watching Bell the day she interviewed for the nanny position. Morrison had never seen the kid before in the neighborhood, and the teen could have matched the description of their thin, taller killer—the one in the boots. The guy had been wearing a hat that day, and he'd been too far away for Morrison to see clearly, but the bike... Someone had reported a bike at Dylan Acosta's school the day he died. They'd presumed an adult killer, but teenagers were very similar in stature. They could be looking for a kid—an impulsive, murderous, psychopathic kid. And if he'd been watching Shannon, watching Bell...he might have been watching the other candidates too. Maybe one of them had seen him.

Morrison got out and closed the gap between Petrosky's car and his own. Maybe Alyson Kennedy could help him nail this fucker to the wall.

If she was still alive.

26

ALYSON KENNEDY'S eyes widened when he introduced himself. "Mr. Morrison?" She clapped a hand over her mouth. "I wasn't supposed to start this week, was I? Oh my god, I thought—"

"No, no, you're fine. Next week."

"Well...um..." She peered behind him at the street where his car was parked half on half off the lawn at the curb.

"I'm not here about the job. There was an"—*our first choice nanny was brutally murdered, and I thought he'd killed you too*—"an incident. Near our home the day you interviewed. I thought I'd come by and ask you a few questions. Routine."

"Oh." Her eyes remained tight, but she stepped aside so he could enter the apartment. The hallway smelled like coconut. She didn't invite him inside farther. Did she think he was there for...what had the caller said? A little side action? *No...strange. A little strange on the side.*

He backed up a step and kept his voice brusque. "When you arrived for your interview, did you notice any other vehicles in the area? A bike?"

Her brows knit together. "Uh...no, I don't think so. Just your car in the driveway."

That had been Shannon's car in the driveway—he hadn't even been home yet, something Kennedy'd surely noticed. Either Kennedy was unobservant or lying. Probably the first. But...what had McCallum said? That female pedophiles are...*babysitters. Nannies.* Maybe she'd purposefully come before Morrison arrived—then he wouldn't have recognized her voice when she called pretending to be Bell. But there was something slightly nasal in her register that didn't fit. Not her, of course, it wasn't her. Had he really expected her voice to match? That he'd walk in here and find Shannon tied up in the living room? What was wrong with him?

He cleared his throat. "How about this guy?" He held out Jenny's rendition of the tattooed man and Reynolds's composite sketch.

Kennedy shook her head, nostrils flaring as if the photos themselves were distasteful. "Nope. He looks kinda...dirty, so I feel like I might have noticed that. You live in a nice neighborhood."

A nice neighborhood. Where bad things didn't happen—unless the bad weaseled its way in.

Morrison watched her face, the set of her shoulders: uncomfortable, but she seemed confident that she didn't know the suspect. He put the pictures back into the file and tucked it under his arm. He didn't like the way she was clenching her jaw. Nervous? Maybe she was ready to toss him out along with his troubling questions before the wrong word shattered her illusion of safety.

"What about anyone else outside?" he asked. "Someone walking a dog or looking out from a window?"

"A window?"

"A house window. A car. Anyone." The kidnapper could have planned everything from a distance, but maybe the man who'd taken Shannon looked like he belonged there. "A kid in a ball cap?"

She shook her head. "No. I was kinda nervous about the interview, so I wasn't really looking." She shrugged one slender shoulder, and Morrison narrowed his eyes. Pretty, lithe—Kennedy was Roger's type. And they might have met when she worked at the hospital morgue. Unlikely, but—she might know Roger enough to hate him.

"Where were you on Monday night?"

"Oh, uh..." Her face reddened and she crossed her arms. "I went dancing with friends. Stayed at my fiancé's after with another girlfriend who didn't want to drive home." A little defensive maybe, yet Kennedy didn't seem worried. Her alibi was easily verifiable. But had Kennedy mentioned that she was getting married?

"I'll need those names. From Monday night."

"No problem." She gave him the information while her index finger tapped a steady rhythm on her elbow. No hesitation. She wasn't a suspect. He was being an idiot. But the paralyzing waves of fear were washing his brain clean of all thought, rendering him ineffectual, useless against a kidnapper. Against a killer.

"Do you know Roger McFadden?" he blurted.

"I know who he is. But we've never met." It rang true. And he'd come here to get information and protect Kennedy, not accuse her... Were they watching her the way they'd watched Bell, the way they'd watched Shannon? Had he just signed Kennedy's death certificate by showing up here? *Did I kill my wife?*

Her face had hardened. Was there really anything else to ask? "Thank you for your time, Ms. Kennedy."

"Oh, sure. And um...I'll see you next week?" Her arms stayed crossed. He knew by her posture that she wasn't coming next week or the week after.

Not that it mattered. He might not have a child for her to watch.

The hour after he left Kennedy's passed by in a numb haze, the street signs approaching impossibly slow, road and cars in front of him wavering like a mirage, only blackness in his peripheral vision. Patricia Weeks wasn't home. Morrison didn't recognize what he was doing until he was pulling into his own driveway, the file with the drawings of their suspects held against his chest.

He strode to Mr. Hensen's porch on autopilot as if the nerves that tied the actions to his brain had been severed. He glanced back at his car, registering that he'd left the door open, but not able to manufacture a reaction. Even the cool breeze elicited no goose bumps. Morrison grabbed Hensen's door knocker and let it drop. The first time he'd met Hensen, the man had said, "Good work, son, you do good work," though he probably had no idea what Morrison's job entailed.

He'd find out today. At the very least, he'd have something else to gossip about.

The spider veins on Hensen's nose glared at him, purple and red streaks that screamed the truth: bodies eventually give out, and no one gets through it alive. When Hensen smiled, Morrison's agitation spiked as sharp as the fine points on the man's canines. "How are you today, son?"

"Fine, Mr. Hensen." If the dead could speak, they'd sound like Morrison: voices a mere shadow of what they once were, every utterance strange and flat and hollow. "Just wondering if you'd seen anything strange around lately. A car that didn't belong. Maybe a teenage boy on a bicycle Monday morning?"

Hensen cocked his head, and the lines spiderwebbing their way across his nose went from horizontal to vertical. "No, but my days aren't spent by the window. I been seeing that nice woman you set me up with from a block over. Ms.—"

"Mayfield."

"That's the one." He furrowed his brows. "There some kind of trouble?"

"No, no trouble. Just trying to find someone."

"Someone who was at your house?"

"No, just..." *This is a mistake.* "How about him?" He opened the folder and showed Hensen the photos.

Hensen shook his head. "No, can't say I've seen him. I don't like his look, though."

Me neither. "Okay, well, thanks for your time."

"Son?"

Morrison turned back on the top stair.

"Thank your wife for the soup the other day. She sure makes a mean chicken noodle."

He swallowed hard. "I will."

Eight more houses on that side yielded nothing better. He was considering heading for the precinct when he saw Kathryn Welks on the stoop across the street, blowing bubbles for her two-year-old son, Shane. Shane's dark hair blew in the breeze as he giggled and leaped, the bubbles floating above his head and out of reach. Morrison dragged his eyes to his own vacant lawn, straining his ears as if he might catch Evie's laugh on the breeze.

Kathryn was waving when he turned back to them, using her hand as a visor to block out the afternoon sun. "Hey! How's Shannon's trip going?"

He'd nearly forgotten Shannon was supposed to be gone. "Oh... good." Something sharp stabbed at Morrison's gut, and he inhaled, inflating lungs that couldn't seem to recall how to breathe. "Listen, question for you."

She smiled. "Shoot."

"You seen anyone strange around our place lately?"

Her almond eyes widened, and she glanced up and down the street. "Strange? Like how?"

"Anyone you didn't recognize? Maybe a teenager on a bike?"

"I see people all the time while I'm out front with Shane. No one that looked suspicious or anything." She shrugged. "Why, has there been another one of those car break-in things going on like last summer?"

"Nothing like that." He opened the folder for her and held the pictures in front of his chest.

She bent closer, squinted, and when she straightened, her easy smile had fallen. "Haven't seen him, but I know the cases you work. You'd tell me if I should be worried, right?"

"I'd tell you."

"Are you sure? Another neighbor was over here last week asking if it was a safe place to live. I feel like I'm missing something."

"Neighbor?"

"I don't think she's bought the house yet. Just looking at the area. She asked..." Her mouth stopped moving as if she'd realized something critical. "She asked if there were any cops in the neighborhood, like patrols. And I...I said one lived right across the street, so we didn't need patrols." She looked back at the photos but shook her head.

"What, Kathryn? What else did she say?"

"She asked what the going rate was per square foot. If it was a good neighborhood for children. If there were bus stops."

That sounded like a homebuyer—not abnormal. But it wasn't like their suspects would walk through the streets, sneering, waving around someone's severed dick.

"She did mention liking your place," Kathryn said slowly. "Asked whether I thought you'd sell it."

That was strange. They'd had no sign in the yard, despite their conversations about moving. Yet someone had been asking about their house. Watching.

"I said I didn't think you were putting it on the market, but that I knew a realtor if they needed one." Her eyes were saucers. "They didn't want the name. Said they had one."

They. "What'd they look like?"

"She was our age, pale, thin. Reddish hair, kind of big eyes. Really pretty. Her husband was in the car, too, but I couldn't see him as well."

"You're sure this isn't him?"

"Positive. He was bald, not like that guy. But he had on sunglasses, kept his eyes out the other window, so I didn't really get a look at him."

So he wasn't the pedophile who had raped Acosta and Reynolds. But they still had the booted man who had killed Acosta and Bell, and the woman who had called Morrison from Bell's cell phone. Three killers. He'd considered the possibility before, but confirmation that there were three people wandering around stomping kids to death and stealing others for sport—it was unheard of. Ridiculous. What was this, some kind of fucking cult?

His heart quickened. "Tell me more about him. Tall? Short?"

"Just average. He was thin, though." She frowned. "I do remember being worried because of his neck. Looked like he had chicken pox or something, and I didn't want Shane exposed, but it was probably just acne."

Thin. Acne. That did sound like a teenager. Maybe the same one he'd seen on a bike the morning of the nanny interviews.

"What day was that, Kathryn?"

"Last Thursday, maybe?"

Thursday. Before he'd even gone back to work, they'd been watching.

"I mentioned it to Shannon, but she didn't seem to think much of it. Just laughed about selling, what with the market like it is right now."

Of course she hadn't thought much about it. Asking about housing prices wasn't threatening—but it did give you an awful lot of information if you asked the right questions. Acting normal made you invisible. Unless...they really were just a couple looking for a house.

"Any way you might come to the station, give me a sketch?"

Her mouth dropped. "What's all this—"

"Missing persons case. Nothing to do with us, just thought she might have been seen in the area. I'll explain later. Promise."

She looked at her son, who was spinning in circles in the yard, and back to Morrison. "Okay, I'll head out in ten."

He glanced up and down the empty road. "I'll follow you."

Kathryn bit her lip, grabbed Shane off the lawn, and disappeared into the house, leaving Morrison staring down the street, waiting for a man with a bald head and covered eyes to appear with Shannon's corpse.

27

AT THE PRECINCT, Morrison led Kathryn into the conference room and used the main line to call Crystal Irving, local artist and their resident sketcher. He took Kathryn a drink of water, barely registering the worry lines on her forehead, her frown, and the way Shane was already rubbing his eyes. *Does Evie need a nap too?* But the thought belonged to another man entirely, a stranger concerned with sleep schedules and diaper changes instead of starvation and death. He closed the door on his way out with a shaking hand.

Petrosky ambushed Morrison just outside the room, his breath fast, eyes blazing. "Where the fuck have you been all afternoon? I thought you went rogue or some shit. Not that I'd have blamed you, but..." He swiped a hand across his beet-red face.

Rogue. If only Morrison knew where to find these bastards, maybe he would have hunted them down himself. Morrison filled Petrosky in on interviewing Alyson Kennedy and the neighbors, realizing just how little he had to go on besides Kathryn's memory. If only he'd been there to see the suspects in that car. "Most of the neighbors weren't home," he finished.

"I'll go back later." Petrosky's face had returned to its normal color. His fists unclenched. "Better if it's someone else, so they don't assume it has to do with you."

It's too late for that. He'd already spooked Kathryn. Had he put his family in danger?

"Heard back from forensics about the copper," Petrosky was saying. "Too common to trace the weapon to a source."

Were they using that weapon on his wife? His daughter?

"Still no hits on our photos either," Petrosky continued, and Morrison imagined the suspects' car in his neighborhood, a killer taking photos of his house, of his family. Were they still watching his place? No...they had what they wanted. They had his whole world.

Petrosky coughed once, pointedly, and Morrison focused on his partner's troubled gaze. "The entire city's out looking, Cali. Including Decantor and your buddy Valentine."

Decantor. Valentine. *Fuck.* "Decantor say anything about Shannon? I mean, he already knows that her car's been found and—"

"I told him we had it under control, nothing to worry about. That Alex went to get her, and it was all a big misunderstanding. Unless he actually calls Toledo and talks to the techs over there, Decantor won't know any different until they show up here to investigate. And I made sure the Toledo PD has my name as their go-to."

"And Valentine?" Valentine and Lillian would be all over Morrison and Petrosky if they thought something was wrong.

"Told Valentine the same. He might call out of concern, but he'd talk to you about it before he acts. And I gave him The Face."

Morrison nodded. The Face was usually reserved for perps, but it was just as effective for getting other cops to walk away. He'd call Valentine later if the man didn't come to him first.

"Detective?" Crystal. Curly black hair, eyes like midnight, sketchpad in hand.

"Thanks for coming," Morrison said.

She smiled—"Anytime"—and brushed past him into the room with Kathryn and closed the door.

Petrosky gestured in the direction of the bullpen. "You know the FR software best. Get that going on all three sketches, see what you come up with."

FR. The facial recognition software, the one thing the chief had made sure they had a budget for. He'd start with Zachary Reynolds's rapist—but he really needed to ID the people Kathryn had seen in front of his house. *Please let us get a hit.* "Might just be people trying to find a house to buy," Morrison said.

"You don't believe that."

"No, I don't."

"Call if you get something." Petrosky headed for the stairs.

Morrison hovered outside the room, willing Crystal to hurry, rubbing a throbbing nodule in the crook of his arm. *Find the killer. Find the woman. Find my family.*

WITH THEIR FACIAL RECOGNITION SOFTWARE, each photo came back with a list of the top fifty potential matches. Not the best program, but it was what the powers that be said they could afford. Usually, half of the matches were dubious at best or just felt wrong. The closest to Jenny's picture was a man who'd been killed in a car wreck two years back, so he hadn't attacked Acosta—and even with that one, the nose was a touch too pointy. Either the guy they were looking for hadn't ever been in trouble, or he'd been in trouble somewhere that the database wasn't active.

Morrison tossed aside the sketch and headed for the conference room in time to see Crystal emerge, shoving a pencil into her handbag.

"Thanks again for coming." His words sounded insincere even to him, though he thought he meant them.

"Sure thing." She handed him two pages and took off down the hallway as Morrison peeked into the room to see Kathryn, still at the conference table, Shane asleep on her shoulder. Comfortable. Safe.

He backed away from the door before the clenching in his gut became an ache and glanced at the first picture—the man. Nose too thin for his round face, skinny shoulders, fragile-looking jaw. Sunglasses that covered half his cheeks. And the rash on his neck: not chicken pox... acne. Were they really looking for a kid, or did he only look like one from afar? If he was the kid Morrison had seen on the bike Monday morning, then the guy would have had to kill Acosta and hightail it all the way over to Morrison's place immediately. Was he watching to see if Morrison caught the homicide call? Or just watching? Did that mean Natalie Bell was in the wrong place at the wrong time—an impulse decision when the killer saw her get out of her car?

He flipped the page and frowned at the black-and-white image of the woman Kathryn had seen: wide, light eyes, freckles over the bridge of her nose, and a tiny crescent scar on her chin, though that might have been a shadow or a dimple.

Something about the photo niggled at the back of his brain. He tried to picture this woman with the reddish hair Kathryn mentioned. He imagined her with glasses, with darker eyes. Imagined her without the scar. None of these mental pictures seemed quite right, but still, an insistent awareness was creeping up the back of his neck like ghostly fingers trying to break through to the living's plane of existence.

I know her.

Kathryn exited the conference room with Shane on her hip, his head lolling on her shoulder, and he felt a pang of jealousy. Her eyes were tight, mouth drawn. "Listen, I thought of one other thing. The woman... she said something about our neighborhood being close to her job, said that was the reason she wanted to move there. If she has a job around there, it'll be easier to find her, right?"

If she worked nearby, there was a good chance someone knew her. Maybe that was why she looked so damn familiar. But if she was scoping out his house with intent to harm, she wouldn't have told Kathryn the truth. *Hey, just stopping in to stalk a woman so that I can kidnap her and her child someday. And, by the way, let me tell you about my job.*

"Yeah, that helps. Thanks so much for coming down."

She nodded, said nothing. Morrison left her standing in front of the door to the interrogation room, cradling Shane to her chest.

Back at his desk, he loaded Crystal's rendition of man number two into the system. Their pedophile's slightly taller buddy yielded another fifty photos. He pulled the top ten, then ruled out half due to stature because of the footprint indentations left at the crime scene—their killer was only five-nine at best, and thin. Probably why he went after Bell and not Patricia Weeks: that stocky old broad would have kicked his ass.

Morrison ruled out another set of suspects due to incarceration and one due to death. But the remaining two—either could have been their guy. He pulled up birth certificates, driving records, last known addresses. One, Walter Gomez, had been given a ticket three days ago, the day of Natalie Bell's murder, in Arizona.

And then there was one.

Richard Carleson stared back at him with beady eyes and a grin too easy for someone having their mug shot taken. His face wasn't a perfect match—he looked too old, for one thing—but he'd been arrested twice for fraud, once for identity theft, and once for assault and battery during a bar fight. Last known address was in Florida, nearly ten years ago, so he could easily have moved here and committed the attacks while flying under the radar. Didn't need much else if you had cash—just don't get arrested for anything. With his identity theft history, it wasn't unreasonable to think he was living here under an assumed name.

Which meant he'd be hard to find unless someone recognized his photo.

Morrison watched Carleson's information print achingly slowly and stared again at the woman's image. Even if she'd told Kathryn the truth, she could work pretty much anywhere. He'd get her loaded into the computer, check for any hits, and then start showing her picture to local businesses, maybe near his house again. But how long would that take? *I'm grasping at straws.*

He needed help. He needed more cops to canvass. But even Decantor and Valentine would want to call in the Feds. He couldn't get assistance without admitting what was going on and putting his family in more danger—by the time they had anything to go on, Shannon and Evie could be dead. He ripped the sheets from the printer, headed back to his desk, and loaded the woman's photo into the facial recognition database.

Nothing fit well; the pictures weren't quite right. If she'd been arrested, she'd have been in the database, so she couldn't be a perp Roger had put away. How did she know him? He squinted at the photo. Different hair? Skin tone? He looked back at the screen. She seemed familiar in a way that neither of the men had. Then he changed the brightness on the screen, and something snagged inside him, jolted his memory. He bolted upright in his seat.

No. *No way.*

Karen? The nose was different—too wide here—and he didn't recall her having freckles, but maybe she wore makeup. Did she have a scar on her chin? He'd seen her numerous times over the last year, outside the courthouse, at the restaurants near the precinct, and once in a dark bar, back when she was still dating Griffen.

He traced the line of her jaw on the screen. Probably her. But...*why?*

Griffen had been sick, obsessed with Shannon to the point of hurting her and those around her, but he'd had a brain tumor. Delusions. He'd heard voices, and his actions were a desperate cry for help. What were the odds that his girlfriend was just as crazy? And Griffen had never hurt a child. If Karen had taken Shannon and Evie... Maybe she was more ruthless than Griffen had ever been.

"What've you got?" Petrosky's voice didn't jar him as it had earlier, and Morrison tapped the screen. *Unreal...*

"Griffen's girlfriend, maybe? It isn't the best rendition, but—"

"Now, wouldn't that be something?" Petrosky's jaw worked overtime in his fleshy face. "Can't imagine that she just happened to pick up where Griffen left off."

"Maybe she snapped."

"Or maybe she was the voice in Griffen's journals."

Morrison tried to conjure images from the notebooks Griffen had left behind. Griffen had mentioned hearing voices. Doing things...for *her.* Said that *her voice* was stronger than all the others. They'd assumed it was nothing but hallucinations, all of it, but what if some of it had been real? What if *her voice* had actually been— "You think Karen manipulated him? To go after Shannon?"

"I can't imagine why that would be true. Just throwing out ideas, California."

But there'd been no trace of her at Acosta's rape-homicide, nor at Bell's house. The men were the ones who'd killed, who'd raped. Not Karen. Had she become involved with one of them inadvertently? Morrison flipped to Carleson's picture. Or maybe she'd sought them out on purpose, knowing they were as sick as she needed them to be. Knowing that she could mold them. Maybe she'd wanted someone harder, more psychopathic than Griffen, since he wasn't able to pull off what she wanted—since he hadn't been able to kill Shannon. But why?

Feeding people ideas. Something she'd know how to do from years of working in the rehab center. But what did she want now? To hurt Roger, but—

"I'll grab Griffen's file. Wish I could remember Karen's last name." Petrosky already had his phone to his ear. He headed for the stairs, and Morrison threw the papers together and followed him through the bullpen. "Good afternoon, I'm looking for Karen," Petrosky said. "I believe she's one of your therapists?" He paused. "Oh, really? That's too bad. Thank you." He turned to Morrison. "She doesn't work there anymore."

But Morrison had seen her at the courthouse. He saw her all the time. Maybe she was only there because he was. His heart shuddered to life.

Once you remember me, you'll know exactly how to find me.

Petrosky shoved the phone into his pocket. "Looks like we'll be grabbing that file—see what we have on Karen. Then we'll pay a little visit to the rehab center's HR."

THE RECEPTIONIST at the rehab center had a sore on her lip, a dour expression, and skin nearly as sallow as the Formica countertops. She grimaced when Petrosky flashed his badge, but called her boss and gestured to a waiting room outfitted with vinyl chairs and green linoleum. They stood against the wall beside a framed print of a pasture.

"Some shrink probably said, 'You know what would calm these addicts down? Pictures of fucking meadows,'" Petrosky muttered as the head of HR emerged from the back. Black suit. White blouse. Straight, fifties-style bangs.

Marie Silva's office was decked out with the same green floor, though some effort had been made to pretty the place up with an Aztec wall covering. "So, what can I help you with?"

"Looking for a Karen Palmer."

"Oh. Well..." Her gaze darted around the room. "What's this regarding?"

"We just have some questions for her in an ongoing investigation," Petrosky said. "No bearing on the facility, mind you, but without your assistance, we might be forced to look more deeply into your organization to rule out culpability."

Her lips formed a tight line as she appraised them. "Her reasons for dismissal are not protected by law. But I must say that—"

"Sorry, ma'am, but time is of the essence. We're on the same side here." But Petrosky's tone was more confrontational than friendly.

She crossed her arms. "She was let go for a violation of ethics."

"The Griffen case."

"She was dating a patient during the course of treatment." Her words were clipped. "Clearly a violation of ethical boundaries and contradictory to the agreements she signed at the outset of her employment."

Petrosky nodded noncommittally and opened the file. "Can you take a look at these photos? Tell us if any of these individuals have been in treatment here?"

Silva shook her head and pursed her lips. "Now that I cannot do.

Patients are protected heavily by HIPAA laws. I'd lose my job and my license."

Petrosky pulled the male suspects' pictures out anyway and set them on the desk side by side, but she pushed them back toward him without so much as a glance.

"You can help us, or we can come back with a court order."

They didn't have time for a court order.

She leveled a hard stare at Petrosky. "Do that."

Fuck.

"Can you tell us whether they've ever worked here?"

"Half the people who work here have been in treatment. Peer support is great for addiction centers, and our programs push rehabilitation and job seeking as a part of continuing sobriety." Her back straightened, proud. "We practice what we preach, which means we pay now-sober ex-patients to provide mentoring and to help with groups. That makes what you're asking a gray area for us, and ethically I cannot—"

"What about the basics? Recent terminations? Anyone else that Karen took a special interest in?"

Her eyes narrowed. "No. If I'd seen her taking an *interest* in anyone else, I would have put a stop to it immediately."

Petrosky leaned in and spoke quietly. "Ma'am, we all have the same goal here."

She sighed. "Listen, I can give you dates of employment, titles, and salaries, but I'm not comfortable giving out every employee's confidential information without a warrant."

"A list of employees for the last year. I'll get those before we leave, and we can come back with follow-up questions."

She glared at Petrosky like she wanted to slap him.

"For now, let's stick to Karen Palmer," Petrosky said.

Her mouth stayed tight, but she leaned back in her chair as he slid the pictures back into the folder.

"How did Karen meet Frank Griffen?"

"I can't comment on Griffen."

"He's dead, ma'am."

"That doesn't mean he has fewer rights, Detective."

Petrosky's jaw was as hard as the stone crushing Morrison's chest. Petrosky was trying not to push her—trying to get what they needed without losing his shit. But the boss was getting angry. The next words from Petrosky's lips would probably get them thrown out, and they needed to ask about Karen anyway, not patients.

"What did Karen do here?" Morrison's voice sounded strange to him as if it had come from someone else. Silva seemed equally surprised to hear him speak, her head jerking his way as if she'd forgotten he was there in the presence of Petrosky's bluster.

"Mostly intake," she said.

"Was she a clinical therapist?"

"No. She was in her last year of school for her bachelor's in social work, some online program. Had me fill out forms saying she was here as part of an internship." *Probably for a school that didn't exist.* "All she did was the initial contact and the first set of paperwork: financials, legal issues, basics on what they came in for. Shortly after Mr. Griffen's…uh… death, an act unrelated to this institution, our investigation found that she had been dating him. Which was quite surprising to those of us who knew her and not only because of her position with the center."

"Why was that, ma'am?" Morrison asked.

She leaned over her clasped hands. "Because, last we knew, she was dating Roger McFadden."

28

Every bump in the road sang through Morrison's body like a voltaic jolt. Behind him, the sun sank into the blackening troposphere, and dusk crept over the road now washed in amber from the streetlights.

You'd better be home, you fucker.

He tried to calm the heat in his chest as he pulled up. Roger's lakefront property was more ostentatious than it should have been for a public servant's salary. Red brick columns flanked a deep front porch with floor-to-ceiling windows on either side of an oak door. Above, the second story balconies provided cover for the porch, reaching from one side of the home to the other. Trees lined the edges of his property, their trunks silent and gray as prison bars in the gloom. And so quiet. Even the water behind Roger's house had ceased to lap the shore, though it still shimmered red and orange like fire under the setting sun.

No one would know Morrison had been there.

Roger answered the bell still dressed in his suit, though he'd loosened his tie. It lay against his button-down like a failed hangman's knot. "Back again?" Smug as hell. "Ready to apolog—"

"Do you remember Karen Palmer?"

Roger's eye twitched almost imperceptibly, but enough that Morrison knew the answer before he said it. "Vaguely."

Bullshit. Morrison sucked a breath through his nose. "You dated her last year. At the same time Griffen was dating her."

His mouth tightened.

"Why didn't you tell anyone, Roger?"

Roger paused, then sighed and backed into the house. Morrison followed him into the living room across light oak hardwood floors. A deer's head glared at him from over the fireplace, though Shannon had once told him Roger didn't hunt.

Roger made himself a drink from a bar cart in the corner: scotch on the rocks. He didn't offer one to Morrison. "Dating Karen wasn't relevant," he said finally. "I date lots of people. And so did she. Obviously." But the last word was laced with malice.

"Not relevant?" Morrison snapped, but he inhaled sharply and leveled his voice. "She was feeding you information about me, telling you that I was taking advantage of those in rehab, lying to you about people under her care." And Roger had bought it all, not thinking for a moment that she might have been covering for Griffen or even egging him on.

"So what?" Roger jerked back hard enough that scotch splashed over the rim of his glass. "She was crazy, but she wasn't a killer. He was the whack job."

"If she was so crazy, why didn't you give a statement after you found out about Griffen? You could have mentioned she seemed unhinged."

Roger slugged back half the drink and pointed at Morrison. "What happened with Griffen wasn't my fault."

"Shannon was attacked while I was in jail. If you knew your girlfriend was messing around with an unstable guy who was close to Shannon during that time, you had an obligation—"

"I didn't know Karen was with…him." He spat the last word, eyes tight as he downed the rest of the drink and poured another. "Not until it was all over. And once he was dead…" He shrugged.

Based on the journal entries, Griffen had no idea about Roger—your girlfriend banging someone else was worth writing about. Had Karen manipulated them both? If she'd convinced Roger of Morrison's guilt when she and Griffen were the ones involved in the crimes, maybe she'd even been the one to plant the murder weapon at Morrison's home. And Shannon—

"Did she ask you to hurt my wife?" The last words escaped Morrison's lips with an intensity beyond his control. He tried to calm his shuddering insides, but it felt as if his entire being were trapped in an earthquake.

Roger balked at the accusation, or maybe at the reminder of what he'd lost. "Don't be ridiculous. I wouldn't have let that slide."

But just this week, Roger had refused to even listen when Morrison told him Shannon had been kidnapped. "How could you not know Karen was dating Griffen?"

"It wasn't like we were in an exclusive relationship. She was young. And…flexible." The smirk was back for only a fraction of a moment, and then it was gone. Roger's eyes went as fiery as the lake behind his house. "I had no reason to think she was seeing anyone else."

Maybe Roger really hadn't known. If he'd been aware, he would have cut it off. "Roger, I think she manipulated Griffen. Sent him after Shannon. Now she's after you. And she was in my neighborhood the other day, just before Shannon was…taken."

"If you're trying to fuck with me, you're doing a—"

"Call the Central District Station in Toledo and ask about Shannon's car."

"What?"

"Found abandoned. Blood on the headrest. No leads yet."

Roger still didn't look convinced, but the heat in his eyes had mellowed. "A prosecutor, kidnapped? That's big news."

"The people who know about the car think it was a misunderstanding." Morrison stood and took a step toward Roger and the bastard flinched. "Goddammit, Roger, I'm not making this up. There's no way in hell I'd be speaking to you if it wasn't necessary. And I swear to god I wish it was my life on the line. I'd gladly give it to get my family back."

"Karen was just a piece of ass." Roger's face did not change, but his voice almost sounded…remorseful. Maybe he'd figured out why this woman was pissed at him. Maybe she had a good reason.

"Did she know about the safe deposit box, Roger?"

"Everyone has a safe deposit box."

"Does she have reason to think you had something questionable inside?"

Roger's lips were nearly white from pressing them together so hard. "No."

The hairs on the back of Morrison's neck stood, but he had expected nothing less than a lie. "I have a list of questionable activity taken from your accounts, much of it in the form of irregular deposits." Morrison nearly whispered the accusation, but Roger reeled back as if it had been shouted at him.

"You didn't have a warrant for that."

"No, I didn't. It was acquired over the course of the Griffen investigation when we considered you a suspect. And now with the knowledge that your girlfriend was also Griffen's—"

"That's a fucking illegal search, and you know it. I should have you—"

Rage flamed through his chest, and his vision went red. "Have me *what*, you entitled fuck? You want to charge me with getting this information illegally? Just a rumor would spell the end of your career, and you know it. I'm not going to hold my fucking breath."

Roger sat heavily on the couch, the scotch slopping over the side of his glass and darkening the oak floor. His face hardened into a stony mask. Morrison was losing him.

"Griffen's journal entries," Morrison said in a calm, measured tone. "He wrote about a woman's voice, telling him to do things, and comforting him after he killed Johnson. We assumed that voice was a hallucination, maybe even Frieda Burke, the social worker he dated before Karen. But…what if it was *her*? What if Karen is pulling the strings now, but with a more dangerous crew?"

"That waif of a woman? You're out of your mind." But Roger's confidence seemed to have cracked. His voice was tenuous, his gaze exploring the ceiling as if he was considering something.

"Roger? What?"

"She asked about you. A few times. I thought it was because of her work, the rumors she said she heard about you during the Griffen case." Roger set his glass on the end table, and it clattered briefly like his hand was shaking. "She was nuts. Intense. But I didn't think she was lying."

"You found out afterward, didn't you?"

"I couldn't verify what she said, but that didn't mean she was wrong. And by then, Griffen was already dead, and the case was over."

Know your opponent. Know your killer. "What did she do that was so intense?"

"She was a good fuck, did everything I wanted her to do. Threw herself at me the night we met, all over me in the parking lot after we'd talked for like twenty minutes. Begged me to take her back to my place, all glassy-eyed like she'd lose her shit if I refused."

Maybe Shannon had done that too. Morrison averted his gaze before he puked all over Roger's lap. *Don't think about her in his bed. Focus.* Morrison's fist clenched, and he tried to relax his grip as he asked: "What'd you do?"

"What the fuck do you mean? I took her back to my place. Figured it'd be a one-time thing."

"But it wasn't," Morrison said, muscles taut, ready to throttle the asshole. "You did something to make her angry. She isn't after you for nothing."

Roger shifted in his seat. "The next day, she seemed to think we were together. I didn't call her for a few weeks, but she kept showing up places where I was, and eventually, I took her out. That first night at dinner, she waited until I ordered, then asked me to order her the same." He snorted, and it was a derisive sound. "When it came, she said she was allergic to shellfish and refused to get anything else. Weird shit. And the next week, I saw her in court, and she asked if I liked to ski, suggested we go onto the slopes. She had no idea what she was doing, almost broke her fucking leg. Two dates later, and she started accusing me of bullshit, and I broke it off. Wasn't like we had an actual relationship."

"What'd she accuse you of?"

"The usual. Looking at other women."

"That doesn't seem that strange." Morrison's voice was colder than he'd intended, but he couldn't seem to connect himself to it. And Roger probably *had* been looking at other women: his continuous infidelity was one of the reasons Shannon had left him.

Something flashed in Roger's eyes—angry, incredulous—and disappeared. "She tried to kill herself when I broke it off, screaming and threatening me on my voice mail, and then just hung up, like that's supposed to make me want to call her. How's that for crazy?"

Morrison glared at him. *How fucking stupid is he?* "Why wouldn't you say something about that before? We're talking about her being unstab—"

"I didn't think that much of it, I guess. Not the first woman ever to go stalker on me."

"What did you do when she threatened suicide?" But he already knew the answer—he'd have known if Roger had called the police.

Roger shrugged. "Told her to fuck off. Put a block on my phone."

Blocked. That must have pissed her off, especially if she'd planned to use him for more than just a fling. But...that didn't make sense. This wasn't just a fatal attraction. She hadn't kidnapped Shannon for being Roger's ex, or she would have done that long ago. She wanted to hurt Roger, but...he was a bonus. Instead of going after Roger when he'd hurt her, Karen had just kept dating Griffen. And continued to pursue Shannon.

And Shannon had been Griffen's ultimate target, and maybe Karen's too—she'd spent a lot of time filling Griffen's messed-up head with hatred if the notes in his journals were any indication. Shannon had been the one in danger then, and she was the one in danger now. Maybe Karen had given Morrison this futile mission because she wanted a reason to kill Shannon—to do what Griffen couldn't.

But why?

He was missing something. Something big.

"Where does Karen live, Roger?" They hadn't been able to find a recent address.

Roger glanced at the mantel—at the framed photo of himself and Shannon on their wedding day.

Morrison's heart seized, and his body seemed to come back to life, every nerve ending alight and singing with desperation. "Please, Roger. Don't let Karen kill Shannon."

When Roger turned back, his eyes were glassy, mouth hard. *He loves her.* For all his narcissistic bullshit, Roger really did love Shannon. He always would. If Karen, unstable as she was, had sensed Roger's devotion to his ex, she would have had ample reason to hurt Morrison's family.

Roger blinked rapidly and lurched to his feet so fast Morrison jumped. "I'll go with you," he growled. "I want to talk to that bitch myself."

The address Roger had for Karen was a handsome colonial on the outskirts of Berkley, a place not listed in her employee file. The couple who answered the door had bought the home six months before. They didn't know Karen and had no idea who the previous tenant might have been. He'd look into that.

But if Karen was hiding, she probably hadn't left a forwarding address.

Roger stared out the side window on the way back to his house. "You're not fucking with me? She's really gone?"

Morrison kept his eyes on the road in front of him, avoiding Roger's face.

"She is." But not forever. *Please, not forever.*

"Why don't you call in the FBI?"

Petrosky had found no bugs in the car, and the killers couldn't hear him with the phone off, even if they had it tapped. Still, he shoved his cell deeper into his back pocket and leaned his weight against it. "I don't want her to get hurt. And I think Karen...wants *me* to find them." On the phone, Karen had said they were waiting for him, saving Evie for when he got there. If the FBI came barging in, everyone was dead. If he went alone...hope burgeoned in his belly.

"Why would anyone want Shannon?" Roger said, slowly but pained as if he still couldn't accept the truth of it. "She doesn't have much of a past."

No, she didn't. A dead brother. Alcoholic parents, deceased. But nothing about this case was normal. Had Shannon prosecuted someone close to Karen? Convicted one of Karen's family members, maybe another lover? Morrison shook his head. That theory was what Petrosky called "Maury Povich shit," but it might make sense here. Karen was calculating. Ruthless. She'd killed Abby's kitten last year for fuck's sake—or rather encouraged Griffen to do it. She had wanted to make Shannon suffer. This was personal.

Roger cleared his throat. "But you do."

What was Roger talking about? "I do what?"

"You have a past. I investigated you, too, remember?"

Morrison clenched his jaw and drew his eyes back to the road. "Not a past that most would be interested in."

"Come off it, asshole. You and your fucking partner do all kinds of shady shit. Petrosky's known for being a loose cannon—picking up hookers, paying their bills."

"How do you—"

"I get around too." Roger raised an eyebrow. "Maybe some of their pimps don't fucking like that. And anyone watching him would know he's close to your family. He's probably into other things too, that drug-addicted—"

"No." Rage bubbled in Morrison's belly. "Petrosky isn't on drugs."

Roger snorted. "No one tried to take her when she was married to me, *Curt*. No one but you. And you didn't get over your past. No one gets over their past. We all are a certain way. Just because you go around convincing everybody that you're better doesn't mean you are."

"I've never—"

"No, but you think it, don't you? Every time I saw you with Shannon, it was all, 'Hey, Roger, how's it going, Roger?' Showing me, you didn't care how pissed I was about you hanging around her. Showing me, you thought you were better. Challenging me all the time. And you know what? Congratulations. You provoked me until I got angry. And I scared her off and gave her to you with a fucking bow on her ass." Roger grunted as if that had all been part of his master plan. "And the second you saw the opportunity, you took it. You took her."

"That wasn't about you, Roger. Shannon and I were friends."

"Of course you'd say that now. But you saw her, and you wanted her, and you couldn't go about it the reasonable way, the honorable way. Like I did. I didn't have to steal her to get her to marry me."

Morrison's wife, his baby, had been *kidnapped,* and Roger was trying to make this about himself? *He's fucking with me.* Shannon had told him many times about the way Roger could turn things around, make everything about him. And right now...it was. He needed Roger no matter how much he wished that weren't true. Roger might be the key to getting Shannon and Evie back.

"You wanted her, and you figured you'd try to hurt me." In the space of that sentence, Roger's tone went from vulnerable to acidic. From victim to aggressor. "But you can fucking have her, especially now that you have someone else pissed at you. Tell me, how many other women have you taken? Who else might want to get back at you?"

I don't steal women. And no one but Roger would think he had, of that, he was quite certain. But Morrison couldn't leave things this way—he needed Roger's help. "The better man doesn't always win."

Roger said nothing, but Morrison could almost hear him smirking. He swallowed his pride and the lump in his throat and headed over the amber streets toward Roger's house by the lake. The house that would have been Shannon's now if she'd stayed married to Roger. Maybe Roger was right. Maybe this was all his fault. Maybe he should have looked out for her better. Protected her.

If only she'd never met Roger.

If only she'd never married me.

BY THE TIME Morrison returned to the precinct, the bustle of the early morning hours had been replaced by a solemn nighttime shuffle of people disappearing one by one back to their families. Because they still had families. Even Petrosky was gone, and Morrison felt the absence of his own family as vividly as if he'd been boiled alive, his skin raw and exposed and utterly defenseless.

He needed to talk to Shannon. To hear her voice. To prove to himself, there was something there for him to fight for. To prove they weren't dead already. *Find her.*

Roger'd already checked social media—all traces of Karen gone—so Morrison sat at the desk and searched for Karen Palmer's driver's license from the state of Michigan. *Strange.* She should at least have a photo ID, but according to state records…nothing. No records at any nearby university, despite her employer's claim that she'd been in school. He flipped open her employee folder from the rehab center—nothing but a state ID from New York. Forged? Wouldn't the center have double-checked?

He grabbed the phone, and a quick call to the rehab center told him that while they ran the names for background checks, they just ensured the licenses were valid. The out-of-state license wouldn't have been an issue unless it had been suspended. Not unusual, but…

The New York State database, then. This time he got a hit. The address, the date of birth, everything matched the license photocopy in the file…except for the picture. Dark hair. Wide nose. No freckles.

It wasn't her.

Heart in his throat, he clicked through to the national databases and on to birth certificates. Using the New York driver's license, he found her: Karen Palmer, born in 1985 in California, in a city ten minutes away from Morrison's hometown. And died…no, that couldn't be right.

Karen Palmer had died eight years ago in New York, the records said. Cause of death: suicide. Maybe she'd faked her death? Gotten plastic surgery? No, that was real Maury Povich shit. And Karen Palmer's information had been out of circulation after she died—until the kidnapper had resurrected her four years later.

Which meant Griffen's girlfriend had been someone else until a few years ago. And she probably hadn't known Shannon until she'd arrived here—otherwise, his wife would have remembered Karen when she met the woman again as Griffen's girlfriend, especially if "Karen" was someone with a reason to be angry.

So Shannon hadn't known her, but this was no new wound. It was something deep and primal and feral. Based on old hurt. Not something Shannon had done in connection to Griffen or Roger or anyone else. Maybe not even something Roger had done since she hadn't gone after him until now. Was Roger just a bonus too? But Karen had definitely gone after Shannon. And she'd gone after…Morrison. Had him arrested.

He stared at the state of birth.

California.

Karen Palmer had been born in California. The kidnapper had taken her place. Had the kidnapper known the real Karen Palmer? Had she known...him? And if so...

Shannon's kidnapper had come to Michigan for him. And he couldn't for the life of him remember why.

> "In our endeavors to recall to memory something long forgotten, we often find ourselves upon the very verge of remembrance, without being able, in the end, to remember."
> ~Edgar Allan Poe, *Ligeia*

29

SHANNON'S ARMS ACHED, every muscle burning from the position she'd had to take, balled in the corner of what used to be a closet. No straitjacket now. Her breasts throbbed with unexpressed milk, nipples itchy and raw from letdown, and the dried fluids on the inside of her shirt.

Panic came and went in waves, and more often than not, she felt the tug of depression: the desperation, the hopelessness. Like now.

She hadn't fed Evie in what had to be days. Sometimes she heard her baby crying through the wall when they opened the door to toss in a bottle of water. Her own stomach was gnarled with anxiety and hunger, and her nerves were so frayed that it felt like she was brushing up against raw wires in the walls. But she could perceive nothing with her fingertips even when she scratched so ceaselessly at the cement she swore she was exposing the bones in her hands. And sometimes the shocks seemed to originate inside her head, an electric pulse in her brain.

She was probably losing her mind. Maybe had already.

Shannon leaned her head against the back of the closet, the cement board cold and hard and surely insulated well enough to muffle the sound of her echoing sobs. The air reeked of vomit and shit from the bucket in the corner. She had never considered that she'd long for the cold, barren bedroom where she'd awoken. But every piece of her ached for that freedom…and for the ability to see her baby girl whether she could touch her or not. Was Evie alive? *Stop, don't think.*

In this dark chamber, time stretched and compressed and bent on itself—she couldn't be sure if it was day or night. But Karen came to see her regularly, her full lips whispering poisonous words into the dark. Always at the strike of a grandfather clock somewhere in the house, as if the woman had a planner and at seven and twelve and three o'clock each day she'd written "Fuck with Shannon" in scrawling red ink. Karen told her all kinds of things. That she was still angry at Shannon for breaking her collarbone the night she'd attacked Shannon by the lake. Shannon thought it was Griffen she'd fought off that night, but not according to Karen, and Shannon had no reason to disbelieve her. Nor did she disbelieve it when Karen hissed that she'd helped Griffen frame Morrison for murder last year. That Griffen had never set out to harm anyone, that he had flown off the handle and broken a man's head, but that he'd lacked the guts for premeditated murder. Griffen: Shannon's friend for more than a decade. Her friend that she'd *killed* because he'd been sick—he'd been a murderer. Though maybe he hadn't. And if that were true, what did that make her?

Karen was playing on the guilt that had been eating at her every day since she'd put a bullet through Griffen's eye socket. Maybe Karen had gotten into McCallum's files—besides Petrosky, who had taken the fall for Griffen's death, only the psychiatrist knew what she'd done. Even Morrison didn't realize she was a killer too. She'd have to tell him she was sorry. And he'd tell her there was no sorry, only love, but...she'd lied to him. He might not forgive that.

Even as Shannon rationalized each issue away, new ones were introduced. Karen whispered about hurting Morrison. She said Shannon's husband was a murderer—that she wanted him to suffer, to make him feel helpless too. But none of it made sense, not any of it.

Visit after visit, Karen asked her how it felt to be without Evie. Told her that her baby girl was starving as they spoke, as milk stained Shannon's clothes and soaked her front. Evie would be better off without her, Karen said, and maybe they'd kill her baby girl just to spare Shannon the trouble of doing it herself: "Isn't that what you want, Shannon?"

Maybe Karen was messing with her head, but Shannon felt the correctness of each lancing blow in the deepest parts of her soul because she'd said those words to herself. Every fear she'd ever had, every irrational thought embedded itself into her consciousness—as though these terrifying convictions were right in a way that McCallum and her husband couldn't see. Maybe Evie did deserve better than her. Evie might still be fine at home if she'd had a different mother. Shannon tried to tell herself it was the depression talking, but she was having trouble believing it. The days were bleeding into one another, the darkness and lack of life rhythm pulling at the edges of her thoughts until she feared it would drive her mad. Though insanity would surely have been preferable to the hopelessness encroaching on her like a malevolent fog, cocooning her in despair, imploring her to give up.

What kind of mother was she? She wasn't even *trying*.

She stared across the closet—the dungeon—but everything was just black. Above her, she knew, hung a huge wooden strut attached to either end of the closet with brackets. If she could loosen it, perhaps it'd make a good weapon, but it was at least a foot square and too cumbersome to swing at her jailers from the confines of the closet. And with any action she took, there was risk. She could not leave without her child. Would they kill Evie if she tried to escape?

She prayed Evie was asleep. Babies slept through worse in third world countries, right? And when the man in the boots had come to take Evie away, he'd seemed rather...uninterested. He hadn't hurt Evie, hadn't even looked at her daughter, just took her. If he wanted to hurt her, he'd have done it in the room, made Shannon watch, wasn't that what psychos did? She might be wrong. Maybe even now they were burying Evie out back, alive, her tiny body being slowly covered with dirt until it filled her lungs and—

Her empty stomach clenched, and she heaved, gagged, but nothing came up.

Evie. She could almost feel her baby's breath against her neck. Surely if they'd killed her child, she'd have felt it—a snapping of her own lifeline, deep in her gut like the very cord that had tethered them to one another for nearly a year before Evie's birth.

No, Evie was alive, Shannon was sure of that. But she was being hurt, traumatized, if only by her mother's absence. Her sweet baby girl! And Karen didn't give a shit. Nor did the man outside the closet.

The door was thick, but she knew he was there. She could feel him. Smell him.

Milk dripped onto her jeans from below the hem of her T-shirt, but she made no move to wipe it away. Even her body knew Evie was still alive. And Evie still needed her mother. "Please let me feed her," she called into the darkness. There was no response, not that she had expected one. He couldn't hear her through the padded walls, but she was almost certain that he felt her too—surely he must sense the rage that was growing in her belly like a demon ready to emerge and slash at her captors with razor-sharp teeth.

"Hello?" she cried out, louder this time, and again her plea went unanswered. "I know you're there!" Panic mingled with desperation, and then it was there, the fury, a storm brewing without means for release. Her arms and legs twitched with anticipation.

She clawed her way to standing along the wall, probably leaving more trails of red from her already weeping fingertips. Dizziness pulled at her, and she grabbed the beam, wrapping one shoulder over it. The fury burned, hotter and blacker until it cloaked her entire being in unbridled hatred. If they wanted to kill her, then god-fucking-dammit, they needed to just hurry up and do it. She wasn't about to starve to death in a tiny closet, wondering if her child was already dead.

Please don't let her be dead.

She kicked the door with her bare foot, a move gleaned from years of CrossFit and kickboxing, but the door wouldn't budge. She'd tried this before—the space wasn't large enough to get leverage. The sound of her kick thundered back at her, reverberating in her ears as her heel burned deliciously from the exertion.

"Fuck you!" she screamed, then kept screaming it over and over: "Fuck you, you piece of fucking shit!" She kicked the door again, the dull thud of the impact jittering through her leg bone and into her hip, a welcomed sensation after the black numbness of rotting on the closet floor. Again and again and again, she kicked, tears sprouting in her eyes at the pain of the impact. At the helpless fury writhing in her gut.

Then...something. A sound, a scrape, and the light came then, so glaringly bright that she was forced to squint into it or go blind. And a silhouette in the now open doorway: Karen, red hair engulfing her face like hellfire.

You fucking bitch. Shannon tried to lunge under the beam, but the world blackened at the edges, and she had to hold on to avoid falling. She couldn't fight Karen. Had they put something in the water? She shivered in her wet shirt.

"Why are you doing this?" Shannon whispered, straining to hear Evie—a cry, a coo, anything to hint that she was alive. But there was only Karen's breath, steady and soft above the frenzied throbbing of Shannon's heart.

"Your husband is an asshole."

Shannon tried to let go of the bar again, but her legs shook, and she tightened her grip.

Karen smirked, teeth yellowed by the dim light. "Let's call him, shall we?"

Shannon tried to nod, scanning the room behind Karen for something she could yell out to Morrison, any clues that might give him some idea of where she was, but there was just the black bed, its pillows dark as night. No sunlit window. Nothing to indicate direction or location or even the type of building they were in. For all she knew, she could be locked in a high-rise.

Karen was holding her cell, tilting it back and forth like a snow globe. "Let's see if he killed your ex yet."

"Roger?"

Karen smiled, venomous, a look that Shannon had once thought beautiful, but now it radiated malice—hatred. And then Karen froze, staring at—

He loomed just outside the closet doorway, terrifying with his bald head and thick boots, and the room felt heavier with his presence. And with that awful mask, more frightening than it had been the first time because she knew, she knew he'd keep her here, knew he didn't want her to see his face because he was going to do atrocious things to her. He was bare-chested today, thin, scrawny even, but wiry—probably stronger than she'd guessed from his height alone. The scars of what looked like small puncture wounds, maybe burns, maybe an ice pick, glared at her from his stomach, and in the trail of hair on his lower belly the wounds were deeper, larger: some old and healed, others fresh, gaping stains like drips of black oil across his torso.

It must be morning. He only showed up in the morning, or so she thought because he usually came with coffee and a bagel, watching to see if she'd beg for a bite of his meal. She never had. And he'd never given her any.

Karen smiled at him and straightened her shoulders.

Shannon eased her weight onto her jelly legs and tried not to wobble.

Karen whirled on Shannon, her eyes narrowed, lips still smiling, which was more unnerving than if she'd snarled. "You come at me, and I'll kill Evie in front of you."

"I won't. Please." Shannon eased her weight back onto the bar, her head spinning. Somewhere in the house, a clock chimed, again and again, but Shannon couldn't concentrate enough to count the hour.

"Why are you talking?" He spoke to Shannon, maybe, voice muffled under the leather, but it sounded oddly careful. One of his fingernails worried at the molding around the closet door, and he was staring at Karen from inside the mask. His angular shoulders were slumped like an old beaten dog, though he outweighed them by at least fifty pounds.

From the next room, a whine blossomed into a wail, one thin, long howl of exhausted hunger. *Evie. Alive.* Blood pumped into Shannon's legs, urging her to run to her daughter, to take her from this place. *Can't run. They'll kill us both.* She held the bar tighter as the man straightened, muscles corded. He glanced toward the door, toward Evie's screams.

"Please—I can make her quiet," Shannon said, hating that she sounded like she was begging, but she *was* begging. *God, please let me feed her.*

"I can make her quiet too." His voice was more menacing now as he dropped his hand from the wall and advanced. Unafraid of her, apparently, only wary of Karen. Because they were…together? Because she'd seen him without the mask?

"I'll get her quiet," he said, and he turned to the door.

No, oh Jesus, don't hurt her. "She's hungry, just let me—"

"Her agony is well-deserved."

Her agony. Was he enjoying watching Evie starve? He had laughed their first night here, laughed at Shannon's screams as he held his blade over her daughter. He wanted to see their misery. "Hurt me instead."

He turned to her and lowered his face so he could look into her eyes. His irises shone even in the dark of the mask as if madness could escape through his pupils. Where Morrison's pacific blue lenses were always so full of hope and promise and kindness; behind this man's eyes, lay only the glittering promise of pain.

"She doesn't understand what you want," Shannon said.

"Then she'll learn," he said with a lilt that made it sound like he was smiling.

"No, she won't," Karen said suddenly, her bottom lip between her teeth. There was something strange happening, a discontent, an aggression building between her captors—he took a step backward, away from Karen, shoulders tense like a kid being admonished by a parent. Was he...young? Was Karen his mom? *How can I use this to get us out of here?*

"Children don't learn from pain the same way adults do," Karen said. "Like that boy who *never should have happened.*" She glared at the man in the mask, and he shrank farther from her.

What boy? *There have been others.* This wasn't a new game to them; this was an old game, and Shannon and Evie were only new victims. Perhaps the boy was buried out back. Maybe he was in another room like hers, hanging by his ankles from his own wooden beam. And...this man's boots. They'd been covered in blood, hadn't they?

Karen stepped over to the masked man, and he flinched. Then she ran a hand over his abdomen, hooking a fingernail under a scab near his belly button and slicing it off. He grunted and righted himself, taller suddenly, muscles rippling as the wound welled and blood tricked toward his belt line.

Karen's face cleared—no longer angry, or perhaps she'd decided there was a better way to accomplish her goal. "The kid will just cry more. We'll never get her to shut up. But this one..." She gestured to Shannon, and Shannon's blood ran cold. "She'll never bother you again with her whiny bullshit." Karen's eyes were dead, stony, the beauty draining from her face as the blood drained from the masked man's wound.

He appraised Shannon, fingers practically vibrating with anticipation, and left the room.

Oh god. Shannon's heart throbbed, and each beat drove a spike of fear into her chest. Was he going to get that barbaric weapon with the hooked blade? Was he going to cut her open? Would he...cut Evie? *No, please, no.*

Her eyes darted around the room, peering at the doorway. "Please, Karen..." Could she overpower her? But in her weakened state, she could never take on both of them...and the masked man had her child. *Evie—*

She heard him then, his footsteps growing louder, returning, and every muscle in Shannon's body quivered. *Please let us go. Please don't hurt Evie.*

Then he was there, brandishing a small cloth bag in one hand. In his other hand, a collar, the inner part of it, the part that would touch the throat, glinting with what looked like razor blades.

Shannon's mouth filled with cotton, and her throat constricted painfully. The masked man stepped in front of her, his leather face turning this way, then that, the spines on top of the mask stabbing at the sky above him, the vicious beak sharp and deadly. One head butt and she'd be gone. Every panel of the mask seemed to leer at her of its own accord. *Fuck, fuck, fuck.*

I don't want to die.

He reached for her, and she stepped away, almost fell, but he wasn't after her, not yet. He attached the metal clamp to the front of the beam by threading a bolt through a small hole, securing the collar to the post.

"In."

She stared at the blades glinting evilly from the inside of the collar. "But it'll…" *Slit my throat.*

"In. And don't move."

Her eyes filled. Then she saw *her.*

She hadn't noticed Karen leaving, but now the woman walked into the room carrying Evie, her daughter barely struggling in Karen's arms. Evie cried weakly. Shannon's insides leapt and flipped, and she shook with the effort not to run to her.

The man turned his head to look at her daughter, then back. "In the collar, you can hold her, feed the bitch, whatever. You're going to make good on your promise."

Her promise. Shannon's lip quivered, but she stiffened it. *Fuck you.* She watched him set the bag on the beam next to the collar and open it. A sewing kit. Curved instruments glinting in the light, though dimmed by the closet's oppressive shadow. *What the hell is he going to—*

The thought froze in her brain as he produced an upholstery needle, the tip glistening like a shard of broken glass, and it felt as if he were going to stab her with a piece of her own shattered sanity. And…*would* he stab her? Would he shove it into her eyeball, blinding her? Every muscle in her body tightened in anticipation. *Run. Run!*

She dragged her gaze from the needle as Evie kicked one foot, weakly, her tiny mewl tugging at Shannon's gut more fervently than any instrument of torture he could dream up. She steeled herself, glanced once more at Evie, and stepped to the post. As carefully as she could, she leaned her neck against the back of the collar, where there were no blades.

He smiled. And clamped the thing around her neck.

One blade pierced her immediately, on the right side, just below her lymph node, not the fire of real injury, rather the sting of a paper cut. She adjusted a touch to the left, trying to avoid the blades on that side. She felt them, cold and sharp, but they didn't cut her. *Yet.*

His breath was faster, excited, and every exhale amplified by the mask like the hoarse rasp of a dying man. He moved aside, needle held up in front of his glass eyehole as Karen placed Evie in her arms.

Her baby's face was scrunched up. She was suffering—couldn't even raise her limbs to reach for her mother.

"Oh, baby," Shannon whispered. "Sweet girl."

Evie opened her mouth and wailed, but the sound was far smaller than it should have been. Careful to avoid jostling her own neck, Shannon lifted her shirt and pressed Evie to her breast, trying to do everything by feel since she couldn't look down.

Then he was there, staring into Shannon's eyes, running a finger over her lower lip, looking for her fear as he raised the needle. The thread was black like his fucking heart.

She stared back, eyes narrowed. But oh god, the needle. And he'd said...he wanted to keep her quiet. And as she watched his gaze lock on the lower part of her face, realization dawned with a wave of electric horror: he was going to sew her mouth closed. She'd feel every stitch, the blinding pain as he stabbed the needle into her. But if it kept Evie alive... *Come at me, fucker. Do it.* Just like getting your ears pierced. Except she'd not be able to speak.

To breathe.

Evie stirred. She clasped her daughter to her chest. "I love you, Evie, Evie."

He grabbed her face with one hand and stabbed the needle into her lower lip.

She wanted to cry out, but her air was gone as the needle rammed violently through her lower lip and pierced through to the top, the pain sharper and more vital than she'd imagined. *Stay still, keep quiet*—she had to keep her daughter from falling. She pressed her neck against the back of the collar and clutched Evie to her breast. The thread, bloody now, slid more easily than the needle, but it burned like a hot poker through her face. *No, please, no!* It stopped abruptly, a knot maybe and he was bringing it down to do another—*Fuck!* She wanted to scream, couldn't scream, she'd tear her lips apart and—she stared at his face, his mask, listened to his heavy breathing, tasted blood and salt on her tongue as the rage replaced the fear. He didn't deserve to have her cries to jack off to later.

Help me, please, someone, help. But there was no one else—only her. And...Evie. She inhaled deeply, shifted Evie to one arm, testing her strength, and raised the other hand to the beam.

He paused. "What are you doing?"

"Staying...steady." Talking from one corner of her mouth was painful, and she sounded like she was numb from a dentist visit. But he'd apparently understood and approved for he didn't respond, just stabbed the needle into her lip again, rougher this time. *Breathe, just breathe.* Tears welled in her eyes with the searing pain that radiated through her mouth into her cheeks, her ears, finding its way into every nerve ending in her body.

Her milk let down, and Evie was making tiny, sweet noises of contentment, and Shannon desperately wished she could see her face. *I'm a good mother god-fucking-dammit. I will get you out of here.*

Karen's eyes were alight with excitement—at Shannon's distress or maybe at the way the masked man was panting, every muscle in his arms twitching with anticipation. Karen approached behind him, ran her palms over the flat surface of his shoulder blades. *God, please let him stop, please let her take him away, please.*

Shannon snaked her hand toward the top of the beam. Karen didn't respond to the movement, fixated as she was on the stitches, or maybe the misery in Shannon's eyes or maybe on the man himself. His breath in the mask came faster, and she could smell it—hot and sour, though that could have been the smell of her own rank fear.

Another stitch. Panic seized her, a fresh wave ripping through her from toe to brain, begging her to run. *Run, Shannon! No. Not now, no!* She whimpered involuntarily, and it seemed to excite him further, his breath coming faster, hissing from behind that horrid mask as if the thing had come alive—a beaked monster of leather and metal. And then Karen was beside him, working his belt and his zipper—*not her son, definitely not*—and she knelt, out of Shannon's view, and he moaned into Shannon's face as he stabbed the needle into her lip again. And again, through the top, slower now but violent, the thread tugging not only through her flesh, but pulling her toward him as if she were a bull being led to slaughter by a ring in her mouth.

Don't move, Shannon. Almost finished. Don't move. She breathed heavily through her nose, fought the wave of dizziness. If she fainted, she'd be dead in minutes, her jugular shredded by the blades.

And Evie... Shannon tried to focus all her attention on Evie and the gentle pull of the baby at her breast. *Evie will be okay.* Tears stung her eyes.

Karen was standing, wiping her mouth, and he was growling into Shannon's face, the beak of the mask at her nose, and when it touched her, it sliced her right nostril, though that pain was dull compared to the stinging needle piercing her lips.

At the closet door, Karen pulled out the phone. Pushed buttons. Watched Shannon, practically panting. She put the phone to her ear. "Hello, Curt. The stakes have changed. Your partner's over at the rehab center. He's going to stay there."

Stay there? Why would they want Petrosky in rehab? But with the panic zinging through her body, her brain could only focus on the pain, could only scream inside as she watched the needle approach again. Her chin was wet, spit and blood dribbling down her chin, onto the arm that held Evie. Blood dripped onto her baby's head.

"What's to understand? Breckenridge Rehab has a reservation for one, Edward Petrosky. I'd hurry."

The man had paused, needle in hand, Shannon's blood on his fingertips, so much blood and was it hers or his or maybe both, and maybe she'd catch some crazy disease, *oh, fuck.* The dizziness pulled again until she feared she might not be able to hold herself up this time. He turned and stared at Karen, head cocked as if he were a student listening to a lecture.

"Please nothing," Karen snapped into the phone. "You're good at hooking people. Dragging them down to your level. Just be the same asshole you've always been. And they need a positive test for a same-day admission, so make sure your partner's good and dirty."

This bitch wanted Petrosky to—

The man turned back to her, peered into her eyes through the glass lenses of the mask as if he could see directly into her soul. His breathing turned everything inside her to ice.

"It's in your glovebox," Karen said. "Manila envelope. Get him to do it with you, or wait until he's asleep, then shoot him up and take him in. Do you understand?"

She couldn't think, couldn't focus. Something dripped onto her upper lip from the tip of her nose. More sweat. More blood.

Her torturer pulled his face back from Shannon's, and the air felt cooler, crisper. Then he chuckled like she'd told him something funny through her punctured lips. She ground her teeth together to keep from screaming.

"Roger taken care of?" Karen said into the receiver.

The masked man turned back to Karen again, and Shannon reached the corner of the sewing kit with her pinky finger. Ring finger. Then—

A sliver of metal, cool against her fingertips as the hooked beak swung her way again, but his eyes did not look at the beam or the kit, just at her as if trying to stare into her head. Sensing her pain. Enjoying it.

He made a noise like a groan, and for a moment, she feared he'd seen her hand in the sewing kit in his peripheral vision, but then his hand was flying toward her face, and he stabbed the needle deeper, higher, harder into her top lip; white-hot agony shot through her brain as he hit something, a nerve, a piece more crucial than before. He turned away. Done or waiting?

Don't move. Shit, don't move. Evie. Stay with Evie. Sweat rolled down her back and into the waistband of her pants.

A frown deepened on Karen's face. "Get the deposit box, his logbook. That's all you need. Or just shoot him in the face. But you better hurry. Women like your wife weaken fast—either we'll break her, or she'll break herself. Soon."

They would. They'd break her. Leave her in the dark, deprive her of her child, make her watch Evie weaken and succumb. *Come on, Morrison, come on.*

"I want to watch *you* suffer," Karen spat into the cell. "Like you watched Danny. Then I want you to watch the people you love die like you watched Danny die. And I'm going to love every second of it."

The man turned slowly, almost reverently, and her insides roiled, but oh god, she couldn't throw up, not anymore—she'd choke to death on her own vomit. And he was there at her mouth again, stabbing once more at the last remaining corner of her lips, and when he tugged the thread this time, it was as if he were trying to force her face into a grotesque joker's smile.

"I don't need rumors," Karen said. "I saw you."

The masked man cut the thread with the tip of his beak, and Shannon shuddered. The point of a blade from the collar pressed to her neck, and she felt the warm wet roll down to her collarbone. She'd cut herself. Hopefully, the wound wasn't too deep. *Or I'll die, I'll die, and Evie...* She forced her spine against the back of the beam again.

He snatched the sewing kit. Snatched Evie off her breast, the suction breaking and the sound slapping against the walls of the cell as Evie whimpered, then wailed.

"No, please, she's still hungry," Shannon wanted to say, but she couldn't say it, couldn't say anything. *Give her back to me!*

He put Evie on the floor outside the closet, roughly, as if she were a suitcase and not a living, breathing person, close enough to Shannon that she could only make out her daughter's kicking feet. He tossed the sewing kit beside Evie, his fingers still glistening red with Shannon's blood. The needles...so close to her daughter. *Oh god, not Evie, please don't hurt—*

"You've got a limited amount of time, Curt. She falls asleep, and she's done for," Karen told the cell. "And if she hasn't already killed herself, tomorrow night, I'll help her say goodbye."

*If I fall asleep...*oh, god...they weren't going to let her out of the collar. If she nodded off, she'd slit her own throat. No, shit no, she'd never make it through the—

But she couldn't tell them, not that they'd notice her trying to speak. Karen had dropped the phone, and the man was tearing at Karen's clothing, tossing her shirt and skirt aside as she grabbed his shoulders, wrapping her naked legs around his waist. He slammed Karen into the still-open door of the closet and entered her, thrusting into her again and again, right above Evie's head.

"Told you about the phone," he growled.

"You're good," Karen said. "We were made for each other."

"My number one girl." He shifted his weight, looked once more at Shannon, and hammered Karen into the wall. Shannon tried again to see Evie, but could only make out her baby's feet, no longer kicking so ferociously. Slowing down. Shutting down. Was it starvation? Trauma? *Oh, baby, please be okay.* On the floor lay the phone, still on, the time ticking away, upwards and onwards. And she knew Morrison was there too, listening to Evie scream, listening to the man's grunts and Karen's moans, hearing the sounds of sex and his screeching daughter and dear god, what he must think.

The man walked Karen to the bed and threw her off him, onto the black sheets. Then he returned to the closet, his erection at his belly, and there was...a tattoo. On his penis. A medieval sword, but terribly done, faded and pixelated like he'd done it himself. He paused at the doorway, and for one breathtaking moment, he studied the infant on the floor, his eyes behind the lenses wild with anticipation.

Please, no.

He pulled his eyes from Evie, and then the door was closing, encasing Shannon in perfect darkness, Evie's wails fading, and then gone completely, though she could still feel her daughter's frantic energy on the other side of the door. Shannon pressed her neck as far back as she could to avoid the blades. Blood trickled steadily down her chin. But in her palm, she tested the sharp point of the needle she'd stolen, hoping it'd be enough.

30

Karen's words echoed in his brain, mingling with Evie's screams and the sick grunts of pleasure. Morrison threw the phone to the floorboards like it was a ticking bomb. His baby girl. Not his baby.

Through the windshield, sunrise pinkened the bruised early morning clouds. One more day, two at most. And it was Saturday already: day four.

He'd run to his car when the call came in, his arm half-asleep from passing out at his desk, the remnants of a dream still thickening his mind.

Me first.

No, me.

A hallucination, or maybe a sliver of memory—girls laughing in his head, and Danny bleeding, and Shannon was bleeding too, covered in ants, just like—

He pounded the steering wheel with his fists.

Escalation.

These other assholes Karen was with had begun smaller—a rape, a little pressure on the neck. But Karen had started with murder in mind. His fist clenched, and he resisted the urge to punch the steering wheel. *Think.* What had driven Karen to embrace such savagery? If he knew her motive, would he be able to find her? To find Shannon? Was Evie still okay? Were they alive?

The cold. Keep the cold. But the fire and ice were fighting, sizzling, boiling, and he couldn't control it for much longer. He needed time. She wanted Roger punished, but he knew Roger wouldn't admit to anything. Fabrication of evidence? Frame him? He could do that. He could always clear Roger once his family was safe.

But Petrosky. Dragging him into the hell that was heroin...

The drugs were probably tainted. They were going to make him kill his best friend. Make him choose—Petrosky, or Shannon and Evie.

And with Petrosky gone... But why didn't Karen want him to drop the case? To clear her or whoever she was with for their other crimes? Instead, Karen had told him to keep going. Without Petrosky.

She wanted Morrison to find them. *Him.* No one else.

She wanted him there so he could watch Shannon die. So he could watch his child bleed.

She wanted to punish him.

Find the cold. Stay with the logic. Run from the heat.

The heat would kill them all.

He replayed the conversation. The voice wasn't familiar, but she seemed to know him. Had known him back when he was using to escape, when the only thing that made him happy, made him whole, was the needle.

I don't need rumors. I saw you. And she'd used Danny's name. Shannon didn't know about Danny. Not even Petrosky did. But Karen—she'd seemed familiar the first time they'd met, though he hadn't known her before, he could almost swear to it. Then again, the flashes of memory from the night Danny died told him next to nothing. Only that Danny was dead. That it was probably his fault.

Murderer.

He'd always suspected karma meant that mistakes simply repeated until you learned, and he hadn't needed a second chance to avoid repetition of that event. But perhaps karma was vengeful. Like a god. Like a jilted lover.

Think. What else did he know?

He had tried to start over. He'd tried to move on, to be better. To forget. But someone hadn't forgotten Danny, after all this time. Karen hadn't forgotten.

Maybe she'd been biding her time until he had something worth taking.

Evie's wails grew louder inside his head, and Morrison's heart threatened to implode. There was too much pressure in his chest. The world tilted and spun. Shannon and Evie couldn't pay for his mistakes—pay just for knowing him.

Unless that was all bullshit. Pretending to know him. Just part of the game.

You see me, but you don't. But you'll figure it out—you'll remember me. And once you do, you'll know exactly how to find me.

And she'd said Danny's *name.*

The phone on the floorboard buzzed. He shook as he collected it. Dropped it. Turned it over. Text: a picture.

No. Shannon. Fuck. His wife stood with her neck locked in some kind of collar, hands gripping a wooden bar on either side of her head. Shirt, stiff-looking, half of it riding high over her bare breast, the other half slumped to her waist. Blood coated her chin, had dripped down her neck from under the black collar. And her mouth—*oh god.* Ragged black stitches secured her lips together, her beautiful, perfect mouth swollen and angry and mangled and—

No Evie.

The air had disappeared entirely. And below the image, one word.

"Hurry."

Morrison hit his thigh on the wheel at the sudden thud against the driver's side glass. Petrosky's nose touched the window, hands cupped around his eyes as he peered inside. Morrison squinted at the sky, the bruised clouds solid now, the sun higher. How long had he been sitting there, staring into space?

You need to go into rehab, Boss. You need to become...an addict. He needed time. Petrosky would be an easier sell than Roger, but for someone already struggling with addiction, the pull of heroin would be strong. Morrison rolled down the window. For someone whose demons never went away...it would be an invitation to death.

Morrison shook his head, tried to refocus, tried to pull in the cold air that he couldn't taste or smell. He needed to ice the fire in his heart.

Tomorrow.

One way or another, by tomorrow night, this would all be over.

But he couldn't save them. Not like this.

He finally looked at Petrosky's face but couldn't discern individual features, only grainy beige fuzz and a pulsating movement where the boss's mouth should be.

"Nothing else at the center—she was a recluse, according to the staff. Morrison!" Petrosky clapped his hands, and Morrison blinked hard to clear his vision. The old man's brows were knitted together like they'd never come unstuck. *He knows.*

"What the fuck happened?"

How to buy the time he needed? Even if he could locate Karen, or whatever her name was, how could he find her in a day? Morrison swallowed hard, tried to ready himself to answer, but Petrosky was already hurrying around the car and sliding into the passenger side.

"Tell me, right the fuck now."

Morrison handed him the phone, open to Shannon's picture.

Petrosky froze. "They make more demands, or was this in response to Roger still being free?" His jaw was tight, every knuckle white and hard.

"Both." Morrison put the car in gear, certain that the hands gripping the wheel belonged to some other being put there to drive them away.

There was no high road to take. This was life and death. Shannon's life. Evie's life. "We need to talk."

Morrison drove them to the edge of the river, where no one could approach without being seen. Few buildings to spy from, and before them, just the endless expanse of water until it butted up against the opposite shore in a haze of gray fog. He parked on the bank.

"So what's—"

Morrison pulled his phone from his pocket and tossed it into the console, then exited the car and headed for the water's edge.

"Morrison?"

No Surfer Boy. No California.

California was dead.

"I—" He'd rehearsed it all the way here. "I need you to check into Breckenridge."

No expression on Petrosky's face.

"Listen, I know you don't like the idea of—"

"I'm clean. Have been since the wedding. You see some fucking sign on my head that says 'user?'"

The air thickened around them until Petrosky's face softened with understanding. "She didn't like that I was at the rehab center, huh? Not that I found anything—no sex offenders, no violent offenses just a few burglary charges. No one that matches our descriptions."

What the hell was Petrosky babbling about? "Boss, they want you out of the way. They want you strung out. I figured maybe if you act the part, we can make it work. I'm just not sure what to do about the drug tests."

Karen probably still had access to the online medical records, so if they started switching up passwords, she'd know something was up. He could try social engineering...calling up there, tricking someone into coughing up their password, but either way, Karen had someone on the inside—someone who'd told her that Petrosky was there asking questions. "If I hacked their system, I could enter a positive drug screen," Morrison said. "But it's a newer system. One wrong move and the whole thing will shut down."

And Karen would know.

Then what next? They were already fondling Shannon, tearing at her clothes, sewing her fucking body parts together, and doing god only knew what to Evie. Had they raped her? Sewn her lips shut like they did to Shannon? He was panting through his nose, and Petrosky's hand on his arm brought him back.

The cold. Find the cold.

"Fucking technology." Petrosky's voice held not a trace of irony, only sad acceptance. "If she has someone on the inside instead of just online access to the medical files, I could sniff them out."

He'd thought the same. But he couldn't figure out a way around the screening tests. "Right, I know you'll find them. But you can't get in for a same-day admission if you're sober."

"Guess I better get un-sober. Liquor store around the corner, right?"

Morrison searched his face, trying to figure out a way around it, but he came up empty—there was no other choice that he could see, and he only had until tomorrow night. *I'm sorry, Boss.* "She...wants you doing more than that." Morrison gestured to the car, and Petrosky followed his gaze. "Glovebox," he said quietly, hoping that the package she'd mentioned wouldn't be there.

But it was. Petrosky returned with an unfamiliar envelope, a jagged construction paper *#1* taped to the cover. It looked like someone had carved it out with a kitchen knife instead of scissors. *Jagged cuts hurt more.*

"I'm number one, eh? Romantic." Petrosky opened it. Powder. A spoon. A syringe. A rubber band, not that the band would do much to assist with isolating a vein. Had she never used herself? And if that was the case...did they really know each other? The spaces in his memory were usually drug-induced voids: places where few, or any, sober people were hidden.

I don't need rumors, I saw you.

You see me, but you don't.

Petrosky opened the bag and poured half of the powder onto the spoon.

"What are you doing?"

"Checking. Don't need it all to get stoned. But if it's dirty, I'd rather know now." He handed Morrison the syringe, and it seemed to vibrate in his hand.

Checking. Not using it. *Checking.* He fought the urge to throw it into the river.

Petrosky pocketed the rest of the powder and pulled out his lighter, and they both watched as the mixture liquefied. Morrison's veins sang with electricity as if the drug were speaking to his cells directly, calling them to it.

"You know we can't get a warrant," Petrosky was saying. "And those fuckers at the center won't give up what we need without it. I might do better figuring this out on the inside anyway."

"Yeah, right." The vibration in Morrison's palm danced through his wrist, up his arm, spreading through his body. Warm. Enticing. Euphoric. Just one little prick, that's all it'd take, and he'd remember. *I don't need rumors, I saw you.* "State-dependent memory" McCallum had called it. He needed to be in the right state of mind to remember Karen. Then he'd be able to find his family.

Petrosky took the syringe from Morrison's hand. "Roger going to help?"

"If he won't, I'll force his hand. We both know he's dirty. There has to be a way to at least get him hauled in for questioning, which should buy us time." But Morrison didn't have enough evidence for that. There had even been an investigation last year, and Roger had come out ahead, all accusations deemed erroneous. But Morrison had to do better—frame him maybe. But that would take time Shannon and Evie didn't have.

"You'll find a way."

He didn't like the way Petrosky put it. *Just me? I'll find a way?* Morrison shook. This was all on him. His balled fists left tingling imprints on his thighs. They had her. Shannon. Shannon's lips. They were torturing her. Torturing his baby. He couldn't breathe.

Petrosky positioned the needle, drew half the liquid into the syringe, and held it up to the light, flicking it with his index finger: clear liquid tinged with brown. "This was your thing, California?"

Yes. "Not anymore, Boss."

"They know you. Knew you then."

"I assume she thought I'd go back, that I'd use again." She knew his weakness—there was a reason she'd chosen smack.

"You'd think she'd realize you wouldn't force this on anyone."

She had to know if she knew anything about him at all. But the more he played her words over in his mind, the more they branded themselves there along with the certainty that she had not been speaking in generalities. She knew something about him. Something he couldn't recall. *Be the same asshole you've always been.*

Morrison forced an inhale through his nose, noticing a slight vinegary tang. The scar at the crook of his thigh pulsed and shuddered. "Either they think I'm a...monster who will do whatever they want," he began slowly, "or they think I won't, and they want a reason to hurt Evie and Shannon...and me by default. To punish me." He ran his hand through his hair, and a few strands clung to his fingers as he pulled his hand away.

"What'd you do, California?"

Everything was hot, tight. "I hurt someone. At least I think I did. But I can't... I'm not sure who this woman is." He needed to remember. He had to find a way to remember, but the hurricane raging in his chest prevented any rational thought as if his abdomen were a vortex where the heat and the pain and the fear had collided with enough force to make his chest cave in.

My turn. No, me! And Danny's head, bloody and gaping to the bone, and the ants, everywhere, on his pants, crawling up his leg—

Cold. Feel the cold. He imagined the breeze off the water singing into his veins, flowing through him and calming the electric peal of panic, the desire for the drug. "If I can figure out where she is—"

"You don't need me to find her."

"I do." He couldn't do this. He didn't even know who she really was. But if he did everything she asked of him, maybe he wouldn't have to find her. *You'll remember me. And once you do, you'll know exactly how to find me.*

"You'll figure it out, Cali. And from the inside, I can help more than I can out here."

"That's not—"

"Decantor's a smart guy, Morrison. And he's on your side. You've got Valentine, too, if you need him. You know he'd do anything for you and Shannon." *Morrison.* The name sounded strange coming from Petrosky's lips, as did the compliments he was paying the other officers. And Morrison knew both Decantor and Valentine would be on the phone with the Feds the moment they found out Shannon and Evie had been kidnapped. Was he trying to tell him they *should* go to the Feds? He didn't need the Feds or Decantor or Valentine. He had a partner. Just not his family.

He gazed out at the water. "There has to be something else we can—"

Petrosky brought the needle up, stabbed it into his thigh, and emptied the syringe.

No.

The needle and the spoon with the remaining drug dropped to the earth.

"Petrosky!"

"You and Decantor will be fine. If the kidnappers want me in rehab, there's something there that I missed. I'll find it. And we'll find her. Now get me back to the car, Surfer Boy." He took a step and stumbled, one arm shooting out to steady himself as if his legs were turning to jelly, though it might have been a muscle spasm after the needle stick. Still better than the vein—shooting into the muscle tissue gave a more mellow buzz, less chance of overdosing. Had Petrosky known that when he'd shoved the needle into his thigh? He shook off the thought that Petrosky's addictions might be deeper and more varied than he'd realized. His boss was an addict, but there was nothing like heroin. *Nothing.* And Petrosky had many demons to silence.

Please let him make it. Morrison put his hand on Petrosky's arm, leading him, hoping he wouldn't have to carry him. Hoping Petrosky's heart wouldn't give out. Hoping—

"Aw, fuck." Petrosky reached the car and slumped against the door. "Get me to Breckenridge."

The receptionist's eyes widened in surprise when Morrison walked into the rehab center, supporting Petrosky under the arm. Twenty minutes in and Petrosky was fully under heroin's spell, head lolling as if he'd been reduced to a sack of skin, his essence sucked from his marrow. A shadow of himself.

Another woman came out to take their basic information. Petrosky leaned heavily on the counter and gawked at her and the receptionist, who tapped diligently on her keyboard while Petrosky muttered half coherent responses.

The computer. Was the receptionist in on this? Was she the one who'd called Karen the moment they'd headed back with the HR director? Her squinty eyes danced over her screen. The boil on her lip was no longer as innocuous as it had been earlier—it stared at him like a third and horribly misshapen eyeball.

Petrosky listed Morrison as his emergency contact. Though Morrison had been the one to put him here in the first place.

Then there were no more questions. Orderlies, slim but strong, emerged through the door and took Petrosky's fleshy arms, one on either side. Neither looked suspicious with their sympathetic smiles, but smiles hid a great deal. He knew that all too well.

The younger, blonder one nodded to Morrison. "We'll take good care of him, sir," he said as he hooked his palm under Petrosky's elbow.

Petrosky tried to shrug them off, but as they started for the metal doors, he stumbled, and then the three men were heading back whether Petrosky was ready or not.

At the double doors, Petrosky turned and looked at Morrison one last time, eyes unfocused but wet. "Get 'em, Cali."

He had no choice. There was no time. Morrison walked away, convinced he'd just left his best friend in the care of a murderer.

31

THE DRIVE back to the precinct was unnaturally silent but blessedly short. Morrison headed through the bullpen and found Decantor at his desk, nose in a file, cell by his palm on the desktop. He looked up and grinned as Morrison approached.

"Hey, man! Glad you found Shannon! Women, huh?" He shook his head.

Morrison opened his mouth in shock. *Right.* They'd told Decantor that Alex had picked Shannon up—that she was safe. "Yeah. That was something else." He tried not to envision her in the collar; mouth sewed up like Frankenstein's monster. He rubbed at his temple hard enough to chafe the skin as he tried to push the images from his brain.

"Where's Petrosky? He finally take a Saturday off?"

It's Saturday? Morrison cleared his throat. "No. Just out looking into a few things."

Decantor cocked an eyebrow like he knew Morrison was lying. But there was no logical reason for the man to believe his suspicion was true, and as expected, Decantor's face softened. "Want to brainstorm in a few, then? Or should we wait for Petrosky to get back?"

No time. They'd taken his family. They'd taken his partner. Decantor didn't have what he needed anyway—it was locked in his head, hidden by sobriety. *You'll find a way.* And when Morrison found these fuckers… he wasn't going to bring them in. He'd get his family back, and Karen and her fucked-up partners would die. "We'll wait for Petrosky," he said.

Again with the eyebrow, but Decantor recovered faster this time. "Sure. Just let me know when he gets here." He stood. "I need to grab a few sheets off the press."

"Sounds good. I'll be at my desk looking over your notes." As

Decantor walked away, Morrison slid Decantor's phone off the desk, clicked it to vibrate, and dropped it into his pocket.

THERE WAS little new information in Decantor's case files, and the notes Petrosky had taken at the rehab center earlier didn't give Morrison anything he could use to jog his memory.

Once you remember, you'll know where to find me.

But he couldn't remember. He'd never remember if McCallum was right about the state-dependent memory. If he knew her when he was high, the memory was gone—while he was sober.

The woman who'd kidnapped Shannon had known Danny personally, maybe intimately. And though Morrison hadn't known everyone Danny had been with, she'd been insistent that he should remember her. They'd met. He'd thought hers might have been one of the disembodied voices he heard when he slept, keening to him from the night Danny died—*Me. No, me!*—but with the rubber band, he wasn't sure she'd ever been a druggie waiting for her turn. Maybe she'd been there in some other capacity the night Danny died. Maybe not. None of it helped him unless he got stoned, and his partner was already high enough for the both of them. Morrison couldn't afford to fuck it up. He couldn't take a chance on the needle.

I can't afford not to.

Something the kidnapper had said was irritating his brain. Something about...women like Shannon weakening fast. And the original Karen Palmer had killed herself—had she been driven to suicide? Or had she been murdered?

Who are you?

He'd start with the name she'd taken.

Karen Palmer, the real Karen Palmer, had been born to Hillary and Sherman Palmer. Her mother was easy to locate: address in upstate New York, listed phone number. According to her Facebook page, she headed an anti-bullying organization and was involved in another group dedicated to suicide prevention. On their own, either organization might not have struck him as profound—but together, they invoked the image of a harassed child, driven to escape the cruelty of the world by her own hand.

He put Decantor's phone to his ear.

"Hello, you've reached Hillary." Her voice was high, lilting, not weighed down by grief as he'd expected it to be. Not like Petrosky's. Maybe Petrosky had always sounded like that. "I can't come to the phone right now..."

He waited for the greeting to finish and left his name and credentials along with Decantor's number, and re-pocketed the phone.

Karen or whatever her real name was—she'd had a long time to plan. To disappear. She was calculating, too, like the psychopathic stab-fanatic who had brought a murder weapon to the Acosta scene and stalked and butchered Natalie Bell. But the pedophile who had raped Acosta and Reynolds was sloppier, leaving his DNA all over the place—and it was a lonely world for pedophiles. Decantor was chasing down leads on Bell. Petrosky was on the lookout at the rehab center. *Acosta.* Find the boy's rapist, he'd find his wife.

Morrison logged into the chat rooms one more time, scouring for clown-obsessed pedos, pedos discussing how to incapacitate their "lovers"—*victims*—particularly references to T-shirts or the woods or the *#1*. Though Reynolds had not received that brand, Acosta and Bell and Petrosky's drugs all had. Nothing. He dug deeper. Some websites were encrypted, and others needed passwords, but Morrison was better than that. Ten minutes to hack into one. Four to hack into another, twenty minutes the third. And as he read through each, the dread in his belly grew.

"The kid loves me, I know it…"
"I took him to a ball game…"
"Her parents seem upset, but we're in love. They of all people should understand that."

Morrison's breathing echoed long and loud in his ears, yogic breathing, the only way he was able to keep his shit together. He tried to tell himself that these sick bastards were not the ones holding his family prisoner, but it didn't help, not enough. The vein in his thigh throbbed once, and Morrison flashed to Petrosky on the shore, stabbing the needle into his leg, and he didn't feel guilt, didn't feel anger, just the searing burn of jealousy. His thigh. The one place no one ever thought to look. And they wouldn't start looking now.

He shifted his weight, letting his pants rub against that forever-tender spot in his leg. In the oblivion, he'd find his family. And if he didn't find them in time, he'd release himself into the oblivion, heaven or hell on the needle; it didn't really matter so long as he didn't have to consider the world without his family in it. Without Shannon. Without Evie.

He was almost panting now, the dizziness pulling at him, tunneling his vision until he sucked in a thick burst of oxygen. The agitation lessened. And then, there on the computer screen, large as life: The Juggler. Morrison's breath caught. Lots of child abusers. Fewer with a penchant for cult bands and bloody clowns. But with that name…

He scoured The Juggler's pages, poring over chatrooms, conversations.

"He was so sweet. I really think God made them adorable to tempt us

—and that's not a bad thing. Even the priests get away with it. They know these boys were meant to be loved."

Translation: "I'm entitled to rape. It's their fault for being appealing." Morrison pictured Evie's beautiful little face and covered his retching with a choked grunt. Decantor turned and looked across the room. Morrison swallowed hard and went back to the computer.

He clicked on the bar to message users privately, picturing the man on the receiving end: scraggly hair, sneering at the screen, Shannon locked up in the background, lips mangled and swollen and bloody. He paused, his trembling fingers poised over the keys.

Finally, he typed:

"The jugglers were always my favorite at the circus."

Morrison consulted the song lyrics from his desk drawer and finished:

"Don't get under those knives, motherfucker."

He hit send.

Somewhere, a phone rang. Morrison jumped, touched his pocket where Decantor's phone rested—it wasn't buzzing. Nor was his own cell. The words on the computer screen were hypnotic, pulling his attention from all else.

He searched through more of The Juggler's pages, looking for IP addresses or anything else he could use to track him. But The Juggler was well protected. Firewalls. Encryptions. Rerouting mechanisms. This asshole wasn't living in Kazakhstan, that was for damn sure—he was craftier than Morrison had given him credit for. Even his profile picture gave nothing away: a mask like one from a Mardi Gras parade, white, porcelain maybe, with black checks around the eyes and fangs, much like the clown face on the cover of one of the CDs he'd seen. In one thread The Juggler had bragged:

"Made it myself."

The bag that Xu had mentioned seeing the guy handing off…had he made a mask for a friend and taken it to him? Morrison tried not to picture that hideous mask. He didn't want to imagine that mask being the last thing his daughter saw before she was stomped to death.

Focus on the clues. Find them.

Morrison went back to the private message screen and typed:

"Also, I love your profile picture. Do you make masks for other people, too? If so, I'd love to buy one."

Cold. Find the cold. Too forward? Would he scare the guy off? He squinted at the computer, willing a response. Nothing. The words ran together on the page, swimming, then solidifying, wooziness pulling at him the more he stared. *I can't stop until I find her. I'll never stop.*

And these bastards wanted to be found, didn't they? Karen did, anyway. *Work your cases. You'll know where to find me.* That's what she'd said. So Morrison was supposed to find them. He'd be walking into an ambush, but he had no alternative.

Find him. Find them. Think, Surfer Boy.

Somewhere nearby, a phone rang again. Morrison eyed the phone on his desk, patted his pockets. Not his. He rubbed his eyes with his palms. He needed coffee. *No.*

He needed heroin.

One little prick and he'd finally remember how he knew Karen. But it was an excuse. Or was it? He could stop again—he'd done it before. And no one would ever have to know.

But Shannon's voice pealed through his head: "Evie needs you. I need you." Could he do that high? *Yes*, the drug whispered. *No*, he whispered back, less convincingly, his veins practically trembling with the memory of the drug, craving it, begging for it.

He was losing his mind. The phone rang again, and he looked up. The phone. Petrosky's phone. He leapt from his seat, stumbled over Petrosky's chair, and threw the receiver to his ear.

"Detective Petrosky?" Music blared in the background over the voice, a male voice, gruff and thick with what might have been liquor.

"This is Detective Morrison. How can I help you?"

"This is Zach."

Zachary Reynolds. The Juggler's first victim that they knew of and a connection to the kidnappers. A connection to his little girl, to his wife. Morrison sat at Petrosky's desk and opened the top drawer, rummaging for a pen and something to write on. He snapped open the drawer on the other side and found a nub of a pencil. No paper. "What can I do for you, Zach?"

"I found something. Or...maybe. I mean, I don't know if it's something, but Detective Petrosky asked me about that number."

"The number one." Morrison pulled a fast food bag from the first drawer and turned it inside out, throwing an old french fry to the floor and crushing it underfoot as if it were The Juggler he was stomping to death. The way Acosta had been stomped to death.

There was a sharp inhale on the line like the kid was smoking, and Morrison gritted his teeth against the pause, every synapse in his brain firing with impatience.

"Got this box in the closet. Shit I wanted to forget about. The scans and pictures of me in the hospital bed." Cancer. The kid had beat fucking *cancer* only to be raped and strangled. Some luck.

Another inhale on the line, this one longer, sharper. "Had some toys in there, things I forgot about. Cards and little teddy bears and shit. But one of them was this little brown bear with a Get Well Soon balloon sewed to his chest."

Morrison's nub of a pencil trembled over the bag.

"The balloon says 'You're number one.'"

Probably commercially produced, but... *Too much coincidence.* Morrison's heart palpitated, growing bigger with each beat, but his rib cage squeezed tighter and tighter around his lungs. "Zach, do you remember who gave it to you?"

This time the exhale was hard, as hard as if he were blowing up a balloon. "I don't know. I was out of it."

Morrison's stomach dropped. "Would your mom know?"

The music changed, and the bass vibrated through Morrison's hand and up to his elbow, rattling his already frayed nerves.

"Nah, she wasn't there all the time."

"Wasn't where?"

"At the hospital. Where I got it." Zach's voice was vaguely defensive.

Shit. He'd missed it. Hadn't Dylan Acosta's mother mentioned him being in the hospital, too? If that was how their pedophile was choosing his victims, grooming the kids while they were sick and vulnerable... "Emerald Grace, right?"

"Yeah." The music stopped so abruptly that Morrison felt he'd been pulled into an alternate universe where the world was wrapped in cotton. "You think I'll go back?" Zach said, his voice so low that Morrison had to strain to hear him.

"Back to the hospital?"

Zach was silent on the other end. Then: "I'm just tired of being scared." The line went dead, and the pressure in Morrison's chest erupted with heat. The kid was going to fucking kill himself.

32

Strings of multicolored Christmas lights and the finger paintings strung from the hospital walls did little to mask the scent of rubbing alcohol and some kind of lemon cleaning fluid. Morrison kept his eyes on the center of the corridor, footsteps echoing back to him in time to his heart. Both too fast. At least a phone call had verified that Zachary Reynolds was not in immediate danger from himself or otherwise: his mother was home with him, and he was most certainly fine—physically, anyway.

The halls in the children's ward were empty. Maybe morning rounds. He peered into the nearest room at a little black-haired child, scrawny body wasting away under a thin sheet. Air hissed through a tube into a cannula held under his nostrils by a piece of clear tape. At the kid's bedside, his mother slept, face planted into the foot of the bed, one hand on the child's leg. Connected.

Shannon was stuck in a collar. And Evie was alone.

The next kid was just as asleep as the first, the gentle glow from a light in the corner glistening on her bald head. Maybe the stabby killer worked here and shaved his head as a way to connect with the kids. A doctor maybe. A nurse. An orderly. Or maybe their rapist had shaved his scraggly hair, which is why no one recognized him now.

"Can I help you?" A young nurse with butterfly-print scrubs and an afro approached him: L. Freeman, according to her name tag. "Visiting hours don't start until ten, but if you want to wait in the cafeteria downstairs for fifteen minutes—"

He flashed his badge. "I'm not visiting. Looking for information."

Surprise registered in her eyes. "On who?" she whispered. "Are you family?"

Zachary Reynolds had been there too long ago for most current staff to remember any pertinent details. But Acosta—they might get lucky. If he could get her to cooperate. "I'm looking for a killer."

Her mouth fell open. She closed it again.

"Dylan Acosta was a patient here a year ago. Did you know him?"

She crooked a finger, and he followed her to the main desk where another nurse—short, thin, brunette—was bustling around with files. Morrison startled when a buzzer sounded, and the other nurse glanced at him, then rushed off to attend to it. Freeman watched her go.

"I...saw on the news what happened to Dylan. Killed at school, right? Just horrible." Her voice shook with emotion. She *had* known him.

"I need to know who he would have been in contact with," Morrison said, as softly as he could manage. "His doctors. Staff who had access to him."

She shook her head, crossed her arms—preparing for battle. "I'm sorry, I can't give that kind of information out. I'm not even supposed to tell you if he was a patient here."

She was right. But he didn't have time to waste on a warrant or on a fucking release from Dylan's mother. So why the hell was he here? He could get all the information he needed on the doctors just by looking at the hospital website. Same for the nursing staff. Maybe if he hacked into the database—but no, hospital websites were notoriously tricky. One wrong move and he'd shut the whole thing down. He didn't want to give the killers a chance to sew any more of Shannon together or carve her up like they did to Bell.

"But..." the nurse began, glancing over her shoulder, "if you can give me a date, I can tell you who was on duty without discussing individual patients." She punched a few buttons and looked at him expectantly.

He opened his mouth to talk. He had no idea. But it wouldn't have been just one day. It would have been multiple days. Acosta and Reynolds had been admitted with cancer, not broken bones.

"Dylan Acosta was here for a few weeks." And in that time...had the pedophile given him a gift? Like he had with Zachary Reynolds? Other parts of The Juggler's pattern had remained consistent over time. "Specifically, ma'am, I'm looking for someone who gave Dylan a toy. A teddy bear, maybe."

"A teddy bear? Sounds pretty common. They sell them in the gift shop downstairs."

"Outside of parents, are there staff members who sometimes give toys to the kids?"

She squinted at him. "Sometimes? Most of the kids need a little distraction, so that wouldn't be out of the question."

"Anyone who does it routinely?"

She shook her head.

"What about someone who takes a special interest in certain children? In Dylan?"

She studied the ceiling, the wall, then her eyes widened, and Morrison's heart picked up. *She's got something.*

"Actually...nothing out of the ordinary, mind you. But we have people who come in to cheer the kids up, and those are the ones whose job it is to distract, to play. To take an interest. It's not that we don't, but we can't always take the time to play as much as we'd like."

"No one's accusing you of being inattentive."

Her shoulders relaxed, but her mouth stayed tight. "The people I'm thinking of are volunteers from a company called Winning with Grinning. Incredibly nice, all of them. So kind to the kids."

"How often do they come?"

"Once a week. Usually Mondays. Sometimes they do puppet shows here in front of the reception desk...or magic. And they always bring something for the kids who're here—books or toys or games."

These people wouldn't be protected by HIPAA—they weren't patients. He had every right to their files. "Do you have records for the group? Names, addresses?"

She nodded slowly. "They would in HR. Anyone who has contact with our patients has to have a file. Background checks, vaccine records, all that. Especially with how ill some of our kids are."

Morrison glanced at the clock on the wall, ticking away precious seconds of his family's life. Felt the file under his arm. He'd almost forgotten.

He pulled out the photos and composite drawings and handed them to Freeman. "Any of these guys look familiar?"

She frowned at the bald man and shook her head. But slowly.

"Are you certain?"

"I'm... No. There's something familiar about him, but I can't place where I know him from. Maybe he was here visiting someone? But we get lots of people in and out. He definitely wasn't here regularly." Freeman flipped to the second photo, the scraggly brown hair, squirrelly face, and her eyes lit up. "This one, I know. He's here like clockwork. Missed this Monday, though."

Because he was busy behind Dylan's school—he was busy raping an innocent child.

She shook her head again. "But you can't possibly be looking for him. He's amazing. So sweet and always makes everyone laugh." She beckoned him around the counter and over to a back wall with a bulletin board covered with photos. In one, a guy in dreadlocks and a magician's hat held up a deck of playing cards, his face every bit as animated as the children who sat in a circle around him. In another, a woman had a puppet on each hand, mouth open, apparently talking in what looked like a silly voice for the green caterpillar on her right fist.

And...*him.* Morrison's heart skipped a beat.

He was cleaner than he'd been in Jenny's rendition of him, and his thin brown hair was covered with a yellow wig, though a few strands had come loose and were plastered to his cheek. His light eyes were just the right shape. His mouth. But in this photo, his squirrelly nose was covered with a red foam ball.

The Juggler was an actual clown.

33

An hour and a half later, Morrison had a photocopy of a driver's license with Michael Hayes's face on it—a face that looked like their suspect. And Hayes was here. In the city. With Shannon. With Evie.

According to the volunteer records pulled by the harried head of HR, Hayes worked full-time at a plant that manufactured nuts and bolts for the auto industry. More telling was Hayes's website: Paraphernalia for Performers, which offered custom masks, shoes, boots, and even puppets, all made to order. Looks like they could guess what he was bringing to his buddy outside of Xu's nail shop. He'd been married and divorced in the same year about four years ago—maybe his ex-wife had discovered his little fetish. His sickness. He'd look for her too, just in case. But later.

Now he drove.

Every traffic light seemed to take extra long, and he flipped on his flashing red and blues and shot through the intersections in a blaze of angry horns despite the police lights.

Fuck them. Fuck everyone. When he found the kidnappers, he would stomp them to death with their own fucking boots.

Michael Hayes's neighborhood was good, not great, with smooth asphalt and adequate streetlights but noise pollution from the nearby freeway. The house was just another two-story colonial on a block with a hundred nearly identical colonials, but The Juggler's house was somehow more formidable than the rest, despite its white aluminum siding, brown shutters, and curtained bay window. It was the basketball hoop—probably there to tempt neighborhood children onto the property—that seemed to buzz with the energy of a thousand angry hornets. On the backboard was a painting of a clown, its fangs dripping green venom into a puddle just below the ring.

How many kids had Hayes taken? How many had he raped? Killed? Morrison glanced up and down the street as he drove by, but no one was out besides the brilliant midday sun searing the new growth on the lawns. His chest tightened. At Hayes's home, the grass was newly cut, though not edged. Bushes grew too tall against the house, but the sides had been trimmed back from the walk. Someone lived here. He looked again at the backboard clown. The Juggler lived here.

Morrison drove by the house twice, then parked in a neighbor's driveway where four newspapers sat piled on the porch. They were probably on vacation. He shut the car off and got out, then climbed into the back seat, so he could watch, hidden partially by the headrest and the shadow of the carport, looking for...what? He tamped down thoughts of the blood on Shannon's seat back. Her head. And then her mouth... *Oh, fuck, stop thinking*. He breathed in the cold, let it take the fire from his belly.

Karen had taken her time kidnapping his wife—she was patient. Calculating. It had been a year since her first attempt to harm Shannon during that bullshit with Griffen. And Karen was smart enough not to hold Shannon here, in the middle of suburbia, with a highly visible creepy clown in the driveway.

He shouldn't be here. This wasn't the place. His wife, his child...they were somewhere else. Had to be.

But he couldn't stop himself. He was being pulled by something deep and wild—the house called to him. And while Shannon might not be here, he'd get The Juggler—Michael Hayes—to tell him where she was. Unless...Hayes was with Karen, with Shannon, in another location. A storage facility. A warehouse. He'd never find them then.

But someone had cut the grass recently—if it had been a lawn service, they would have completed the edging too. Someone *lived* here. With another glance down the road, Morrison exited the car and crossed the street. The air was still heavy and wet with yesterday's storms. Had that been only yesterday? It seemed like an eternity had passed.

He hooked around the garage and pressed his body flush against the wall, creeping slowly past two garbage cans to the back of the property. The stink of rotting trash singed his nostrils. When was trash pickup? He wished he could see inside the garage, to know whether the car registered to Hayes was here. He'd find out soon enough.

Behind the cans, he scaled a chain-link fence and crossed a cement patio to the first window. No noises came from inside—no scuffle of a shoe, and though he held his breath, he heard no cry that might have been Evie. Stomach twisting, he scanned the bottom of the building, seeking glass block windows, a vent, anything to indicate a basement. Nothing but a slab foundation. His family wasn't being held below.

Slowly, Morrison leaned his forehead against the glass and peered inside. He was looking into a laundry room, dim with drawn blinds. Plenty of grime on the window, but from what he could see through a gap near the sill, the room was empty. He strained his ears, squinted up at the second story. There'd be a couple of bedrooms up there, maybe a bath. But when he stepped back, he saw that the windows were open, just like those in front, curtains swaying softly in the warm breeze that was rotting the garbage. *They're not here.* It would be too easy to overhear the wails of a starving baby, the muffled screams of a woman having her mouth sewn—he retched, swallowed. No one would use this place as a dungeon.

He crept across the cement, thankful for his stealthy Toms. On the other side of the patio, he could see into the kitchen, lit by the sun, see the bowl on the countertop, fruit flies and fat houseflies buzzing around something on a cutting board. Something...wet. Dark. *Please let it be animal meat.* Bile rose in his throat, and Morrison visualized the cold coming back in before the panic pulled him from what he needed to do.

He ducked under the window and around to the last section of the house, where the home protruded farther over the cement. A glass door opened onto the patio, blue light flickering from a television inside. There were no other lights on inside that he could see. He peered around the corner, hearing only silence, and crept closer to the glass door. With one final inhale, he peeked into the living room and—

The phone in his pocket buzzed suddenly, and he snapped his head back so quickly he was certain that the sound of his temple cracking against the brick would rouse the man from the couch.

A mere six feet away. Michael Hayes. He looked exactly like Jenny, the tattoo artist, had drawn him.

Plan. You need a plan.

Making as little noise as possible, Morrison flew back along the patio on his tiptoes, then leapt the fence and ran around the garage to his car. They had cameras on this place. They knew he was there. Hayes's friends were killing his family now, were calling to tell him his family was dead.

The cell buzzed a third time.

But no, it was Decantor's phone, the caller ID blinking with a New York number. The phone Morrison had taken so anyone watching his cell would not know he'd contacted Karen Palmer's mother. He slammed the car into drive, trying desperately not to squeal the tires or call any attention to himself before he had a chance to think. He'd found the bastard. He'd go back to Hayes's while the man still lay on the couch. If he could do it without anyone knowing he was there, he wouldn't risk his family's life. He'd search to make sure the other suspects weren't there with Hayes, then look through cupboards, drawers, closets for clues to his family's whereabouts.

But if he found nothing, he'd need a bargaining chip. Could Roger help? It was the only card he had left to play, the only other thing she'd asked him for.

The phone. "Detective Morrison." He turned down another side street and headed toward the main drag where he could blend in with the other motorists.

"Yes, my name is Hilary Palmer, and I received a message from you earlier. Something about an identity theft case?"

"Thank you for calling back, Mrs. Palmer." *Don't sugar coat it. No time.* "I'm sure this seems a bit out of the blue, but I'm working on a homicide that seems to be linked to your daughter's identity."

Silence.

"Mrs. Palmer?"

"My Karen?"

"The woman I'm looking for is using your daughter's name. Has been for a few years. I believe she stole your daughter's identity after she died."

The silence stretched, amplifying the sounds around him. A car backfired somewhere up ahead, behind the shrill squawk of a bird. Had she hung up?

"I know who took her identity."

Morrison's hand cramped around the receiver. "Who?"

"Do you know why I got involved with Moms Against Bullying?" Her voice was cold, harder than before—and there was the longing, the grief that he heard every day in Petrosky's hello, in the way his partner asked about lunch. Palmer wasn't hiding it now, not like she was on her voicemail recording.

Tell me who! He stopped at a red light and put on his blinker, looking for a parking lot where he could pull over inconspicuously. "No, ma'am, I don't know why you got involved with them." And it occurred to him that he should have known. He should have dug deeper. Which meant he'd missed something critical. *You see me, but you don't.* The light changed, and Morrison put his foot on the gas, resisting the urge to tell her to hurry up. To hurry because something terrible could be happening to *his* child right now.

"Karen was such a happy child," she said. "She played in the band, worked after school, had friends. Her best friend, though...she was something else. Got her involved in little petty trouble. I got a call one day that they'd been shoplifting. *Shoplifting.* Karen said Janey wanted to see if they could get away with it."

Janey. The name pinged a little memory somewhere in Morrison's subconscious, but he couldn't place it. His brain was scrambled. *Think, or you might as well let them die.*

"Janey what?"

"Krantz."

His heart hammered against his ribs. Danny's last name. But Danny didn't have a sister, and she was too old to have come around after the fact. A niece? Cousin?

Palmer coughed, and it was a phlegmy sound as if she was swallowing tears, but when she spoke again, her voice was harder—angry. "I tried to keep them apart, but they gravitated toward one another. And then they started college. My husband and I were moving to New York, so Karen decided to come, go to college there. Janey stayed back in California. I thought that'd be the end of it."

The cell buzzed in his pants pocket, and it took him a moment to register that he had Decantor's phone in his hand already. His own cell phone was ringing. No...not a call. A text. *Shit.*

Palmer blew her nose. "Karen had a hard time; depression, anxiety, you name it. Then Janey cut her wrists, ended up in the hospital. And it seemed like"—her voice hitched—"like Karen blamed herself. After Karen died, I found messages from Janey to Karen. Awful things. A few little knocks here and there, but later, the texts were blatantly aggressive, encouraging her to hurt herself. And she listened. Karen took sleeping pills, but she never made it to the hospital like Janey did."

The phone buzzed again—*oh, fuck*—and he tried to grab it out, but the blare of a car horn made him swerve back into his lane. He fumbled his cell to the floor. *Fuck, fuck, fuck.* What if it was Shannon? Or the kidnapper? But this woman was telling him about the kidnapper. Palmer might hold the clue he needed to find her, to find his family.

"I tried to file charges against Janey," Palmer was saying, "but bullying isn't really a crime." She sniffed. "Janey should have to pay for what she did."

So what was he dealing with? Psychopaths didn't usually try to kill themselves—they didn't feel enough pain to merit escape. Narcissists didn't often commit suicide either; if a narcissist made a threat or slashed their wrists, it was probably to manipulate someone else, not because they truly wanted to die. But Karen—Janey—wanted him to suffer because Morrison had hurt someone she'd cared about. Narcissists might pretend to care, but they typically lacked the empathy for any meaningful bond to form. But this Janey woman—she felt. She felt everything too deeply.

Janey had manipulated people in the past, driven them to the edge, and pushed them off. And if she had emotionally tortured Karen from the opposite side of the continent, what was she doing to Shannon, right now? She knew how long it took to weaken people. How long it would take her to weaken Shannon.

Ahead, a driveway approached, a dry cleaners. He put on his blinker, resisting the urge to blare the horn at the driver in front of him. Shannon didn't deserve this pain. Evie didn't deserve to lose her mother. Evie didn't deserve to die.

But then again, neither had Danny. And Janey wanted to avenge his death. For years, the madness must have grown, festering like his dreams until she'd embraced the ferocity inside her, birthing cruelty and aggression until there was nothing left but revenge. She'd found Morrison, stalked him, taken her time planning her attack. She'd convinced Griffen to channel his rage into Shannon, into Morrison, to destroy their lives. And when Griffen failed to do it…

Now Janey had sought out men who really were capable of murder. Men who hurt others for the fun of it. And she'd turned these maniacs loose on his wife. She'd had them take his baby. His hand, wet with sweat, slipped, and he gripped the wheel so hard his knuckles ached. If he burst into Hayes's house, gun drawn, and hauled the man out—Janey would surely have a contingency plan. She'd take it out on his girls. He needed to find where they were before he—

"Detective?" Palmer's voice was tight, worried, but he couldn't find a way to respond. He screeched into a parking lot, slammed the car into park, and scrambled for the phone.

Text message:

"Roger's gone, or she's gone. You want them back, you do it tonight."

And below it a photo.

Oh, god, no.

Evie's onesie. Torn in half. Streaks of red covering the arm, the side, the neckline. Blood? They were going to kill his baby. Maybe she was already halfway there, the life ebbing from her drop by drop.

He felt it then, a swelling in his belly, the blistering fire that he'd hidden, the one he'd tried to keep dulled with drugs, the one he'd stomped out again and again and again since the day they'd found his father dead, shot by some asshole who just wanted the store register. The beast was waking up. But he had to keep going. Pretending. Pretending to be normal. Pretending he wasn't carrying a monster within him.

He needed more time. He needed to go see Roger.

"Detective?"

He hung up the phone.

Arrest him…or kill him. Janey didn't care, and as Shannon's bloodied mouth flashed in his mind's eye, as Evie's wails of pain lit up his eardrums, neither did he. *Work your cases.* She wanted to put him in an impossible position. Needing to fix it and being unable to do a fucking thing. He'd felt that same sense of helplessness too, so many years ago, staring down at Danny's lifeless, broken body. And so had she.

But she would feel helpless again when he watched her bleed.

He would kill Karen, Janey, whatever the fuck her name was. And so help him, if they'd hurt his family, not a one of them would get out alive.

"I BECAME INSANE WITH LONG INTERVALS OF HORRIBLE SANITY."
~EDGAR ALLAN POE TO GEORGE W. EVELETH, JANUARY 4, 1848

34

Janey downed the rest of her wine and sank into the bathwater, listening to the footfalls in the next room, the telltale clack of the boots Adam always wore. The water suddenly felt too warm as if she were heating it with her fury.

The rage never went away, not anymore. She inhaled the scent of soap, trying to ground herself in the moment, but her back stayed rigid. *Fuck.* Danny had been perfect—the only one who'd ever understood her. He might as well have been her brother the way he patted her hand when something inside her snapped out of nowhere, and all the feelings burbled angrily to the surface like froth, seeking escape. And the depression that would follow those episodes, the ugly hole that would open inside her—every time, she saw it coming, knew it was coming, yet still couldn't avoid falling into the darkness. And he would just sit. Hold her hand. He was the only thing in her life worth clinging to.

And Curt had taken Danny from her.

Danny had said they were family, and his shining eyes had made her believe it. But the others—those who had loved Danny too—grieved him and ignored her, ostracized her, even. Everywhere she turned were such hateful people, trying to hurt her in one way or another. They said she was crazy. That she was broken. They left Danny's photos lying around just to taunt her, to make her cry.

And worse, they blamed her—for not acting sooner, for not calling an ambulance, for lying down beside his cooling body and falling asleep. It wouldn't have mattered. They hadn't seen his face. His blue lips. His body, broken on the floor of his bedroom, a few stray ants from the shattered tank still struggling in his blood. They hadn't seen the congealing gore clinging to the corner of the end table.

She had tried to become someone else so many times, altering every little snippet of her personality, every little quirk, convinced each was the cause of her misery—and every time, Danny held her hand when she realized she'd been wrong. Again. If Danny had lived, she'd have found peace by now, surely. She'd have been a better person. The day her last husband left her, she had decided: Curt had destroyed what she could have become by taking away her lifeline. Now he would pay.

She had moved to Ash Park. Gotten a job. And watched. Waited. Once, while following him, she'd come face to face with him in the grocery store, and there had not been even a flicker of recognition. He'd forgotten her, discarded her as completely as if she were a piece of trash. He'd destroyed her life and didn't even remember her. How it had stung.

But now he'd never forget—not as he had before when she was just Janey, useless to him, not even worth remembering. Now she had something of his that was just as dear to him as Danny had been to her. And now she had help, help more reliable than the insufferable Frank Griffen.

Somewhere in the other room, something shattered, and her heart rate climbed. Adam hadn't once tried to hurt her, but she'd seen signs of his rage simmering below the surface, seen the way he became silent and still when she tried to tell him how to do something, the way he froze and averted his eyes when she said anything, *anything* he didn't agree with.

She tried to make it up to him on those black sheets, but he closed his eyes there too—couldn't even get hard. The day he'd sewn Shannon's lips shut was the first time he'd actually responded to her sexual advances, stayed with her, looked at her when he came. Better than what Roger had done—he'd whispered Shannon's name once while they were fucking. Even if Curt had ended up marrying someone else, she would have killed Shannon anyway.

She rolled onto her side and submerged her face in the water, feeling the pressure of the liquid as her ears filled, the water muting the sounds in the house. Bubbles escaped from her mouth and crawled along her skin toward the water's surface like fingers tracing a path from her lips to her ear where the bubble burst above water.

Her lips. Blessedly untouched by a needle. But she had other scars, and her lover liked them. His eyes had lit up the day her sleeve had hiked a touch too high, and he'd seen the butterfly bandage on her wrist, though he hadn't said a thing. He'd been too timid.

He'd gotten over that, it seemed. She'd wanted help hurting Curtis Morrison, but he might no longer be there for the sole purpose of meeting her needs. He might be there for the blood. And if that were true, she would never be able to control him. And she didn't want to bear the brunt when the last of his anxiety melted, and the hostility in his eyes was stoked into an inferno.

He'd told her he had an errand Monday morning, that he was going to the store to get coffee. When she came home that evening, his boots had been in the bathtub, covered in mud. And there'd been no coffee. Just the newspaper the next day, the boy at the playground, found dead. But it didn't make any sense. The kid had nothing to do with her or with their goals, and the paper said they were looking for two killers—she didn't know anything about another guy. Was Adam working with someone else too? Or did he...like boys? Was his lack of sexual interest in her because he was a pedophile?

She couldn't even consider it. That wasn't in the plan.

Then there was the girl he'd told her about, whispered it like a confession while he picked at her lower back with his fingernails. Said he did it for her, but she didn't know the woman, only that he'd followed her home from Curt's. He'd insisted they needed the phone to punish Curt more, mess with him. And Adam had looked so...concerned, practically begging for approval with those big puppy dog eyes. But she knew his motives were deeper than wanting to help her. The night after he'd killed that girl, she'd heard him moaning while he dreamed.

Had Adam fucked her? Rage simmered in her belly. She'd kill him if he had.

The mask stared at her from its stand on the sink, and her heart quickened. He'd told her it was a symbol of status, an updated replica of a doctor's mask that had been used during the black plague. But when he wore it, it was as if he became someone else. Without it, he chewed his fingernails. He couldn't meet her eyes. As soon as it was strapped onto his face, he stood straighter, as if the mask made him feel different, made him feel worthy.

Made him feel strong.

35

They hadn't come back, not once since they snapped her photo. Karen smiling over the smartphone screen, the beaked man—gone. Evie, gone. And Shannon felt herself creeping ever more quickly toward the brink of madness.

She could not hear her baby. She could not feel her baby. But she *could* feel. God, how she wished she couldn't.

Her lips throbbed, hot and painful with every beat of her heart, each pulse bringing with it the sweet, putrid stink of coming infection—though that might have been her imagination. Her legs were rigid with the strain of holding herself upright, frozen brittle with terror, and her arms ached from fruitlessly picking at the lock. For hours, maybe days, she had tried to free herself from the evil contraption on her neck, bloodying her shirt still more every time she shifted to pick at the lock from another angle.

The needle dug violently into her palm now, but she was unable to loosen her grip as if the sharp prick of pain would tether her to the closet, to this world—a lifeline, capable of keeping her awake and vertical. But so far, the needle hadn't helped her escape. And there was no way to hang from the collar unless she wanted to slit her own throat or strangle to death. No chance for reprieve even for a moment.

It would be so easy to take a step forward, neck against the blades, and just be done. Who knew what other atrocities they were capable of? Morrison should have been here by now, but they wouldn't keep her alive unless they knew they wouldn't be found. She was on her own. And whatever they had planned—it would surely be worse than death.

The air hissed through her nostrils, but it hitched occasionally as if trying to tell her to stop breathing, to just let go. The blackness in front of her eyes called to her, the quiet void of eternity, and she envisioned herself walking toward it, a sharp pang in the throat, warm, soft wetness, and then—

The sour reek of milk from her shirt called her back. Her daughter needed her. Evie could not escape without her. She gripped the needle still harder, the metal digging into the meat of her palm, and gritted her teeth against the scream that desperately wanted to escape her sutured lips. *Evie.* She imagined her daughter's face, her legs, her smile. Her tiny feet, barely kicking. Barely moving.

Shannon raised her aching arms and jammed the needle into the lock.

36

The house was colder than it had been yesterday. Damper too. Morrison's cheeks were wet, though he wasn't entirely convinced they were his cheeks and not someone else's. His eyes watered feverishly. Aggression? Sadness? *Madness.* It was irrelevant. Nothing mattered, nothing but this.

He walked into the living room and opened a window. The screen was tight, but not stuck, and he removed it and set it on the floor. The couch Roger had sat on yesterday seemed smaller, or perhaps everything else just loomed larger now as if his world had shrunk with Evie's desperate wail. *She isn't dead yet; she isn't dead.* Morrison's ear was bruised and sore after that last call from Janey, from pressing the device so tight against his face that he feared he'd break it.

The photos on the mantel belonged to another life, another world—Shannon and Roger, both smiling with un-sutured lips and very much alive. Beside the photo, an angel holding the scales of justice. The one from Roger's office? Had he taken it home from work and stuck it there, or did he have one in every room, holding court over every place he was? Roger had probably always seen himself that way—not simply a purveyor of justice, but justice itself. But justice was dead. The deer above the mantel glared.

Morrison picked up the statue, leaving streaks of blood across the figurine's white marble skirt, marring the mantel, too, with gore. He walked the statue to the body and dropped it. It rolled from chest to arm to floor, dully clicking as it caught the button on Roger's shirt. Justice was rarely clean, but the once pristine statue settling among the carnage —that was the last thing he wanted to see here tonight as if Lady Justice herself was admonishing him, condemning him for what he'd done, for the butchery. Not that it mattered.

He'd done it for Shannon. For Evie. And now he would find them.

He started at the back of the house with the gas can, fuel spreading in heady, oily snakes over tile, carpet, wood. The fumes turned his stomach, made him dizzy, but no more than anything else he'd seen and done that evening. He gagged. But the dizziness, the nausea, the burning in his gut, all of it belonged to someone else.

He could almost pretend that he wasn't really here. He could almost pretend that the deep crimson shimmering on his hands was just paint.

But it wasn't.

In the kitchen, he emptied the gasoline over boots, jeans, a button-down shirt. Roger's cufflinks glinted accusingly from the floor, just outside those dead wrists, but Morrison didn't look, just spilled, splashing the fuel over the floor, over the body, and onto the towel he'd used to conceal the man's face. For though Morrison was desperate, he could not bring himself to stare into those eyes—swollen and wide and dead. Just like Danny.

He turned his back on the body and grabbed the files from the deposit box, then set the packet on the floor beside the blood-soaked towels, pouring gasoline over all of it, watching as the papers absorbed it like they were thirsty enough to chug the poison, knowing it would be their end. A few renegade drops of fuel flitted through the air and struck the cabinets, streaking the cupboard doors. Leaving the finish in ruin. He tossed the empty can to the floor and walked out back.

The glass bottle was where he'd left it, filled with fuel, a rag protruding from its neck. Morrison lit it, waited a moment for it to catch, and then hurled it through the open window as he backed away down the walkway to the side yard and into the trees. He was parked one block over, well behind the lake where no one would see him.

Not loud, a subtle clank, a whoosh, a crackle. Soon it would roar, but he'd be gone before then. Shannon. Evie. *I'm coming, baby.*

Sometimes justice was nearly silent. Morrison took off across the yard, choking on unshed tears.

37

"It's done. What's the next step?"

HE SAT on the floor in his bedroom, guitar at his side, absently plucking at a single string. Waiting for them to call.

He texted again:

"Can I come to get them now?"

Nothing.

He tried calling next, but no one answered. Shannon's voice-mail greeting made tears prick in his eyes. Janey wanted to tell him where Shannon was, didn't she? But the phone stayed silent, save for Decantor's calls from his precinct extension—probably about brainstorming the case. He let them roll over to voice mail.

Janey had said to take care of Roger if he wanted his family back. But it had been hours now. He was no longer confident that she'd tell him where to find them, or whether she'd text him with other instructions. And was there anything at this point that he wouldn't do? He was already in too deep—whether he got his family back or not, he was in a lot of trouble. But Shannon and Evie were all that mattered. If he couldn't get them back safely, what happened to him was irrelevant.

The drug called to him now like a song in his heart. She'd said that once he knew who she was, he'd know where to find her, but all he knew was that she had cared about Danny. That she blamed him for Danny's death. He'd gone back to the hospital, in case, but no one recognized her photo. And Janey Krantz didn't come up in any birth certificate searches —she wasn't Danny's sister, and there were no other family members with that name. Had Janey always hidden her real name? Must have. But how? Why? She'd been a kid then. If she was adopted, her records might be sealed, but...

Janey had his family, and she was trying to punish him. And he couldn't even fucking remember her, other than a vague scratching in the back of his brain, an answer just out of reach. If only he could recall—

You can't get your family if you're all fucked up.

But the whisper of sweet relief had swelled to a dull roar, and every word had teeth, gripping him and pulling him in. He needed her name. Needed to know who she was. And if it helped him remember...

He had the remnants of the baggie, still had the syringe Petrosky had used. Sweat popped out on his forehead, and slices of memory teased at the edges of his consciousness. He leaned his head back against the bed. *You can do this. Remember her. And if you can't, if it doesn't help, you can go back out and keep investigating.*

He'd been sitting on the bed in Danny's bedroom. There was an ant farm on the end table. A few schoolbooks.

And they weren't alone. There were other voices, girls.

My turn!

No, I'm next.

Two meaningless lines, innocuous and on a continuous loop as if someone had broken a DVD and sent it spinning over this same swatch of memory again and again and again. But no new information, no images of family or friends or lovers. Where had Danny met them? Had he said?

One little prick of the needle.

He was rationalizing. Trying to find a reason why using would make sense.

And those reasons did exist, though he'd tried not to consider them. Tried and failed, oh so many times. State-dependent memory. Some people reported miraculous recoveries of memories long forgotten—once they were in the right state.

But he feared the blanks in his memory were far too wide. And were the blackouts due to trauma or the drug? He'd tried once before to recall that night, hopped up on booze. It hadn't been the same, though he hadn't been in the same panicked state as he had been the night Danny died.

He was plenty panicked now.

Outside his window, the night thickened with darkness, his hope dwindling as dawn crept toward him, the phone utterly silent. He only had one syringe—not that Petrosky was diseased. Hell, it probably didn't matter. *What's a little blood shared between friends?* They were all one step from the grave anyway.

Morrison's cell rang. He jumped at it, but it wasn't Shannon's number. It was one he didn't recognize.

He put the phone to his ear without saying hello.

"Need you over at Roger's, Morrison." Decantor. Borrowing someone else's cell to call him. "There's been an incident."

An *incident*. Not an *accident*.

Yes. There had.

THE REMAINS of Roger's home glistened under the street lamps and spotlights, each beam catching water droplets left behind by the firemen. The front door, once so thick and imposing, had been reduced to a blistered, splintered pile on the porch, blackened with char and water. While the brick columns and window frames were still intact—strong and sturdy behind the soot—the windows themselves lay in shards on the ground surrounding the house, and the vacant openings left by their absence were like eyes, glaring at Morrison, judging him for what he'd done.

He ducked under the remains of the entryway, ignoring the protests of the firefighters, and followed flashlights and voices into what was left of the kitchen, where the corpse was being loaded into a black body bag. A charred finger peeked out from between the teeth of the zipper, accusing him. Morrison wasn't sure if he was sorry. He stared at the finger until the tech closed the bag and loaded it onto the gurney. The body moved with improbable lightness, and Morrison realized it was because the fat would have sizzled off in chunks and melted into the wood floor.

"Definitely arson," Decantor said. "Motive's unclear, but it isn't like Roger had no enemies."

"Was he dead before the fire?" Morrison asked, even though he knew the answer.

"Have to wait for the ME on that one."

Morrison toed the broken glass figurine and wondered how long he had before they figured out it was him. When he looked up, Decantor was eyeing him, an unlit cigarette perched between his lips. Since when did Decantor smoke?

"I can let you know when they have forensics back on it," Decantor said. "On him. Couple days. Hopefully, there'll be a trace of whoever did this."

There probably would be. But according to Janey, he only had one more day. And if he failed, nothing else mattered anyway.

Decantor was staring at him. Morrison nodded and turned to leave.

"Wait—"

Morrison's back stiffened.

"You get a hold of Shannon?"

No. "Yeah."

Decantor cleared his throat. "I never heard back from her. To get her statement about Natalie Bell." Decantor was scrutinizing him, and Morrison didn't like the look in his eyes.

"I'm sure she forgot," he said carefully. "Vacation and all." *And her lips are sewn shut.*

"Right." Decantor did not look convinced, just stared at Morrison as if the gaze could crack him. *He's suspicious.*

But Morrison was beyond that. He'd already cracked open, and the secret, brutal parts of himself had been unleashed. He glanced in the direction they'd taken the body bag.

"If you hear from her—"

"I'll have her call you. Until then, let's concentrate on Bell and Acosta. And now"—Morrison gestured to the charred remains around them—"this."

"Any progress on the case?" Decantor asked. "Missed you yesterday, I thought we were going to brainstorm. I called you a few times last night."

Yes, he had called. And Morrison had ignored him.

"I went to bed early," Morrison said. "I have a whole lot of nothing anyway." He paused at the smile lighting up Decantor's face. "Did you find something?"

"I got a hit on one of the sketches—our rapist. Guy at the automotive plant said he works with him over there. And get this—there's no record, but this guy from the plant said he heard a rumor that our suspect's wife divorced him because she caught him abusing her daughter, his stepchild. Elementary school age. Sick fuck."

Michael Hayes. The Juggler. Morrison's throat closed.

"Want to take a ride over there?"

He shook his head. He already knew what they'd find at the house. Morrison's phone hung, heavy and silent, in his pocket. *I did what the fuck you asked, why aren't you calling me?* He needed to think of a plan in case that call never came.

Decantor leaned close, away from the techs bustling around on what remained of the floor. "Listen, I heard a rumor. About Petrosky."

Of course he had. "You don't say."

"Hey man, what's going on with you?" Decantor squinted, his brows furrowed. "You're not...yourself."

None of them knew who he was. What he was.

Neither did he.

38

Edward Petrosky started the day with a shivering in his muscles, rancid liquid in his bowels, and bile streaming from his nose.

Fucking hell.

He'd told them that he'd used. Told them he needed help. He didn't—one use didn't do jack except make you want more of it.

And he did want more. There had been two blessed hours where he'd felt something other than the crushing despair which followed him every day like a shadow that had the ability to stab him in the fucking face. The heroin hadn't made him happy; it had made him better than happy. It had detached him from the pain that'd been wrapped around his throat since Julie died.

And the pain was back, especially now that they'd swiped his cigarettes. Since when was smoking forbidden in a rehab ward? If he wanted to kill himself slowly and perfectly legally, that was his own fucking business. When he got out, he was going to haul one of these twatweasels up on charges just for fucking fun.

The irritability was probably a side effect of withdrawal, but the pain in his chest was not. Walking Shannon down the aisle had been one of the happiest moments of his life since Julie was born and by far the best thing that had happened since Julie's death. When he'd held Evie the day she was born, still pink and warm from Shannon's body, he'd finally had a family again. And now that family was going to be taken away while he rotted inside this prison.

He hauled himself to the bathroom and did his business, his jaw clenched tight as his stomach lurched. Back by his bed, he drank the tepid piss they called coffee and nibbled a slice of dry toast. He never thought he'd miss Morrison's granola, but holy fuck did he ever. He'd keep that to himself once he got out of here.

And he could walk out. Sign himself out AMA. But if the kidnappers—murderers—wanted him here, then they surely had someone on the inside monitoring him. Probably enjoying the shitshow. But all the diarrhea and irritability in the world weren't going to keep him in his room while the day passed him by. Not while Shannon and Evie were in danger. Not while Morrison was in danger.

The common room was already bustling with residents as Petrosky settled onto a threadbare couch, probably riddled with dust mites and years' worth of imprints from other users' asses. Against the wall was some skinny twerp, maybe a coke head, sitting next to an overweight dude who was probably here as a function of probation, his cocky gaze showing everyone he didn't need no fucking help, though he was probably the one who'd end up needing it most in the end. It was always the ones who went down slow who seemed to forget that life existed somewhere else.

All the shuffling addicts were trapped there together, yet no one spoke. Three men in the corner stood close enough to strike up a conversation, but each merely stared in a different direction like some wholly depressing Renaissance painting. And none of them so much as glanced his way. If one of these guys was the informant, they'd at least have been interested in Petrosky's presence—after all, it was their fault he was here. Without his fucking cigarettes. He swallowed bile and headed to the nurses' station.

The on-duty nurse was young and pretty, with teeth that stood out brilliant white against her skin. But the bags under her eyes revealed her exhaustion. Watching people destroy themselves all goddamn day wasn't easy.

"Good morning, Mr. Petrosky."

"Detective."

Her smile faltered. "Of course, Detective. Did you need your pills?"

They wanted him to take some drug that would help with the tobacco cravings, but goddammit, they could kiss his ass. "No thanks."

"Sir, part of the program is—"

"I understand. You want compliance. But I don't want to take more drugs to get off the first ones, all right?"

"Detective, tobacco and heroin withdrawal can be—"

"I appreciate your position. But I'm okay. I'd have symptoms if I weren't." And he sure wasn't about to tell them how he really felt—the sick nastiness in his guts. "I'll let you check my blood pressure all day long." He leaned toward the window. "You could let me have a cigarette."

"Nice try." She shook her head and smiled kindly, probably trying like hell not to roll her eyes.

"Just one."

She looked past him into the room. Looked down. Wrote something on a piece of paper. Looked up again and met his eyes. "Oh, you're still here?" Now her smile was sarcastic. "Answer's the same." She waved him away, this time with her middle finger.

He liked her better every minute. Even better than he had yesterday when he'd sat in the back of the room trying to figure out how to get into the locked cubicle she was in now, where the computer was. She'd just sat there, pretending to ignore him but watching him out of the corner of her eye. He could always tell.

"How about a deck of cards?"

She appraised him. "Have you checked the table in the back?"

"I will now. Thank you."

He felt her eyes on his back, probably trying to tell if he was wobbly on his feet like he had been last night. Maybe wondering if he was about to have a heart attack or a goddamn seizure. He strode to the back of the room, taking extra care to walk square and stiff and probably looking like a fucking penguin, trying as he was not to shit himself.

The cards were on the back table right where she said they would be. He pulled them from the pack and shuffled, attempting to look nonchalant to conceal the fact that he was scoping out the other residents. There was a cocky-looking asshole in the back who didn't meet the description of any of their bad guys, and he was way too overtly jerky to be playing low-key. Petrosky turned his attention to the guys in the front corner, still all standing with slack expressions and pock-marked faces. Probably on heavy legal drugs, helping them come down from even heavier illegal ones. Not a good choice for an inside informant, but this Karen girl wasn't necessarily smart. Just manipulative. And patient as fuck.

He dealt solitaire.

He hated solitaire.

He fucking sucked at solitaire.

Three games. Four. Five. The nurse caught his eye, and he lifted the deck and nodded to her. She smiled and went back to her prescriptions or whatever she was doing behind the counter. Would she make a good informant? Probably.

Hell, probably not. She seemed too…genuine. He'd met a lot of perps, and he could see guilt like he'd be able to see a third nostril, knew whether they deserved to be handcuffed before he could tell you what they'd done. And the hairs on the back of his neck prickled now at the sound of another person breathing behind him. He resisted the impulse to turn around and look.

"One of my favorites." The voice was low, hoarse, the sound of someone who had damaged his vocal cords smoking bad crack or who'd had an unfortunate run-in with a kung fu master and got sucker punched in the trachea.

"Not mine," Petrosky said, dealing the cards again. "Turns out playing against myself, I can't win for shit." A steady *shh shh* crept into his awareness behind him, and he glanced down and saw the head of the broom, sweeping breakfast crumbs from under his seat into a messy pile next to the guy's shoes. No, not shoes. *Boots.* Like biker boots, but not—high from the outline through his taupe uniform pants, made of faux leather and adorned with buckles across the top of his foot. Treads bigger than were necessary for any self-respecting man. Not that this meant much— Morrison's hair was longer than any self-respecting man's should be, though at least his hair didn't look like it could leap from its owner and stomp you to death. Unlike this asshole's fucking boots.

Petrosky glanced up at the medication window and waved to the nurse again, who was now watching the pair of them from under a cocked eyebrow.

"No one likes to play alone if they don't have to, I guess." The man spoke softly, but there was a note of agitation to it. Irritation or fear? Their suspect had a fear of rejection, got worked up about challenges to his masculinity if McCallum was right. Petrosky stiffened and stared at his own feet again, keeping his face placid as he could manage. *I know what you are, fucker.* And soon as he was able, he was going to take this jerkwad down.

The man made no further effort to correct the mess on the floor but shuffled around the table toward the other chair. Petrosky squinted at the boots again. On the inside, near the heel, a set of hammered copper panels were sewn to the boot, mud or dog shit squished between the panel and the boot tread in the tiny, imperfect crevice. *Fucking fancy.* Looked homemade, too. Petrosky wondered if he knew how to make spikes. But surely, he did. He was flaunting it, teasing him. It was a slap in the goddamn face. He had to know Petrosky was aware of who he was, and the fact that he didn't seem concerned made Petrosky's heart rate climb. If this guy didn't care about getting caught—was the damage already done? Were Shannon and Evie already dead? Was the guy on a suicide mission? What?

Unless he was just there for Petrosky. Maybe he wanted to spill. From the sounds of his heavy breath, the guy was practically salivating with the thrill of *almost* discovery. Almost. This dude was a fucking idiot.

Dude? Now he was thinking like Morrison. His heart seized at the thought of Shannon and Evie, and he resisted the urge to grab the broom and shove it up the guy's ass for what he'd done to Shannon's face. Hopefully, this bastard hadn't done worse since that photo on Morrison's phone. And if he had... Petrosky's fist clenched, but he released it, sighed far more loudly than was necessary, and collected the cards into a pile. "Want to play? I can't do this shit anymore."

A *thunk* noise, wood on mortar, probably the broom being propped against the wall. "I suppose," the guy said softly. "I am due for a break."

Petrosky finally glanced up as the guy circled the table. Bald, shorter than Petrosky, thin— he'd fit the stats of the booted killer at the Acosta scene. No visible tattoos, but a stippling of pockmarks ran along his jaw. Some might have been pimples, even infected blackheads, but others were deeper as if he'd been digging for something in his face with a needle. Sicko had probably enjoyed that shit.

But his most striking feature was the lack of wrinkles—not a single age spot. This guy was *really* young, nineteen or twenty, especially with the acne. Just a fucking kid. He *had* been learning—McCallum's shrinky ass was right. He'd been watching the pedophile. Maybe watching Karen. His gaze was dead and dark, even when he smiled, but his black eyebrows had a touch of blond coming through at the corners like he'd done a shitty dye job. That explained the half-blond-half-black hair at the Bell crime scene, the one they'd used to type his DNA. The guy's gaze flicked to the nurses' station, and when the nurse looked their way, he sat quickly, averting his eyes though he could not hide the brief quiver in his jaw. Fearful. But as Petrosky watched, the man's face hardened—fear and *rage*. McCallum was fucking good.

A badge on his shirt said *Adam: Xtreme Clean Janitorial*. Fake name? Probably an independent cleaning company, unrelated to the rehab center. Looked like the center paid ex-patients for mentoring and not for cleaning up—or maybe they just hired out on the weekends. Still, if HR had been more forthcoming, maybe Petrosky would have been able to snag this bastard before he'd ended up in this shithole. Bunch of fuckheads, all of them.

Across from Petrosky at the table, Adam's eyes glittering darkly but still with a telltale tremble at the corners. "So, what are you in for?"

"Heroin."

"Mm-hmm." No shock. No surprise. He already knew.

Petrosky dealt out gin rummy. "What about you? Dabble a little on the side?" He leaned in conspiratorially and tried to wink, but his eyelid just twitched like he was hopped up on crank.

"I don't do drugs. Tried a few in my day, but…you know."

Yeah, he did know. This guy wasn't an addict. This guy had no demons that bothered him enough to drown them in liquor or drugs—inside, he was already numb. Some people were born that way.

To the left of the table, a tiny smear of mud from Adam's boot marred the linoleum. Petrosky nodded toward it. "Better wipe your shoes, or you'll be here all night cleaning up after yourself." He waited for a telltale grimace or a frown, and the guy didn't disappoint. His nostrils flared, and he kicked the mud with the toe of his boot. The walkways outside the rehab center were cement. He must walk to work, or maybe he biked it through the park. Explained the mud. Forgoing car ownership would also mean one less thing to buy—one less record to have.

Petrosky picked up his cards, and the guy did the same.

"Looks like it's been a hard road for you, Detective." The guy's chest puffed out, almost in challenge.

Petrosky resisted the urge to remind the guy that he hadn't told him he was a detective, and instead chose a card, then laid another down. "You look a little tired yourself, Adam."

Adam did not respond to the use of his name—maybe not his name at all—just shrugged and played his turn, laying his discard down. Thin fingers, fidgety. Eyes darting all over the fucking place as if he was trying to decide how to act. At his temple...bumps—*hives?*—were appearing, swelling, working their way across his skin. Adam scratched the back of his neck.

"Bet it's hard, this line of work," Petrosky said. "All the bitches coming in and out every day, the nurses giving you shit. Having to *wait* on them like you don't even exist."

Adam's jaw worked, and his chin was suddenly pinker, angrier—definitely a rash. He clenched his fingers. What the fuck was wrong with this guy?

"Bet it keeps you up at night. You've got bags under your eyes: trouble sleeping, am I right?"

Adam's gaze darkened, but the corner of his mouth twitched almost imperceptibly. "Not really from this. More the cats. They claw the windows at night or fight on the lawn." He stared at the cards, perhaps unsure about his next move. "Any ideas for getting rid of them?"

If he had cats at his window, he probably had a one-story house. A one-story house within walking—or biking—distance. Petrosky wracked his brain. He'd lived in Ash Park for twenty-five years. He could think of two neighborhoods that were likely. But how to discern the exact property?

Petrosky pulled an ace and discarded it. "You got awnings? I'd think if you hung something from them, you'd make it uncomfortable for the furry fuckers. Strings of beads or something heavier that will sit against the sill. Block them out?"

Adam shook his head. "Nope. And the shutters are old as shit, and the worst piss-poor green you've ever seen."

Green shutters. This fucker was brutal but not smart—or maybe he was just too damn excited. The look on his face was closer to "come at me, bro" and less "holy shit, I'm about to get caught" like it should have been.

"Sounds like you need an upgrade."

"Or a better job," he spat.

Angry again. *Fuck.*

"And it's right across the road from some moron with an American flag that flaps all night long. Can you believe that? Not even sure how anyone can fly it all proud like that these days." His eyes flicked to the nurse and back. "What do you think, *Detective*?" His words dripped bitterness. He was telling him on purpose. If Petrosky hadn't asked a single question, this guy would have brought it up anyway. And if Petrosky hadn't been coming down off heroin, withdrawing from nicotine, and clenching his ass cheeks together, maybe he'd have noticed sooner.

He could find the place now. Probably rather quickly. In an hour's time, they could be walking Shannon out—so long as this guy was giving him the correct location, and Shannon wasn't locked in a storage shed somewhere, which was entirely possible. But the moment Petrosky checked himself out of this hellhole was the moment this fuckhead called his partner. Called Karen. And once that happened, Shannon and Evie were dead. Maybe he'd find their bodies full of holes like those in Dylan Acosta's back.

Adam smiled, but his eyes were menacing, not friendly. Adam was giving him this information because he wanted Petrosky to screw up. He wanted a reason to kill Shannon and Evie. Maybe he was tired of the game. Bored? But if Karen had another goal in mind—going after Morrison and Shannon both, as she had when she was with Griffen—she wouldn't be ready to give up yet. What had McCallum said? That their guy was afraid of women. That he'd been rejected. Maybe Adam was tired of playing the game, but he couldn't confront Karen directly, so he was forcing her hand by ending the game himself.

The guy was staring at him, not at the cards. He knew Petrosky was trapped. Phone calls were monitored here, and Petrosky was certain there'd be no home registered in this guy's name. Nothing to make the process faster. Even if the asshole weren't lying, they wouldn't be able to scout the neighborhood, let alone pinpoint to the correct house before Shannon and Evie got hurt.

Adam smiled at him. He'd been fucking with Petrosky the whole time.

Petrosky gritted his teeth and laid down his cards. "Gin."

39

Morrison turned the phone over and over in his hand as if that would make the text message different somehow. But every time the cell came to rest face up in his palm, the message was the same.

He had texted:

"It's done. Watch the news."

Janey's reply:

"Now to watch them suffer the way I watched Danny suffer."

The pictures she'd sent earlier practically leapt off the screen, and he couldn't stop looking. Shannon, the bottom half of her face covered in spit and gore, her lips surgically zipped together with blood-soaked sutures. Evie's onesie, drenched in blood. But no photos of his daughter. He could not allow himself to consider what that meant.

He had done everything he'd been asked to do, and he knew now what a grievous mistake that had been. This was the reason you didn't give in to demands. This was the reason no panicked spouse was allowed to decide whether to give kidnappers what they wanted.

He had settled some old drama she'd had with Roger. He had hurt his best friend—maybe irreparably. But the suffering wouldn't end there. He hadn't begun to suffer yet. That had been the point all along.

And after all of it, he still didn't know who Janey really was. *Once you remember me, you'll know exactly where to find me.* Was she full of shit? Didn't matter if she was—he had nothing else to go on and if he didn't do everything in his power...he'd never forgive himself. He was no longer concerned with the possibility that she was lying.

What if she wasn't lying?

Morrison leaned back against his pillow and dropped the cell to his side, picking up the photo of Evie they'd always kept beside the bed. Newborn, pink. Before she had known pain. Before she'd been taken. Before she'd been…abused.

His gut clenched, trying to force bile into his throat. He had to get her back.

I'm coming for you, baby, baby girl.

But what else could he do? He'd scoured all the newspaper clippings from around the time of Danny's death. Obits, headlines, every local high school yearbook that he could find online. No Janeys that matched the description he was looking for. And Danny had no family left that Morrison could ask—Danny's father had died before he'd met Morrison, and his mom'd had a heart attack nearly six years ago. No siblings. Even Mrs. Palmer had no idea who Janey's family had been, though she'd looked—had to be a runaway or adoption —and the cell Janey had used to text Karen Palmer was a throwaway. He'd looked at birth records from 1983 to 1987 for fuck's sake—no Janeys listed. Jenny? Janet? Jane? But there were too many. And he had no more time.

You see me, but you don't. Because she had been there that night. She'd watched Danny die. She blamed Morrison now, whether it was because he'd brought the drugs or left without getting help, or because she'd watched him beat Danny to death in a moment of drug-induced rage—he had no idea. He couldn't remember a fucking thing—or at least nothing that would make all of this click. But just because he couldn't recall it didn't mean he hadn't done it. And no matter how often he told himself he didn't want to know…he had to find out. Or he'd fail. He'd lose Shannon. He'd lose Evie.

He'd lose everything.

The needle called to him. There had been too much in that bag for Petrosky alone, way too much. And that was the point, wasn't it? That was why she had put him through all of this. To bring him to this place where the drug spoke louder than everything else, where the drug would talk, and he'd listen because he had nothing and no one else.

His wife was gone. His baby. Petrosky. All because of him. They'd never forgive him. And they shouldn't—he couldn't forgive himself.

The comforter, once so soft, so sweet, felt rough and full of sharp edges under his bare legs. No matter how slowly and purposefully he inhaled, the air did not restore his calm—it was a roaring ocean, trying to drown him. It had all been a carefully laid trap. She'd set out to destroy him from the very beginning.

And she would. Tears fell onto Evie's picture, still clutched in his hand. "I'm sorry. I'm sorry, I couldn't save you."

One last chance. One last shot.

The spoon, cooling now but not yet cold, sat next to him, staring accusingly. He palpated the vein in his thigh, and it sang with anticipation. *I'm ready*, it called. *No one will ever know.*

He'd always know.

Not that it mattered anymore.

He barely registered filling the syringe, but now it was loaded, liquid and sweet, and more vital than it had ever been. He leaned back on the bed, widening his legs, staring at the vein where his leg met his torso. The old mark could have been an ingrown hair or a little pimple, but now the scar appeared like a target—an evil eye. *Nothing to worry about, nothing at all.* He picked up the needle and brought the point to the center of the scar, but the tip wouldn't stay still; his hand shook with such force the needle scraped along his inner thigh, leaving a thin, angry line.

Just one little injection, and his head would clear. Just one prick, and he'd be ready to go back out and find them. He'd know who Janey was. Where Danny had met her. He'd know what to say to her. He'd know where to find her. Maybe.

He brought the needle back, pressing the pinky side of his palm against his thigh, trying to force his hand steady, but it was no use. His hand vibrated. The needle shook.

And if he missed...he had no more. One chance to do it right, that was all he had.

He brought the needle to his chest and laid it against his heart. The plastic was frighteningly cold next to his sweaty skin, though maybe not for long. Would the drug stop his heart on the first pull? Probably not, but it wasn't impossible, and he knew it. Had always known it. And it had never stopped him before, either.

Back then, it wasn't that he didn't care about death. More that he didn't care about life without the drug.

But now he did, didn't he? He gasped for air and held Evie's photo in front of his face. Her pudgy cheeks, her wide, innocent eyes so like his in color and shape. His baby girl. He could almost hear her laughing. She was why he had stayed clean. He'd been clean before her, but after, there was no greater reason in all the world than the remotest chance of looking into her eyes again. Even now, she was probably crying, needing him. He wasn't there.

Those fuckers. *That bitch.* Torturing his little girl.

He screamed at the ceiling, unleashing a string of profanities, resisting the urge to fling the needle across the room and watch the case splinter against the doorframe, soaking the carpet in the precious, vile liquid.

He would not let them win.

But if he didn't do this, he might lose.

He looked once more at Evie's picture, steadied the needle, and slid it into his vein.

40

THE COOL of the liquid quickly morphed into a glow that spread through his legs, his belly, his chest, wrapping every part of his body in a pleasant tingly warmth. The world around him mellowed into pure love, and he could have kissed his creator the moment the euphoria flooded his brain. The nods came fast then, perfect and quiet, a heavy, peaceful sleepiness that drowned the pain, the helplessness, the terror. He felt his eyes flutter open—had he closed them?—almost of their own accord. He didn't want to miss anything of this glorious world. He was back with the family who'd been there for him when he had no one else. He was home.

His head dropped back against the pillow, and the ceiling was the purest, most perfect shade of white he'd ever seen, clear and clean and utterly devoid of color. Then his eyes were moving, his head lolling to the side, and he rejoiced, sure he'd see the window there, the awesome rays of light borne by a glorious midday sun.

But he didn't.

It was Evie. Evie's picture, crumpled in his fist on the other pillow, illuminated by the garish light. Her tiny face was creased and marred with hairline cracks, red drips coating her eyes like she was the devil incarnate. Blood? Had he hurt her? And in his leg, a sharp pain—the syringe had broken. He stared at it as if it were something entirely foreign to him. And smiled.

Until he remembered. Even as tears of joy sprang into his eyes, even as his chest vibrated with glee—he remembered. They were gone. Shannon and Evie were gone. And pain collided with the pleasure, euphoria slammed by panic so intense the buzz almost silenced itself. But only for a moment. Then it was nothing but a slight dampening around the edges of the blissful cloud he was riding, a storm under him that he'd surely have to acknowledge once he fell, but now—he was untouchable.

His eyes fluttered closed again, and he rode higher and higher, pleasure shutting out the world, and the blackness cocooned him in the deepest peace he'd ever felt. A name came from below his cloud, and one small whispered word carried on the breeze as if by angels: "Danny."

The dark around him began to gray at the edges, and then images shuddered to life: a curtain rustling in the breeze though he could see no window, a bedspread with a comforter as ice blue as Shannon's eyes. He could feel his wife there too, loving him, her presence wrapping around his heart and squeezing until he was certain the adoration would cause him to burst, and he'd finally succumb, leaving the world with her name on his joyous lips. The green walls pulsed, glowing with the vibrant energy of new spring buds. The wood floor was a sea of honey beneath him, sweet and ripe.

And...the ants. Ants all over, tiny, persistent soldiers forming impossibly ordered lines. They were trying to fix something, helpers, and he wanted to reach out to them, to help them too, for their nobility was like nothing he'd seen, each and every one of them a hero. Or a martyr. He smiled at them, and they seemed to smile back at him, and he felt their adoration as clearly as if they had whispered a collective, "We love you." And he smiled at Danny. At Danny's blood? Or maybe it was his own blood, running even now over Evie's picture.

Danny.

I killed him.

The room was alive, swelling and shrinking with violent gasps, the now heavy curtains whispering to him about the blood that snaked across the earth, vast and wet as the ocean, and each crimson wave murmured sounds of serenity in his ear. And Danny: a bump on his forehead, the center of the welt split open like a shattered egg, clear to the pure, peaceful white of his skull.

Danny's lips were bluer than the most beautiful cerulean sky, and Morrison rejoiced, for they too seemed to want nothing more than to wrap him in a glorious mist of everlasting unity. And he was so overcome by the elation at being near his friend that he wept. Wept for Danny's beautiful lips, for his pure alabaster skull, for every ant on his face, for the way he was looking at Morrison now, eyes glassy and so full of love that Morrison had to turn away lest he be blinded.

And behind him...voices. Girls.

"My turn!"

"No, me next."

It was like a VCR tape rewinding, scrambling backward over time and space, and all he could see was a screech of blur and color. But then part of him was outside himself, a conscious splitting as if someone had taken a divine ax and severed his soul from his physical being. The calm peace that had wrapped him remained thick and heavy in his body, but the other him, the one that walked away now—*his* heart was frantic. *He* was choking.

"My turn!"

"No, me next."

Morrison tried to see who was speaking, but the room was filled with fog and smoke. He twisted a little more and caught sight of them: they were laughing, their faces hidden behind dark, silky curtains of hair, and they were beautiful. And he saw himself, the other him, sitting on the bed, back against the headboard. Not looking. Maybe he'd never seen them—maybe he'd already been in the cloud when they arrived.

Morrison closed his eyes and let the cloud take him again, inhaling the mist into his core and releasing it.

"Goddammit, give it here!" A girl.

Danny: "Shut up, dicks, you'll wake up my cousin, and then we're all fucked." Morrison's eyes flew open, and there was Danny, standing at the foot of the bed, and there were no ants on him, and Morrison wanted to cry with relief. But the world was sideways. How had he gotten here? Was he lying down? Then came a scuffling sound, the swishing of fabric, and Danny approached the foot of the bed, by Morrison's feet, holding the syringe. Danny shoved it into his own arm, pulled it out and wavered, and she—long hair but she was all black and white and misty—grabbed the needle from Danny. Then Danny whipped around and faced Morrison, and here was the part where he'd get upset, where Morrison had surely beaten him to death, and Morrison wanted to stop it, but the heaviness in his arms and the calm in his chest kept him down. He just watched. Danny smiled, and his lips were moving—"Fucking A"—and then he was stumbling toward the bed, tripping, grabbing at the mattress where Morrison lay, but missing, crashing. His head connected with the end table, a book flipped up, the green ant farm tumbled, and Danny hit the floor with a hollow-sounding *thud*. Morrison giggled softly to himself, the crash and the thud and all that tinkling glass such an improbable, comical thing to happen, as if every hilarious thing he'd ever seen, ever done, ever felt, was multiplied a thousand times over.

And then his perspective changed again, and he was watching from across the room. Watching himself wake up on the bed. Other Him looked awkward and lonely, and decidedly not high—though This Him still felt really fucking high.

Danny. Other Him didn't say it, but Morrison heard it in the air as Other Him peered over the side of the bed at Danny's face, at Danny's closed eyes, that sleepy fuck. And then Other Him had the bedsheet —*what the fuck?*—and he leapt off the mattress and held it to Danny's head. Danny was going to be pissed about the sheet. Danny was going to punch Other Him in the nuts. And then something slammed into Morrison as if he'd been thrown into a wall and Other Him was gone, and it was just Morrison, staring at the floor, staring at the comforter, staring at Danny and his glassy eyes and the ants. Morrison's hands were wet. Why were his hands wet? And they were red…and the sheets were red…and he could smell it, stronger now, the iron in the air, thick at the back of his throat—rust, metal, death—but his body wasn't sure what to do. Laugh or cry, maybe, but neither seemed quite right even when the ants swarmed Morrison, crawling up his legs into his pants. And then they kept coming, pinching jaws attacking his flesh over and over again. He remained still, unable to move, unable to run, not even really wanting to, but his heart was seizing, throbbing with the panic that was slowly creeping in through the haze of the drug. He had to get out of there. Someone would come soon, and they'd see that he had done this, that he'd fallen asleep while his best friend bled to death on the floor.

Morrison looked at the ants. At his crimson palms. He ran to Danny's adjoining bathroom and let the water pour over his hands, icy and sharp, the sink turning first red, then pink. When the water ran clear, he wrenched a towel from the hook over the counter, twisting it around his hands as if it were a tourniquet, and he was the one bleeding. But the world was still foggy around him, and the panic pulsed and retreated as if it were merely a butterfly alighting on a flower, then fluttering off.

The girls were gone. He'd never known them, never seen them outside of their curtains of dark hair. Janey had to have been one of them, but he was no closer to an answer. *Find them.* He ran for the bedroom door—four feet away, three—then the knob twisted of its own accord, and the butterfly of panic returned, beating its iridescent wings until the air itself was alive with horror. The door squealed and came toward him before he could hide.

Her.

Tiny, twelve years old, maybe, red hair, freckles, eyes wide, smiling. "Dan?"

Morrison put his finger to his lips, shoved past her, and tore down the stairs, and he was tumbling, falling, head over heels over head, the world cartwheeling away from him in a perfect spiral of white and black and—

He opened his eyes. Evie's photo was stained a brilliant cardinal red. He could still smell the blood. Danny's blood? No. This time it was his.

Who was she?

Shut up, dick, you'll wake up my cousin, and then we're all fucked.

Cousin. Was Janey Danny's cousin? He'd already investigated immediate family, anyone nearby he might have met, but maybe he hadn't gone far enough. He wanted to be angry about this, knew he ought to feel incensed by his own incompetence, but his limbs were too heavy and too loose, and he was just too fucking blissed-out to care about anything.

He could almost smell Evie's hair. Feel Shannon's hand on his arm, soft and warm and loving.

The cloud was still there, promising respite. Morrison breathed it into his lungs and walked into the mist, letting it consume him.

41

The phone pulled him from his nodding—insistent, a harsh and angry buzzing. Voice mail from Decantor. He'd missed three calls from Valentine, too. He touched the screen and put Decantor's message on speaker, his palm sticky and bright with injuries that were only now beginning to sting. He turned his hand over, appraising the hash marks on his palm.

"Morrison, we've gotta talk. I just got back from Michael Hayes's place. Someone filleted his ass. All we found were swaths of...flesh. Someone tried to skin him alive." Decantor coughed, gagged. Maybe he was still there, looking at the mess. "Fucking horrible. Listen, I'm going to head your way in a little bit. Hope you're around."

Fuck. Morrison headed for the living room on shaky legs, the wavering of the world pulling at him a little, but mostly he felt...dreamy. Sleepy. He'd been so stupid. And already, the promise of more pleasure was taking root in his head. He'd be good for a few days, and then he'd—

He punched the wall on his way down the stairs, letting the drywall crack and shower to the carpet as if he could obliterate his thoughts with a left hook. Photos of Shannon pregnant and Evie as an infant rattled in their frames as he pulled his hand free, knuckles smarting, but at least this time, it was his own blood on his hands. He squared his shoulders. He would get his fucking family back, and he'd move on like he always did. Shannon and Evie would be his bliss.

But not like heroin. Nothing was like heroin. *Nothing.*

Morrison almost tripped down the last of the stairs, caught himself on the railing, and stumbled into the kitchen. Coffee. Then research.

Janey. Danny's cousin. Danny's last name had been Krantz, and that was the name she'd given Palmer, but Janey Krantz didn't exist. He pulled Danny's parents and grandparents, but there'd been no adoptions, and Danny's father hadn't had brothers—no one to pass on the family name. He frowned into his coffee cup. No Krantz anywhere. He cross-checked birth certificates for each aunt and uncle, then cousins, then second cousins. No Janeys, but...

There she was. She'd been right there all along.

Janice Lynwood. Danny's cousin once removed. Parents deceased, automobile accident, the year before Danny died. Though she never was formally adopted, her school records indicated she'd lived at the Krantz house since the death of her parents—but she'd gone to a middle school and later a high school nearly an hour away. Problems in the nearby school? But there was no record of her enrollment there at all. Had Danny's parents tried to keep her with the friends she'd had before her parents died? Either way, it explained why she was able to use whatever name she wanted when she met Karen Palmer—if they went to different schools, Karen would have been none the wiser.

But...Janice had been a child when Danny died, and she'd only gone to be with his family the year prior. They were too far apart in age to share much more than blood. Though from Roger's description of her, Janey was prone to obsession and a self-righteous rage, as though she were intent on having someone else pay for the shitty hand she'd been dealt. He considered the suicide attempts, the threats she'd aimed at Roger. Maybe she was just terrified to be alone, to be abandoned. Under most bad behavior is fear.

Morrison understood loneliness well, and a tiny part of him just under his heart tightened with sympathy, but he crushed it, smothered it with the heat of fury when he pictured Shannon's skewered lips. After he'd lost his father, and years later, when he'd found his mother on the living room floor with her brains bashed in, he'd felt the same. Anger. Abandonment. Loneliness. And if he'd found the asshole who had done it, he'd have sent him to meet his maker just as quickly—back then, anyway. Over time, he'd been able to let the anger go and move on.

But Janice still blamed him. She had no one to blame for her parents careening off a rain-slicked road, but she did have someone who would pay for Danny's death: the man she'd seen that morning, and everyone he loved, innocent or not.

The doorbell rang. Morrison jerked his head toward the entry hall—woozy, he was so damn woozy—then kept typing. Searching. Janice Lynwood. No brothers, no sisters. The bell rang again.

Once you remember me, you'll know exactly how to find me.

Four marriages. All out of state. No children.

Pounding, incessant, on the front door.

He typed. The knocking stopped, but he could feel someone out there. Decantor—of course it was Decantor—could probably hear the clacking of the keyboard.

House deeds. Mortgages.

Morrison's cell buzzed. He took it from his pocket but didn't answer, just set it on the table.

A text came through:

"It's Decantor. Where you at?"

"Out to lunch. I'll meet you at the station."

Morrison searched property listings and deeds in the names of any of her immediate family. No current properties listed for any of the living family members within five hundred miles. *Click, click, click.* The cell pinged again.

"Who are you eating with?"

Morrison had left his car in the driveway. He should have put it in the garage.

He stabbed at the phone:

"Sister-in-law."

Did Decantor know Shannon didn't have a sister?

"K. An hour?"

"Sounds good."

Morrison wouldn't make that appointment either. Nor would he have his cell with him when Decantor called to ask where he was—not if he figured out where Janice was hiding. *Where is she?*

He tried Janice's mom's name. Nothing. Her dad—

Theodore Lynwood. He stared at the property listing, called up a map. The house was right in Ash Park. She could walk to it from the rehab center. And mortgages weren't kept up by dead men.

Morrison tore up the stairs to throw on a pair of boots and grab his gun.

He left his badge on the dresser.

THE SUNSET HAD STAINED the road with shapes like the splatter left behind by a gunshot wound. The adrenaline in his veins had burned off the dizziness, the nausea, or maybe he just couldn't feel anything beneath the ragged panic that even now scorched his insides. Perhaps there would have been a chance for recovery had the slightest hint of blue still streaked the sky, but as it was, the tree branches blackened all but the pattern of angry red gore.

The metal against his hip was a comfort. What would he do once he arrived?

He wasn't sure. Didn't know. But it felt right.

She wanted him alone. She wanted him to suffer. She wanted him to watch.

But she didn't know he was coming.

The house crawled by on his left, dark shutters of gray or green, a green door, a sparse garden in the front where haphazard tulips strained through overgrown grass. No vehicle in the driveway, but a one-car garage. The ripened sun turned the windows into blazing orange eyes.

His chest heaved as he lost sight of the house—like he was abandoning his family again. He parked around the corner, well out of sight of the place, just in case they looked from behind the smoldering windows to peer down the road. The pavement was still bloodied by the setting sun.

I'm coming, Shanny.

He switched the safety off his gun, climbed out of the car, and started around the block so that he could go in the back way.

Tonight, he wasn't a fucking cop.

He was a monster forged of rage and desperation and steel. A monster they had woken.

And Janice would pay.

42

Petrosky sat on his bed, his stomach aching, his ass still half-numb from the rock-hard, torture device of a chair he'd been in all day. And while he'd sat in the common room, Adam, the agitated boy-man, had watched. When he'd left the table to take a shit, the perp was waiting outside. For every meal Petrosky ate, that asshole was there with his shiny, bulging forehead.

That was his job. Not the sweeping that he probably got paid some paltry amount for. His real job was to make sure Petrosky was stuck in here with critical information he was helpless to transmit—impotent to assist Morrison. Or Shannon. Or Evie.

He didn't want to think about the drug either. But he did. Jesus, he did. It was the happiest he'd been in as long as he could remember, and he had little to lose, if anything, once Shannon and Evie were safe.

He had been refused phone calls twice, thus far. Against the rules, they said—fearful he'd be contacting some dealer to hook him up when he got out. Inpatient rehab was meant to disconnect you from every aspect of your outside life. Old lives were ready triggers, old friends were eager enablers. They'd told him that in group therapy this morning, some sour-faced man with a cross around his neck wearing goddamn purple argyle. *Argyle.* Checkers were bad enough, but he didn't trust a man in fabrics with more depth than your average perp.

Petrosky shot to standing at a knock at the bedroom door—it'd be the therapist, or maybe the nurse. "Obstinate" and "uncooperative" they'd called him, respectively. Not that cooperation had been a prerequuisite for this part he was meant to play; whoever had Shannon didn't give a flying fuck if he was actually recovering. They'd probably be happier if he weren't. They wanted him to hurt. They wanted to bring him down.

Karen...and *Adam*. But that couldn't be his real name; it was too easy. From the moment the name passed his lips, "Adam" seemed a little too confident like he figured once Petrosky got out of rehab, he'd seek him *only* by name.

They'll never find me! They think my name is Adam!

Fucking idiot. Though who knew, this might be part of his game. This fucker seemed to get off on giving away his hand, exposing critical information, and then...watching.

For now, Petrosky needed a better plan. The phones were locked in the nurses' station and in the main offices, but a few more hours and the majority of the staff would go home. Ghost staff overnight. He had a filed toothbrush that he could use as a pick, very prison-esque, but everything here was prison-esque. Not like he could throw a fit, pull his badge, and sign himself out—not if he wanted Shannon and Evie to live.

The doorknob turned, and Petrosky reached for the twentieth time for his holster but touched only cloth. Bullshit jailhouse pajamas. Scratchy and considerably less comforting than the cool heaviness of his Glock.

An orderly, skinny and irritatingly young—though still older than Adam—peeped his head into the room, then swung the door wider and took a few steps forward, holding a black plastic sack. Probably here to tell him it's therapy time, it's game night, or something equally asinine.

"Hope you're not here to get me for something stupid. I don't have time for that bullshit. But if you can get me a phone—"

"I have to take you out. Discharge."

Petrosky froze, not comprehending. "I'm in recovery here."

The orderly shrugged. "You've got to see the nurse." He handed Petrosky the bag. "I'll wait outside."

Petrosky opened the sack. His clothes. He was leaving. Was he supposed to be leaving? He had a sudden urge to take a shit.

But this had to be good news, right? Morrison had found them. Morrison was here to get him, and maybe Shannon and Evie were with him, or they were going to go together to the hospital. The girls would take some time to heal, but dammit, he'd be there to help them. They were okay.

Dressed in minutes in the sour duds he'd come in with, Petrosky followed the orderly to the nurses' station. Her smile was tight as she handed him prescriptions through the window.

"Why am I being discharged?"

Her smile went from tight to nonexistent. "I'm... You can speak to the gentleman outside."

The gentleman. Not "your friend."

"Listen, I'm not trying to be difficult here."

She pushed one last script through the slot. "Go talk to him. He can answer your questions."

But her eyes were narrowed—she was worried. They were trying to keep him calm. It wasn't his partner out there, ready to take him home, friendly and excited. Why would you try to keep someone from rehab calm? It wasn't like they'd be discharging him into the care of their psychopathic janitor. "I don't understand why—"

"It's not up to us." She sent a form through the slot. "Sign this, please."

Only so many things could upend recovery. The only time they released like this was…if someone was under arrest. If they thought the patient was dangerous. If it was an emergency. But who would be here? Decantor? And if it was Decantor…Shannon and Evie were probably dead. Morrison too.

He signed the sheet and shoved it back through the hole, heart hammering in his temples. It had to be good news. *Please let it be good news.* But when was the news ever good for him? It was over. If he was out, it was over one way or another.

He followed the orderly out of the common room and through the main hallway toward the exit. The orderly took forever fiddling with his keys, his badge, to get them the fuck out of there. The door finally swung open, and Petrosky bolted to the kid's agitated: "Hey wait, he said you're under arrest!"

The orderly's cry fell on deaf ears. Petrosky froze just outside the door, staring at the man who'd come to claim him.

Roger cocked his head. "What's up, Detective?"

Definitely not good.

"Your partner isn't home," Roger said as he slid into the car and slammed the door.

Petrosky closed his own door, feeling like more of a prisoner than when he'd been trapped in his room filing toothbrushes into lock picks.

"He running?"

"Running?" What in the ever-loving hell? If Roger wasn't here to get him because it was over—"Wait, do they still have Shannon?"

Roger shrugged.

"What the fuck does that mean? Are you trying to get her fucking killed?" Petrosky's fist clenched, wanting desperately to drive it into Roger's already crooked nose. How long did they have before Adam found out and called his partner at the house?

Roger was appraising him—apparently, he didn't trust that Petrosky was actually dumbfounded. "Morrison and I had a deal," he said sharply. "He was taking care of something for me. Supposed to turn himself in this morning for arson."

Arson? "Taking care of what?"

"Don't worry about it."

Morrison had taken care of...incriminating evidence against Roger? But why would he do that when the assholes who had Shannon wanted Roger locked up? *Arson.* What the hell was going on?

"I went over there," Roger said. "Your boy's gone. Figured you'd know where." He narrowed his eyes. "And if you fuck with me, I'll make sure—"

"Shut the fuck up, Roger." Petrosky buckled his seat belt.

Roger froze, keys raised halfway to the ignition.

Petrosky punched the dash. "Drive, motherfucker. We don't have all day."

"We going to get Morrison?"

"We're going to get Shannon before they kill her."

Roger opened his mouth to say something else, but Petrosky put up a hand.

"We find her, and we'll find Morrison too." He reached over and took the keys and shoved them into the ignition. "Let's go."

THE DESIRE TO cut and run was strong, not because he had any intention of abandoning Morrison, but because Petrosky was certain Roger was a fucking twat. You don't go into battle with someone who doesn't know what the hell they're doing—you leave their sorry ass at home. But Roger refused to be left, even after a cruise through the first neighborhood seemed fruitless.

"I don't know how you can rule so many out," Roger grumbled.

"No flags."

"So what? You can't be sure that he even told you the truth."

But Petrosky felt it. The hairs on the back of his neck hadn't risen when that dickhead was telling him about the cats, bitching about the screen and his neighbor's patriotism. And Adam hadn't flinched once. Dangling the truth in front of Petrosky, taunting him with it—that had been part of the game. Part of the excitement. Adam probably *was* his real fucking name. "He told me the truth."

"I can do all the shit you guys do and better. I'd have found her three days ago."

"Then why didn't you?"

"If she wanted someone to get the job done, she'd have stayed with me."

But the edge in his voice betrayed his concern. God forbid someone got rid of her before she could fall into Roger's arms and tell him that he was clearly the superior model, that she'd made a huge mistake in leaving him. Petrosky appraised him. His furrowed brows. His knuckles, white against the steering wheel.

Roger wasn't a prosecutor today. His interests might be selfish, but at least they were aligned with Petrosky's. With Morrison's.

And with Shannon's.

"There's that jackass's car," Roger said and went to pull beside it.

Petrosky shook his head. "For fuck's sake, Roger, drive around the block."

"But if he's here—"

"He didn't park in front of the house and go in rampaging. He's not an idiot." *Unlike you.* "But the place has to be close."

Roger's mouth tightened, and Petrosky gestured through the windshield at the road. "One block, two at the most." Morrison would have been in a hurry. "Drive around the right side first."

Roger ran a stop sign and hooked a right into the blinding sunset.

43

Morrison's breath was hot and fast, every sense acute, magnified by the thrumming of his anxiety. He could almost feel the sun being siphoned from the sky in measured increments like water sucked down a drain. The chirping of the crickets was deafening.

But still, he could hear.

The window was closed, and all he could see was a black curtain, yet muffled sounds came from within—more a feeling of movement than an actual noise. He brought his face closer to the window. The curtain was stiff, plastered against the glass. No one looking from the street would notice a difference, but there was no way the window covering was free and loose on the inside. Pressed to the window with cinderblocks? Spray insulation? Surely they had insulated the windows and the exterior walls. Unless...that was why they'd sewn Shannon's mouth closed.

The cold. It burned.

But he heard her. No, it wasn't Shannon, not the right timbre, just the tickle of a female voice, no discernible words.

Then the wail. A baby. His baby. Evie was surely screeching, but if he hadn't had his ear so close to the window, he wouldn't have heard her at all.

I'm coming, baby girl.

Every muscle ached with the desire to crash through the window and snatch Evie to him before he blew Karen—*Janice*—away. But he couldn't be sure of what was on the other side. Was it booby trapped? What if he knocked something over and hurt Evie instead? And if there was insulating foam, it might take him all day to saw through it and actually get inside, depending on how they'd secured it. Just the foam, cool. Bricks? Bad news.

He was still squinting at the corner of the window when he registered the sound of feet swishing through the grass, somewhere near the front of the property. The house was small, maybe thirteen hundred square feet. Was it Janice's sadistic partner? He pressed himself under the window, hoping they wouldn't come around. A dozen steps and they'd be on top of him.

Then the clack of shoes on the porch. So close.

Knocking echoed through the air, and he could feel the vibration in the house itself. The front door. Who was out there? Was Janice's accomplice insecure enough, afraid enough of Janice, that he'd knock every time he showed up?

In the room, the voice went silent. Evie continued to cry, but it was faint enough that it might have been his imagination. A door slammed, closer to him this time, but muffled, thick. Then no more cries.

The knocking came again, hard and fast, carrying through the air around the house, the shoes on the porch eerily silent. And a squeal of hinges, again from the front of the house, far more distinct than anything he could hear through this window.

"Hey, there." *Roger?* Morrison bolted upright, almost smashing his forehead on the exterior windowsill. *Shit.* Janice would know he lied about getting rid of him.

"I hope you don't mind me coming by, but I've been thinking about you lately. I've missed you."

Even from here, Morrison could hear the anxiety in her voice, though not her words, just a rapid stuttering of sounds. Had Roger spoken loudly on purpose? Did he know Morrison was there? Did Janice?

Morrison held his breath, the only sound a haunting moan of wind through the trees as if even the air could feel the gravity of that moment and was distressed by it. Roger could not let her go back inside. Could not let her get to Evie, to Shannon. Janice would hurt them.

Janice would die first.

He slid Petrosky's pocketknife from his back pocket—the one left on the passenger seat the day Morrison had driven him to the rehab center. From the front of the house came Roger's muffled voice, and hers too, not quite arguing with Roger, but raised higher than it had been moments ago. He took off for the back door. It was less likely they'd be watching that as closely as the rooms where they held captives. This door they'd need for escape.

It took mere seconds to reach his destination, and only seconds more to wedge the knife beside the jamb. A ray of orange sun clawed at his hands as he jimmied the back door, turned the knob, and pushed.

But...resistance. Not a deadbolt. A padlock? He couldn't crack a padlock from the outside, and if he broke the door down, he might not be fast enough to get to Shannon—he didn't even know where Shannon was, or if she was in a different room from Evie.

And then the yelling. Somewhere nearby, a thunk—sharp but muted. Not the front door closing shut, but maybe the door on Roger's shoe or against his shoulder if he was attempting to bully his way inside. Was he trying to be a hero? And if so… Oh shit, if he was, and Janice's partner was in there with his family—

He raced back to the window. He'd have only moments, but it had to be enough.

Had to be.

Janice was still talking, arguing now, louder than before. If there was someone else in the house, wouldn't he have come to her aid? Morrison heard no other sounds from within the home, and no other male voices save Roger's on the porch—though a man terrified of rejection might be cowering in the bedroom instead of assisting. There was no way to tell for certain. And Morrison was out of time.

The noise from the front was enough to cover Morrison breaking the back window with an elbow wrapped in his jacket. Sound suppression goes both ways, and while they might have heard it from the front if they'd been quiet, Roger's voice kept booming over the splintering of glass and the tearing of Morrison's knife across the curtain and into whatever was behind it. Foam insulation. No bricks.

He sawed through it, the Styrofoam-like material squalling like nails on a chalkboard though the argument out front did not stop—so the noise couldn't have been as deafening as it was to him. The foam peeled from the window frame, and he tossed the pieces behind him into the grass, until he had an opening he could shove his hand through. There was pink fiberglass insulation behind the foam, but no resistance beyond that, and he sliced cleanly through the material, ripping chunks of foam and fiberglass from the window opening, each piece like a bit of hope he was stealing back.

Roger yelled something that sounded like "goddammit," and Morrison pulled himself halfway into the window, trying to see through the hole he'd made. Tight, but doable, and nothing below that he could see in the dim light, no child to be injured if he lost his balance and tumbled into the darkness.

From the front, something banged again. *Out of time.* He was up and over the sill in moments and had wiggled through the hole in even less, trying not to care when he heard the knife slide off the outside sill and into the grass. He heard another sound behind him, but didn't stop to think, didn't stop to see, just moved. Someone behind him. Someone after him. But if he could get to Evie and Shannon first…

The dimness of the room stretched around him, but the last blush of twilight through the torn window covering gave him enough light to see there was no crib in there, no mattress. Just a table against the far wall that held…bottles. A glass cup. A pet carrier crate in the corner of the room with a handle on top.

Did they have a guard dog? He had not considered coming up against an animal, but surely the beast would have heard him and growled by now or attacked Roger if it was in the front end of the house. In this room, he was the only beast. For now.

Evie had quieted, and for once, he wished she was crying—he couldn't discern her silent breathing above the sound of his own heart and the muffled voices out front. Where would she be? Where would they keep her? In the picture Janice had sent of Shannon, she was in a room, attached to a beam, but behind a door. Like it used to be a—his eyes locked on the folding doors along the far wall.

He ran to the closet, the treads on his shoes soft and supple and above all else, silent. He paused as an image of Evie, suspended from the clothes rod, smashed into his brain: his baby girl hanging from a T-shirt around her throat, her skin blue and cold and dead. He inhaled sharply, reaching for the knob. And opened it.

The door creaked just a touch, but there was nothing inside that hinted at his family, only a few boxes of electronic equipment, empty bags, and a fast food-cup as if someone had gone shopping and deposited everything, including their snack.

But Evie had been here. He'd heard her. Janice hadn't taken her to the front door, had she? No, she wouldn't have let Roger see her. Morrison turned, scanned the walls, the floor, the—plastic pet crate.

Two steps and he was at the pet carrier. He gingerly lifted the crate, rushing back to the window as he did so that he could see inside it. She was there, barely moving, wearing only a diaper, one tiny fist opening and closing. "Baby. Oh, baby."

At the front of the house, a door slammed. Evie mewled weakly. *Fuck.* He tried to wrest the carrier door open, and only then did he see the padlock on the front. Opening the crate would take too long, and he'd risk hurting her if he smashed it.

A shadow fell over him from the window, and he shifted the crate into one hand, grabbing his gun with the other. *Die, motherfucker.* So help him, he'd—

"Give her here, Cali," the silhouette in the window whispered.

He didn't lower the gun.

"For fuck's sake, Morrison—"

He heard them then, the footsteps approaching the door. "I love you, baby. Daddy'll be right back." Morrison handed the crate to Petrosky and ran for the bedroom door.

44

Janice didn't have Shannon with her—the padded sounds of her feet on the floor were too quick, too clean. Purposeful. And then the steps just... stopped. Morrison flattened himself against the doorframe, waiting, listening for one harsh inhale, a gasp to indicate her understanding that he was there for her ass. Nothing. He held the gun trained on the crack above the doorknob. If she opened the door, Janice wouldn't have time to speak.

But the knob did not turn. She knew he was there. She was listening, trying to hear him breathe even as he was trying to hear her. Perhaps she had a gun on the other side of the door, waiting for him to open it, ready to blow his face off too.

Perhaps she'd change her mind and go after Shannon instead.

He strained his ears for sounds of her feet on the wooden floor. If she stepped away from the door, he'd fling it open, go in low, and shoot for the knees, the belly. Even if he missed, a wild shot or two might throw her off balance so that he could cap her in the back of the head before she could get to Shannon.

And her ability to focus might be impaired—she'd be angry now. Angry that she might not be able to complete whatever sick goal she had in mind. Angry he hadn't killed Roger as he'd said. That she'd been tricked by the story in the paper—a story he'd leaked the day he'd carved the tattoos off the already dead pedophile and left him in Roger's house to burn.

But now, instead of the crackle of flaming wood and cloth, he heard only her breath. Whisper quiet, but there. Fast. *She knows.*

Then a step, just one, then another, and he yanked the door and fired into the hallway, low, so if he missed, it'd lodge in the floor and not ricochet into another room where he might accidentally murder his own wife with a stray bullet.

A scrambling, a thin squeal.

He got his head around the doorframe in time to see her foot, clad in a fuzzy yellow sock, disappearing into the next room. He leapt for the door, for her ankle, grabbing at her but coming away with only a few threads of yellow fuzz. He lunged again, trying to keep his head behind the frame, wanting to drag her out. His fist connected with ankle bone, and he gripped her foot so hard he thought he'd break it. He yanked her to him.

Pain, white and hot, shot from the side of his hand and up his arm, forcing him to release her as she swung the lamp again, the base heavy and metal and dented from the first blow to the back of his hand. He rolled in time to avoid it, clambering after her into the bedroom. She skittered back on her butt, and he reached again for her leg, but she was faster, scrambling for the closet on the far side of the room, pressing numbered buttons on a padlock.

He couldn't move his pinky finger. From the corner of his eye, he could see that it was bent at an unnatural angle. But he wouldn't need it to fucking kill her.

He leapt to standing at the same time she did. She threw the closet door open and ducked behind—

Shannon. *Oh, dear god.*

Her eyes were red-rimmed, her face haggard. Around her throat was the collar: heavy, metal, black like iron, bolted to an oiled wooden beam that ran horizontally through the closet five feet off the ground. Her hands appeared to be free. But she made no attempt to grab the woman —her fingers were locked around the beam on either side of her iron-clad neck. And her lips—*oh, baby, I'm so sorry*—angrier in person or maybe simply infected by now, congealed blood and yellowed pus clinging to the sutures, black thread piercing her lips from top to bottom like a huge, grisly zipper. Janice had done this to his wife. Put his baby in a cage. Hatred burned hotter than any flame. *I will fucking kill you.*

"Come closer, and she's dead. I'll slit her throat." Janice remained low, but shoved Shannon's legs from behind, just a touch. Blood trickled from somewhere behind the collar. Her neck had been sliced. *Shit, no, no, no.* Shannon whimpered, her eyes wide, moving her hands to the collar itself as if trying in vain to stop the bleeding from her neck.

The collar. Blades or something inside it. But it didn't matter what— he couldn't get near enough to free her, and as he peered closer, he could see the bolts and the lock attaching the collar securely to the beam. He'd have to coax Janice out, have to—

The collar swung open, and Shannon was free, and she stumbled forward against the closet door and pivoted, trapping Janice behind her near the beam.

Janice's jaw dropped, and she put her hands up, trying to block Shannon's knee as it connected with her chin. But Shannon was weak, off-balance, maybe she hadn't eaten or slept, and she fell to her knees, a piece of curved metal falling from her hand to the carpet.

Janice reeled forward, teeth bared, and punched Shannon in the belly.

Fucking bitch.

Morrison jumped in front of Shannon, hauling Janice from the closet before she could attack his wife again. He threw her against the wall, watched her mouth move, knew she was saying something, but he couldn't hear a word, couldn't hear anything but the ragged hiss of air through his teeth. Or maybe he was just far beyond listening.

He wrapped his hands around her throat. The broken bones behind his pinky and ring finger poked at the skin from the inside like spiked alien parasites. His tendons, swollen and bright with agony, screamed as he tightened his grip.

He didn't fucking care. He squeezed.

45

She fought him, slashing at his hands with her nails, every attempt to free herself, stoking the fire in his gut. *You fucking deserve this.* Streaks of bloody red welled on his fists and dripped onto the floor, but he did not relent. Nor did he stop when pain careened from his hand to his wrist and shot into his brain like lightning, an electricity composed of concentrated malice.

Her face reddened, then went purple, her eyes bulging. But her mouth... It wasn't the shocked *o* he'd expected. And though her survival instinct was kicking in, she was no longer pulling from him, pulling away—trying to escape.

She had expected to fight him. She'd invited him here. *Once you remember, you'll know where to find me.*

"You don't want this." Morrison heard the words but did not see the speaker, and though he knew it was Petrosky's baritone, it seemed to come from Shannon's mouth, and—*oh dear god*—she was on the floor, her lips unmoving, sewed together like a voodoo doll, and still, the voice came again: "Morrison, this is what she wants."

He squeezed harder, watching Janice's face as her lips turned blue, the veins in her temples bulging like fattening worms as she crept toward unconsciousness, toward death, the only fitting punishment for what she'd done.

"Morrison!" Now Petrosky was there, at Shannon's side, tugging her shirt down, and Morrison caught a whiff of her, the harsh metallic tang of the collar, maybe Shannon's blood, maybe his own. He squeezed until he was sure he'd tear a muscle in his hand.

"You're not a killer. She wants you to be."

Shannon. Shannon's voice. He jerked back to her. Petrosky stepped away from her, a knife in his fist, and Shannon opened her mouth, her lips bleeding and swollen and cracked. Speaking—or whispering—but she might as well have been yelling at him, for her words were all he could hear.

Petrosky touched Morrison's elbow, not trying to impede him, just letting him know he was there, and then Janice was falling, this bitch who'd tried to take everything from him, who'd tried more than once to kill his wife, who had tortured her, who had taken his daughter. A woman who'd followed him, hunted him, plotted against him, with nothing but vengeance in her heart.

She hadn't won. But if he killed her, he was exactly what she believed him to be.

Janice was in a heap on the floor, unconscious, unable to stop herself from smacking her head on the boards, and then Petrosky was there, cuffing her arms behind her.

Morrison watched, dumbfounded. It was over. But no, it wasn't. They were missing one. "He here?"

Shannon's gaze darted to the door. He knelt beside her, and her hair smelled of grease and gore and the must of body odor and piss and rank, spoiled milk. And it was the most beautiful thing he'd ever smelled.

"Evie," she said into his chest, her voice trembling with terror that the news was bad, that she'd lost her daughter.

"She's okay. She's okay." Morrison jerked his head toward Petrosky.

"Roger has her," Petrosky said. "He's driving her to the hospital with a police escort. Figured it was safer than staying here, in case there was any...trouble." He hauled Janice to her feet, and her eyes rolled around, but she stood, wavering ever so slightly. Her face was returning to a furious shade of pink.

"Your asshole boyfriend on his way here?" Petrosky asked Janice. When she didn't answer, he jerked her arm, and she stumbled, almost fell, and caught herself against the wall with one shoulder.

"Fuck you." Janice's voice was hoarse, but she could still speak. Morrison should have squeezed her throat harder. Or sewn her goddamn mouth closed. He glanced at Shannon, who was running her tongue over the sutures, the ends of the severed threads poking from her torn lips.

"I sent Decantor over to the rehab center," Petrosky said. "That's where these douchebags met, where Adam still works. If he's there, Decantor has him."

Morrison eyed the door behind them, straining his ears, listening for the telltale sound of the latch on the front doorknob, a boot in the hall, the clink of spikes ripe with purpose and violence. Morrison would show him fucking violence—he'd ram those spikes down his throat. But there was no noise besides the far-off clang of a grandfather clock striking a quarter past the hour.

"We'll get his ass, Morrison. Now let's get Shannon to the hospital. Put your family back together."

Relief shuddered through Morrison in waves, one after another. He wrapped his arms around Shannon again, trying to be gentle. She was so weak, so beat up, so bruised. She'd suffered because of him.

"I'm so sorry," he whispered into her hair.

"You didn't do anything wrong," she said. "There is no sorry here."

"Only love," he finished. But he felt the guilt, tearing through his gut, that heavy aching sorrow he feared would never disappear. And one day she'd resent him for it—for all of it. She'd leave him. Take Evie.

And then he'd only have the drug. The vein in his thigh throbbed, one slow, deep pulse, then stilled. But when she put her injured lips to his neck and kissed his throat though it must have hurt like hell, he knew he'd endure.

"Only love," she said. "You didn't cause this. But you did save us."

His heart swelled and throbbed, harder than the vein.

The drug could kiss his ass.

46

The room was dim when Petrosky awoke. Not the mellow dusk of a day's end, but that brassy half-dark of another day trying to creep in when you're not yet ready for it. He rolled over and tried to push himself to seated, his tongue rank and sour from last night's vomit, shoulder still tender from the tattoo he'd had Jenny ink on him last week. Julie's face, memorialized. Maybe it would always hurt.

And that was difficult to take.

Each day he drew closer to an unknown conclusion. But he didn't want to get there. He eyed the gun in its holster, hanging innocently over the chair as if it had no intention of luring him with that quick, easy path to peace. Petrosky reached for it, comforted by the hardness of it, wondering if he'd register the moment he died as a flash of light, a deafening crack of lead as his soul left his body, or if it would be only silence and floating. He wasn't much for religion and the afterlife. If he'd believed in a heaven where Julie waited for him with open arms, he'd have put a bullet in his brain a long time ago.

He put his feet on the floor and heaved his doughy body off the bed. The room shuddered violently around him, the edges wavering, then solidifying like he was exiting a tunnel or a horrible nightmare. He might as well have been.

Another day, another dollar. Another day of wondering: *Will today be the day someone shoots me?*

Like he'd be that fucking lucky.

He met Morrison and Shannon at their house, the leaves already falling to their deaths on the front lawn. Helicoptering red and orange skittered across the driveway, and he kicked them aside on his way to the stoop.

Everything died, and today just happened to be their day. Petrosky envied them.

Morrison greeted him with a warm smile and a worried look, though he said nothing. He never did. Petrosky was thankful for his silence, though perhaps Morrison simply knew that the moment he opened his mouth, Petrosky would cut his ass out of his life. Not like Morrison and his family needed Petrosky's bullshit.

Shannon was already at the table, their newest addition at her heel, his ears pricked and alert. The dog appeared to relax when it saw Petrosky, but he knew it was from the gentle command Shannon had whispered. One word and the German shepherd would rip his fucking throat out, as would the other two who were probably in the backyard now, patrolling.

Shannon spooned eggs off her plate with a pink plastic spoon and grinned at Petrosky as he entered the kitchen. Petrosky tried to smile back.

Her mouth turned down, and the tiny marks where her lips had been sewn together dimpled just a touch. Almost healed now, but still a little pink, a little angry. "You look like shit," she said.

No wonder they'd sewn her mouth closed. "Nice to see you, too."

Evie gurgled and waved her arms, spraying eggs across the highchair tray and into Shannon's hair. Shannon ignored it, just frowned at him. She'd gone from tough to fucking badass after the kidnapping. Maybe being locked in a closet for a week made you realize what was important. Maybe she was on guard in case Adam Norton came back for her, though he was surely long gone by now.

And Janice had been little help. She'd met Norton at the rehab center, and swore she'd never met Michael Hayes, the guy who raped Acosta and Reynolds. Further investigation had determined that Norton and Hayes had met at the hospital, Norton working with the cleaning service and Hayes volunteering as a clown. Both of those jackoffs seemed so fucking fragile he couldn't begin to determine who had approached whom, though from everything they had found online, Michael Hayes seemed the less violent one—creepy tattoos, and a rapist, though not a killer.

But Adam Norton—that motherfucker was vicious. Dangerous. And impulsive, possibly because of how young he was. At least Norton's DNA information was in the computer now, so they'd find him when he did it again—it wasn't like he'd be able to stop himself.

And he could be anywhere. The trail had dried up. They'd chased down every futile lead, and, through it all, Morrison had kept that stoic, cool-collected façade, as if this shit had never happened. Like it didn't bother him.

But Morrison had bought the dogs.

Petrosky squinted back at Shannon's narrowed eyes. Still watching him, possibly for tremors or looking for needle scars. His ankle twitched, and Petrosky shifted his weight. At least she didn't look scared. Maybe it was the canine unit.

Maybe she'd stopped giving a fuck too.

Petrosky waited for her to say something else, but she turned back to Evie and offered her another bite of eggs.

Morrison approached with two stainless-steel coffee mugs and handed one to Petrosky. "What the hell is this?" Petrosky said, frowning at the garish blue peace sign on his mug.

"Present." Morrison smiled.

"Liar. You just wanted a new mug and were afraid your wife would say no." He cast a sidelong glance at Shannon, who raised an eyebrow and went back to feeding Evie. "Give me the other one, Surfer Boy. Then we can swing by the donut shop and get a few crullers."

Morrison exchanged cups with him. "You sure you need all that sugar, Boss?"

Speaking of not giving a fuck... "Damn sissy beach boys and their peace signs and their *kale*."

"If we go, maybe we can bring some to Roger."

That asshole. He had come in handy even if he was a lying sack of shit. Even if he'd just done it for the headlines that came out right afterward: *Lead Prosecutor Rescues Ex-Wife from Homicidal Kidnapper*. No mention of the fire. And before the press got wind of Morrison's role, coercion and duress had cleared Morrison as well, though it had been touch and go for a few weeks: he'd found Michael Hayes dead in his home, suicide by pills according to the ME, probably guilt over Acosta's death. But filleting the tattoos from his dead body to purposefully mislead police was something the taxpayers would have been pissed about—it would have been a public relations disaster. In the end, Morrison had walked away with five thousand dollars in fines and some restitution to Roger. Insurance had rebuilt the house. And the extenuating circumstances were enough to keep Morrison out of jail, off probation, and still on the force.

Roger had applauded Morrison publicly for finding Shannon, which, for Roger, must have fucking hurt. But it was surely worth it—all the critical information Morrison had on Roger, everything in the safe deposit box, was gone along with his dining room table and the last of Roger's goddamn dignity. Fucking shmuck. Maybe he'd stay on the up and up. If he didn't, Petrosky had no intention of giving him another chance, regardless of his partner's opinion.

Morrison was still looking at him expectantly.

"Fine, goddammit, we can bring some breakfast to your new best buddy."

"Not exactly best"—Morrison winked—"but I figured we'd butter him up before Shannon goes back next week."

Petrosky gaped at her.

She smiled. "You look like you've seen a ghost, Petrosky."

"I thought you were going to wait an extra month or so."

"I thought so too, but even McCallum says I'm doing awesome. I think I'm ready." She drew her shoulders up, proud maybe, or maybe trying to seem stronger than she felt. "And Lillian, Valentine's wife, is going to take Evie during the day to play with her little one. Starting tomorrow, actually. Get her adjusted before I really have to leave."

"Is he going with you?" Petrosky gestured to the dog.

"I'll have Ozzy with me, and Floyd and Prince will be at Valentine's. At my husband's insistence." Shannon rolled her eyes, but she was still smiling. "Don't look so worried. You're as bad as Morrison."

Morrison shrugged one shoulder. "I thought she'd wait longer too. But you know...prosecutors."

"Fucking lawyers," Petrosky agreed.

"Evie's going to be talking soon," Shannon said. "Watch your mouth."

Morrison was gazing at his wife with that adoration thing he did. Shannon ate that shit up, and she looked at Morrison the same way. He was glad for them, he really was. Or as glad as he was capable of being.

His ankle itched again, reminding him that the bliss never lasted long enough. And every morning, awakening felt worse than it had the day before—more desperate. The world was tightening around him like a tourniquet.

"Lawyer or no, there's no stopping Shanny when she gets something in her head," Morrison said.

"Women, am I right? Always doing crazy shit...stuff," he amended when he saw Shannon's raised eyebrows. Petrosky headed for the door.

"Screw you, Petrosky," Shannon called as Petrosky touched the knob.

Screw him indeed.

"This story is told through the eyes of a madman, who, like all of us, believed he was sane."
~Edgar Allan Poe, *The Tell-Tale Heart*

EPILOGUE

The last stone brick went in more easily than the one before as if each new support was begging to be a part of something great. And great it would be, now that he was free of Janice—of her *restraints*—though he'd been too cowardly to take care of her himself. He'd left that to the police. They might still be looking for him, but they'd not find him here. *Happy, happy, happy.*

He adjusted the fiber optic camera behind the brick and applied mortar to the last section of wall. He was tired of being afraid. He was also tired of being invisible, but he wouldn't be for much longer—at least, not to his number one girl.

He'd paid his dues, lying low under the radar, mopping up the puke of degenerates. He was capable of more. He deserved more. And now he knew how to get it.

The mortar complete, he dropped the trowel and turned to the back wall of the room, a checkerboard of heavy iron bars from floor to ceiling, and shackles practically begging to be filled. He inhaled the steely scent deep into his lungs. None of that plastic zip-tie bullshit: this equipment was harsh, substantial, from back when they used to make things that lasted. Before people had the luxury of escape. Shannon had stolen from him, gotten out using his own needle, but he'd have no more surprises, not here. He'd watch every movement. The house upstairs held enough food for months, if not years.

In the corner of the room, the dress waited, satin of a vibrant red, the color of wealth and status. A belt of gold ovals circled its waist. Every stitch of cotton puckered ever so slightly, bringing with it the memories of the night he'd sewn it. It was all his. He'd built this. He'd built her.

And she would be perfect.

He approached, his breath quickening as each stitch came into clearer focus. He glanced at the tools in the corner but did not reach for any, though he was tempted by the billhook, a gleaming machete-like tool that boasted a curved blade along one side and an evil-looking hook at the top.

Later.

He traced his finger down her cheek, and the plastic of the mannequin caught ever so slightly. Dry. Not like skin, especially once it bore the blush of amour, the inevitable sheen of excited sweat. He ran a hand over the waist of the gown, and the gathered petticoat. He could almost feel the promise of her flesh.

But it wasn't time yet. She wasn't ready, didn't deserve to wear it. The girl still looked at him with blazing hatred in her eyes, a defiant rage that made his breath catch, his heart race. He deserved better. The men of their world deserved better. And if the women would not acquiesce, he'd bring them back to a time before they had a choice. When real men made the decisions.

I'm a real man.

He walked back to the iron cage and stopped just before the bars, where a large dog crate sat waiting. He bent and peered inside.

She was on all fours; her hair damp with sweat and oil—limp and disgusting. But it was red like Janice's—the color of power, of wealth—and glowing like the girl's eyes. She glared at him, and her cheeks flushed like she was ovulating, making his stomach drop and squeeze until he feared he might vomit. His jaw prickled with that old, familiar itch, and he resisted the urge to run for his needles and release the pressure by gouging the infernal boil. Too many, and he'd look like the savage he was. He wanted that to be a surprise.

Perhaps he'd grab the billhook after all. Nothing was too good for his number one girl.

But no...it was not time yet. Impatience was for weaker men, and though Michael had been weak, he had shown Adam how to bide his time. A gift here. A kind word there. Not that Michael hadn't made mistakes: he was so kind, so diminutive that the Acosta boy hadn't even remembered where he knew him from. But done right, you could draw a woman closer, closer, and they'd never suspect—they'd follow you wherever you went. He could be as patient as Janice, that fucking cunt. The reward would be that much greater.

He glanced at the stone wall. Patience. She'd give him what he was owed.

Near the stairs, it hung on a hook, the death mask, nose long and thin to protect him from her stench—pheromones could make a man insane, and he feared that heady stink as much as he feared the accusatory gleam in their eyes. Did they think they had the right to accuse him? If so, the mask would make them reconsider. The leather was thick and heavy and still smelled of the souls of the creatures it had been. One corner of the mask called to him, a tear he'd intended to fix. He wiped his hands on his pants and chose a shimmering needle from the kit, then ran his middle finger along each spool of thread. *Ahh,* the taupe was the one for the job: the hue would stand out nicely against the leather. His heart fluttered as he threaded. Perfection.

He shoved the needle into the corner of the fabric. It stuck. He pushed harder, feeling the stirring in his belly as he forced it, and when it gave, he sighed the needle through, watching the puncture deepen, the hole form. Like the boy. He'd felt the pierce of the spike, the initial resistance, then the give—and it might as well have been his own body entering the child. It had been the same with the woman. He'd taken the spike right off his boot for that one.

He plunged the needle into the mask again, and his dick got hard. He could almost feel the sword he'd tattooed there swelling, sharpening. He considered fucking the girl in the crate to teach her a lesson, but he didn't really feel like it. Sex was boring without blood. He glanced at the gown in the corner again, but went back to the needle, relishing the sharpness of it. Seamstress was synonymous with sissy, but the entire occupation was slashing and violence and stabbing. Was there anything more manly?

The tear was repaired in five stitches, and he carefully knotted the thread and replaced his tools. Then he lowered the mask over his face.

Much had changed since medieval times, but he could almost feel the ghosts still there, imprinted on the material of the mask, every soul sucked from a body via a too-thorough bloodletting, from plague, from childbirth, from injuries still ripe with complications and the promise of certain death should infection set in. He wished he'd been there to witness medieval life in all its glory. Sometimes he missed those days like he might miss a severed limb.

He bent to the cage again, seeking her face, and her eyes widened with fear and excitement and longing. The beaked doctor's mask was a symbol of status, and she surely knew it. Or perhaps she could feel how close she was to those who'd gone before, their souls almost touching her through the metal tip of the mask's nose, still stained with Shannon's blood. Maybe she was excited by the jester, superimposed over beak and hide, grinning at her with its fanged mouth. Hidden beneath the mask, he smiled.

Happy, happy, happy.

YOUR NEXT BOOK IS WAITING!
**Get *HIDDEN*, the next book in the Ash Park series,
at MEGHANOFLYNN.COM.**

PRAISE FOR THE ASH PARK SERIES

"Dark, gritty, and raw, O'Flynn's Ash Park series will take your mind prisoner. This series will keep you awake far into the morning hours."
~Kristen Mae, bestselling author of Red Water

"Haunting...the Ash Park series should be everyone's next binge-read."
~NYT bestselling author Andra Watkins

"Visceral, fearless, and addictive, this series will keep you on the edge of your seat."
~Bestselling author Mandi Castle

"Cunning, delightfully disturbing, and addictive, the Ash Park series is an expertly written labyrinth of twisted, unpredictable awesomeness!"
~Award-winning author Beth Teliho

"Intense and suspenseful...captured me from the first chapter and held me enthralled until the final page."
~Susan Sewell, Reader's Favorite

GET THE ASH PARK SERIES AT MEGHANOFLYNN.COM.

HIDDEN

AN ASH PARK NOVEL

HE'S BACK.

DETECTIVE EDWARD PETROSKY has always felt the pain of the world like a razor blade in his gut, even more so when he considers the killers who have escaped conviction. But he can't let that stop him, not after a grandmother is found murdered on her front lawn, the victim of some machete-wielding psycho.

The case is strange from the outset: no one heard a thing despite the public nature of the crime. An unknown child's footprints cover the property without a trace of the kid. And a grisly discovery in the basement has the entire police force stunned. Nothing makes sense. Whatever secrets their victim had, she'd taken them, quietly, to her grave.

But when another woman's corpse turns up with a familiar brand on her rib cage, Petrosky realizes the horrible truth: a killer he'd thought was long gone from Ash Park has remained, lurking in their midst. And who knows how many victims this butcher has collected? For those he's kidnapped, any day might be their last, imprisoned, unseen, with only their screams and a deranged lunatic for company.

Now Petrosky must risk everything he holds sacred to track the most sadistic killer Ash Park has ever seen, a man whose thirst for carnage extends far beyond mere bloodletting. But saving innocent lives will require an unbearable sacrifice.

One from which he may never recover.

GET YOUR COPY OF *HIDDEN* AT
MEGHANOFLYNN.COM

SHADOW'S KEEP

A NOVEL

For William Shannahan, six-thirty on Tuesday, the third of August, was "the moment." Life was full of those moments, his mother had always told him, experiences that prevented you from going back to who you were before, tiny decisions that changed you forever.

And that morning, the moment came and went, though he didn't recognize it, nor would he ever have wished to recall that morning again for as long as he lived. But he would never, from that day on, be able to forget it.

He left his Mississippi farmhouse a little after six, dressed in running shorts and an old T-shirt that still had sunny yellow paint dashed across the front from decorating the child's room. *The child.* William had named him Brett, but he'd never told anyone that. To everyone else, the baby was just that-thing-you-could-never-mention, particularly since William had also lost his wife at Bartlett General.

His green Nikes beat against the gravel, a blunt metronome as he left the porch and started along the road parallel to the Oval, what the townsfolk called the near hundred square miles of woods that had turned marshy wasteland when freeway construction had dammed the creeks downstream. Before William was born, those fifty or so unlucky folks who owned property inside the Oval had gotten some settlement from the developers when their houses flooded and were deemed uninhabitable. Now those homes were part of a ghost town, tucked well beyond the reach of prying eyes.

William's mother had called it a disgrace. William thought it might be the price of progress, though he'd never dared to tell her that. He'd also never told her that his fondest memory of the Oval was when his best friend Mike had beat the crap out of Kevin Pultzer for punching William in the eye. That was before Mike was the sheriff, back when they were all just "us" or "them" and William had always been a them, except when Mike was around. He might fit in somewhere else, some other place where the rest of the dorky goofballs lived, but here in Graybel he was just a little…odd. Oh well. People in this town gossiped far too much to trust them as friends anyway.

William sniffed at the marshy air, the closely-shorn grass sucking at his sneakers as he increased his pace. Somewhere near him a bird shrieked, sharp and high. He startled as it took flight above him with another aggravated scream.

Straight ahead, the car road leading into town was bathed in filtered dawn, the first rays of sun painting the gravel gold, though the road was slippery with moss and morning damp. To his right, deep shadows pulled at him from the trees; the tall pines crouched close together as if hiding a secret bundle in their underbrush. Dark but calm, quiet—comforting. Legs pumping, William headed off the road toward the pines.

A snap like that of a muted gunshot echoed through the morning air, somewhere deep inside the wooded stillness, and though it was surely just a fox, or maybe a raccoon, he paused, running in place, disquiet spreading through him like the worms of fog that were only now rolling out from under the trees to be burned off as the sun made its debut. Cops never got a moment off, although in this sleepy town the worst he'd see today would be an argument over cattle. He glanced up the road. Squinted. Should he continue up the brighter main street or escape into the shadows beneath the trees?

That was his moment.

William ran toward the woods.

As soon as he set foot inside the tree line, the dark descended on him like a blanket, the cool air brushing his face as another hawk shrieked overhead. William nodded to it, as if the animal had sought his approval, then swiped his arm over his forehead and dodged a limb, pick-jogging his way down the path. A branch caught his ear. He winced. Six foot three was great for some things, but not for running in the woods. Either that or God was pissed at him, which wouldn't be surprising, though he wasn't clear on what he had done wrong. Probably for smirking at his memories of Kevin Pultzer with a torn T-shirt and a bloodied nose.

He smiled again, just a little one this time.

When the path opened up, he raised his gaze above the canopy. He had an hour before he needed to be at the precinct, but the pewter sky beckoned him to run quicker before the heat crept up. It was a good day to turn forty-two, he decided. He might not be the best-looking guy around, but he had his health. And there was a woman whom he adored, even if she wasn't sure about him yet.

William didn't blame her. He probably didn't deserve her, but he'd surely try to convince her that he did, like he had with Marianna... though he didn't think weird card tricks would help this time. But weird was what he had. Without it, he was just background noise, part of the wallpaper of this small town, and at forty-one—*no, forty-two, now*—he was running out of time to start over.

He was pondering this when he rounded the bend and saw the feet. Pale soles barely bigger than his hand, poking from behind a rust-colored boulder that sat a few feet from the edge of the trail. He stopped, his heart throbbing an erratic rhythm in his ears.

Please let it be a doll. But he saw the flies buzzing around the top of the boulder. Buzzing. Buzzing.

William crept forward along the path, reaching for his hip where his gun usually sat, but he touched only cloth. The dried yellow paint scratched his thumb. He thrust his hand into his pocket for his lucky coin. No quarter. Only his phone.

William approached the rock, the edges of his vision dark and unfocused as if he were looking through a telescope, but in the dirt around the stone he could make out deep paw prints. Probably from a dog or a coyote, though these were *enormous*—nearly the size of a salad plate, too big for anything he'd expect to find in these woods. He frantically scanned the underbrush, trying to locate the animal, but saw only a cardinal appraising him from a nearby branch.

Someone's back there, someone needs my help.

He stepped closer to the boulder. *Please don't let it be what I think it is.* Two more steps and he'd be able to see beyond the rock, but he could not drag his gaze from the trees where he was certain canine eyes were watching. Still nothing there save the shaded bark of the surrounding woods. He took another step—cold oozed from the muddy earth into his shoe and around his left ankle, like a hand from the grave. William stumbled, pulling his gaze from the trees just in time to see the boulder rushing at his head and then he was on his side in the slimy filth to the right of the boulder, next to...

Oh god, oh god, oh god.

William had seen death in his twenty years as a deputy, but usually it was the result of a drunken accident, a car wreck, an old man found dead on his couch.

This was not that. The boy was no more than six, probably less. He lay on a carpet of rotting leaves, one arm draped over his chest, legs splayed haphazardly as if he, too, had tripped in the muck. But this wasn't an accident; the boy's throat was torn, jagged ribbons of flesh peeled back, drooping on either side of the muscle meat, the unwanted skin on a Thanksgiving turkey. Deep gouges permeated his chest and abdomen, black slashes against mottled green flesh, the wounds obscured behind his shredded clothing and bits of twigs and leaves.

William scrambled backward, clawing at the ground, his muddy shoe kicking the child's ruined calf, where the boy's shy white bones peeked from under congealing blackish tissue. The legs looked...*chewed on.*

His hand slipped in the muck. The child's face was turned to his, mouth open, black tongue lolling as if he were about to plead for help. *Not good, oh shit, not good.*

William finally clambered to standing, yanked his cell from his pocket, and tapped a button, barely registering his friend's answering bark. A fly lit on the boy's eyebrow above a single white mushroom that crept upward over the landscape of his cheek, rooted in the empty socket that had once contained an eye.

"Mike, it's William. I need a...tell Dr. Klinger to bring the wagon."

He stepped backward, toward the path, shoe sinking again, the mud trying to root him there, and he yanked his foot free with a squelching sound. Another step backward and he was on the path, and another step off the path again, and another, another, feet moving until his back slammed against a gnarled oak on the opposite side of the trail. He jerked his head up, squinting through the greening awning half convinced the boy's assailant would be perched there, ready to leap from the trees and lurch him into oblivion on flensing jaws. But there was no wretched animal. Blue leaked through the filtered haze of dawn.

William lowered his gaze, Mike's voice a distant crackle irritating the edges of his brain but not breaking through—he could not understand what his friend was saying. He stopped trying to decipher it and said, "I'm on the trails behind my house, found a body. Tell them to come in through the path on the Winchester side." He tried to listen to the receiver, but heard only the buzzing of flies across the trail—had they been so loud a moment ago? Their noise grew, amplified to unnatural volumes, filling his head until every other sound fell away—was Mike still talking? He pushed *End,* pocketed the phone, and then leaned back and slid down the tree trunk.

And William Shannahan, not recognizing the event the rest of his life would hinge upon, sat at the base of a gnarled oak tree on Tuesday, the third of August, put his head into his hands, and wept.

GET *SHADOW'S KEEP* AT MEGHANOFLYNN.COM.

ALSO BY BESTSELLING AUTHOR MEGHAN O'FLYNN

STAND-ALONE THRILLERS
The Jilted
Shadow's Keep
The Flood

THE ASH PARK SERIES
Salvation
Famished
Conviction
Repressed
Hidden
Redemption
Recall
Imposter
Composed

SHORT STORY COLLECTIONS
Aftertaste
Listeners
People Like Us

DON'T MISS ANOTHER RELEASE!
SIGN UP FOR THE NEWSLETTER AT
MEGHANOFLYNN.COM!

ABOUT THE AUTHOR

Meghan O'Flynn is the bestselling author of *The Flood, The Jilted, Shadow's Keep*, and the Ash Park series, which includes *Salvation, Famished, Conviction, Repressed, Hidden, Redemption, Recall*, and *Imposter*. She has also penned a number of short story collections including *Aftertaste* and *Listeners*. Her husband still hasn't decided to sleep with the lights on, so he's either very brave or very silly, her children remain unimpressed with her practical jokes, and her dog hasn't stopped side-eying her since she hid all the dog treats. There shall be mutiny before the year is out.

Sign up for Meghan's newsletter at meghanoflynn.com to be first in line for new releases and get a **FREE SHORT STORY**. Guaranteed spam free. And if you want to give back a little, leave Meghan a book review. She'll be so psyched that she might even give those dog treats back. Make a puppy happy, people. *Happy, happy, happy.*

Want to connect with Meghan?
meghanoflynn.com